Q-16
and the Eye to
All Worlds

A.A. Jankiewicz

For Expo 2024

Q-16 and the Eye to All Worlds

First published February 2015

Second Edition: 2017

ISBN: 978-0-9959080-1-7

www.aajankiewicz.com

To the kids in the corner of the schoolyard, for starting the adventure,

To my family; Mom, Dad and my brother Adam for supporting me through the quest even on the darkest of days,

To my loyal friend and editor Anthony Geremia, the Sancho Panza to my Don Quixote who sallied forth with me on my expedition,

To Ashlee Terlicher for bravely tackling the voyage of beta reading,

And to the staff of the Contemporary Media Production program at Durham College for helping me reach journey's end.

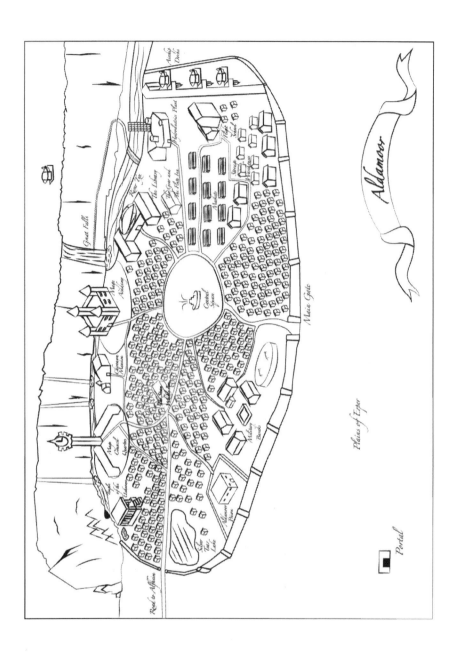

4

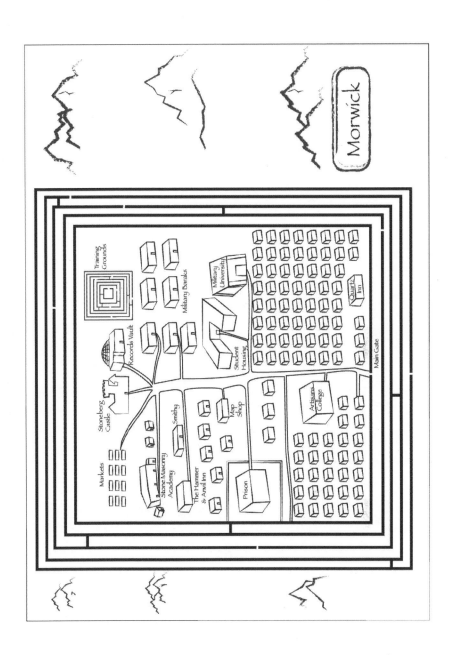

Morwick

Training Grounds
Military Barracks
Records Vault
Stoneberg Castle
Markets
Stone Masonry Academy
The Hammer & Anvil Inn
Smithy
Map Shop
Prison
Military University
Student Housing
Artisans College
Quartz Inn
Main Gate

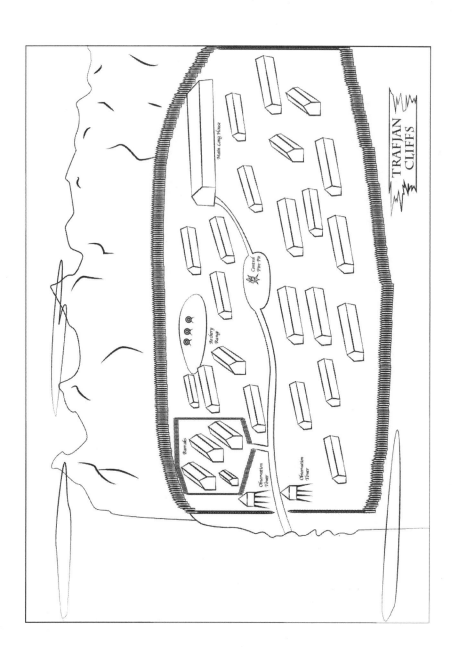

TRAFJAN CLIFFS

Main Long House

Archery Range

Central Fire Pit

Barracks

Observation Tower

Observation Tower

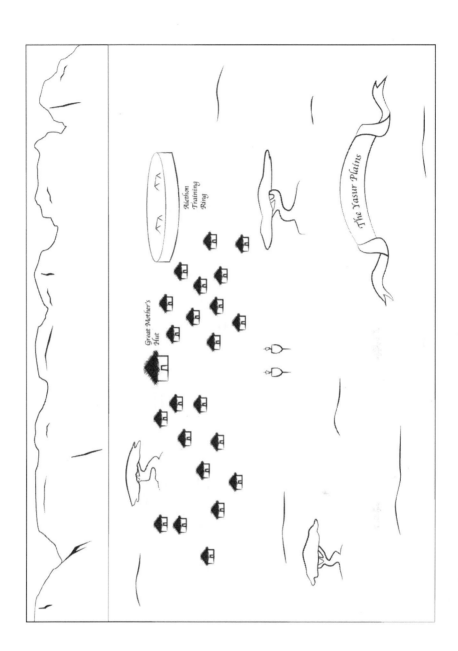

Auction
Training
Ring

Great Mother's
Hut

The Yasur Plains

7

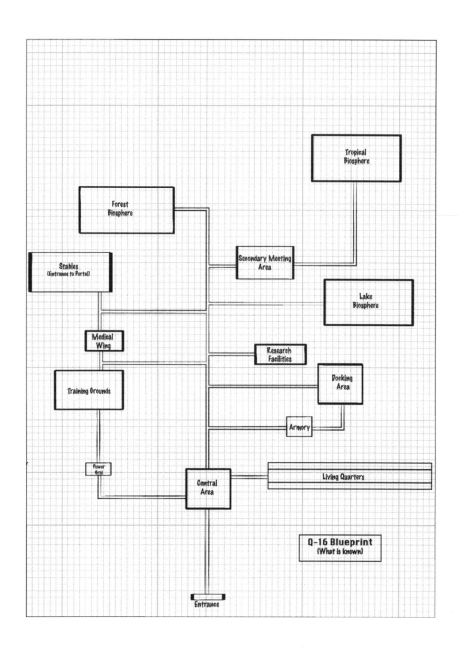

Tropical
Biosphere

Forest
Biosphere

Stables
(Entrance to Portal)

Secondary Meeting
Area

Lake
Biosphere

Medical
Wing

Research
Facilities

Training Grounds

Docking
Area

Armory

Power
Grid

Central
Area

Living Quarters

Q-16 Blueprint
(What is known)

Entrance

8

Myth can only ever stay myth for so long. The world always moves towards progress, an everlasting cycle more ancient than the earth and sky. As this progress is made, myth is lost, and so is much of the magic about the world. Stories can be forgotten, but that which writes itself on the hearts of the seas, the wind, the fire, and the stone will remain forever. It will be retold as long as the ancients keep the Earth turning, as long as at least one wishes to seek out the truth, and as long as they believe in it.

80C3

Prologue

From behind towering white castle walls, a red sun rolled, capturing all in gold and crimson hues. The day was almost at its end, and the tattered flags upon the four cerulean tower heads seemed to wave goodbye to the last of the fighting that had occurred hours before. The ancient structure had stood witness to many such battles over the years, and would stand for many more. Somewhere out on the field, amongst the ruins of broken spears and fallen soldiers, a mountain of a man swung a twin bladed axe, finishing off his final opponent. His wild silver hair and beard were covered in the grit of battle. From beneath a beaten helmet, a pair of blue eyes scanned the area for intruders. But no one dared to stand before him.

Lord Orbeyus Severio laughed, his eyes filled with the bloodlust of battle. He shook off a glimmering mix of sweat and dirt, taking a deep breath. The Four Forces had won the last encounter against Mordred the Conqueror. Orbeyus looked to his right to see his son, Arieus. He smiled at the memories that swam within his mind each time he saw him. He remembered having a little boy at his side, and teaching him to ride a horse and shoot a bow. Before him now he glimpsed the man that had come out of those lessons. He was tall and broad of shoulder, with short messy copper hair, like that of his mother. The man in his late twenties reminded the older Severio of himself when he was young.

"The Unknown shall be proud," Orbeyus said to him, removing his helm to reveal a head of close-cropped grey hair. "We have won a great victory."

Arieus nodded, holding a bloodied sword in his one hand, and a tower shield in the other.

The man grinned at his father, his coppery-brown mustache covering half of his mouth. His youthful face was filled with vigor for life, while Orbeyus's displayed ageless authority. Though they looked different, one could tell that Arieus was Orbeyus's son by his stride and the power of his sword arm.

"It will be talked about for ages to come," Arieus told him, "The day when the armies of Lord Orbeyus the Axe vanquished those who threatened the lives of-"

"My dear lad, no one in our world will ever know our stories," Orbeyus said, smiling at him sadly. "Not in the time we live in."

Arieus sighed, admitting his father was right. He looked around at the multitude of races that surrounded him. There were bull-headed Minotaurs, wolf-headed and eagle-winged men called Soarin, reptilian Ogaien, and blue-eyed Water Elves, as well as men and women just like him. The world Arieus lived in did not know they existed. Truly, it had forgotten the ways of the sword, of chivalry and honour. In its skies rode great birds of steel, and horses with rubber hoofs charged through its land. In the world Arieus lived in, he was a factory worker, and his father was a businessman. It was a world so far ahead of itself that no one ever stopped to think that there was something more to it, and only by using the portals at Severio Castle could Arieus still be free. He hoped that someday others would believe in his world once more.

Orbeyus, on the other hand, masked his sadness with laughter, and looked back at his allies that had survived the onslaught.

"But it shall be remembered by those who stand here! Come! Tonight we feast so that tomorrow those here can spin stories to tell for generations to come," he said, as those around him banged their weapons together in approval.

A short time later, the Great Hall of the castle was lit up with the splendor of feasting and the scents of roasted meat wafted through the air. Food and drink were provided in abundance, and the walls echoed with the chattering and laughter of those gathered. The various races of the Four Forces filled the tables, different in appearance, but united by the spirit of brotherhood. Orbeyus sat at the head table with a large goblet in hand, chuckling as he watched his comrades enjoy themselves. Their toils had been long and laborious. Their rejoicing came to him as a reminder that the peace they had sought to bring was well worth it. His eyes then turned to

Arieus, who sat eyeing a woman at another table. She sat beside her companions, gentle featured, pale skinned, and graceful in her motions as she spoke. She wore a dark blue, high collared dress trimmed with white and her chestnut hair was in a thick long braid running down her back. Her name was Aurora Pelleio. Orbeyus knew that she had been the object of Arieus's affection for many years. Yet Orbeyus never informed Arieus he knew this.

"Has something caught your eye, my son?" Orbeyus asked him.

"What? Oh, nothing, it's just-" Arieus began to say.

"Is that the woman who has captured your heart, and who you have been courting all this time?" He questioned his son while pouring himself some more mead.

"Yes, father. But she...Well, she insists I find someone up to my standards but I-" Arieus started to explain to his father, who clearly was not in the mood for long conversations.

"But you love her." Orbeyus stated rather than asked. He could see in his son's eyes how much the woman meant to him. Who was he to make his son find something else, when he had already found what he wanted most?

"Yes, I have strong feelings for her," Arieus said quietly, uneasily shifting in his seat. "We both do... for one another."

"Feelings like you have not had for other girls? It's called love. People try to rationalize it as something else, but it is not. You can't fool me, Arieus. I may be old, but I'm not thick," Orbeyus snickered as he watched the other soldiers enjoy themselves.

"But what am I supposed to tell her to change her mind?" Arieus gazed into his father's eyes, trying to find an answer.

"The truth. Go and tell her what I just told you. Arieus, we live in times where status has nothing to do with how we feel. It's only when we sit at this table that we seem different from the outside world. When we go back to it, we're back to being the same as everyone else," Orbeyus explained to him. "The only true form of anarchy that ever existed is love."

Arieus nodded, taking in what his father had just said. He rose from the table slowly, adjusted his tunic, and made his way over to the table where Aurora sat.

Orbeyus glanced over at his son and watched in interest as the scene unfolded. After a minute, a hulking creature with the ears of a rabbit, the mane of a lion, and the snout of a badger flopped into a chair on his left. It was very easy to hear it approach, for in both ears there was an assortment of jingling silver hoops.

"Has the lad finally puckered up the courage to ask that bonny lass what be on 'is mind?" the creature asked, leaning in beside Orbeyus.

"Patience, Brakkus. We will soon see," the older man said with a smile.

He was unable to hear anything over the feast's clatter, but he could tell from the slowly softening expression on Aurora's face that she was having a change of heart. His suspicions were confirmed when the young couple sealed the deal with a kiss. Grinning, the two of them made their way over to Orbeyus, who tried to look as oblivious to having looked in their direction as possible.

"Father, we are going to marry!" Arieus told him, beaming with excitement.

"Well then! That was to the point." Orbeyus laughed as he ran a hand through his thick beard. "Looks like I need to get this lot's attention."

Taking the hilt of his axe, he slammed it into the floor, making a thunderous echo across the hall.

"My dear friends!" he shouted, "I have an important announcement to make before we continue on with our festivities. My son Arieus is to be married to Aurora of the house of Pelleio. I would like to wish them well, and I hope I get to become a grandfather sometime soon!"

Those assembled in the hall chuckled at Orbeyus's comments, and clapped for the couple. Orbeyus was a fierce warrior, but it was well known that he had a soft spot for children. They knew he was waiting for Arieus to find himself a girl so he could steal their youngsters away and assume the duties of a grandsire.

The celebrating continued late into the night. There was not a moment of sorrow in the eyes of those present. They all knew they would have to leave in the morning to return to their lands, some of which would never hear of their triumphs. They knew, however, that as long as those who were there in those moments remembered the war, it would not be forgotten.

⁖⁗

Three years later…

It was another hot day of summer in Severio Castle. Orbeyus worked on fixing one of his horse's shoes in the stables. It had been a long time since he had maintained any of them, and they were beginning to get worn down. There was something relaxing about working with the magnificent beasts, and Orbeyus enjoyed doing it, despite having others who could do it for him.

Elsewhere in the castle, Arieus played with his year-old daughter, Annetta. Though she was small, Annetta already had her father and grandfather's sharp blue eyes, which observed the world around her with curiosity and wonder. He smiled, watching her tiny hand grab hold of the poppy in his hand. He understood more each day why his own father loved children so much.

Arieus's eye contact with Annetta was broken when he heard his father howl in pain. Instinctively, Arieus grabbed his sword in his free hand, and rushed to where his father had been fixing the horseshoes. He found Orbeyus lying on the floor in a pool of blood, his shirt slashed open. Horrified, Arieus knelt beside his father, Annetta crying in his arms.

"Father?" he asked, seeing if he was alive.

Orbeyus coughed, looking up at his son, barely able to move. He grabbed Arieus by the shoulder, looking at Annetta.

"Fate is a funny thing," Orbeyus croaked.

"Father, let me get help," Arieus said, tearing up at the sight.

"You can't help me. The poison is already too far spread. Not even magic can stop it now," Orbeyus wheezed, grabbing hold of Arieus's arm.

"Father, no, I'll send for Puc," Arieus protested, trying to rise, only to have his attempt thwarted by Orbeyus's hand clasping his forearm in an effort to keep him where he was. The elder man's breathing was labored now, and it was getting harder by the second for Arieus to resist the urge to call out for aid.

"I can die a peaceful man, Arieus. I watched you grow up, get married, and start a family. I have also seen the rise of the future, and of the one who will stop all of this." His gaze turned to the little girl in Arieus's arms. She clutched the withered poppy, sobbing.

Arieus's eyes narrowed as he looked at the child. The girl quieted down upon seeing the protective eyes of her father watching over her. The man then understood what his father spoke of, and putting all the pieces together in his head, all the cryptic words, he realized there was no other route to be taken, for everything led back to that one finite end. He looked back at Orbeyus, seeing the thin film of death begin to fill the man's eyes as he prepared to pass on.

"No," he half whispered, "she can't be."

"A love of battle...born of the axe of ancients, but it is in her father's sword that shall be born battle's desire. All the signs point to it, and it cannot be-" Orbeyus coughed up blood, but continued. "You cannot stop it Arieus, it was written-"

Before Orbeyus could finish his sentence, his eyes rolled to the back of his skull. Anything that would have been said was overpowered by Annetta's cries.

Arieus thought long and hard on what had just transpired in that moment. The shock of his father's death was mixed in with the revelation of words that he and his father had spent most of their lives trying to understand. They finally made sense to him, and he knew one thing for sure. He was not going to let his daughter get involved in any of it. A graver thought crossed his mind as he looked upon the broken body of his father. He would not bury his firstborn. Taking Annetta, he ran to another room in the castle.

The room's walls were covered with tapestries, save for one taken up by a vast open window. In the center of the room sat a large pedestal on which were etched four symbols: One of three water drops, one a three peeked mountain, one of a gust of wind and one of a tongue of flame.

Coming to a halt, Arieus placed his daughter on the ground and took out his sword. He gazed at the gleaming blade a final time, then at his daughter. The girl had calmed down and looked up at her father in confusion as to why he had let her go.

"One day you will understand why I did this for you," he said quietly. Taking the sword into both hands, he approached the pedestal. "I swear, upon all Severio lords past, never to lift a blade in battle. I do this for my daughter."

Arieus took the sword and slammed it into the pedestal with all his might, encasing the steel within it. The glow from the carvings around it disappeared, and the weapon seemed to fuse with the stone. Arieus sighed. He may not have been able to save his father, but he was able to save Annetta, and the future was what mattered.

Chapter 1

Fifteen years later…
Toronto, Ontario

A shaggy head of dark reddish-brown hair peered over a blue-skied horizon, plodding across a grass-covered hill. Annetta Severio headed home from school on foot. The afternoon sun beat down on her slightly oversized jean jacket, making it uncomfortable to wear. She wouldn't take it off, though. It had been a present from her father after she'd brought him her first A on her report card. She'd always wanted one, but her mom said jean jackets were for boys, and that girls should wear dresses. However, her father knew how much she wanted it, and he made the deal. It had taken a long time, but after much hard work, Annetta had managed to get the A in her English class, and the first thing she did was race home to show her dad. They'd picked it too big on purpose, so Annetta could grow into it, making it last longer. Of course they had over estimated her growth spurt, and it was still too big, but she didn't mind.

Usually there was a light step in Annetta's gait as she walked home, particularly when it was this close to summer. But that day, she walked slowly and lazily, trying to prolong the walk. She had been in a fight, and didn't want to confront her father on the matter.

Reaching the parking lot of the apartment building, she pulled out the key to unlock the door of the lobby. Opening it, she went to grab an elevator, the last wait before the inevitable talk with her father. Annetta sighed and watched the elevator lights as they came to a halt on the tenth floor, and the door slid open. Shuffling out, she made her way to the apartment she lived in with her parents and younger sibling. She turned the knob quietly and walked inside. Fortunately she didn't see her father in the living room.

The apartment was neither the smallest in the world, nor was it the biggest. Two bedrooms could be found on the right when one walked in, along with the bathroom all neatly packed into a row, while on the left was the living room, the kitchen, which was walled off from it, and the dining room beside it. Annetta had always found it a cozy living space, with enough room for all four members of her family. Her gaze turned quickly to the large painting of the castle that was located over top of the bulky wooden entertainment system, a piece of art her parents had in their possession as long as Annetta could remember. There was something warming about the tall, white walls and surrounding greenery that made her smile and forget all of her cares each time she looked at it. Snapping out of her trance, not wanting to be caught, she began to make her way to her room.

"Annetta," the familiar deep male voice called from the kitchen. Were Annetta a dog or cat, her ears would have flattened against her skull and her tail would have been tucked tightly between her legs. She could tell without looking that his blue eyes were boring their way into her back.

"Yes, daddy?" she answered, the way an obedient sixteen year old would.

"I received a call from your teacher saying you were involved in a fight at school. Is this true?" Arieus stepped out from behind the kitchen wall to look at his daughter. Age had taken its toll on him, and he was no longer the young man he once was. His hair was beginning to grey, but there were clear laugh lines around his eyes.

"I...Uhm...well...no, not really. I mean, Finn pushed me first, he called me a coward," Annetta answered him, spinning around to face her father. Her eyes met his, and it was clear she was her father's daughter. Her small, sharply defined face peered into his definitely upon the accusation made at her, reminding the man more of his wife than himself, even if everyone he knew claimed she looked just like him. The largest difference, people claimed, between them was their hair. While Arieus's had a deep copper tone, Annetta's was slightly darker red like her mother's.

"And you let a little comment like that get to you?" he questioned, moving past the living room area, and standing a few feet from her near the entrance. He could see her clearly now, the tousled up hair, the worn, large jean jacket and the run down blue sneakers she loved to wear, all traits of his little girl who's erratic behavior was slowly becoming harder to handle.

"Well, yeah, they were all laughing at me..." Annetta felt ashamed, conceding that she had a hot temper.

"Annetta, I think I have taught you better, have I not?" Arieus spoke to his daughter gently, yet firmly enough to let her know he was being serious.

"Yeah but, they were all looking at me, waiting for-" Annetta began as she took off her shoes and placed them in the appropriate place in the closet.

"Waiting for you to fight back? Annie, sometimes it takes more skill to lift your head high and walk away than it does to raise a fist and cause a scene," her father stated.

"He still would have beaten me up if the teacher hadn't shown up," she muttered, feeling defeated. She finished undressing by hanging the jacket on a hook beside the door.

"Annetta, my dear, if you only knew of the power inside you that will one day emerge," Arieus sighed.

"Uhm...dad, are you giving me or Xander a pep talk? 'Cause you do realize I'm a-" she looked at him as she did her best to play charades and give him clues to the last word in the sentence, which was, of course 'girl'.

Arieus smiled. Her mother desperately wanted Annetta to be more of a girl instead of the tomboy she had embraced. He knew he was partly to blame by reading fantasy to his young daughter instead of normal bedtime stories, but part of him could not help it. In some way, he wanted to be able to pass on a little something to her, even if it was just make believe.

"Yes, sorry dear. I'm just a bit caught up in my work, and wasn't thinking," he said to her, smiling lightly. Before he could say anything, the door opened again, and in came Aurora.

"Hey everyone, I'm home! Annetta, what happened, sweetie? You look like you got in a-" Aurora looked at her daughter, raising an eyebrow.

"I did, Mom...but Dad already talked with me about it, so..." Annetta felt like flattening her ears again as she prepared for another lecture.

"Oh, well, in that case you're spared from further speeches. Any plans for tonight?" her mother asked as she put the groceries down in the kitchen.

Annetta looked at her mother, startled that she had gotten off without even a comment about how it wasn't lady-like to get into a fight. She decided to make nothing of it. Maybe her mom was in a good mood, and did not feel like lecturing. It had happened before.

"I think I'm gonna go see a movie with the guys. I'll take Xander if he wants to come along, too," she told her parents.

"As long as it's not a horror movie. Do you remember last time what happened when he went to see one," her mother told her.

"Yep, no problem." Annetta smiled and went to the other room to grab her little brother.

Alexandrius, or Xander Severio was five years younger than Annetta. Like his sister and parents he had blue eyes, but his hair was jet black and his frame was of a wiry build like a runner. Despite his lanky build, he still had the round face of a child. He was currently glued to the screen as he watched his enemies fall in a video game. His brow furrowed as his hands jumped across his controller. Annetta watched him play for a few minutes before she decided to make her presence known.

"Hey Xan, want to go see a movie with me and the guys?" she asked him.

Xander looked over at his sister with a huge excited grin.

"Okay!"

"Alright then, come get your shoes on," she beamed to him, dropping her bag off and leaving the room.

ॐ

Jason Kinsman, known as J.K. to his friends, had received his nickname when his mother had labeled his lunch in his first year of high school with the initials, and his friends had teasingly started calling him that instead of his full name. Presently, he waited outside the theater located in the plaza close to where they all lived with Annetta's other friend, Darius Silver. The two of them were not the closest, keeping up a friendly act for Annetta's sake. Jason thought there was something very dark to Darius's nature, and he did not mean his hair, or eyes, or even his pointed and slender featured appearance. He meant the way Darius spoke and perceived the world. Jason sighed, trying not to dwell on his dislike, not wishing to end up in a losing fight with the taller boy. He ruffled his uneven brown hair, and scanned the area with his large green eyes. His broad face attentively looking around for any sign of his friend. It was still light outside, it being just after four o'clock and the parking lot across from them teemed with life as people pulled in and out with their vehicles.

"What's taking them so long?" Darius broke the silence.

"She's probably taking the heat for that fight in school today," Jason answered, not really paying attention to Darius.

"Oh, yeah, they were really at it today. I almost thought Annetta would beat him a few times. Too bad the teacher broke it up." Darius smirked, leaning against the side of the brown brick wall of the theater.

"I didn't think she would beat him. I knew she would," Jason stated boldly. He'd known Annetta far longer than anyone else. The two of them had met in kindergarten, and had been best friends ever since. He sometimes liked to think he knew Annetta better than she knew herself. It may not have

18

been true, but he did know her well enough to see when she would win or lose.

"You're crazy. He's way stronger than her." Darius glared at him, then ran a hand through his shoulder length black hair. "Should we maybe call to see if she's grounded? It's really taking a long time."

Jason was about to answer Darius when he noticed two people coming towards them on the sidewalk. He instantly recognized the swagger in Annetta's stride created by the billowing of her jacket.

"How's it hanging?" Annetta smiled as she approached with Xander.

"Not bad. You got off easy after the whole scrap with Finn?" Jason greeted his friend.

"Bit of lecturing, nothing massive. Even my mom was in a no-speeches mood today." Annetta grinned.

While Jason and Annetta talked, Darius turned his attention to Xander, who seemed left out. Darius had always liked the boy. He reminded him of the younger brother he never had.

"Hey little man, you decided to come hang out with us even after the horror movie fright?" He winked at him.

"Yeah, but my mom said not to go to another one," Xander answered plainly to which the older boy chuckled at his frankness.

"No worries, man," Jason said, butting into the conversation. "There aren't any good ones out, and I don't think your sister liked them much either."

"Ha ha ha," Annetta deadpanned. "You were the one with dark circles under your eyes the next day, right?"

Darius, turning away from his conversation with Xander and noting the time, looked at the two of them.

"Can you guys chat about who was the bigger pansy later? We've gotta decide what show to go to," he reminded them. He was not a fan of walking into the theater late, mostly because he hated it when he was stuck sitting too close to the screen.

Annetta and Jason nodded and looked up at the sign above the theater, taking a minute to read the titles over.

"Which one was the fantasy flick again? I feel like swords and horses tonight," Annetta thought out loud. Titles made no sense to her without posters.

Jason smiled to himself. He knew she was going to ask that. If Annetta ever passed up a fantasy film, he would need to make sure she was not an evil clone. Not that he minded, since they both shared a passion for those sorts of things, which was why they had become so close in the first place. To Jason, Annetta was the only girl he knew who was actually fun to be around, and who shared his interests. Everyone in school thought they were weird for liking what they did, but Jason felt that, as long as they had each other to talk about it, then it didn't matter what everyone else thought.

"Anne," he said, "you always feel like swords and horses. You should be feeling like princesses and castles."

"I like castles, I just think the dresses that princesses wear are too...impractical? And what's this about me having to like one thing over another?" Annetta teased him.

"I'm just pulling your leg. It makes you who you are. You guys up for the fantasy one?" Jason turned to the others.

"Works fine for me. What about you, little man?" Darius looked at Xander, who was fully focused on the names of the different movies. After a long pause, Xander turned to his sister and her friends with a very serious look on his face.

"As long as it's not a horror," he said.

&oq

The movie was typical. Dark creatures crowded the screen as a hero appeared to vanquish them. This time, to Annetta's delight, it was a female hero, a woman in her early twenties liberating the people of the imaginary country from a spawn of darkness. The concept wasn't very original, but it still brought a smile of satisfaction to her face. She liked the idea of magical creatures and heroes that came to the rescue of those who needed it most. To her, the sad part was that it was not the way things worked in the real world.

Having lived her whole life in Toronto, she was well aware of how harsh reality could be. Though her parents taught her to be kind to others and to defend what was right, it was hard when everyone was out for themselves. On top of that, no one believed in the existence of anything remotely magical in the world, either. Of course, she knew nothing like that existed, but what was the harm of dreaming about it sometimes?

The film came to an end, and the lights went up. People began to leave as soon as this happened. Annetta, Xander, Jason, and Darius lingered for a little while, hoping there would be extra scenes after the credits.

"What did you guys think?" Annetta asked, breaking the silence.

"Not bad. The chick was bad ass." Darius grinned.

"I liked the dragon. It was awesome," Xander responded. "Especially when he roasted the bad guy at the end."

"Yeah, it was pretty awesome," Annetta agreed with her little brother.

"You guys still want to do something, or we gonna split?" Jason questioned his friends.

"Nah, I think I've abused my parent's good graces as it is. The movie was way longer than I expected," Annetta said. "Plus we have a minor who needs to be home."

"Aw… but I wanna go out and have fun with you guys." Xander made a sulking face.

"Later, in the actual summer," his sister promised him.

"Cool," Darius said. "Well, I'm gonna split then if that's the case. See you at school tomorrow." He waved to his friends as he got up and left.

Jason felt his face heat up a little when the other boy left. Both Darius and Annetta lived in the same building, yet he had not even bothered to walk back with her and Xander. It was things like that, which made him dislike Darius.

"I'll walk you home, I guess," Jason said to the pair as they headed out the doorway.

Chapter 2

The walk home was filled with chatter on all three ends. Jason could not get over the visual effects, while Annetta continued to ramble about the plot. Xander would sometimes pop in with his own points, but was distracted by the fact that he was walking around at dusk with only his older sister and her friend.

"Say what you want, but that last fight scene, with the dragon...It looked amazing. It felt like it was real," Jason beamed. "They're really making some advances in CGI. I felt like...like it could be something that could pop out from under that rock over there."

"Stuff like that doesn't exist," Annetta said, trying to keep her friend's feet on the ground. Despite her fantasies about such things existing, she knew better, and always made sure to remind others of it, even if only to reassure herself.

"Yeah I know. But I can dream, right?" Jason grinned at her.

Annetta smiled back at Jason. No matter what happened, he always had a positive attitude towards the situation he was in. He'd had a lot of practice over the years. Jason's family had a very unpleasant history. His father was a war vet who had lost one of his legs and had spent years ranting and raving about how a similar fate would befall his son. One day, his mother could no longer take it. When his father was drunk to the point of passing out, she called for him to be taken to a mental institution. He hadn't been heard from since. She told Jason and his younger brother Liam that their father had simply moved away on business. Jason had learned the truth when he accidentally picked up a letter to his mother from the institution.

A few years later, in a fit of rage, Jason admitted to his mother that he knew the truth about what had happened. She had explained to him that it was for their protection, but part of him had never forgiven her. For a long time he'd been very quiet when the subject of his family came up, but he learned to cope with it. Now, he did not allow his sadness and anger to show through. Instead, he attempted to smile back in the face of his misfortunes, knowing that no one else would live his life for him if he didn't do it himself.

Annetta then noticed that Xander had stopped ahead of them and was looking up. Perplexed by the odd behavior she paused, and looked around herself but saw nothing.

"Hey, little buddy. What you looking at?" Jason asked, walking up to Xander, who was still frozen.

"Up there," Xander said dimly, as he pointed up in the sky.

Jason looked up at where Xander was pointing. At first, he didn't see anything that could have caught the boy's interest, not even a plane or a star in the sky. Squinting his eyes harder at the dark blue skies, he then saw it, and it felt like his whole world had frozen around him.

"What you guys looking at?" Annetta asked, walking up to the two boys.

For a long moment, Annetta also found herself staring up into the heavens looking for an answer, until she finally saw it. The navy blue evening sky seemed to darken as heavy clouds rolled across it. Annetta felt adrenaline rush to her head. The pace at which it was happening was not a natural occurrence. Clouds did not move that fast, except when a tornado was coming. But it couldn't be, it wasn't possible. They were in Canada, after all. Her heart pounded in her chest as lightening flashed across the heavens and the sky turned an even angrier violet. She could either run home, or stay and risk getting crushed by a large tree when it fell.

"Guys...I think we should go," Annetta said, not wishing to abandon them. "I'm pretty sure standing under trees during a storm isn't safe."

Before either of them could respond, the wind began to pick up. Annetta felt the muscles in her legs coil up. Whatever was going on was far from normal, and she had no intention of finding out what it was.

"Run!" she screamed.

The trio took off towards the building the moment Annetta's voice rang through the air. The wind howled around them like a wild animal as they tried to reach the front gate. As they ran across the parking lot, a bolt of blue lightning struck one of the parked cars, causing it to burst into flames. Annetta was thrown to the ground by the blast, tearing her jeans and scraping a knee. Cringing, she tried to get up, but every part of her body seemed to be paralyzed with fear.

"Annetta!" Jason ran over to her after getting himself up. "You alright?"

She nodded weakly while the lightning bolts hit the ground a few more times. The girl was not prepared for what she saw next, and she bolted up to a sitting position.

Two balls of glowing blue light had formed behind them, illuminating the night like two tongues of fire off the tips of candles. The two oval shapes then began to take more specific forms. The blaze shrunk away, leaving the shape of two large exotic birds. One looked like a phoenix, with a red body covered in smooth plumage. It had a long graceful neck, and peacock tail feathers that turned into flames at the end. The other bird sat perched on the remnants of the exploded car, and looked like a large yellow vulture. Its feathers formed into spikes all over its body, which ended with a tail that looked like a ball with the same gold feathered spikes all over it, like a morning star. The two creatures stared at the children with an almost controlling force, their beady feral eyes analyzing them in a predatorily manner.

Annetta could not believe what she saw. She almost thought that the two beasts were some kind of animatronics project, and that they happened to be in the wrong place at the wrong time. Maybe this was why her father hated her going out so late at night, for fear of being eaten by giant robotic birds. By this point, Jason had turned around, and was also staring in disbelief.

"Whoa…Must have hit my head pretty-" Jason began to say.

"Silence, mortal!" The wings of the yellow bird flapped as sparks of blue lightning surrounded it. The bird had not spoken, yet words had come from it, and it was hard to tell if it had spoken them with its enormous curved beak, or simply thought them.

"…Damn…hard." Jason finished his sentence, unable to say anything else due to his astonishment.

Annetta managed to shake off some of the paralysis. She tried to see where Xander was, hoping her little brother had not been hurt by the explosion.

"Bwiskai, do not frighten them." The phoenix-like one turned to look at the thunderbird, then back to the children. "Greetings, she who is severed, and he who fights like a lion of hell. I am Fulgura." Its voice sounded strangely feminine, while Bwiskai's was male.

"Who…What are you?" Annetta managed to ask the most basic of questions as she crawled closer to Jason, who was still on the ground.

"We are angels, come to deliver that which is by birthright yours to hold," the one called Fulgura said to them.

"Angels? I thought they were supposed to be-" Annetta trailed off, afraid to anger Bwiskai, in case he should create more displays of his dissatisfaction.

"There are many different angels. Not all look as you mortals portray us," the phoenix answered her gently.

"Enough explanations, Fulgura. We cannot linger here for long." Bwiskai glared at his companion with his black eyes.

"So if you're angels, then we must be dead, right?" Jason asked in a serious voice, slightly panicked.

"No, mortal. You are still very much living, I can assure you of that," Bwiskai snapped at him. "Now, as I said before, we come bearing a message of great importance."

"Okay," Annetta managed to say in a small voice, not really enjoying Bwiskai's harsh tone, "what is it you have come to tell us?"

"Unto you the keys are to be given, as is the power to protect those who cannot protect themselves, and the knowledge of what lies beyond this world," Fulgura said to them. "We come with a plea from those with no voice, to take up arms."

Annetta stared at the two birds. The whole scenario was so bizarre to her that she almost wanted to laugh and walk away, even if the one called Bwiskai would most likely strike her down with lightning.

"This is....absurd. Something must have hit me on the head, things like this don't just happen..." She began to rationalize.

"Do you doubt what you see, she who is severed?" the phoenix questioned.

"My name is Annetta Severio, not...what you just called me. And yeah, I think this is all really weird, and I have a hard time believing it. You and him and..."

"You doubt the power of the supernatural?" Fulgura looked into the eyes of the girl.

Annetta looked right back at the creature as she recited to it what her world and everything in her life had told her.

"The supernatural does not exist," she said to it. "There is no myth and magic here. That's why none of this is making any sense."

Fulgura looked over at Bwiskai, who seemed calmer, but worried by the girl's words. The two of them looked at the children again.

"Annetta Severio, daughter of Arieus and Aurora Severio, she who is severed, your name speaks everything about your character. You have been cut out and taken away from things which are as old as time, things in which you still believe, deep down inside yourself. Is this not so?" Fulgura continued to speak in its feminine voice to her.

Annetta looked over at her friend for support before answering with a shrug. "Maybe."

"Then why is it so hard for you to embrace what you see before you?" Bwiskai spoke. "Young Annetta Severio, there is such magic in this world. One only needs to look from beyond the glass of false reason in order to see it."

"Look, all this stuff isn't supposed to exist. I go to high school, I read about this sort of thing for fun, and yes, on occasion I wish it was real, but up till now it hasn't been, and I was cool with that. Now all this gets thrown at us, how exactly do you expect us to react? I think I speak for J.K. and myself when I say this is all a bit much," she began to rant.

"The first step is to believe," Fulgura interrupted, the long neck swimming towards Annetta in order to look her in the eye. "A foal cannot run without the belief that it can first stand."

Annetta exhaled roughly and looked at Jason once more for help. The boy was in as much shock as her from everything that was transpiring, yet he could not help but want to know more about the reason for everything that was happening.

"You mentioned something about protecting those who can't help themselves. Say we walk away from all of this, say we decide not to take whatever it is you came to give us. What happens then?" Jason asked.

The two birds glanced at one another as a sad look came into their eyes. They turned back at two children, almost with a look of mourning.

"Then the world we speak of," Fulgura responded, "shall be without defenders. We have a glimpse of what is to come should you refuse to accept, for note that evil is on the horizon, and soon someone will need to rise to challenge it."

Fulgura spread her wings to reveal a bright red belly. Standing up from where they were, Annetta and Jason looked at it, feeling almost hypnotized by the flame-like red feathers. The feathers soon became reflective, like a mirror. The children looked at their reflections until they disappeared. They were replaced with a landscape unlike any they had seen before.

The sky was filled with dusty clouds, while strong winds pushed against the remains of trees across a desert scene. No living thing could be seen anywhere. As they looked closer, the trees morphed into metal beams from the wreckage of buildings, and the children realized that this was their beloved city they were staring at, torn to shreds.

The setting then changed. As everything was consumed with flame, people, among them Annetta and Jason's families, were dying as monstrous shadows attacked them in the fire. An army of fiends approached, in the middle of which stood something that resembled a man with a feline face. He seemed to stare at the youth from beyond the mirror, and with a feral roar, ordering his troops to kill.

"Stop!" Annetta shouted with tears in her eyes as she pulled back and glared at the two creatures.

"Are you saying if we don't do what you ask us, then everyone is going to die?" Jason looked up at them. "What kind of choice is that, then?"

"We never said there was a choice. We but ask for your help to prevent this," Bwiskai reminded them. "This is what will come to pass. It is no lie that grave things are coming Earth's way, and only you two hold the power to keep them at bay."

Annetta quietly looked down at her feet. She loved the idea of fantasy and magic being real, but she had forgotten an important part of it. People got hurt, there were always struggles, and sometimes people died. The tears dried on her cheeks as she continued to look down, lost in these thoughts.

"We're just kids. We have no power," Jason protested.

"You have the power of belief," Fulgura said to him. "You have stayed this long because you believe in what is being said, and because you believe that what you do will have a great impact on both your future and that of the entire world. If you did not have this, then you would have already left."

Annetta felt her insides twist. The images she had seen in the mirror felt so real, it was like she had already been there. She could feel the heat of the fires on her face, taste the coarseness of the sand in her throat, and worst of all, she could feel the predatory gleaming eyes still glaring at her. Everything about it screamed at her to run, to not get involved, but there was something to Annetta that always made her do the opposite. It was the same thing that always made her stand up to those who hurt others, and it was this same thing now that pushed her towards the two beings with her final decision.

"I'll do it," she said, barely audible.

The two birds, not having moved from their original places, looked at one another, then turned to the girl.

"What was that?" Bwiskai asked her.

"I said I'll do it," she said, more confident.

Jason looked at his friend. She was not even trying to fight what they might be getting themselves into. But he knew after what he had seen that she had a reason to say so. He also knew that he had promised to be Annetta's best friend in every situation. He was not about to back out on her because he did not know what was waiting on the other side.

"Okay then. Me too." Jason looked at them. "If Annetta is in, then so am I."

The two birds glanced at one another with their dark eyes before looking back at the children.

"May the Unknown bless thee, young Annetta and Jason," Fulgura said. "Unto thee are given the keys. May you serve the Earth with the strength of your forefathers."

The two birds then spread their wings and gave loud, glass-shattering screeches. The earth began to tremble below Annetta and Jason's feet as a white light emitted from Fulgura and Bwiskai.

Before they knew it, Annetta and Jason were alone in the parking lot, with no sign of any of the damage caused by the birds' arrival. Even the burnt car looked as if nothing had touched it. At their feet, however, were two metal card keys. Engraved on them in heavy block lettering was the phrase 'Q-16'.

"Q-16? The hell is that supposed to mean?" Jason asked Annetta, trying to shake off the shock.

"I don't know, J.K. but I think I may know someone who does," Annetta replied, having caught on to the forefathers bit in their speech. Picking up the piece of flattened metal she turned to go to the apartment building she lived in.

Chapter 3

The moment Xander burst into the apartment, his instincts led him to his father, who was sitting on the couch reading a book. Xander proceed to tell him what he had seen outside. It did not take Arieus long to figure out what had befallen his daughter and her friend. By the time the two of them made it upstairs, he was prepared with an explanation. After giving Xander a comforting speech and sending him to his room with a glass of milk, Arieus sat in his armchair in the living room and waited. It seemed like an eternity. Then the door crept open.

"Dad?" Annetta's voice rang from the hallway as she took her shoes and coat off.

"In the living room." His tone was serious as he called out, much more serious than he had intended, but it was too late to fix it.

Annetta and Jason then came out from around the corner. Arieus could not see the card keys anywhere, but he was certain the children had them, probably in their pockets. He knew they would be shaken after what they had just seen, especially since they were brought up not to believe in such things.

"I never wanted this for you, Annetta. Nor did I wish this fate for anyone else, J.K... but I suppose I've no choice but to explain now," Arieus sighed. "I had hoped this fate would not befall either of you, and for that, I am sorry."

The two of them froze in their tracks as they approached the elder Severio, a confused look spreading on their faces. Neither of them had expected this reaction.

"What are you talking about, Dad?" Annetta asked, slightly confused.

Arieus could tell she was aware of what he meant, but was not sure of his involvement in all of it. He leaned back slightly on the sofa, adjusting his grip on the dark crimson fabric of the left armrest.

"I know what you saw. Xander told me, and there is no need to hide it. Now where are they?" he asked them, shifting in his seat again.

Annetta and Jason looked at one another. Though they could see he knew what had happened, they could not help but fear it was all a trick. How could they even begin to tell Arieus what had happened? They'd be grounded and separated for the rest of their lives, or else put on so many prescription pills they'd be seeing rainbows and unicorns.

"Where is what?" Annetta looked at her father.

"The card keys. May I see them?" Arieus answered her.

Finding it pointless to argue with her father, Annetta surrendered her card key. Jason did the same, and Arieus accepted them. He sighed as he looked at the two pieces of metal, running his fingers over the embossed letters. They were just the same as he remembered them.

"Oh, my dear little Annetta. I wish I had explained this all before. But I suppose now is as good a time as any." He looked down. "I have prayed for years that they would never come. But alas, the Unknown had other plans for you both, and I can do nothing to change it."

Annetta raised an eyebrow. She had never heard her father speak like this.

"Sir, are you saying you know about what-I mean, all that stuff that happened?" Jason asked him.

"I do. The question is, will you believe what I have to say?" Arieus looked at the pair.

"Well, it can't get any crazier than a pair of giant talking birds calling themselves angels...can it?" Jason looked at Annetta's father, whose calm face had become very solemn.

Before Arieus could say anything else, the door opened. In came Aurora with some shopping bags.

"Hey, everyone." Aurora began to greet them when she noticed the card keys in Arieus's hands and nearly dropped the bags, causing an array of fruits and vegetables to scatter on the floor. "Where...where did you get that?"

"They came," Arieus simply said to her.

Aurora looked at her husband, still standing in one place, "But you said that-"

"I swear I had nothing to do with this, and clearly it was not enough to stop them," he explained to her, raising a hand. "Now that this has happened, even against my own wishes, there's nothing to do but to clarify as best we can. Sit down."

Aurora nodded, picking up what had dropped and put the groceries down in the kitchen. She came to the living room and sat down on the sofa beside him. Annetta looked at her parents. For a brief moment, they almost resembled a king and queen in a castle, despite the four of them being in their living room. Night was beginning to fall, causing everything around them to take on a dark blue hue as though someone had airbrushed everything with watercolors. Aurora moved to turn on the lamp beside her, filling the room with golden light.

"A long time ago," Arieus began, "before you were born, Annetta...my father, your grandfather was in charge of...many, many soldiers, who served to protect the Earth. Now...what you truly need to understand before I go any further is that our world, this world, is very different underneath the surface. There are many dark and ugly things that hide in the shadows, and someone needs to be there to protect others from them."

"Like grandpa and these soldiers did?" Annetta questioned him.

"Yes, that's exactly right. For a long time before you were born, I did the same thing," he said to her.

Annetta looked at her father with furrowed eyebrows. He had always been an ordinary man to her. He went to work in the morning, came home at night, and went over bills at his desk, making sure they had enough money to live another day.

"So, who's protecting everyone now?" she asked him.

Arieus felt his pride being stung by his daughter's words. Had he been a younger man, this would have been an insult, implying that he was not doing his duty. Instead, age had granted him the right words to say back.

"No one. Because I chose to protect you instead," he answered her.

"But aren't I part of everyone else, Dad?" she continued asking her father.

"Yes Annetta, but...someday you will understand. What you need to know right now is that the team your grandfather led had a secret base where they all stayed. This card key opens that base," he explained to her.

"That's all good, but why did I get one?" Jason finally broke his silence.

"Your father was among those soldiers," Arieus said to him. "He was a great man, and a good friend, despite what your mother tells you about him. He saved my life more than once. But he was unable to accept the world we live in now. His mind wanted to believe that there was only the other world we defended, and that this one here was nothing more than an illusion."

Jason nodded. It gave him some comfort to know that his father was not all crazy. He hoped to be able to speak with Arieus one on one to learn more about him. Maybe even someday he would go visit his father on his own.

"So the reason we were left these card keys to this base is because no one is defending it?" Jason followed up with another question to break the silence.

"Yes, that's right. The base has been undefended for a very long time. You were too young before to even be asked to consider such a task," Arieus said to him. "And in my opinion, you're both still too young to be asked to do this."

Annetta felt the need to jump in upon being called too young. "But Dad, stuff has to be getting bad if we got these now. Maybe there's something Jason and I can do to help. Granted, I have no idea what that could be."

Arieus turned to his daughter, who had fallen silent, and was sitting on the sofa beside them with Jason. He sighed at her stubbornness, his shoulders slumping forward in the heaving motion.

"This isn't like your movies and games. It's a lot more complicated than that," he began once more, the copper mustache on his face twitching with irritation, only to be interrupted by Aurora's hand landing gently on his own in an effort to calm him down.

"Your father is right." Aurora nodded. "There was a reason we left, and it was the same reason Jason's family left. It was to protect you both."

Jason had a hard time comprehending why such a thing was left without anyone to look over it. It seemed selfish to him. "Okay, but if this was all so important, why did all the people defending this place leave?"

"The company fell apart. There was simply no one left to fight," Arieus stated, still with a sour note. "The rest either got old or were too weary to do it anymore."

Annetta could feel something was not right. Her father seldom lost his temper, and she could see he was getting agitated. One thing was clear, though. Whatever it was that was in this base, it was significant.

"Then I will do what no one else wants to do. I choose to fight." There was no hesitation in the girl's voice.

Arieus looked at his daughter once more, the resolve on her face reminded him of another person in his life and he knew he had little choice in what to say next.

"Just know that what you are getting yourself into is not all fun and games. It is a responsibility that should not be taken lightly," he told her again. It seemed only days ago when he was holding her in his arms and playing with her on a lookout tower in a castle. Now here she was, his mirror image, saying yes to a challenge she knew nothing about. He felt fear. He wanted to brush the truth away and hide her from it a little longer, but he knew it was no use.

"Since there is no changing your mind, come with me and I will show you the entrance," he said, getting up from his seat.

Everyone who was present in the room followed Arieus. They all stopped briefly in the hallway by the door, while Annetta and Jason put on their shoes and slipped on their jackets.

"Is it like... in the middle of some abandoned warehouse?" Jason asked, hoping it was like in old spy movies.

"It's actually a lot closer and less elaborate than that," Arieus said as they walked to Annetta and Xander's room.

Their room was not very large. At the far side stood a burgundy laminated wooden dresser with a television and game system on it, and beside it was Annetta's bed. Next to that were her desk, filled with thick novels on its shelves, guarded by figures of knights and dragons as well as papers sprawled out all over it, then Xander's desk, neatly organized with his action figures and videogame cases, and then his bed. The beds had been placed this way so Xander would not spend all night playing video games, since he would wake up Annetta, who'd throw a fit. The room seemed far too ordinary to host a hidden passage to an underground base.

Xander sat on his bed glued to the television screen, trying to forget what he had seen outside. He could not help but turn around when he saw his sister and her friend safe and sound.

"Hey, you guys are okay! What happened out there?" he asked, pausing the game.

"I don't think you'd believe us if we told you," Jason grinned.

Arieus stopped and stood beside the rectangular mirror that hung beside the entrance of the room.

"What you need to do is swipe the card key along the side of the mirror from top to bottom to activate the teleporter," Arieus instructed.

Annetta and Jason examined the mirror, then traded a confused look with one another. It had been there as long as they could remember. They'd assumed it had been placed there when Annetta was a little girl.

"Wait, what? Teleporter? I thought you said that-," Annetta protested.

"Remember what I told you about our world not seeming like what it really is? Well this is one of those things," Arieus explained to her. He looked at his son. "Remember what I told you before?"

"Yes Dad," Xander nodded, "Don't tell anyone what you see happen in the room, except Mom because she might get worried."

"Who says I'll get worried if I'm right here?" Aurora asked as she came into the room. It was starting to become crowded.

Arieus smiled at his wife before turning back to the children. "I think you should try to go down individually before you attempt to go down both at once. It can be a little exhausting on the body if you are not used to it."

Annetta nodded, taking a step towards the mirror. She took the card key from her father's hand and swept it quickly. Almost instantly, a platform materialized underneath her feet, and a flat circular disc appeared above her head. A small rectangular keyboard and screen also appeared, floating on the far end of the platform, asking the amount of people who would be traveling in green san serif lettering. Annetta looked up at her parents hesitantly, uncertain where the next move would take her. The excitement of the unknown that coursed through her body was enough to calm her remaining fears.

Chapter 4

As soon as she hit the enter button on the keyboard it began. Annetta fell for what seemed like an eternity. As she plummeted, she felt as though she was being assaulted by ocean waves all around her. The next thing she knew, she was on a steel floor, completely dry. Getting up and feeling a little disoriented, she looked at her surroundings. They were extremely plain, covered in the same silver steel plating as the floor. She turned around to see a massive door, marked with the same font as the card key, also spelling out 'Q-16' in large characters. It looked like it took a dozen men to move.

There was a light hissing noise. Moments later, Jason materialized on the floor behind her. He got up and shook his head as though he had a bad fall, then looked around with wide eyes.

"Wow, this totally beats what I pictured," he said to Annetta, then noticed the door she was looking at. "Uh…that the way in?"

"I guess so," she responded, "But I don't see how we'll be able to get in anyways. I mean…it's so big. I don't think any of us can move it."

"That's kinda obvious," Jason snorted. He began patting the cold steel with his hand. "Maybe there's a switch or something we gotta press, or a password."

"But don't you think my dad would have said something about it?" she asked him.

"I don't think your dad was too keen on us coming here in the first place," Jason said as his brow furrowed. "Although if that was the case, then he could have let us know how to get back. I don't see anything to swipe this thing on here either."

Annetta felt a surge of panic go through her. She had never been placed in a situation where going home was not an option. Now the concept of it was frightening. Amidst her thoughts, she heard something shuffle lightly, making her heart race even more.

"To open the gates of old, use that which the mind has bestowed," an eloquent male voice said from the shadows.

Annetta and Jason both jumped upon hearing it, realizing they were standing in a large hallway and not just a small square of metal. However, neither of them wanted to explore the dark without a flashlight.

"What the hell is that supposed to mean?" Jason grunted, trying to be tough.

Annetta scrunched up her face in concentration and mulled over the words in her head, realizing they were being given a riddle. She'd read plenty of books where speeches like this were used in challenges or in prophecies. With everything that had happened, why not have a riddle get them through the door?

"Uhm…is it reason?" she asked the voice.

"No, use that which was given to you through birth right," it answered her.

"Intelligence? Brains? What? There are only so many words I can think of for a person's head. What do you expect us to do, open the gate with our minds?" Annetta questioned the voice, hoping for a more straightforward answer. Maybe what was written in fantasy books was overrated.

Before Jason could say anything to his friend a tall man with shoulder length black hair came out of the shadowy hallway. He was dressed in robes of deep blue that were piped in gold. He carried with him a large gnarled wooden staff, the tip of which was covered in what looked like a fine green moss. He was the palest person the children had ever seen, which made his angular featured face all the more frightening to look at. Even his deep-set eyes were a shade of blue that looked almost inhuman.

"Something like that...they did teach you how, did they not?" he looked at Annetta and Jason, examining them both. "I was expecting you'd both be older when we would meet, but I suppose the Unknown had his reasons for sending children…"

The man circled the two of them and took a step back so he could study them both again. The youth huddled closer together when he did this, not feeling comfortable at the two sapphire spheres glaring back at them. They felt unnerved by this, Jason, more so than Annetta.

"And who are you? Pretty sure there's no magic conventions around here, so why are you dressed like-," Jason went on the defensive. He did not like being called a child.

"I am Puc Thanestorm, also known as Puc the Mage, Water Elf of Aldamoor, and former advisor to Orbeyus of the Axe, Lord of Castle Severio and protector of Earth," he announced, "And you will do well to remember that."

"An elf? I thought they were all blonde, skinny, and super tall with pointy ears, right?" Jason snorted.

"I would have you know, boy, that elves do not have pointed ears," Puc said, sternly. "Otherwise people would be easily able to distinguish us from them. In these times that is not wise. And save the childish commentary for the schoolyard."

Jason smirked and rolled his eyes, before slouching against the wall nonchalantly. Already he didn't like Puc. He'd been down there waiting for them, and had clearly expected them to be something different, and this rubbed him the wrong way. He firmly believed a person should be all they are and not be looked down on for it. This was why he and Annetta had become such good friends in the first place. Despite his family's situation, Annetta was his friend because of who he was, not who he could be or should be.

"Have you finished?" Puc looked at him.

The boy looked around as though he were waiting for someone to tell the elf the answer to his question. Seeing Annetta do nothing but stand there in waiting, he shifted and stood up straight.

"Yeah, I think I'm done for now," Jason answered.

Puc moved from where he stood and went to examine the massive doors, running a hand down the cold dark metal plating as though he were looking for a hidden switch.

"Good. I am assuming by your lack of general respect that you have no idea what I was referring to before," the elf stated, continuing and turned again to gaze at the children.

"Nope, not a clue," Jason answered him in the same casual manner as before.

While Puc and Jason bickered, Annetta had been focusing on Puc's words. What he had said about using their minds to open the gate had reminded her of something from her childhood.

ကြ

Five years earlier…

A much younger Annetta played with Xander in their room in the apartment building. Back then, it was only filled with action figures of knights, ogres and dragons. They were one of the few things the two of them could agree on playing with together, so their parents allowed Annetta to indulge in her boyish playing habits. The two of them sat on the floor around a large toy castle. Xander played with a knight on a white steed while Annetta played with a red dragon, pretending to fly over the fortress.

"BOOSH! BOOSH! RARGH! Now I am king of the castle!" Annetta grinned, setting the dragon on one of the towers.

"You can't climb the castle and just say you're king. You need to go in," Xander said matter-of-factly to her, as he continued to pretend to make the knight on the horse gallop around the castle.

Annetta tried to withhold what she felt inside her. She knew he was younger and so she did her best to be the big sister and let him have his way. There were times however when she got tired and she wanted him to be on the same playing field as she was. Her grip on the dragon tightened slightly as she held her tongue.

Xander placed his knight in front of the gate, pretending to block Annetta's path.

"Now you can't get in. I win," he smiled.

The words made something stir inside Annetta. They upset her to the point where she was no longer able to let Xander have his way. Why should she? Was she not allowed to win from time to time too?

"Oh yes I can!" she snapped at him. At that moment the little toy gate behind the knight Xander was holding opened.

∾∿

Annetta stood before the massive steel gate with her friend and the elf. Puc and Jason continued arguing amongst themselves while she looked up at the large block lettering on the doors. They seemed so big and overpowering that Annetta was not sure anything could get through them, let alone someone like her. Thinking back on the incident with the toy castle, she knew something strange had happened that day but the problem was she had no idea in the world how to make it happen again.

"What about telekinesis?" Annetta asked Puc, "Moving stuff with your mind? It sounds silly but I've read about it in books and seen it on television…"

Her voice died down, it was absolutely the most absurd thing she could think of but it fit what Puc had said.

Puc and Jason stopped arguing, hearing what Annetta had just said.

"You gotta be kidding me right?" Jason blinked a few times before turning to look at Puc, who gripped the staff with both hands while he observed the youth with a calculating gaze. "Besides, wouldn't we have like…tapped into them by now if we'd-,"

"Your powers were blocked until your first descent here," he answered them, "Both of your fathers were accomplished psychics who could move objects with their mind as well as many other abilities, that of course take a lot of practice and are for another time to discuss all together."

Puc moved closer to Annetta and Jason as he spoke, his staff hitting the metal floor created a hollow wooden sound that echoed all around them.

"You are both inexperienced but the matter of the fact is that you have the predisposition because your parents knew how to harness this gift. It will take both of you to open this gate," he said to them.

Annetta and Jason looked in shock and surprise, first at Puc, then at the gate and then at one another, before turning back to the mage.

"You're saying this like it's an everyday thing," Jason grumbled. "No wonder people thought my dad was crazy."

"It was an everyday occurrence long before you were born. It has simply been lost with time." Puc stated. "Now, both of you. Turn towards the gate and focus your thoughts on it."

Annetta and Jason rotated hesitantly towards the gate. They felt silly doing this but something inside them, bade them to obey the strange request. The way Jason saw it, Puc would probably turn them into toads if they did not do as he said.

"Okay, now what?" Jason demanded of the mage.

"I told you, focus," Puc said to him in a stern tone, crossing his arms as he spoke.

"If it were that easy, don't you think doors would be opening on their own all the time?" Jason sighed.

"Not everyone is a psychic. Now focus, boy. I'm getting bored waiting for you to accomplish this simple task," the elf fumed, losing his patience with the doubtful youth.

Annetta shut her eyes and faced the gate. She tried to think of how she felt when playing with Xander and tried to picture the small castle doors flying open. The memory was faint from the passage of time. Yet she kept trying, recalling it over and over again, until it felt like she was back in that moment.

On the other hand, Jason thought Puc was a crazy man who'd somehow gotten trapped wherever they were. Who was he to make them think they had psychic powers? As far as Jason was concerned, the two of them were regular teenagers from Toronto who were in way over their heads. His train of thought was interrupted when Puc's staff made contact with his back, hard enough to make him feel it but not enough to do any real harm.

"I said to focus, not think about how you'd rather be at home playing video games," Puc sneered, "I might not be able to read minds, but I can tell you don't give a damn by the way you're staring vacantly at the floor. Now hop to it, or the next time I'll make sure to leave a lasting impression of my staff on your backside."

"You know that's called child abuse," Jason blurted out.

"Not down here it isn't. I'm afraid, Jason Kinsman, that you are a far way from home, and what simple taps you call abuse in your world down here, we call motivation and discipline. Now, stop stalling, and do as I have asked." Puc instructed.

Jason sighed, not really convinced but still trying to focus on the door. Out of the corner of his eye he saw Annetta, completely oblivious to what was happening as she concentrated. She had stuck her hand out and pressed it against the gate, as if hoping the gesture would move it. He almost wanted to laugh at how ridiculous she looked, but something inside prevented him from doing so. Closing his eyes, Jason pressed his own hand against the gate. He allowed his thoughts to flow into it, as though they were a single force that could open it.

With her eyes closed, Annetta was not really sure what had taken place between Puc and Jason. She'd heard Puc get angry with Jason about something and threaten him. Ignoring it, she focused on opening the door. She felt heat rising into her palms from the force she was pushing into them but nothing seemed to be happening, and it was beginning to make her panic. Wasn't she supposed to be able to make it budge just a little bit at least?

Puc watched the children for a while longer before coming to a conclusion, something he had once heard from Arieus himself.

"Let's try a different approach," he suggested. "I want you to pick a moment in your life where you were very angry at someone. I want you to focus on that and then release that anger on the door."

Both the children opened their eyes and looked at Puc, slightly confused.

"You want us to hit the door?" Jason asked.

"Metaphorically," Puc stated. "Seeing as you are both new at using your abilities, I think it is best to assume that you can only harness it through intense emotions for now and since anger is more powerful than sorrow we will use that. Trust me and try it."

Annetta closed her eyes again and allowed herself to get lost in the memory of playing with her brother.

"You can't get in," his voice mocked her, "You can't get in."

She did not hate her brother. She'd hated the situation itself. She always had to let people have their way. In a fight, she wasn't supposed to fight back. Playing with someone, she had to let him or her win because she knew it was the right thing to do. She wished she didn't have to constantly let things slide. For once, she wanted to be the one on top.

"You can't get in."

As the thoughts ran through her head, the frustration began to build up inside of her. It was getting hard to breathe, to even be in the same skin as them. She wanted to escape. She wanted to make a difference.

"You can't get in."

The pressure continued to rise in the girl to the point where it became an uncontrollable force. Unable to contain it all any longer she opened her eyes, trying to escape the memory and then something occurred that the girl had not thought was possible.

Jason opened his eyes and jumped back, hearing sound of the enormous steel door as it opened. He looked over at Annetta who seemed to be in a trance, before she collapsed onto the ground.

Puc smirked thinly, then looked at the boy.

"Observe and learn," he said, before going over to help Annetta up to her feet. "You did very well. I was not expecting you to open the entire gate in one shot. I was hoping for a tiny creak at most."

Annetta groaned, she'd never experienced anything like that pass through her body. It felt like she had run a marathon. Every muscle in her body seemed to ache, even where it didn't seem possible. Disoriented, she looked around at her surroundings, her head still spinning.

"What...just...happened?" she moaned.

"You tapped into your powers," Puc said, as he reached into his robes and produced a vial filled with dark blue liquid. "Drink this, it should help a little bit."

"What is it?" she asked, taking it from him.

"An energy potion. A very minor one. I'm not sure how your body will react to anything stronger," he explained.

"And I thought these only existed in video games," Annetta muttered before opening the cork and downing the potion. She regretted it moments later. Her face curled up in disgust as the flavor hit her. It tasted like someone had urinated into her mouth and tried to mask it with a very poor imitation of blueberry flavoring.

"What...should I even ask what's in this?" she cringed.

"Ginseng extracts," he said. "What were you expecting? Eye of newt and bat wings?"

Before Annetta could say anything, she noticed Jason was missing from the scene. She looked around and noticed his faint outline in the darkened room on the other side of the doors.

"There a light switch anywhere?" he asked.

Puc walked into the dark in long strides. Annetta attempted to follow his pace, nearly tripping over her sneakers from the fatigue. Once inside, Puc tapped his staff lightly against the ground as a small ball of flame formed above its head, providing a little light, but not enough to see very far into the shadows.

"The generator is off. We will have to get to it in the central control room," he told the children as he continued to walk into the dark.

Annetta and Jason followed, doing their best to keep up with the elven mage while trying to catch a glimpse of the obscure dark shapes around them that were half illuminated by the tiny flame as they passed by.

"So...where are we exactly? I mean, where is this place?" Jason questioned, since the task of getting inside was complete.

"Geographically, we are located under the Atlantic ocean. Now, stay close to me. If the portal forcefields have weakened, there may be some fairly dangerous things lurking about," Puc said, more to himself than to Annetta or Jason.

This was getting more complicated by the moment to Annetta.

"Portals? Forcefields?" she wondered aloud.

"I...You really don't know anything, do you?" Puc smirked, slightly amused.

"Well no," she admitted, "this is all kinda new to us. You're talking to a couple of kids. We don't slay dragons or whatever you expect us to do."

"Yes, of course," the elf nodded his head, "Very well. I suppose I should explain then." He delayed while putting his thoughts together. "A portal is like a gateway to another time and place. The problem is that this base is linked with Severio Castle, which belonged to your grandfather Orbeyus. The reason this is a problem is that Severio Castle was built in a place which acts as a conductor for other portals, which means it is sensitive in picking up links to them and allowing other things to unintentionally cross over."

Annetta and Jason looked at one another before looking blankly back at Puc, trying to piece together what he had said. Annetta paused from walking for a moment, mulling everything over in her brain.

"Wait...my grandfather didn't just have an underwater base? He also had a castle?" Annetta raised an eyebrow, "Did he also have a spaceship and animal-man guards?"

Puc chose not to answer and simply glared at the girl.

"Okay, maybe I shouldn't have asked," she said quietly. "But I was serious about the part with my grandfather having a base and a castle."

"Your grandfather was a resourceful man," Puc said. "He did not believe in completely sticking to the old ways. He believed that there should be a balance of the old and new. The castle itself has been in your family for generations, passed down from Severio to Severio. It was built by your ancestor Lord Adeamus. This base, Q-16, was a more recent addition."

"You mentioned the castle linked to portals," Jason said, "and that Q-16 was connected to it. And that things can come out of the portals without us knowing. Isn't there anything we can do about that? Shouldn't there be a spell or something to block them? Or some kind of border patrol?"

"As I said before," Puc continued to explain, "there is a forcefield in place. Or rather, one was raised when someone was maintaining the base. But it has weakened since then. I have tried to use spells but they are like small bandages pressed over a large wound. They keep out infection, but if the wound keeps bleeding then the blood will seep through. The magic in the portals is far too ancient and powerful to be contained by anyone. It's what makes Severio Castle so precious to those who would conquer it. To have control over these portals means you control all worlds and have access to them at will. The forcefield was designed through science instead of magic and was maintained continuously unlike a spell, which is cast once and does not renew automatically. It served very effectively, which is why we must reach the main control room and restart it."

After a long pause, Annetta tried slightly changing the subject, feeling overwhelmed by the information. "So... how did you know my grandfather was Orbeyus?"

"I knew your father. For a short time, I knew you as well. After Orbeyus's death, your father withdrew from our world. You know the rest," Puc answered the girl's question.

Annetta didn't like how Puc made assumptions about what her and Jason were suppose to know and not know. Thinking back on her father's advice about not fighting however, she held her tongue as best as she could and continued to follow without a word. Jason had similar feelings to her but was being held interested by the concept of the forcefield and wanted to know more about it.

"So these forcefields. They make sure nothing gets in here but since no one has been around stuff might have gotten in, right? So how do we get rid of it?" Jason looked at the elf.

"We fight," Puc said, as he continued to walk.

Before anyone else could speak, there was a stirring in the dark, and something metallic hit the floor. The youth stayed behind Puc, uncertain of what to expect. The elf raised his staff defensively, and muttered an incantation as an orb of blue light formed around them.

"Whatever you may be, come forward. Show yourself and perhaps I will be courteous with a gift of mercy," Puc growled. His brows knotted as he gripped his staff tighter, ready to defend his new charges.

There was a long pause before anything happened. Time seemed to slow down around Annetta and Jason as they watched the elf glare into the dark in full concentration. Moments later, there was then a growl as a pair of large yellow eyes looked out at the three of them from the dark. Annetta felt her heart jump to her mouth.

There was a howl and the thundering noise of something charging at them. The muscles in Puc's arms coiled as he prepared to fire an offensive spell.

Annetta and Jason watched as a creature resembling a big burly man with a canine head came at them and was hit straight in the gut with a blue fireball, knocking him flying across the darkness. Instead of hearing another howl and charge, deep rumbling laughter could be heard from where the dog-man had landed.

Puc removed the orb from around him and the children, loosening the grip on his staff.

"What was that? Was that...a laughing spell?" Jason asked incredulously.

"No...I-," Puc was about to explain as the creature came into the light of the staff's fire again.

This time, Annetta got a good look at the creature. He was at least seven feet tall, and just about the widest being she had ever seen. He was not exactly fat she could tell. He had a pair of large muscular arms that were exposed without a shred of self consciousness and all he wore on his chest was a cuirass to protect his large belly. He also wore dark brown legging of a thick hide material tucked neatly into his boots. His face resembled a badger's snout, but with long rabbit-like ears with large silver earrings in them. Topping this off were lots of sharp crocodile teeth coming out from his mouth, which was covered with a thick beard that blended into his mane-like hair. He also carried a large broadsword that now hung from his right hand.

"Oh yer a big ninny, didn't shoot the full spell at the last minute," the beast said, grinning at the three of them with its large snout.

Puc looked at the creature, not shifting his cold demeanor and only fixed the out of place sleeve on his arm.

"I thought you were a hobgoblin. And weren't you supposed to be clearing the creatures off the grounds?" Puc scolded him.

"If ya haven't noticed, laddy, I am a creature. Technically, so are you. And how could ya confuse me with a hobgoblin? I've got these big bloody ears an-," the creature ceased to ramble when he noticed Annetta and Jason hiding behind Puc. "Well bless me whiskers, so that's what you've been protecting so fiercely. It's the granddaughter of Orbeyus and the son of Arcanthur." He spoke with a hint of an accent from somewhere in the United Kingdom. If she'd only had his voice to go on, Annetta would have assumed he was Scottish.

The creature smoothed its hair and ears back with a massive paw, "I'm Brakkus the Hurtz and I'm here, ready to serve ya, my lord and lady, be it by my life or death. That's my word to ya both as it was to those who came before ya."

Annetta looked at Brakkus and raised an eyebrow, "Uhm...we...we don't need your life. But it would be nice if someone could show us around. We need to get to the control room to restart the forcefield."

Brakkus looked at the young girl with his gold eyes, nodding his head and causing all his earrings to jingle in the process, "I can do that, just follow me and stay in the light. I can see in the dark, but I'm not so sure about you three."

"And here I thought elves could see in the dark," Jason muttered, only to be caught by Puc's piercing gaze.

"I may be a different species, but I am not superhuman," the elf grunted at him and followed Brakkus.

The walk to the control room was fairly quiet, the group only pausing when a suspicious noise was heard. It seemed to take an eternity. From what Annetta could see, they might as well have been walking in circles since the floors looked identical, for it was all covered in large metal panels that seemed to turn a slight shade of blue from the light of the staff.

"Here we are," Brakkus announced as they finally came to a halt.

"So...how come you guys didn't turn on the forcefield before?" Jason asked.

"Because someone related to Orbeyus or someone else of the proper authorization in the alliance is needed to do it," Puc stated opening, the door to the control room and going inside. "I was not granted authorization by Orbeyus before his death. Brakkus and I simply remained here when Arieus and Arcanthur chose to leave, which happened rather quickly. We've been here waiting for a long time for the return of the heir of Orbeyus and the son of Arcanthur. I have been using magic to keep this place from collapsing in on itself. Quite literally at times."

The room looked like nothing Annetta or Jason had ever seen in their lives. The area was closed off with what looked like walls of glass. A few freestanding glass walls also were dispersed around the chamber. There was no monitor, button or knob to be seen. Everything was covered in dust and cobwebs and looked like it had not been used in years. Puc walked over to the other side of the room, idly dusting off a large flat, rectangular table, which lay at the front of the room.

"This is what turns on the forcefield," he said. "It was designed so that only those who were meant to command the base would be able to do so.

Put your hand anywhere on the table and it scans it. If your DNA matches with one of our former leaders, the power will return."

Annetta and Jason nodded their heads and then looked at one another, each expecting the other to move.

"You can go if you want," Annetta said, finally. "I did sort of open the door."

"Alright." Jason placed his hand on the table. Nothing happened for a few moments. After an awkward stretch, the first signs of power returned when a light bulb overhead began to flicker to life. The sound of a generator springing to life could be heard somewhere far away as the remaining lights turned on. The glass walls flickered and came to life displaying an assortment of information and what looked like multiple screens. Annetta saw brief flashes of startled creatures scurrying away as her eyes darted from video footage to video footage, unable to keep up with the amount of information displayed before her.

"Ohohooo, now we're talking business," Brakkus grinned. "I see all 'em little bastards and where they be hiding. My sword is tingling for a fight."

"Well," Puc agreed and moving his hands in a swiping gesture across the screen he watched as the information changed, "That should prevent anything else from getting in. Looks like there are only a few hobgoblins, maybe an ogre or two." He dimmed the light on the tip of his staff.

Annetta continued looking at the different videos. The base was more massive than she had imagined. From what she could see, there were training rooms, a library, a work area with smelting equipment near some kind of aircraft hanger, and a collection of greenhouses.

"Welcome home, heir of Orbeyus and son of Arcanthur," Puc said, watching the wonder in the children's eyes.

Chapter 5

In a tall, dark, expansive room with many large windows, a warlord watched the blue planet go round day and night from his throne in the fortress high above it. He was not a being of Earth but a creature resembling a man dressed in a long dark tunic with golden embroidery all along the sleeves and a dark blue cloak. However, he had the face of a cat with sable fur and a pair of vicious green and yellow eyes. His feline features were filled with memories of a past defeat. Not his own, but still a defeat. He had traveled a long way to this planet, and spent many years building an army to claim the greatest gift in all the universes, the Eye to All Worlds. He remembered the castle stronghold well, the white walls contrasted by green fields that haunted his every dream. He had vowed long ago it would be his no matter what it cost him.

A wiry man entered the room, his white hair going out in all directions as though it had not been combed since the day he was born. Though it was white, Lloyd Abner seemed no older than a man of thirty Earth summers. The word going around on Valdhar was that Mislantus's fits of rage were the cause of the peculiar hair colouring. Drawing close, but not too close to the pensive creature he bowed low. Clearing his throat, he lifted a file from under his arm. The tyrant turned to address him, a smile visible on his face.

"Ah, Mr. Abner, what news of Pessumire do you bring?" he asked.

"The veil-tearing cannon is near completion Lord Mislantus," Lloyd said, nodding. "But the sample we recovered from your fathers' time cannot be used to calibrate the correct portal. It's simply too old. You know how fragile these dimensional portals are? It's like an ocean and nothing ever stays in one place when you want to make a direct link. I mean, you could tear up the entire fabric of time and space if you leave it in one place for too-,"

Mislantus raised a hand to stop the man from rambling. Specifics did not interest him.

"This is why I have you and your little lab rats to figure it all out," Mislantus said as he rose from his throne and began walking towards the large wall of glass. "There are many beings in the multiverse, Lloyd. Some are men of learning such as yourself. Some are followers, doing simply as they are asked, some are warriors who serve the greater good, and some never realize their potential, trying day in and day out to find out who they really are. But some of us are leaders of worlds, destined to become gods."

Lloyd watched the back of his lord and master. Mislantus was not someone to be crossed. He was quick to anger, and rarely ever went back on his decisions when he made them. The scientist had served under Mordred, Mislantus's father, and the one thing they both shared in common was their drive to accomplish their goals.

"What is your cultural division's progress on locating the descendants of Orbeyus and Arcanthur?" the warlord asked, turning back around.

"Yes sir, I came here with that subject in mind. They have succeeded in putting together a package as you've requested, with photographs we managed to find on the human information center known as the World Wide Web. We did have a slight problem gathering the exact location as to where they live. Something has been preventing us. And by that I mean some nasty little being has magic or science surrounding them and scrambling our signals." Lloyd handed the carefully-made package of notes to Mislantus, who began looking through it. Coming across the pictures of the two children Mislantus snarled, recognizing the features of each from their predecessors. "A general area has been pinpointed though, yes?" he asked, wiping the scowl from his face and turned to his subordinate.

"Yes, my lord. It is small enough that it should not take long to find them," Lloyd answered bluntly.

"Good," Mislantus closed up the file. With a single gesture he ordered one of the guards who stood at the door to come before him, "Bring Matthias to me. I have a mission for him."

"Yes, Lord Mislantus," the serf answered obediently and left the quarters.

Mislantus watched until he left, then turned back to watching the planet from the window, oblivious to Lloyd's lingering presence. His mind went back to the day of his shame and defeat as he ran a hand over his feline face. He would make the descendants of those who opposed his father's rule pay, and he would establish his place as ruler of all worlds.

෴

Within the lower levels of the fortress sat a tavern that beamed with the life of off duty soldiers. In this bar, a pair of azure eyes watched everything pass by them in silence. That silence was a trade of Matthias Teron. He was well known to many in the room as a psychic assassin, and rarely put to the test, lest they longed to breathe their last breath. He sat in his usual spot, a corner overlooking everything around him, cradling a goblet between his fingers. Though he rarely finished his drink due to being always on guard, he enjoyed coming to the small establishment the soldiers had been granted by Mislantus. He took pleasure in being able to see the rabble in their most natural state, as nothing more than the ever-consuming life forms they were. That was, after all, the fate of a soldier. To kill, consume and conquer.

Ever vigilant, Matthias watched out of the corner of his eye as two creatures blundered towards him. One was gigantic, resembling a rhinoceros, and was called a Verden. The smaller companion in tow behind him was a purple, reptilian creature with a beak called an Imap. They were but two of the races that served on Valdhar, the floating castle of Mislantus the Threat. Both races had pledged themselves to the tyrant they had viewed a god upon his arrival.

"What you lookin' at, chump?" the slurred words came from the obviously drunk Verden as a beefy hand slammed down on the shoulder of the assassin, "Ya white skinned little ape."

Matthias made no moves as he did his best to ignore the encounter. The situation had happened all too often to him in the past when new recruits came to the bar and indulged. It generally had only two ways of ending, neither very pleasant. Taking a sip from his goblet, he disregarded the creature and continued to watch everything else around him.

"Me thinks him deaf, Dirik," the Imap chortled, "He ain't talking nothin'. Maybe he's dumb too."

"Ain't there a rule about the strong conquerin' the weak, Jepa?" the Verden leaned more on the straight-backed assassin who sat at his table without a sound. "What say we show him how it's done?"

The two drunks continued their tittering amongst themselves as Matthias casually put his goblet down on the table, only to have it knocked over by the Verden named Dirik. The contents of the glass spilled on the assassin's boots in a slow and steady stream of golden red liquid. Matthias's eyes landed on the puddle on the floor, then shifted towards the two laughing companions.

"I believe you just spilled my drink," he said in a calm and serene tone, still sitting down.

"Eh? What's he sayin?" Dirik turned to look at the seated man, fully oblivious to the serious expression upon his face.

"You have spilt my drink," Matthias repeated louder, rising from his chair.

At this point many of the patrons sitting closer to them moved, well aware of who was being agitated. Jepa and Dirik were ignorant to the events unfolding, their glazed eyes focused upon Matthias standing before them, dressed in a black gambeson with three elongated pentagonal metal plates upon his chest and a blue cape, the symbol of his office as the head assassin.

"Oh boo hoo! Ye spilt yer drink, big deal," Jepa waved him off, almost falling over from the gesture and spilling his own tankard, causing the Verden to laugh at him.

"I can help you find it if ye want runt," Dirik grinned, cracking his knuckled and pacing towards the assassin.

Matthias sighed, not wishing the encounter to end in such a way, but there was no choice in the matter. Having seen the Verden's meaty fist coming towards him, he dodged with minimal effort and teleported behind him. Before the creature could even react to the move, Matthias activated the hidden claws within his gauntlets. Wrapping an arm around the lumbering creature's neck, he pierced the side of its throat, ending the wretch's life. The Verden fell to the ground like a sack of grain, leaving a very terrified and sobered up Imap standing before him, trembling. Retracting the claws and shaking the blood from his still curled hand as though nothing had happened at all, Matthias stepped towards the cowering reptilian creature.

"Never spill a First Assassin's drink without offering to buy him another. Remember this rule well, little one," he patted the shoulder of the shaken soldier.

"Is Matthias Teron on the premises?" a voice came from among the silenced crowd.

The assassin turned from where he was standing and faced the door where the caller was.

"I am, who calls for me?" Matthias straightened his posture.

"His lordship inquires for you. You are to follow me at once," the guard stated.

"Hm. Finally some real action." Matthias smirked and then turned back to the Imap, still standing beside the fallen Verden in a state of shock. "Make sure you clean the spilled drink from my table. I'll be back for a refill."

Mislantus did not need to wait long for the guard to return. Matthias was hard to miss with his dark blonde hair, goatee, and blue eyes. Compared to the band that commanded his fortress, he looked more like a prince from a fairy tale than a murdering assassin. That was one of his advantages and made him a formidable weapon for the warlord.

"My lord, you summoned me?" Matthias knelt before him, not daring to look his master in the eye without permission.

"Rise. I did," he replied, turning around from the window and casually walking over to the throne. "I summoned you because the moment for which you have been trained all your life has finally come."

Matthias rose slowly from his submissive stance as the breath in his lungs released itself slowly. His blue eyes were a pair of flickering orbs ablaze.

"The heirs. The ones you spoke of. They have been found?" he asked in a hushed tone.

"They have," Mislantus grinned with his pointed cat teeth. "But this will be more difficult than striking someone in the dark. The base requires a key, and only the heirs will have it. You will need to get close to them and gain their trust before you are able to get your claws dirty. Someone needs to have access from the inside."

"That will not be a problem, I assure you my lord," Matthias looked up at his liege. "I'm told I can look very trustworthy."

"Which is why I am sending you there," the tyrant said, handing Matthias the file. "Basic information has been compiled, as much as the science and observation division could gather. They seem to have magic shielding them, and he won't allow just anyone to get too close."

Matthias took in the information and allowed it to sink in. He knew of the one Mislantus spoke of. Everyone on the ship knew of the mage who was responsible for disfiguring their lord, the one they called Thanestorm.

"A mage does not frighten me," Matthias stated coldly. "What's he going to do? Throw fireballs at me?"

The tyrant chuckled upon hearing the tone of his soldier as he took a seat on his throne, fixing his cloak.

"Oh, I do so enjoy your confidence, Teron. But still I caution, be wary and be prepared," Mislantus warned him. "Once your task is complete, show no mercy. Kill them all."

"Yes Lord Mislantus. I will not fail you." Matthias bowed deep.

"Good. You have come far in the years you have been in my service. You are one of my finer warriors and now my number one assassin after the untimely demise of your mentor." The cat face grinned viciously, "You are dismissed."

Matthias nodded once more and turned on the heel of his boot, making his way for the door in a quick but sure stride. Mislantus watched him leave, the mechanical door gliding shut behind the assassin. He turned his gaze back to the small blue world floating innocently in space below, its inhabitants unaware of the predator that lay in wait above.

෩

Matthias walked down the corridor, his mind on the task that lay ahead of him when his train of though was interrupted.

"And where are you going?" the voice of a young girl questioned.

The assassin turned to see the owner of the voice, which was a young girl dressed in black leggings, high boots and a light brown tunic with a wide ornate belt. It was Sarina, the daughter of Mislantus. Unlike her own father, Sarina could pass for an Earth dweller with her deep auburn hair and large almond shaped brown eyes. She was about sixteen years old, unlike Matthias himself who was approaching thirty. Despite this, the two of them were close friends and Matthias regarded Sarina as his younger sister when Mislantus was not looking. His face did not however betray this notion when he turned to face her without a trace of emotion, said for stern discipline.

"I have been given orders to go to the planet Earth by Lord Mislantus," he stated.

"You mean the planet below?" Sarina asked with a spark of excitement in her eyes. Ever since they had entered orbit around the blue planet she had been filled with curiosity, studying as much as she could about its mysterious ways.

"Yes. I am to go on a mission to help in completing the quest our lordship embarked on so many years ago," he said, and then added, "It is our reason for being here and no, do not ask to come along. I can't afford to have any setbacks on this one. We are not here on vacation, much as you like to think that sometimes."

"Meanie," Sarina groaned over dramatically. "What happened to the old Matt? The one who used to be more fun?"

"He got old, I guess." Matthias stated, the corner of his mouth curling upwards ever slightly upon hearing Sarina call him by his nickname.

"And boring," she giggled. "Why is this mission so important anyways? From all of the others, I mean."

Matthias paused and took a minute to look around before turning back to the young girl. "Come with me to my quarters."

୫୦୧

Before more could be exchanged between the pair, Matthias and Sarina were in Matthias's quarters. The room held nothing significant about it with its dark grey walls and it almost looked dreary were it not for the large circular wall lights that illuminated it from all four corners. A large metallic dresser sat in the far corner of the room, across from which was a large black metal desk. Beside both of these was the bed, which the assassin sat down on. The files he had been carrying from his meeting with Mislantus were spread out on the covers moments after.

"So what's so secretive about all of this that you had to invite me into your room?" Sarina said as she took a seat on Matthias's bed.

"Because I am not sure if your father will approve of you knowing about this mission," he answered, flipping through the files. "Do you remember your father talking about the castle which is the Eye to all Worlds?"

"It's all he ever thinks about these days and his stupid plot to get revenge. I mean C'mon, he owns like over a dozen planets with loyal followers, what more does he need?" she snorted but seeing the look of disdain on Matthias's face made her change her tone, "Well, what about it?"

Matthias looked through the files and pulled out two photos, then handed them to Sarina. One was of a girl her age with chestnut hair and blue eyes. The other was of a boy with brown hair and green eyes. The two of them looked quite content, and she wondered why her father would want two children no older than herself assassinated.

"What's so dangerous about them? Do they sprout fangs and horns when no one's looking? They don't seem like much of a threat."

"They literally hold the keys to the kingdom," Matthias explained. "And they know where it's located. Castle Severio is its name, and those two are heirs to it. I need to get close to them in order to extract the necessary information about getting into the castle, and then eliminate them."

Sarina studied the pictures for a moment longer, pursing her lips in deep thought.

"You're going to need my help if you want to do that. No offense Matt, but you can come off as just being scary sometimes."

Matthias glared at her as if he did not understand what she meant. Her father had moments before said how trusting he looked and that was why he was sending him.

"You wear gauntlets with retractable claws," Sarina continued, "and a cape. You have a goatee and cold blue eyes. They don't exactly spell friendly if you get my drift. How do you expect to get close to people my age if you look like-"

"An assassin?"

"Exactly. That's why I should go with you. I can help you with this. I look way more innocent that you do."

"Out of the question," Matthias growled. "Your father would have my head on a spit faster than I can say die."

"Not if I suggest it," Sarina grinned, getting off the bed. "I'll go speak with him about it. Make sure my things are packed and ready to go, will you?"

Chapter 6

Annetta and Jason had split up to look around the base, Annetta going with Brakkus while Jason went with Puc. Though it was far too large to see in one night, they figured they would make the best of it and see as much as could be seen in a few hours.

Annetta walked alongside the large creature called a Hurtz. She'd learned that he was similar to the Bugbears or Hobgoblins in human folk-tale stories. They had existed on Earth as long as humans, but had nearly gone extinct in the middle ages from knights hunting them down as a perceived threat. Annetta could see why people would be afraid of someone like Brakkus, but she found it unfair. Already he was the friendliest and biggest chatterbox she had ever met.

"Do ye like horses, Annetta?" he asked, interrupting her stream of thought.

"Uhm. I guess, they're pretty cool," she said quietly.

"Well then this might interest ya." The Hurtz grinned as he opened a large steel door.

For a moment Annetta thought she was going to vomit from the smell. Then she realized where she recognized it from. It was the smell of a stable, like the one she had visited when she had gone on a trip with her class long ago to see harvesting in autumn. Brakkus went through the door and held it for Annetta, who stepped inside to see the entire interior was a wooden stable. Had Annetta not seen the room she was in before, she would have thought she had set foot in a farm in the middle of nowhere. Inside each of the stalls a horse's head watched the new arrivals with curiosity.

"These here are the descendants of yer grandfather's horses, who served him while he and your father looked after Severio Castle. Which I think I may need to take ya to once ya learn to ride," he said. "I'm guessing daddy never took ya to riding lessons did he?"

"We live in the middle of the city. Where would I find a horse?"

Brakkus said nothing to the comment and only smiled again. "A valid enough reason as any for not knowing how."

Annetta's eye was drawn to a beige horse in one of the further stalls. He seemed to be looking straight at Annetta as though he knew her.

Brakkus glanced over at the horse Annetta was gazing at and drew his mouth into another grin.

"You've a good eye, Annetta. That be the descendant of your grandfather's horse. His name is Bossman."

Annetta looked up at Brakkus then at the horse, who tossed his blonde mane and whinnied.

"What kind of a name is Bossman?" she asked.

"Well I could ask ya what kind of a name is Annetta," the Hurtz chuckled. "It's the kind of name the horse of the boss man has."

Annetta realized the pun and smiled a bit as they approached the horse. Bossman poked his head out of the stall and looked at them as they advanced. He snorted when he looked at Brakkus and tossed his head about.

"Oi! I know what ya want," Brakkus reached into his pocket and pulled out a sugar cube that he gave to him, "Never miss an opportunity do ya?"

He turned to Annetta after giving the horse the cube. "What do ya think about me teaching you to ride?"

Annetta looked up at the horse and then back to Brakkus. Though she was slightly intimidated by the massive beast, she had a feeling there was no turning back at this point and she would have to grab the bull by the horns...or the horse by the mane in this case.

"I say go for it," she grinned.

The Hurtz smiled back at her with his large pointy teeth. "Truly the granddaughter of Lord Orbeyus Severio."

ೋ೦ಇ

Jason and Puc walked through the base together in silence, their earlier spat hanging over them. It was not even that either of them wanted to hold a grudge, it was just that neither of them now knew where to start over. The only noise to be heard as they walked was the rhythmic hitting of the staff on the steel floor.

"So, you knew Annetta's grandfather and her father?" Jason finally broke silence.

Puc did not even turn to look as Jason as he walked and continued onward but spoke none the less, "Yes. And I knew your father as well, an accomplished warrior and psychic."

"Okay, but here's what I don't understand. If my dad is such a great warrior and such an accomplished psychic, then why is he locked up in an asylum right now and why was he a useless drunk when I needed him." Jason couldn't keep the bitterness out of his words.

Puc paused dead in his tracks and looked back at Jason, staring him down with his pale blue eyes.

"Some people cannot handle learning of this life and being given the right to be here, then learning they must go back to the reality they are from. Your father, brilliant as he was, could not take it any longer. He had seen things most people only confront in their dreams and nightmares. In order to forget, he turned to drinking. At first it was once a day, but I was there and I saw it escalate into him wanting to be numb all the time in order to escape his demons."

The elf looked out into the open space before them. Nothing could be seen for miles around but the cold blue steel walls and floor of the corridor in which the two of them stood.

"You see Jason, when you entered into this knowledge, the world around you changed. From the moment that one knows anything is possible, a whole new world of fear opens up right before their eyes. Some are able to cope with living in both worlds, but others are unable to stand with one foot in either world. Your father could not balance both, and began to believe that only one world could exist and that he should be the one to make it so."

Jason looked down at his feet. If what Puc had said was true and his father had been unable to live with the knowledge of another world, then would the same thing happen to him? Maybe he'd made a mistake by going along with Annetta.

"Is something the matter?" Puc asked him breaking the silence.

The boy shifted uneasily, "I was just thinking. What if I'm just like him?"

"You fear that you will crumble? Like father, like son? No, I do not believe that will be the case. You are already aware of what happened to your father. You know it drove him insane. I see by the way you think, the way you try to make light of everything, and the way in which you speak of your father that you are stronger than he was. You are also aware of the danger which will help in safeguarding you against it."

Puc then continued to walk forward towards their destination.

"And remember, you have others to whom you may speak about whatever it is that bothers you. A faithful friend is a strong defense."

Jason looked up at the elf and nodded before continuing to follow him.

"To your left, that corridor leads to the training grounds. That is where I shall be instructing you and Annetta on using your abilities. Past that is the medical wing, let's hope you do not end up there too often. Straight ahead is what we call the common room, a big area with couches and tables where people would socialize. There are other corridors that lead to exits to other areas around the world, but those will be of no use to you until you learn to teleport on your own. It would otherwise take days to get there, and I would rather only use portal magic when necessary, for it could attract the wrong types of attention. If you go past the common room, there is the armory to the right. Beyond that the spaceship docking area, close to which is the actual laboratory, and to the right is another key feature, the living quarters. This is where you may stay, if you so choose."

"Geeze, with all the gadgets here it's like a mad scientists lab you'd think," Jason said looking around.

"Well Orbeyus did always call it his 'lab' when referring to it in casual conversation so those around him would not know what he spoke of," Puc stated as they continued walking while deep in thought, "A practice I would advise both you and Annetta to adopt for safety reasons. No one and I mean no one must know of this."

Nodding, Jason followed Puc down the hallway where he had pointed out the living quarters. Nothing seemed unusual about the hallway from the rest of the base. Were it not for there being slight creases in the metal on the walls Jason would not have noticed that there were doors. He looked further down the wall to notice a block sticking out with a flat dark glass surface on it.

"The rooms are customizable," Puc explained. "You place your hand on the glass and once the door opens everything you need will be inside as you wished it to be."

"You're kidding me, right?" Jason blinked looking at the block, "So this thing. It reads my mind and when the door opens my room has everything I want inside of it?"

"It reads what you require to have in your living space, so I suppose you can say that," Puc said. "Orbeyus made them this way so that his warriors would have all they needed to prepare for battle. For example, when I created my room I required spell books and other mage materials which would be otherwise very hard to acquire."

Jason nodded, looking at the little silver box. He wanted to know how it worked, but all the questions piling up in his head were overwhelming. He was still having a hard time accepting it all, and part of him just wanted to yell at everything and to make it stop. But he knew that Puc was not interested in listening to him whine about how this was all too much for him, so he did his best to keep up with the elf.

"So I just put my hand on it?" Jason asked, reaching out towards the block.

"Yes, it uses the subconscious to pick out what is needed. You may find things in the room you had not even thought would be useful." the elf told him, leaning on his staff.

The boy nodded and placed his hand on the cold block. There was a momentary flash of blue over where he'd placed it. Seconds later, the steel door slid sideways out of view. Jason stepped through the doorway, into darkness. He looked from side to side and saw the silhouette of a light switch, then flipped it on.

It felt as though he had stepped into a dream. The walls were a deep red covered with what looked like graffiti designs. To one side there was an enormous television screen, and on the other wall was a large bed with deep blue sheets that contrasted the red on the walls. On the far wall there was a large bookshelf filled with books and cases of films, things Jason had always wanted to have. He stared wide-eyed for a few moments, taking in everything he was seeing. It was how he had always wanted his room to look back in the home he lived with his mother and younger sibling.

"You've very colorful tastes," Puc finally broke the silence as he came inside, "The rooms I was accustomed to seeing were much more...war ready. But of course, I forget that you are still a young boy. No matter. The rooms warp and change as you get older and become filled with what you desire and need."

"It's incredible," Jason breathed, looking at everything. He walked over to the bed and flopped down onto it. "I wish I could stay here, but I know my mom will get worried if I do."

Puc stood some distance away, still close to the door as though the sight of the room made him uncomfortable. After a moment of thought, he looked at the boy and said, "She will worry more once she sees the card key. She knew your father, and all his secrets."

Jason looked up at the elf from the bed. "Really? Then how come she called the nut house to get him taken away?"

"It is not that simple." Puc peered at Jason with genuine concern. "This is something no one will ever tell you face to face, but I will if only for the sake of getting to the point. Your father did not know when to stop when it came to his obsession, and it reached a point where he was a danger to himself and to his family. It needed to end, but your mother could not go through with it. She knew that if people thought him insane his ranting would go unnoticed, and he would be able to live along with all of you. She made the greatest sacrifice there is in the name of the people she loved to keep all of them safe."

Jason sat up on the bed, listening. In all honesty, this didn't sound much like the mother he knew. She was harsh and she was strict. It was a miracle he was even friends with Annetta, the way his mother hated her. He was now beginning to understand why. She did not hate Annetta or his father. Instead she hated the world she was forced to acknowledge because of them. Though Jason tried to hold it back, he felt tears well up in his eyes. He always had to be tough, but he just couldn't take it anymore. Folding his head into his hands he tried to hold back tears.

Puc, not sure how to respond to such an outburst of emotion, kept his distance while he analyzed how to respond to the situation. He usually strived to stay away from them, his mind more focused on the rational in a situation. He walked over to the boy and placed a hand on his shoulder in an effort to comfort him.

"Let it out," he said, uncertain of the right words.

Jason did his best to regain some of his composure, but the tears kept flowing from his eyes and so he did not look up at the mage when he spoke, "She always acted like she couldn't even stand to think of him."

"Sometimes, when you truly love someone, you need to let them go," Puc told him. "She loved your father just as she loves you and your brother, but she knew that if he stayed you would all be in danger. She had to make the sacrifice of letting him go in order to save you."

"She's always acted like she hated him. Like she hated me for being friends with Annetta. But now it makes sense. I-I feel like such a child..."

Puc sighed and rubbed the boy's shoulder, the motion so foreign to him that he felt the need to stop and turned to look at him.

"You are still a boy, Jason. Even in older age you will find that there will be mistakes that are made. What you must be able to do is pick yourself up and seek forgiveness."

Jason looked up through his tear-streaked face at the elf, still shaky from the revelation. There was something comforting in the cold tone of voice.

"Yeah, I guess," he said quietly. "And I take it back, you're not so weird after all."

"Well, that's progress, then," smirked the elf.

Chapter 7

Having put on one of her finer dresses, a high cut dark emerald gown decorated with blood red stones and a pale green shall to go along with it, Sarina waited for the guards to come back with her father's reply about an audience. She sighed, remembering the many times he had dismissed her without even laying eyes on her. Sometimes, it was because he was having a bad day. Mostly, it was because he was reliving memories of the past. She was used to it. The only daughter of Mislantus the Threat had to be. Smoothing out the creases on her dress, she looked down at her feet and heard the sound of a mechanical door gliding open moments later.

"Lady Sarina, Lord Mislantus will hold audience with you now," the baritone voiced Verden announced as he bowed low to the princess, locked up in the confines of her room.

Rising, Sarina put on the metaphorical mask she was expected to wear, and looked at the rhinoceros-like creature.

"About time you blundered back," she hissed. "Didn't they ever teach you a lady does not like to be kept waiting?"

The Verden soldier began to loosen his jaw in response, before the fiery brown eyes of the princess ensnared him once more.

"I will have your head for this when this meeting is through," she snarled. Storming out, she made her way down to the throne room where her father spent the majority of his time.

ഇരു

Mislantus sat on the throne with his eyes closed. He did not need to wait long to hear the sound of the door gliding open. His cat ears pricked up, followed by the dilating of his slit pupils as a huffing and puffing Verden soldier entered the room, covered in sweat.

"Your lordship...Lady Sarina...has arrived," he wheezed, trying to get everything in with one sentence.

Mislantus ignored the sloppiness of the soldier and dismissed him with the wave of a hand, feeling it unnecessary to waste any energy on the brute who would sooner or later end up dead anyways. His eyes then focused on the door, as a specter in dark green entered the room, her skin pale as a ghost.

Curtsying, Sarina rose to face the man who wore the title of her father. No more a man but a creature half feline, and half of what he once was.

"Good evening father," she bowed her head low, not looking into his eyes, never once daring to challenge them.

"Sarina, my most beautiful flower veiled in thorns." He grinned viciously. "Tell me, what brings you here?"

"A request, my lord," she said, her eyes still averted.

"Speak your terms and perhaps it shall be granted," he spoke quickly, his vision wandering away from his daughter and out the large glass windows as dawn lit the blue planet anew. "What is it your heart desires so?"

Sarina bit her lip as the tension lifted from her body as Mislantus's gaze wandered. It gave her a moment to compose herself and to think about what needed to be said next. Words needed to be chosen carefully when dealing with him. Smoothing out the long dress again, she glided towards him and seated herself like a child on the steps leading to his elevated throne.

"My heart yearns for knowledge of the enemy we face," she said. "I wish to know who it is that pains you so, even after all these years and all the triumphs Valdhar and her master Lord Mislantus have risen to."

"Then go to the cultural division of the science department and research there," Mislantus answered promptly. "Do not come bothering me with idle questions."

Sarina sighed. The first approach having failed, it was time to activate her second plan. Her stare momentarily shifted to the silhouette of the blue planet, the intense rays of the sun causing it to look black in the lifeless space around them. She turned back to the man who was her father, his feline eyes locked upon the shape. She needed to get his attention now, while the hypnotic link between voyeur and object was still relatively weak.

"I know about the two children," she spoke sharply, rising to stand beside him.

"What of them?" Mislantus huffed, his gaze not moving.

"I know for a fact that Matthias will fail if he does not take me with him because he does not stand a chance of getting half as close as I can if I am there with him." Sarina bit her lip repeatedly as soon as the sentence left her. This was as close to honesty as a conversation with her father would ever get.

Mislantus's eyes widened, the cat head whipped to the side locked upon her, a predatory gaze transfixed in them.

"And where did you hear about that? That was classified information," he snarled.

"Father, you forget that I'm your little girl sometimes, don't you?" She smiled, innocently. "I overheard Lloyd talking to someone when I was, as you said yourself before, researching who it is we are going up against."

Mislantus's jaw slacked as he leaned back in the throne, his quiet contemplation taken away.

"And why is it exactly you think the plan will fail, since you know all about it?" Mislantus asked, focused upon her.

"Simple, they're young like me," she said, weaving the words in an intricate blanket of thought as she went along. "If you had to choose between trusting a person who was similar to you, or someone older and different, whose interest in you baffles you, who would you chose? I would trust someone closer to my age over someone who is a lot older and could be a threat if they do not act the right way."

"Not a problem, we can de-age Matthias to look younger with a spell," Mislantus said in a dismissive manner.

"Magic guards them, or something does at least, does it not?" Sarina interrupted. She knew she was overstepping her boundaries, but it was the only way. "If there is magic, who is to say the wards you place on Matthias will not diminish? It could cost you your best assassin. Let me prove myself to you, father. Let me go with Matthias to this strange blue world. Let me do what you never had a chance to do for your own father. I yearn for approval, and sitting locked up in my room gives me none. Let me plunge the dagger into the heart of the heir of Orbeyus."

Seeing she had not driven the point home just yet, she pushed further. "I yearn for the blood of your enemies."

The green and gold feline eyes looked at the girl in judgment. The gears in Mislantus's head then clicked into place. Rising, he walked over to his daughter and placed an arm around her shoulder. He pulled her into a one armed embrace, caressing her hair gently with his fingers.

"Sarina, my dear little gem, if there was one thing Orbeyus and I agreed upon, it was that children are truly remarkable beings," he said to her in a low tone. "We do not realize they are making grown up decisions until after the fact. If blood is what you yearn for, then I give you my blessing to go forth and claim it."

⚘

Since the day was almost done, the four companions met up at the gate to see Jason and Annetta off to the Severio apartment. Annetta and Brakkus had made it to the gates first and were chatting together. Puc and Jason arrived later, more quietly than the Hurtz and the girl.

"Oh there you guys are. What took you so long?" Annetta greeted them.

"We had a bit of a delay," Jason told her. "What happened to you?"

Annetta smelt of a barn. On top of that, she looked like she had been thrown about, seeing as there were bits of hay in her hair. Despite this, there was a big grin on her face.

"I was trying to put a saddle on a horse and then get on it. It's a lot harder than it looks in the movies," Annetta laughed, "And once you're up there it hurts just to sit. I don't know how people ride horses."

"Ya forget they have tons of practice," Brakkus chuckled. "Don't worry, little lass. I'll make a rider of ya yet."

"Uhm, okay," Annetta cringed pulling out a piece of hay from her hair. "Just one step at a time if you don't mind."

Jason chuckled, happy to see his friend was having a good time. He turned to Puc. "So how do we get back? I don't see anything that would let us use the card keys."

"The teleporter to go out is not located outside the doors," Puc explained. "A secondary precaution in case someone who was not meant to come down did."

He then walked over to a slanted rectangular block that seemed to be welded into the side of the metallic frame. It looked like the hand-scanning device Jason had encountered, only taller and with a slit going through the side of it.

"Swipe your card along the side of the frame and the teleporter will take you home. I advise you to go one at a time until you are used to the sensation."

Jason and Annetta nodded before turning back to the block. Annetta swiped her card, then watched the two pads appeared before her like in her apartment. She took a final glance at her new friends and at the world that had become a part of her own.

"I guess I'll be back tomorrow." She smiled lightly.

"Tomorrow it shall be." Puc nodded, bowing. "But before you go I have one important thing I must impose on the both of you."

The children turned around to face the ever-stern elf.

"I know full well the vision you received from the angels, you're not the only ones they came to and I request that for the time being, you do not tell your parents of what you saw this day," he said with utmost seriousness, "Not a single word. It is important that they do not know of it."

"Why not?" Annetta asked.

"Unnecessary worry about things which can still be changed and therefore will not come to past," he explained, "There is no point about worrying about a future that shall never be."

Annetta and Jason nodded their heads in understanding, Annetta's gaze then falling on the Hurtz.

"And be ready," Brakkus said, grinning a toothy grin. "I'll be teaching ya to ride tomorrow."

"Until tomorrow then, rest easy," Puc acknowledged their leave.

Saying nothing more, Annetta entered a single digit on the keyboard. Closing her eyes, she felt a sensation like falling down a roller coaster. For a moment it became so intense she thought she would vomit. Fortunately, it was over quickly. Opening her eyes, she found herself standing in her room in the dark. Remembering Jason would be there moments later, she moved over and watched as he appeared in the same spot.

"I'm not sure what's worse, going down or coming up," he said, squirming as he held his stomach.

"Maybe it won't be so bad once we get used to it." Annetta smiled weakly, trying to reassure her friend.

Her father walked into the frame of the door. "How was the trip?" he asked.

"Surreal," Jason answered, still feeling queasy. "Could I...please use the bathroom?"

Arieus nodded and entered the room, flicking on the switch as the boy passed him. He grinned at Annetta, still covered in hay. "You need a shower before you even think about going to bed, miss."

"I wouldn't have it any other way," she replied. "Smelling like horse all the time isn't fun."

"You get used to it after a while," he sighed. "I assume you met Brakkus."

"And Puc, too," Annetta told him.

"Puc is still around?" Arieus raised his eyebrows. "I could have sworn he said he wanted nothing more to do with the Lab right before I left. I guess your grandpa had something to do with it."

"He seems to have a lot to do with things," Annetta muttered as Jason came out of the bathroom. "You okay?" She added.

"Yeah. Just need to practice going up and down is all." He groaned before looking at his watch. "Oh man, I need to get home. My mom is going to kill me."

"I'll drive you home. You can tell your mom the movie ran late," Arieus told him, "Unless you want her to know the truth."

"Thanks. I think I'll stick with the alibi for now. I'm not sure how my mother would react to finding out I'm becoming involved with the very same thing that locked my father away."

"Understandable." Arieus nodded, casting down his eyes as he did so and then turned to his daughter. "Annetta, will you be coming with us?"

"Uh. Yeah, sure. If it's okay that the car is going to smell like a stable."

"That's what air fresheners and windows are for," Arieus chuckled, taking out his keys and heading for the door.

∞∞

No one spoke of the events that had happened that day. It could almost have been a normal car ride were it not for the card key in Jason's pocket. At that moment, he was trying to think of a way to sit down with his mother and talk of what he had learned about his father. The subject was taboo to her. He needed a strategy to let her know that he knew the truth and that she did not need to hide it anymore.

Annetta also was swimming in her own thoughts, too occupied to be in any sort of conversation with Jason or her father. She appeared to be adjusting well to the situation, but there was much in her head that felt out of place. She didn't want to make Jason feel the same way, so she hid it. She had enjoyed learning about horses from Brakkus, who really was a gentle giant, but she wasn't sure of what lay ahead. She had said yes of course but she had not comprehended what everything meant until she was standing before those doors. She was after all, a sixteen-year-old girl in the middle of her high school education. What did she know of the supernatural world? She had read and daydreamed, but that counted for nothing. Deep down inside, she was scared, and simply tried to act tough.

"There we are," Arieus said, attempting to break the silence as they pulled up to the townhouse where Jason lived. "Much faster than walking, I like to think."

Jason snapped out of his train of thought and looked over at the still pensive Annetta. "Yeah, definitely faster. Thanks, Mr. Severio." Jason smiled at Arieus then turned to Annetta. "See you tomorrow at school."

"Yeah, have a good night. Are we going down tomorrow?" she asked, trying to sound casual.

"As long as my mom doesn't find out, and doesn't ground me or anything."

"Just tell her we have a project or something."

"Yeah, that's always an option. Night." Jason closed the door of the car and walked up to the building.

Annetta sighed when the door shut and felt a wave of tension hit the car. She realized it was coming from her father. He'd been hiding it since she had come home with the card keys. Now in the privacy of the car without her friend present it was finally coming out.

Arieus shifted the gears into reverse and did a three point turn out of the parking lot in silence. His face illuminated by the streetlights, as he drove out onto the road, seemed much older and wearier.

"Dad...is everything okay?"

"Yes, everything is fine. Why?" He avoided her gaze as the car passed by an array of streets.

"You seem upset. I mean, Mom was upset when she saw the card keys. She said something about you saying it was over."

Arieus sighed as they rolled up to a stop sign. He looked over at his daughter in the other seat.

"Your grandfather didn't die of natural causes, Annetta. He was murdered. I was out with you when it happened and it was only because he was nearby that I heard the yelling. But when I got there it was too late." He said all this extremely quietly. "There is much you need to learn about the Lab and about everything you are getting involved in. It is not something that can be learned in one day, but one thing you need to understand is that this is not a game and it's not like in the books you read."

"But Dad, I don't get why you're so worried. I mean, nothing bad really happened after you left. Didn't you say grandpa protected the world from evil? As in stopped it?"

"Annetta, there is always evil in the world. That is the first thing you need to learn. There can be no good without evil to stabilize it, nor any evil without good to defy it. That is just the way of life. It lies dormant now, but sooner or later you might be asked to do exactly what your grandfather and I did. Believe me, Annetta. I don't know what I would be capable of if anything ever happened to you or Xander or your mother."

Annetta felt the same sensation she had before of her ears flattening against her skull if she were a small animal and looked over at her father then down to her feet, trying to think of what to say to him.

"I'm sorry I'm such a disappointment, Dad." She exhaled deeply.

"Disappointment? Where did that come from, Annie?" he raised an eyebrow, still keeping his eyes on the road.

"For not being stronger. For not being more prepared for this," she muttered.

"Annetta, I left all of that so you would not need to be stronger or prepared for it. Why would I expect something like that of you?" Arieus pulled into the parking lot beneath the apartment building and parked the car before continuing.

"I will admit, the part of me that's your father is not very happy. But you need to understand, it's because I'm worried for your safety. But I'll always worry for you until the day I die. It's my job."

Annetta lowered her head upon hearing this. She felt horrible for making her father feel this way. Even if he was saying it was not her fault.

"I will say, however, I am very proud of you. I never thought I would see that card key again, much less in your hands. I will do my best to be there and help you through this when I can. You need to know, though, that most of this needs to be done on your own. This is your quest and I cannot take it from you."

Annetta nodded her head. Her father had been the one to introduce her to the world of fantasy and medieval history when she was a little girl. He had also taught her the importance of a hero's quest. She could tell he was talking about it now. The quest tested the hero in various situations and it was meant to shape who they would become in the future.

෨෬

After showering, changing, and saying goodnight to her parents, Annetta settled into bed. But she couldn't sleep. She thought long and hard about the events of that day. The angels, the Lab, Puc, Brakkus, and the truth about her grandfather were all overwhelming. On top of that, she would have to go back to school tomorrow and still pay attention to what the teachers were saying. Forcing her eyes shut, Annetta tried to go to sleep and allow the things she had discovered to be taken over by dreams.

ℬℛ

Once both children had left the Lab, Puc strode back into the depths of the base, followed by Brakkus.

"Lovely bunch of kids, don't ya think? I like that Annetta, she's a bright one." Brakkus grinned to his companion. "Doesn't say no, no matter how hard."

"Keep in mind this is just the beginning. You will see how their demeanors will change once the thrill wears off." Puc warned him as they continued to walk. "It is nice to finally not be tripping over ones robes, though."

"Ye don't dress practically is all, mage. I'd send ya into the trenches and see how long yer skirt would last." Brakkus couldn't help but burst out laughing from the last part, evading a hard slap from the lower part of Puc's staff.

Puc rolled his eyes, knowing his bestial friend's intentions were only meant to lighten his spirits. Hearing something faint resembling footsteps, however, the mage stopped and turned around, silencing the Hurtz. Gripping his staff with both hands, he dropped into an attack position, along with his companion. Thrusting the staff forward, a ray of light emitted from its tip illuminating the area. He withdrew moments later when he saw who it was.

"My apprentice," Puc said, lowering his guard and the staff. "What brings you down here at this time?"

The youth standing before him nodded, handing Puc an envelope. Puc accepted the package and opening it, he found himself looking at photographs of space. At first the images were faint, only a blur of stars. It was not until he began flipping to the enlargements that he noticed what the reason behind the visit was. Though small and distorted, it was the shape of a fortress Puc had grown all too familiar with. The elf felt the blood drain from his face.

"Not now," he managed to say.

Brakkus took in the images on the photographs, the long ears flattening at the sight of them. He knew what it meant.

"He's here," the apprentice assured his master.

Chapter 8

Annetta and Jason spent the next week venturing into Q-16 to meet with Brakkus and Puc, learning small bits and pieces of their abilities and their inheritance. Before they knew it, both of them were able to manipulate objects with strong emotional force, and not very effectively. They were able to communicate with one another through the use of what had been explained to them as being telepathy. Though it was all done in a magic controlled environment under Puc's supervision, it was a start, and enough to make the mage promise to start training them seriously, instead of offering cryptic instructions. It made Annetta slightly worried, though. If what they were trying to learn now was horsing around, then what would they be learning when their proper training began? One night, Jason had accidentally thrown Annetta into a wall while trying to pass her a ball using only his mind. She was lucky to not have broken anything, but she had bruised quite a bit.

Their mornings however, were no different from the days before this had begun. Annetta's mother finished coffee and toast before running off, while Xander chomped on his cereal. Her father had already left for work and Annetta tried to make some lunch for school while the commotion went on around her. The events of the day before would be all but pushed to the back of her mind like some surreal dream in a dream. She was reminded of the reality of it when she went to grab her bag and saw the card key on her dresser.

Later in the week, while grabbing her coat and keys, Annetta rushed out of the apartment, pulling on her sneakers as she went, to get to the stairs in order to avoid waiting for the elevator.

"Hey sis, wait up!" Xander called, trying to catch up.

"You gotta be quicker than that," she sighed, holding the door for him as he went into the stairwell.

"I know, but I had to finish eating."

"Did you at least brush your teeth after?" Annetta raised an eyebrow as she adjusted her t-shirt and jean jacket from under her backpack. Xander only grinned sheepishly, then stuck out a piece of gum on his tongue to show her.

"One of these days you're going to get cavities. You know that, right?"

"I know, but I didn't want to walk by myself to school, it's more fun with you, sis."

"You need to know that I have to get to my school on time, so I need to leave early. You also need to get used to the idea that I'm going to have to go away university or college in a few years. It's not going to be a two minute walk from your school to mine, then what are you going to do?"

"I'll go to college with you?" he grinned again and ran ahead on the stairs in front of her, "Race you to the bottom!"

Before Annetta could open her mouth, Xander was already three flights of stairs ahead of her. From above, he looked like a black haired bobbing head with a bulging backpack that swayed behind him as he ran.

"Not fair! You had a head start!" Annetta glared at him, then followed.

Xander waited for Annetta while she caught up with him. A triumphant smile plastered across his face in the form of a wide grin.

"You lost, I win," he beamed.

"More like you cheated," she growled.

Darius waited in the lobby, observing the two of them as they came out of the stairwell. "What's taking you guys so long? By the time we get there people are gonna be lining up to get inside."

"Why are you so eager to get to school all of a sudden?" Annetta asked him.

Darius adjusted his bag as they began walking to the entrance and looked over at her, "To avoid running into Finn outside."

"Why? It's not like you're the one he got into a fight with." She followed him as they exited the building and headed to the school.

"I know, but your dad wasn't too happy about you getting into a fight with him."

Annetta rolled her eyes at the comment, brushing it off. "Thanks for the concern, but I can take care of myself if you haven't noticed."

"I have, I'm just saying it's an option." Darius stated, and making their way past the last set of doors they wandered outside into the streets.

Annetta said nothing back to him and continued on her way to school. Darius had the irritating habit of trying to sound smarter than her, despite stating the obvious most of the time. Today she was not in the mood to listen to him, especially with recent events occupying her thoughts.

Silver Birch High School was like any typical high school in the greater Toronto area. It consisted of an immense industrial building with a large track towards the back of the structure, and portables located close to the rear exit of the school.

After dropping off Xander, Annetta and Darius came out from the rear entrance that separated the townhouses with a fence from the outer area where the track was located. If they zig- zagged through the townhouses, a shortcut would present itself. They'd discovered the path in their first year of high school and had been using it ever since in order to avoid the crowded long way which was usually filled with more students coming from other areas of the surrounding houses.

"You guys are early today. What happened?" Jason greeted them once they had reached the inside of the fence.

"Trying to avoid an encounter with Finn." Annetta said. "You seen him around?"

"No, I think he might have gotten suspended, actually. You okay after last night?" Jason asked.

"What happened?" Darius prodded.

"Nothing. We just ran into some guys after school who weren't too nice." Annetta quickly came up with the story before Jason could say anything.

"Did you get into another fight?"

"No, they just said some things to us. But we didn't pay attention to them-," Annetta was saved by the bell ringing, and began walking inside.

Darius frowned and looked at Jason, silently asking what happened. But the only response he got from him was a shrug of the shoulder, before he moved forward to catch up with Annetta.

ഇരോ

After reaching their first period English class, Annetta did her best to pay attention to the announcements on the PA system, and stood tall during the national anthem. But her mind was racing, traveling back to the events of the days before and to what the future held that night after school. She understood why people might lose track of reality when they had knowledge of the other world. It was far more appealing than sitting in a classroom learning how to write an essay. After the anthem finished, she sat down. Pulling out her agenda, she began doodling in the side margin while she waited quietly for the teacher to call her name. Annetta had always loved to draw, especially when she got to draw anything fantasy related. Of late, she had been practicing drawing people, never having been good at human anatomy. A certain figure had become her muse. She was a tall woman, with long hair past her shoulders. She wore silver armor and wielded a long sword. Accompanying her was a great fire-breathing dragon with bat wings and massive curved horns.

"Annetta Severio?" the teacher called out, checking the attendance list.

"Present," she managed to say, almost lost in her own thoughts.

The teacher, Ms. Quixote, a woman in her mid thirties with fiery curly hair, green eyes framed in thin black horn rimmed glasses, and a pin stripe suit, looked up at her for a moment, noting the dazed response, but shook her head and moved on.

"Please pull out the written assignments due today, and I will have a few of you read them to the class."

Annetta felt herself freeze as she went for her English folder. Had she done the assignment? She barely even remembered getting it. She scrambled through the mass of papers in the folder, but found nothing. Finally it came to her, and she slipped out of her desk to the back. She carefully unzipped her bag and took out her nearly identical Math folder.

"Is something the matter, Annetta? I don't remember giving you permission to go to your bag," the teacher said, looking up at her as a few of the students snickered in the background at the flabbergasted girl.

"Oh, sorry Mrs. Quixote I mixed up my folders." Annetta made a quick recovery as she looked innocently at her teacher, waving the assignment to show as proof.

"Very well, would you like to share it with the class, since you're already up?"

Annetta looked at her peers and swallowed hard. She was not popular with them, due to her unique set of interests, and her head always being in the clouds. It wasn't that she was particularly picked on, despite the occasional fight. She just knew where her hobbies were not welcome. Her teacher however left her little choice.

"Sure, I can read my assignment."

She shuffled to the front without another word, listening to the buzz of her classmates chatting amongst themselves, showing no interest. Standing at the front and moving the hair from her face, she sighed and looked to her teacher for the sign to begin.

"Whenever you are ready Annetta," the teacher said from her desk, looking down at her marking sheets and giving a short glare to the class, who now sat quietly.

"Okay, I did my descriptive paragraph on a castle." Annetta introduced her assignment in a shaky voice, then looked down at the paper and started to read. "The outside of the massive stone structure towers over all that lies around it with its impressive frame of grey granite and veins of mortar, which bind it to the earth it inhabits. Around it lies a moat of still, crystal clear water, and the only way to get inside is through an immense gate of solid ancient oak which has stood as its guard for hundreds of years."

Annetta continued to read the paragraph, but her mind was still focused elsewhere. This time, it was not because she longed to go back to Q-16. This time, it was in order to avoid the humiliation of having to read her homework to a classroom of peers who viewed her as strange. Finishing up the last sentence, Annetta looked away from her paper as fake applause came from her classmates. A sigh escaped her lips as the pressure of the moment passed.

"Very well written, Annetta. Have you ever been inside of a castle?" her teacher asked.

"No, Ms. Quixote, I haven't," Annetta answered. "I've only read about them in books and seen them in movies."

"Well you have a very rich imagination then, Annetta, I've been inside some of the castles in England, and they're just as you described. Thank you for sharing. Now who would like to go next?"

Annetta took no more than a few seconds to go back to her desk and slump back in her seat beside Jason. He smiled at her, and then turned back to the front to listen to the other presentations. Annetta slouched and rested her chin on her arms while she looked at the picture she had been doodling earlier. Picking up her pen she went back at it trying to forget the embarrassment from moments before. A piece of folded up paper landed beside her hand and picking it up she opened it to see the words 'good job' written in crooked writing across it. She smiled, looking over at Jason who gave her a thumbs up. Deep down, she was sure she would have lost it already if she didn't have him for a friend.

ʔʘ⊃⊂

The bell rang for second lunch and everyone piled out of the classrooms to go to their next destination. Annetta and Jason fought their way through the crowd, having just come out of history. They did their best in trying not to be pushed around too much and to not come into contact with any of their peers whom they had just been in class with. Annetta especially was not in the mood for confrontation, still dwelling upon the morning class. Stepping outside the red doors, the two of them made their way towards the track to their usual back corner where they had lunch when the weather was nice. The different parts of the school held different kinds of people. The popular kids usually occupied the portables and the area behind the school. The sports fanatics who usually played some form of soccer when the weather was warm occupied the middle of the track, while younger students usually occupied the corner of the track beyond the ditch close to the parking lot. The corner by the fenced entrance usually remained empty as anyone seen there without a note saying they could leave school for lunch was automatically suspended, so Annetta and her friends were left with the other corner of the fence in the very back to themselves.

Coming to a halt, Annetta leaned against the fence, looping her fingers through it.

"She always does that to me," she growled, her thoughts going back to the morning.

"It's because she likes your work. Don't take it as a bad thing," Jason told her.

"I don't like reading it, because I know the others don't like it."

"Well, screw them. Besides, we got two more years here and we're done, off to university or college and half of those guys are gonna be working in fast food or pumping gas for customers for the rest of their lives."

"I know but-," Annetta was cut off when she noticed someone coming towards them. He had messy black hair, and his bronze skin could be picked up almost anywhere around the school. Richard Finn had a reputation as the kind of person who picked fights with those he viewed as less than himself, particularly students in younger grades. Annetta had of late become a thorn in his side, preventing him from doing this and thus solidifying her place in his mind as his antagonist. Sighing, they turned to face him.

"Thought you were pretty smart talking about the castle, didn't ya?"

"What's it to you?" Annetta gave him a cold glare, "Not my fault all you know how to describe is the sound of your face hitting the pavement when this is over."

Before Finn could say anything else, Jason shot them both a glance, then motioned towards the vice principal chatting away with some custodians close by about branches that needed to be cut from some of the trees because they were too low. Both of them froze where they stood, shifting the looks on their faces to more pleasant ones, like they were engaging in civilized conversation. They had all learned that fights were best left between students. Once the vice principal was gone, the two of them picked up where they left off.

"I remember I had you cornered last time." Finn glared at her, fists balled.

Annetta ground her teeth as she tried to think of a rebuttal fit for pushing Finn over the edge, proving he knew nothing but how to use his brawn. Sadly, nothing was coming to mind and her pride wasn't allowing her to back down.

"If you want a rematch, fine. But we're gonna do this without any teachers interfering," she said. "After school, meet me at the back gate."

"Sounds good to me. I'll be there." Finn smirked as the bell rang and students walked back towards the school. He went with them, paying no more attention to Annetta and Jason.

"Are you nuts?" Jason glared at her as they walked towards the crowd that was heading in. "He's going to kill you and this time there's no teachers to bail you out!"

"He's not killing anyone. And he's going to get exactly what he deserves."

"How exactly do you plan to do that?" Jason stopped dead in his tracks.

"With a bit of psychic intervention." Annetta grinned.

"What? But you don't even know how to use it fully," Jason said, pushing through the crowd.

Annetta turned her head slightly so she could see Jason's face and cast her eyes down to a discarded old soda can. The can flew across the yard and hit a portable.

"I can't always control it. But I kinda know how to make it work," she said to him as they began to move inside.

"What? I'm pretty sure someone is going to notice if there is a guy flying across the school yard."

"Not if I make it look like he's just being hit by me."

"I don't think this is a good idea, Annetta. And I'm pretty sure Puc won't like it either if you just go around blasting people across school property."

"Puc doesn't need to know anything. Besides, how's he going to find out when he's at the bottom of the ocean?" Annetta stated as they entered the classroom.

"I guess. But I still don't think it's a good idea. We should just take the long way home and avoid running into him."

Annetta glared at Jason. It was the look she gave when she was not going to give up or back down from a challenge. Exhaling in resignation, he said nothing more to her as they climbed the stairs to their next class, Science.

Settling back into their desks, the two of them tried their best to pay attention in class. It proved to be a difficult task and the hours seemed to drag by endlessly.

Chapter 9

The moment the bell rang, Annetta and Jason headed for the door with their coats and bags. Annetta looked back at Jason as they moved through the busy hallway towards the exit, students' faces blurring around them into a single mass of varied colour, making sure not to lose her friend. His choice of clothing, a worn green zip up hoodie and washed out jeans, made him blend in too much so she had to be careful not to get separated.

"You don't have to come watch if you're so worried, you know," she told him as she pushed open the doors.

"Are you kidding? I wanna see the look on his face when he flies into the wall." Jason grinned, shouldering his bag. "That and when have I ever left you to fight alone?"

Annetta smiled at this, continuing to walk towards the back of the school, preparing mentally for what she had to do. She knew how to trigger the psychic energy, but she was not sure if she could command it as she pleased. Making a tight fist with her right hand, she tried to focus on what she had to do once she got there. Lifting her blue eyes up, she scanned the back entrance for any signs of Finn. There was none, strangely. When there was a fight, Finn was always the first to arrive. What she did notice was a man waiting just beyond the gate of the schoolyard.

He was wearing large rectangular glasses with golden rims and his mouth was almost covered with a thick mustache and beard. His skin had a dark tan, the kind one got from spending years in the sun, and there were tattoos made in rich dark ink all over him. He wore large silver rings on both hands and two silver earrings in each ear that were barely noticeable through the long strands of black hair. He reminded Annetta of a biker.

"You two, come with me," he said to them when they came close enough.

As soon as he spoke, Jason and Annetta stopped dead in their tracks, recognizing Puc's voice.

"Where's Finn?" Annetta asked him as he grabbed her and Jason by the arm and pulled them along one of the side streets.

"I dealt with him, and I was watching you both the entire day," he said, sounding very cross. "What you were attempting to do just now was very irresponsible."

"I was just trying to give him what he deserved," Annetta protested.

80

Puc veered around to look at both of them, sheer rage visible on his face.

"That does not matter. Do you have any idea what you could have done? You could have risked exposing our entire world to other humans. Do you know how hard your grandfather and father both worked to make sure such a thing would never happen? Do you know what could have happened to you or Jason if you attempted what you did or what would have happened were you to not succeed? You could have been seriously injured in your hasty attempt to try being a hero."

"I was not trying to be a hero. I was going to give a bully a taste of his own medicine," Annetta snapped.

"You were to shine in a so called hour of darkness in the schoolyard, which is not always the best approach. That is what you were trying to do, was it not?" Puc glared at her, taking off his glasses and staring at her, his lips pulled back in a snarl.

"So what if I was?" She glared back as he held her by the arm.

"You would be locked away and treated like a lab rat if they found out what you are. That is what humans do to things they cannot explain. This goes for you too, Jason. Never use your abilities in public, or risk your exposure as something supernatural. I don't care how well orchestrated you think your plan is. Believe me when I say there are many who would hunt you down for what you are, and many races that will defend the secret of their existence."

Puc's grip loosened, and he let the two of them go. The anger on his face lessened, cooling back into his usual composed state.

"After dinner the both of you will report to the Lab to begin your training. The sooner you learn to understand your powers and what you can and cannot do in public, the better. Your time of innocence is at an end." As soon as he finished, he spun on his heel and set off towards the building where Annetta lived, before she could even tell him to wait.

Annetta turned back to Jason, who simply shot her an 'I told you so' look and adjusted his bag on his back.

"I guess I'll see you later then?" she smiled at him weakly.

"Yeah, hopefully my mom will let me go," he said, before turning to go his own way. "Later, Annetta."

"Bye," Annetta waved, and then ran to catch up with Puc, already across the street.

"How did you know I was going to do that? And why are you dressed like that?"

"I was posing as your uncle. Who is not a force to be reckoned with," Puc answered simply. "And I have been watching your activity since last night using an enchanted mirror."

"Those really exist?"

"Young Annetta," he said, shaking his head, "You have still much to learn about the world you have become part of," Puc smirked as the two of them continued to walk together.

——

After dinner Annetta waited for Jason to arrive at her apartment. She'd already confirmed on the phone that he was able to come over. He had decided to stick with the alibi of a school project, instead of revealing to his mother his knowledge of their legacy. Jason had told Annetta that he thought it would take a bit of time before he was bold enough to tell her about it. Sooner than Annetta could dwell on the subject, there was a knock at the door and she was up answer it. But it was not who she had expected.

"Hey Annetta. How's it going?" Darius greeted her with a suave grin on his face, dressed in dark jeans, a white shirt and light grey cardigan. Were it not for his long hair, Annetta thought he looked sort of like a student teacher.

Annetta bit back the urge to yell at him to leave, or else she'd have an angry elven mage to deal with. Instead she smiled back as quickly as she could.

"Same old. Just waiting for Jason to get here. We've got an assignment to work on for class." She said, stepping outside into the hallway and locking the door behind her.

"Oh yeah? Quixote working you to the bone? It's a shame you guys are in a different class than me. I wish I was with you guys this year," he sighed. "So what's it on?"

"Short story unit. We need to present a short story together. You know, different themes and stuff."

"Ah, yeah." Darius went silent for a moment, looking down at his feet. "So I heard you and Finn were supposed to fight again after school. You don't look like you were in one."

82

"I wasn't. The fight never happened," Annetta said, trying to make the conversation go as fast as possible, while looking to see if Jason was coming from the elevator.

"Huh? How come? I could have sworn I saw you and Jason going out to the back after school, where the fight was supposed to happen."

"Yeah, well it never did. My uncle came by and broke it up before it began." Annetta shifted uneasily on the spot.

"You have an uncle here?" he asked.

"No, he just came to visit, and my mom had him pick me up from school, and he went to meet me at the back gate. He found out about the fight when I got there, and then he told Finn to hit the road or he'd call the cops." Annetta weaved the story together as quickly as her mind could go.

"Really? You know that's just gonna make Finn go after you again tomorrow, right?" He leaned against the doorframe.

"I know, but I had no say in the matter as soon as my uncle heard 'fight'."

"Yeah, I hear ya. Parents don't know much about what it's like to be in school nowadays."

The elevator door opened and Jason came out. Turning the corner to Annetta's apartment, he noticed Darius in the door-frame. At first, he looked unsure about what was going to happen, since they were supposed to be departing. After a moment, he made a decision, and kept walking without hesitation.

"Hey guys, what's up?" Jason asked, coming towards them.

"Hey J.K., I was just telling Darius about the English project Ms. Quixote gave us in class to work on. And how my uncle got me out of the fight with Finn after school."

"Oh yeah?" Jason said. He caught the alibi, and then turned to Darius. "You should have seen the look on Finn's face when her uncle showed up. It was pretty priceless."

"Yeah, I bet it was," Darius said, shifting towards the exit. "Well, I guess I should let you guys get going on the project. I just wanted to make sure you were okay, Annetta. Later, J.K."

"See ya, Darius," he answered and watched him descend the stairs before he turned to Annetta. "Good call with the assignment."

"Yeah, let's just hope he doesn't come back while we're down there asking for us. That would really suck." She said, as she opened the door and went inside closing it behind Jason once he came in.

"Who cares?" Jason replied. "We could have stepped out for some fresh air. I'm sure your parents can think of something."

"True. Ready to get this over with?" She asked, taking her card key from its hiding spot inside the pocket of her jean jacket once she put it on again with her shoes.

"Yeah, wonder what we're gonna have to do."

"One way to find out," Annetta answered him as the pair walked into her and Xander's room. Taking the card key, she swiped it along the mirror in one fluid motion.

The platforms appeared instantly, along with the keyboard. It was still hard for Annetta to grasp that this had been right next to where she'd slept for her entire life, and she'd never even noticed.

"Want to go together or separately?" She asked.

"Separate." Jason scrunched up his nose. He was still getting used to the trips down alone.

Nodding, Annetta stepped onto the platform, and entered the number one into the keyboard. She braced herself for the sensation of being swallowed by waves of water to take hold of her body. Before she knew it, she was on the cold steel floor of the base again. Raising her head, she saw the immense doors staring down at her like gods from another world.

"You are late, Annetta." Puc's voice came from across the hall. Sure enough, the pale elf, now back to his normal self, was watching her.

"Sorry, ran into a bit of a problem up above." She grinned sheepishly as Jason appeared moments later on the floor with a sour look on his face.

"No matter, you are both here now," Puc said before looking at the gates. "Now, as a warm up, you will open the gate. But I want to try something different instead of having you both do it together."

Jason looked at Annetta, who furrowed her brow as she stepped forward.

"Jason, I want you to do it alone this time," Puc instructed.

Jason glanced up at the elf, "You're kidding, right?"

"You are both on the same level with this. You've both grown confident working as a team, but this will not always be the case. Annetta managed to do it alone before, and now I want you to do the same. You also

84

have the advantage of a good batch of training behind you, unlike what she had the first time. Now, focus!"

Jason groaned and stood beside Annetta. "So how did you do this?"

"I think you just really need to concentrate on whatever it is you're trying to move, except you need to use your emotions to push the object. You can't just think about it." Annetta tried to explain as she closed her eyes.

"Enough chit-chat about the theory. Get on with it." Puc folded his arms, watching the two of them.

Closing his eyes and biting his tongue back, Jason tried to put what Annetta had told him into practice. He remembered the way the gate had blasted open that first night, the way the immense structure had bent to the will of his friend with nothing more than a mere thought from inside herself. He knew what needed to be done. Now all that remained was to find the emotions to force open the gates. He had a lot of things he could use. All he had to do was reach for them. All he had to do was think of how his mother had locked his father up, the fighting at home, the way she despised him but really loved him. It all welled up inside him until he felt as though he would black out.

"That is enough!"

Jason felt his entire body lock up. He opened his eyes. It wasn't just him who couldn't move. Everything around him was motionless. The only movement came from Puc, who stood before him and Annetta, pointing his staff at them. Around the mage, particles of dust were suspended in midair. When Jason looked beyond Puc, he saw the massive gates broken off their hinges, frozen in mid-flight, in the process of being torn into pieces. He looked over at Annetta, who also seemed to be still, though she could move her eyes about.

Puc shifted from his defensive stance. He raised a hand and waved it before Jason and Annetta, who immediately unfroze.

"I fear I may have miscalculated how much power lies inside both of you for novices to the art. Clearly opening a door is no task anymore." Puc looked back at their handiwork then turned to Annetta. "And now another lesson. Can you put back what you have just done?"

Annetta's eyes widened as she looked at the unmoving doors in the air.

"Don't worry," Puc reassured, "it won't go anywhere. I've frozen it. Your next lesson is to put the door back together."

"That's impossible," Jason snapped. "It's shattered. Besides, you said being a psychic means you can move objects. Not fix something that's busted."

"And I did say to put it back together, not fix it. I will do the fixing. All you must do is to rearrange the particles as they were before you tore the door from its hinges. Can you both do that?"

Jason looked at his friend, who seemed to still be dazed. He could not blame her for he felt the same as she confronted with the new task.

"So you just need us to take the doors and put them where they were before?" He asked.

"Yes. I could do it myself, but I feel it will be a good exercise for the both of you. You never know when it may come in handy."

Jason nudged Annetta, who snapped out of her own world.

"Think we can put humpty dumpty back together Anne?" He grinned.

"We're not all the king's men, but let's give it a go," she chuckled turning back to the frozen doors.

Puc folded his arms into the sleeves of his robe and watched. He had weakened the spell enough for the children to be able to try and move them but not enough to continue the fall.

Slowly but surely, the large metallic slabs began to move through the air in a clumsy sort of ballet as they made their way back toward each other. Even the little screws that reinforced the doors floated backwards, like snowflakes.

Waiting for the right moment when everything was back in place, Puc grabbed the staff and pointed it at the doors, muttering a spell to undo the damage. He then removed the freezing spell completely.

"Well done, not a single scrap out of place," he nodded, turning back towards them. "Shall we? Try doing it once more Jason."

"Breaking down the door?"

"No, opening it. And hurry up. I'm sure Brakkus heard the commotion and will have a million questions, and the Unknown knows I am not in the mood to answer all of them," he said, and waited for Jason to open the doors.

The boy raised his hand and retreated back into his thoughts, trying to repeat what he did before with less force. Moments later, the massive gates creaked open and Puc walked through them. Annetta and Jason both hurried after him, unsure of what the erratic elf had in store. As Puc had predicted, the large form of Brakkus, with his sword out ready for combat, stopped him. The Hurtz looked over at the children, raising his large ears slightly.

"I heard one bloomin' loud noise! What happened?" he asked the elf as the children caught up.

"Nothing spectacular, they just blew up the front gate."

"Blew up the front gate? How in bloody...Oh, learning to use their powers, are they?"

"And rather quickly," Puc said, looking at the two of them and tilting his staff in the general direction of the training grounds. "After you. You have a lot of work to do."

"I won't keep ya then. Good luck," Brakkus chuckled, then added, "If you get tired of Puc's bantering I'll be with the horses."

The children watched as the giant creature walked off in the opposite direction to where the elf had told them to go.

ഇരു

The training room, as Puc had called it, was actually an assortment of a few connected rooms. The furthest one resembled a gym filled with different kinds of training machines and free weights. The room in the middle looked like a large hockey rink with no ice. On the floor were markings showing a rectangle, which outlined the whole room. Puc called this the sparring room, where warriors would train against one another with their weapons. The third room was the largest. The walls had thick plates of glass all around them. Though Annetta and Jason had been inside, they had never come back to it since the initial viewing.

"This is the arena. It is where warriors could train using magic and psychic abilities. Often it was used for exhibition matches and for duels. We will use this room from now on as it has the necessary protection in case anything goes wrong."

"They look the same to me," Jason said, gazing up at the tall ceiling.

Puc pointed his staff and aimed at one of the windows. A blast of green light shot from it and hit the glass. The wall shimmered white for a moment, then went back to normal.

"It is not glass you are looking at, but Calanite diamonds, an elven material able to absorb most forms of energy attacks. When fighting enemies who wield magic and psychic attacks, it was once common to use shields made of this substance," he explained. "Many shields in the armory were once of this material."

"We have an armory, too?" Annetta asked, raising an eyebrow.

"First and foremost this was a base for warriors." Puc stated. "There are several different abilities all psychics possess, some more defensive than others. They are telekinesis, the ability to move objects which you already know a little about, telepathy, the ability to speak to someone through the use of thought alone, projection, the ability to show visions of what one has experienced to another person, teleportation, which is simply traveling from one place to another, and psychic fire, an offensive spell that allows one to create blasts of energy, but that is something you will not worry about for a very long time."

"Aren't psychics supposed to be able to read minds, too?" Jason asked.

"That practice is a forbidden one, Mr. Kinsman. The invasion of ones mind is reserved for the Unknown alone and no one else. To learn such a feat could become the cause of one's demise. Now, shall we begin your lessons?"

Annetta glanced over at Jason to see what his reaction would be. After a split second, the two friends both nodded their heads.

"Very well," Puc said. "We will start with the basics, and that is moving objects. I know you have both proven your ability to do so, but you must learn to be able to employ that talent at will, not by chance. But before we begin, I must strongly emphasize once more how serious it is that you never under any circumstances use these powers in the outside world. If you are caught, no one will be able to help you, especially if something that does not want the existence of such a force known finds out."

"What are you talking about?" Jason asked. He was getting fed up with Puc's cryptic warnings.

"Lets us just say angels do not always bring good news," Puc stated. "Some worlds they are meant to know about certain things and in others they are not. Life is not about being fair but about everyone getting what they need and let's say some worlds are not ready for certain kinds of knowledge, they need to grow into it. It is a way of keeping balance and should balance be disrupted before the time is right there can be dire consequences which I will not dive into."

Jason looked away, dissatisfied with the answer. But he was getting better at reading Puc, and he could tell right now that the elf was not trying to be sarcastic, so he left it alone.

Puc turned his attention to preparing the first exercise. He waved his staff, and watched as two round stones appeared on the ground before him.

"This exercise will help you regulate the amount of force you use while moving a given object. You may find yourselves in situations where you do not need to send things flying across a room, but simply move them a few paces." He explained this to them, then used the bottom of his staff to draw a line a few feet away, using an incantation to mark it in red. "You are to move the stones onto this line. They must be exactly centered, and not an inch out of place. Is that clear?"

Annetta looked at the stones, then over at the red line marked on the steel floor. How hard could it be?

"Yeah, we got you," she answered, and took a step forward to attempt the task.

Puc said nothing more and moved out of the way. He nodded his head, silently telling them to begin.

Annetta was the first to attempt the exercise. She lowered her body so she could see the stone better, and then focused all her attention on it. She watched as the stone began to hover a bit above the ground. But when Annetta attempted moving the stone to the line, it went flying into one of the Calanite walls. Sparks of electric current seemed to engulf the small rock for a moment, and then it fell to the ground.

"What?" Annetta narrowed her eyes in outrage. "But I had it!"

"It seems to me that you did not, as you say, have it." Puc stated and moved it back to its original spot with the wave of his hand. "Try again."

Annetta felt the back of her neck heat up as she glared at the stone. This time, she sent it flying so hard it became embedded in the wall.

Puc frowned and muttered under his breath as he took the stone out of the glass wall, repairing it in the process. "Anger will get you nowhere. You must focus and not allow your emotions to take hold."

"Hey, it's easier said than done, okay? Besides, why don't you do it if it's that easy, Mr. All Wise One."

While Annetta ranted, Jason worked on trying to make his stone hover as high as he wanted it to go. It started off only an inch above the ground. He lowered it back down, and then lifted it a little bit higher each time. However, the stone still went flying when he tried to move it to the red line.

"I would watch your mouth if I were you," Puc snarled at Annetta. "I have trained some of the greatest psychics that have ever lived and your father was among those ranks. I cannot even begin to believe you are both related, seeing how stubborn you are compared to him!"

"Well excuse me, but my father was born into this. I'm just finding this all out now. It's a lot of to take in at once!" Annetta snapped back.

Taking in a deep breath, Puc attempted sympathy. "Look, try again. Not even your father got it the first time. There is no shame in making mistakes."

He then turned to Jason, who had grabbed the stone from where it had landed and put it back in the original spot. He was attempting to move it again using the same technique.

"I do not wish you to make the stone hover. I want it moved across to the line."

"I know, but you never said how you wanted us to get it there."

"As you will have it. Continue, then." Puc sighed and moved to the other side of the room, watching them continue training.

☘☙

They had stayed three hours in the room practicing moving the stone across to the red line. By the end of it all, Annetta was mentally and physically exhausted. She was learning that moving objects with her mind would take a toll on her body. She also felt frustrated with how often Puc reminded them of the many psychic warriors he had trained, and how they all appreciated his teachings. She was not trying to be disobedient on purpose. The pressure of knowing there had been others before her that were successful with less attempts bothered her.

"I'll get it tomorrow," she muttered to herself as she headed towards where Brakkus had said he would be. She had separated from Puc and Jason. They had gone back to the gate to send Jason home, despite Puc wanting them to stay together. She knew it was dangerous, but she also knew if anything came near her she could send it flying far enough to be gone when it returned. That much she was good at for sure. Coming to the stables, Annetta pushed the door lightly, only to be blasted with the usual smell.

"I don't think I'll ever get used to this," she said to herself, trying to desensitize her nose. She spotted Brakkus on the other side of the stable and waved to him. The giant creature looked up and smiled with his sharp teeth.

"Oi! What are ya doing walking about the Lab by yourself, Missy? Could be nasty beasties wandering about and ya don't want to be snatched up by one of those. You won't even hear em coming."

"I'm pretty sure I can take care of myself now, Brakkus."

"Oh, can ya now?" The Hurtz raised his eyebrow and chuckled. "I'd like to see that if ya don't mind me asking."

"Probably not a good idea, I haven't perfected my range of motion."

"Ah, hitting everything with full power, then?"

Annetta grinned and nodded sheepishly before Bossman nudged her in the back of the head with his muzzle and interrupted her.

"I dare say I think he likes ya," Brakkus mused, "Are y'alright for another lesson?"

The leftover strain from the lessons with Puc made Annetta want to genuinely say no and give up for the evening, but as she looked up at the ferocious yet gentle creature, she knew she could not disappoint him. Besides, she'd always wanted to learn how to ride a horse.

"Let's give it a go," Annetta smiled, "I'm not making any promises about how long I can last. I'm pretty tired from the lessons with Puc."

"I won't push ya today. Let's see whatcha can remember from last time. Ya remember how to put the saddle on?"

Annetta paused for a moment, thinking long and hard. "Yeah, I think so."

She looked at equipment he had laid out, and proceeded to go for the brush.

"First," Annetta began, trying to remember all of the details, "You need to groom the horse and check for hair clumps, mud, or dirt that can irritate the horse when you place all the equipment on. The only time you don't is if there's a call for battle or an emergency, but a horse should be groomed regularly anyways so there should be no issues. The second thing is you need to check for sores so you don't hurt it further. If it's an emergency use extra padding. Saddling is done from the left side and you begin with the blanket-,"

"Good so far," Brakkus interjected. "I've just finished grooming Bossman and he's in good shape with no sores, so ya can start from the steps after and tell me what yer doing as you go along."

Annetta nodded, put down the brush, and went to go get the blanket she had used last time.

"You need to make sure the blanket is free of dirt, and dry," Annetta repeated from memory, looking over at Brakkus for approval.

"Good. And how do ya put it on?"

"When you place the saddle blanket, it needs to be well towards the front, so the front pad rests just in front of the horse's withers. The back pad should be facing forward, and when you slide it to adjust it make sure it goes in the same direction as the horses hair."

"Right, and ya need to make sure the blanket ya use is big enough so it shows all around the saddle of the horse, or it'll irritate him. Don't forget that," Brakkus reminded her.

Annetta nodded. She took a second glance at the blanket before deciding it was big enough, then went over to get a saddle.

"When you're placing the saddle on the horse," she continued, "You need to make sure none of the parts from the right side hit it when you lift the saddle to place it on the horse. You can make this easier if you hook the right stirrup over the saddle horn. That way it's held in place." Annetta kept talking as she grabbed a stepping stool, "And if you're short like me you grab a stool so you can reach over the other side of the horse."

"Aye, good, though once you learn to use your powers you can just have the saddle float up over the horse and ya won't need a stool," Brakkus commented. "Go on, keep going. You're doing really well so far."

Annetta continued, and placed the saddle on Bossman, who didn't mind the girl's presence one bit.

"The fork of the saddle needs to rest directly over the withers. Next, you need to go on the other side of the horse and place the right side of the saddle correctly, which was flipped up before so it wouldn't hit the horse."

"Make sure you're touching the horse when ya walk around him, you don't want to startle him or he might bolt or kick ya," Brakkus chuckled.

"Right, I almost forgot." Annetta felt her ears turned red, feeling the pressure of trying to remember everything, "Uhm, when you put the other side of the saddle down, you need to make sure you don't throw anything down because you don't want to hurt the horse. Once the blanket and everything is centered you create an air pocket where the withers are and the blanket-,"

Annetta paused again, it was time to tie the girth on. She reached over to grasp the girth, but her palms started to sweat a little on the leather as she tried to recall how to tie the knot. She had never been good with remembering knots. It was the only thing she had hated in girl guides when her father had signed her up one year.

"Is something wrong, lass?"

"I...I can't remember how to tie the knot," she blurted out, feeling the skin on the back of her neck heat up. She almost had it memorized, but the pattern of tying the knot had just not stuck in her head.

"Ahh. Well then, no need to fret, took me a few good times before I got it myself. Do ya remember how many times the tie strap goes through the ring?"

"Twice, right?" she asked as Brakkus took her small hands, and began guiding her on how to tie the knot. Despite their size and clumsy look, Brakkus was able to help tie it with ease, and without his massive claws getting in the way.

"I'll finish up. Next time ya can do it by yerself. Practice makes perfect," the giant badger-head grinned at her.

"I wish Puc would see it that way," Annetta grumbled, watching him finish tying the other knots and secure the saddle on the horses back.

"Oh, he giving you a hard time? Want me to smack him about for ya?"

"Well no, I just...I don't think he gets that J.K. and I are just kids. We've never done this. We weren't even supposed to believe stuff like you or him even existed. I mean, if he'd give us some time to get used to it, and-"

Brakkus turned to look down at the young girl after finishing with the horse.

"Puc may be strict with ya, but it's 'cause he worries. Ya saw those creatures in the screens the first day ya came here, right?"

Annetta nodded.

"If anything were to happen to me or to Puc, you'd be defenseless against 'em. He just wants ya to be prepared."

"But didn't you guys get all of them?"

"There's two of us, and who knows how many of them, lass," Brakkus told her then looked back at the horse, "Ready for a riding lesson?"

Annetta looked up at the horse, remembering her lesson the last time. She shifted the weight on her legs, both still hurting and bruised from sitting in the saddle the previous time.

"I'll even give ya a boost this time," Brakkus teased. "I know you're tired but ya need to keep at it."

The girl sighed and placed one leg in the stirrup, and a hand on the horn. "I think I can do it on my own."

The Hurtz watched as she hoisted herself up, making sure she did not fall. Once she was on, he went to grab his own horse from the stall.

"Now, ya remember the command to get him to start?"

"Is it F-L-Y?" she spelled the word out.

"Only if you're in a hurry. Ya want to start slow, right?" he reminded her.

"So it's just a nudge?"

"Aye, that would be correct," Brakkus nudged his own horse.

Annetta followed his lead as they both rode into a grassy area on the other side of the stable. Puc had told her that the Lab contained biological spheres, artificially created habitats containing all sorts of animals. Her grandfather believed in preservation, and had them built in case anything ever happened to the habitats on Earth. Creating things was a hobby of his, she'd learnt.

She had so many questions about her grandfather that she wanted to ask Brakkus, Puc, and her own father. What was he like as a person? Was he patient? Was he talkative? Did he like children? Did he have a sense of humor? How did he learn about this world that she was becoming a part of? At times when she thought of these questions, a feeling of loneliness crept in over her. She felt alone, like someone had abandoned her, someone who she barely knew. Now she was in this new life that sometimes made no sense to her. She felt like it was her duty to have known about all of this, and she was a terrible granddaughter for being ignorant. But how could she have known?

"How ya holding up there?" Brakkus called from his saddle.

"Sore, but okay I guess," Annetta admitted, snapping out of her thoughts.

"Think we can speed it up a bit?" he asked.

"I guess so, but what can I say besides fly-," Annetta was cut off as Bossman went from slowly trotting to a full gallop, not even thinking of any speed between the two.

Annetta clung to the horse for dear life as the creature kept going faster and faster. She didn't even care where it went. She was so scared of falling off that she even forgot how to make him stop. Somewhere in the distance, she heard Brakkus's voice beyond the gusts of wind swirling past her ears, but it was nothing more than a blur. Closing her eyes, she hoped the animal

94

would run out of steam or room to run. Moments later, a strange feeling came over Annetta, a feeling similar to using the transport in her room, only this time it felt like her whole body had caught fire for a split second. She shut her eyes tighter, and then a miraculous thing happened, the horse stopped.

Annetta opened her eyes a little, seeing blurred green shapes. When she was sure she was not dead she opened them some more, trying to sit up in the saddle. As she came to her senses she saw the horse was standing at the edge of a cliff made of limestone rock, but what was beyond that stumped her completely. There, nestled in a valley among mountains, in all of its fortitude and prowess stood a castle. But it was no ordinary castle. She was looking at an exact replica of the one that was in a painting her father had in their living room.

"Severio Castle, also called the Eye to All Worlds," the voice of Brakkus announced as his horse stopped beside Annetta. "The only way the castle can be reached is by riding through the sealed exit inside the Q-16 base on horseback."

"You mean the one I just went through?" she asked.

"Aye, the very same," the Hurtz grinned, looking down at her and then back at the castle, "For centuries people have tried to take the castle for themselves, to gain access to the ability to travel to different realities. The castle is not only a fortress but also a gateway filled with portals leading to different dimensions. It stands upon a spot where all worlds are weakest, where tears in the multiverse have been created through the wear of time."

"So it's almost like a bridge?" she raised an eyebrow.

"Aye, in a way. It has been yer family's duty to help protect it so that no harm would ever befall any of the creatures found on the other sides of any of the portals it's linked to. It's also the resting place of all Severio's past."

"I've only ever seen it in a portrait before," Annetta said, spellbound. "My dad has a painting of it in our house. He never mentioned it being real or that.... it was ours."

"Do ya know why yer father never mentioned it before or why he chose not to continue living linked to this world?"

"Is it something to do with my grandfather's murder?"

Brakkus was silent. For a moment there was no sign of the good-natured creature that Annetta was used to seeing. Lines of worry and grief on his face replaced happiness.

"When yer grandfather passed away, your father denounced his duty of protecting the castle. He vowed never to be involved in this world again, for fear of what might happen to you or your brother or yer mother if he stayed here."

"So he chose a normal life to save us instead of the world. That's selfish."

"Nah, it's the decision a parent makes," Brakkus responded, "I know. I had a daughter once and she died because she'd been in a fight, helping me of all people."

Annetta was flooded with a wave of empathy when she heard this and looked up at the big creature that sat in the saddle beside her.

"I'm sorry, Brakkus," she whispered quietly.

"Aye, it's alright lass. It happened many years ago. Ya would have liked her though, she loved horses as much as you do."

"I'm sure I would," Annetta smiled back.

Brakkus said nothing for a moment and simply patted his horse's neck before sighing.

"Well, I think that's enough of a lesson for today. Ya must be drained. Perhaps when J.K. catches up to ya we can all go to the castle so ya can get a better look."

"Sure, I'd love that."

"Aye, well, back to the Lab then with ya for now," the Hurtz motioned towards the back and veered his horse around in the direction they'd come from.

Annetta turned around and then saw what she had come through. Before her was an enormous wall of what looked like black and red water.

"That would be a glimpse of yer first portal," Brakkus told her. "Some can be kind of painful to go through, others not so much. Some portals are made while others are natural tears in the world. Severio Castle was built where the fabric is weakest in all worlds so nothing harmful can come through."

"I thought Puc said anything can come through them," Annetta questioned.

"Aye, things can go through but it doesn't happen often. Remember, not all places it links to believe in magic or portals, like yer world. Generally, portals do not happen in places with a lot of organic activity as well."

Annetta nodded. The concept of other worlds, other dimensions with their own solar systems, planets and whole functioning societies similar to her own was comforting. The thought that somewhere out there was another little girl just like her going through the same thing she was made her feel less alone.

છાબ

Upon returning to the Lab, Annetta and Brakkus unsaddled their horses and put them in their respective stalls. The girl didn't say much, but it was not an uncomfortable silence. In fact, it felt like the sort of silence that existed between two good friends.

"Aye, well, we best be getting you home," Brakkus said once he finished up with his horse. "Don't want yer father upset that yer missing sleep because of old me."

"What was my dad like back then, during the war?"

"A good man who never left anyone behind. He always had a smile on his face, especially when he saw yer mum," the Hurtz answered, opening the door for her.

The two of them walked out and made their way towards the exit of the Lab. Since the generator had been turned on, it was much brighter and easier to get around than the first time Annetta made the journey through the steel corridors.

"How did you and Puc live down here when there was no power? And how long were you down here for?" Annetta inquired.

"Took turns keeping guard and killing beasties. As for how long, I'm not sure. Nothing to keep track of time … except killing beasties I guess," Brakkus laughed, unsure of how to answer the question. "War hardens ya to live with just the essentials. The small things we needed, Puc was mostly able to provide or we had the sleeping quarters. He didn't show ya those yet I'm guessing."

"Jason said something about them. Rooms that adapt."

"Aye, that be those. Back up power in those so they never die, not till the end of time would be my guess."

Annetta nodded as they approached the exit, but she was stopped when Brakkus's massive paw-like hand gripped her shoulder. She looked up to see his long ears twitching as though they were picking up sound, then she heard something metallic clash against the floor. In an instant, the Hurtz had drawn his sword and stood in front of her, his animalistic face wrinkled.

Before Annetta could react, Brakkus leaped forward and grabbed a shape from the shadows. He slammed it into the floor, his sword aimed to kill. The girl ran forward to see what the threat was, only to be surprised at what she found.

It was a boy. Granted, he did not look like a normal boy. He had fair skin and a square jaw, which paired with his thin lips and high cheekbones made him appear to look more sinister than was his intention upon a first meeting. He was dressed in a tabard, with a chain mail shirt beneath it. In one hand he held an ornate buckler, red and studded with silver. The other was empty, but only a few feet away there was a sword. The youth sneered at Brakkus, his gray-blue eyes focused on his enemy, his dirty blonde hair tied in a ponytail falling away from his face, revealing a circular crescent scar across his right eye.

"How did ya get in here!" The Hurtz bellowed, pointing the edge of his sword into the boy's neck. "And answer me quick or I'll cut yer liver out!"

"Just try, beast, and it'll be the last thing you do! Now get off me!" The boy snapped back, trying to reach for his sword.

"Oh ho ho, big talk from a lad like you," Brakkus smirked humorlessly. "Who sent you? It'd be wise to answer me."

"No one sent me, and that's all I'm saying until you get off me!"

"Well, considering yer life is in my hands, I say ya have to listen to me. Speak or die, boy. Ya got two options."

The boy struggled, but the pressure on his neck from Brakkus's sword only increased. Any moment there would be a pool of red on the floor. Annetta shifted uncomfortably where she was standing. She was not ready to watch someone die.

"Brakkus?" A voice called from behind.

Brakkus's huge head turned back to see Puc standing behind him. Paying to more attention to the boy, he withdrew his sword and gabbed the youth by his shirt, lifting him off the ground as though he were nothing more than a rag doll. The captive struggled vainly to be free as he tried to get a better look of those around him, his eyes now wide with panic.

"Yes, mage?" the Hurtz answered.

Puc glanced at the struggling boy Brakkus had gripped in his hand, noting his clothing and the buckler that still dangled attached to his one arm.

"What is that?" Puc said, casually.

"A boy and he just don't want to talk, which means I think he wants to die." Brakkus lifted his sword again.

"No, stop it!" Annetta finally broke out, unable to watch Brakkus.

"Have you tried diplomacy, Hurtz?" Puc said to Brakkus, who has lowered his sword when Annetta cried out.

Brakkus looked at the boy, who was finally noticing Annetta.

"Yer lucky the mage showed up when he did, lad, so I'm forced to ask again, who sent ya?"

"No one sent me. I don't even know how I got here. Now can you put me down?"

"Not unless I got your word you won't try to run anyone through with the sword you got laying over there," Brakkus glared at him.

"You pinned me to the floor I wasn't going to run anyone through. I'm just trying to figure out where I am," the boy had calmed down now that his ordeal was partially over.

Brakkus lowered him and let his prisoner drop from his grip, still keeping a wary eye on him as the youth went to get his weapon and put it in his scabbard.

"My name is Lincerious Heallaws," he said. "I'm a militia in training from the Gaian forces. Or, well, I was until I got here. Uh, I prefer to be called Link for short."

Puc quickly whispered something into Brakkus's ear that Annetta did not catch. It was significant enough to make Brakkus put his sword back into its scabbard. The Hurtz crossed his massive arms across his chest as he watched the youth.

"A warrior in training who has lost his way. I would have filleted ya if ya were under my command," Brakkus smirked.

"It doesn't matter now," Link said, looking down at his boots. "Even if I did return, I'd be killed. I know it's been too long since the exercise began."

"They would do that? That's terrible," Annetta said in disbelief. How could you kill someone just because they were late? Granted, the looks Ms. Quixote gave could kill when one came late to class.

"It is the rules of training," Link explained, responding to her silent question. "And if you don't mind me asking, who are you? All of you, actually."

"I am Brakkus the Hurtz, this here is Puc the Mage, and this is Annetta Severio."

Link looked at the girl, his eyes widened.

"If I am where I think I am, then that means that you must be related to Lord Orbeyus of the Axe Severio." The youth knelt down instantly, and took out his sword, which he offered to Annetta. "I am at your command, m'lady."

"Uhm, that's great but, uh, I don't need to command anyone," Annetta said, feeling embarrassed.

"Lord Orbeyus of the Axe has traveled as a legend through my people, as one of the greatest warriors of all time, it would do me a great honor-," Link was cut off as he collapsed mid-sentence.

Annetta noticed a bloodstain on his tunic, and drops that had begun to fall onto the steel floor. She glared at Brakkus.

"I didn't do that, lassie. That was already there."

"He needs medical attention," Puc said, examining the wound and putting the boy's arm around his neck. "Come with me, Annetta."

Annetta picked up the sword and shield the boy had dropped. "I uh...right."

Chapter 10

After returning from the Lab, Jason had come home and retreated to the room he shared with his brother. His encounter with his mother had been a brief one. After he had hung up his coat on the wall of the narrow hallway, all that had been exchanged was a quick 'school was great, project is coming along well.' He knew that was all she expected. Talia was a tough woman, and the last thing he wanted was to get on her bad side, especially now that he knew what had happened to his father. Leaving his shoes on the well worn wooden shoe rack in the closet, he proceeded onwards, taking note of the deep chocolate colored walls around him, which seemed to make everything seem darker than it was outside.

Closing the door behind him, Jason noticed his brother Liam, a scrawny boy of about ten years old with scruffy short brown hair and big green eyes, sitting on the bottom bunk of their bunk bed, his sock covered feet curled up close to him, hugging a pillow. Liam was the same age as Xander, and the two often played together, but like all boys they sometimes wandered off with other groups of friends, one wanting to play tag and the other soccer in the field. It was on those days Liam found himself feeling lonelier than usual, and it was then that he was quieter after school. Noting this behavior from his generally hyperactive brother, Jason decided to investigate.

"Hey Liam, what's up?" he asked, throwing down his bag beside the closet.

"I don't wanna talk about it," the smaller boy murmured in a strained voice, burrowing his brown messy hair into the pillow to hide from his brother.

"Did you get in trouble by mom or something?" he asked, flopping down beside him. "You can tell me, you know. I'm always here to listen and I won't tell mom if you don't want me to."

"J.K...where's our dad?" Liam sniffled.

Jason sighed, looking at his own socks as he went over the well rehearsed story in his mind, the one he had always been told by his mother when he was younger. The one he now found most appropriate for Laim.

"I told ya Liam, he's working. He's working so we have money to live." Jason sputtered out the lie as quickly as he could.

"But why can't he work and be here with us?" the younger boy asked. "Why can't he be like all the other daddies and stay with us? Did he leave because he didn't love us anymore?"

Jason sighed as he felt his heart break, watching his brother cry. There was very little he could do, and he hated the feeling. It was this part of coming home that he hated most, but he knew he had to, for Liam's sake.

"Liam, that's not true, our dad loves us very much. If he could, he would be here all the time, but he can't because he knows he needs to work hard so we can live here and not have to worry. He works so we can have all of that, because that's how much he loves us. He loves us enough to be able to let us go so we can be happy." Jason felt the wounds of revelation from earlier in the week reopen, but somehow when he spoke the words to Liam they didn't hurt as much. Somehow when they came from his own mouth, it was alright.

"Will we ever see him? People were making fun of me today for not having a dad and....I didn't know what to say," Liam responded, somewhat calmer after the explanation.

"Next time they bother you, you tell them your dad is off fighting bad guys." Jason smiled lightly and looked over at a pile of building blocks in the corner. He had an idea. "Hey, Liam? You wanna see something cool? You have to promise not to tell anyone though, not even Mom."

"Yeah!" he grinned in delight.

Jason nodded and crept out of the room to check on his mother. When he was sure she was asleep, or at least passed out in front of the television, he set straight to work. He put the blocks on the floor at the foot of the bed and walked to the other end of the room where his desk was located. Standing there, he tried to lift one of the blocks and put it on top of the other. It required complete concentration on his part. His hand reached out, but his body not moving, he struggled to make the block rise up off the floor and hover above the other. It successfully landed on the other one.

Spellbound, Liam sat on the floor beside the blocks, wide-eyed after having seen the move.

"How did you do that?" he gasped.

"Magic," Jason winked.

Jason decided to make things more interesting, and he looked at the pencil beside him on the desk. Moments later, it lifted off the desk and hovered, before he floated it on top of the blocks. He made it twirl as it stood erect on the second block. Liam giggled, seeing the pencil perform acrobatics. Smiling, Jason turned to a blank piece of paper on his desk, which folded itself into a paper airplane and took flight inside the room. Another piece of paper became a boat, another a crane, and they all began to float in the air. Jason watched as the world of paper toys danced around him, allowing himself to get lost in their innocence while Liam jumped up, attempting to touch them. For that moment, the world seemed perfect.

"Jason, I wanted to talk to you abou-" the voice of his mother interrupted his stream of thought. Talia Kinsman was a tall, thin woman with long brown hair, a sharp pointed chin and sunken green eyes that seemed as though they never slept. She was the sort of person that seemed as though she had dried up from living too long, despite not been that old. Unfortunately, she had already entered the room, and saw her son standing in the middle as the array of paper objects floated about him and her youngest trying to catch them. The peace he had known moments earlier crashed to the ground along with everything else the moment Jason heard her voice.

"I can explain-," he started to say.

His mother was far from listening. Instead, she stormed into the room and began throwing his things around, searching, Liam getting shoved to the corner by her as she stormed past him.

"Where is it?" she yelled.

"Mom! Mom did you see J.K. make magic?" Liam tried to get his mother's attention.

"Where is what?" Jason asked, doing his best to appear like he didn't know.

"Liam, go downstairs now, I need to talk to your bother alone." Talia gritted her teeth as Liam shuffled out of the room obediently, before she tossed the boy's mattress to the ground, "Don't play stupid with me! Where is it? I thought this would be all over if he were gone. I thought we would be left alone!"

Jason looked down. The card key was securely on a chain around his neck and under his shirt, where she would never find it. He placed his hand to his chest, feeling its cool surface press against his chest as he did so.

"Mom! Can you just relax and tell me what this is all about?" He said, trying to act calm and clueless.

"The card key! Where is it?" She screamed at him, gripping his arms with her hands.

"You're not going to find it," he said, as calmly as he could manage, which wasn't much and pulled away. "And even if you do, you can't take it from me. I won't let you."

In his repressed anger, the computer monitor on Jason's desk flew across the room and hit the wall right beside his mother. Talia's face went pale as she looked at her son. It was too late to turn back.

"It's all because you hang around that Severio girl! I knew this would happen. I should have never let you be friends with her. I should have forbid you from-" his mother collapsed on the floor, slamming a fist into the wooden floor in frustration, beginning to sob. Jason stood awkwardly on the spot, not sure how to react.

"Mom, me hanging around Annetta had nothing to do with this. And I know who Dad really was, Puc told me everything, and I know what you did was really painful for you-,"

"You were never supposed to find out. I sent him away so you and Liam would be safe."

"I am safe, Mom. The Lab is the safest place there is."

"Jason, you have no clue what's out there." His mother wiped the tears from her eyes. "You think the Lab's this great place now, but what they didn't tell you when they handed you the card key is what it can do to you and the secret it protects. How people have fought for generations to-,"

"Mom what are you talking about? So far no boogiemen have shown up."

"Maybe none have yet. But as soon as someone finds out you have the keys you and your friend will both be targets."

Jason watched his mother slowly compose herself as she began to speak with more clarity. Why was she so worried that someone was out to kill him and Annetta? He brushed off the thought focusing in on his mother's concern stricken face.

"Look Mom, what's done is done. I know about Q-16, about who Dad was, and about him being a psychic and passing it on to me. You can either support me in my decision, or I can leave, because the rooms in the base are really nice."

Talia stood up and looked at her son. He was right, there was no turning back. Even if she tried to forbid him from this world, it was done.

"I will not kick you out of his house because of this," she stated. "But you should know that I will have no part in this. I said no to that world the moment you and Liam came into our lives."

"That's fine, Mom. I understand, but there's one thing I want."

"Yes?"

"I want to visit Dad."

There was a long silence as Jason's mother looked at him. Her green eyes, his green eyes, stared down at him trying to make a decision.

"I will see what I can do," she said, leaving the room. "And fix your bed."

ဆဝ

Annetta sat on a stool in the emergency ward as Puc worked away on Link's injuries. The boy had fainted from blood loss during the process. After seeing the amount of blood coming out of the gaping hole in his side, Annetta nearly felt the same way and turned away. Thanks to Puc, the hole was now barely visible and she was able to sit facing the sleeping youth.

She decided to break the silence. "What was it that you told Brakkus earlier?"

"I told him that the unit the boy belonged to was a friendly one," Puc said. "It seems he is hiding something, though. That scar on his eye wasn't caused by battle it was caused by magic. I can feel it as I'm trying to mend the other wound."

"You mean like a curse?"

"Yes, something like that." Puc paused his train of thought and then looked at the girl. "Under no circumstances are you to be alone with this boy at any time until we know his intentions. Do you understand, Annetta?"

"I uh, yes I do. But I mean… Even if I am and he does try to attack me, can't I just throw him half way across the world or something?"

"You can. However, if he knows magic or is a more accomplished psychic than you are, you would be defenseless. The fact that he knew of your grandfather and wanted to serve you makes me doubly suspicious." Puc finished mending the wound and put away one of the vials he was using back on the shelf. "There is also something else which bothers me, has been for some time."

"What's that?"

"I think mine and Brakkus's darkest dreams are coming to pass," the elf breathed uneasily. "A long time ago, your grandfather and your father faced an enemy who nearly defeated them and took control of the castle. His name was Mordred the Conqueror. He was a warlord who traveled through space taking over other worlds, hoping to become the supreme ruler of them all. And then he found out that he could cross dimensions into other universes where he could practically make himself into a god. What you need to understand is that not all universes evolved the same way ours did. Some are younger than our own and some being far more ancient. And so he became even greedier. He was defeated, but your grandfather showed mercy and let his son, Mislantus, escape, something we were all against. The reason I bring this up is because he was known for his floating fortress, Valdhar. A few nights ago, I spotted what looked like a floating castle in the sky. If I saw it correctly then Mislantus has returned to extract revenge and is searching for you and Jason."

Annetta sat very still, looking at her feet, trying to find comfort in the worn sneakers, taking in everything he had just said. She felt goose bumps form under the denim fabric of her jacket. A floating fortress, a warlord, it was starting to get a little out of hand.

"The time of innocent play is at an end, if it was ever truly here. The time of action will now be close at hand." Puc interrupted her stream of thought.

"And what exactly should I do?" She asked, looking up at him, the mage sitting in the armchair, his gaze penetrating her small form.

"If it is indeed Mislantus, we will need to increase the intensity of your training, and Jason's. We will also need to try and reform the Four Forces; they are the alliance your grandfather created in the defense of the Eye to All Worlds. Mislantus doesn't operate alone. He will have an army to back him up, some of the most skilled mercenaries there are. Do not doubt for a second that he will also have spies, which is why you must be wary of this Link character."

Annetta nodded her head, "Okay. What about my parents? Is he going to go after Dad?"

"There is a possibility," Puc admitted, "but he will be more concerned with you, since you now hold the key to Severio Castle."

"Can't anyone get there?" She frowned.

"The only way to Severio Castle is on horseback through the portal you took by accident with Brakkus today."

106

"So they need to have access to the Lab, and since Jason and I have the keys we're the targets."

"That is correct," Puc answered.

"Does Jason know? And...what do I tell my parents?" She asked. "I mean I can't just miss the last few months of school because of this."

"You will not miss any school," Puc said. "You finish in about a month's time correct?"

"Uhm, no. I just started. I have almost a year left."

"Until then we train, and collect allies as we go. Mislantus has no clue who or where you are. We have the advantage here. As for Jason, I think now is the time to use another psychic ability that we practiced before. Telepathy."

"You mean mind speech?" Annetta asked, feeling a little uncomfortable at the idea. She had practiced using the ability in the past week, but her actions were in a magically protected environment where no one could get hurt. Even though she had some degree of faith in herself, she did not feel at ease using the skill out in the open just yet.

"Yes, exactly that." Puc nodded. "A person trained in telepathy can project their thoughts to another psychic from afar. Remember what I taught you. Hone in and find the person you want to contact. In this case, Jason. Close your eyes and focus your thoughts on him, what he looks like, and where he lives."

"Just focus." Annetta breathed deeply, closed her eyes and then opened them again, "But if it's that easy shouldn't we have been able to do it on the first go?"

"They did not build the Lab in a day, and neither are seasoned warriors into full regalia set in a single dawn without training of any kind. Now form a mental picture of him, and think his name," Puc instructed.

Annetta nodded and closed her eyes. For a moment, all she saw was a still picture of Jason smiling in her mind's eye. But then something happened. She could see him in his room, cleaning up broken pieces of a monitor from the ground.

'J.K.?'

Jason stopped and looked up at the ceiling like a frightened animal.

"Annetta? Is that you?" he asked out loud.

'Yes.'

"Where are you? I can't see you but I can hear you like you're talking to me right here."

'*I'm not, I'm in the Lab still. I'm using telepathy.*'

"Okay. This is weird... it not being in the Lab I mean." He raised an eyebrow.

'*Remember the lessons? Just focus on me and then don't actually talk, just…think of talking,*' she tried to walk him through it.

Jason nodded and closed his eyes. He tried to think of Annetta's appearance, how he saw her when they were together. He thought of the times they had gone to the theater and the times they had hung out at school, but that was all he was getting.

'*I'm not feeling any different-,*' he started, but paused. He found himself seeing Annetta in the Lab, standing beside Puc. '*Oh…am I doing it right?*'

'*Yeah. Now listen because Puc asked me to tell you a lot. Everything just got more complicated.*' Annetta stopped and looked over at Puc, "Do you want me to just tell him everything?"

"Yes," Puc said, "But you do not have to communicate in this way, remember? You can send each other mental images of what you have seen or heard, projection. A skilled psychic can use this method to tell his life story in a moment to another psychic. Focus on the conversation we just had. Remember what I told you, it's like handing a ball to someone."

Annetta nodded, still in trance. It was a lot easier to operate psychic abilities once someone had already tapped into them. She found it similar to cooking with her dad. He had recipes he followed but he was not afraid to go beyond what he knew. Most of the time they turned out okay.

Jason stood in his room, waiting to get something from Annetta.

'*Annetta? You still there?*' he asked.

Just after saying that he felt himself knocked back against a wall as a stream of images hit his brain. He was seeing things so fast it made him feel dizzy. He wanted to scream to make it stop but he knew there was nothing to be done. Clutching his head, he tried to steady himself.

Puc pulled Annetta back from where she was standing to take her out of it. Muttering an incantation under his nose he quickly cast his own version of a telepathic link to the boy and to Annetta, so they could all hear what went on.

'*Jason, are you alright?*' he asked.

Jason struggled to sit up and felt his nose, pulling his hand back to see blood on it.

'*I think I've been better. Hey, how come I can hear-,*' he began.

'*It's a spell. It will cause you no harm,*' Puc reassured him. There was an edge of frustration to his voice. '*You children are too young to be learning this, much less fighting a war.*'

'*There's no war yet,*' Jason groaned as he sat up on his still overturned mattress '*I think I got everything you and Annetta said. Man, though. Man.*'

'*You mean it worked?*' Annetta asked, looking at Puc.

'*Apparently so. Your throw may have been a bit much, however. I should have warned you about that.*'

'*Oh, sorry,*' she grinned.

'*We will work on that,*' Puc continued. '*We will need to if we want to have you both with your brains intact.*'

Puc then spoke through the connection he set up. '*Do you understand the risks that are now coming into play?*'

'*Yeah, I do,*' Jason replied, '*and I still stick with what I said before. I'm not leaving.*' He paused for a moment, before adding, '*My mom found out about me knowing about the Lab. She caught me using my psychic powers. It didn't go down to well. The good news is she might let me see my father in the asylum. If he fought alongside Orbeyus and Arieus he could have some information on how to defeat Mislantus.*'

'*I see,*' Puc said, nodding. '*Then we will need to act quickly with this. The sooner we have more information, the better. Now, as your mentor I must urge you both to go and get a good nights rest. If time permits tomorrow, we visit the interior of Severio Castle. But you have still much to learn, both about keeping our world secret and about using your abilities.*'

Jason smiled sourly. '*There's no extra homework, is there?*'

'*Not unless you wish it upon yourself. Good night, Jason Kinsman.*' Puc said and then muttered a counter to the spell and it dissolved.

Annetta had remained quiet the entire time. The fact that she had almost killed her best friend was not something she wanted to speak about right after the fact. It angered her that such a thing had been risked. Puc had said it himself. She was only a kid. Stuff like this had to take years of training, didn't it?

"Come, Annetta. I will take you back," Puc finally stated.

She looked up at the elven mage and nodded, still occupied with own thoughts. She looked over at the boy they had brought in. They had completely forgotten he was there. If he was the enemy, wouldn't that have been the perfect time for him to strike? She found it hard to imagine that the youth meant to cause harm to anyone, his chest rising slowly in a rhythmic balance as he slept. Puc nudged her with his staff to get her attention. They then began to walk towards the exit.

෨෬

The entire trip had been silent. Puc had nothing to say to Annetta, and she had nothing to say to him in turn. From her perspective, she was not sure if this was a good thing or not. Unlike when she walked with Brakkus or her friends, she felt like she should be talking to the mage more than she did.

"I should not have let you use that technique yet," Puc finally said as they closed in on their destination. "It was my mistake to assume you were ready."

"I managed to get it done though, right?" Annetta looked up at him.

"Yes, but you almost dashed his brains out. Were I more analytical of the situation we could have avoided that. And now, I also have to have a firm talk with Jason. And you too, I suppose. As I said before, you are not to use your powers anywhere outside of here. Even at home, you run the risk of being seen by an outsider or even a spy," he explained.

"I guess I can see your point," she muttered. She was still disappointed that her new means of defending herself was largely useless.

"Annetta, magic and telekinetic powers cannot solve all of life's problems," Puc said, looked down at her. "A sharp tongue and mind however, can work wonders."

"Right, like that'll work on Finn," she replied, rolling her eyes.

"You can land a punch on a person's face and make them bleed for a while, or you can injure their ego and make it bleed far longer."

They stopped at the gate. Annetta took out her card key and swiped, not really wanting to say anything else.

"I wish you a safe trip to the surface. Be here tomorrow again at the same time," were the elf's last words as Annetta was teleported back home.

Chapter 11

Far in the sky above Earth, on Valdhar, Matthias walked down the vast corridors, making final preparations for his deployment. The halls around him were illuminated with lights on the floor and rooms were bustling with soldiers and scientists as they went on with their everyday tasks. Each knew full well to get out of Matthias's way when he was close.

The assassin had needed to make multiple aliases for his stay. This included identifications and currencies. For the most part, he would be a college student since, according to the cultural historians, that was the demographic he best fit. Heading back to his room from having received all the paper work, he looked through to make sure everything was in place.

"Matthias," a cold voice rang from behind him like a dagger of ice piercing his back. He spun on his heel to face Mislantus, his cat eyes observing him with intent.

"My lord, I had no idea you were-," Matthias bowed down, ashamed to have been at the same level as his superior.

"Rise," he ordered, watching the young man. "I wished to speak with you about the mission that you are about to embark on."

"Of course." Matthias was back to his confident self after the momentary lapse of balance.

"My daughter has requested my permission to go visit Earth. She finds it a fascinating planet and wants to learn more about it. I think it will also be beneficial for you to have her along as a cover, providing a more fleshed out background for yourself."

"I... sir, is it wise for you to be sending her with me?" Matthias looked questioningly at him.

"It would be if I did not trust you." The cat teeth flashed a smile at him. "Carry on with your preparations, and you may brief my daughter on the situation."

The assassin nodded in obedience to his master and turned on his heel to continue walking, only be cut off by the voice again, "And Matthias, if any harm befalls my daughter; know I will have your head."

Standing at attention, the warrior responded without hesitation, "Yes sir."

છજ

Sitting on the large four metal-posted bed in her room, Sarina stared out her circular window watching the stars glisten in the distance, along with the satellites above Earth. She found the floating objects interesting, and wondered about each one's purpose. Shifting to make herself more comfortable she sighed looking at her surroundings. The bland, plain room, looked no different than that of Matthias's with the large round lights on all four corners of the grey walls and the exact same arrangement of the desk and dresser. The only major difference was the size of the bed. Despite hating her room, for at times it seemed a prison when she was not allowed to leave, it was also the only room where she could truly be alone without being judged by others.

Moments later a knock came from the door.

"Enter," she said, turning her head to see Matthias step inside.

"I don't know how you did it, but I am now to officially brief you on the mission," he announced. "You are coming to Earth with me once the shuttle is packed."

A smile spread on Sarina's face at the news. For the first time in her life, she was going to be able to leave the castle. Part of her almost didn't believe it was happening.

"I told you if I talked to him he would let me go. He just needed to realize I wasn't going to be a little girl forever. Plus I told him I wanted to be personally involved in his revenge."

"You are beautiful and brilliant," Matthias chuckled. "Someday, you will break some poor man's heart."

"I thought that was a good thing to do. At least father tells me," she smirked.

Matthias grinned back, then put on his business face.

"Go down to the cultural historians and have them help you pick out some clothing appropriate for Earth. We will buy what we need as we go along, but we need to look normal from the start."

"What's wrong with what I have on now?" she asked.

"I can't tell you that, only the cultural historians can," he said. "I will go and have your identification set up in the meantime, and procure some additional funding."

Sarina rolled her eyes. When Matthias was in business mode he did not stop for anything. It was his way of distancing himself from her, letting her know he was still a soldier even though they were friends. She understood why, though. If her father thought the two of them were too close, he might have had him executed for it. That was what bothered her most out of her confinement, that she was unable to have normal friendships because everyone was either seen as a threat or inappropriate. Her friendship with Matthias was kept secret, and she was lucky enough to be able to choose her own bodyguards when she went places. Still, she craved a real friendship with someone who would not be worried about her father having his or her head lopped off.

"All work and no play," she said, smiled sourly.

"I'm sorry, you know how it is," he said over his shoulder as he left the room.

Chapter 12

The next morning, Brakkus waited for Link to wake. His massive paw-like hands rested on the hilt of his sword as his eyes watched the boy for any signs of unusual movement. He did not trust the youth. Something was definitely amiss with the scar on his eye and the armor he came dressed in. Something was wrong, and he intended to find out what it was, or at least get a sense of his intentions. The way he'd sprang up and offered his services to the granddaughter of his long lost comrade was fishy. Having spent the long years in the Lab during what was now deemed 'The Blackout' had made the Hurtz wary of anything that seemed out of place, and the youth who held the name Lincerious Heallaws was just that.

Link's eyes shifted rapidly underneath his eyelids as he began to awaken. He wasn't expecting to see the enormous furry muzzle glaring back at him, and so he naturally cried out, and leapt back on his bed in fear.

"Relax laddie, I ain't gonna hurt ya, unless ya give me reason," the Hurtz told him.

Link calmed down, but still looked cautiously at the massive two-handed sword the creature had with him. It looked more like a butcher's cleaver than a sword due to its width and the jagged nicks that decorated the well used blade.

"Has the patient awakened?" the voice of Puc echoed from beyond the door as he entered.

"Aye, but he's the quietest little bugger I've seen. Least quieter now than he was last night," Brakkus chuckled.

"I would be too if I woke up having your old mug staring at me," Puc said dryly.

"Ohoho, you hurt me bad," Brakkus laughed. "Then again, not like your face is any prettier."

Puc rolled his eyes, letting his friend take the victory in the quarrel before turning his attention to Link, who was sitting in silence watching them.

"His odor is worse than his bite, ignore him," Puc said to the boy, hearing Brakkus snort in response. "How are you feeling?"

"Better. Well, better than last night at least."

"Good, then I suppose you will not mind answering a few questions for us, such as who sent you. And answer honestly, or by all that is holy not

114

even the Unknown will help you." the keen eyes of the elf glared at him, all trace of humor instantly gone.

"I told you before, I was training. I was part of the Gaian military," Link explained again.

"I think there is more to it than that, boyo," Brakkus said, leaned on his sword. "Puc, why don't we do this the Hurtz way, and every time he lies I take a finger?"

"Because that would be barbaric," Puc stated as Link cringed and turned to the boy. "But I do agree that you are keeping something from us. Your cloak is far too tattered for you to have been in the military recently, even if you have been wandering about here for days. I suggest you answer now, and answer honestly."

The boy looked from the creature that called himself a Hurtz to the man named Puc and back. He swallowed hard and breathed out, before speaking again.

"It is true I did not tell you everything," he began, "but I am not lying. I was part of the military until I ran away. Not because I'm a coward. I was called to leave. I just… I suppose I didn't want to sound crazy. But these two creatures, two birds, one of fire and one of thunder, which called themselves angels appeared. They spoke of a castle in the sky and a girl who needed my help. They called her 'the one who is severed,' like the name of that girl, Annetta Severio. They said if I did not find her then terrible things would come to pass, so I agreed. They said that the fates would guide me and before I knew it, I was here. Then I ran into you."

Brakkus and Puc looked at one another, then back at Link, who was attempting to take off the bandages on his side. Puc struck his hand away from them.

"Leave those. You're saying they visited you with this message? Where did you get that scar, then?"

"I don't know. I've had it as long as I can remember. My father had one just like it, if that helps," Link said, running a hand down it self-consciously.

Puc glared long and hard at Link for a moment, before looking at Brakkus, whose gaze was also fixed on the boy.

"I believe you," the elf finally said after a pause. "I suggest you rest for now. I healed most of the wound, but it will still take a few days to fully recover. I will check in with you tomorrow. Oh, and keep your sword close, you never know what can pop out of the shadows. And I do not mean Brakkus."

Getting up, he made his way to the door. Brakkus followed, saying nothing to the boy.

"Spit it out, what is it?" Brakkus demanded, once they were far enough away that Link would not hear their conversation, "I saw the change of tone, ya can't fool me."

Puc continued to walk in silence, ignoring the Hurtz.

"Oi! I'm talking to ya!" Brakkus grabbed Puc's shoulder pulling him back.

"Do you remember when Arieus swore off being part of this world and in anger I vowed to leave, to have nothing more to do with any Severio as long as I lived?"

Brakkus's ears perked up as he took his hand off of Puc's shoulder. The events after Orbeyus' death had never left his memory, not in all of the blended-together and confusing years lived in the de-powered Lab.

"Aye," he answered.

"I never told you why I changed my mind and stayed behind, did I?" The elf looked back at his companion. "As I began to pack my things, as I got ready to leave here forever, I was approached by those creatures, these angels as they called themselves, the same that came to the boy, the same creatures which came to the children and told them of this place." After he'd started, the words had simply begun to pour out of him. "They told me about the heirs of Orbeyus and Arcanthur, about my need to stay behind and wait to train them, that this was the will of the Unknown, and if I did not then this whole world would be engulfed in flame as would all others, because there would be no one left to defend the Eye to All Worlds."

"But there hasn't been a defender in years, it's just been us down here-," Brakkus interrupted.

"Let me finish, friend. It is just us, but you forget that the only way to get to Severio Castle is through here, and who else has been down here but us. We have been defending it. Granted, poorly, but better than nothing."

Puc began pacing, leaning on his staff as he did so.

"They asked me for two specific card keys. The ones that Arieus and Arcanthur used. I refused, until I saw it."

The Hurtz's ears shifted, causing the earrings to jingle as he stared at his friend. "What did ya see? Well come on, out with it!"

116

Puc stopped pacing, a tortured look in his face. "I saw him. I saw Orbeyus shrouded in blue light, the light of the Unknown. He told me to do as they commanded, and that he was doing well where he was now. I needed no further explanation and I knew it was no trick. That feeling of being overwhelmed by seeing someone's spirit... it was like nothing I have ever felt before. I felt at peace when I saw him, but at the same time I fear that I was seeing something I should not be able to see. He told me to stay, if not for the sake of the Unknown, then as his last request as a dead man, to stay and see to his granddaughter for him."

Brakkus's ears lowered and wolfish mouth turned downwards. He could see the pain etched onto his friend's face. But there was still something that bothered him. Had Puc chosen to stay only because of an apparition or because their friendship forged on the plane of battle had meant something to him?

"I thought ya just stayed because you changed your mind on your own," the giant said quietly.

Puc sighed, realizing the magnitude of his words on his friend. "It was the best decision I ever made, Brakkus. I know our friend can rest in peace. And I never really did plan to leave anyways."

"HAH! I knew it, ya were just jabberin' when ya were yellin' at Arieus," Brakkus said, grinning victoriously. "I knew ya'd stay here with me."

"Did I ever leave you during the war? Don't start doubting me now," the elf said as he rolled his eyes. "I just want you to know that...well, there was simply more to it, and I think there is more going on here than we both know."

"You think the Unknown himself is somehow involved in all of this?"

"No, I don't- well not directly anyways. Why would he care about such a minuscule planet when he oversees the entire multiverse?"

"He sent angels to get the card keys, didn't he?"

"Well, he could have, but it could have just been another angel who wanted it done, I don't know," the elf answered, feeling frustrated.

"I think he did," Brakkus said. "Anyways, what do we do with the boy?"

"I stand by not leaving him alone with Annetta or Jason until we know what that scar represents, or if it is magical. He said his father had the same one, and it is beginning to sound more like a curse to me, but what for and why I do not know. I will need to do research in the library, and those kids need to find time to get to Severio Castle. That schooling of theirs keeps interrupting. We need to find a way out around that. Until then, we must both be vigilant. It could just be a bad luck charm or it could be a lot worse."

&OCR

Somewhere in the deep of night, the shuttle from Valdhar touched down on Earth in silence. Only the sea of grass blowing in all directions betrayed its landing. Stealth was something Mislantus valued. The last thing needed was for the natives to notice a spaceship landing on their planet and making a huge commotion about it. He had a cloaking device placed on all his ships, rendering them invisible to the eye. Inside, Matthias sat in the cockpit with the pilot and scanned the readings on the various computers, checking the air composition, the temperature, and the location of where they had landed. Sarina was asleep in the seat beside him. She hated descending into the atmosphere and had wanted to be knocked out for the process. Once Matthias was sure everything was set, he nudged his companion.

"Wake up, we're all clear," he said to her.

Sarina's eyebrows furrowed, the eyes shifting beneath the lids as she stirred and finally opened them. Through the darkness, Matthias's hair reflected the green lights of the inside of the craft, making him appear more angel than assassin.

"Where are we?" she grumbled, stretching.

"Western coast of a country called…Kanadia?" Matthias glanced at the geographic locator and tilted his head, reading the name listed above it. "Canada…strange name."

Sarina looked outside the window. Around her were trees far taller than she'd even imagined possible, and all around them was green foliage as far as the eye could see. It was too dark to see much else, but she still could not tell what her father found threatening about this planet. It was beautiful.

"Alright. We need to move into the city," Matthias broke the silence once he had all the necessary information about the area they were in. He turned to the pilot. "We will take it from here."

"But I don't see any people outside," Sarina complained, as the pilot nodded, adjusting his monitor with the information needed to return.

"The shuttle landed us in an isolated area so we would not attract attention. This is the landmass where unnatural activity was spotted by the

118

ship a few months ago, that storm that happened and then disappeared faster than a storm on this planet can form and disappear. Although," Matthias paused to look at his files, "we should be closer to the east coast than the west. But not to worry, that's a problem easily fixed."

Getting up from his seat, Matthias strode to the back of the ship, where his duffle bag was located. Opening it, he took out his gauntlets. He had been ordered to take them off for the mission in order to blend in, but Matthias had his own agenda when it came to being parted with his favored weapon. It went something along the lines of 'till death do they part.' He had already dressed on the ship to blend in with the population of Earth, wearing jeans, a green sleeveless shirt, and a black leather jacket. The sleeves of the jacket hid the gauntlets well enough, so he pulled out gloves he had been given to go with the jacket and put them overtop. He looked over at Sarina, dressed in a pair of light blue jeans, a salmon button up shirt and a long black spring jacket that the cultural committee on the ship had deemed appropriate for her.

"How are we going to get to the east coast from here? You going to answer me or what?" Sarina looked at him with her hands on her hips.

"Easy there, princess. I'll tell you." He grinned and walked further to the back of the ship, once he had taken all the papers he needed out of the bag. He came to a large object covered with a protective tarp. He removed the tarp, revealing a sleek blue sports motorcycle underneath. He'd driven similar vehicles on other missions and felt more comfortable riding something small. He'd been taught how to drive it beforehand; an easy task for someone used to driving a spacecraft. He seated himself in the seat, put on a helmet, and looked in Sarina's direction.

"You coming?"

Sarina raised an eyebrow, looking at the bizarre metallic beast before her.

"What? On that thing? Do you even know how to operate it?"

"Yes, as a matter of fact I do. Now come on, we're wasting nighttime," he growled at her.

Sarina said nothing more and ran over to the motorcycle. She paused again, not sure what to do next.

"Put this on and hop on behind me," he explained, "like on a hover bike, it operates the same way, and it just...doesn't hover."

"Oh. Well that's dumb, who would make a bike that doesn't hover?" she asked, climbing on behind him.

"Backwards alien technology? I don't know," Matthias shrugged and opened the rear hanger. As he turned the key, the engine roared to life, and they took off out of the ship. Matthias maneuvered the motorcycle around and looked back at where the shuttle was. All that could be seen was the inside from where they had come out. The cloaking device was still in place. As soon as they were out, the hanger closed and the ship began to take off. The only sign it was moving was the sea of grass below it rippling from the power of the engine.

"Hang on tight." He looked back at Sarina before revving the machine and taking off into the forest.

As they continued to accelerate, the unmade path ahead of them became bumpier and harder to stay on.

"Matt! We're going to crash!" Sarina cried into his ear holding onto him tightly.

"Not yet, not on my watch," Matthias gripped the handles and focused his mind on the picture the cultural institute had shown him of where the activity had taken place. To an amateur, teleporting was no easy task, and could easily result in death. But to Matthias, a seasoned psychic warrior and veteran in the arts, it came as easily as snapping a finger. As he allowed his mind to recreate the image of where he wanted to go, he felt the motorcycle, Sarina's fingertips and his own flesh become engulfed in the transferring energy created. When he opened his eyes again, he was moments away from colliding with another giant metallic beast and swiftly evaded the crash.

"You okay back there?" he shouted over the commotion, to which Sarina only murmured an exhausted response, "Good, I'm going to try and locate an inn, so don't fall asleep on me yet. I know teleporting the first time can be exhausting, but trust me, it gets easier."

80C3

Matthias parked the motorcycle beside one of the inns listed as a location they could stay at. It was not the largest, or most elaborate of hideaways, he thought wryly. Mislantus may have sent out his daughter with him, but still did not allow his best assassins cover to be blown.

"Whatever you do, do not speak until we are in the room. Let me handle this." Matthias instructed Sarina, who was picking at the foam on the inside of the helmet she had been wearing.

Entering through the door, they came into the lobby of hotel. A vibrant carpet greeted them in an array of rich reds and yellows that had not been cleaned in years. Above, dim lights shone onto it, causing the fabric to look more stained than it was. Behind a large desk sat a bored looking older man with short grey hair, reading a paper of some sort, not even noticing that the doors had opened and closed before him.

It being Matthias's first encounter with a local, he walked over to the desk and waited, until he was asked what he was required. It took the man a while before he noticed Matthias was standing before him, but once he did his demeanor changed immediately. With a cough, the paper was folded neatly in half and a salesman smile crossed his face.

"How can I help you, sir?" he asked in a gruff but polite voice.

"I would like to get accommodations for my sister and I," he said, motioning to Sarina who stood beside him, not making a sound.

"Okay, I think I got just the thing for you," the man moved over in his wheeled office chair, and punched in a few things on a keyboard hooked up to a large rectangular monitor. "I got a two queen bed room in the non smoking zone...er... Mister?"

"Repronom. Matthias Repronom," The name rolled oddly off his tongue, but he had no choice in using it, with all his documentation saying it was his name. Those in the cultural division had chosen it, and they did not really have a grasp on reality at times he felt.

"Foreign name. I like foreign guys, they work harder than most of the locals. Feel like they got to prove themselves or something. It's a good example, I just wish others would see it that way," the man said. "I'll need your credit card for holding, in case anything breaks, you know? One of those rules."

Matthias nodded silently at the man's pathetic attempt to seem hospitable. Pulling out the requested card, he slid it along the table to receive the keys. Taking them, he picked up his duffle bag, ready to leave.

"Room is on the second floor to your left. Have a happy stay," the man replied, but Matthias was already gone, heading towards the stairs that led up to their room.

Coming to the room number assigned. Matthias paused and examined the little key in his hand. He was used to card keys and punching in sequences of numbers whenever he went on missions.

"Truly backwards technology," he sighed, and put the key in the hole. He had to turn it a few times in order to get it to open and nearly broke down the door the third time, were it not for Sarina telling him to calm down and trying herself.

After much trial and error, the door finally came open and they stepped inside the room. It was dark and it took Matthias a moment to switch on the light, after which the room was flooded with a deep yellow hue. Sarina took in everything she saw: The dark wooden desk, the drawers with a strange rectangular object sitting on it that resembled a monitor, and the beds that seemed to be made with such precision it put all the beds in the barracks to shame back in her home.

"They should really take some pointers from these Earthlings on cleaning back on Valdhar," she muttered out loud, taking a few steps forward to familiarize herself with the room.

"It's not your quarters in Valdhar, but it will have to do for now until I acquire lodgings for us," Matthias informed her. "For now, I suggest you get some sleep. Tomorrow we start scouting the area looking for lodgings and looking into the schools, and I want to get an early start. The less time I have to spend on this backward pile of dung, the better."

"Matt, you're so mean sometimes, they can't help being where they are," Sarina scolded him.

"And you're too nice for the daughter of Mislantus the Threat, and that's something you need to learn. You can't become too familiar with the enemy. The moment you do, you see them as more than a target. This is something you need to remember on this mission. Yes, you need to get close to the heirs but never, ever see them as more than a job. Do you understand?"

"Yeah, yeah. Pieces and not people," she sighed. "Anything else, Commander Teron?"

"No, you are dismissed," Matthias answered, and watched the girl leave into the bathroom, located by the door to change.

Taking off his jacket and flinging it on the desk, then removing his boots, Matthias flopped down onto the bed. He looked out the window into the setting sun. Somewhere deep down, he felt it had been a mistake to allow her to come along. On his own, he was able to watch his own skin, get close to the target, and strike. But now with Mislantus's daughter with him, he was vulnerable. He did not like the feeling. He had not felt this way since his early days in Mislantus's service, a time blocked from his memory simply because of those feelings. Weakness and defenselessness were things long ago wiped from his mind and body. Discipline was the only thing he was allowed to know, along with the cold killer's instinct and responsibility to his one true lord and master. When he spent time with Sarina, even on the ship, he felt those things go away to some degree. He almost felt carefree and part of him could not help but remember that somewhere in his past there had been a little sister just like her, someone he had loved unconditionally. Another part of him knew the bond he had with her was dangerous, because it would eventually cloud his judgment, and perhaps even lead to his downfall. Swimming in these thoughts, Matthias closed his eyes and accepted the inevitable.

"Duty above all else."

Chapter 13

One month later…

Annetta had come down to the Lab as per routine, and waited for Jason. She had managed to master opening the two great doors using telekinesis, without as much struggle as before. Once inside, she leaned against one of the walls, allowing the cold steel to seep past her jacket and shirt. It only took moments for the chill to touch her skin, causing goosebumps to form on her arms.

'*Annetta?*' the voice of her friend rang in her mind.

'*Yeah, I'm here, what's the hold up?*'

'*I can't make it today. Some stuff is going on at home and I need to stay behind to help with my brother.*' Jason's voice echoed, his tone tense. Annetta figured his mother had been upset about something again, and he didn't want to leave his brother alone with her.

'*Okay, I'll let Puc know you're not coming today, I'll see you at school tomorrow.*' She sent the message to him and felt the connection break between them, before she took off towards the training room.

Despite her increasing skill with her powers, and the decreasing amount of monsters lurking about the Lab, Annetta still hated traveling alone. Each time she did, it felt like something would pop out of the dark and grab her. This feeling made her run to the training room instead of walking. She could not wait until Puc taught her and Jason to teleport, cutting their journey from the door to the training grounds short. He'd explained to them that teleporting was not the same as portal travel. It only worked for shorter distances within the same world, and you needed to know where you wanted to go. It was similar to telepathy and projection, but was more difficult because they would be physically throwing themselves into a different space.

Annetta continued to jog as the motion sensing lights turned on in each area. She was so paralyzed by the fear of running into something that she didn't notice Link when he stepped in front of her. She rammed into him full force, knocking them both to the ground.

"Oww… hey," Annetta rubbed her temple as she looked over at the boy with the crescent moon scar across his eye.

"Hey to you too," Link grumbled, brushing his hair out of his face and getting up, holding out a hand for Annetta.

"Sorry about that, I don't like walking alone down here," she explained quickly, feeling the need to justify her reason for running in the first place. "The silence is kind of creepy."

"It's okay," he smiled at her.

Annetta noticed he was dressed differently than when she had first met him. He was wearing a black t-shirt tucked into a pair of jeans and a jean jacket of a similar shade to go with it. His dirty blonde hair was tied in a braid and hung down his back like a tail, with his bangs parting on the sides and flying loose. He still had his sword, which now hung in its scabbard from the baldric fastened to his torso along with a pair of brown leather gauntlets hidden behind the sleeves of his jacket, making them look like regular fingerless gloves. She'd never really gotten a good look at his face before, not while he was awake. Over the last month, she'd only caught glimpses of him from time to time, since Puc made sure they were always busy. Despite all the warnings the mage had given her about not being alone with him, his face seemed warm and non threatening. His gray eyes told the story of someone who had been forced into a life of fighting from an early age, something Annetta had read about in fantasy books but never seen in real life.

"You're looking better since the last time we met," Annetta smiled back at him, not sure what else to say.

"Yeah, Puc has been helping me adjust a bit to things here on Earth. Uh, clothing-wise and stuff," he said, motioning to his outfit.

"I think he forgot to mention that we don't carry swords where I come from," she said, smirking.

"Oh, yeah, that. Yeah he did, this is a precaution. Brakkus told me about things being loose in the Lab during the 'Blackout,' so I've had my sword with me."

Link took the baldric from his shoulder and held the sword in his hands, balancing the scabbard on his palms. Annetta examined the finely detailed hilt of the sword, which was designed to look like two wolves sprouting from the blade, creating the guard. The hilt itself was wound in black leather with silver wiring wrapped carefully around it. It looked more refined and delicate than the blade Brakkus carried around with him. It had an air of dignity about it.

"It's beautiful," Annetta said.

"It was my father's once, passed down from generation to generation. My great grandfather foraged it out of a meteor that fell to our planet. At least, that was what my father told me when he was alive." Link paused, looking at the sword in his hands.

"I'm sorry," Annetta said, looking down at her feet awkwardly, not sure how else to respond to the sudden personal information.

"No, its okay," Link said. "He's better off where he is. My people believe death is the release of the soul from all its worry. You become completely free when you die, and you get to meet the people who have already gone before you. It's sort of going on a vacation you never come back from."

Annetta looked back up at Link's honest face. He truly believed it.

"That doesn't sound like such a bad thing," she responded, a light smile forming on her lips as she adjusted her jean jacket on her back.

Link nodded and pulled the baldric over his shoulder again. They stood quietly for a moment, not sure what to do next.

"Say... you think you could teach me how to use a sword?" Annetta asked breaking the silence.

"You want to learn to wield a sword?" Link raised an eyebrow. "Well... I guess if Puc and Brakkus don't have anything against it, I'm willing to teach you all I know. I mean, I was sent here to help."

Annetta could not help but smile a little wider. She had already learned how to ride a horse and take care of it. Learning to use a sword was something else she had always wanted to do, as old fashioned as it was. In the world she lived in guns and machinery had taken over war, but she found something elegant in wielding a blade. It was a dance with death the other methods were far too clumsy to appreciate. She then remembered something else Link had said.

"You said you knew my grandfather. Or of him, anyways," she looked over at Link hopefully, who nodded.

"Lord Orbeyus Severio," he explained. "Sometimes also called Lord Orbeyus of the Axe for the twin bladed axe he wielded. All of our people know of him. He is said to have been the son of a king, but instead of ruling, he chose the path not often taken, and dedicated his life to defending the universe from threats. He was a protector of the weak, and his name is known far and wide across the various worlds."

126

Annetta shifted the weight on her feet hearing this, the more she found out about her grandfather, the more surreal he seemed and the more intimidating of a person he felt to her. There was no way she was going to be able to match up to him in her lifetime.

"You know a lot more than I do about who he was," she said, smiling weakly. "All I have is a few photos. I was always told he was some kind of businessman who died having a stroke, until now anyways. My father told me a few months ago that he was murdered."

"I'm sorry." Link paused and then added. "At least you know now who he really was."

"That's true," Annetta said, looking up at the fluorescent lights high above her head for a moment, feeling the blindness creep in on her from looking at them too long. She looked back down, seeing the faint blue blotches in the corner of her eyes as she faced Link again. "You must get really lonely down here. I mean, we've hardly ever talked aside from that first night."

"It does sometimes. But I don't mind it."

Annetta nodded her head. An idea then came to her, "Well, if you leave the sword down here, maybe you can come hang out with my friends and I? We could maybe go see a movie?"

Link looked at the girl, confused, raising his scarred eyebrow.

"Do you guys not have movies where you're from? Moving pictures on a screen? They tell a story and you go into this big dark room to watch them? It's like...uhm," Annetta scratched her head, at a loss for words.

"I would be glad to come with you to one of...those." Link said, awkwardly.

"Awesome," she smiled and began taking steps in the direction of the training grounds. "I should get going now, Puc is probably worried sick."

"I'll go with you," Link blurted out. "I mean, if I go with you then you won't get in trouble as much."

"Oh. Okay, good plan. Thanks."

Link nodded, following her to where Puc and Brakkus were already waiting.

After a few hours of learning to use projection with better accuracy, Puc decided it was time to call it a day. He was not pleased that Jason had been unable to show up, but he understood the boy's predicament, simply

127

saying he would need to stay longer the next day. Annetta told him she would relay the message, and headed for home.

ഏരു

The next morning, Annetta awoke in her bed and got ready for school, leaving with Xander to meet up with Darius on the ground floor of the apartment building.

"You know, I hardly ever see you guys outside school and the morning," Darius commented as they exited the building. "It seems like you and Jason are always busy doing something together. Are you dating? Did I do something to offend you?"

"Uhm," Annetta was slightly taken aback. "We aren't dating and we're not avoiding you. We're just busy with class projects." Annetta wrinkled her nose at the thought of kissing her best friend, "Actually, I was going to ask. Would you wanna go see a movie tonight? Like how we all used to? I have a family friend over, and he's from out of town. I thought it would be fun if we all hung out together."

"Sure, that sounds like a plan," Darius smiled.

The rest of the walk to school was a quiet one. Once they reached the back gate, Jason was already there waiting. He waved and ran up to them, with his backpack hanging from one shoulder.

"Hey guys, how's it going?" he greeted them.

"Good, same old, you?" Annetta managed to say before the bell rang. "What? Already? We must have walked slow today."

"Yeah you guys did take a while. You sleep in, Annetta?" Jason asked as they made their way to their first period class.

"A bit, that lesson took me right out last night." She paused, blinked, and then continued. "I mean with the tutor. The math tutor's lesson took me right out."

"You're failing math?" Darius looked at her.

"Not failing. Just having a hard time with it. Algebra isn't my strongest subject. I find it kind of confusing so my parents got me a tutor," Annetta quickly wove a story together.

"Well, if you had trouble I could help you," Darius began. "I'm pretty good with it."

"No, its okay. The tutor knows his stuff," Annetta cut him off as they began to go inside.

128

As they turned the corner leading to the second floor of the school, Annetta caught sight of someone talking to the principle, with his hand on the shoulder of a young girl about her own age with dark brown hair and big eyes. He was a young man with light brown hair, wearing a tweed blazer and rectangular glasses. The goatee under his lower lip made him seem like he was trying too hard to be an artsy teacher, but his face suggested he was no older than his late twenties. He gave off the aura of an overachiever and a suck up, which Annetta instinctively disliked. The moment his azure eyes turned to look at her, she hurried up the stairs.

"What's wrong?" Jason asked, looking back to see Annetta straying behind.

"Nothing, lets just get to class," she answered.

೮೨೧೪

After school, Annetta rushed back home to get changed and have dinner before heading down to the Lab to find Brakkus, Link, and Puc. Brakkus could be found in either the stable or armory, where he sharpened his sword or mended the other weapons and armor. He said it gave him a sense of peace because he could focus on the task and nothing else when he did it. Puc, on the other hand, was always at his books, whether scribbling something down or reading. Annetta understood the desire to read and learn, but the way Puc did it took things to a whole new level. Link was a bit more difficult to locate. He generally wandered around the Lab with his sword at an arm's reach. It was still hard for him to take the fact that he was miles from home and unable to return on pain of death. It was difficult for Annetta to comprehend what it felt like sometimes, but she did her best to understand.

Turning the corner, she moved to where Puc usually sat reading and that was his office. Despite the Lab being as modern as possible with its large metal panels and enormous fluorescent lights, Puc's room was the opposite. It was filled with huge wooden shelves that seemed to hold more books than Annetta had ever seen in one space. On a few smaller tables in the far left corner were what the girl made out to be as supplies in jars and empty vials along with other tubes that seemed like they belonged in a science classroom in her school. In the center was a large rectangular wooden table on which were generally a few big candles, quills and other writing materials. Stooped over a book and sitting in a large ornate chair was the mage.

"Hey Puc, have you seen Link anywhere?" she asked.

The elven mage looked up from his task. "I have not."

Annetta nodded and turned her heel ready to leave.

"And where are you going?" he demanded in a stern tone.

Annetta's sneakers made a squeaking noise as she pivoted back to facing the mage.

"Well...to the movies with Link, Jason and Darius," Annetta responded.

"And what of your training?"

Annetta didn't know how to reply to his question, it was true that Jason and her were supposed to come down each night to hone their skills.

"Can't we have a day off?" She looked at him, shoving her hands in her pockets as she leaned against the doorframe.

"And will those pursuing you take a day off? Or will they keep going until you and Jason are eliminated?" Puc rose from his seat. "This is not a game. You need to know how to use your abilities at the snap of a finger, and use them efficiently. The enemy never sleeps."

"Oh come on! One day! A few hours won't make a difference."

"It can make all the difference in the world in a life and death situation, Annetta Severio," barked the elf. "I do not think that you and Jason are taking this very seriously."

"Or maybe we're trying to live two completely separate lives, which is really hard!"

Puc fell silent, observing Annetta. He curled his lip slightly as he thought of a rebuttal to her argument, which did have some validity.

"You may be correct," he said, finally, sitting back down in his chair. "There needs to be more balance. Go and enjoy yourself tonight, but in the near future I may request to pull you from school for a day or two to make up for it."

The girl shifted the weight on her feet again as she got ready to take off again.

"He's in the mountain biosphere," Puc added after a moment. "And before you leave, that sword comes to me."

Annetta nodded once more before taking off to find Link, while Puc returned to his books and his writing. Moments later, Brakkus walked in on the mage and his work.

"What was that all about?" he asked.

130

"Defiant youth, let her win the fight but the war shall be mine," Puc said threateningly, not looking up from his books.

"Yer being pretty rough on 'em, ya know. They're just kids." Brakkus pulled up a chair beside him.

Puc stopped his work and looked up at the massive creature sitting beside him.

"Kids or not, they are in danger. That castle is up there, watching this planet. For all we know, the Lab could already be infiltrated, and they are just waiting for the right time to strike. Look what happened to Orbeyus, and he was a seasoned warrior."

"I still say yer overreacting," Brakkus scoffed. "Look how far they've come since we met 'em, and it's only been a couple months, not a year or decade or nothing. Ya need to give them more credit. Yerself, too, 'cuz what happens when the time comes and the enemy is at hand? You said it yerself, we won't always be there for 'em, and sometimes there's not enough training in the world to prepare ya."

Puc let out a sigh as his shoulders relaxed slightly from their hunched position. He closed the book before him.

"So you're saying just let it happen and not train them?"

"No, I'm saying yer training them like oxen when they're the heirs of Orbeyus and Arcanthur. What do they really know from being cooped up down here, learning to levitate stones? Orbeyus left ya in charge of this because he knew ya'd teach them more than just controlling their powers. Ya'd teach them what's out there, that it's not just black and white, that there's something more to it."

"Sometimes I speculate if maybe he meant to leave you in charge, the way you talk," Puc snorted and got up.

"No, no, I got left to take care of the horses cuz Orbeyus knew you always hated the stables an-,"

"And don't you dare finish that sentence," Puc glared at him, and grabbed his staff as he walked out of the room, followed by Brakkus's booming laughter.

৪৹ৈ

After dropping off the sword with Puc, Annetta and Link made their way to the exit leading to her apartment. It would be Link's first time out, so Annetta tried to explain the things he would encounter, like streetlights and cars and her friend Darius, who would be told that Link was her friend from out of town. Luckily, her parents were not home so she did not have to go through awkward introductions. They left, locked the door, and headed over to the theater. Jason and Darius were already there.

"Hey guys, what's up?" Annetta interjected, looking at them both curiously.

"Not much," Jason said. "Just talking about what to see." Jason paused, realizing that Link was standing right beside Annetta, and he wasn't supposed to know him. "So, is this your friend you were talking about?"

"Yeah, this is Lincoln Johnson, but everyone calls him Link for short." Annetta smiled as Link extended his hand to him.

"Jason Kinsman. But everyone calls me J.K. instead." He smiled, and then noticed Darius eyeing Link suspiciously, focusing on the crescent scar across his eye. Jason nudged him quickly to get him to stop staring.

"Darius Silver," he said, introducing himself. "Sorry for staring, but how did you get that scar?" He tried to sound polite while shaking Link's hand.

"Sort of a funny story actually. I took a bottle to the face when I tripped and fell into the corner of a coffee table."

"I see. It's just very.... well… noticeable," he said, and then turned to the others. "Let's get going then shall we?"

Annetta noted the change in Darius's behavior, but did not think much of it.

"Okay cool, let's go grab tickets then so we're not late," Jason turned and began walking to the sales booth reaching to grab his wallet from his back pocket.

Darius seemed detached to Annetta as he motioned with his head for everyone to get in line after Jason. He continued to throw glances every now and then at Link as they bought their tickets and walked to the theater.

Once inside, Annetta sat beside Link and Jason, while Darius sat beside Link with the same scowl on his face, as if something was not right.

"You okay?" Annetta leaned over from her seat.

"Yeah, I'm fine. Why?" Darius peered over at her.

"You just seem upset."

"Nope, I'm fine. Just peachy," he said as the lights dimmed.

80CB

After the movie, the four of them exited the theater and began to walk towards the residential area nearby. They liked to take the alleyways, so they could talk and joke in peace. It was still light outside, but fading fast.

"Meh, same thing as always, when are they gonna think of something new?" Jason groaned.

"I enjoyed it," Link said after a moment. "Particularly the car chase."

"Yeah that was well done," Annetta said. "I mean, it wasn't realistic, but it was fun to watch. Especially when the guy was using the broken door like a skateboard, then climbed into the villain's car by kicking the driver."

Jason scratched the back of his head. "Yeah, I did like that. You gonna head home now or do you still wanna hang out a bit? It's a Friday after all."

"I guess we can. What do you think, Link? You want to hang out a bit or go home?" Annetta looked over at him.

Before Link could respond, he turned to look back at Darius, who had stopped moving. Annetta and Jason followed his glance. Darius stood a few paces behind all of them, staring at his feet as though he were a robot that had shut down.

"Whoa! You okay dude?" Jason asked, and then noticed Darius's fingernails had grown into thick black claws. His breathing too had grown heavier and almost inhuman.

Sooner than anyone could say anything else, Darius leaped at Link, sending them both flying into one of the alleyways. Annetta and Jason ran after them. What they saw shocked next them both. Facing them stood something that looked like a huge black panther with the body of a man. The creature, standing on its hind legs, was at least eight feet tall. It towered over Link, who lay in a pile of cardboard boxes that had broken his fall. Its powerful muscles coiled under the fur in its arm as the claws extended. Link slowly shook himself aware as he looked up at the creature.

"What the hell?" he groaned.

"It is my duty to protect the heirs. Now answer me truthfully, where did you get that scar?" the creature growled.

"What? I've had this long as I remember!" Link yelled at it.

"Liar! I can sense the magic coming off of it. Do not take me for a fool." the panther bared its fangs, then struck at Link's chest with its massive paws, leaving four large gashes in his torso.

Annetta cringed, but tried to think of a solution quickly.

'Can you distract it?' She sent her thoughts to Jason.

'I can try, what are you pulling?'

'Just trust me and get its attention, okay?'

Jason nodded and stepped behind the beast.

"Hey! Hairy! Over here!" Jason waved to it.

"What do you want, Kinsman? I'm busy," the creature growled.

"Darius? It's you in there? The kitty thing looks good, but you need to trim your nails. Someone could get hurt."

The panther ignored Jason's taunting and continued to glare at Link, its green eyes fixed on the boy. "Who sent you here? I fail to believe you just happened upon the two of them without any-"

Before the creature could finish its sentence, it found itself six feet in the air, thrown like a rag doll across the alley into a pile of garbage disposal units. Having hit its head on the metallic surface, the beast fell unconscious and turned back into Darius. Annetta ran towards Link with Jason, helping him to his feet.

"You okay?" she said, taking his arm and wrapping it around her neck for support.

"I think so." Link cringed, getting to his feet. "It's not that deep."

"We need to get moving before he wakes up," Jason said as he got on Link's other side and took a look at the gash in his chest.

"What? Wait! We can't just leave Darius here alone," Annetta protested, only to have Jason grab her arm.

"Uh, yes we can Annetta, he just turned into some weird panther thing and tried to turn Link into canned tuna," Jason reminded her.

Annetta bit her lower lip, though Jason was right about what happened she still did not feel they should abandon her friend. The pulling at her arm from her friend however made it hard to argue any further, this was not her choice. Looking over at Link, who was clutching his torn shirt, further cemented this fact. Darius had indeed attacked them, a question they would need an answer to later, and perhaps it was one they could find in the Lab.

"Fine," she muttered.

"You think we should call your dad for a ride?" Jason glanced over at Annetta as they began to walk towards the apartment building.

"No, I think we'll be okay as long as we stay in the open, where there are cars and people." She paused for a moment. "But with Link in this shape I don't know if that's such a good idea, people might try to pull us over and get him to the hospital." She thought out loud as they continued to walk. "Hang on, stop for a moment, guys."

Annetta got in front of Link and took off her jean jacket, which she wrapped around Link's wound. She then buttoned up his unstained jacket over it. Link watched with a stiff expression as the girl worked. Every muscle in his body seemed to turn into a repelling stone substance at her touch. He didn't enjoy it. He didn't enjoy being the one that was taken care of.

"It's the best I can do," she said, looking over her handiwork. "At least it doesn't look like you're bleeding."

Link nodded and took his arm off Jason's shoulder. "I think I can manage for now. Thanks, though. You know, I was sent here to help you. Not the other way around."

There was a look of failure in his eyes as he kept walking. Annetta raised an eyebrow then looked at Jason for clarification.

"I guess where he's from they haven't heard of the self-rescuing princess yet," Jason said trying to break the tense atmosphere.

"Princess? Pfft! Never!" Annetta shook her head at the thought of being locked in a high tower and wearing a pink ruffled dress. "You would have to give me some serious brain damage before I'd become that."

§Ω§

While Annetta was gone, Arieus and Aurora had come home from their shopping. They were told by their son of the strange young man who had come out of the Lab with Annetta and gone with her. It worried Arieus, who was suspicious of anyone but Puc and Brakkus. His children were his most treasured possession. He would never deny them anything, but he would also never allow them to fall in harm's way. After helping his wife unpack the groceries, he sat in his armchair with a mug of coffee in his hand, deep in thought.

"Arieus, what's wrong?" Aurora came out of the kitchen.

"I worry for her when she is down there," he answered stiffly.

Aurora looked at her husband. Of late he had come to worry more than before, especially when it came to Annetta and the Lab. They shared their concerns, but Arieus was a bit more verbal on the subject.

"We both do. But she made her choice."

"I should be down there with her..." He trailed off. "But I can't. I can't go down into that infernal place where all of those memories are stored," he sighed. "But I still feel guilty for not being the one to teach her to use her abilities, to be the person she can turn to. It feels like I've been stripped of my fatherhood."

Aurora sighed as she looked at the man she had once fallen for many years ago in a far different time and place. She knew full well why he could not return to Q-16, having witnessed first hand the many sleepless nights her husband had endured after his father's death.

"Arieus, you are no less of a father to her." Aurora placed a hand on his shoulder. "Besides, it has been years since you have even tried to tap into your abilities, or used them for anything serious."

Placing the cup down and getting up from his seat, he walked over to the balcony and looked down into the darkening surroundings.

"Look at us, Aurora. It's hard to believe that we once fought in wars. Actual wars. Now we go to the grocery store and live an ordinary-" he was cut off by his wife's hand entwining with his own as she came up beside him.

"It is hard to believe, but we are together and it is a peaceful existence. I would not have wanted it any other way for all of us." She kissed him on the cheek. "And you need to trust your father a bit more. He would not have left things the way they are if he didn't have faith in Annetta."

Arieus nodded, a serious look still etched on his face. "I cannot help it, Rory. She's my little girl no matter what my father had to say about it."

The door crept open. In came Annetta and Jason with another boy. The couple walked back from the balcony to see whom it was. When Arieus noticed the scar on the youth's face, he paused. He knew all too well scars like that were only caused by a curse and meant the bearer had committed something terrible.

"Hi Mom, hi Dad. This is Link-," Annetta greeted her parents.

"Lincerious Heallaws," the youth introduced himself with a bow.

"Heallaws...I know that name from somewhere," Arieus searched his mind. "Say, where did you get that nasty scar?"

"I don't remember actually. My father had the same one," Link explained, running his fingers down the crescent across his eye. He then cringed and clutched his chest. Annetta rushed over to his side.

"What's wrong?" Aurora asked.

"We... we got attacked." It wasn't easy to say. Annetta hated worrying her parents.

136

"What! By who?" Arieus's eyes set ablaze.

"That's what I don't understand. It was Darius. He changed into this creature. It looked like a panther except he was bigger and could stand on two feet like a person. He just attacked Link out of nowhere after the movie. I need to get him to Puc, Dad. He's really hurt."

Arieus turned to Jason who was standing there silently. "You need to get home. Your mother is almost certainly worried about you."

"You're probably right sir," Jason nodded before turning to Annetta. "I should get going. Will you be okay getting him to the Lab?"

"Don't worry about us, we'll be fine," she stated. "Go before your mom thinks something happened. That's the last thing we need now."

Jason felt a bit reluctant to move at first. He did not want to abandon his friend.

"You're sure?" he asked again.

"Yes, go." she rolled her eyes.

"Alright, see you in class," he said, "Bye, Mr. and Mrs. Severio."

"Bye Jason," Aurora replied as the door shut.

"Are you sure you can take him? Your father could go down, too," Aurora then turned to her daughter; ignoring the look her husband had shot her.

Annetta looked at her feet for a moment, not wanting to answer how she truly felt. She decided to be honest. "I don't think I will be able to. I'm still not used to going down on my own."

Arieus, signed and rose from his seat. "I will go. Just let me get my shoes."

Annetta nodded and led Link to her room, then waited for her father to come in.

Arieus put on the shoes, doing up the laces on each foot slowly. Aurora could see the taxed look on his face. A pang of guilt surged through her, not having thought about what she was asking of him until it was too late.

"I'm sorry. I should have offered to go down myself. Are you sure about this?" she asked him.

His eyes hardened as he looked at Aurora, "I'm her father. I was sure about it as soon as she came into the world."

Aurora knew what he meant and said no more as he went into the room. Moments later the familiar noise whisked both her husband and her daughter deep beneath the Atlantic Ocean.

Annetta had already contacted Puc, sending him a psychic message as she had been walking home, and he was waiting at the entrance with Brakkus at his side. Annetta's form appeared on the floor, followed by Arieus and Link. The moment Arieus appeared Brakkus fell to his knees and bowed his head.

"My lord," he said. "It has been a long time since ya last graced us with yer presence."

Arieus sighed, looking down at the Hurtz. "Rise. I only came to aid my daughter in getting her friend down here. My decision not to return still stands. I washed my hands of this place many years ago."

Brakkus nodded as he grabbed Link's arm to support him while Puc took off the two jackets, handing them to Annetta so he could examine the seriousness of the boy's wound.

"Will ya ever return?" Brakkus said, turning back to the man.

Arieus looked down at his daughter, who stood silently in the midst of the conversation. "In some ways, I already have. If you're asking if I myself will return, that is something I cannot answer."

"Scratches, nothing more. You will live," Puc told Link. "We should get you to the hospital wing regardless."

Arieus glanced at Puc. Upon feeling his gaze pierce him, Puc stood up, and then almost immediately cast his eyes down. He would not face the elder Severio for what he had done, the aged anger from long ago visible in the elf's face beneath the curtain of black hair.

"I hope you are not boring her too much," Arieus said. "Teach her who my father was and of all aspects of our world, not only the grim coldness of it."

Puc's pale eyes lifted up to stare at him with a vacant expression. He had no love for Arieus for the treason he had committed in his eyes as a former Defender of the Eye to All Worlds. Yet what the man said had a subtle impact on him. It was not long ago that he and Brakkus held a similar conversation about how he was treating the youth. He knew he was working them to the bone, but he felt it was for their benefit. Brakkus argued for him to show them some of the good of the world. Now the son of Orbeyus himself commanded the same.

"So it was said, so it shall be done," Puc said, nodding as he gripped his staff and straightened his posture.

Arieus took a moment to look at his surroundings. Wherever he gazed, ill memories began to appear. He shook it off, and made his way back to the teleporter. He stopped when he realized he did not have a card key anymore. Annetta noticed him looking for it, and swiped her own to activate the device. He stepped onto the platform and looked over at his daughter. The shadow of the man he once was lingered in his eyes.

"I wish I was the one taking you through all of this Annetta. But I gave up my life here to keep you safe. I love you, and I will stand by you as much as I can, sweetheart. But for now…it's too much for me to be down here. I will see you at home." Arieus then disappeared before her eyes.

Annetta stood there for a moment after her father had left. She then looked at Puc, whose eyes were still cast down as he thought about what had just transpired. He felt the young girl's eyes upon him and looked up to face her.

"Your grandfather, Orbeyus of the Axe Severio, was murdered inside Q-16 when you were but a little girl. He was killed with a weapon of foreign origin, and with a poison so powerful that he was dead within minutes of the attack. We never found out who or what it was, and the reason your father left was because before your grandfather died he told him that he knew the answer to the prophecy, which foretold the coming of the ones who would become the new defenders of the Earth after his death. Whether his interpretation of the text is true or not, we never found out. What Orbeyus told Arieus was that all the signs pointed to you and Jason." Puc told them. "Arieus would not have it, he did not want any more wars, anymore fighting and so he left. The Unknown however has had different plans since you are both here. The words to the prophecy went like this."

He then began reciting the lines that had long been etched into his memory.

'The axe no longer in hand will sway,
And though darkness be a thing of far away,
Its shadow will stain.
The threat is a creature very vain.

Descendant of the axe step forth,
And take the mantle up into skies north.
Through the sword of thy sire,

Shall be born battles ancient desire.

Descendant of the mace step forth,
And follow the mantle up into skies north.
Though love and servitude be two things,
Separate cannot be these beings.'

Annetta absorbed the words. She could see why her grandfather was so obsessed with it. But one thing scared her. She was not a hero. Despite working on controlling her psychic powers and learning to ride a horse, Annetta knew full well she was a girl from Toronto. Granted, she happened to know how to throw people seventy feet through the air with her mind, but only if she then ran away. She did not know how to take a mantle up into the sky or fight battles like the ones she read about.

"Puc.... I don't think I can do something like that," she whispered, feeling a chill go down her spine.

Puc looked over at Brakkus, whose ears pricked up alertly upon seeing the girl's reaction.

"What happened to the girl who accepted the card key?" Puc began.

"I'm not a hero, though.," snapped Annetta, "I can fistfight a guy in class who's being a jerk, but I'm not some Amazon warrior chick who can stop an entire legion of-,"

"Annetta, we won't ask you to take down an entire legion, and we know full well who you are. These are just words and I wanted you to be aware of them. We do not even know their true meaning. They were laid out long before any of us were born. People have been interpreting prophecy for thousands of years and the truth is only the Unknown knows their full meaning."

"Aye, and when something is older than the mage here, it's old." Brakkus chuckled, only to be countered by a nasty glare from Puc.

Annetta furrowed her brow regardless. The whole thing disturbed her, and she was beginning to regret taking the card keys from the angels. She shifted uneasily as she let the information pass through her. She wanted to quit in that given moment but as her eyes landed on Link and wandered to the faces of those gathered there, she stopped herself.

"If you say so," she answered.

"Prophecy is just a bunch of strung together words that people try to make sense of," Link said, trying to be encouraging. He cringed slightly, grabbing at his wound as it burned him.

"I think that there was a bit much," Brakkus said, pointing at the wound and wrapping his arm around Link he helped him begin to walk. "Let's get ye checked up."

As they left, Puc breathed out, letting his shoulders sag. The Lab around him seemed to dim as soon as the trio was a few feet away, allowing the mage to sift through everything that had just happened. For a moment he felt more alone than he had in years. Teaching a child was simple. They would believe whatever they were told. Meanwhile, an adult had composure and understanding, which also made them fairly easy to teach. But a teenager had issues with finding their place, doubts about their abilities and plenty of other things he was not used to dealing with. He traced the contours of the grip on his staff, examining the living moss that grew around its tip in perfect harmony with the wood.

"Orbeyus, what sick and twisted humor did you have, leaving me in charge of your heir at the age she is?" he groaned, following his companions.

ഔരു

Link woke up to a bright light hanging over his eyes. The last thing he remembered was being brought to the hospital wing of the Lab, and Puc mending his wounds. Exhausted, he'd fallen asleep during the process.

He tried to move, but was in a lot more pain than he remembered. Shifting his eyes to scan the area, he saw the entire room was dimly lit, the typical blue hue from the steel walls illuminating everything to match. The only things around him besides the hospital bed he lay on was a solitary desk, with what looked to be a glass of water on it. He also noticed the wounds on his chest had been attended to fully, feeling the thick bandages under a new black t-shirt. No one seemed to be present, but then he felt something like a light fan on his palm. He looked over to see Annetta fast asleep at the side of his bed, her reddish brown hair falling into her face and moving gently with the rhythm of her breathing. His head fell back into the pillow as he looked at the girl who had saved his life along with her friend. It was not that he did not appreciate being alive, but others had too often saved him, and it bothered him to be the one in need of help. When he had been with the army, he had more than once been saved by his commanding officer, Layla. But Layla was not here, and it seemed that Annetta had stepped in right where she had left off.

"She wouldn't leave, ya know," the voice of the Hurtz echoed from the other side of the room. "She said she wanted to wake up to apologize for upsetting ya by saving ya from the creature."

Link looked over at the giant beast. His striped badger muzzle looked down at him with a straight face, the elongated ears with silver hoops twitching from time to time as though they were picking up sound from all around him. It felt as though he was looking into the face of the Unknown, about to lay down his final judgment on his soul. He swallowed, trying to think of something to say back to him, but could not. The Hurtz took the initiative to speak.

"Now why would a pretty little thing like that need to apologize to the likes of ye?" His massive form crossed the room and sat down on the other side of him. "Or rather, I should rephrase that and ask what ya did to upset her. And answer wisely, because I have a sword that's out of practice."

"I may have gotten upset about her saving me. It's just that-," Link licked his lips nervously as the rabbit ears of the Hurtz pricked up, waiting for an answer, "I prefer to fight my battles alone."

"And alone ya will die if that is the route ya choose." Brakkus's massive finger pressed lightly against Link's chest, causing him to cringe. "How in the Unknown's bane ya served in the army and didn't learn to fight as a unit with others is beyond me."

"I didn't join to fight like a unit. I joined to become a warrior," the boy scoffed.

"Ah, and now the truth of it comes out. So ya want to be a warrior, little Lincerious Heallaws? And what does this warrior-ing of yours mean?"

Link's eyes gazed over to Annetta's sleeping form. She was oblivious to all around her, and the only thing that kept her from looking like a complete statue was the slow and steady rising of her back from breathing.

"I want to protect those who cannot protect themselves," he replied.

Brakkus looked over at Annetta, who stirred a little, muttered something under her breath, and continued to sleep. His large canine head then turned to Link, who was lying in bed still watching her.

"I can assure you she don't need much protecting, since I reckon ya saw what she did tonight," the Hurtz said, after a moment.

"I know. But I couldn't do anything to it." Link tried again to pull himself up higher and cringed. "I need to be stronger. Strong enough to beat anything that stands in my way."

Brakkus gave out a soft laugh. "No one is strong enough to beat anything, but if ya wish to become a better fighter, then I think I can help ya with that, if yer willing to follow my instruction."

The boy looked up at the creature, then down at his hands on the white sheets. He had heard stories of the Hurtz, a race of creatures so fierce that sometimes even the name itself was enough to drive the enemy to retreat. They could destroy trolls in a few swings of a blade, and some were so powerful they could take on dragons all by themselves. To be in the presence of such a fearsome fighting machine was an honor, to be given the opportunity to learn from one even more, for they rarely opened up to those who were not their kin.

"Yes, I am willing," Link said, then remembered his manners. "Please? It would be a great learning experience."

Brakkus studied the boy for a long moment with a serious expression, taking in his features as though he were analyzing his soul. This made Link feel unnerved but the feeling passed as soon as a toothy grin appeared on the Hurtz's face.

"Right. I'll help ya when yer better and healed, but for now," he got up and walking over to where Annetta was laying and gently lifted her up, "I need to put this one into a proper bed. I'll check on ya later."

Link nodded in response, and watched the massive creature walk out with the small sleeping girl in his arms before himself drifting off to sleep.

Chapter 14

Annetta stirred under the covers of the bed, then woke up, realizing where she was. Her vision came into focus momentarily, and she saw she was in an unfamiliar room. The sheets she was under were bright orange. They were soft enough to make her want to stay under them for an hour longer, but the distress of being in a foreign room made her want to get up and explore.

She looked first at the nightstand by the bed, on which rested a glass of water, an alarm clock with big red numbers on it, and a small silver lamp. She moved up to look at the walls, which were painted a rich maroon color, the kind she had always wished she had in her own room. This made her realize she was in one of the rooms in the Lab that adapted to its owner's needs. Sure enough, on one wall there were shelves filled with books and movies, while right across from her bed was a television set.

After finding a fridge, along with a bowl and some milk and cereal, Annetta got changed into a fresh t-shirt and jeans, brushed her hair and headed out the door to figure out who had placed her in the room, and what had happened to Link.

What she came across next came to her as a complete surprise, Puc arguing with none other than Darius Silver in the corridor. The conversation seemed very heated, almost to the point where a violent outbreak could occur. But there was something about their body language that suggested a bond between the two. Annetta crept closer to listen.

"You said protect! He was a threat! How in hell was I supposed to-," Darius snarled at the elven mage.

"Simple, you contact me. And you did not do so." Puc glared at the boy with his eyes blazing with fury.

"I tried, but-," before Darius could answer he noticed Annetta, standing some distance away.

Puc looked over, his arms stiff by his sides from suppressed rage. "You can come over. He won't bite you."

The girl shifted from her spot and moved towards them, uncertain of what to make of it. The fact that Darius was there was one thing. The fact that he seemed to know Puc was another. She was feeling betrayed, but somewhat relieved that she did not have to lie to him anymore. Still, the betrayal seemed to sting more and with each step closing in it rang in her ears.

"Well, I suppose since we are all here," Puc said after a moment of silence, "Annetta, this is my apprentice, Darius Silver. I've had him watching over you and Jason for quite a few years now."

Annetta bit her lip, processing the information as her mind raced, placing Darius at various events in her life. One of the more recent ones stuck out. "So wait, were you the one who told Puc about the fight with Finn?"

"You were threatening to expose the secret," he said, bluntly. "My orders were to keep such a thing from happening, to keep you and Jason safe at all costs."

The girl felt her ears heat up so much steam might as well have come from them. She turned abruptly to Puc, who stood stone-faced, watching the tantrum.

"Let me guess. He was the "magic mirror" you watched us with. And you were lying when we got here. You knew who we were all along." she snapped.

"Sarcasm, and some secrets are best kept intact until the appropriate time. There is a reason to all madness."

Annetta felt even more betrayed. What hurt most was the idea that Darius had simply been sent to her as a bodyguard, and was not her friend by choice. She tried to keep calm, but the emotion was starting to show on her face. She balled her hand up into a fist in order to suppress it.

"So when you attacked Link last night..." She trained off.

"I did it because of the scar on his face," Darius answered her quickly. "A scar like that is only caused by a curse. I was following orders to protect you and Jason."

Annetta wanted to punch someone, and could not decide which of the two deserved it more. Her blood boiled and she wanted justice, right away. She then turned to Darius who had spoken last, Darius who through all the years had been part of her life as someone he was apparently not.

"Let me guess, being my friend was part of your orders too," Annetta snapped, before spinning around and stomping towards the exit.

Puc watched her go in silence, figuring it best to give her space, while Darius jogged up to her.

"Wait, Annetta!" he called out with exasperation.

"What the hell for? So you can lie to me some more?" she stopped in her tracks with her back to him.

"No, so I can tell you the truth. You are my friend because I wanted to be yours. Otherwise I would have kept my distance."

Annetta felt heat rising in her as she listened to him. He sounded true, but she still felt hurt. She clenched her fists together, tighter, looking at the floor beneath her.

"I took the time to get to know you," he continued, softly. "I saw how warm you could be once you let your guard down, and how great it would be to hang out with you."

She finally looked up, and turned around to him. He held an apologetic look in his eyes, and seemed to be searching for more words.

"He speaks truth, Annetta," Puc called out from where he still stood down the hall. "Whatever blame exists can be cast upon me. I sent him in the first place. His only orders were to watch over you. Befriending you was his choice."

Darius stepped a bit closer, and held out his hand. "Will you forgive me?"

Annetta looked at his outstretched arm for a moment, before reluctantly taking it. "I guess I can let it go. You were trying to protect us and all," she muttered. "What… are you then, exactly?"

"A mage in training," Darius answered. "If you mean by species, I'm a Water Elf like Puc."

Annetta looked over at Puc, still standing in the same position, unmoving, his burning blue eyes watching the exchange between them. She looked back at Darius, whose eyes were almost jet black.

"You don't look anything alike, though." She frowned.

Darius put his hand in front of his face and muttered something under his breath. When he removed his hand, his eyes were the same shade as Puc's.

Annetta shifted uneasily. The feral blue eyes on Darius made her a bit uncomfortable. Seeing a feature like that, on a face she knew, change was strange. "So then," she said, "how old are you really?"

"Do you really want to know?" he smirked. "I'm twenty three years old but because elves age slower I don't look much older than sixteen like you. We elves can slow down or speed up our aging as we please. We can live for hundreds of years looking no older than a teenager if we want."

Annetta looked over at Puc, still as a stone. She studied his features carefully, from his long robes to his pallid, sharp featured face and black hair. She had never asked him how old he was. He didn't seem very old, but when they first met he had told her that he had served her grandfather. Darius caught her looking at his mentor and smiled.

"I wouldn't ask that question of him," he chuckled. "He might get offended," he chuckled.

"Enough idle chatting," Puc said, finally came towards them. "Annetta, I need you to contact Jason and get him down here."

"Are we going to have to train again?" She groaned. "It's Saturday, you know."

"No, we will not be training today. Not now at least. Today, we set out to Severio Castle." He came to a stop before the two of them. "Brakkus and Lincerious have been getting the horses ready for the journey. Will you be joining us, my apprentice?"

"Yes, master. If you wish it," Darius replied, suddenly very formal. "Though I dare say Lincerious and I are not on the best footing at the moment and I don't think-,"

"Leave the boy to me," Puc replied. "He will understand when he learns the reason for your attacking him. You may both go to the stables. I will wait for Jason to come down here. Have you reached him yet, Annetta?"

"Yeah, he's on his way to my house now," she informed him, snapping out of her trance.

Puc gave a swift nod of the head and was off before Annetta could say anything else. She looked up at Darius, still standing with her.

"Do you want to get going?" He asked after a moment, then paused seeing her still gawking at him with a bewildered expression. "Right...I forgot," he said to himself.

He covered his eyes again, muttered the spell under his breath, and when his hand came down they were dark once more.

೮೦೮೩

Link assisted Brakkus in saddling up the horses for the journey to the castle. From what had been explained to him, the Eye to All Worlds was an entry point to alternate universes. For this reason it was guarded with more ferocity than anything else for fear of foes taking of the castle, and using it to achieve dominion over all of creation. In his books back home, the castle was said to be a myth. Of course, if people thought that, no one would bother looking for it. Puc had clarified that much to him earlier in the morning after healing his wounds to have him prepared for the ride.

"Oi, that'll be the last of 'em," Brakkus said to the boy, finishing up with a saddle. He looked around as if something was missing.

"Is something wrong?" Link asked.

"One thing I forgot." Brakkus left the stable for a few moments, then came back with a giant backpack, and plunked it down beside Link. "That'll be yers."

Link scoffed at the massive backpack, almost two feet high and twice as wide as he was. "What's this for?" he asked.

"A warrior carries the weight of the world on his shoulders. I figured it would be fitting for ya to start with something a bit smaller and more manageable," Brakkus chuckled. "Yer training starts now."

Link blinked a few times, trying to figure out how to put on the massive pack. After some struggling, he managed to get to his feet with it on his back and his sword on his belt. Just as he accomplished this, in came Annetta and Darius. Hot fury spilled through Link's veins as he attempted to leap at his attacker from the previous night, but the backpack caused him to trip over his own two feet. Seeing what happened, Annetta rushed to his side instinctively.

"You okay?" she asked as Link groaned and got up, not responding to her.

"What the hell are you doing here?" he tried to snarl at Darius through his panting.

"I could ask you the same question with that giant scar on your face." Darius bared his teeth at him.

Link's muscles coiled, getting ready to pounce, when he felt something touch his arm. He looked over to see Annetta's hand on him, her face stone cold as she looked at the both of them.

"I don't want any more fighting. It was a misunderstanding, okay? Darius was just trying to protect me. He's been under orders from Puc to watch Jason and me. He was just doing his job." She tried to summon authority into her voice. "Maybe now, since we all know we are on the same side we can start over?"

Link stared at Darius, who stood before him, unmoving. He sensed animosity coming from the boy, and it was not a pleasant feeling. The apprentice extended his hand towards him, but not out of genuine peacemaking. It was an act to show he was the bigger man in front of Annetta. Link simply smiled at the challenge and shook his hand as firmly as he could.

Annetta sighed in relief, and released her grip from Link. She then turned to Brakkus, who had watched the whole ordeal without interfering.

"Well then, back at it," he said, before getting back to work on the horses.

Annetta's gaze lingered on the two boys, before she moved to help Brakkus, and occupy her mind instead of thinking about the encounter that had just taken place.

Link and Darius continued to observe one another in silence for a little while longer.

"So," Darius said, "why are you carrying that backpack? You going camping or something?"

"A warrior needs to learn to carry the weight of the world on his shoulders," Link grinned, puffing his chest as Darius rolled his eyes.

A few minutes later, Puc entered the stables followed by a breathless Jason, who froze the moment he saw Darius standing beside Link.

"It's quite safe, Jason," Puc explained. "He will not harm you if he knows what is good for him." Puc glanced at the brown haired boy, and then turned to Brakkus, "Are we all ready?"

"I'd say so," The Hurtz answered. "Horses are prepped. It's all up to you lot. What say you? Are you ready?"

"I am," Annetta answered without hesitation. "I can't speak for everyone, though."

"I stand ready." Darius nodded, as did Jason and Puc with him.

"As long as someone can hoist me up onto a horse, I should be good." Link shifted his backpack.

"All on yer own, little warrior." Brakkus lifted his leg, and got onto his horse. "Or ye'll never learn," he added.

Darius picked a sturdy grey mare and mounted her, after shooting Link a smirk of triumph that only further infuriated the boy. It made him climb his own horse to the best of his abilities, and fall over on the first attempt from losing his balance.

Annetta, Puc, and Jason all got on their horses and waited for further instruction from Brakkus, who seemed to be in charge of leading the party onward at this point. Once they were all set, Brakkus nudged his horse gently and they proceeded.

After a good five minutes of riding on a grassy pasture set against a clear blue sky, they came upon the massive portal leading to the castle. It was the same red and black wall Annetta had gone through before. The surface moved like liquid, ripples being created in various spots.

"Best way is to power through," Brakkus told them. "The magic word to make the horses go as fast as they can is F-L-Y. They'll stop as soon as they get through, so don't worry about the cliff on the other side. That said, Annetta, ya did well the last time, will ye go first?"

Annetta nodded, and patted Bossman on his neck for encouragement. "Fly."

The horse bolted for the black and red wall of water, only to be engulfed by it. Puc followed, and after him went the others. Once the feeling of extreme heat passed, they found themselves on a cliff facing the castle known as the Eye to All Worlds.

The castle had not changed since Annetta had last seen it. For miles around the castle, there seemed nothing but a flat plane of rich green grass. Further in the distance, it was surrounded by walls of shining white limestone mountains far as the eye could see, with deep emerald forests scattered upon some of the mountain ranges like a platoon of soldiers surrounding their king. The feeling it gave Annetta could not be compared with anything she had ever felt. Jason was also taken aback, seeing it for the first time in his life.

"Hey...isn't that?" he whispered to Annetta, who nodded her head in agreement.

"This is it? The Eye to All Worlds?" Link asked, looking down at the castle. "Who would think to build a fortress in the middle of a valley? It's absurd, and against all tactical-,"

"With the amount of allies, and with defenses in the mountains around it, it was impenetrable," Puc cut the boy off. "It still would be if our allies remembered the old code. The castle was built where the tear in the fabric of worlds is weakest. It is not meant to defend people, but to defend the gateways to other worlds. Now hurry along. We are wasting daylight."

They rode around the mountains until Puc located the pass used to go down to the castle. It was a steep and dangerous road. There was only room for one horse at a time, so Brakkus made them tie a length of rope around their waists. In case one person fell, they could hoist them back up. Once they reached the end, they untied the rope and rode together until they came to the gates of the castle.

The castle looked even more impressive up close. Its four enormous white towers capped with tiled cerulean roofs stared down at its visitors in judgment, awaiting their next move. They had been able to see it clearly from far away because the castle itself was up on a hill of limestone, invisible from above due to the castle walls blending in with the stone, making them seem as one with each other. Seeing this made Link quiet down about the castle having been built in a place that would be hard to defend.

"The Severio clan have been warriors for generations, Lincerious," Puc stated, "not just architects. They would have thought as you think." He got off his horse and headed for the front gate, two massive doors created from dark wood and heavy metal hinges.

"How are we going to get in? It must take at least ten men to open that gate-," Jason began, and then remembered. "Oh. Right."

"Actually, the gates will not open through the use of psychic abilities alone," the elf explained, "There is an enchantment on them, which allows only those loyal to the Severios to enter."

He turned to face Annetta, "The only Severio here is you, Annetta, and it is to you the oath must be sworn."

Puc got down on his knee before Annetta, and placed his staff over the other. Brakkus did the same and placed his sword in the earth. Link and Darius followed, leaving Jason as the only one standing.

"You're serious?" he raised an eyebrow, "I gotta swear an oath of loyalty to my best friend?"

"The spell requires the exact words to be spoken," Puc said, sternly. "So go on."

Jason muttered something under his breath and did as he was told.

Annetta felt awkward having people bow before her, and waited for it to end. She did not feel comfortable being the object of attention. She was used to being the shunned one. She had learned to stay in the shadows, off in her own world, only fighting when necessary. She felt at home without special treatment, and getting the opposite felt out of place. It was like someone had put a spotlight on her when all she wanted to do was escape.

"Repeat after me," Puc said. "In the one who is severed we trust. Our lives to you until we are dust. What is ours we give unto you to use, our strength and wisdom use as you choose." The mage closed his eyes and spoke the words with great reverence.

Annetta felt goose bumps form on her skin as they all repeated the words Puc had first spoken. Once they had finished, everyone got up.

"Uhm. Do I need to say anything special to accept?" Annetta asked.

"As long as you believe the words we have spoken to be true, then we should all be fine."

Brakkus placed the sword back in its scabbard and turned to Puc, "Well, we gonna get going?"

Puc nodded and placed his hands on the gates. He pushed them open with ease, the oath having worked.

"Enter, and welcome to the Eye to all Worlds," the elf spoke as they led their horses into the courtyard.

Annetta and Jason looked at the pure white and blue stone structure with awe. It was one thing to see it from afar, but something else to be up close and personal. Every stone and brick seemed to come to life and speak for itself as they passed by, greeting them. They noted it was also warm, much warmer than back home as if summer had already been here for a long time. Once they had tied their horses up in the stables they walked towards the main building of the castle.

"So, where are all of these portals the castle is supposed to be protecting?" Jason asked.

Opening the ancient wooden gates of the main building, which creaked with age, Puc turned to the youth. "Portals are a one way door. The chambers within the castle contain the portals to destinations where previous generations of Severios catalogued a return route. They are among the oldest, dating back to the time of Lord Adeamus Severio. Those on the other side are not always aware of their existence, most have forgotten. As I said before, however, Severio Castle is located in a spot where all dimensions seem to tear. New portals are often here created because of this and with it new doors as well for an enchantment was placed upon the building once it was complete to create a new chamber each time a tear occurs in order to conceal it within the castle walls. Not all of them are catalogued because of this and we have no way of telling what is on the other side. Having the portals behind these doors also creates a shield, not letting anything pass through. Sometimes portals are created outside the vicinity of the castle, in these cases it would be the job of magic casters to find them and seal them off, otherwise what happened in the Lab during the blackout would occur. It is rare that it happens but I dare say I have my work cut out for me because at least one has been created in all this time. The portals which have been catalogued have a carving of some kind marking it, in most cases a gateway of stone, telling of what lies on the other side."

"So at any moment I could end up in a completely different world by stepping through a portal?" Annetta raised an eyebrow, trying to absorb everything Puc had just said.

"Not quite, Miss Severio, you can see a portal before you approach it, or at least feel a strange presence before you, and you can choose to go through it," the mage answered, "Tears in dimensions can sense places where little activity exists, and like a worn out rug will tear over time in those places as a way to release the stress created by that universe. Some worlds have maybe one such tear, a place where things disappear and no one can explain why, others that are more ancient can have multiple tears leading to different parts of the multiverse. These are, as I said, not as common as you may think. Otherwise everyone would be getting sucked into portals all the time. A new portal may be created only every hundred years."

"How many different worlds are there?" Jason looked over at the mage as they made their way down a corridor.

"They're countless. Only The Unknown knows how many there are," he responded. "And they are not worlds per say but completely other dimensions. It is accurate to say world, though, for no one has ever explored all the different universes entirely, but has simply caught a glimpse of one particular world nestled within it. We live in a multiverse. We have our entire universe with its own solar systems and millions of planets, but coexisting with us on other planes of existence with thousands of other universes just like our own. Some are coming to an end, some are in the same era as our own, and some barely having even begun. This is what portals lead to, not just different worlds, but worlds in different universes."

Annetta felt her head spin, like she was absorbing so much information her brain could not store it all. She decided after a few minutes of struggling to put it aside for another day to digest and continued walking, admiring the insides of the fortress.

They all stopped upon coming to the end of the corridor. The first thing Annetta noticed was a pedestal in the middle of the room on a raised platform, with a sword lodged inside it. A surge went through her body the moment she saw it, like an electric current. She was almost instinctively drawn to it, and took slow steps towards it.

"Through the sword of thy sire shall be born battles ancient desire," Puc intoned.

Annetta stopped dead in her tracks, and turned around.

"What?" she asked.

"That is the very same sword upon which your father swore to keep you and your brother away from all of this in order to give you a normal life in the world you live. It is also his sword he used in battle. You feel a need to draw it from the pedestal, do you not?"

"Well... I guess I sort of do," she said, raising an eyebrow, "Isn't that what everyone feels seeing a sword lodged in a pedestal? I mean...it's the whole sword in the stone thing right?"

Puc simply motioned for Annetta to follow him. He turned briefly to Brakkus. "Take them and scout out the castle to make sure all is still in place. I must go honor my words to Arieus."

The Hurtz shook his head and looked at the boys. "Right. You lot, follow me. We can go and have a look around."

Darius and Link followed Brakkus without hesitation. It was only Jason who waited until the last moment with a look of isolation on his face before following.

After they vanished, Puc spoke. "He feels you are both drifting apart. He can sense the parts you have to play are different and that you are no longer in this together as you were in the beginning."

"What? No," Annetta looked up at him, surprised. "We're still in this together."

"You are, but I can sense the jealousy he is starting to feel. A castle, an oath of loyalty, and a sword with a history. He feels he is no longer the hero of this adventure."

"But he is. The angels came to both of us, not just to me."

"They came because you are both part of this. But your roles will be different as things play out," Puc stated plainly.

"Whatever," Annetta groaned, tired of arguing with the elf. "Jason is my friend. Simple."

154

Trying to distract herself, she walked up to the tapestry hanging around the room, circling the walls like a large blanket. Its border was made to look like rose vines, while the tapestry itself depicted scenes from battles. There were men and women fighting alongside strange creatures, the likes of which Annetta had never seen.

"Not all in the Four Forces were human." Puc answered her silent question. "The other races in the alliance were the Water Elves, the Minotaur, the Soarin, and the Ogaien. All of which pledged allegiance to your grandfather, Orbeyus Severio, and to your father."

"You're talking about an alliance and battles. What for?" she asked.

"If one world was threatened, then others would come to its aide. Your grandfather wanted to protect those who could not protect themselves, those who did not know of the existence of universes outside their own and the threats that came with them. Could you imagine the chaos if a world born into ignorance came into contact with the world of magic and advanced technologies? It would be a disaster, likely ending in their extinction. He believed each world should be given its own chance to grow, and only if their growth threatened the well being of others should something be done to correct it. The last war, the Great War, was because of one such individual who threatened this. His name was Mordred the Conqueror, a being who wished to have all universes bow to him, and was close to doing so until your grandfather stepped in. He took those who were still free and those who would not be controlled, and he fought back. The final battle was underneath this very castle, when Mordred tried to take it and gain access to all worlds. He was slain by Orbeyus himself. Those who followed under your grandfather's colors were named the Four Forces and were sometimes called the Alliance of the Axe, for that was your grandfather's favored weapon, and the one thing that set him apart on the battlefield from all other men. For years after, peace remained and those worlds which were enslaved were freed from Mordred's grasp."

Puc paused, then continued, quietly. "Your grandfather had few weaknesses. One was that he was a merciful man. He let Mordred's son Mislantus live, in exchange for me placing a curse on him, so that wherever Mislantus went, he would be seen as nothing more than the animal he was. It was believed for a long time that Mislantus had perished, but the castle in the sky I saw not long ago confirmed my fears. He has come back to finish his father's business, and he comes with a burning vengeance in his veins. That is why we must summon up the old alliances once again."

Annetta felt a chill go up her spine, but tried to look like what he was saying did not faze her. She climbed to where the pedestal and the sword were placed, noticing four small carvings in the stone, each bearing a symbol. They were simple in design, as though a child had drawn them in the sand. One resembled three drops of water, one a flame, one a three peaked mountain, and one three wavy lines representing the wind.

"Though Orbeyus's axe was what he used in battle, this sword held more meaning than anything. It was a re-foraging of Lord Adeamus's blade that had lain unused in the castle until your grandfather began to gather alliances from other races. The sword was then taken by the races composing the Four Forces and re-forged to create what you see here. It was meant to show a combining of efforts to create a weapon to unite them. It was hoisted into the air before each charge, each of which was victorious. Some said it had mythical powers that ensured victory, others simply found it inspiring to see a weapon that they had contributed in making. Your grandfather only used it for a short time before giving it to your father, their future leader as a symbol that their alliance would last through the ages. It is called Severbane, and it stood as a beacon of hope in darkness."

Annetta placed her small hands on the massive leather hilt of the sword and tried to pull it out, but it did not move an inch.

"So, is this like in one of those King Arthur myths where only the worthy one can pull the sword out?" She gave it another tug. "If it's supposed to be me, we're all screwed."

"Well, you didn't think it was going to be that easy now, did you?" Puc pointed at the engraved symbols on the pedestal. "The sword can only be pulled from the pedestal when the Four Forces are restored."

"You keep saying that name. Who are the Four Forces?" she looked at him.

"The Four Forces are meant to represent the elements each race is associated with, water, stone, wind and fire. The four forces in nature. We will need to visit and ask them to pledge allegiance to you. When your father left and placed the sword into the pedestal, it voided the alliance. They will have to swear the same oath that we swore to you, acknowledging you as the heir of Orbeyus."

156

"Well, that doesn't sound too hard." Annetta stepped down from the pedestal. "I'll do it as long as I know where I'm going. How do we get to where they are?"

"Portal travel," Puc answered. "Of course, we will need some proof to show that you are indeed Arieus's daughter, and that Jason is the son of Arcanthur. They are stubborn, and will not help just anyone. But I think I have just the place we can go to partially solve that dilemma."

Puc took the lead and left the room, his billowing robes followed him like a tail. Annetta followed as fast as she could. Her previous dread had been replaced with excitement. She was going to see new worlds, things that until now only existed in the books she so loved.

Chapter 15

Brakkus, Link, Darius, and Jason walked along the halls of the castle exploring its interior while Brakkus commented on the things they passed. Link and Darius seemed genuinely curious, asking Brakkus a constant stream of question. Jason, on the other hand, was in a world of his own. He had not liked the fact that he had been pulled away from Annetta, and it stung him that she had not said anything to Puc about it.

"Oi! J.K. are ya with us here?" Brakkus called to Jason, who had stopped in front of a coat of arms without realizing.

"Hm? Oh, sorry I was just thinking about something else," he responded, and kept walking.

"I think we gathered that much," Darius said, having diverted his attention from looking out a balcony. "What's going on?"

"It's nothing," Jason answered walking, over to them, "I'm fine, this is just all a bit much for me to take in."

Darius frowned, not buying it. He was about to say something when he noticed Annetta and Puc coming up the stairs to the tower.

"Have you enjoyed your exploration?" the elf asked, coming to a halt.

"They can barely contain themselves, methinks," Brakkus smirked. "You lot done?"

"Yes, I was just explaining our situation to Annetta," Puc began.

"Which I think everyone has a right to know," the girl interjected.

Puc raised an eyebrow and looked at the young girl, her shaggy locks of hair out of place from having run up the stairs, and her blue eyes set on her friends. He smiled, remembering seeing Arieus like that when he was her age. But he saw more in that moment than just her father. He saw a future leader.

"A long time ago, before we were here, there was a Great War in which my grandfather, who I know nothing about other than what everyone has been telling me, killed a warlord who wanted to take over all other existing universes. But my grandfather let the son of this warlord live, and now that son is back, and wants to finish what his father started." She took a moment to collect her thoughts before continuing.

"Here comes what I think is the important part, guys. No one but us knows he is back, and no one is going to stop him because everyone who was defending the castle is either gone or doesn't know what we do now.

I'm going to go and ask the races that formed the Four Forces for help. I'm not asking any of you to come with me. What we'd be getting involved in is bigger than anything we have seen up to now, but I'm going to fight, because no one else will."

The room was silent after she spoke. The eyes of the three boys wandered across each other's faces as they searched for something to say. The finality of the words reverberated in the walls around them. The Hurtz was the first to step forward from the group, breaking their ranks.

"I'll go with ya to the end, little Annetta," Brakkus said. "I said when we first met I'd serve ya life or death, and I meant it."

The mage was the next to speak, leaning on his staff as he observed the girl, "I served the Severios, and the rulers of this castle for many years. I do not intend to quit now."

"And where my master goes, so I follow," Darius added. "But not only because of that. I'm going because I'm your friend, Annetta, and I'll do whatever it takes to prove that to you."

Not missing a beat, Link also stepped forward, "I was sent to help you, Annetta Severio, descendant of Orbeyus of the Axe Severio, defender of the Eye to all Worlds. I will not back down from what was asked of me by the Unknown himself."

All eyes then turned to Jason, who still stood in silence, not having spoken a word. His eyes locked with Annetta.

"I didn't think I needed to say anything at all." He blinked a few times. "I'm always going to be there with my best friend, no matter what."

The boy's gaze shifted more directly to Puc in defiance; "No matter what any of you think."

Annetta could not help but smile when she heard them all agree to go with her. Puc then walked a few more paces towards the door and turned on his heel to face them.

"Well, lady and gentlemen...to arms."

☼☾☾

Annetta and her friends followed Puc down the stairs of the tower, the staircase spiraling below them as they went. Exiting the tower, they headed down another corridor, until they ended up at another massive wooden door.

Puc flung the doors open to reveal the destination of their trip, the armory. The first thing they saw was a rack filled with different melee weapons. They slowly filed in and began admiring the different weapons and armor stored in the room.

"You could arm...an army with this," Jason exclaimed, finally feeling a bit more enthusiastic. He picked up a sword, only to find it far heavier than expected. As he dropped it, it almost cut Darius in half.

Annetta laughed, seeing her friend enjoying himself, but then stopped, feeling someone staring at her. She turned to the left to see something on the far wall of the armory. It was the portrait of a man whose blue eyes gazed back at her with deep authority. His formerly black hair and beard were almost completely covered with silver. Had they not been trimmed neatly it would have been hard to find his mouth, curved in a victorious smile. He sat on a throne. Across its length, he held a massive twin bladed axe. His other hand served as support for his chin. He seemed to be in thought, yet causally observing those who looked upon him at the same time.

"That is your grandfather," Puc said as he came up behind her.

A chill went down her spine as she looked at the portrait, into the face of a man she had never truly seen, yet had left her more than she could ever have imagined. Her parents had kept few photos, blurred and distorted. She walked closer to the painting, her small fingers tracing the heavy golden frame.

"Was he always so serious?" she asked.

"No, that is just how the portrait was painted. Your grandfather had quite the sense of humor when he was not on the battlefield." The elf stood beside the girl and gazed up at it. "He was only a fighter when it was necessary. More than anything, he loved life. That was why he fought."

"If all of this was so important to my grandpa, then why did my dad throw it all away?"

"I cannot say for sure what went through Arieus's head when his father died right before his very eyes," Puc said, pointedly. "He was a father as well, with a little girl who he wanted to protect more than anything else in the world. Even more than the world itself."

"You said that before, but I still don't see why." She frowned.

Puc simply shook his head. Sometimes, he forgot Annetta's age. He crossed the room, to a row of armor suits on stands that had collected a fine grey layer of dust, making them seem covered in wool. He picked up a large rectangular wooden tower shield off the wall, and wiped down the front of it. Upon the crimson backing was a black rampant lion behind which were a sword and a mace that crossed one another as well as an axe, which seemed to spring up from among the two of them.

"Your father's shield." Puc carried it over to Annetta. "It saved him many times in battle, and was well known by the races of the Four Forces."

Annetta reached out and took the shield from Puc, only to realize how heavy it was, nearly dropping it. She grabbed onto its sides as tightly as she could, and lifted it up in front of her, sideways.

"Ya building a wall there, young lass?" Brakkus called, seeing the whole shield cover Annetta almost entirely.

"You will get used to it," Puc observed.

"Get used to it? This thing weighs a metric ton!" Annetta peeked over the top of the shield on her toes, "This thing is way too heavy to be made of wood!"

"It is not as bad as you make it out to be, you will get used to it in time. You just need to put your mind to it," Puc stated.

"This another mind over matter thing?" she groaned.

"Something like that, yes," the elf nodded his head as Brakkus came up to him.

"So, we've searched high and low, but I can't find the Kinsman mace, Helbringer," he reported.

Puc frowned and buried himself in his thoughts, going back to the last time he had seen it. When he finally managed to track down the memory, it was fuzzy and obscured by anger.

"I was here the last time Arcanthur came to the castle," Puc recounted, "after Arieus gave up his place. But I cannot for the life of me remember where he placed it. We may need to go and speak with him in person to find out its whereabouts."

"Uhm," Jason interrupted. "In case you haven't heard, my dad is locked up. The only way I can see him is with my mom's signed permission, which even though she promised she hasn't given me yet."

"You mean with the permission of a guardian, correct?" The elf glanced as the boy.

"Well, yeah, but I mean, my mom is the only guardian that I have." Jason bit his lip, not sure where the conversation was going, "She hasn't mentioned anything about going to see him recently either."

"What about a long-lost uncle?" Puc smirked. "You forget I am more resourceful than I appear, and can blend in quite well with your world."

Jason could not help but curl his lips up into a faint smile, remembering his encounter with the disguised Puc.

"So, what are we going to do now, master?" Darius asked, digging his hands into his pockets, as if the action could come up with an answer before Puc would.

"I will need to make the necessary arrangements to see Arcanthur with Jason before we venture forth. In the meantime, we will continue training."

Annetta and Jason both groaned. They were sick of lifting stones.

"What will it take for you to let off on the whole training thing?" Annetta sighed, looking over from the shield she was still holding.

"When you are able to produce psychic fire, of course," Puc answered. "Unfortunately, that can take years to accomplish, and as you know we do not have years, we have months at most before they find us."

"Psychic fire?" Jason scrunched up his face in question. "Did you just make that up on the spot?"

Puc looked the boy in the eyes. "Does it look like I make up any of the things I speak of, Jason Kinsman?"

Jason decided to shut his mouth. Instead, he looked at Annetta, waiting for the next move. He knew there was no point in throwing arguments at Puc. He would simply deflect them as though they were dull arrows.

"Well, I think we are done here, for now." Puc fixed his sleeves. "Annetta, you had better take that shield with you. You will need practice carrying it. And by carrying it I mean properly on your arm, not making a wall of it."

Before they got ready to leave, Puc selected a sword and a mace from the wall, giving them to Annetta and to Jason respectively. "In addition to your lessons, you will also learn to use these. Brakkus will instruct you, and I can assure you he will be no less hard on you than am I, correct?"

"Yeah, yeah, course." The Hurtz grinned at him.

Annetta muttered something unpleasant under her breath after taking the sword and adjusting the belt over her shoulder. She tried to slide her arm through the tower shield, grabbing hold of the grip inside of it. She hoisted it off the ground, only to feel her entire arm start to throb in moments. It felt like it would simply fall out of its socket, but she said nothing and clenched her teeth.

"Ya think that's hard, lassie, wait till ya start swinging a sword," Brakkus chuckled seeing her locked up expression. "I'm just teasing, we'll make a fighter of ya yet."

"I'm never going to look at fight scenes in movies the same way again," she sighed as they walked out of the armory.

∞⊗

Link remained behind for a little while. He'd noticed something once Puc had lifted the shield for Annetta. Picking it up, he began brushing the mass of cobwebs and dust from it. After a few minutes of tedious work, worn black leather began to show.

"Oi! Lincerious! Ya coming?" Brakkus wandered back into the armory, noticing the youth inspecting something. "What ya got there?"

"I'm not sure. It was behind the shield." Link handed the leather scraps to the Hurtz.

Brakkus took the object gently into his massive paws and began examining it, his ears twitching inquisitively as he tried to figure out what it was that the young Gaian had stumbled across. Coming to a conclusion, both ears shot up erect, causing his earrings to jingle. "Oh, I know, it's the scabbard...well er...what's left of it, that is."

"Scabbard?" Link looked at the thing questioningly. "A rag, more like it."

"Well, ya leave leather unattended to, and where pests can get to it then that's what happens," the Hurtz explained. "Well, I guess I got me work cut out for. We'll need a new scabbard to be made for when the blade is set free...like I don't have enough to work on now."

Link took another look at the beaten piece of leather. Underneath the outer layer, rotting wood could be seen protruding from it, its dark brown decomposing state suggesting there was no hope for it. The more he looked at it, the more the gears in his head began to spin.

"We could work on it together," Link suggested. "I used to get stuck working on sword belts and doing repairs to weapons all the time...mostly for being too late or too slow. I've helped make many scabbards before."

Brakkus snorted humorously. "This ain't gonna just be any old scabbard. It has to be perfect. The sword it'll hold will represent all of us when the time comes."

"What makes you think I won't take making it seriously?" Link shot back at him.

163

"Never said you wouldn't, just saying there's no room for mistakes," Brakkus stated, walking behind the youth and thrusting the remains into the already heavy pack he carried. "And I ain't got extra time to be making this thing, so it's going to be your task. I got tools ya can use back in the Lab, but my priority be the horses and safety. So ya best do yer best work."

"Hurtz! Hurry up, we're leaving!" Puc's voice boomed from the entrance of the castle like a bell.

Brakkus turned once more to Link, "Yer task, on yer own time. Not mine."

Pivoting back once more, he left to join the others, leaving Link standing where he had been. Pondering the words, the youth smiled. Hoisting the heavy load more evenly on his shoulders, he took off to meet with the rest of the group.

🐒🐓

The return to the Lab was briefer than the process of going to the castle. The excitement had worn upon the youth, creating a much less energetic atmosphere, as everyone seemed to dwell on the sights they had just seen. It was not until they arrived in the stables again that the silence was broken.

"We've still a fair bit of daylight left," Puc said as he dismounted his horse. "I propose we start having you learn another vital skill, teleportation."

Annetta and Jason frowned, looking at one another. Both of them were tired from the long ride, and mentally exhausted. Puc ignored the unrest in the duo as he handed the reins of the horse to Brakkus, already busy with leading the beasts to their stalls before he would check each of them.

The elf turned to leave, his dark hair sliding over his shoulders as he looked at them from the corner of his eye. "I will meet you in the training grounds. Do not dally too long here. I wish to look into starting to make arrangements to visit Arcanthur."

"Oi! Ya lads going to just stands there bland-faced, or are ye gonna help here?" Brakkus called over from the stables, looking at Link and Darius, who had both seemed to blank out. But upon hearing the Hurtz's booming voice, they sprang back into action and went to attend the warrior.

Handing their reins to Link and Darius, Annetta and Jason began the journey to the training grounds, the thudding on the metallic floor their only companion to the sound of their breathing as they walked. Emotions of weariness boiling within her, Annetta huffed, breaking the steady pace of sound around them.

"I thought we weren't gonna do anything today," she groaned under her breath as she trudged with the shield still in hand, switching arms whenever they began to hurt too much.

"Same, although you gotta admit, if we learn to teleport, it would save a lot on time and bus money," Jason joked. "I mean, think about it. You gotta get somewhere, you run late, so all you do is teleport into the bathroom of the place and-"

"And you get caught doing it, and then Puc wrings our little necks," Annetta cut him off. "You remember how mad he got with the whole thing with Finn in school."

"Yeah," he sighed, throwing up his hands behind his neck to stretch as they continued to walk. "But we can still dream. It would be cool, though, right? I mean, to use these powers out in the open. We could be like superheroes."

"Yeah, and then one of us goes nuts and tries to kill the others, like in that one movie we saw." She chuckled darkly.

Jason laughed a little uneasily, the thought leading him to think of what had happened with his own father, and how he had become the unstable one.

"Would you actually do it if it came down to that?" he asked.

"Do what?" Annetta stopped and looked over at him questioningly.

"You know…kill me if I turned evil or something. I mean, I don't think I would have it in me if you were the one who went all crazy," he said.

"You ought to know my answer then. It's the same as yours. That's like asking if I could kill my dad if he turned out to be like…I'm a murderer, join me."

The look on Annetta's face confirmed it all for him as she spoke, and a sense of warmth returned into Jason's fingers as they reached the Calanite Diamond walls of the arena. Puc stood at the far end of the grounds, leaning on his staff as he watched them approach. The two continued to walk towards him without a care in the world until Jason, who was walking slightly faster than Annetta, walked straight into what seemed to be a barrier. Shaking off the shock, he tried to walk again, hands in front of him, braced for impact. Feeling the resistance once more, he began to knock on the air before him.

"It is an invisible wall. Don't try to get through it, because you can't." Puc stated. "There is only one way to get through, and that is to teleport."

"You expect us to be able to teleport on the first try?" Jason snapped at the outrageous proposal.

"It's not much different than any of the other powers you have been learning to harness," the mage explained as he walked closer to the wall, until he was standing before them. "You only think it is difficult because it seems to be a different power, but the basis of it is the same. You are commanding your body with your mind to do something. It's no different than picking up a pencil and learning to draw really if you think about it."

"Uh, yeah, there's a big difference," Annetta muttered as she thought back to her own doodles.

"You practice the skill to maintain it, do you not?" Puc sighed as he stressed the point. "Even a mage must practice, re-read, and study to keep his mind sharp. Now, enough of this incessant whining. Teleportation is exactly what it says it is, moving one's body from one place to another, but there are rules to the skill, the most basic rule is not teleport into a place you know you cannot survive. If you can't breathe underwater, then don't go there. I have seen many attempt the feat, and it is not in your best interests unless you wish to be seriously harmed. Same goes for space. Simply...don't do it. Secondly, one cannot teleport to a place where they do not know what it looks like. This works exactly like telepathy. You need to be able to picture where you want to go, just as you need to be able to picture the person you want to speak with. You can be shown a place on a photograph and go there, but it generally is not a good idea, especially if it is a highly populated area, or a place with much motion to it, or severe weather. Now, your task is simple, and that is to pass this barrier."

"Can't we just save it for tomorrow?" Annetta groaned, still holding the shield. "I'm just really sore and exhausted right now."

"Pain is weakness leaving the body. Walk it off." The elf glared at her with his icy eyes. "Drop the shield at the entrance, and focus."

Seeing as there was no way of winning with the mage, Annetta nodded her head and left the shield where he had asked her, before she returned to her previous spot.

"Your destination is here where the floor is marked," Puc instructed, as he used his staff to draw an 'X' on the floor in red. "I put the barrier up so you would not cheat by moving forward on failed attempts. The room is also protected so that you cannot teleport out of it, so do not worry about ending up on the other edge of the Lab. You may start when you are ready."

Jason and Annetta looked at one another in confirmation, as the mage headed back to his original spot on the other side of the room. Taking a few paces back, the two friends did their best to relax and focus on what was being asked of them.

"Focus upon the place you wish to find yourself in," Puc instructed from the other side. "Close your eyes if you must the first time, but focus, and then place yourself there."

Annetta snorted at the words. How could it be possible for someone to just will themselves over the other side of an invisible wall? Still, he had been right about how to get the door open, and she tried to keep that in mind as she tried her best to think of nothing else but the place she wished to get to.

Jason followed Puc's instructions and closed his eyes. He had not yet figured out how his powers worked, but he understood that it required his full attention to whatever task he was trying to perform. It was then that he felt something tug at the core of his being like a pulsing fire that ignited each time a task needed to be completed.

Fire... he felt it take over his whole body, his being burning as he thought of nothing else but the place he wished to go, the place marked with an 'x' that he wanted to attain. His body became warmer and warmer, to the point of discomfort, and then it stopped. Opening his eyes, Jason looked down at his feet, his knees shaking. Looking back, he saw the marking on the floor just a few feet behind him. He then looked up to face the mage before him, a smirk upon the elf's face.

"Well, that wasn't so bad, was it?" Puc strode towards him, then looked behind the wall where Annetta still remained. "Your turn now. Come along."

"It's easier said than done!" snapped the girl, so tired she could not focus on where she needed to go, the pain in her arms made her aware of anything but the destination she wanted to achieve.

"Pain is weakness leaving the body," the elf repeated again. "You can do this. You will have to one day, and you could be half dead when the need arises, but it could save your life."

Jason turned around to face his friend, who seemed paralyzed to the spot. "Come on, Annetta. It's easy. You just gotta focus."

"Will you shut it? No it's not." She snapped. "Plus I'm tired, okay? All we ever do is train and train."

Without warning the mage moved forward, his heavy robes gliding all around him like thick smoke. Stopping before the wall he aimed his staff at the girl, a blast beginning to charge at its tip. "Then you leave me no choice."

Jason felt fear grip him as he looked at the battle ready stance of the elf, and began to move forward.

"I would not do that, Jason Kinsman, if you value your life," Puc warned him in a threatening tone, then turned his attention to Annetta. "Now, you will teleport, and you will do so before the blast hits you, otherwise I can promise it will hurt very much. Do you understand?"

Jason felt his muscles tighten as he fought the urge to tackle the elf into the ground, for he knew he stood no chance against him. He took a few more steps forward, his fists raised in resistance, only to be caught in the icy stare of the mage. Ignoring it, he plodded forward, only to feel moments later as though his legs were caught in cement. Unable to move, he looked at Puc, questioning.

"I told you that you would regret it, Kinsman. This is not your quarrel," the elf said to the boy out of the corner of his eye, then turned his attention back to the girl.

"I will fire, I warn you." Puc hissed a second warning. "You have three seconds."

"Wait, this isn't fair! I don't even know how," she protested.

"Three," the mage stated, eerily calm.

Jason licked his lips nervously, "Just think of where you want to go. Any place but where you are!"

"Two," he continued.

Annetta felt the reality of it set in as she looked at the tip of the staff that was pointed at her, gathering light. Her heart raced from her chest to her throat as it grew brighter and brighter. She looked around frantically at the arena, and then shut her eyes. Out of fear, she remembered the shield, and shakily, using her abilities, she summoned it to her, hiding behind it.

Stopping the count, Puc furrowed his eyebrows at the sight, and withdrew a hand from the staff. He threw his arm vertically to the side at the same time, causing the shield to be knocked from Annetta's hands. "You will not always find yourself with something to hide behind."

Without further speech, the mage fired the ball of light at the girl. Jason let out a scream as the other side of the field was consumed by light. Feeling his legs set free, he leaped at the mage, only to be gripped by the shoulder with inhuman strength, and forced down. Twisting free, Jason growled and threw himself once more, only to be pushed off again with ease.

"I told you not to interfere," spat the mage.

"If you killed her, I swear I'll-" Jason threatened, his voice stopping in his throat as he locked eyes with Puc.

The mage veered his head to the side, glaring back at the boy, "And should a time come when she needs to teleport to save her life, what then?"

The boy curled up his fist and slammed it into the ground causing vibrations to go through his entire hand. He really did not care for the mage's reasons. Standing up, he got ready to slam into his teacher once more.

"J.K.?" a voice called from behind.

The boy's guard dropped as he turned around. Behind him, Annetta leaned against the wall, holding the tower shield awkwardly in both hands by the edges. He felt his pulse return to normal, and his muscles relax at the sight of his friend. He exhaled in relief, but then turned to face Puc, who seemed unmoved.

"Are you nuts?" Jason threw his hands up into the air. "You could have killed her!"

"Actually, my assumption-making pupil that was simply a blast of light. Its only purpose is illumination, so I could not have killed her. I would not have even left a scratch on her. Motivation is given when needed, and I do not deal well with whining when I am trying to teach you how to save your own skin. You need to take these lessons more seriously, and if that means having to threaten you with a blast, then so be it. I will not be held responsible when you are on the field of battle, and I have failed to teach you everything I know."

"You could have still warned us," snapped Jason.

Anger seething through the mage, Puc strode forward until he stood right in front of Jason, towering over him, his dark robes making him appear even bigger than he was, "In battle, there is no warning but the sound of the first arrows flying your way, and the moments you have before their fangs find you."

He then turned to Annetta, "We are done for the day, and we begin tomorrow anew. You are dismissed, Miss Severio. Jason, come with me, as we need to prepare for visiting your father."

The mage strode out of the room, dissipating the invisible wall, leaving the two on their own.

"You okay, Anne?" Jason asked after a moment.

"Yeah, I'm fine, I guess." She said quietly. "Thanks, though."

"Any time," he nodded. "I better go before he gets mad again. I'll see you later."

"Bye," Annetta managed to say as she watched her friend follow Puc out of the room.

She remained where she stood, and dwelt a bit on what had transpired in those moments as the staff was aimed at her, the fear and the helplessness she felt. Silently vowing to herself, Annetta took the words Puc had said to heart, and promised herself to do better the next day. Gripping the shield in one hand, she began walking back in the direction of the stables.

Ⅎℬ

Arriving in her destination, Annetta encountered Brakkus, Darius, and Link at work, making sure everything was in order from the day. When Annetta asked if any extra help was needed, Brakkus waved her off with his massive paw, saying he enjoyed spending time with horses and that the boys could leave, too. Not waiting for second thoughts, Link was more than happy to drop the remainder of the work and take a break, even though Brakkus did not allow him to leave his backpack. When Annetta and Link's efforts to coax Darius to do the same showed to be in vain, they were forced to stay and watch for a while seeing as Puc still did not want Annetta to be alone with Link at any point in time. Seeing that both Darius and Brakkus were paying little attention however, the two of them soon decided to leave regardless.

Their traveling with only the blue tinted walls and the sounds of their feet pounding on the metal floors seemed eternal. It was only interrupted when they thought they heard something. Link led the way, having had more time to explore the Lab than Annetta, choosing which corridor to turn into and which one to avoid. There was no need for words in their silence, only the companionship of each other. They continued on their way in this manner, eventually coming to one of the biosphere openings.

"Hey, I never got a chance to say I was sorry about what happened back at the movies." Annetta broke the silence.

Link stopped in his tracks, and looked over at the girl beside him carrying the shield, her hair disheveled from the long day. She watched him waiting for an answer. The boy ran a hand through his own hair as though he were raking through it to find the right words.

"Don't worry about it, I guess I overreacted," he said quickly.

Annetta nodded and catching herself staring at the boy's face too long, her eyes darted away. The two looked around for a moment, unsure of what else to say to one another.

"Have you even been in here before?" Link asked, hoisting the backpack he had been carrying over his shoulders.

"No," Annetta shook her head. "Puc always has Jason and I training, so I don't really have time to be going anywhere around here."

"Well, you have to come see at least a bit of it," he smiled. "Plus, you'll get to put that shield down. If we have time I can show you how to spar a bit, too. I mean, if you want."

Annetta's eyes lit up at the opportunity to learn how to sword fight. The fact that her arms were hurting seemed to disappear instantly.

"Yeah, totally, let's go," she answered, as Link walked up to the clear glass doors and opened them.

The biosphere they walked into was a mountain region similar to the one around Severio Castle. Tall green grass surrounded them, and on the horizon Annetta saw more limestone mountains. The wind on her face felt so real she almost forgot she was in a man-made environment. The two of them walked a little, Link leading the way once more, until they came upon a small stream that seemed to fence the area off by dividing it in two.

"I think we can stop here. I've never gone any farther in case I'd get lost," Link said, setting his pack beside a large fallen log.

"Fine by me. I don't think I can carry this thing any more." Annetta dropped the shield on the sandy banks of the river.

Link climbed up on the log and looked out beyond the river at his surroundings. The reeds in the water and the grass beyond them swayed to a silent melody for miles around. Above and beyond this, scattered trees broke the horizon line, their branches waving in the wind.

"It's hard to believe someone made all of this," he said, "But I can see why they would make it."

"Why would they?" Annetta jumped up on the log and sat beside him.

"Because the moment you come into this place, you forget about everything that's on the other side of the glass dome. This world is perfect because it's untouched by society's greed and vanity." he grabbed a small stone that was beside the log and tossed it into the stream.

"Sounds like you don't like people too much," she said, picking up another stone and tossing it in as well.

"I do. It's just... I feel more connected to this sometimes. When I was younger I would spend all of my time outside wandering in the woods by my house. I had a chance then to watch everything that was going on around me, and I never felt angry or sad. Everything just sort of happened, and I felt at peace and just... happy I guess," he explained.

Annetta nodded her head and looked out at the water quietly, tossing another stone and watching the ripples.

"Apparently my grandfather was the one who built this. But how could he be able to make something this beautiful and real?"

"That's easy. Magic." Link stretched out on the log, leaning back and looking up. "We may be in an underwater base that seems to be filled with nothing but technology, but don't doubt for a second that magic is at work in half of the things going on here."

"Isn't magic just undiscovered science, though?" she looked over at him.

"Uhm, no. It's-" Link paused, trying to think of an answer. "It's more complicated than that. I'm probably not the right person to explain it. If you want a real answer you need to talk to Puc, but the way it was explained to us in the training camp is that science is a physical and practical approach to things, and magic is more about spirituality and believing in what you are doing. It comes from the heart instead of the mind."

Annetta nodded her head and held her knees to her chin, watching the grass move like a great sea in the wind. A chill went through her spine when an unexpected blast of cold wind passed her, causing her to hug her knees closer. She watched some sparrows in one of the nearby trees fluttering about. They didn't even take notice of her or Link, and continued on their business, chirping at one another and flying to where they needed to get to. Watching the scene, she understood a little of what Link had said before, but her further train of thought was interrupted.

"So, you wanna get started?" Link said, stretching his arms a bit.

"Sure," Annetta took the sword Puc had handed to her out from its scabbard.

"Whoa, what are you doing?" Link raised an eyebrow. "I don't think it's smart to start with real swords just now. Have you even used a sword before?"

"Does it look like I would have?" Annetta returned his quizzical gaze, waving the weapon around in small circles with her wrist, to drive the point home.

Link walked around the riverbank until he found two sticks that had been smoothed out from having been close to the water. He then made sure that they were thick and long enough to serve as swords, testing them against a large stone by the shore. Sure of his choice he turned back to Annetta. "Then for safety's sake, let's start with these. This way, no one gets hurt too badly."

He handed one of the sticks to Annetta, and got into a defensive position by slightly crouching and holding his in front of him. Annetta thought he looked ready to play a round of tennis, rather than teach her how to fight. She was disappointed as she looked at the piece of driftwood, her eyes wandering to the sword instead. Sighing, she shook it off and got ready for instruction, remembering what she had promised herself earlier in the evening.

"You don't want to be too planted in one position on your feet ever," Link explained, "because you need to be alert to what is going on around you and you need to be able to move quick if someone is going to come at you, especially if they're bigger and slower. I use this stance when I start, but that doesn't mean you have to do the same thing I do, especially when you're using the shield. You need to find something comfortable for yourself, so you can spring to action."

Annetta nodded, and put her focus on her feet. She tried to imagine them being light, and attempted to find a position that was comfortable for her to stand in. Both hands gripped the pseudo-sword over her head as she shifted her feet in the sand, waiting for instructions. Link observed what she did with curiosity, analyzing all the weak spots he had been taught to seek out in his training.

"You sure you want to start in such a vulnerable position?" he inquired, not breaking his concentration for a second as he spoke.

"What's vulnerable about it?" Annetta asked, going back into a neutral stance with the stick at her side.

"Well it's just that they... never mind, do what's most comfortable for you," Link said. "If anything, Brakkus will be training us so he can fix whatever he thinks is wrong. Okay, so to be fair I'll let you go first and attack me any way you want. All I'm going to do is block. Got it?"

Annetta nodded her head and went back into the position she had chosen. Her blue eyes set intently on Link, watching even his slightest movement. After a moment, she rushed and attacked, the branch coming down with lightening speed. Evading, Link moved to the side quicker than she could comprehend, tapping her lightly on the arm with his stick.

"Well, you're dead," he said, grinning. "Nice try, but you gotta be faster than that."

Annetta took a step back into the same position as before. She exhaled, trying to relax a bit, and ran at him again. She brought down the stick once more, this time using only one hand while using the other to balance herself with. Her stick came into contact with his.

"Good. Try again because, if I'd really wanted to-," Link pushed his stick forward, causing Annetta to stumble as it reached her neck. "I could have gotten you again."

Annetta growled as Link chuckled, twirling the branch in his hand.

"I've had more practice than you. It's nothing to be ashamed of. I'm just trying to point out what you're doing wrong."

Annetta said nothing in return, using her stick to get up as she got back into her fighting stance, her eyes flaring with determination.

"You ready again?" he inquired.

"Yeah, just do me one favor?" she said in a focused tone.

"What's what?" Link asked.

"Don't patronize me!" she charged again and slammed her stick into his own. Link pushed back, but this time Annetta was prepared, and drove her entire body mass into her weapon. The boy brought his pseudo-blade down in order to get away, but the moment he did Annetta came at him again and again. She had no intention of stopping until she had knocked the branch out of his hands or until she had scored a hit.

"I can see what Brakkus meant by being able to defend yourself," he huffed, blocking her attacks.

"Why? Did you think I wouldn't hit the stick on the first go?" Annetta grunted, laying on as many attacks as she could.

"To be honest, yes," he smirked, which only made Annetta more furious.

They continued to spar in this way until, by sheer luck and total obliviousness, Annetta managed to hit Link square in the gut. He cringed a bit and losing his balance collapsed on the sand. Feeling terrible for what had happened, Annetta rushed to his side to help him up.

"I'm sorry, I got carried away...are you okay?" she asked.

"I'm fine, I just-," Link groaned, then looked up at the sky, noticing a crescent moon and the stars glittering overhead. "I need to go."

"Huh? Did I crack a rib?" She looked at him curiously.

"No Annetta, I just...please you need to leave, I need to get out of here." he said nothing more and took off, running past the stream and into the forest beyond the tall grass.

Annetta watched him go until he disappeared, and almost went after him until there came a noise that sounded like something between a howl and a scream. Startled, her legs instinctively began carrying her in the direction of the cry. Picking up the shield despite her fatigue, she put her free hand on the pommel of the sword and began making her way towards the noise, only to find her shoulder latched into a vice grip.

"And that, lass, is as far as ya go," Brakkus's voice said from behind.

"Let go! I need to go after him!" she protested, gritting her teeth, "Link went out on his own, then there was a scream. He could be-,"

Brakkus's hold tightened on her shoulder until it was almost painful, "You leave him be lass. He knows what he's doing, now come with me."

"But he's in-," Annetta snarled, breaking free only to find herself propelled into the air moments later.

Brakkus grabbed the young girl and threw her over his shoulder as though she weighed nothing at all, "That wasn't a request, lassie, but an order. Now yer coming with me."

෫෨ගෑ

Kicking and protesting the whole way, Annetta was carried into Puc's room. The mage sat around his large wooden desk, parchment and tomes spread all around him in an assorted mess. The elf did not bother even acknowledging their entrance until the frantic objecting of the young girl bashing the shield into the Hurtz's side was too loud to ignore.

"Is there a problem?" Puc looked up, his eyebrows still knotted in a semi-concentrated look as he glared at the sight that was Annetta and Brakkus.

"You bet there is!" Annetta roared as viciously as before. "Put me down!"

Seeing as there was no room to run, Brakkus obeyed, placing the young girl on the ground. He still stood by the door in case she decided to double back. His eyes then fixed their gaze upon the elven mage, awaiting a command.

"I suggest you calm yourself, young Severio. Rage never did anyone any good." Puc observed the tantrum with distance. "And once you are done, with your little fit, I can proceed to help you. That is of course, if you tell me in a civilized tone what is going on that has brought you such distress as to have Brakkus carry you back here like a savage."

Annetta bit her tongue, trying to prevent herself from blowing up completely, but she was enraged. Anger surging through her like hot water, she made a move towards the door only to have Brakkus's bulky frame fill it. A snarl rippled through her teeth. "Let me go."

"Not in yer condition, lass," the Hurtz stated. "As the elf says, calm down."

The girl was so mad she found herself shaking, the after effects of her rage visible on the trembling shield in her grasp, which she had to finally rest against the ground to prevent it from pulling her down completely. Focusing her eyes upon Puc she began to try and formulate words. "Something happened in the mountain biosphere. We were sparring and then Link just took off out of the blue and then there was this...howl or a scream...I'm not even sure, but he never came back after it and I have to go find him."

"That is not your concern at this point," Puc stated coldly.

"Yes it is, he is my friend," she snapped at him, her arm having recovered enough that she grabbed the shield yet again. "And I'm going back to find him whether you like it or not."

Turning around she found her way blocked by Brakkus. "Ye ain't going nowhere lassy," he said, sternly.

"Friend he may be, Annetta," Puc began, "But my responsibility is to keep you safe, and safe is exactly how I am going keep you. You also disobeyed my orders on going alone with the boy and I will not tolerate that."

The last bit felt like a hand wrapping around Annetta's throat, suffocating the girl.

The elf wasted no more words on her and looked up at Brakkus. "Find Darius, go check out the biosphere and make sure nothing has gotten loose that should not be in there."

The Hurtz looked up at the mage, taking in the order and nodded his head. His gaze then shifted to the concerned girl before them. "I'll find him lass, on my honor, but ya stay here as Puc commands."

Helpless, Annetta watched the hulking creature as it left the room, leaving her alone with the mage. She turned around, her full attention on Puc who watched the scene from the array of gold light the candles around them were creating. She was not sure why he insisted upon reading by candlelight when good old-fashioned electricity ran through the entire base. Surrounded by thick leather-covered books and the orange glow, Annetta almost felt as though she were back in the castle and not Q-16 itself.

The mage's gaze finally locked with Annetta's. He could still see the doubt within the girl's eyes about the safety of the Gaian youth. "He had his sword with him, did he not?"

"Well I...yes, I think so." She frowned.

Puc closed the book he had been pouring through as if to summarize a point. "Then he will be fine. He was in an army, and I am sure that he can fend for himself. He did, after all, survive within the Lab for a period of time before he ran into us."

Annetta felt all arguments stop within her throat. Looking down at the shield she had dropped, she suddenly felt very childish. She hoisted it over her shoulder once more.

"Well, now that you are somewhat coherent again, I can escort you to the exit. Leave the shield and sword here. I don't think your parents would react too kindly to you bringing them home." Puc picked up his staff and began to make his way out of the room, his robes trailing behind him like smoke.

Despite most of her inner fire being quenched, Annetta still had part of her soul tugging at her against all reason to go after Link. She was certain the scream she heard had belonged to him, no matter how inhuman it had been. But she knew better than to try arguing with Puc, because he seemed to be eternally right. Whether that was true or not did not matter, because no one would listen to her anyways.

"I might be heir of Orbeyus, but no one around here is obeying me about anything," she muttered under her breath, following Puc.

Chapter 16

The next day, Annetta woke up and got ready for school like nothing had happened. She had to act this way, at least while she was around her parents. They had not been happy about her not coming home the night she had gone down to the Lab with Link. Upon returning the night after, she'd had to explain to them why she had not come back until the next evening. She did not tell them about her practicing sword fighting with Link, or about the howling, not wanting to worry them more. The less they knew it seemed, the more tolerant they were of her going down, and that was what Annetta wanted most. Getting her things together, she walked out the door with Xander to meet up with Darius.

Darius stood at the foot of the stairs leading to the exit, with his bag thrown over his shoulder, leaning against the wall in a casual manner. Despite all they had gone through over the weekend, and everything Annetta now knew about him, he seemed unchanged.

"That was quick," he said, shifting the bag as he began walking towards the door.

The girl stopped upon descending the last stair and looked at him with a pleading expression, her younger sibling passing by her in obliviousness. Darius found the look of concern foreign on her face.

"Did you find out anything about Link?" were the first words she said to him.

Darius took a moment to gather all his thoughts, connecting her bizarre behavior. He put a hand on Xander's shoulder, stopping the boy from leaving without them and then turned his attention back to her.

"No, we checked the biosphere, but we never found anything. I did hear Puc speaking with Brakkus this morning as I was leaving. They mentioned his name, but I never heard what they were talking about," he answered. "I never even really found out what went on. Brakkus just came and grabbed me and said we had to look for him. Did something happen last night? You weren't attacked by anything, were you?"

"Not me, but I'm worried something might have happened to him," she said quietly.

Darius opened the door for her, and thought of something to say that would not betray the fact that he could care less what happened to the Gaian soldier.

"He'll be fine. I'm sure it was nothing, and you'll know by tonight," he reassured her as they walked outside.

"I hope so," she muttered under her breath.

"Who is my sister talking about?" Xander finally decided to make his presence known to his sister and Darius.

"He's a guy your sister met down in the Lab, and she loooooves him." Darius smirked. Annetta tried to hit him with her bag on the shoulder.

"Do not!" she hissed.

"That's not what your face says," Darius laughed.

"Well, I don't and that's that," Annetta growled, throwing her bag back on and stormed ahead.

"Oh hey, it was only teasing Anne," Darius said, as he ran with Xander to catch up with her. "Besides, you were spending a lot of time with him last night, and you keep sticking up for him. As your guardian mage-in-training, I think I have a right to know if something is up."

"I'll tell you what's up, my hand about to smack the back of your head if you don't let up," she sneered, finding the conversation less humorous by the minute.

"Okay, okay I'll stop." Darius shoved his hands in his pockets and continued walking without another word.

There was silence until they got to the back gates of the school after dropping Xander off. Jason waited for the three of them. Reunited, the trio wandered off to their corner in the school to talk before the bell rang. They quickly went over what took place while they had been separated in the castle, and about what had happened in the Lab when they arrived and wandered off again. Jason informed them that he would finally be going to see his father once Puc had sorted out all of the details.

"They have an entire machine down in the Lab for creating fake passports and stuff so you can get in anywhere. Puc showed me last night. All I can say is holy crap, the F.B.I. has nothing on what we have down there." He was full of enthusiasm as he talked about what he had seen. "I'm starting to have a hard time imagining what else we've got down there lying around that we don't even know about yet."

"Well, it was once a military base of sorts. That kind of stuff is standard," Darius answered.

"Maybe, but I've never seen anything like it before," Jason stated.

Annetta had zoned out of the conversation. Her thoughts were still set to the time she had spent with Link and the horrifying scream she had heard after he had run away. As those thoughts faded, her mind focused in on when she had spent time speaking with Brakkus and Puc. Anger began to roil inside of her, a fist forming at her side as she remembered being ordered to not go and look for him. He was her friend and she had not been strong enough to stand up and help him.

As she stared into space, she noticed a girl sitting under a tree reading a book on the other side of the schoolyard. She looked familiar to Annetta, and then she remembered seeing her that day walking up the staircase with that young man that looked like a college student trying too hard. Before she could say anything to Jason and Darius, the bell rang, and the students began shuffling into the building. As the crowd moved, Annetta noticed the girl talking to her teacher, but paid no more attention to her as her class went upstairs.

ಬಂಭ

When they reached the classroom, everyone took their appropriate seats, and grabbed their English folders. They then waited for the national anthem and the morning announcements to come on the P.A. system. Once the tedious routine was done, everyone took their place and the teacher walked to the front of the class with the girl from under the tree. The girl had brown hair pilled-up in a bun and wore an emerald dress that Annetta thought was far too elegant to be worn to school as she looked down at her own worn blue sneakers and dark jeans.

"Class, we have a new student who has just transferred to our school. I would like to introduce you to Sarina Repronom." She smiled, introducing the student quickly to the classroom. "Sarina, if you like you may take a seat beside Jason over there."

The girl called Sarina nodded her head and glided over to her chair beside Jason. Jason could not help but gawk at the girl dressed in such an exquisite dress sitting down beside him.

"Hi...I'm Jason," he said almost instantly and robotically, taking his hand out to shake hers.

"Sarina," she said, smiling back at him.

Annetta watched the scene unfold beside her, almost feeling nauseous.

"Boys." She rolled her eyes and flipped to her last homework assignment.

The lunch bell rang, and the halls were once again buzzing with the sound of students. Annetta exited the school and headed for the corner with her hands shoved into the pockets of her jean jacket. Despite it being an incredibly warm day for that time of year, she refused to part with it. As she came to the ditch she usually crossed to get from the track to the outskirts, she looked up to see Jason already there with the new girl, talking away. Annetta frowned. All she wanted was to talk to Jason and see if he had heard anything from Puc about either the trip to visit his father, or about what had happened to Link. She was in no mood to pretend to be entertained by small talk when larger things were at stake. She sighed and put on her best smile as she walked over to the two of them.

"Hey guys, what's up?" She greeted them.

"Oh, hey Annetta, not much. Uhm, I asked Sarina to hang out with us on break, you know, since she doesn't know anyone, and kind of isn't dressed to be sitting on the bleachers with the other kids in our class." Jason waved as she approached them.

"Okay, fine by me," she said, leaning against the fence and tried enjoying the sunlight. "So…Sarina was it? What school were you in before this?"

"I was in school for a few years," she explained, "before my parents died. I was very little. Then my big brother home schooled me. Now that he's started University, it's hard for him to balance teaching me and doing his own studies, so we decided it was time for me to go back to school again."

"Oh…I'm sorry to hear about your loss." Annetta suddenly felt bad about being so callous beforehand. She shifted her weight from one foot to the other, as she tried to think of something else to say to the girl, but could not come up with anything.

"Hey, look! You guys got a new member!" A familiar voice yelled from the track. Annetta looked over, half blinded by the sun, barely able to make out a familiar silhouette; Finn.

"At least we're intelligent enough to meet new friends," Annetta called, doing her best to keep her cool.

"Real funny. Come say that to my face, eh?" Finn grinned, challenging her.

182

Annetta eyed him with disdain, crossing her arms across her chest. She recalled the talk she had with her father about being able to walk away as well as what Puc had said about being able to injure a person's pride. She figured it was time to put into practice their preaching.

"Thanks, but no thanks," she answered. "I can see your face just fine from here, any closer and I might get a heart attack, mistaking you for an ogre."

Sarina and Jason laughed hearing the comment. Finn smirked, kicking up some loose gravel on the track as he paced eyeing her like a trapped predator. Annetta could see he was getting antsy. She was seeing Puc's words in effect.

"You think you're funny? Who's been feeding you this garbage? We've always got a middleman when we do this, someone I was having a bit of fun with before you stumble in. I'm giving you the chance here and now without anyone in the way to get hurt." Finn spat. "Take your shot Severio."

Annetta felt every nerve in her body begin to pulse as she fought the urge to use her powers and fling him across the schoolyard. Her first curled up at her side and inhaled deeply as it became harder and harder to breathe the air around her. She could end him in a moment.

Jason noticed the rising tension in his friend's face and got ready to step in.

"You know antagonizing someone like that is a form of harassment," Sarina said, interrupting Finn's rant, her voice strangely calm. "And there are two witnesses here to stand against you, not good odds. I can bring the teacher over if you like to make it three."

Finn stopped in his tracks after what Sarina had said, like a deer in headlights. No one other than Annetta had dared to talk back to him before, especially so eloquently. No girl, anyways. He was about to say something back to her, but the teacher came around the track on duty and he was forced to leave in order to avoid getting into trouble.

Instead, he shot Annetta a glance. She had won the round, but not the war. Annetta exhaled and looked over at Sarina, unclenching her fist.

"Thank you," she said, honestly. "You kinda saved me from getting into trouble over there."

Sarina smiled and nodded her head. "It was nothing. He was being a bully, I just called him out on it."

"Yeah, let's hope it doesn't backfire after school," Jason told her. "Finn has a reputation of following you home."

"Yeah, I don't want to be the bearer of bad news," Annetta added, "but he may try something after school. Where do you live? If you want, we can walk home with you so he doesn't."

"Oh, don't worry about me. My brother will be picking me up after school," she said.

"Okay, perfect," Jason said. "If you want, we can wait for you by the drop off area so you're not alone. And if you want, you can hang out with us next break."

Before Sarina could answer, Darius ran up to the group, out of breath.

"Hey guys, sorry I was over by the portables, Nathan and Tom wanted to show me an article about the new gaming system they just announced," he said.

"Well, you missed Finn getting told by Annetta and Sarina," Jason motioned to the girl in the dress, who curtsied lightly upon mention of her name.

"Darius Silver." The other boy extended his hand to her. "Clearly I need to tag along with you guys more often. I keep missing all the good stuff."

"That's what you get for trying to be everybody's friend." Annetta smirked.

೫೦೧೪

After the final bell of the day rang, Sarina, Annetta, Jason, and Darius exited the school and waited by the pick up zone for Sarina's brother to come and get her. Cars of every design and color drove into the school parking lot to take students home, making the small area appear almost like a conveyor belt from the traffic.

"So, how did you like your first day?" Jason asked, breaking the silence between them.

"Oh, it was wonderful, just what I've wanted for a long time." Sarina smiled. "I've been away for so long from people my age, I've forgotten how enjoyable it is."

"That's good. Well, we'll have more fun as the week goes by. Too bad you didn't get here any earlier in the school year. The break starts in a few months, so school is going to be over then, but I'm sure we can hang out in the summer," he added.

Sarina nodded as a black sedan pulled up to the curb of the entrance with tinted windows. Sarina almost looked shocked, but did her best to stay stone faced, seeing Matthias's form in the drivers seat of the rolled down passenger window. It looked brand new, as though it had just come off the production line. The trio had never seen a car like that pull into their shabby school parking lot. Even the other students turned to stare at the intimidating vehicle.

"That's my brother, I've got to get going," Sarina told them, taking her backpack and slinging it over her shoulders delicately. "I'll see you guys tomorrow!"

"Later!" they all called in unison as Sarina disappeared into the black car.

ഇരജ

Matthias sat in the front of the car, his gauntlet-clad hands on the wheel, observing the parking lot while Sarina got in and shut the door behind her. She dropped her bag on the floor, and put on her seatbelt. She looked around the interior of the car, taking in the scent of the new vehicle with unfamiliarity and fascination.

"Where did this come from?" she asked.

Matthias stayed focused in the front seat, checking around to make sure he did not run into any of the teenagers crossing the lot. "I bought it. I figured if I came by the school, a motorcycle would not exactly spell dependable older brother, so I decided this would do instead. I must say human beings are a silly race. The more of their currency I threw down, the faster the little man behind the desk said the vehicle would be ready."

Sarina could not help but chuckle a little as she settled into the seat and looked out the window, watching everyone leave the massive building while they waited for the line up of cars to move along. As the silence grew more explicit, Sarina finally exhaled in an effort to break it.

"You were right. I was overdressed." She sighed as Matthias cracked a wicked grin, visible in the rear view mirror.

"I told you," he chuckled, "That kind of dress is something worn on special occasions, not for a school day."

"You were only going on intuition," Sarina sneered, shifting in her seat uneasily. "Besides, father never lets me wear dresses like this anywhere, except when I hold audience with him."

"Ah, so this is to spite your father, not to look out of place in a school setting, is it?" Matthias teased her, keeping his hands on the wheel as he exited the parking lot and headed for their house. They had acquired it just a few days beforehand and had not wasted time in getting everything else set up so their pseudo-life would seem somewhat realistic to those peering in from the outside.

Sarina could not help but laugh at Matthias. His sense of humor had gotten more relaxed since they had come to Earth, and he seemed a more pleasant person to be around, instead of the cold, uptight one she was used to observing on the ship. She was glad to see him as he acted when they were alone together, where he would tell her all about his missions, about the places he had been to. Out here, they did not need to hide from her father's ever-present gaze that forbid her from ever knowing what friendship was. She wished the mission could last forever, and that she would never have to go back to the confinement of her tower in Valdhar, but she knew it was only petty wishing. Once they gained access to the Eye to All Worlds, it would all be over.

"So, did you meet anyone who you think could be the descendants?" Matthias asked, changing his tone of voice along with the subject. "We're running out of schools in the area to check."

Sarina's heart sank. She knew full well who it was that they searched for. She knew them by photograph and by name. By fate and by the Unknown's will she had ran into them. She had spent the whole day associating with them, and even came to like them a little. She wanted to lie and tell Matthias she found nothing, but she knew if she did she would throw away her only lasting friend. Weighing the consequences, she decided.

"I may have found them. I met a boy today named Jason Kinsman and a girl named Annetta Severio." She said the names quietly.

Matthias slammed his foot into the break pedal, bringing the car to a halt in the middle of the street. Car horns blared behind him, but he did not care as he turned around to face Sarina.

"Are you sure those were their names? Are you absolutely sure?" he asked.

"Yes, those were their names," she answered, still quietly.

Matthias laughed as he took his foot off of the brake pedal and began to drive faster.

"This is brilliant! Do you know what this means?" He grinned wildly. "We finally found those runts! Now we just need to figure out how to gain access to the castle and all my problems will be over."

He drove silently for some time, lost in his own thoughts as he tried to think of a way to get them to confess their knowledge of the Eye to All Worlds and give them access to it. Sarina smoothed out her dress in the back seat, trying to think of what to say next in order to keep conversation flowing.

"I could...pretend to become their friend," Sarina suggested to him as they pulled into the driveway of the house. "Maybe if I knew them well enough they would let me in on it. I mean, that is the reason father sent you on this mission. You cannot enter the Eye to All Worlds without swearing the oath to the Severio descendant first."

Matthias put the gears into park and turned off the engine. He sat in the drivers seat, stroking the hair on his chin, thinking of what approach to use. Killing the children would do him no good, not right away at least, for he needed to swear that oath. He also needed visual confirmation for himself. It was not that he did not trust Sarina. But this was his job and it needed to be flawless for the glory of his lord and master. He took her offer into consideration, though.

"How long will it take you?" he asked.

"I don't know, but I will do my best to get as close to them as I can," she answered. "The boy, Jason, seemed to take a liking to me more than that girl, Annetta, did. I could maybe focus on just becoming his close friend if need be."

"Perhaps you wearing that dress was not completely in vain after all," he chuckled, exiting the car.

Chapter 17

Annetta came home from school to hear distinct chatter between her brother and a voice she had not heard in her room before. Though she was aware Xander was home early from a half day due to testing, she had not expected any other company.

"So when you get to the lower level, you need to jump there," Xander instructed, over music coming from one of his games on the television.

Dropping her bag, Annetta crept around the corner of the room to see Link sitting in a chair facing the television, awkwardly holding the videogame controller in his hands, his fingers trying to coordinate the miniature knight on the screen, who promptly fell off a cliff while viciously stabbing thin air.

"No! B is for jumping, not the X button." Xander growled in frustration, grabbing the controller from him, "Ugh…fine. I'll get over it."

Link couldn't help but chuckle at the boy getting so worked up. He looked over at Annetta, who watched them. A smile spread across his face in greeting.

"Hey, how was school?"

Annetta shook off the shock of seeing him sitting so casually with her sibling, almost like he belonged in the room. She walked rapidly towards him, nearly tackling him in the process from relief, "I'm fine, great!" She said, flustered. "How are you? Are you okay? I was so worried when you took off last night."

"I'm okay," he said wide eyed, watching Xander leap over the ledge and shoot him a prideful glance. "I saw something watching us in the grass. It was a Baba Yaga, a forest witch. I was worried it might try to attack you. That's why I made you leave as soon as possible. I got Puc and Brakkus to come with me and help me get rid of her."

Annetta raised an eyebrow, watching his face. He knew she was capable of taking care of herself. The story felt invented, but she knew Link had no reason to lie to her, so she brushed it off. There was a lot she still did not know. He was fine, and that was what mattered. However, she continued to glance at him, and then looked questioningly at Xander playing the videogame.

"Oh, right. I got my own card key now, Puc sent me to tell you that you and Jason won't be focusing on psychic abilities today. You'll be working on combat training, so he wanted you and Jason to dress comfortably. Your parents went shopping, and I'm learning the refined art of video gaming from Xander."

"And he sucks," Xander muttered, handing the controller back to Link and proceeding with his own character across the screen.

"And he couldn't contact us himself because?" She raised an eyebrow again. "Besides, I never dress uncomfortably. That's the last thing on my mind."

Her stomach continued the conversation for her, arguing against further interaction, "Sorry, human needs." She blushed a deep red.

Since her parents weren't home, Annetta left Link and Xander to their game and went over to the fridge. She heated up some leftover chicken, rice and steamed vegetables from the day before. Wolfing down the contents of the plate quicker than she thought possible, she wandered back into the room.

"Since we're waiting for J.K. to arrive, why don't you throw on the multiplayer, Xander?"

"I did, you gotta join." Her brother pointed to the "press start" option at the top of the screen.

"Right, awesome." She nodded and pressed the button. Annetta found herself entering a world all too similar to the one she now knew existed.

The game had a simple objective: Kill as many monsters as possible before getting to the main boss at the end of each stage. A team of up to four heroes could play at a time, with classes varying from generic warriors to spell casters. The attacks were all one or two button combinations, and as long as a person never got hit or jumped off a cliff it was fairly easy to stay alive. Players also got to pick up loot and customize their character along the way. Annetta always found herself immersed in the world she was playing in, and could not help but pretend to be the barbarian on the screen charging into battle and taking down half of the enemies in one swing. There was something about it that appealed to the side of her that wanted to save everyone.

"None of this is realistic at all," grumbled Link, fidgeting with the joystick as he ran into another monster and lost some health, "I would have pulled out my sword and slayed him then and there, not walked into him."

"It's not supposed to be real, it's a game." Annetta reflexively twitched, moving her whole body with the controller as she ducked and rolled from an attack, "It's meant to be fun."

"Well, it's not real at all." Link wrinkled his nose. "And I don't see what's fun about it. You're cooped up in a room looking at a screen. You could be outside, or-"

Annetta pulled back the curtain in their room, standing up on her bed and cocking her head to the side as her eyes wandered to look outside. Curious, for his only encounter with this world had been at night, Link stood up on the bed beside her and looked out down into the horizon. Before them was a forest of grey and red brick buildings, mixed in with an assortment of little houses sprawled out like bushes in the forest of stone columns. Interlocked with this were black roads on which cars zoomed by faster than Link could catch the colour on them. Blinking, the Gaian youth looked back at Annetta, wanting an answer.

"Do you see my world?" she asked in a saddened tone. "There's not much that's pretty about it. Now look back at the screen."

Link did as she asked. The brilliant green of the pastures they found themselves on far outshone anything he saw out the window. Even the little green park across the street seemed dull in comparison.

"It's an escape," she continued, pulling the curtain back over the window. "An escape from the world. The only world I ever knew existed before everything that happened. There's no heroes, no monsters, sometimes there isn't even a line between right and wrong, so you just shut your eyes and look the other way."

The youth looked at Annetta and nodded, a mutual understanding having been reached. It was something that he had not thought of when they had been going to the movie. This was why Annetta wanted so badly to learn of the world he had known his whole life. It was escape. Sitting down, the two of them continued on with the game without another word for a long while.

"Hey, when do I get to go down the cool portal thing, Anne?" Xander interrupted.

"When you're older," Annetta informed him. "Mom and dad won't let you right now."

"Man, I never get to do anything cool." Xander frowned.

190

"Well, if you get to do everything now, then what will you get to do later when you're my age?"

"I don't know. More cool stuff," he responded, and then turned to Link. "Can you take me down with you? Please?"

Link smiled a little at Xander's puppy dog expression. "I can't. Sorry. You don't want your parents upset, do you?"

Furrowing his brows, Xander turned around, clutched his controller, and mumbled under his breath about how life was not fair. Before they knew it, a knock came at the door and Jason had come to join them.

Jason gave a short laugh, seeing the three of them gathered around the game. "I see you're taking time to enjoying the finer things in life."

Link looked at the game, not picking up on the sarcasm until a moment later. "Xander was just teaching me how to play while we waited for you to arrive. I was sent by Puc to let you guys know we're going to be doing some weapon training today, so dress comfortably."

Jason looked down at his faded jeans and red hoodie. "Why would I dress uncomfortably?"

Annetta raised her arm and pointed at him, curling her lips in an 'I told you so' smile. Link shook his head in turn.

"Right, well, let's go, I guess." Link pursed his lips and took out his card key, then slid it down the side of the mirror to activate the teleporter.

The scarred Gaian turned back to Xander, looking at the silver platform with hope. "I'll come back to visit you soon. We can level the characters together a bit. How does that sound?"

"Okay." Xander sighed with longing. "You promise?"

"I give you my word." He winked, and within moments was gone to the depths of another world, followed by Annetta and Jason.

‍ℬℭ‍

Arriving in the Lab with the same ceremonial thud, the trio quickly opened the door and began to make their journey inside. Annetta still felt the strain in her arms from carrying the shield back when they had recovered it in the Castle, but she knew there was no use in complaining to Puc. The mage would hear nothing of it. Puc never paid any attention if they were sore or tired. Even if Brakkus tried to tell him to stop he would push them harder than before. Thankfully, the psychic lessons were becoming less wearisome as the two of them were building up tolerance to the repetitive tasks Puc had them do. The two of them had learned to use projection, telepathy, and telekinesis within the few short months they had been down at the Lab training with Puc. It was only a matter of time before they were able to teleport, and perhaps someday to use psychic fire, which they both had yet to witness. However, shrugging her shoulders and flexing her back muscles, Annetta admitted to herself that she would have taken psychic training over combat at that moment.

"Pain is weakness leaving the body." Jason quoted Puc jokingly from one of their previous lessons. "Walk it off."

"Yeah, I'll walk your head off when I shield bash you." Annetta frowned as she stopped to stretch, Jason plowing on ahead of her and Link.

"Golden advice either way," Link stated, standing beside her, "You can't gain anything without pushing yourself. Trust me, I've been training with Brakkus."

"And how are you still standing, and not in pain?" she huffed.

"I'm a good actor," the youth said turning to face her, his bangs falling into his face as he looked down at her.

Jason stood a bit farther back, watching the exchange of emotion between the two of them. From the smiles on their faces, something began to boil inside him that vaguely reminded him of jealousy. For years, he had been Annetta's best friend. They confided in each other with everything, and now he was seeing this display of affection towards someone she barely knew. He did not like it, but he did not show his dislike, either. Another part of him simply thought he was overreacting, and that the friendship he and Annetta had could never be replaced, no matter what. He was so off in his own world that he did not notice Annetta and Link walk right past him and continue on without him.

"You coming?" she asked, turning back to look at Jason who was frozen like a statue.

"Yeah, sorry I was just thinking about some stuff," he said snapping out of his trance as he caught up to them, "So what kind of weapons you think we will be learning to use?"

"No clue," Link answered as he took the lead to the training grounds they always went to. "I was just told to come get you guys so we can start as soon as possible."

"I wish we could do more fun stuff, like going to visit the castle," Annetta grumbled. "I'm tired, and it's either train like this or train like that.

It's like Puc doesn't understand the meaning of stop. If you're tired then just keep going."

Jason looked over at Annetta. He rarely heard her complain. She had to be really tired if she was resorting to it.

"I don't think that's the issue here," Link answered as they walked on.

"What do you know?" she glared at him.

"I don't know for sure, but it feels like Puc might be trying to overcompensate for something. I think I know what, too," he said.

"Overcompensate?" Jason raised an eyebrow. "By making us work like dogs?"

Link stopped in his tracks and turned on his heel to face the two of them, his feet sliding gently on the metallic floor.

"Puc probably believes if he had been there, Orbeyus would not be dead. Now he's doing everything in his power to have you two prepared for anything that could come your way, in case he is not there to help you."

Annetta looked down at her feet. It made her feel rotten, speculating Puc's only reason for training them so hard was because he was worried about their safety. Still, she felt he had an odd way of showing them he cared. He never really praised them, and when they did well on something, it usually meant the task would become even harder.

"He's got a weird way of showing he cares," Jason voiced both his and Annetta's thoughts.

"I know, it might not even be right as I said," Link said, "but I've heard him fighting with Brakkus and that was brought up a few times. They also fight about how he never gives you guys any time to rest or explore the Lab. I mean, I bet you guys don't know about half of the things in here, do you? There's a spaceship dock if you go the opposite way of the training grounds."

"A what?" Annetta looked at him.

"A spaceship dock. Come on, I'll show you. I don't think Brakkus will care if we're a little late." Link took the lead down the massive steel corridor.

Annetta was amazed at how easily Link was able to maneuver through the identical metal hallways. Even though she only took one route to get to the training grounds, she still managed to get lost at times, and had threatened to post pieces of paper on the walls with directions. There were no windows anywhere, and there were no signs on any of the blue-tinted silver metal panels that made up the walls and floor. It was almost like going through an animal burrow. It astonished and saddened her when she thought about how many people could have been staying at the Lab, and how now it was only them.

After a good ten minutes or more of walking, they made it out of the corridor and came to another larger opening. The cavernous room was unlit, and there were massive objects underneath grey tarps. Feeling his way, Link walked over to the side and pulled a switch on the wall. The lights turned on to reveal that the entire room was littered with the enormous tarp-covered things.

Annetta's jaw dropped as she shuffled over to the nearest covered object. They were all at least over thirty feet tall or larger, towering over everyone. It made her feel like an ant. She pulled one of the tarps off using her psychic abilities, revealing what lay underneath it.

She had half expected to see a flying saucer or a sleek rocket. What she found instead was what appeared to be an old navy ship. Triple mast-ed, with detailed carvings, it almost looked like a vessel that had been once in a bottle, lying casually on its side. Frowning, she looked closer. Although the ship looked to be made of wood, it was, in fact, made out of metal that had been painted to look like wood. She had never seen a paint job that was so accurate. Annetta reached out to touch the surface, and was reassured at the panels were indeed made out of cold metal.

"It looks like an old pirate ship." Jason took a few steps back to get a better look.

"You didn't think everyone flew in modern spacecraft from day one, did you? Some of those races wanted to keep their space flight secret from superstitious locals." Link chuckled, "This is a Gaian warship. From the looks of it, it was meant to blend in with its surroundings at the time."

"Maybe at a carnival, but not out on open seas," Jason said.

Annetta ignored Jason's comment as she paced around the ship, only making it a quarter of the way in one direction before pausing to look at it some more. She put her hand once more on the ship, reassuring herself it was indeed made of metal and not wood.

"Why would someone build a spaceship to look like this?" Annetta said. "I mean, wouldn't anyone on this choke from lack of oxygen? And wouldn't there be like...an issue with gravity?" Annetta continued to walk around the massive structure. She paused, noticing writing on the side of the ship. "The Flying Dutchman?"

Jason ran up to where Annetta was standing. Reading the words, his eyes almost popped out of his head. "Nah, it can't be the one."

"There only be one Flyin' Dutchman from where I come from," a gruff voice called from their entry point. Annetta turned to see Brakkus resting his hands on his massive twin bladed sword.

"You're telling me my grandfather owned the real Flying Dutchman, the ghost ship?" Annetta raised an eyebrow.

"Oh, no, he didn't own it, it's been in yer family for generations. But if ya must ask, it is the one and the same." The Hurtz wandered closer to the children.

"So my grandfather owned the Flying Dutchman," Annetta said, pointing at the ship.

"It was passed down, so yep," Brakkus said. "One of yer ancestors got it as a gift when the Gaians were paying tribute. She still works. Yer grandfather loved working on this ship. Keeping it in running order. He said it was an important artifact for the future to preserve."

"So all those legends about the Flying Dutchman glowing and being seen at sea-," Annetta looked at the Hurtz.

"I think I can explain that," Link cut in. "Gaian ships rely on a special type of energy called Beta. It's harvested from Beta dragons on our home planet. It protected everything onboard the ship from the lack of atmosphere and gravity in space. We still use it to this day, but the ships are a bit more modern-looking than this one here."

Annetta nodded her head and looked up at the ship with a sort of longing. The more she learned about this world she was part of, the more she seemed to not understand how all of these things she once thought she knew worked. Now, in addition to castles and swords, there were spaceships and universes far beyond her own that seemed inaccessible to her. She thought back to the portrait of her grandfather in the castle, his blue eyes watching her from his throne high above. How much more was hiding behind those eyes of his?

"Aye, well, we ought to get going and training. Annetta, ya need to get yer shield and the lot of ya need to get yer weapons. Come along before Puc comes in." Brakkus broke the pensive silence, picking up the sword and slinging it back into its scabbard.

Jason and Link followed Brakkus without so much as another glance at the ship, while Annetta took another moment to take in the sight before her.

She'd never known her grandfather, and now more than ever she found herself wishing he were there to explain these things to her. She sighed, feeling very much alone and then followed her friends.

Chapter 18

Far above the Earth, Mislantus waited for news from Matthias about his progress. So far, each school they had gone to with Sarina held nothing. As time went on, he began to grow impatient with lack of any good news. He had waited years, assembling an army to be ready to take on the heir of Orbeyus. The warlord yearned to get his revenge for the death of his father, and his own disfigurement.

The tyrant sat in his throne room with his fingers entwined, waiting for the servant he had sent out to return with his report. His cat slit eyes watched the world below go about its business. A crooked grin crossed his face at the realization that the little blue planet had no idea of what was going on above them.

A creature resembling a fawn with blood red skin walked into the room. It wore a grey tabard with Mislantus's emblem, a black dragon with seven heads, arched and breathing fire, around it ten stars circled the heads. It was an old crest and well respected in space for it had belonged to his father and all those who knew of the seven-headed beast of Valdhar knew to fear it well. Mislantus stirred from his resting place as the creature knelt before him with no eye contact, knowing better than to look its master in the face.

"Speak. Are there any updates from Earth?" he commanded.

The servant bowed as low as it could, its cloven hooves trembling on the cold steel floor. "Sire, we have received no transmission as of yet from Matthias Teron or from Sarina."

Mislantus's patience had drawn the line. He slammed his fist into the armrest of his throne and gave an animalistic hiss of displeasure. Rising, he walked towards his serf, wanting with all his heart to kill him. But he knew it would do him no good, aside from being a momentary distraction. The creature hunched over even more, its face nearly touching the ground as it did its best to stay where it was. The tyrant snarled, doing his best to keep his wits about him as he walked past the creature over to the window. He kept his back turned, the pale blue light shining on the outline of his mantle.

"Go. And keep waiting! I fail to believe one of my greatest assassins has been taken out by a bunch of children!" he sneered.

The fawn quivered and bowed the entire way out, only turning heel once he was at the door to run.

Mislantus closed his eyes with a growl, searching for a solution in his head.

"Might I be able to offer some assistance, your grace?" A low deep voice came from the dark. "I did, after all, train the boy in all he knows, and I can assure you I am well enough to undertake this mission and see it carried out till the end. That is, if it will please you, my lord."

The tyrant opened his eyes and turned around to face the direction the voice had come from. The gleam of a metallic object was barely visible from the reflection of starlight coming through the window as a man stepped forth. A silver mask that formed the shape of a five-pointed star covered his face. The two lower points were longer than the rest, making them look like fangs, leaving his lower jaw exposed. The place on the mask where his right eye was had been destroyed, and the skin beneath was burned. His eye was no longer functional, a pale and lifeless thing which saw all and nothing at once. White hair stuck out behind his mask and came past his chest, making it look like a lion's mane. Along his arms he wore vambraces of leather dotted with little silver studs, and he wore the same tabard as the servant, only in black.

"Amarok Mezorian." Mislantus faced him with a smile. "My eternal shadow."

"Always, my lord." Amarok gave a low cackling chuckle. "I hear that my old student is not fulfilling his duty, is this correct?"

"He has not reported in the last few weeks," the tyrant said, still facing the window. "I am getting ready to send another in his place, for I think we underestimated the children."

Amarok's good eye glistened at the statement. The elder assassin moved closer to his master, getting a better look at the feline facial features that seemed to be drawn into deep thought on the subject at hand.

"As I said earlier, my lord, I am well and ready to go back into the field. I would gladly go to Earth and get what is required for you. After all, I did dispose of that oaf who led the Alliance, did I not?"

Mislantus looked into Amarok's good eye and studied him intensely for a few moments. He was the best of the best among psychic warriors, which is why it was hard to give him up. After Amarok sustained his disfiguring injury, Mislantus had him posted as his bodyguard. It proved handy when you wanted no one to know you had one, but could snap your fingers and make people drop dead. Still, what he desired most was hidden on Earth, and if sacrifices needed to be made, he was willing to make them.

"I will have a ship prepared to take you to Earth. In the meantime, I will need you to find a way to blend in, seeing as you are not subtle in the looks department anymore." Mislantus snickered.

Amarok took a low bow and then looked up. "I could say the same thing about you, my liege. I'm not sure those whiskers would go over well on Earth."

Mislantus let the insult slide. He had known the assassin for years. "Off with you."

The assassin said nothing more, and left the room with a grin on his face. His chance had come.

෴

Amarok exited Mislantus's throne room and headed to his own quarters. Joy gleamed behind the mask. He existed for the purpose of being able to take lives without the victim knowing he was there. He relished the wait for the pulse to stay steady and only rise at the very last moment, when his prey realized there was nothing that could be done to prolong life. But what he loved more than the moment of the kill was the dance with death, the time in which he hunted his victim and locked onto it. Picking the right moment to silence someone was an art. He continued to walk, engrossed in his thoughts.

"Well, don't you look just smug there, Amarok," a female voice called to him from behind.

He turned around to see a woman with pale green skin, dark green hair, and large blue eyes smiling in his direction teasingly, wearing a black tabard as he did. He turned to face her, all thoughts from before vanishing.

"Nanika, a pleasure to see a familiar face." He bowed.

"The pleasure is all mine." She curtsied. "Amarok Mezorian. We thought your recovery from that fight was just a myth. A lot of people around here have been trying to obtain your position as Mislantus's favorite, but I guess there is no longer a point, is there?"

"Not from where I stand, although I know there will be some morons who will still try it, thinking me a cripple." His good eye gleamed at her wickedly from behind the silver of the mask.

Nanika laughed and moved closer. She took one of her fingers, tracing the contours of his mask slowly. "I think the whole masked man thing suits you very well. Makes you more…mysterious."

Amarok stood in place like a stone as she drew closer and ran a hand down his armored chest, smiling and playing with his hair teasingly. He was growing more annoyed with her by the moment. Seeing him not respond, she withdrew a little.

"What's the matter, Amarok? You seem tense." She grinned.

She reached for his arm, and before she could respond, Amarok triggered the armor with his mind, and it shot to life. Dozens of small, sharp spikes punctured her body from the places were the studs sat on it. His psychic-responsive vambraces were his favored weapon, ornate and intriguing to the eye with the little metallic dots, but when activated, a mass of spikes that he could manipulate with his will. Amarok moved his arm as the limp corpse slid off of the barbs. He glared at her and then kicked the dagger out of her long sleeve.

"Imbecilic wench," he sighed. "Never could keep it in her pants."

Chapter 19

After another evening of weapons training, Annetta and Jason split up for the night. Jason headed home earlier accompanied by Puc, while Annetta decided to stay behind and chat with Link. The boy tried to think nothing of it, but it was beginning to bother him. He wanted to be included in everything his friend was up to. He shook the notion from his head as he walked, and turned his mind to other matters.

"Have you managed to get everything in order so I can go see my father?" he asked the elf.

"It will be done by tomorrow, I promise you. Creating a false identification for the world you live in isn't as simple as you think it to be," Puc answered, "I will be there to pick you up after school."

Jason nodded and continued walking silently, listening to the sound of their footsteps and the thud of Puc's staff on the steel floor.

"There's something else I've been meaning to ask you, and it's bothered me ever since. Well, two things, really." Jason looked over at him.

"Speak, and I may be able to answer." The elf stopped and faced him.

"Well, okay. First of all, with all this training we've been doing to learn to use our psychic powers and all, how do you know about how to use them? And secondly, why are we learning to use swords and maces if guns would be more effective?"

Puc seemed impressed. "Valid questions, indeed. I am not a psychic myself, but the way mages use magic is very similar to being a psychic. You need to be able to focus in order to use your abilities, and a person must be born with the predisposition to use either gift."

The two of them walked until they came to another open area. It looked similar to where they had found the Flying Dutchman earlier that night. Puc looked around the room and tore down one of the tarps, revealing what lay underneath it. They stood in the shadows of a large armored vehicle made out of a beige metal, with numbers printed on either side in bold red, lacking wheels of any sort. A rifle protruded from the top of it. There were all kinds of strange machines like this scattered all over the Lab under gray tarps. Jason hardly paid attention to them anymore, since he had no use for them and no knowledge of how to operate them. He doubted Puc and Brakkus did, either.

Puc walked closer to the tank and faced Jason once more.

"As for why bullets and projectile weapons are useless, allow me to demonstrate." The mage stretched out his hand and muttered something quickly under his breath. His eyes glowed a pale green for a split second, and then the tank began to shrivel inwards like it was being sucked into a black hole. The noise of metal being crushed together so quickly made Jason cover his ears, and before he knew it, the massive tank was nothing more than a wrinkled ball of metal the size of a soccer ball on the floor.

"Magic renders guns mostly ineffective in war. It is far easier to kill your enemy with the skill of your blade and mind. A spell known as a defense aura slows bullets and arrows down to almost a stand still. When this spell was created, it changed the rules of combat. There are, of course, spells which can counter this, and can be etched into projectile weapons, but these take much time to make, and so many have simply abandoned making them. Larger weapons such as this battle tank can also be taken out with ease using magic, or even simple telekinesis. Speed is of the essence when fighting a psychic, or a magic-user. If a gun jams on you for a moment, it could mean your end. You will find guns in the armory here, and you are free to learn to use them. However, they are useless to you for the most part. The sort of foes you may find yourself going up against will be far easier to defeat with melee combat than ranged."

Jason walked over and tried to pick up the crushed ball of metal, but it weighed a ton.

"When can I learn that? You know how much time that would save on the road when we're late going somewhere with my mom?"

"Kinsman, do not even think about trying to use your powers in the outside world. But if you are asking when you will be able to do that, give it a few more weeks and you should be ready." He answered starting to walk again.

"Really? Sometimes it feels like we're not learning anything at all." Jason frowned, kicking the metal ball, and regretting it moments later when the pain became present in his toes from the impact, causing him to hop in order to walk it off.

"Have you ever heard the words mind over matter?" Puc asked, continuing to walk.

"Well, yeah, but what does that have to do with anything?" Jason followed, still limping.

"Everything. When you are doing your exercises, what do you focus on the most when you see the objects you use?"

"Well…the size and the weight of it, and then what I have to do with it," he said.

"Remove the first two from that equation, and you are left with what you must do with the object. This is what I have been trying to teach. Being a psychic means being able to suspend all doubts about the size of an object or its identity. It simply comes down to what you want to do with a given object, or if necessary, person."

Jason nodded his head. He'd trained long enough with Puc that he understood what it was that he was trying to explain, even if the small thought was hard to put into practice when on the spot. They reached the exit to the teleporter, and the boy turned to face the elven mage.

"Hey, listen, me and Annetta know why you're doing all of this… why you go overboard with the training and stuff. It's not your fault Orbeyus died when he did. I mean, it's not that we don't appreciate what you're doing for us but…we just want you to know that we know you weren't responsible," the boy said. "I mean, I don't blame you, and Annetta doesn't, and I know that for sure."

Puc looked at Jason slightly, raising his eyebrow at the odd conversation. He curled his lips as if to form a word to back it up, only for a sigh to escape as he turned away.

"You had better get home now before your mother starts to worry," was all he said. "Good night, Jason Kinsman."

Jason watched as Puc headed back into the shadows, his robes billowing behind him, the thud of his staff echoing on the metallic floor. Guilt passed through the boy for having brought up the topic but there was nothing he could do to take it back now. He thought nothing more on what had happened, and slid his card key into the slot.

ಸಾಂ

As the school day came to a close, Jason waited in the parking lot for Puc to show up. He was not sure what to expect of the elven mage, since when it came to blending into the real world, he had a strange way of accomplishing the feat. Annetta and Darius waited alongside him. Sarina had been there, but her brother had already picked her up. Jason sighed and leaned on the fence, guarding the lot as he watched cars go by and pick up students.

"He said he would be here. Chin up." Annetta leaned on the side of the large blue box that contained road salt for the winter. "I don't think Puc is one to go back on his word."

"He never does," Darius confirmed with a straight face. "I've known him for years. When he says he'll do something, he goes through with it."

Jason nodded and continued to watch the parking lot. The afternoon sun beating down on his spring jacket was making him feel drowsy, and he would have happily laid down on the pavement to sleep. Just then, the roar of an engine interrupted his stream of thought, and a vintage car pulled in.

All the boys who were still waiting perked up their ears at the sound, and looked up to feast their eyes on the red and black paint job of the car. Even Jason had to stop and stare at the vehicle that stood in the front of them.

"He's not very humble when it comes to his choice of alias," Darius sighed. "Yet he insists on being as unfriendly as possible in his disposition."

The window came down. Puc wore a pair of sunglasses and had the same makeup on as before when he had stopped the fight between Annetta and Finn. Jason almost wanted to laugh, knowing that underneath it all was the stern, attentive, and very studious Puc.

"Get in, Jason.," he said in a gruff voice, his hands fastened to the steering wheel.

Jason looked at his friends, and without saying much else, he opened the passenger side of the car and sliding in, shut the door behind him. Annetta, still standing outside with Darius, gave a small wave of goodbye to her friend, and the car sped away from the school just as quickly as it had arrived.

ೲഌ

Jason sat uncomfortably in the vast leather interior of the passenger seat as Puc drove onward to their destination. He was not sure what to make of the whole situation, so he resorted to looking out the window for a long time before deciding to hold a conversation with the elf.

"So, can I ask why you put on the whole tough guy act when you're not in the Lab?" The boy looked in his direction.

Puc glanced over at Jason and took off his sunglasses. His pale blue eyes contrasted sharply with his fake tan.

"It's easier to look unapproachable than approachable here in this world. I don't think people would show me an ounce of respect if I walked around in a dress shirt with my hair combed to the side."

"Well...no, but you could...you know, dress normal. You don't have to be one extreme or the other."

"I don't enjoy engaging in conversation with humans who know less about the world than a goblin who's been trampled by too many war horses in his life and doesn't know left from right," Puc growled again, "And that's that."

Jason blinked a few times, trying to imagine what a goblin trampled by war horses would look like, but simply shook his head and looked out the window again at the blurred mix of apartment buildings and stores as they came out onto the main road. The boy looked at Puc who kept a straight face the entire time, his focus being his driving, which the mage seemed to do with ease.

"Jason, you need to know that there is a reason your father is where he is today," Puc spoke after the long silence. "He is not stable, and unable to handle that some worlds are not ready to know about the existence of others. It was his belief that everyone should know about the Lab, the castle and portal travel, things which, if known about, could send this world into turmoil."

The youth shifted in his seat, hugging his bag closer to him as he took in all of the information.

"I don't see why that would be such a bad thing," Jason answered. "A lot of people could be helped by some of the things that are down in the Lab, and people are always searching for answers about if we're alone or not."

Puc continued to lead them to their destination, switching lanes when necessary and stopping when the lights told him to do so. Jason was having a hard time comprehending that the elven mage actually could get around on their human roads so well when all he seemed to do in the Lab was very medieval in nature.

"There is much good in the Lab, but can you imagine the fear of knowing there is something else out there, and the potential evil that is down in the Lab? You have seen the weapons and you know what magic can do as well as the power of psychic abilities. Humanity is not ready, not now at least." Puc stopped as the car came to a halt. "We're here."

Jason looked out the window again as they came to a large, sterile building. The color gave a white tint to everything in the vicinity, almost making Jason want to turn back and never go in, because it reminded him too much of a hospital and of sick people. Though the building looked safe and secure, it was a little too much so for Jason's liking, like a mother coddling her child. It felt like the last stop on a long journey, and the doom about the place was overwhelming.

Puc said nothing to the boy as he paid for parking, and then locked the car. The two of them strode to the lobby, where a few receptionists sat on stools organizing files and answering phone calls. One of them stopped after feeling the icy glare of Puc's eyes bite through the protective wooden desk.

"Hi there, how can I help you?" A young woman with pale blonde hair tied into a bun answered with a flash of teeth white enough to have been part of the walls.

"I have an appointment to see Arcanthur Kinsman today. Name is Puc Kinsman," he said, looking the woman directly in the eyes.

"I'll need to see some I.D. Mr. Kinsman," she said, and then looked at the boy. "Is he going with you? If so, I'll need to know his relationship to the patient, and he needs a notice from his guardian with permission to be here."

Puc took out a thick envelope and handed it to the woman. "I believe all you need should be in there."

The receptionist looked through the paperwork Puc had given her, crosschecking to make sure everything matched up, and entered a few things into her computer, updating the patient notes. Jason stood anxiously beside the elf. He was so close to being able to see his father that everything else had stopped mattering to him. Even what Puc had said to him back in the car lost meaning.

"Okay, you guys are good to go. If you turn left there's a lounge area there and wait for an escort to call you to go through another security check," the woman said.

Puc nodded and placed a hand on Jason's shoulder, guiding him towards the door.

ॐ

After the security guard checked them once more, and they went through the metal detector, Jason and Puc were led to where they were to wait while Arcanthur was prepared for their visit. It reminded Jason of a questioning room in a criminal investigations TV program. Usually there were two people in the room who questioned the suspect, plus the person's lawyer. The more the boy thought about it, the situation was eerily similar.

Jason's palms began to sweat as he looked down at the squeaky clean white paneled floor.

"Will he even know who I am?" he asked as he sat down beside the mage.

"He will remember," Puc said calmly, showing no emotion in his face. He was here for a reason, not to play friendly with Arcanthur and reminisce about old times.

The doors opened and a man in scrubs wheeled in a rugged-looking man in a wheelchair with cuffs on his hands and a leather restraint around his waist. He was chained to the chair and covered with a baby blue quilt that smelt strongly of bleach. He had a square jaw, the kind a football player would sport and brown hair that went past his ears lined with grey. His straight nose appeared as though it had been broken and never fully set into place. He seemed like he would have been a tall man should he had stood up straight by the length of his legs coming our from under the covers and the size of his shoulders. His eyes, green like Jason's, darted back and forth as he breathed heavily, his hands wrenching together in an unsure manner.

"See, Mr. Kinsman? Your brother Puc and your son Jason are here to see you. Remember like we talked about?" The attendant in the coat told the man on the wheelchair as he was wheeled to the table.

"My name is Arcanthur Lackfoot! Lackfoot!" the man in the wheelchair hissed. "And I have no brother named Puc. Puc was just a bloody elf who took orders from Orbeyus like a lapdog!"

Jason's jaw almost dropped when he heard the gruff tone coming out of his father's mouth. He had pictured their reunion a thousand times over, but never did it start out in this manner.

"Alright sir, he is not your brother, but your little boy Jason is here," the man said to him in an effort to calm him down, before looking up at Puc. "I'm sorry. He's having an off day."

"That's alright." Puc nodded his head.

The man in scrubs took a few paces back when he was certain Arcanthur was secure. "I'll be right outside with security, just look into the camera and we will come to get him."

Puc nodded, staring down the man as he locked the door, the magnetic locks pressing down, meaning they were inside with no way out.

Arcanthur grunted and looked in Jason's direction and stopped fidgeting.

"My boy? Jason?" Arcanthur twitched with joy. "Is that...is that you?"

The shackled hands reached out for the boy, but the man was too far away across the table. Jason was not sure how to react. He helplessly looked to Puc, whose expression showed nothing for him to read into. Acting on his own impulse, Jason got up and walked to Arcanthur, then embraced him. For an instant when the calloused hands wrapped around him, Jason felt a sense of safety he had never felt around any adult. This was what he had been searching for, but just as quickly as the feeling came, it left as the man let go and gently pushed him away, his green orbs gazing back at Jason and then quickly fixing themselves on Puc.

"As grateful as I am for you bringing my son to see me, what in hell are you doing here, mage? How have you come to know my son?" Arcanthur glared at Puc and let go of Jason.

"Much has happened, Arcanthur. What Orbeyus wished has come to pass and both your son and Annetta Severio know the truth. We have come here today because your mace, Helbringer, is missing from the castle," Puc answered.

"Severio!" the man snarled, and pulled his son in closer. "Listen to me, Jason, and listen good. The reason I am here is because of a Severio, and I will be damned if I ever see you in here as a patient. Never trust a Severio. Never!"

Arcanthur was breathing heavily at this point, frustrated and paranoid by the turn of events. He touched his son's arm gently to have him come closer without the security guard outside being roused.

"The thing you seek," he whispered, "and let it be only for your own protection, lies in the one place all secrets are kept about one's true identity. The one place a person is always meant to unwind. There, under the third board, you'll find him. Keep him safe. He will be your most loyal companion through all time." Arcanthur looked his son straight in the eyes, darting to Puc briefly, then back again.

"I'm going to tell you a story, Jason. No, a warning about the true nature of Severios, and how the only thing they are good at is taking the glory but not doing the work. Your friend's father, Arieus, is the reason I can no longer walk, and the whole reason why everything in the Lab fell apart. He washed his hands of it all after Orbeyus was murdered. He said he was done. He abandoned everything we had worked for. He didn't even stop to think the Lab would no longer function, and he had forgotten all about our dream..."

"Arcanthur, I think that is far enough." Puc pushed the conversation away from what it was veering towards. "Now where is the mace? We need it to call up old alliances. We need proof that Jason is your son."

Arcanthur simply shushed Puc with his finger. "How can they not know he is my son? He has my eyes. But if you must ask, I just told him where Helbringer rests."

"I heard full well what you said, Arcanthur. You forget I am an elf," Puc sneered. "We have no time for this, so you tell us, and you tell us now where exactly it is."

"What's this, the great Puc Thanestorm cannot take on a riddle?" scoffed Arcanthur. "And here I thought Orbeyus made you his lapdog just for that precise reason."

Puc sat rooted to his chair, without any emotion aside from the stern look upon his face to indicate his feelings on the situation, while Arcanthur bellowed a laugh from his gut.

"It is in his room under the third floorboard, safe and secure. I'm not a moron, Thanestorm, though according to you I am crazy." Arcanthur twitched again and laughed. "Oh yes, we had a dream with Arieus, to let the world know what's out there, that there's hope for something more than the conformity of our miserable lives here on Earth. But in that last moment, when we were about to tell everyone, he changed his mind. He decided that it should be kept secret."

"And with good reason, Arcanthur! You know the consequences we'd have to deal with!" Puc finally blew up, annoyed with Arcanthur's ranting.

Arcanthur spoke only to his son. "Never trust a Severio, my boy. They have their own agenda, and if you do not comply with them, they will leave you to die in the dust. You must look out for yourself. I lost life and limb because of that wretch. Do not let my fate be your own." As he spoke, tears began to form in his eyes.

Puc pulled the boy back with a quick jerk. Jason looked up at the elf questioningly.

"I think it is best that we leave," he said. Making eye contact with the camera, the magnetic doors clicked open.

"You think you can just get away and leave me in here!" howled Arcanthur. "Remember what I said, boy! Never trust a Severio or their lapdog elf!"

"Oh my, he really is off today," the attendant shook his head as he took hold of the wheelchair and began wheeling him away.

Arcanthur grabbed hold of the sides of the wheelchair. Hoisting himself up slightly, he slammed down onto it with his entire body mass making it come to a halt, "You will not interrupt the Lion of Hell!"

The attendant sighed behind Arcanthur. Pulling out a prepared syringe from his pocket, he checked it to make sure it was the correct one. He then spoke in a bored tone, having heard the ranting all too many times. "Okay, that's enough of that Mr. Kinsman. We all know you are a fierce warrior who saved many a kingdom."

"They were not kingdoms you moron, but worlds! Universes!" Arcanthur shrieked as he turned to look at the man with a scowl, and then whirled his head back around. "What is the use of talking to the likes of you, anyways, when you've scarcely begun to understand your own puny existence on this vast terrain known as-,"

There was no finishing of the sentence for Arcanthur as the syringe entered his neck and forced all the anger and contempt to leave his face. Peacefully, he drifted off into an artificial sleep with the help of the tranquilizer.

Having finished the deed, the attendant turned to Puc. "I'm so sorry about that, Mr. Kinsman. I didn't think it would get so bad today, otherwise I would have cancelled the visit all together and rescheduled for another day."

"That's quite alright, perhaps we can come back another time," Puc answered in an emotionless tone before turning to the boy. "Are you ready to go?"

His mind still swimming in the events of what had just happened before, Jason looked up at Puc, the pale blue eyes judging what now flowed within him. "I...uh...yeah I'm ready."

The attendant smiled an overly fake smile to the boy. "Okay, you can both just exit using the door behind you. It has been unlocked."

Jason watched as the shell of the man he called his father rolled out of the room unconscious with the attendant in tow. He had imagined many things about his father, how he was a great man who was simply troubled, how he had to be here because of something that was not entirely his fault but the result of a psychological condition. Listening to his words brought forth some tiny form of doubt. This was not the meeting Jason had been hoping for when he was younger.

"We're just going to leave him here like that?" he questioned in a small voice, turning to Puc. "No one is going to say anything about the things he was talking about?"

"It is a mad house, and so all in here are mad," the elf retorted, ending the discussion.

Forlorn about the encounter, Jason scarcely felt Puc's arm on his shoulder as the elf escorted him out of the room and down the hall to the main lobby. He did not even remember the blonde-haired receptionist telling them to have a nice day, or how they had managed to get to the car. All he remembered was snapping out of his trance when the car engine started and they were already off.

"This is not how I imagined any of it." Jason finally uttered a sentence.

"He's there for a reason," Puc answered, without any sympathy. "He put everyone in danger by his actions and this was what it led to in order to keep him alive."

"He talked about Arieus betraying him," Jason said, "and how they were going to reveal everything to the world."

"It started off as no more than drunken talk between two good friends. They'd known for years that no one could ever know of our world, in fear of the damage it could cause. But your father grew to believe that it was possible, that they could change the world if Orbeyus or his own father were no longer around to press upon them the importance of keeping it all secret. When Arieus left Q-16, Arcanthur confronted him, and in a fit of rage when things did not go his way he challenged him to a psychic duel in the middle of the city. In the end, it cost Arcanthur his mobility, his power, and his sanity. That is all you need to know of it, for it is not my tale to tell," Puc told him.

The story caught Jason's interest, and the moment Puc stopped his disappointment at the events of the day grew tenfold. He turned his attention instead to the slowly speeding landscape outside the car, losing himself once more in the contemplations about what he had learned from his father on that very day. His accusations against Annetta simply for being a Severio angered him, and even at the time of him saying it had made the younger Kinsman want to lash out against his father. He could, however, not help but question Puc and everything else that he had learned about the Lab. Perhaps it was not Annetta that was the cause of it, but he felt like he couldn't fully trust the others involved. The thought vanished as quickly as it was produced, and Jason found himself looking upon a familiar sight as Puc pulled into the parking lot of the townhouses he lived at.

"The mace will most likely be in its dormant state. It will look like a simple wooden carving on a leather cord. This prevented Arcanthur from parting with it in this world. I trust you will be able to find it." Puc broke the silence as he shifted the gears in a fluid motion into park. "Or am I making assumptions and will you need me to go in and assist you?"

"No, I think I'll be okay." Jason nodded and then took one final look at the car, "Say…how are you going to get this thing back down to the Lab?"

Puc reached into the glove compartment of the car to produce a few documents, "I am not, for that would be too complicated. There are many things you can lease and borrow in this world. A vehicle is one of them. Unfortunately, a driver's license is not."

As Jason opened the door of the car to get out Puc called after him, "I expect you at the Lab this evening. No exceptions."

Jason closed the door behind him and gave a nod. The car reversed out of the lot and sped away as quickly as it had come for him.

ಬಿಐಚ

In no time, Jason found himself at home. Slinging down his bag in its usual spot, he locked the door. His brother sat downstairs mesmerized by the television, and his mother was out somewhere, so there seemed no better time to look for the mace. Standing before the entrance to his room, he counted the floorboards thoroughly in order to find the third one from the door, before kneeling down before it.

Running his fingers along the finish of the panel, Jason found a weak spot. Gripping the wood with his fingers, he pulled with all of his might, but nothing happened.

"Maybe he was just being a crazy old man," he grumbled to himself under his breath. Still, he tried again until he felt like he would tear his fingernails off.

212

Huffing, Jason sat on the floor in front of the board. Then the obvious dawned on him. Hoping his mother would not walk in on him again Jason tapped into his abilities. Within seconds, the board floated away from where it had been placed and landed on the floor a few feet away. Crawling closer to it, Jason noticed a small wooden box where the slab had been, and for a moment hesitated to reach for it, worried about some sort of trap. Shaking off the disillusion, he levitated the box out of the crevice and covered it up. Finally, when he felt all was safe and sound, he picked up the box on his own. It seemed lighter than he expected. Opening it up, Jason found himself looking at a small wooden object on a leather string. It was far more intricate than any carving Jason had ever seen. Each of the four blades on the head of the mace seemed to be carved into the silhouette of a lion. He could not wait to see the full-sized object.

At the same time, Jason found himself once again dwelling on darker thoughts, like how his father had said to be wary of Severios. He wondered what his life might have been like if his father had obeyed, had not crossed Arieus and done what he did. What sort of father would he then have been to him? His stomach muscles tightened as he contemplated. Shaking his head, he put the leather cord over his neck and tucked it under his shirt.

"I'll play along with Brakkus and Puc, I guess," he sighed out loud, comforting himself with the sound of his voice. "I'll play along to be safe. But I mean, Dad was wrong, Annetta's not a bad person. She's my friend and she always has been. She'll back me up in a fight no matter what."

Jason looked out the window in his room; a faint ghostly reflection of himself could be seen on the glass. "No matter what."

Chapter 20

While Jason and Puc had been off to see Arcanthur, Annetta and Link had their own adventures down in the Lab. Brakkus was busy, and Darius was nowhere to be found, so Annetta and Link set out to explore more of the biospheres, picking one they'd never been inside. Though they both knew Puc would be fuming if he found out that they had gone off alone again, the scolding was worth the prize of one another's company.

The biosphere they had chosen was a vast forest filled with a variety of tall deciduous trees. Everything on the ground seemed to be filled with decomposed leaves, and in some places tall, thin grass sprouted up, providing green patches, adding life to the floor like a multicolored carpet. Link walked in front of Annetta, scouting out the area and talking from time to time about the woods. Annetta remained quiet, enthralled by everything around her. She had never been in a real forest before. Save for the small tree-infested area close to Jason's house, Toronto was not exactly teeming with woodlands.

The air was rich with the smell of soil, and the only thing that could be heard was the occasional cracking of a dead branch under their feet, or the sound of birds overheard heralding their arrival in the area.

"I wish we did more stuff like this," Annetta said after another long silence between them.

"Well, that's what we're doing right now, isn't it? Taking advantage of the fact that Puc isn't around to tell you to get on the training wagon," Link said, before stopping. "This place goes on forever, I think I'm gonna climb up and have a look to see if everything is just forest or if there is anything else. Otherwise we might as well head back."

Link looked around and found a tree that had branches low enough for him to climb. He quickly set to work, his arms grabbing hold of the lowest branches, hoisting himself upwards with ease as though he were born for climbing.

Annetta waited on the ground, amazed at how quickly he disappeared into the dense array of leaves that seemed to create green clouds overhead, letting in sunlight only slightly. She looked around the forest every few seconds to make sure nothing else was in sight. Though she knew they were safe, being close to the exit, Annetta still felt on edge in an unfamiliar location. She was beginning to understand that she needed to expect everything and anything.

Moments later Annetta, heard excited muttering from the top of the tree, followed by Link sliding down the trunk as though it were no more than a child's slide in the park.

"Come on! You gotta see this, but you need to be really quiet, okay?" he said to her.

Annetta nodded her head as he grabbed her hand, walking as quickly as he could without dragging her behind.

"So...what is it exactly we're going to see?" she asked, still being dragged.

"You said you wanted more stuff like this? That you wanted to know about the world you're part of? Then come with me and I'll show you," he answered. Arriving to their destination, they stopped.

Link crouched down and motioned for Annetta to do the same, though instead of letting her do it herself he pulled her down in excitement.

"Link could you calm-" before Annetta could complete what she was saying, Link had clasped his hand over her mouth and shushed her. Annetta wanted to say something nasty to him, but was interrupted when she notice what it was that Link was hiding them from.

The first thing Annetta thought she saw was a herd of white horses grazing on the clumps of grass. They looked small and sturdy. Brakkus would have probably said they were no taller than thirteen to fourteen hands high. They had been startled by something and were looking about curiously for whatever it was that had caused the noise. After deeming it harmless, they continued grazing, and the most curious thing happened. A bright blue light formed at their foreheads, and when the shine passed each horse had a single white horn. Annetta felt faint from excitement.

"Unicorns?" Annetta whispered, once Link had let go of her.

"They've adapted to hide their horns when they feel threatened," Link explained. "I needed you to be still in order to see them for what they really are."

Annetta smiled and nodded, watching the creatures go about their business, chomping at the grass happily. Sometimes, when one got spooked, the horn would disappear in a puff of light, and then reappear moments later.

"I'm guessing we can't get any closer, right?" she asked.

Link shook his head. "Not this time. But if they stay here and we keep coming back, maybe eventually. Unicorns are just like other animals, really. You need to earn their trust by showing them you mean no harm. If you do that, they'll treat you like one of their own. They were once fairly common on Gaia but are now considered a protected species, we had a heard that lived close to my home."

"So do we like...bring them sugar cubes and stuff?" Annetta raised an eyebrow.

"I think for now we can just watch them a little bit." Link smiled as the two of them turned their attention to the white creatures grazing in the forest.

Time seemed to slow down when they watched the unicorns and after a while the two of them even sat in the open some distance away to get a better look. At first, the horns had disappeared, but seeing as the two of them hardly moved, the creatures soon forgot they were even there and went about their business. Annetta and Link continued to watch them for a while longer, but their peaceful activity was short lived. There then came a crunch as though someone had stepped on a large tree branch, and the unicorns looked up, freezing where they stood, their horns disappearing instantly. Link looked around, trying to determine where the sound was coming from.

"What was that?" Annetta looked around in confusion.

"I don't know, but whatever it is the unicorns don't find it to be friendly, so neither should we." Link rose quickly. "We need to head back."

Annetta got up from where she was sitting. The unicorns behind them reared and took off, nothing more than a blur of white among the green and brown foliage of the woods. The crunching became louder and louder, and the sound of trees falling now accompanied it. Link grabbed Annetta's hand and bolted for the exit, not even bothering to tell her to get a move on, his brain racing faster than his mouth. Annetta was not one to argue.

They ran stumbling through the woods on uneven ground, their feet getting caught in the tall lanky grass, which seemed to wrap around their ankles. They dared not to look back at whatever it was that hunted them. Hearts pounding in their throats, they stopped in front of a massive log that seemed too large to either climb or go around.

"Which way?" Annetta breathed heavily, looking up at him.

A roar came from the trees and before Annetta could say anything else, Link pushed her to the ground and his sword was out before him, his eyes focused on the blurred shape bounding towards them.

Link's arm muscles coiled as he braced himself for impact. Sure enough, moments later, a large club came hurdling down at him. His blade cut into the wood, but made no significant damage. He glanced at his attacker. It was a full-grown Forest Giant. Its skin was the deep brown color of the soil with a bark-like texture, and its thick hair the green of the trees as it swung its club again at Link and Annetta. The tiny dark eyes beneath a large knotted brow glared at them both in primal anger.

Link pushed Annetta to one side, while quickly rolling the other way in order to divert the thing's attention from her. He ducked again as another swing from the giant attempted to sweep him from his feet. Link began to panic inwardly as he tried to think of a plan. He was not sure how long his luck would hold out without one.

Annetta groaned, shaking the dead plant life off from her shirt, and then looking over to get a better look at the thing that was attacking Link. She scanned the area quickly, then realized there was a solution to the problem: the tree trunk. Closing her eyes, she did her best to focus on the massive object before her, trying to make it rise from the ground, but the sound of the battle meters from her side was making her shaky.

"Damn it...come on, Anne," she growled at herself. Taking a deep breath, she tried to block out all of the sound around her. She was beginning to understand why Puc's training was so important.

Link continued to dodge the blows, parrying with his sword from time to time. He knew he did not have the strength to take on such a massive opponent. His only ally in this battle would be his wits, most of which were shot from the shock of the assault. He'd only read about Forest Giants in his texts, he had never expected to encounter one in real life, more so in an underwater base that was completely cut off from the world. Still, he had sworn to protect the heir of Orbeyus, and he would do so to the best of his abilities. Dodging again, he tripped on an uncovered root and braced himself for the next attack.

The sound of splintering wood came from behind Link and flew over his head as the log that had been blocking their path collided with the Forest Giant, and sent him to the ground with an inhuman howl. He looked to the side to see Annetta standing with her arm outstretched as though she had thrown the log herself.

Annetta's knees buckled, overwhelmed with the effort of her attack.

"You okay?" she called, "What is that thing?"

"I'm fine, and it's a Forest Giant. They're not usually dangerous. They're forest guardians. It must think we were threatening the unicorns," he answered, picking himself up.

Annetta nodded, but before she could say anything else to him the pile of decaying wood thrown onto the giant began to stir. Bunching her hands into fists, Annetta stood in the same place, unmoving. Despite how large and terrifying the creature was, something inside of her had snapped, and she wanted this fight, even if she would get hurt. The adrenaline coursing through her veins gave her courage and that was all she needed.

The creature rose from its wooden grave and roared in anger, raising its fists into the air.

"Come on, I'm not afraid of you," she whispered, gritting her teeth.

Before the scene could unfold any further, there came another howl crashing from the trees, more frightening than that of the Forest Giant. There was a quick flash of steel, and the giant fled deeper into the woods. Link and Annetta looked up to see Brakkus mounted on a warhorse. His eyes flared with bloodlust, the massive twin bladed sword resting at his side as he gripped the reins with his free paw-like hand. His ears remained flattened against his skull as he calmed down, observing the area.

"Are ye both alright?" he grunted, to which all they could do was nod their heads in unison. "Good, then follow me. We got a lot to talk about."

Annetta ran quickly to catch up to Brakkus and walk beside the slowly moving horse. Link took his time sheathing his sword, waiting to make sure the giant did not come back. Hearing nothing from behind them, he went to follow the Hurtz and girl.

ഈര�

Annetta waited quietly some distance away with Link while Brakkus unsaddled the horse he had rode to their rescue. Despite nothing being said between them, Annetta was well aware that he was not happy with them having wandered off. It was the same silence that went on between her and her own father when he was angry at her about something.

"Do ye have any idea what ya could have cost us?" Brakkus finally spoke, having finished what he was doing.

"We just wanted to take advantage of the fact that Puc wasn't here and we didn't need to train," Annetta began to explain.

"Ya could have asked me to accompany ya," Brakkus snarled, "Ye may think the Lab is all safe, but it's not and don't even get me started on how ya ain't supposed to be going off alone with the lad. I don't get mad easy, lass, but if we lose ya then all hopes go down the drain!"

"Brakkus, I'm sorry I-," Annetta struggled to say something she was cut off however by Link's hand on her arm.

"It was my fault," Link said "If anyone's to blame, it's me. I took her into the biosphere. I took her to see the unicorns. The giant was probably protecting them."

Brakkus's rabbit-like ears flattened against his skull as he glared at the boy, trying his best to suppress his rage.

"At least ya own up ta yer mistakes, boy," he growled, "I forgive ya, as yer both kids. I just want ya ta let me know where yer goin' in the future."

Annetta nodded. She understood his concern, even if she did not fully agree with it. Despite her fear at the time of the attack, she was now confident enough to believe that she could have taken on the Forest Giant without much trouble.

The trio left the stables and entered the common room area of the Lab. The common room would have once been the equivalent of a great hall in Orbeyus' time. Chairs and sofas lay scattered about in the large vicinity, but Puc had made Jason and Annetta clear the area of seats they would not be using with their abilities. The majority of the room was now an empty steel hall with chairs and sofas pushed to the sides of the walls, and only a few left in the middle arranged in a rectangular position.

Before anyone could make themselves comfortable, the sound of feet could be heard pounding on the steel floor, and Puc came to the entrance, still in the leather jacket and jeans, rubbing off the fake suntan from his face with a cloth. He seated himself in one of the large armchairs and threw the cloth to the side once he was done with it, proceeding to peel off the fake beard, wincing as he did so.

"Why do you torture yourself so much with that disguise?" Annetta couldn't help but stifle a laugh, even though she had seen him dressed that way before.

"I do not wish to be bothered with people, therefore I make myself inhospitable," he stated coldly, and then noted Brakkus's discontent face. "What ails you?"

"I found a Forest Giant that was trying to attack 'em in one of the biospheres," he grunted. "They got lucky I could hear it from the stables, and that Annetta thought quickly enough to throw that rotting log at it when she did."

"How far can you hear, then?" Link glanced at the Hurtz as Puc sat in silence.

"Very far, lad." He glared back.

"You wandered off without Brakkus or myself with you?" Puc shot ice with his stare at the both of them, "You both realize it is still very dangerous here, correct? You know we are still not certain if everything that got in has been purged, and yet you insist on such volatile excursions in order to sate your desire for adventure. You have also once more violated my rule of going off with the boy alone."

"And nothing happened," growled Annetta as she rolled her eyes.

"Silence! You have no idea what could have gone wrong you arrogant adolescent," the mage gritted his teeth as he glared at Annetta and continued to rant, which the girl then blocked out.

She hated when he started scolding in his brooding, sarcastic tone. She did not mind being yelled at. But being belittled, that was something that made her want to punch holes in the steel walls around her. It was not enough that she spent almost all of her free time in the Lab. Now she was not able to have anything remotely close to leisure time.

Puc's face became less tense despite the news he had just heard, and he leaned back in the armchair like an old king would. Had it not been for his lack of grey hairs and a beard, Annetta would have said that he looked similar to the painting of her grandfather in the armory.

"Well, no matter. In the days to come I think you will get your share of adventuring. Jason and I have been successful in recovering Helbringer from its previous owner. The most important part of the journey now lies before us, reuniting the Four Forces by convincing them to reform old alliances with the heirs of Orbeyus and Arcanthur."

"What are ya thinking of?" Brakkus asked his comrade.

"My apprentice has gathered useful information regarding Mislantus, a threat that if left unchecked will spread like wildfire." Puc rose from his seat. "Come, Annetta. You may have proven to be quick today, but you must learn to be efficient as well."

"Aren't we going to wait for J.K.?" she asked.

"He will join us when he gets here. We have wasted enough time as it is," were the last words the elf said before wandering off.

Only nodding in obedience, Annetta exchanged a quick look with Link before bounding off behind the mage to continue her training.

Brakkus flattened his ears against his skull in acknowledgement that they were going and got up to go back to his chores. Link watched the Hurtz go and then decided it was time to confront him. Getting up, he followed the massive creature.

"You still doubt my abilities no matter how much I hone my skills, don't you?" he interrupted the silence.

"Why would you say that?" Brakkus stopped in his tracks and looked at the boy curiously.

"I thought it would be obvious. You called me a child," Link snapped at him.

"It is what you are, is it not boy?" the creature looked at him, "How old are ye? Seventeen? Eighteen summers at most."

"I have trained and fought in the militia camps on Gaia. People younger than I have gone off to war and never come back. That has to count for something."

"Aye, the haughtiness of a race to send children out to do an adult's job," Brakkus sneered, "In my eyes, yer a boy and nothing can change that."

"I'll fight you if I have to, so I can prove I am not a child who needs to be taken care of." Link drew his sword.

Brakkus's eyes widened with curiosity as he watched him, his thumbs stuck under his belt. "Ya sure that's wise, lad? Ya do know what I am, right?"

"I know full well, but if this is what it takes then I am willing to go through with it." Link stated, going into a fighter stance. "I am sick and tired of being treated like some brat who cannot take care of himself or those-,"

Before Link could say anything else, Brakkus was upon him, the twin bladed sword out, impacted into Link's stomach hilt first. Link fell to his knees, holding his torso in pain. Brakkus grabbed the scruff of his neck and glared at him.

"The only thing adult about ya is yer pride. It's killed plenty of warriors on the battlefield," he grunted. "Until ya learn to control that and do more than ya speak, I will never accept ya as a warrior or a man. In my eyes, ya'll always be a boy, and nothing more."

The Hurtz sheathed his sword and continued on his way, leaving Link on the steel floor to contemplate the events that had just occurred.

Chapter 21

Having left what was not needed at home and taking only the necklace and card key with him, Jason set off to Annetta's apartment building. The walk usually took him a good half hour, as his mother refused to drive him or have any part in his involvement in the Lab. It was tough at times, and it was not like he could keep relying on Annetta's parents to pick him up all the time, so he set out on foot, putting some headphones on in order to make time fly by faster.

He could not help but feel as though someone or something was watching him. But each time he looked over his shoulder there was no one in sight. Maybe it was like Puc had said, and it was those nebulous lurking things that did not wish to be seen. Maybe he was more in tune with them now that he had begun honing his psychic skills. He continued to walk, trying to ignore the feeling, but the closer he got to Annetta's building, the stronger it became.

Finally, it hit him like a cold knife in the back. Jason took off his headphones, and looked around at his surroundings, trying to find what it was that was staring him down. He then noticed a figure, a man, walking in the shadows of the parking lot lights.

The man looked like an eccentric detective from a film noir, except for the long white hair that stuck out from underneath his fedora and cream-colored trench coat. The other curious thing about him was the red bandana on his face, concealing everything but his eyes, which Jason avoided, trying to seem unaware of his presence. Something did not seem right about him, and Jason quickened his pace to the building. Though the man showed not even the slightest bit of interest in him, Jason could not help but be paranoid and kept moving quickly, his legs pumping with adrenaline. Going into the lobby, he called the Severio apartment to get inside. He knew once he crossed the door the man could not follow him anymore, or would at least have a tough time of it.

"Severio residence, Aurora speaking," a voice said through the intercom.

"It's Jason, Mrs. Severio. Could you let me in?" he asked, his heart racing behind his ribcage.

"Sure thing, J.K. . Just a moment." there was a pause, and then a buzzing sound filled the room. Jason opened the door and shut it behind him, running to the elevator without looking back.

৪৩৪৪

Mislantus stalked through the barracks of his castle, on one of his unannounced inspections. He liked to keep his men on edge, and so these inspections came random and often. A fit soldier was one that was ready for war at any moment, someone who was not simply going about a routine.

The soldiers, all of different species and size knelt beside their beds on either side of the room, facing the center as Mislantus passed by, looking at each bedside and each fighter. He would stop from time to time, lingering over soldiers, particularly if they exhibited any signs of being nervous. A weak-witted soldier was useless in war, and these were usually the ones that got called out.

As he reached the end he paused at the bedside of a humanoid solider with stark white hair. He was a novice, and clearly worried about something. The sweat on his brow made him look as though he had just gotten out of the rain. Mislantus stopped and stood before him, watching as the shaking increased.

"Are you ill, boy?" he asked, for the white haired individual was no more than eighteen summers of age, in accordance to Mislantus's calculations.

"No, my lord," he responded.

"Then why do you sweat like a swine about to be roasted on a spit?" Mislantus neared the soldier.

"I do not know my lord," the man shuddered.

A something heavy landed on the man's shoulder. He looked from the corner of his eye to see Mislantus's clawed hand.

"I think I have a good hunch. You fear death." The cat slit eyes stared down at the man. "But that is alright. We all fear something."

The shoulder of the man in Mislantus's grip loosened a bit, becoming less tense at the sound of the soothing tone of voice.

"But, we will need to do something about it. There is no room for fear in these walls. One needs to be able to conquer their fears, and I think I have the perfect way for you to conquer yours." Mislantus fell silent.

Before the man could even dare to look into the face of his lord and master, a fist drove itself into his chest, shredding the heart still inside his

224

ribs. The corpse collapsed to the ground, Mislantus standing above it with a bloody fist.

"Death," he sneered, and with the whirl of his cape left the barracks, pulling out a handkerchief as he left to clean his hands. Sometimes it was good to instill fear and be made known as someone who did not simply rule over everything, but was also capable of being lethal himself.

"My lord, Amarok wishes to speak with you," a servant said, approaching the tyrant humbly. "A voice conference has been set up for you in the throne room."

Mislantus casually tossed the bloodied rag on the ground as he walked and only slightly inclined his head to the servant, "I shall go receive it now. Tell no one to interrupt me. This conference takes top priority over all," he spoke.

"Yes my lord," the serf nodded his head and went away, leaving Mislantus to pace the halls of his fortress.

ಬಂಣ

Once in his chamber, the warlord seated himself upon his throne after having washed his hands more thoroughly in a basin and continued to wipe the blood clean from them with another piece of cloth. Blood was a hard substance to remove from skin, once there it stained and became an inconvenience of the deeds done in the past. He waited as the screen came to life, acquiring the transmission from Earth. The familiar masked face of Amarok became present on the screen, gleaming like the visage of death itself.

"I have them, my lord," he said to him, "Now how is it that you wish me to go about this?"

"We will need to find a way into the castle. Remember, there is an oath that needs to be sworn to a Severio in order to even enter it," said Mislantus. "You were able to enter once before by means of a card key looted from a corpse, but you said that moments after you left, the key disappeared from your hands, correct?"

"Yes my lord," he answered. "It must have had something to do with Orbeyus' demise. I may have scared the boy today as well so that limits my way of getting inside. I must try to approach the girl, or her father."

"I would not trouble yourself with Arieus. We've not seen or heard from him since the fall of Orbeyus. From the looks of it, he has nothing more to do with the base, as rumors said. He may, however, be useful leverage in the future if push comes to shove..."

A beeping interrupted their conversation. Mislantus noticed that another transmission was trying to get through from Earth.

"Stay on the line, Amarok. I think Matthias has finally remembered who his master is," he said, and switched transmissions by flipping the switch on the control panel.

The face of Matthias Teron appeared. He inclined his head to indicate a bow.

"My lord. I apologize for the absence in reports, but I wished to wait until I had something valid to say instead of interrupting your busy schedule with empty words," Matthias greeted him.

Mislantus leaned back in his chair, curling his whiskers with his fingers, trying to get a reading on Matthias's true intentions. He could detect nothing but honesty from his face. Eloquent as ever in his greetings, the younger warrior had a way of smoothing out any sour mood the tyrant found himself in. He was not sure why this was, but it was a talent that had prevented Matthias from being the object of his wrath many times. A glance, a gesture, and a smile, and the feelings seemed to diminish. Mislantus often wondered if it was because he saw some of himself in the man, or perhaps the son he would never have.

"Go on," he said.

"I have located the heirs of Orbeyus and Arcanthur. Your daughter and I have been working on infiltrating the base. It may take a little longer than expected, but Sarina has told me she is swaying the boy and befriending him. If she succeeds in doing so, we'll have a way paved in gold to the castle and nothing can stop us."

"And what if she is unable to do so? Have you a back up plan if this does not work?" The tyrant leaned forward.

Matthias stood in silence before the screen. Mislantus felt his fears come to life, but they showed only by the slight twitching in his face.

"We will not fail, my lord. The plan is already set into motion, and I have managed to find useful information about Arcanthur that will further strengthen our position," he said. "Arcanthur was sent to a long term psychiatric facility. Apparently after it all happened, Arieus was the one responsible for locking him up, and by means of magic, stripping him of his

226

powers. If the boy were to learn of this betrayal, this information could be used to fuel distrust between him and the girl..."

Mislantus calmed upon hearing the plan, and leaned back into a relaxed position. There was still a seed of doubt planted in the back of his head about it all, but it all seemed more solid with the data provided.

"You want to use this to turn them on one another and to stick my daughter in the middle of his wound. That is quite a plan you have concocted, Matthias. I never pinned you as the conniving type, not to this degree anyways." The cat face grinned. "Very well, continue on with this plan. I request you report to me in a week, progress or no progress at all. I wish to be kept up to date."

"Yes, as you wish my lord." Matthias bowed again.

Mislantus nodded in acknowledgement and turned off the transmission. He switched back to Amarok, who had been waiting patiently for his lord to turn his attention back to him.

"It was as I expected," Mislantus stated. "Matthias decided it was time to report back. Though his reasoning seemed honest enough for not having done so before, I cannot help but be suspicious of his actions. I did not get this far by putting all my faith in a single entity that is not myself. It is why I lead armies. Should one fall, ten shall take his place. Your task for now is to remain and watch Matthias. If there is any indication of him wishing to betray us, kill him, and bring my daughter home safely. I have read far too many sagas and legends where the assassin has a change of heart. I cannot allow for this pattern to happen here."

"Do you not trust him then, my lord?" Amarok asked.

"I trust him about as much as I trust all of my soldiers out in the field," he sneered. "To add to the matter, these are no ordinary children and anything and everything can happen. I refuse to let anything stand in the way of accomplishing my father's dream and my life's ambition."

"I will see to it that all goes well, my lord. I was there when the Axe fell, and I will be there to see that his offspring breathes their last breath. You have my word on this." Amarok bowed his masked head. "Be it in my life or in my death, I will see your kingdom rise."

"Go to your task then." Mislantus dismissed him and turned off their transmission.

He sighed, leaning back in his throne staring into the eternal dark of space, dotted with stars. His dream was so close at hand. Yet the closer he got to it, the more he feared something would fall through, something would go amiss, or someone would stand in his way. He had always in the back of his mind planned to send Amarok to Earth with Matthias, it was only a matter of waiting for his injuries to heal. His confrontation with the assassin had simply pressed the final buttons. The more pawns he had out in the field at one time, the better his odds. Every piece counted when cornering his prey. Sighing, the Lord of Valdhar looked over at the cloth that lay discarded on the floor, painted a faded crimson with blood. He had learned first hand, only the strong survive.

Chapter 22

Jason exited the elevator and headed down the corridor to Annetta's apartment. Knocking, he fixed his half-tucked in t-shirt, not wanting to look like a complete slob.

Aurora opened the door, beaming with a smile.

"Hi J.K., Annetta is already inside," she greeted. "I'm just on my way out with Xander. If you need anything, Mr. Severio is there."

Xander scooted past Jason and raced to the elevators to be the first to press the button, since it always took a while before one showed up.

"Sure thing. Bye, Mrs. Severio," he said back.

Aurora nodded. Picking up her purse, she followed her son and waited with him. Jason waved and closed the door. He took a moment to orient himself, and then he saw Arieus sitting on the couch reading a book, absent from the world around him.

It would have been a lie for Jason to tell himself that what his father had said to him had not taken hold in his heart. He had questions for Arieus, questions that needed answers if he were to be able to look his best friend's father in the eyes again. But along with that was a rooted fear, which would not escape him. He was not sure how much he could ask, or what he could ask without poking a metaphorical sleeping dragon that could potentially put him in the same place his father was now. These feelings were not whole, however. They were mixed and muddled. Each time he looked over at Arieus, he could not help but see the man who had told his daughter she could venture into the Lab, even though he himself would not enter. He could also not forget the fact that Arieus was the only other male role model he had ever interacted with, for his own father had never been there. But the fear was bigger, fresher, and it placed doubts within him. Still, the need to know drove him past it.

"Hi, Mr. Severio," he said, unsure if Arieus had seen him enter or not.

Arieus lowered his book and smiled, "Hi, J.K., Annetta is already in the Lab."

"Yeah, Mrs. Severio told me that already…" Jason nodded his head. He should have left at that moment but something rooted him to the spot, "Sir…could I ask you about what happened between you and my father?"

Arieus placed the book on the coffee table before him gently, and sat up straight on the sofa, his blue eyes studying the boy.

"Of course, J.K. What is it that you would like to know?" he asked.

"Well it's just that... I visited him today with Puc and... he told me some things about what happened after Annetta's grandfather passed away. Did you...did you know what would happen to the Lab if you left it unattended?" Jason continued with no hesitation in his voice.

Arieus sat in silence for a moment, as though someone had taken a hot iron glove and slapped him across the face with it. There was a realization that dawned over him as well as much pain.

"Jason...do you remember what it is like learning to ride a bike? The first time you fall, you cry and you leave the bike not wanting to try again, ever." The man looked at the boy. "Try to picture that same emotion, but instead of falling from a bike you lose one of the most important people in your life. Also, I had no idea of the consequences of my leaving, nor did I care at the time, and after it was much too late to go back."

"But sir, after a while a person learns to get back on the bike. Why didn't you go back to take care of Q-16? Why didn't you go back to defend it like you always did with my dad? Why did you abandon Puc, Brakkus and your father's dream?" The questions flowed out of Jason like well-seasoned blows from a sword.

"Because I had children, Jason. I had to protect Annetta." Arieus was getting a little irritated. "I could survive my father's death, but the death of my daughter who had barely begun to live, I could not. There is one thing you need to know about parents Jason and that is we never wish to see our children six feet in the ground before it is our time to go."

"But my father had me at the time and never gave up after what happened," Jason continued. "He could have quit just as easily, given up to be with us but he chose his duty to the Lab."

"What your father did and what I did are our own decisions," Arieus stated coldly.

"If it was his decision, then why did you disable him when he tried to show the world what really lay beyond its borders? Why didn't you let him do his job and let people know what was out there so they could at least try to defend themselves against it if you weren't going to help?"

It was the final blow. Arieus rose from his seat, his eyes blazing with anger. Whatever was left of the warrior inside him had been forced to awaken.

"Because this world is not meant to know about it, Jason Kinsman," he snarled. "This world is meant to exist without magic and without the technology that lies within the Lab, until the time the Unknown sees fit for this world. Your father is lucky to be alive for what he did."

"And who are you to know when the time is right, or this Unknown guy? How does anyone know? People are dying everyday all because of simple things. I bet you anything there are things down there that could really help them. Is that why you wanted to keep it secret? You want to keep it all to yourself?" Jason glared at him in defiance. "I get it, you have the power to change the world but you refuse to. You were never really about defending the Earth, you were about ruling it! Controlling it like the Lord Severio you are."

"Jason I am warning you-," Arieus raised a hand as if trying to calm the boy but really he was trying to calm himself.

"What? If I disagree with you, are you going to lock me up, too? You had no trouble doing it to my father." Jason sneered.

"Now you are just putting words into my mouth that were never there, boy." Arieus snapped, "And if I wanted to rule so badly I would have never given up the Lab. Listen to what you are saying. I stopped Arcanthur from bringing about the apocalypse on this world. If people knew about everything it would make them a more attractive target to species from other worlds."

Arieus breathed out heavily. "Until you understand that sometimes decisions need to be made for the greater good, we have nothing to speak of. I chose my loyalty to my family, to protect them. Perhaps when you have children of your own you will understand. Yes, there are things in the Lab that could benefit this world greatly; I know that, we both knew that. Arcanthur and I spoke of it often. But the sordid truth is that the more people know about the world around them, the more danger they put themselves in because they do not fully understand everything about what they are tampering with. So when Arcanthur decided to do a public demonstration by dueling me in the middle of the streets to prove the existence of psychic abilities, the agents of the Unknown, the angels, gave us a choice. They were to kill your father for what he had done, or the alternative we decided on. Puc and I had no choice but to disable him and bind his powers for good. The rest was taken care of by the angels. Just know this. I never wanted your father to suffer such a fate, but it was the only way I could keep him alive. It was the only way I could save my best friend."

Jason could not take listening to Arieus. The last line tore deep inside him, a scenario he had not wanted to picture, the choice between life and death for a friend. Arieus was right to some degree, but what Jason felt in his heart pulled him in the other direction. More personal and painful thoughts tore at him. He thought of how he and his family struggled, how other kids made fun of him at school. If he could have shown them who he was, impress them as being the son of Arcanthur that could have changed. Turning on his heel, Jason headed for the door. He did not want to stand being in the same room as the man who had taken his father from him.

"You would have been kinder to kill him instead of making him live like that," he said through his teeth, and left without another word.

Chapter 23

As darkness crept over the Toronto skyline, with the CN tower leading its charge, so too did darkness began to creep into the memories of Arieus Severio. The man's conversation with Jason had brought back things he had long since buried deep within the chasm of his mind. He held a highball glass filled with a golden spirit and ice that he swirled in his hand from time to time, trying to distract himself from his thoughts. Sitting alone in the dim room, facing the windows beyond which lay the balcony however, Arieus recounted what had taken place so many years ago, and what, to that very day, he would never be able to forgive himself for.

୫୦ରଃ

A few years had passed since the burial of Lord Orbeyus Severio. Arieus had tried his best to forget the whole ordeal, to move on with life and not dwell on the past, but the past was never far behind. He worked in a warehouse, his trade being construction, making sure the best supplies went out to customers. He had just finished inspecting a pallet of bricks, when an all too familiar hand grasped his shoulder, and Arieus found himself staring into the green eyes of Arcanthur Kinsman.

"Airy, long time no see, buddy!" The man grinned with genuine happiness.

"Arcanthur?" Arieus raised an eyebrow, surprised to see his old friend after such a long time.

"Same old, same old," he beamed, putting an arm around his friend, "Where have you been, buddy? It's like you dropped off the face of the planet."

"Busy. Life caught up to me, I guess," Arieus responded quietly. "Having a family isn't an easy task."

"Oh yeah, I bet," Arcanthur chuckled. "Annetta, was it? How's the little bugger doing? Boy I bet she's gonna be a man killer like her-"

"She's doing good, she's growing quickly," he replied, stiffly.

"Yeah? That's good, that's good." Arcanthur nodded. "My boys are doing good, too. We just had another one with Talia. Liam's his name. You on break now?"

"Finished my shift, so I'm done for the day," Arieus told him.

"Excellent, okay, so you gotta come down with me to have a drink! We need to catch up!" Arcanthur wrapped his arm around Arieus's shoulder, as the two of them walked out of the warehouse.

శోళ

The Black Sheep and Knight Pub was among Arcanthur's favorite spots to go out with his friends. They had come here often when they were younger, starting when both of them as teenagers could hoist up a legal driver's license and grin with their still child-like faces. It was a small establishment located on the lower level of a plaza, with red brick stone walls, and squat dark wood tables filling its interior. On each of the tables, a red candle stood lit, wax dripping into the holder, causing them all to look well used.

Accepting a pint of dark frothing beer, both men thanked their waitress, and turned back to their heated conversation.

"And you remember that time we stole Kaian's horses from his carriage? I never thought it possible for an elf as pale as he to turn purple with rage," Arcanthur chuckled. "He was so pissed."

"Not as mad as my father was." Arieus smirked, taking a sip of his beer.

"Yeah, he was." Arcanthur sighed, taking his beer and polishing off the half glass. He placed it back on the table, watching the foam in it slide down the glass and dissolve upon reaching the dark substance. "And do you remember what we spoke of once, long ago?"

Arieus brought his glass down from his mouth, and placed it gently upon the table, his eyes wandering to meet his companions. Part of him had known this day would come.

"It was all fantasy, Arcanthur," he said, firmly.

"Fantasy, then, Arieus. Fantasy when our old men walked the Earth hand in hand, defending and teaching us what one day would be our right. I say, why not let it be the right of all humans on this world?" Arcanthur brought his finger down for emphasis, and eyeing a waitress from the corner of his eyes, turned to her. "Pardon me, miss. Might I have another pint?"

"Right away, sir," she smiled back at him, and hurried off to the bar.

"There is a reason those rules were put in place, Arcanthur," Arieus spoke fiercely. "We cannot just break them at will. I mean, not everyone here is ready for such a revelation. And I don't think some of the races, would take too kindly to dealing with a bunch of bratty humans. Let's face it. Humans think they are the kings of the universe, coming in and claiming land, taking things that aren't theirs, or trying to establish trade agreements to benefit themselves, or-"

"But think of all the good, Arieus." Arcanthur cut him short. "Think of all the knowledge they could gain, and all the people we could help. I mean, look at us. Look at us poor wretches who slave day in and day out, who die of disease, old age, and natural disasters that we could stop with a single hand, should we have the proper knowledge."

"There is a reason this world is the way it is, and it's not our place to change it," Arieus snarled having heard enough. "I swore that part of my life off long ago for the sake of my baby girl. I want nothing more to do with it. That life is a cursed one, and I wish it for no one."

The second pint was set down before Arcanthur, who thanked the waitress, and stared blankly at the man he had once called his best friend, a man who had practically been his brother for all those long years.

"What's happened to you?" he asked. "You're not the same Arieus I remember. Who is this infidel who sits in front of me, this man who had the marrow sucked from his bones by some dark conjured thing?"

"A ghost and shade who should not have come here," Arieus said. Dropping a ten-dollar bill on the table for the beer, he rose, and moved for the door without a single word.

His jaw open, Arcanthur watched as Arieus left the pub. Quickly downing his second beer, he threw a twenty onto the table, not bothering with the change as he left after his companion.

"Arieus!" he called, running past the crowds in the streets of downtown. "Arieus, please! Wait! What's gotten into you? This was our plan, this was what we had hoped for, and with our fathers gone we could usher in the age of clarity, the age of human enlightenment, just like the prophecy-"

"That prophecy was not meant for us, and you know it, Arcanthur. Tampering with fate is a grave thing," Arieus sneered, continuing on his path to the subway.

"Fate is what we make of it, Arieus, we need to grab the Minotaur by the horns and tell it to submit." Arcanthur reached forward and spun his friend around to face him. "Now answer me already. What happened to the man I was supposed to bring clarity into the world with?"

"He grew up!" Arieus snarled, slapping his hand away. "He grew up, started a family, and wanted nothing more to do with the world that took his father away, and threatened what he considered his entire existence. Now, if you're just going to bring up old war stories and interrogate me about a fool's dream, then I suggest you stop contacting me, for you will get nothing from me. I'm done playing this game."

Their eyes burning with the passion of their decisions and kept the two former companions locked in a staring competition for a few long minutes, before the overpowering sounds of life around them seized their contest. Turning around, Arieus headed for home, thinking no more of the events that had just occurred.

"You leave me no choice then old friend," he said, in a voice loud enough for Arieus to pick up from among the bustle of city life.

Sighing, and ready to retort, Arieus turned around, only to be faced with a much different scenario than he had anticipated. Arcanthur stood a few paces away from him, his palm turned up, with a ball of blue and purple flames hovering slightly above it. Arieus froze with fear, the people around him too beginning to notice the bizarre sight. Sounds and stares of wonder came from those around them, as the immediate area began to clear out.

"Have you lost your mind? Put that away!" shrieked Arieus, walking briskly towards Arcanthur, with his arm outstretched to extinguish the psychic fire in his hands.

"No, Arieus. In fact, I am the only one who stands for any sort of reason here, and therefore I stand alone." He hissed, and whirled the ball at his companion.

Quickly dodging it by landing on his stomach on the pavement, Arieus covered his head as the blast hit an unfortunate vehicle, causing it to burst into flames, while countless others around it set off a stream of alarms. Now the panic truly began, as everyone who had been close enough to the blast ran for dear life, a pack of unruly animals only wishing to live another day. Arcanthur stood in the midst of it all, basking in the chaos he had created.

"You idiot! What did you do that for?" Arieus shouted, rising to his feet, "You want them to call in the police? The army?"

"Let them come. They can do nothing to a god," Arcanthur snarled.

"A god? So now you think you're a god?" Arieus raised an eyebrow.

"We are both gods, you and I, Arieus." Arcanthur grinned viciously. "For we hold the keys to the kingdom, and ours alone on this Earth is the power to level this entire world. We hold life and death."

"No we do not, stop this mad talk," Arieus snapped at him. "Now, come with me. I can try to contact Puc. Maybe he knows how we can fix this."

"I am fixing it, Arieus. I have waited years to fix this." Arcanthur gritted his teeth as he spoke. "I have waited for a long time to be able to walk on my own two feet without anyone else telling me what to do. I already know what needs to be done. The people in this world have a right to know."

"That is not our choice, Arcanthur! You know that! You know full well there needs to be balance!" Arieus hissed at him. "Now come away with me, before it's too late."

Arcanthur glared at Arieus, his green eyes filled with venom as he watched him, the vicious grin spreading wider across his face, until it became a mask of madness.

"It is too late indeed, Arieus," he said, an eerie calm settling over him. "To choose which side of the wall you sit upon!"

Before Arieus could respond, another ball of psychic flame came hurling towards him. Without enough space to dodge, he teleported away before the ball of flame engulfed where he stood moments before. Appearing behind the now steadily floating Arcanthur, Arieus slammed an elbow into his back to get his attention.

"You idiot! You could have killed me!" he shouted.

"If you are not with me, Arieus, then you are against me. Simple as that," Arcanthur retorted. He filled his hand with more of the blue and purple fire, and attempted to shove the ball of flame into Arieus's face, who got out of its way just in time.

Spinning around, Arcanthur attempted to find his prey. Moments later, a fist hit his face, causing Arcanthur to lose complete balance, and fall to the ground. Arieus landed on the ground a few feet away from him, in the midst of their carnage.

"One more warning, Arcanthur. That's all you are getting," he said in a stern tone. "Stop this nonsense and come with me, so we can fix what damage is done."

His pride wounded, Arcanthur rose before Arieus. The fire from the ruins of the car had spread to the point that the blaze was visible even in the cluttered streets of downtown, and the smell was so strong it filled his lungs completely. A fire truck had arrived at the scene, followed by a squad of six police cars. The uniformed men and women behind the safety of their cars aimed their guns at Arcanthur, uttering the same arcane words they always did when one broke the law. The one called Kinsman rolled his eyes.

"Come with me, we can still fix this," Arieus whispered to his friend, extending a hand.

Arcanthur looked down at Arieus's weathered and worn hand reaching towards him like a beggar. Disgust filled him at the sight of it.

"No," he sneered, and began to walk away from the scene.

"Freeze or I will fire!" the voice of one of the policemen carried past the chaos of the scene.

Arcanthur stopped. Cocking his head to the side, he glanced at the man with the gun. "I dare you."

As soon as the words left his mouth, the police cars and the people beside them were swept up in a tornado that appeared to have manifested out of nowhere. Arieus, left with no choice, dove into the fray and began teleporting from one body to another, removing each one from the storm.

Once the deed was done, he turned to look for Arcanthur, only to be struck by psychic fire from the back. Howling in pain, Arieus fell to the ground. The flames burned him and it was only by rolling that he was able to extinguish them before they did serious damage. Looking up, he saw Arcanthur standing atop one of the nearby buildings, looking down at Arieus.

"You should have picked your side more wisely. That was just a warm up shot. The next time, I will show no mercy." Arcanthur pulled out a necklace from beneath his shirt. Moments later, it manifested into a mace. He then teleported from sight.

Arieus rose, feeling his entire upper back still on fire, as though he had lifted the world onto his shoulders. He knew as soon as he saw the mace that he was at a disadvantage, Severbane was sealed years before in Severio Castle, never to be lifted again in battle. He never thought he would have longed to see the blade just once more.

Alert, he teleported into the air just a little above one of the buildings and landed on the asphalt roof. Scanning the area, he saw no sight of

Arcanthur, until he heard the all too familiar whizzing of fire, and dodged a massive blast that had been intended for his head. The collision of psychic energy into the electrically wired building created an even greater blast, knocking an already weakened Arieus out of the air, and almost over the edge of the building. Catching hold of the side of the building, Arieus gripped with his hands as he tried to find a place he could teleport to, his fingers becoming numb from the effort of having to hold on, blasts of fire assaulting the building from all sides from an unseen location.

His luck changed as a powerful grip took hold of his, and hoisted him upwards. Arieus found himself face to face with an all too familiar elf dressed in his usual dark blue robes and armed with his staff.

"Thanestorm?" he asked in disbelief.

"Just this once I will aid you," he said, and thrust a sword into his hands. "It's not Severbane, but it will have to do. Go after him while I try to figure out what I can do about this uproar."

"I am ever in your debt, Puc." Arieus looked down at the weapon in his hands and drawing the blade he readied his battle stance.

"Never you mind. Get out of here!" Puc snapped as a blast of psychic fire came their way, only to collide with a shield the mage had managed to put up.

Tracking the source of the blast, Arieus teleported into the air in pursuit of Arcanthur. Encasing his sword in psychic flames, he slammed the weapon into Arcanthur's mace, sparks flying in all directions. Airborne through levitation, both psychic warriors collided with one another in a series of teleported moves which made them appear to be moving faster than they were, the sound of their weapons ringing against one another the only confirmation of their actual speed.

Breaking the cycle, Arcanthur readied another ball of fire and blasted it at Arieus with full force. Teleporting out of the way of the blast, Arieus slammed the hilt of the blade into Arcanthur's jaw, causing blood to sputter out of his mouth like water. Gritting his bloodied teeth, Arcanthur let out a mighty cry. Summoning all his menace, he created another blast of energy, more devastating than the last. Arieus barely had time to teleport, before the flames collided into a building behind them, leveling it to the ground within moments.

Beginning to tire from the amount of energy used, Arieus looked for a place he could rest just enough to recover his breath, and found himself looking at the tip of an all too familiar tower in the Toronto skyline. Teleporting himself close enough to land just above the observation deck, Arieus hid himself and waited, breathing heavily, his back still aching from the earlier blast. He let out a momentary sigh of relief, only to hear the sound of feet landing on metal.

"You don't think I wouldn't find you up here did you Arieus?" Arcanthur's voice hissed in a slurred manner from the blood on his face. "It's the one place we came to on this world to be truly free."

Arieus did not let out a single sound, keeping himself hidden from Arcanthur, clutching the sword for dear life. He hoped Arcanthur was only guessing he was there. He needed a little more time, if only to think about what to do with the situation.

"Oh, come on, Arieus! Come out! I know you are here. Or do you want me to take the whole thing down with me?" Arcanthur threatened, throwing his hands into the air. "Don't think I won't do it, people or no people."

Arieus bit his lip so hard he tasted blood. Arcanthur was involving innocent people with the whole mess. The stakes had been raised to the point of no return. The acknowledgement of these new facts fueled his strength, and Arieus came into view before his former friend.

"You had fair warning," Arieus declared, blade drawn, a ball of psychic flame manifesting itself slowly in his free hand.

"As did you." Arcanthur widened his stance, gripping the mace tighter, preparing to create more psychic fire. Before he could finish, Arieus teleported from his line of sight.

Arieus wasted no time in reappearing behind Arcanthur, and swung his sword sideways at his opponent. Spinning around, Arcanthur parried the blow with ease, and teleported again to get out of the direct line of fire. Floating high above Arieus, he created flames the size of a soccer ball, and hurled them downwards towards him. Worry for the safety of those below him in the tower took hold of Arieus, and he launched himself into the air, igniting his sword into psychic flames as he sent the blast flying into space.

"Is that all you got?" Arcanthur shook his head and teleported mid-flight.

Gritting his teeth at the mistake of losing his opponent, Arieus began teleporting in a series of small moves around the upper tip of the tower, as he tried to locate him. His prayers were answered when the cold metal of Kinsman's weapon tore through his shoulder. Prying himself away reflexively from the jagged blade, Arieus did his best not to slow. Teleporting to the side, he tried to land a blow on his foe, only to be met by the ringing of steel clashing on steel. The blows continued this way for what felt like ages, teleporting, parrying, occasionally landing a small cut on each other.

Arieus was becoming aware of something as time flew by. With all the injuries and energy he was using up, he knew he did not have long left before he collapsed from exhaustion. He could see the same happening to Arcanthur, even if he was trying to mask it by his rage. Neither of them would last much longer. Someone had to win, and they had to do so soon if they wanted to walk away alive.

Floating back down to the tower, Arieus landed on his feet, only to fall to his knees, breathing heavily. Arcanthur landed a few feet away in the same state, but through stubbornness was able to stay upright completely, propped up on his weapon.

"Give it up, Arieus. You've lost this one," Arcanthur called out. "Go home to your wife and children, and leave me to build this world as it was meant to be."

Arieus heard the words go in one ear and out the other. He was so tired and pained that nothing really mattered to him anymore except winning. Trying to steady himself with the blade he still carried in his good hand, he noticed something on the concrete floor, a reflection. Looking up from the corner of his eye, Arieus noted the sun coming through the dense clouds above them, and an idea was born. His gaze shifted to Arcanthur, who was still speaking absentmindedly about all the things he would change, all the things he would make better through having people know about a the Lab. Hearing him finish, the blue eyed warrior looking up through a bloodied brow.

"You're right, Arcanthur. I should go home to my wife and children," he exhaled in defeat. "But not until I'm finished here with you!"

Twisting the blade so it reflected the sun at the right angle, the glare hit Arcanthur straight in the eyes, causing him to go blind, giving Arieus enough time to teleport away.

Once his vision cleared, Arcanthur looked around, frantically trying to find his opponent, readying a blast in hand to finish him. Just then, the feeling of burning and freezing all at once tore through his left heel. Arcanthur howled as Arieus cut clear through the tendons of his heel with the blade, causing the man to lose control of the psychic fire in his hand, and collapse onto the tower's roof. Having used the last of his strength in the effort, Arieus tumbled beside his lifelong companion, utterly exhausted from the effort of their fight. Neither of them had anything more to give of themselves. The distant sound of a helicopter could be heard closing in.

Finally having caught up to them, Puc came to the roof of the tower, using a spell similar to teleporting. He walked over to the two fallen warriors.

"You couldn't have kept it on the ground?" he snarled, kneeling down beside both of them. "Do you have any idea the amount of damage your little light show just caused? The whole city is in an uproar, and there is media everywhere."

Arcanthur let out a gurgling laugh as he coughed up some blood that had flown into his mouth from his nose. "It's too late now, Thanestorm. I won."

Puc gritted his teeth. Orbeyus had warned him of the consequences of something like this. The Lord of the Axe had been well aware of the never-ending lust for power in the hearts of humanity. When something came along with power, they would all try to lay claim on it. If that failed, they'd destroy it.

"I'm getting you both out of here," Puc said in a hushed tone as he watched helicopters becoming more and more visible on the skyline. "We are traveling to Aldamoor, where I will have Kaian and the elders try to find a way to fix this mess."

"You listen here mage, servant of my father's master. I am not going anywhere with the likes of you," Arcanthur spat. "Not until the heavens-"

As if in answer, the skies went completely dark in an instant, and lightning created white scars in the clouds. Moments later, a bolt struck one of the nearby pipes, bathing the area in white light. Shielding their eyes from it, the trio opened them to see a pair of large birds, one resembling a red swan with exotic tail feathers, the other a yellow vulture with spiky feathers and a long club-shaped tail.

Recognizing who they were immediately, Puc lowered his gaze, bowing before them as low as he could. Arieus and Arcanthur, on the other hand, simply lay exhausted in the same positions as before.

"Defilers of divine powers, they who have broken sacred oath and seal, we come to take that which is needed when life takes life," the phoenix spoke to them.

"What are you two turkeys going on about?" Arcanthur managed to utter before Puc crawled before him, blocking him from their visage.

"Pay no heed to the fallen ones, most sacred angels, Fulgura and Bwiskai," Puc interrupted him. "I, Puc Thanestorm of Aldamoor, ask what is it that brings-"

"You know full well what brings us here, mage," the yellow bird Puc had called Bwiskai answered. "This world is not yet ready for the revelation, yet someone decided to do so, and in a most destructive manner. We have come to correct that error, traced back to those named Arieus Severio and Arcanthur Kinsman."

"There is no error here but truth! Pure truth!" Arcanthur bellowed from behind Puc.

Puc kept his head low. The man was not helping the situation. He had to think fast. Angels were not known for their patience. They brought messages and left.

"Might I speak with you, servants of the Unknown, alone?" he requested.

The two birds looked at one another for a moment, as if exchanging telepathic thought, then turned back to the mage, who still had his face lowered to the floor.

"Permission granted, he who is the storm of warriors," Fulgura answered.

Puc nodded in response. Shooting Arieus and Arcanthur a glare that told them not to move, he walked away with the two birds, still keeping his head low.

Arieus felt himself slipping further and further out of consciousness. An age seemed to pass before he was shaken by a firm grip.

Opening his eyes, everything seemed to have gone back to normal, save for Arcanthur laying at his side unconscious, and Puc looking into the city skyline. He noted both his and Arcanthur's wounds had been tended to in their sleep. Sore, but feeling some semblance of energy returned to him, he attempted to prop himself up on his elbows.

"What happened?" he asked.

"Your life was spared, and the events of today's battle erased from the minds of this world, but at a dear cost," the elf spoke, turning to face him. "I managed to negotiate your freedom. But Arcanthur's, however, I could not."

∞⌘

Arieus watched the ice melt in his glass. He remembered Puc telling him of how his best friend was to be stripped of his powers, and how the angels had confiscated both of their card keys. He remembered having to watch Arcanthur have his foot amputated from the severity of the wound, giving himself the nickname Lackfoot, and finally, the dark day where he checked his friend into the asylum with Talia, who was no longer able to stand his mad ranting and drinking. The sky was already black in the windows when Arieus rose from his contemplative state, and dumped the contents of the glass into the sink.

Chapter 24

Aurora came back hours later to find her husband on the balcony looking down into the city below. He often did that when he was deep in thought about something. After she and Xander put away the groceries, she walked outside to join him while her son retreated to his room.

The wind gently wafted his graying hair, making him appear more like a king overlooking his kingdom than her husband. He had always had that air of authority about him, though, no matter what he was doing. It was the reason she had been reluctant to marry him when he first asked, worried she was not worthy to be with such a man. When she looked closer though, she knew despite his secretive noble birth, they were destined to live out their lives together. She placed an arm gently on his shoulder in order to get his attention from his thoughts.

"What's wrong, Arieus?" she asked.

"J.K. met with his father today," he answered.

"His mother allowed him?"

"No. Talia had nothing to do with it. Puc went with him so they could find out where the mace was kept. Arcanthur told him about what transpired between us. Aurora... was it so wrong to wish for a life without it all? Was it wrong to just leave it all in the dust and not look back? Was I wrong to let Arcanthur live?"

"Arieus, you did what you thought was right at the time. You wanted our children to grow up safe, without us having to look over our shoulder every moment of our lives because something could happen and as for Arcanthur, his life was not yours to take."

"But the Lab was crumbling, Aurora. There was no one left to manage it but an elven mage and a Hurtz warrior. I should have known better, but I just...couldn't stay down there a moment longer." He cringed, thinking of the events that had forced him to leave.

"Arieus, the important thing is that now there is someone to take up the responsibility again, as much as we despise it and do not wish it upon Annetta," Aurora sighed. "To some extent it feels like this is right. She always did love fantasy, as much as I tried to push her away from it."

"I know, but..." He paused, unable to express what he felt.

"But we are parents, and it is our job to worry." She smiled at him.

Arieus looked over at his wife. Even in the darkest of hours, her smile always made everything in the world seem right.

"I suppose that is the way it is," he exhaled, watching the lights in the sky.

ଧୈଓଡ଼

The next morning at school, Jason waited for his friends to arrive by the fence. His head was swimming in a world that was not entirely of his own making. The events of the night before with Arieus were still fresh, and he was not sure he would be able to look Annetta in the face if her father had told her what had gone on between them. He knew none of it was Annetta's fault, and so he held nothing against her, but he was still partially angered with Arieus.

"It's a terrific day to be outside," a voice greeted him from behind. Jason turned around to see Sarina with her bag strapped to her back, smiling at him.

"Yeah, it's really nice." He returned the smile and continued to wait, slouched against the metal fence.

"Everything okay?" she asked.

"Hmm? Yeah, I'm just kind of out of it today. Some stuff happened at home last night and I don't really want to talk about it," he said.

"Oh, I see. Well, if you change your mind and you need to talk about it, let me know. I'm always ready to listen. Sometimes it helps to unload what's on your mind to another person," she smiled again.

Jason only nodded his head, not wanting to talk anymore. He saw his friends from behind the fence approaching the gate. He walked over to them, leaving Sarina.

"Hey J.K.!" Annetta greeted him, Darius in tow. "How come you didn't show up last night? It was so weird having my dad use telepathy to tell me. I almost hit the ceiling when I heard his voice in my head."

"Yeah, uh, some stuff came up and I had to stay home," he said, "I'll probably be over tonight, though, as long as it will be okay with your parents."

"Sure, why wouldn't it be?"

"Uh, no reason," he said, and turned back to see Sarina on her own. "I'm gonna go talk with Sarina for a bit. She doesn't seem to have many friends, and I kind of like talking to her."

"Oh, okay then," Annetta watched as he walked.

246

There was a small tinge of anger inside of her, anger that he had decided not to stay with them so they could speak about the Lab and everything that had gone on last night. She wanted to share her story about the unicorns and the Forest Giant.

"He's just found himself a new toy," Darius muttered. "He'll come back to his friends soon enough."

Annetta didn't have time to dwell on anything as the school bell rang and they all marched to their classes.

ഇ൚ര

The day ran by quicker than any of them had predicted, and again they found themselves on the way back home. Jason had split his break time between spending time with Darius and Annetta and getting to know Sarina, who constantly seemed to have her nose in a book whenever she was not speaking with someone.

After the bell for the end of the day rang, Jason waited outside by the door for Sarina with his bag hanging from one shoulder. Annetta and Darius came outside after him.

"All set to go?" she asked, approaching him.

"I think I'm going to go walk Sarina part of the way home. I'll catch up with you guys later," Jason said looking at his friends.

"Oh." Annetta raised an eyebrow, and then smiled. "Does J.K. have a girlfriend?"

"No! And I could ask the same about you and Link or you and Darius!" he retorted.

Darius couldn't help but stifle a laugh. "I think any guy who speaks with Annetta can automatically be assumed to be her boyfriend, but that's beside the point. If you want, we can all go with you. Or do you just wanna be alone with her?"

Jason looked at his friends. He did not want to hurt their feelings, but when there was more than one person to speak with at a time, conversations became very displaced.

"If you don't mind, I'd rather just walk with her alone. Besides, Puc might be mad if you guys take too long with getting to the Lab. I don't want us all in trouble, I can take my own heat."

"Sure thing, if that's what you want." Darius nodded his head.

Annetta looked over at her watch and cringed. "We should get going. I still have to grab Xander, and who knows what'll happen if he's late for pizza night at home."

She then looked over at Jason one last time, half hoping he would change his mind and just go with them. But it was clear by his unmoving body language that he was set in his ways. She fixed the collar of her jean jacket as a way to postpone her gaze on him.

"See ya later, J.K.," she said, before turning heel and walking off with Darius.

Jason exhaled. Turning back to the door, he saw Sarina come out with a thick hardcover book under her arm and her bag neatly on her back.

"Where are your friends?" she asked, noticing he was the only one of his group left.

"I told them I would catch up with them later. They all headed over to Annetta's right now. We're gonna play some videogames and hang out," Jason explained to her as they began to walk.

"Oh, I see. Do you do this often?"

"Yeah, all the time. We practically live at Annetta's apartment. Her parents are really cool with having us over and it's nice to get away from-," Jason paused as he tried to find the right words. "From stuff at home."

Sarina observed Jason as he spoke about spending time with his friends. He could speak of them without fear of being forbidden to see them, without being told they were a negative influence. Though Mislantus spoiled her rotten, she was always alone, and the one thing she had always wanted but could never get was the comfort of having a peer.

"Things at my home aren't good either," she said quietly.

"Your brother strict with you?" Jason asked her.

"Huh? Well a little yes but-,"

"I can tell, the way you always carry that book around. Does he not let you have any friends or something? I don't ever see you talking to anyone except when I talk to you," he continued as they exited the schoolyard.

"I never spent time with people my age. I was home schooled and after my parents died, remember? My brother, Matt, he just became very protective of me. He always wanted to control who I was spending time with in order to grow up right. He always says stuff like, I can't lose you as well, or you're the only reason I'm alive and I keep going." Sarina twisted the story of her true existence, weaving a tale of fact and fiction. She found it somewhat liberating to be able to talk about it, even if indirectly.

"I can relate to that," Jason said, trying to find something to lighten the mood. "My mom is the same way with my brother and I. We're lucky. At least there are two of us to divide the attention." He smiled lightly. "Well, if you want, maybe one of these days we can all hang out together."

"That would be fun." Sarina looked over at him.

"Yeah, Annetta is pretty cool to be around. I don't talk much to Darius, but he's an alright guy too once you get to know him a bit." Jason kept walking. "Uhm. All this time and I forgot to ask, am I going the right way?"

"Yes, you are." Sarina smiled and nodded.

Jason grinned back, but with an uneasy feeling in the pit of his gut. It was similar to what he'd felt last night, with the stranger in the parking lot. He stopped laughing and looked around, trying to see if he was back, but he saw no one in sight.

"Is something wrong?" Sarina asked.

Jason looked over at her, worry creasing his face, "You don't feel it?"

The girl glanced back at him obliviously, "Feel what?"

"That...I don't know. In my stomach I feel-," Jason was cut off as he saw something move from the corner of his eye.

It seemed like nothing more than a blurred shape, like a squirrel had passed by. Jason's pace was about to quicken when the force of an invisible blow threw both him and Sarina back. Everything around them turned grey, as though the world were drained of all colour. Sarina screamed. Jason could have panicked, but he was used to strange thing happening thanks to the Lab. His heart pounded in his chest as he summoned up courage.

"Whatever you are, show yourself!" he shouted, pulling on his bag in case he had to run for it.

A shape began to form in front of them, as though Jason's words had coaxed it out. It was barely visible, but from the filmy image Jason was able to make out what looked to be the silhouette of a large animal. If he had not known better he would have said it was a ghost. The shape was not clear, and appeared to be made of smoke that swirled within the four-legged form. As Jason tried to analyze the situation, the form focused into a feline shape. A thick mane hung around the creature's neck, but its muzzle was narrower, more vicious looking than that of the lions Jason was used to seeing on television. A long, slender tail swished back and forth behind the creature, as its muscles coiled and moved in a slow prowl towards the youth before coming to a pause. It was almost as tall as the spruce trees that grew beside the houses that surrounded them. He'd been prepared for just about everything, but not that.

The beast glared at Jason and let out a mighty roar, getting ready to charge at both him and Sarina. Jason's heart was in his throat as he tried to think of something, anything that he had learned that he could use to stop it. He got the feeling that throwing it across the field would only annoy it. To top it off, he had someone else there with him. Could he risk exposure? How would Puc react?

Sarina clutched at Jason's arm, her fear causing a mutual paralysis in both of them. There was nowhere to run. Jason looked over at the frightened girl beside him. No, he would have to disobey the mage. His life depended on it. Jason breathed deeply, trying to compose himself as quickly as possible, and lashed out, throwing his foe far enough to give him time to think of a strategy.

The creature dug its invisible claws into the earth, struggling to ground itself, resisting the push of Jason's telekinetic ability before giving out a shrieking roar.

"Sarina, you need to get out of here!" Jason yelled, trying to get her to snap out of her paralysis.

The girl simply looked at him, shivering, unable to say anything. Seeing as she wouldn't move, Jason went back to his main problem, the invisible lion-like beast glaring at him. He looked around quickly, and noticed some boulders that were used as a landscape piece beside the entrance to an apartment building. He had no clue if the rocks would even hit the creature, but it was better than becoming its lunch. Extending his hand, he focused on one of the boulders and flung it at the creature.

The rock smashed into the lion's side and shattered into two parts. The beast roared in anger and began to move for Jason again. The boy grabbed Sarina and teleported behind where the beast had originally stood, causing the thing to stop its charge and turn around to face them yet again. Though the thing was partially invisible, like a statue made of glass, Jason could see the features of its face contorted in fury, every muscle in its body rippling with rage, and ready to kill. It made his heart leap from his chest, before he got an idea. Grabbing Sarina, he teleported again, this time to the top of the apartment building. Moments later, he returned alone, and stood face to face with the beast in the middle of an empty street.

"Here kitty, kitty." He swallowed hard, curling his hand into a fist, doing his best to hold his ground.

The ghost lion snarled and charged, without taking a moment to think its actions over. Jason reached out his hand yet again. Despite what Puc had said about avoiding using one's hands, so as not to give away what the next move would be, he found it comforting. As the beast, perfectly framed in between the two halves of the crushed boulder came at him, Jason waited for the creature to be in the right position, then slammed the two halves of the rock into it, crushing its head.

The beast struggled to move. Jason found it harder than expected to hold the creature and press the two halves of the boulder against its skull. The more the beast struggled to move forward, the more fear rose in Jason, causing him to lose concentration. But the fear of death was stronger than any doubt, and in the end he chose what was most important. With all the emotion in his body, Jason pressed the rocks against the creature's skull until he heard a cracking noise, and the stones collided with one another.

Jason trembled as the body of the creature solidified, becoming a collapsed heap of golden brown fur, the majority of its corpse covered with boulder fragments, and a pool of blood spreading in the streets. Jason couldn't help but fall to his knees, vomiting on the grass beside him. Whatever the thing was, he had killed it, butchered it with a pair of rocks. The boy felt woozy, but remembered he had left Sarina on the building. Gathering himself, he spit out the remainder of the bile from his mouth, and teleported to get her.

Sarina waited for him in the same position he had left her. Her face was completely pale, matching the skies around them. He put his hand on her shoulder. She turned to face him, fear burning in her eyes.

"I...," Jason paused, unable to find the words to say to her. "It's over..."

Sarina nodded quietly as they teleported down to the ground below. They both stood in silence looking down at the carcass of their attacker. The world began to fade back into color and the body of the lion-like creature disappeared without a trace. The boulder too was back in its place, beside the building, as though nothing had ever been touched. Jason looked around in confusion. Had it all been a dream?

"Who are you?" the all too real frightened voice of Sarina asked, affirming that the events had been true.

Jason simply looked at the girl, said nothing back, and took off in a run. He headed for Annetta's building, knowing the further he got from Sarina the safer she would be from whatever it was that had been pursuing him.

Chapter 25

Annetta, Darius and her brother had just gotten home when the phone rang. Seeing as her mother was not home, Annetta went to answer it.

"Severio residence," she answered.

"Anne, it's me, it's Jason. You gotta open the door quick!" He seemed out of breath.

"Uh oh. Did Sarina turn out to be an old hag or something?" Annetta chuckled.

"Shut up! It's not funny. I'll explain when I get there," he snarled, still breathless.

Annetta knew that tone. She pressed the button on the phone that activated the entrance to the building.

"What's up with him?" Darius had heard the conversation.

"I don't know, we'll find out in a few minutes." Annetta wore a serious face as she took off her shoes and bag before heading into the kitchen to pop in Xander's promised pizza. Her younger brother had long since turned on his video games. She knew if she did not put the pizza in, he'd probably starve. That was how important his games were to him.

A few minutes later, there came a knocking at the door. Darius looked through the keyhole and opened it to a panting Jason.

"Took...stairs... too long for elevator," he spoke in heavy breaths.

"I've heard of men running from women who tried to seduce them, but this is the first time I've actually seen it." Darius received a nasty look from Jason.

Annetta came out of the kitchen and sat down in the armchair her father always favored.

"Hey man, what's up?" she asked.

"Freaking...alternate universe, lion ghost monster thing is what is up!" Jason exploded, "I don't know, one minute I was walking with Sarina. Then the next, everything around us goes like... grey, like we got sucked into some kind of black and white movie and this thing that was like a ghost which looked like a lion attacked us and-,"

"Ghost that looked like a lion attacked you in a grey world?" Darius summarized, "Uh...ghosts can't hurt people.

"It wasn't a ghost, I just said it looked like one!" Jason shouted, frustrated with the lack of understanding

"Well, obviously." Darius muttered quietly.

"It, well," Jason continued, "when it died it turned solid with a golden coat."

Darius listened to his ranting. His smile quickly disappeared after he heard the final description.

"A Leonemas." He spoke the words quietly.

"A what?" Annetta looked at him along with Jason.

"Your world only has one account of such a creature, and through translation its name was turned into what you call the Nemean Lion," Darius explained. "But they live on a completely different dimension. They can be summoned through magic, or can come through a tear in their world that creates a portal leading to this one. My guess is it was summoned. Tears in different worlds don't just happen. This could be really bad."

"Do you think it's that Mislantus guy?" Annetta looked worried.

"There's a good chance it is. If so, we need to tell Puc as soon as possible."

ഇൽരു

Puc and Brakkus were waiting for them at the gate along with Link, all with disgruntled expressions due to having been there longer than expected. Their expressions lightened slightly when the first of the children appeared.

"Took ya long enough," Brakkus said as a greeting.

"We've got trouble," Darius reported. "A Leonemas attacked J.K. on his way back from school."

"What?" Puc glared at Jason. "You were attacked and you did not contact anyone?"

"It happened fast," Jason growled. "How was I supposed to know what to do? It's not like what you teach us is meant for high stress situations exactly."

"No training is ever meant to help in that sort of scenario. One only learns from being thrust into the midst of battle," Puc responded. "Did anyone see you use your powers?"

Jason froze. "No, no one was there. It was like I got sucked into another world completely. Everything went grey."

Puc nodded, absorbing Jason's tale, and looked to Brakkus. Furrowing his eyebrows, the elf took a moment to organize all the pieces of information in his mind.

"I fear Mislantus is hot on our trail. Leonemas don't just appear on Earth because they feel like a change of scenery. Preexisting portals are heavily documented and guarded against this, especially in worlds that do not know of their existence. Someone had to summon it here, and whoever it was, clearly had Jason in mind as a target. This only means we need to have you more closely shielded, and it is crucial you stick together. As a group you are strong, alone you may panic and not stand a chance."

Brakkus read between the lines of what Puc was saying, perking his long ears up, causing the earrings to jingle.

"Well I hope ya don't propose I go to that surface to guard em. I don't exactly have the appropriate skin tone." Brakkus flicked one of his ears. "And I don't think ya'd last long without stabbing someone through the heart from being too single minded for ya to handle."

Puc looked at his companion. It was true that the mage did not want to have to walk among humans more than he had to and the only way he could make Brakkus fit in was to cast a spell on him. Puc sighed running out of options, for he knew how the warrior felt about having magic cast on him. He then turned his eyes to the boy who stood with them in silence, his sword strapped to his back, ready for action. The elf shifted his weight from one foot to the other as he leaned on his staff, deep in thought. He still did not entirely trust Link, but it seemed like their only option.

"Lincerious," he said to the boy, "we may have a use for you yet. Once I sort out all of the papers you will be attending school with the others. The larger the group, the less likely someone is to attack."

"You want me to go to school?" Link raised an eyebrow, "You want me to do homework? That kind of stuff?"

"Whatever is necessary to blend in. You said you were sent to protect Annetta at all costs. Consider this part of the job."

Link could not argue with Puc's reasoning, and simply nodded, cramming his fists in his pockets with vague disappointment.

Puc then turned his attention to Jason. "I trust you have brought what we have been waiting for." He looked at him sternly, awaiting only the correct answer.

Jason looked dumbfounded for a moment, and then remembered. He pulled out the mace necklace and handed it to Puc, who looked at the small object between his fingers, gently turning it.

"Hrm. I almost forgot about the dormant state spell I cast so its owner would not have to part from it no matter where he went. I should have known Arcanthur would have left it as such. I will need to find the spell among my notes again. It should take a few days, and no more," he said, after examining it.

"Wait, a mage who doesn't remember a spell?" Jason snorted.

"A mage who has too much on his mind to remember mundane spells," Puc retorted, a sharp edge to his voice. "A mage does not carry a spellbook with them like a flimsy sorcerer who uses up his life force in the process, and neither can we conjure spells out of thin air using a channeling object like a wizard. We draw from our memory, and there is only so much information the memory can store at once. I had no need to remember the spell, therefore I do not remember it."

Jason bit his tongue upon hearing the answer. "Sorry, I didn't know. You said you can find it again, right?"

"If you do not mind leaving it with me, of course."

"No, why would I?" Jason raised an eyebrow.

Puc glared back at him in confusion. "It is the weapon of your father, your heirloom from him."

Jason's eyes wandered to the small piece of wood tied to the black cord that Puc held in his hand.

"As far as I'm concerned, it's nothing more than a piece of wood on a string right now," he responded.

"Wise words." Puc nodded from beneath his pensive face. "For now, you may go about as you please, within a group for safety. I need to work on finding the spell."

"We're not going to train?" Annetta asked.

Puc, who had already turned away in order to work turned back around, causing his cloak to whirl behind him like a faithful dog following its master.

"Annetta, there is nothing more I can teach you at this point," he said to her. "You have both proven able to use your abilities to defend yourself. What you must solidify is your nerve in battle, and for that I cannot do anything to help. You must find the strength in your own heart." He turned once more to leave.

"So why were you pushing us so hard if you're just going to give up?" She watched him, her eyes burning holes in his back with determination.

"For you to have the skills, so you can then hone them in your own style Annetta," Puc said, growing impatient. "Learning to use psychic abilities is like selecting a weapon to favor. Everyone is different, but they first need to be exposed to the necessary skills in order to pick a favorite. This is why we are switching to weapons training instead. If you are so eager to learn, go with Brakkus to train. Now, if you need me I will be at Severio Castle looking through my old notes stored in the library. Darius, I will need you with me."

Darius nodded, and followed his mentor who had already begun to stroll off towards the stables.

"I think ya need a break, least for today." Brakkus slipped his thumbs under his belt.

Annetta shook her head. "I think I'm going to go to Severio Castle too, then," she announced once she had made up her mind. "Anyone who wants to come along is welcome."

"I'm in. Link?" Jason looked over at the other boy.

"I think I may stay with Brakkus, if that's alright. I have a project I'm working on." Link looked over at the Hurtz.

"All settled, then," Brakkus said. "Off ya go to catch up with them mages, while us warriors go off and do warrior things."

Annetta and Jason inclined their heads in a goodbye, taking off to follow Puc and Darius.

"What about the whole safety in numbers thing?" Link stated once they were gone from earshot. "Now there are only two of us,"

"Ya forget, mah boy, that I count as at least three." Brakkus smacked his breastplate.

෨෬

Upon reaching their destination, the four of them let the horses off to roam in the fields. Splitting up on the main floor to go their separate ways, Puc and Darius had long since buried themselves in the spell books of the castle library while Annetta and Jason wandered off to explore towers of the castle. The youth had been warned not to try to open any doors without the mage and so most of their exploring was in the form of trying to find rooms without doors that were the regular sleeping quarters or other rooms that contained no portals. It was a system developed long ago that kept those at the castle from being confused, especially when a new door would appear. Having found a corridor that led up, Annetta and Jason climbed a wide set of stone stairs to the roof of one of the towers. Coming outside, they were greeted by the lazily setting orange sun on a gold sky. Finding a spot which directly faced the sun, they walked closer to the stone railing, coming to a rest to get a better look at everything below them.

"It's so pretty. I wish we spent more time here," Annetta said, closing her eyes, allowing the wind to comb through her hair.

Jason let out a small grunt in agreement and rested his arms on the railing looking down below. He felt a degree of safety being in the massive fortress, like nothing could go wrong. Something from beyond his time there however still weighed on his mind, intruding on his peace.

"It's all really crazy," she continued. "Least the last two days. I mean you got attacked today, then the whole thing when Link and I were in the biosphere. I can see what Puc meant about us not being able to learn to fight only from training. It's way different than just being thrown into the midst of something-,"

"Annetta." Jason interrupted, "If it came down to listening to what Puc says, or what I would say, who would you go with?" The weight of the conversation with his father sank in on him fully as he stood looking at his friend.

Annetta opened her eyes and looked over at him. "Uh, what does that have to do with anything? Did something happen, J.K.?"

"My dad said something when we went to go see him about your father betraying him and sending him there, and Puc was involved in it all. I mean, I know why it all happened, and I don't blame your dad or anything, but I have to ask anyways. If it came down to listening to me or Puc, who would it be?" He looked her in the eyes as he spoke.

Annetta felt the matter come upon her like the wind around them. In fact, she was not sure if it was the wind or the conversation she was feeling. She sighed, running her hand on the rough, sun-warmed stone.

"J.K...I wouldn't betray you like that," she answered, "But sometimes stuff can be complicated, and-"

"So you're saying under the right circumstances you would?" he said, cutting her off. "You would choose listening to him over listening to me?"

He scoffed, shaking his head and looked out at the land around them in silence.

"That's not what I wanted to say." She spoke softly after giving him a moment to cool off. "I was going to say I would not betray you, because

258

we're friends and we stick together, so why are we having this conversation?"

Jason looked back in her direction, the wind playing with her long hair, causing it to fly like a flag behind her.

"Stuff can be complicated," she continued, "but I think since we've been friends for so long, we'd find a way out of any situation. We would talk before acting. Besides, just because stuff happened between our parents doesn't mean it has to be the same with us, right?"

"Yeah, you're right." A faint smile came across Jason's face as he listened to her. Throughout his entire life his mother had told him that his father had been the villain, someone who had abandoned him. To some extent this still remained true. What else was true was that he was standing at the top of the highest tower of a castle in an unknown land with his best friend. She had been there before anything in his life had changed, and she remained the same throughout all the struggles they had faced until now. He exhaled in relaxation, knowing the same familiar face would be there with him the next day.

෨෬

Puc had told them both before they left the Lab the day before to take it easy and relax a bit, and that was exactly what Jason set out to do once school was finished. Annetta had decided to go back to the base and explore, while he had chosen to go to one of the few places he could still think: the forest behind his house.

It was nothing like a real forest, of course. It was just part of a park located behind his home, but there were enough trees growing in all directions without guidance that before Jason had gone into the Lab, it was the closest he had to a real one. He had spent many days playing there with Annetta and children from the neighborhood when he was younger. They built snow forts in the winter, and in the summer would camp in shelters of fallen logs when it was warm enough at night.

Today, however, he did not play with anyone. He walked alone until he came to a clearing with a few moss-covered boulders. Brushing off the fallen twigs and leaves from one of them, he flopped down on top it. He ran his fingers through the coarse moss covering the stone and exhaling deeply. It had been a while since he had last come here, due to always being in the Lab. It seemed like time sped up when all leisure time was gone. He missed the days when approaching summer meant time to spend with friends. Now it just meant more time to be stuck training with Puc. It was not that he disliked learning to use his powers. He even had a better understanding of why it was crucial. But what was the point if it all had to be secret. He closed his eyes and listened to the silence around him.

"J.K.?" His sanctuary was interrupted moments later. Jason opened his eyes and looked to the side to see Sarina standing beside one of the fallen logs. Her large brown eyes looking up at him with curiosity as to what he was doing.

"Sarina?" He looked at her questioningly, jumping off the rock he was sitting on. "How did you find me?"

"I called your house, of course," she smiled. "Your mom told me where to find you."

Jason had to search his brain for a few moments.

"How did you get my number?" he said finally, with a raised eyebrow.

"Oh, I looked it up in the phonebook. I hope that's okay," the girl responded in a meek voice, looking at the ground.

"Right." He nodded, finding it a little strange someone would go through the trouble of doing that when they could have asked instead.

The two of them stood in silence looking at one another in the midst of the woods. The events that had befallen them earlier still lay fresh in their memories, at least in Jason's memories. He was unsure if Sarina actually knew what had happened, or if she even remembered it. He hoped she didn't, and they could leave it all behind. It would make things simpler.

"J.K., I need to talk to you," she said, a serious expression showing on her face, "About what happened yesterday."

Jason felt his skin heat up upon hearing the words as though someone had placed him under a giant hot iron and he had no way of escaping.

"I don't know what you're talking about," he blurted out reflexively.

"I think you do," she said in a stern voice. "J.K. I'm sorry to have gotten you involved in all of this, but with everything that's happened, I think it's time you know my secret, seeing as I know yours."

·About to retort, Jason paused. His entire throat constricted. This was the worst-case scenario. What would the others think? And what would become of her? Could he risk her knowing about the Lab, or would Puc or Arieus lock her up the same way his father had been? Surely a girl with no parents and only an older brother would be easy to dispose of. And what would become of him for being so callous, exposing his powers to someone

260

not of their world? The questions continued to pile up inside of him until it became so hard to breathe that he was forced to open his mouth slightly in order to let air pass through him.

"Jason... I'm not human. I'm a refugee from another planet." She exhaled deeply. "My father was once the ruler of an entire planet, but he had a curse placed upon him by a warlord. Now the same man is pursuing me. Unfortunately, it seems you've been caught in the middle of it all."

"Wait, what?" His eyes widened, absorbing the information.

"I'm being hunted, Jason. I'm sorry to say it, but it seems now my hunters know about you as well."

Jason felt the hairs on his back stand up. Puc himself had stated that those things did not just appear out of thin air. They were sent for people. He had been in the wrong place at the wrong time. The trouble was what his next move would be. Did he tell Puc about the complication, or take care of it on his own?

"So does this mean..." He swallowed, looking down at his feet. "Do you know what I am?"

"I did after you first used your powers," she said quietly. "You're a psychic warrior like my brother."

Jason looked up. "Your brother is like me?"

"Yes, although he is a lot stronger than you. But from what I saw you did a great job with that Leonemas." She smiled lightly. "He's also been training for a lot longer."

Jason looked down again at the crumpled dried leaves and small sticks covering the barren ground. He sighed, letting his shoulders slump down.

"I'm glad I don't have to hide who I am from you," he said, finally. "But no one else can know, none of my friends for now at least. My life is a lot more complicated."

"Isn't everyone's?" Sarina gave another smile. "I didn't even expect you to believe what I just told you. If you want, you can forget all about it and pretend it never happened. I won't tell anyone about your powers either, not even my brother."

He took what she said into consideration and mulled it over for a few moments in his head. This revelation was a bit more than he had expected. He felt somewhat relieved at the way the events had played out, versus what he had pictured in his mind.

"I believe you. I just don't know if I can trust you with a secret that isn't even fully my own," he answered.

Chapter 26

While Sarina was at school during the day, Matthias wandered the city on his own. He could do nothing to help while the children were in the school without causing suspicion, so he took that time as an opportunity to view the world they now found themselves in. He had set the Leonemas on Jason a few days earlier when he was walking Sarina home, to force Jason to expose his secret to her. It was now a matter of all the pieces falling into place. All that was left was to get access to the fortress known as Q-16. In order to do so, they had to gain their trust. He almost felt useless on this assignment. He hated worlds where magic was not supposed to exist. It always made the missions more complicated, and this one was even more so with the targets being children. It almost felt as though Sarina was the one doing most of the work, and he was just there as the muscle when things went wrong. Of course, without her there, he would have no way of getting in touch with them aside from perhaps playing the role of a teacher in the school they attended. There was always the option of capture, torture, and brainwash, but Matthias preferred a clean cut. It was an art to him, the pursuit, the deception and the kill.

Crossing the street in a crowd of other people, he exhaled as these thoughts accumulated in his head. He couldn't wait to actually do something instead of lurk in the shadows. He knew, however, that patience was needed in order to find the right opening to strike. Sometimes though, it was good to vent one's frustration in order to keep patience reserved for the task at hand. Crossing the street, he came to a strip with multiple small stores, all modeled in the same reddish brown brick that seemed to be favored in construction in the area, and in the midst of the shops hung a sign with a green dragon breathing red flames on it; a pub. His attention turning to the sign, he headed straight for the doors below it.

Matthias walked into the local. He had picked this establishment as his usual destination when he needed information because it seemed to be a hub for those who enjoyed conspiracy, magic, and the supernatural. The fact that the pub held the name 'Dragon's Den' might have had something to do with it, but he shrugged it off. He took his regular seat in one of the booths and waited for a server to take his order.

"Whatever is dark and on tap," he said with a slight smile once the waitress came around. He set to his usual task of eves dropping on what people around him were saying. The one other thing he enjoyed about the place was that no music played. It made his task of listening in on people very easy. When he heard something of interest, he would usually see how he could approach the table and chat with those there. It was always easiest if there was a female around. The human women fell for him in a heartbeat. Relaxing in his seat he exhaled as he cleared his mind, only noise all around was the sound of intellectuals deep in their conversations or role-plays. He smirked to himself, hearing dice roll on tables and voices around him. They thought they knew about role-playing, and here he was, the greatest role player of them all.

"Did you guys see what happened to those boulders that decorated the building at Finch?" Matthias's ears pricked up, hearing the words in the booth behind him.

"Yeah, it looked like someone was having fun with a hammer. To move them so far... I mean, guy must have been pretty strong," a female voice answered.

"Nah, had to have been a few of them, I'm yet to meet someone in real life that can haul a rock that big," the voice from before replied back.

"Well, we don't exactly hang out with the most athletic people," the girl snickered.

The waitress came back with Matthias's drink, and set the glass filled with dark liquid before him before bounding off to the other patrons to attend to their needs. Bringing the glass to his lips he took a sip, savoring the bitter taste of the beverage that had been given to him, and continued to eavesdrop.

"Still, for no one to have heard anything? The rock was split in half. Now forgive me if I'm wrong, but I ain't ever heard of a silent power drill," the man replied.

"So what are you saying then? Magic?" The girl chuckled.

"I wouldn't rule it out, even though it is crazy talk," he stated.

Matthias smirked from behind the rim of his glass as he brought it down. From what he had learned in his short time on Earth, human beings banished anything that was not grounded in their little world of science. Even the religious practices of the world were being tried in this area, which Matthias found to be the most ridiculous of all. Faith was a thing not to be tampered with. He saw them as quite pitiful, not knowing about half of the

264

things that lurked beyond the stars or even simply in the dark when they were not looking. They were a primitive race that had lost its true roots.

໖໐໐ສ

Having spent a few hours listening to the conversations around him, Matthias had gathered no new information and decided to call it a night. He could only play with one glass of beer for so long before people began to grow suspicious as to what he was doing at a pub alone, not trying to flirt with any women. Adjusting his coat, he headed out the door and began his walk back home.

"Would you quit it! Let go of me!" The voice of the girl from behind his table rang loud and clear from the side of the building. He had not seen her while indoors, and so had only a voice to run by.

As curiosity would have it, he silently leaned close to the wall on the side of the building and slowly eased in to get a look at the situation. He enjoyed the sound of someone begging for mercy before a kill. Ever since he could remember, he had felt no fear of killing. Instead, he relished it. That was what had made him so valuable to Mislantus. He did not think twice about his target. He did not care where they were from or who they were. To him it was a job.

When he peered around the corner, however, a different reaction occured. The young woman, who had her hand caught by a man, was trying to break free of his grip. Her dark hair, down to her shoulders, swung in all directions wildly, and her brown almond shaped eyes were rimmed with fear. Knowing his better judgment was fueled by his detachment to these people and the world around him, his heels turned to leave, but something prevented him from actually taking the first step. His stagnancy on this mission was getting to him, and the scene fed his taste for action. He wanted involvement in something.

He stepped out from the shadows, the contours of his face lit by the light of the nearby lamppost. His fingers itched at the sight of the man standing there, and he could feel his claws begin to slip from their gauntlets ever so slightly, as if they were coming alive on their own. His eyes wandered to the girl, on the edge of tears, and the claws slipped back in, grip tightening into fists. He was not completely conscious as to why this was his reaction. The alcohol seemed to have relaxed his guard, and his movements were based upon the purest of instincts.

"I believe you need to get your ears checked," Matthias called to him.

"What did you say?" He grunted.

"See, this is exactly what I mean. I said you need to get your ears checked," he said coming closer from the dark.

"Why don't you just beat it and go your own way?" The youth spat, his grip loosening on the girl's hand.

"Well, I can't just leave you here. I happen to be an ear specialist," he said with a smile, coming closer and pausing right in front of him, pulling his hands out of his pockets. The claws instantly came out at his command from his gloved hands. "Why don't you let me have a look?"

The moment the claws were visible from Matthias's hands, the man backed away as far as he could before his back came into contact with a wall.

"Whoa, okay stay away man!" He yelled.

"Hm. Well, you seem to hear me now, so as long as you leave the girl alone, I'll stay away." Matthias continued to keep the slight smile on his face as he spoke with his weapons out.

The man said nothing back. Staggering, he took off in a dead run into the dark of the city. Disappointed with the cowardly behavior, Matthias retracted his claws before turning to the girl, who stood there gazing at him.

"Who...who are you?" she managed to ask.

"Just someone who believes pretty girls should not be hurt." He winked at her. "I suggest you get a cab and wait inside. It's not very safe here once it gets dark."

"Are you like a guy trying to be a superhero?" she called after him.

He turned around once more to face her. "No, I just happened to be in the right place, at the right time and in the right mood." He exchanged one last look with her before vanishing back into the dark.

80CR

The day after his encounter with Sarina in the woods, Jason was quiet all morning, pondering whether or not he should tell the others about who she was, and that she had been present at the attack. He had already lied to them once, dismissing her presence, but the issue had become large. He could not help but think of what would happen to both of them if he revealed everything after the fact. Would she get locked up with her brother, seen as a potential threat? Puc had already assumed the Leonemas was a minion of Mislantus, thinking them to be the center of the universe in all things supernatural.

Jason couldn't help but worry for her now that he knew the situation was and what it could potentially become. Sarina needed help that Jason could theoretically provide if he told the others, but the gap was there, created by the fact that he could not tell them who she was. Sighing in defeat as his head spun, he looked down. He had no power of his own, merely the great deeds of his father looming over him. He desperately wanted to be known as his own person, someone people would speak of unrelated to his father.

His thoughts were shoved aside once he noticed Annetta's head of copper bushy hair approaching the back gate, followed by Darius, and to his surprise, Link.

"Puc got on that identification for him pretty fast," he muttered under his breath remembering how long it had taken Puc to come up with his own identification for when they had gone to see Arcanthur at the mental hospital.

"Hey J.K.!" Annetta greeted him the moment that they crossed into the schoolyard. "Link's going to be going to class with us from now on, Puc managed to get everything in order for him last night, isn't it great?"

Jason shifted from one foot to the other, straightening the straps from his bag as he looked at them, "Yeah, he got it all done really quick. You think you're up to being part of the tenth grade?"

"I think I'll manage," Link said grimly. "I've solved much harder things than what Puc showed me last night."

"Gaia has a much higher level of learning. What you guys learn in ten years, they are forced to learn in....six, was it ?" Darius looked at Link, who nodded.

"What are you guys? Geniuses?" Jason raised an eyebrow, "I still don't get algebra, let alone trying to learn them in the sixth grade. I think my brain would explode. If it came down to it I'd take Puc's training over learning it."

"Which one was algebra again?" Link looked at Darius, confused.

"The one you said no one should have to learn unless they were actually going into a field that required it because it's otherwise considered a waste of time," Darius said solemnly as Link nodded his head in recognition.

"I think every tenth grader would agree with you," Annetta said wryly.

Before they could continue the conversation any further, the bell rang, calling all students back to the building. Jason looked through the sea of heads, trying to spot Sarina, but his efforts seemed in vain. He wondered if what had happened had forced her to flee the area and find another place to blend in. At this point, he was willing to believe anything could have happened to her. He needed to help her somehow. Despite all the confusion that surrounded her, he knew this for sure. Something drew him into her, and it was an instinct he could not fight. It was like what Annetta had always said about fate and being unable to avoid it.

After a moment, Jason spotted her in the side entrance of the school. She was speaking with a young man in glasses who had his arm around her as though he were explaining something of great importance. Jason assumed this was her brother. Sliding off to the side of the crowd, Jason moved closer to the wall in order to wait for her.

"Hey J.K.! Come on!" Annetta called as she was being pushed inside with the other students.

"I'll be right there," he called to her, peering over the corner of the brick wall to see Sarina moving towards the clutter of students. He stepped out from behind the wall, almost slamming into her. "Hey!"

"Oh, hi!" Sarina regained her balance. "I had some stuff I needed to take care of this morning. Sorry I wasn't there, I guess it was a bit rude of me to say all of those things and then just disappear on you like that."

"No it's okay, I understand," Jason felt a pair of eyes on him and looked up to see the young man staring at him from the shadows. His face seemed grim, as though he were ready to attack him at any given moment. Jason took an instinctive step back, and the young man in glasses did the same, becoming darker from the shadow of the building.

"That's my brother, Matthias. But he prefers Matt," she said. "He's just worried about me being around another psychic."

"Yeah, he doesn't look to happy to see me," Jason said quietly, feeling put off by the silent man. "If looks could kill, that would be one of them."

"Like I said, he worries, especially after the Leonemas attack. He even thought you might have been responsible for it, until I told him you didn't use psychic fire to fight it off," she said.

Jason exchanged one more look with the man in the dark before he disappeared behind the other side of the wall completely. He could still feel the heat radiating from the strangers blue eyes moments after they had stopped watching him. There was something very feral about him, despite his well-composed exterior. He figured it was all a disguise, since Sarina had said he was a psychic warrior.

"We should get to class before we get in trouble. We'll talk more at break," Sarina said. Jason nodded in reply and shouldered his bag as they left for class.

∞∞

Annetta had begun to notice Jason was less and less talkative with the group. In fact, he seemed to be trying to get away whenever he could to talk with Sarina at the other end of the school. At first, it had annoyed her. She wanted them all to hang out together to help Link adjust into school life, but Jason had a different agenda. Finally, on the lunch break, Annetta told Jason to just go and talk with Sarina, and come see them when he was done instead of pretending he wanted to be there.

"You did the right thing, though you didn't need to be so forward about it," Darius said later on.

"Maybe not but I've known Jason a while. He'd just keep sneaking off all the time. If he wants to hang out with her, then fine. When she dumps him he'll come back crying to us," she huffed.

"Yeah, but that was still a bit rude either way," Darius sighed, shrugging his shoulders.

Annetta ignored his comment, crossing her arms and leaning against the metal linked fence in their usual corner.

"It feels like he's kind of replacing us, that's all," she muttered under her breath.

"Well, can I say something, as the oldest?" Darius looked at her. "It's not that he's replacing you. He's enticed with a new toy, and, well, I didn't want to talk about this, but you guys are in that age where…"

"So they're going out?" she said plainly.

"Well, no. Not now, at least. But…" Darius pursed his lips, trying to think of how to phrase what he wanted to say. "He's…trying to feel out if Sarina is, you know, someone he would like to date someday in the future. She's not a friend like you that he would care to lose, so anything goes."

At this point even Link turned to look at Darius sideways. "You're making it sound like he's inspecting a horse or something," he said, putting his hands into his jean jacket.

"Sadly, that's how most young men think." Darius seemed to blush a little. "I can tell you I still do it sometimes. What I'm getting at is that Jason won't leave you because you're both friends. But when you eventually get into romantic relationships, you'll both go your separate ways. That's just the reality of it."

Annetta didn't want to think about this. It made her heart break just a little bit. She had been best friends with Jason since the first grade. Her life without him as her friend would become empty. She thought of Link and Darius. Would they go away one day too? If they did, would anyone take their place as her friends? If she did find new friends, what would her life be with them? Would they be able to know of the Lab? The thought of that kind of change made her nauseous.

The bell rang again for them to go back inside. Darius said nothing more and walked off towards the school, leaving Link and Annetta behind.

"Don't listen to everything he says," Link said after a moment of silence. "He thinks just because he's older he knows everything. But really, he doesn't. No matter how old a person is you don't abandon your friends."

Link began to walk to the school, his fists shoved into his pockets, the wind billowing the ends of his jacket.

"I promise you this much, Annetta. I'll stick by you until the end. You have my word as a Gaian." He winked with his crescent scarred eye.

Annetta watched him leave, blushing lightly to herself. It felt nice of him to say what he did. Breathing in the spring air, she shrugged off the thought, and ran off to catch up with her friends.

Chapter 27

Annetta made her way to the Lab where Darius and Link had gone before her. She did not see a point in waiting for Jason. In fact, she was not even sure if he would show up at all given his behavior in school. Walking down the massive steel corridors, she came to the common room area with couches where the elf, two youth and the Hurtz, seemed to be waiting in a clustered group, engaged in deep discussion. She took their ignorance to her presence as a cue to settle in and sit on the arm of one of the sofas.

"Hey guys, what's up?" She greeted them, to which the group stopped their chattering and looked over at her, the atmosphere of excitement coming to a stop.

"Ahoy lass," Brakkus flashed his teeth in greeting.

"Well, someone showed up rather early for once." Puc answered. His face looked extremely drained, like he'd been up all night. Despite the elf always having looked worn and pale, she'd never seen him look like that before. Under his arm, he carried a thick leather bound book that looked to be at least a hundred years old by the wear and tear on it.

"Uh." She stuttered, stunned by the verbal attack. "So, what's going on? You guys seemed really pumped about something."

"Puc found the spell to unlock the mace from its pendant form," Darius summarized.

"The only problem," Puc picked up, "is the only person who can unlock it is Jason. Only the heir of the weapon can bring it forth as a form of preventing it from falling into the wrong hands. Where is young Kinsman, anyways?" the elf asked.

"I don't know, I gave up trying to talk to him when he seemed more interested in talking to some girl he just met instead of spending time with his friends," Annetta stated.

Link interjected the conversation, hearing the hostility in Annetta's voice, "He's just trying to be friendly to the new girl."

"That's all nice and dandy for him, but Annetta may you contact him? There are more important things that need to be attended to now." He glanced back at his book.

"No need. I'm right here," Jason said from behind all of them. "What's going on?"

Annetta turned around to face her friend, who was leaning on one of the couches. She did her best to conceal the betrayed look in her eyes by smiling at him. He might not have even seen it as disloyalty like she did. Pushing the few loose strands of hair from her face, she turned her attention back to Puc, the elf moving past her to the boy.

"Just the person I was speaking about," he said, and held up the necklace in his hand. "I know how to unleash the weapon, but you must be the one to do it. The spell is useless in my own hands."

Jason walked closer to the others who had gathered. He felt a judgmental gaze coming from some of those in the room, but dismissed it, figuring it was simply jealousy. He was about to unlock a weapon wielded by his own father, a vital part of his history.

Puc took the leather string and tied it securely around Jason's neck. "The weapon needs to feel that it is with its owner," he explained. "You must try to not take it off when in its dormant state like this. It allows for the weapon to bond with you. Eventually, your father did not need to even utter the incantation. The weapon would spring to life for him. That was how close he was to it."

"You make it sound like it's a living thing." Jason wrinkled his nose, looking down at the little piece of carved wood. "Here I am having trouble seeing it as more than a toothpick."

"The weapon isn't, but the magic protecting it makes it that way," Puc said. "It is similar to how people say dogs are man's best friend. The dog will be friendly and protective to those who raise and care for it, but will bite off a stranger's hand if he sees fit."

Jason pictured the tiny mace growing a giant set of teeth and chomping off his enemy's hand. He couldn't help but crack a small grin, stopping himself when he remembered that the others were looking at him.

"In order to release it from its dormant state, you need to grip the weapon and say the following incantation: Exorior." Puc instructed and made sure to say the last part slowly and clearly, so Jason could hear him.

"Sounds Latin," Annetta said, shifting in her seat.

"Because it is, or rather what you know as Latin is Elvish. It was adapted by humans when we first started interacting with them hundreds of years ago," Puc replied.

Hearing the language made Jason's eye pop out of his head. Learning to control psychic abilities was one thing. Learning a new language he could barely understand was another.

"Exo-rearor?" He tried to say the word without the necklace in hand, just in case something backfired. He'd seen it happen too many times in the movies he watched with Annetta.

Puc's shoulders slumped as he gave a sigh of agitation. His dislike for humans knew no end for the simple reason that they did not know how to listen and understand magic. Jason had just proven his view perfectly with the iteration. The elf exhaled noisily, knowing the boy was not to blame for his ignorance. His lack of sleep from attempting to uncover the spell was showing and heaving in a great breath the elf tried to do his best to remain calm.

"Exorior. One word Jason. Ex. O. Rior," he said once more in a cold tone, closing his eyes.

Jason caught the word the second time, the shock of hearing a foreign language having worn off. He clasped the small wooden mace in his hand, hoping nothing would happen if he got it wrong. Mostly, he was worried Puc would finally lose it and smack him over the head with his staff. From the way he had reacted moments before, it was a completely plausible scenario.

"Exorior." he said slowly in order to make sure there was enough space in between each sound for them not to blend together. Jason had no idea how magic worked, at least the kind Puc used, or the kind used on the mace. When nothing happened, Jason looked up at the mage in questioning.

Before Puc could provide an answer or a snide remark, an intense light came from Jason's palm, nearly blinding everyone and everything in the room. He covered his eyes with his free hand only to feel the weight of something far heavier in the other than the small carving he had gotten from his father.

Once the brightness dimmed, Jason removed his hand from his face and opened his eyes. At first he almost dropped the weapon out of surprise, but could not bring himself to do so. It lay with its blades to the ground. It was singly the most terrifying and beautiful object Jason had ever seen. Worn brown leather wound around the hilt of the weapon until it reached a metallic guard ringed with spikes. The head of the mace was shaped like four lion heads facing outwards, with serrated blades between them.

Taking the weapon into both hands, he raised it to eye level to get a better look at it. On a small golden band around the middle of it was written an inscription in cursive,

Through hell and back

"That is the motto of your family's house," Puc stated after the prolonged period of silence. "Your ancestors were known for their immense courage. They stood by in battles that seemed hopeless. They went through hell and rose from it again as lions. They then brought that inferno upon their enemies and so the mace became rightfully named Helbringer."

Jason took in the words as he continued to study the contours of the mace. The fine effort put into creating the blades in the shape of heraldic lion heads astonished him. He'd always seen weapons as just that. He had never stopped to consider them as pieces of art. Hearing the part about never giving up brought water to Jason's eyes. His father gave up, and it had cost Jason the knowledge of who he had been, the history of the hero who wielded the mace that now was encircled in his own fingers. Struggling with his anger, Jason eased himself into the knowledge that those here were not responsible, that his father could have brought more harm than good in what he had tried to do. Silently he vowed he would not let this be the fate of his son one day, and that he would be there to tell him all about his own adventures. He would simply have to follow the rules, the rules those around him knew better than he.

"We'll need to think about reuniting the Four Forces, then," Brakkus interrupted the boy's stream of thought as he stroked his beard. "We got Helbringer, and we got Arieus's shield. Think that'll be enough to convince 'em?"

"It will be a start to negotiating with the four races," Puc said. "I suggest we go first to the Water Elves. They are my own kin and will be easiest to gain the trust of, as I have never stopped serving Orbeyus. They are also the ones who helped in building this base."

"Wait, they built the Lab?" Annetta raised an eyebrow. "Aren't elves all like... In love with nature and against technology?"

The mage looked down at the girl, the grip on his staff tightening from the comment and his inability to control his anger due to lack of sleep.

"I think you need to stop reading fantasy novels, Miss Severio," Puc growled, narrowing his eyes in sarcastic anger.

"We're not exactly hippies," Darius said, grinning. "Water Elves are actually the ones who brought about the use of steam for fuel and we still use it till this very day as a source of energy."

Annetta pursed her lips, trying to wrap her head around it, "So...you guys are more like eco friendly dwarves then?"

"Nothing close to dwarves." Puc gritted his teeth, to which Brakkus could only stifle a chuckle as he watched his struggling companion. Annetta looked questioningly at the Hurtz as to what she had said wrong.

"Lass, one thing that is true to yer fiction is dwarves an' elves don't get along," Brakkus whispered to Annetta.

Chapter 28

After a round of phone calls claiming that Annetta, Jason, Darius and Link would not be attending class due to illness, the real work began. Jason and Darius came to Annetta's house first thing in the morning, chatting away about what the elven city would look like once they got there. Though Darius had been away a very long time, he did his best to describe what he could remember. He was dressed in a long black cloak, and looked ready for a medieval convention. When he spoke to Annetta, it sounded like the city was a Victorian paradise full of airships and steam driven vehicles. There was an excited air around the Lab upon their descent. It felt to Annetta as though they were some kind of deranged family going on a trip instead of on a mission.

"Water Elves are the cofounders of Q-16," Darius explained as they walked through the halls once they had descended. "They were well known for their love of creation and their greatest contribution in Orbeyus's time was the Lab. He wanted something that was unseen by humanity in order to protect the Eye to All Worlds. The Water Elves granted him the territory of their fallen city as the site for constructing the base."

"So Atlantis..." Jason began.

"Pretty real," he continued, "though it didn't go down because of any raging gods. In truth, it was never a real landmass at all. It was a constructed bio dome that sunk under the water when a steam reactor melted. I like to think of it as our version of the Titanic, I guess. But yeah, hundreds of years later it was turned into the original foundations of Q-16, and then expanded on over the years."

"How do you know all of this?" Jason asked.

"When you spend enough time with my master and Brakkus, you hear a lot of jabbering." Darius grinned.

Their conversation was interrupted when Link came around the corner with a pensive look on his face. Dressed in his usual attire of a jean jacket, t-shirt and jeans, he didn't look like someone who was about to embark on a journey to another world. A heavy pack swung back and forth on his back and he walked towards them, with metallic pots clattering on its sides.

"Hey Link, what's up?" Annetta greeted him as he came to a halt. He was still staring off into space, thinking.

"Does anyone know where I can find some military grade rope?" he finally asked.

"Did you think about looking in your room?" Jason asked.

Link bit his lip, still in his own thoughts. Anyone who looked at him could tell he was taking the matter of going to visit the Water Elves extremely seriously.

"You know, the sad thing is that I didn't." He cracked a grin after a few moments. "I will be back. Puc and Brakkus are with the horses."

"Okay, see you in a bit," Annetta nodded watching him leave with his clinking load.

"Oh, he's gonna fit in just great with all that metal on him," Darius snarked as they kept walking.

"So, do we need to dress a certain way or anything? Did Puc say anything at all?" she asked.

"I said nothing, because you are going as the heirs of Orbeyus and Arcanthur." Puc's voice emerged before Darius could answer them back. The trio turned around to see him dressed in long black mage robes, lined with silver stitching, "I would, however, request that you go and retrieve your shield for the journey, Annetta. I believe it is in the armory where you last left it. Brakkus has finished polishing it. Jason, you have Helbringer with you, correct?"

As Annetta wandered off to where the armory was, Jason took the small wooden object on the leather cord from under its protective place on his neck, inside his shirt. "Never parted with it. Kinda hurts to sleep with it on, though."

"You will get used to it." Puc's pale eyes affirmed him and then turned to Darius. "Go with Annetta, if you could, to put my mind at ease."

Darius nodded, and turning on his heel he followed her. The girl trudged on in silence through the metal corridors until the boy was right beside her.

"I thought everyone would be more serious about this mission. Instead, it's like a giant field trip," Annetta said. "Not that I'm complaining."

"For Puc it sort of is. The same with myself, actually," Darius replied. "I don't think he's been back to his home city since before the blackout, to be honest. I mean, I haven't either, but I spent so much time here it doesn't matter to me because this is my home. But imagine not being able to go home because you had duties elsewhere. Then, all of a sudden, your duties will take you back there. I'd be kind of excited."

Annetta turned, burying herself in her own thoughts as they walked down the corridors. Despite knowing Puc and Brakkus for so long, she had never really paused to think about the people they may have left behind.

With Brakkus, she knew the situation about his daughter's death and him being alone, but Puc always gave them the cold shoulder, so it was hard to interrogate him about anything of that sort. She felt a sharp pang of guilt about it, but it was diffused when she looked at Darius.

"Do you live with your actual parents, or are they just others who are in on it?" she asked.

"My parents died when I was very young. I was an orphan, and was taken in by the Mage Academy when I showed signs of promise. Some years later, Puc came looking for an apprentice and chose me, so here I am," Darius said, distantly. "Those shades of people you see from time to time are actually a spell. I guess you could call them mirages. It's the reason I never really invited you guys over before. It's difficult for me to maintain it all the time."

Annetta paused her walking for a moment as it all dawned on her. "You're right. I don't think I've ever been to your apartment in all this time. We either go out, or you come over."

"Yep, exactly." he nodded.

"So you've lived there alone?"

"Puc would come visit me from time to time," he said, "There's more than one entrance to the Lab, I hope you know. The one in your house just happens to be the best known. There's one in my house that's portable like the one behind your mirror, and Puc has another one somewhere, though he doesn't say where, and I've asked him before."

Reaching the end of the corridor, they both turned to where the armory was located. Arieus's shield hung in the middle of the room, polished to perfection. The black rampant lion stared back at them in greeting with the shapes of a sword, mace and axe behind it. Annetta took the shield down and adjusted the leather straps on the inside to fit her arm.

"Why does this thing always feel too big for me?" she growled, lifting her arm with it up.

"Well, it's a tower shield, what do you expect?" Darius said. "I say take a sword as well just in case."

Darius walked around the room before selecting a blade from the wall, examining it by taking it out of the scabbard before handing it to Annetta. Taking the weapon, she began to tie the belt around her waist like Brakkus had shown her. Sword belts were not the same as regular belts. There was a whole procedure to tying it up in case anyone tried to disarm you in a crowd. As she did this, her eyes fell and lingered on the dark haired boy in a cloak who stood beside the weapon rack in silence, watching what she was doing.

"You know, I still have a hard time believing that you're way older than Jason and I," she said, finishing the final loop on the belt.

Darius couldn't help but try to hide a grin upon hearing the comment as he looked at his feet and then back up at the girl.

"With all the stuff around you, you have a hard time believing that?" He chuckled. "I thought you'd be more freaked out about being in an underwater base or going to see a whole other race of people, not how old I am."

"I am, and it's all kind of hard to take in but it's just that... I've known you for so long and now all of this comes out." She said adjusting the loops in her belt to make sure it was on tight enough.

"I would have told you sooner if I could. Believe me, it was hard to lie all of these years," he said, looking around awkwardly as he tried to think of something else to say. When it dawned upon him he shared his thoughts. "Think of it this way, at least you know now. I never lied about being your friend. You're a very brave person, Annetta, and you're not afraid to be different in this world. People like that are the ones that will make a difference. They will fight for their beliefs and those are the types of people I'm honored to have a chance to call friends."

∞∞

The journey to the castle had been a silent one. It seemed that everyone's energy was being stored up for the actual journey to the main city of the Water Elves, which they had learned was called Aldamoor. It was there, Puc had explained, he had lived his whole life until he came into Orbeyus's service, as did Darius before he became his apprentice. It was also where the Elven Mage High Council had their stronghold. Coming to the foot of Severio Castle, they stopped and waited for further instruction from the mage.

"We will need to take the horses into the castle," Puc said. "Aldamoor is a large city. It will take a while to walk to our destination which is the Council Tower in the heart of the city, and the more time we have to convince them that you are the heirs, the better for us. Some of the older mages don't take kindly to strangers."

The mage seemed to be the only one to bustle with more energy than in previous endeavors, particularly upon arrival at the castle gates. His frantic movement and continual double checking were making Jason feel nauseous. The boy shook his head and turned away to look somewhere else as he gripped the reins of the horse. His gaze landed upon the heavy wooden front doors, which caused a question to well up inside of him.

"Wait, how are we going to get the horses up all those stairs?" Jason asked as he looked back at the mage.

"There are ramps all along the castle designed for horses and vehicles to travel," Puc explained. "Though knowing your lack of observation, you would not have noticed them."

Unsaddling and opening the gates of the castle, they brought the horses out in single file. Annetta and Jason then noticed steep slopes beside the flights of stairs, almost like wheelchair ramps. They looked so ordinary that it was as if they were part of the architecture itself and could have passed as decoration.

"I thought they were just mindful of the future when they built those things," she said.

"Yes and no. The founding Severios were well aware of the portals and that in order to travel in some, horses or something more elaborate would be needed. Remember, these are natural tears in the world and so one never truly knows what to be prepared for when entering the first time. A powerful spell could create a portal to another dimension anywhere if you knew which world you were aiming for."

"Aye," Brakkus interrupted, "but it's risky and messy. If ya do the incorrect incantation, ya could end up in another world surrounded by some hellspawn, and have yer flesh stripped in minutes."

"Thank you for explaining in detail, Brakkus." Puc rolled his eyes as they came to a halt in front of a large door. The marble and gold arch around it depicted scenes of ocean waves and what looked to be gears enveloped in the water, with fish swimming about them. At the top of the arch were two angelic figures holding a circular object with three water drops in the middle. Annetta noted that it was the same symbol as the one on the pedestal that held Severbane. The mage moved to the front of the door to get everyone's attention.

"Shall we enter?" Puc looked at his companions. "After this, there is no turning back so if anyone wishes to go, you are welcome to leave now."

Everyone looked around before turning their eyes back on him. The elf couldn't help but smirk a bit, seeing no one flinch.

"Very well, your fate is sealed," he stated. Moving his hand over the door handle, it turned on its own, opening.

Annetta had expected a red and black portal like the one that separated Q-16 from Severio Castle. But what lay inside the chamber puzzled her. They were staring into a large reflective surface. It was as if someone had intentionally wedged a mirror large enough to cover the room from head to toe in the space. The companions moved into the room, mesmerized by the bizarre sight.

"Is this...for real?" Link stared up into the massive wall before them.

"Do you recall me saying that all portals looked different?" Puc stated, turning his horse around to face his companions. "Some are easier to tell apart than others. This is partially why the portals were given separate rooms, that and so their origins would not be forgotten."

Link gave a slight shake of the head and turned back to look at the mirror portal. Annetta felt a chill go down her spine. The emotions of her actually going on this venture finally caught up with her. By the look on everyone else's, face it was happening to them as well. Even the horses seemed a bit skittish as they tossed their heads in rebellion and neighed more than usual.

"Everyone head back a few paces. It's best to do these things at a run," Puc warned them as he urged his own horse to walk backwards outside the door.

The others followed his lead. Once everyone was far back, Puc, Brakkus and Darius signaled their horses into a dead run, charging into the mirror before them, disappearing instantly.

Annetta, Link and Jason looked at one another. To Annetta and Jason, a mirror was not something one ran into unless one wanted seven years of bad luck.

"The only way we're gonna do this is with our eyes closed," she said to them. "At least I am. No way am I looking into a mirror as I run straight towards it."

"I'm liking that idea." Jason smiled and made sure his horse was positioned right at the portal. "FLY!"

After shouting the command to Bossman to move forward, Annetta, eyes shut and held onto the horse for dear life. She could feel every muscle and sinew in the giant animal at work as it ran. Then came the feeling of passing through a portal, though it felt different from the one she passed through in order to get to Severio Castle. This portal smelled of steel, and Annetta felt as though she had just taken a bite out of a metal bar, leaving a metallic aftertaste in her mouth. Though the feeling in her mouth lingered, once she was sure that the rest of it was gone, she opened her eyes. They were some distance away from it on what looked like a great plane of tall grass. Beyond, Annetta could see a city before them. In the air flew great zeppelins, previously only found in her history books and fantasy pictures. Tall towers rose from the city, and farther still could be seen a wall of mountains with a waterfall so large that were the sun setting, it would be completely blotted out.

"Aldamoor. The capital city of Water Elves," Puc announced once everyone had made it through.

"Haven't these guys heard of petroleum?" Jason looked at the massive amounts of steam coming from the buildings.

"You mean that substance that is destroying your world both environmentally and socially? You mean that?" Puc glanced back as the boy lowered his head defensively at the comment. "Oh we're very much aware, and choose to use something much more ethereal for energy needs."

"I can think of a few of people in our world who could take some pointers from them," Jason said, whispering to Annetta.

The group then began to descend down the cobblestone road that led to the city, past the plains of grass. The way felt awkward and bumpy under the hooves of the massive beasts. One could tell the animals had not ridden on such rough terrain, and it was just as taxing on them as the riders. It was not until they got to the outskirts of the city that the road became polished and smoother from the constant beating of shoes and wheels on it. The smell of water vapors became overpowering the closer they got to the city. It was not as unpleasant as being in the heart of a city on Earth, but it definitely did not smell like a bouquet of roses.

Once they'd managed to get inside by passing the enormous gates of beige stone, Annetta was able to get a better look at the people in the street wearing their elaborate tailored suits and dresses, though they were somewhat tattered. It felt as though she had stepped into a Victorian painting. The one thing that betrayed everyone was their eyes, which were now fixed upon the newcomers. They were the same feral blue shade that Puc and Darius had.

"Why are the all looking at us like that?" Jason asked uneasily.

"Well," Puc stated, "I think it's safe to say that we stick out like a sore thumb with a large animalistic warrior and three non-elven children riding on horseback. Try your best to ignore it. Our mission is with the Mage Council, not to solicit with the locals."

Annetta gave one long glance at the elves watching her before urging the horse to bound after Puc.

Jason looked at the architecture of the buildings around them. On either side of the busy streets were tall rectangular buildings with slanted rooftops that were squished together as close as possible, tinted in a lime green coating, some in need of a fresh paint job. In each window, something seemed to be going on, be it a couple talking or a woman leaning out the window and airing out a quilt, or children watching the travelers go by. The city, though a little under kept in places, was filled with life in all corners and it was not much different from what went on back home.

"This is definitely not how I picture elves when I read about them," Annetta finally spoke, catching up to Brakkus and Puc.

"Your human writers often confuse us with our forest dwelling cousins," Puc finally said. "Except when it comes to their war scenes in literature, then it is Water Elves they refer to. A Forest Elf would rather hang than lift iron in order to make peace."

"So there are tree hugging elves?" Jason interrupted the conversation.

"Every species has its faults," Darius said, grinning. "They do make some of the most amazing rangers and trackers, though. If you ever are going into a forest and need a guide, it's a Forest Elf you want with you."

"Between you an' me, I'd still prefer a compass. Less chatty," Brakkus whispered to Annetta, holding in a chuckle.

"You got something against Forest Elves?" Darius looked at Brakkus.

"I don't, I just prefer to know my own bearings, that's all." he flashed a grin from his crocodile-like teeth.

Annetta laughed and looked back at Link, who seemed very quiet compared to everyone else.

"What's wrong, Link?" she asked.

"Hmm?" He snapped out of his silence. "Nothing. I'm just... well, I'm a little confused, I guess. I see all of this technology around, and we're going to a Mage Council. Generally, a civilization knows only one of the two and excels in one of the two. That's what they taught us at camp."

"We're one of the rare cases where magic co-exists with technology," Puc said, looking back at the boy. "It is a common rule that civilizations both start with a base knowledge of magic and technology, then either excel in one or the other, depending which way the species evolves over time. Humans evolved technologically, forfeiting their knowledge of magic and the ability to cast it. As you see though, our technology is grounded in magic. The ability to turn water into steam and power a city can be seen as magic if one does not know the process behind it."

"There's a rule where a race can only know magic or have technology?" Annetta asked. "That's stupid. How do you explain the Lab and the Castle Severio then?"

"It is a collaboration between races who know of both. As I said before, there are exceptions to the rule, as there are with many rules," Puc said. "It is foretold, however, that one day, close to the end of the Unknown's time, there shall come the one who will bring light to all races, enabling them to know of both. That, however, is a fable to elaborate on another day. We're almost there. Let's press on."

Puc urged his horse into a run towards the tower, the clattering of hooves overpowering all other sounds for miles around. Brakkus, Annetta and the others followed his lead. Looking up, Annetta noted the many aircraft flying through the sky above them.

"Our airships once served in the War, along with other machines," Puc said over the noise. "Water Elves are known for their love of invention and creativity."

Annetta nodded, looking up in awe. It felt unreal to see such machines overhead, and they almost looked fake to her. On the horizon before them, the tallest structure within the city loomed, a tower that sprang up almost as high as the mountains behind, with a clock face at its peak, and what looked to be a half gear underneath it. Jason was struck by the sight of it, and lifted his head up, not bothering to look down until his horse stumbled in a pothole.

As soon as Puc reached the entrance to the courtyard to the Mage Council headquarters, he dismounted his horse, tying it up at the post next to other mounts. He then waited for the others to catch up and do the same. Around them, other elves nearby stared and muttered among themselves at the newcomers. Once everyone had gathered, Puc led the way towards the door, in front of which stood two guards dressed in long navy coloured coats and high black boots, armed with what appeared to be staves with bayonet knives on top of them.

"We wish to enter and speak with the Mage Council. I am Puc Thanestorm, once advisor to Lord Orbeyus Severio of the Axe." He announced his full title, holding his staff in both hands as if to command authority to make the guards move aside.

The guards however did not move a muscle upon the introduction, but only exchanged a simple nod to one another, and moments later, pointed their bayonet knives at the mage.

"Puc Thanestorm, you are under arrest for the theft of the holy artifact known as Chiron's Toolbox," one of the guards said.

"What?" He raised an eyebrow. "But that's not possible. I've not set foot in Aldamoor for over ten years! Furthermore, what use would I have out of a putrefying old book of history?"

"Drop the staff or prepare to suffer the consequences," the second guard hissed. "Same goes to your friends. All weapons down."

Annetta spun around to note that guards in similar outfits surrounded them all, their staves pointed at them. Link and Brakkus gripped the hilts of their swords, ready to attack on a moment's notice, despite being outnumbered.

"There has to be a misunderstanding. We need to see the Council," Darius protested.

"The Council has no time for foreigners and we're warning you to lay down your arms," the first guard stated. "But we're here on important business regarding the old alliance. Look!" Annetta lifted the shield as high as she could. "I am Annetta Severio, daughter of Arieus Severio and granddaughter of Orbeyus Severio."

The guards grim expressions turned to confusion upon seeing the shield, and the pair turned away for a moment to chat quietly among themselves. Having reached a conclusion they looked back at the group with the same stern expressions.

"This does not change the fact that Thanestorm is under arrest. Take him away," the first guard said, unmoved by the sight of the shield at the door as two others rushed in and grabbed Puc under his arms, taking away his staff.

"What?" Jason blew up, outraged. "You can't just arrest him for no reason! Where's your proof he did it? I mean, haven't you people heard of the justice system?"

"He's right. The gates to Aldamoor have not been opened for many years," Darius added.

"Be silent," Puc instructed them with a scowl on his sharp face. "Silver, do not interfere in politics you know very little about. And you, Kinsman, you're not on Earth anymore."

"But you didn't do it. You said so yourself," he protested, looking at Annetta, who wore a similar expression to his own.

"You were with us in Q-16 the whole time," she added. "They can't just say you did it."

Puc sighed, not having the patience for long discussion, and looked upon the two of them. "Understand this. Sometimes the best way to prove one is innocent is to cooperate. Now, both of you will quit worrying over my fate, which is pointless, and use your minds for something more constructive."

Not given the chance to say more, the two guards holding the mage bound his hands in iron cuffs and marched him away.

The guard at the door then turned to Annetta. "You must disarm before entering to see the Council. The shield may stay, but everything else must be left in the main entrance with our squires."

"What about the mage? Where ya taking him? Answer quickly or I won't be so nice," Brakkus snarled impatiently as one of the guards took his sword.

"He is being taken to the city prison, where you can see him after. Now, if you wish to see the Council, follow me." The guard began to walk inside, while the other soldiers dispersed back to their posts.

Annetta wanted to scream at the guards to release Puc. But she knew that these men would not care for what a young girl had to say, even if she did hold the shield of her father as proof of who she was. It would take a lot more than that. She breathed deeply as she followed her companions, and upon stripping the sword from her being was led to a large set of stairs that climbed high above the lower level she had entered from.

"I think it best if ya address the issues at hand with the council," Brakkus whispered to Darius, "Yer one of them, and Puc's apprentice."

Darius looked over at the Hurtz, his usually calm resolve somewhat faded as the responsibility was thrust upon him. He had always bathed in the shadow of his master and had never walked in the light. He had never been in this sort of situation. The stress of it all rested on his temples, causing them to throb madly as he began rehearsing in his head what to say.

The guard that had been at the door came to a halt on the highest level of the tower, leading them to twin doors, upon which were carved the same scenes as the door inside Severio Castle that led to the portal. They stood at least twenty feet high. All around them were massive windows equaling the door's in size, allowing a view all around of the city below and the machines flying by the tower.

"I will go and inform the council of your arrival. Please wait here," the guard said before slipping inside.

The foreign sentries having left them alone for the first time since they had come to the foot of the strange tower, Link finally spoke up, "They just took him into custody. Why are we all standing here?"

"Because this is what Puc wanted." Darius glared at him.

"I don't think part of his plan included getting thrown in prison, wouldn't you agree?" he hissed back.

"I think you need a little reminder of the fight in the alley." Darius began to roll up his sleeves when Brakkus grunted, standing between them.

"Puc would also not wish you lads both quarreling for nothing," he growled, "Now behave. We need all respectability we can get before that lot."

Link stood down, his shoulders slouching in defeat at he glared at Darius through a thin curtain of his tangled hair, matting the front of his face.

Annetta noted the hostility between the two boys and leaned over to a disgruntled looking Link, "Since when have you been close to Puc?" she whispered to him.

"I'm not, but I never leave a man behind. That is not a true warrior's way." he continued to glare at Darius before breaking his gaze with him.

"You mean a hero. Anybody who can fight can be a warrior." She smiled a bit.

Before Link could say anything, the door opened once more and the guard emerged.

"You may enter," he said, and opened the door wider for them.

Annetta and her companions found themselves in the base of a circular room with a glass ceiling. In rows of seats higher above them were gathered several figures dressed in robes similar to Puc's. In a separate booth on the same elevation was another single chair in which was an elderly man holding a staff more elaborate than any they had yet encountered, with gears and working mechanisms coursing through the crystal head of it. From his clean shaven, sour looking face, framed by graying blonde hair, and the air of authority in his pale blue eyes, Annetta could tell he was the one in charge of everything.

"Enter, those who dare call themselves daughter of Arieus and son of Arcanthur," he spoke in a fluid voice.

Jason and Annetta looked back at their companions who stood where they had entered the chamber. Swallowing hard and taking a deep breath, the two friends came forward into the overpowering light. The elder's pale blue eyes observed them with intense curiosity for a moment, before his gaze shifted to the others standing there.

"You may also come closer, if you will it," he acknowledged them.

After a moment, Brakkus shoved the two boys forward after they displayed a lack of motor functions. Seeing all those gathered below him, the mage rose from his seat.

"Welcome," the man in the central chair said. "I am Kaian, descendant of Chiron the Creator, and First Mage on this council. State your business with the Water Folk, although first I am inclined to ask how it is exactly that you were able to get to Aldamoor when all connections have been severed with outside worlds for over a decade now," he stated.

"We came through the portal located in the Eye to All Worlds, sir." Darius spoke with his eyes on his boots. "I am Darius Silver, apprentice to the one held captive, Puc Thanestorm, also known as Puc the Mage."

"Thanestorm's charge. You ought to be arrested with your master for the heresy lain upon this land." Kaian began to raise his hand for the guards.

"Wait, please!" Darius raised his own arms above his head. "I know nothing of what my master is accused of, and as you said, no one has come or gone since connections were cut off between Aldamoor and all other worlds. My master and I have made our home in the base known as Q-16 since the murder of Lord Orbeyus of the Axe, and we came here to resurrect old alliances, to free the blade Severbane from its resting place so it may yet again meet the forces of darkness, to meet the scourge known to those as Mordred's son, Mislantus. He amasses an army within Valdhar above Earth, which I have personally witnessed. We have come here to ask you to join us in this fight."

Darius's words echoed on the walls of the chamber with firm resolve. Annetta and Jason wanted nothing more than to add in their own voices but heeded what Brakkus had said outside and remembering that they held their composure.

Kaian sat back on his seat, looking down at Darius. He glanced to his fellow mages on either side who chatted quietly among themselves in enlightenment of what they had just been told. Shifting his position in the chair into a more pensive one, the descendant of Chiron let his opinion be known.

"And what proof do we have that these are indeed the heir's of Obreyus and Arcanthur aside from an old shield?" He raised an eyebrow.

Before Darius could speak out again, he was cut off by the sound of thumping feet as Jason raced in front of him.

"You have this. Exorior!" the brown haired boy whipped out the necklace from under his shirt as it began to glow, filling the room with its light until nothing could be seen. Once it had faded, Jason held the mace in both hands before him, and raised it high for those gathered to see. "Given to me by my father, the mace known as Helbringer," he said.

Those gathered in the stands above began to speak among themselves once more in a louder fashion. Even Kaian's expression changed from stern to somewhat angered and shocked. It faded quickly, however, as he collected himself once again in his throne.

"An alliance does not come without a pact or agreement of some sort being made. Unfortunately, we do not have the time to discuss such a thing at the current moment, when all of our attention is devoted to restoring Chiron's Toolbox," Kaian stated. "If however you wish for the allegiance of the Water Elves, then you can help progress this along. Without the Toolbox, we will not pursue anything else. Including an alliance with children."

The last word stung Jason like a burning spike. He knew in truth that was all he was, but he'd gotten this far. He rested the head of the mace against the floor, leaning his weight on it and looked over at the others in defeat.

Keeping a cool head about him in the situation, Link saw it as a good time for him to speak up and take Jason out of the spotlight.

"What exactly is Chiron's Toolbox? What are we looking for?" he asked.

"It is a tome which contains the entire history of the Water Elf race, including the creation of all of our spells and how to cast them," the First Mage answered. "What is unique about this particular tome is that it writes itself. It is said to be the soul of our people. No one has touched it in years, and it is always up to date. Like history, the tome continues on, but unlike history, it stores all of the information, including spells that were cast once and should never be cast again, and are best forgotten. It was kept under strict watch and only a select few could come near it. Thanestorm was one of those people."

Annetta looked down at the shield weighing down her arm as the elf spoke. She'd heard knowledge was power, but never had she thought it could be so literal.

Fixing his cloak which had become tangled in the walk up the tower, Darius looked down at his feet, his eyes locking in on the black marble floors which he finally noticed had fine linings of gold in them. He had only ever been in the audience chamber with Puc and always in his shadow, completely oblivious to the room and the power it seemed to radiate on those gathered in the lower area while the council watched from on high. This pressure was now being placed on him and there was no one he could run to for advice. He had been stripped of that privilege. He did not however need to dwell long on what needed to be done and he hoped it was the same course his master would have taken. There was only one option to take which would satisfy the council and so he turned his face towards Kaian.

"We will return the tome and prove the innocence of one Puc Thanestorm, in exchange for the sworn oath to the descendant of Orbeyus and son of Arcanthur." Darius stepped forward towards Kaian.

Kaian watched the boy in amusement with his pale eyes.

"Oh, this I shall enjoy seeing," the elder scoffed. "Well, I suppose if they truly are who they say they are, then there should be no problem. As I said before, if you wish to assist then start your search within the mage training quarters, for our city guards are occupied sweeping the docks and market. There you may speak with Nathaniel Guildwood. He has been our lead instructor for well over a three hundred years, and was the one to train Thanestorm."

Annetta, not having said much since she came in, wanted to tell Kaian he had no right accusing Puc. Before she had the chance to do so, Darius nodded and bowed, turning around to leave. She was then forced to go as Brakkus's firm hand turned her shoulder to the exit.

As soon as the doors closed behind them, Darius exhaled the deepest breath possible, while Brakkus patted his back, the two of them shuffling off to the side allowing the apprentice to catch his breath, leaving the trio in front of the door.

"The nerve of that guy! Can you believe him?" Annetta gritted her teeth. "He already thinks Puc is the one who did it!"

Link watched as Annetta seemed to turn red with anger. "Well, we just have to find the book and prove them wrong."

Jason furrowed his brows at the simplicity of the Gaian's answer. "Any suggestions, tough guy? Or are we just gonna conjure it out of thin air?"

"Ya did good. He'd be proud of ya," the giant reassured Darius as the boy slid down the side of the wall.

"That must have been the most difficult thing I have ever done in my entire life," he gasped, sucking in air and looked over at Annetta, Jason and Link. "Those mages all looking down. And that power. Couldn't you feel it?"

Annetta looked over at her two remaining companions who shot confused looks back at Darius. None of them had really felt anything but anger while in there.

"I think you're the only one, Darius." The girl shook her head.

"Oh…" He stood up straight feeling slightly embarrassed, "Maybe it was just the air in there, then? Uhm…let's go see to Puc."

Fixing the cloak once again, Darius marched off without another word, while the others lingered for a moment. This was not the adventure any of them had expected to embark upon. Taking one last look at the intricate doors, they then took the long spiral staircase down to the main exit of the building to collect their things.

Chapter 29

After receiving instructions on how to get to the detention center, and multiple pleas with the warden of the prison, Darius, Jason, Annetta, Brakkus and Link were led to where Puc was held. The penitentiary seemed smaller on the inside with the multitude of tiny cells tucked neatly together. The few prisoners there were kept separate from one another, and were often cuffed inside their own cells as though they could do harm within their holdings. The cell walls seemed uninviting, having been smudged in a yellowish-green tint from the fungus and moss that had built up on them from the constant exposure to the high moisture level in the air from the outside.

"The ones with extra holdings on them have protection spells engraved on the cuffs. They are mages or magic users," Darius whispered to them as they kept walking.

Once they had reached their destination, the guard halted before the door and turned to them.

"You may speak from beyond the bars, but no one is to be allowed in with the traitor," he said in a thick, gruff voice. "When you are finished, come towards me and I shall lead you out."

He took a few steps back towards where they had come from, allowing them their privacy. Annetta knew that he could hear everything they were about to say. It was more of a courtesy matter not to be hovering over their shoulder.

Puc sat on a wooden board in his room with his wrists cuffed together and his eyes closed. He remained perfectly still, and did not move until the guard went to stand a further distance away. Once he was gone, the mage opened his eyes, springing to life.

"Thank the Unknown you are alright. Did you see the Council? What did they say?" he asked almost immediately.

"Well, you're accused of stealing a magic book that holds all the knowledge of your people, and we need to find out where you put it, otherwise they ain't negotiating no alliance," Jason summarized. "So, did you actually take the book and hide it?"

Puc exhaled as if he were forced to deal with a human being who did not comprehend the existence of magic.

"As I stated before, no, I never took it. I have been in the Lab all these years. I barely ever left." The mage looked up at them and then down. "If the Toolbox does fall into the wrong hands, this could be very bad, especially if that someone hands it over to the wrong people. All of our weaknesses could be exposed, and every spell ever unlocked. Things that should never be again could walk once more unrestrained. If what you say is true, then this is not good indeed."

The rattle of chains could be heard from beyond the metal bars as Puc hunched over, his icy eyes working at the problem in his head.

"Puc, why would they think it was you in the first place?" Annetta asked. "I mean it's not like someone saw you take it."

The chains clinked once more as the mage rose from his seat, his gaze moving to the guard standing in the distance, then back to his companions. "This is true. Out of all the enemies Kaian could hold, the accusations seem to land upon me. Something does not add up, and it is safest to say you will find something of use within the academy."

Puc then turned to Darius. "Get a list of the most gifted in the arts of disguise and transformative spells. If my hunch is correct, then the culprit will most likely be someone with a talent for such things. To become someone else is not an easy task, nor is it a talent that is left unchecked. All who excel are registered in the school. You remember this well, correct?"

"Yes, master, though if I may dare to ask, is there no other way?" Darius inquired.

"None that are orthodox, and you will do this Kaian's way. There is one thing I know about the First Mage: Not complying with his rules generally makes you the enemy. Now, go. The longer you linger here, the more I have to endure the stench of this hole, and the sight of that ugly brute guarding my door."

The mage then turned to Brakkus, whose ears lay flat against his skull mournfully, feeling helpless at his friend's captivity.

"Assist them in whatever way you can," Puc said. "The sooner this thing is over, the sooner I get out."

"Just give the word, and I'll level this filthy sewer to the ground." The Hurtz pounded his breastplate with his fist.

"That, I feel, would be unwise given the current situation." Puc gave a half-hearted chuckle. "You know as well as I that we're going to need this lot in the upcoming days."

The companions were silent once they left the prison building. There was no merry chatting of any sort like when they had first arrived, just grim faces thinking about what to do. The city around them continued to bustle, taking no further notice of their eccentric presence, save for an occasional stare.

Darius led the way absentmindedly, not bothering to speak with any of the others.

Jason stopped, seeing as no one seemed to be indicating where they were going, "Well okay, we gotta go to this academy place I guess. Darius, lead the way."

Coming into a clearing from the crowd close to one of the buildings, the apprentice stopped once everyone had caught up.

"We're not going," he said grimly.

"What? What do you mean not going?" Annetta protested.

"Now listen here lad, we got a plan," Brakkus began to speak.

"What I mean to say is we are not going yet." Darius turned to face all of them. "This whole thing, it's gonna take way too long, Puc's life is in the balance. If they find more solid evidence, or if Kaian has a mood swing, he could be sentenced to death."

"Oh? We storming the castle then?" Brakkus grinned cracking his knuckles. "I'm liking this plan more."

"Not us." Darius's gaze turned to Annetta and Jason. "They are, so to speak."

"Wait, what?" Jason raised an eyebrow.

"Puc told me once of an ability all psychics can learn called Retrieving," the apprentice said.

"Ya can't be serious, lad. Ya have any idea what kinda consequences teaching them something like that can-" Brakkus interjected.

"I do, and I will do as I must to gain us every advantage in this." Darius glared at Brakkus. "Even if it means fighting dirty."

"Not when it can involve-" Brakkus began again.

"I think the Unknown can turn a blind eye for the sake of true justice," Darius snapped at him.

"Sorry to interrupt, but what are you guys even talking about?" Annetta asked.

"An ability that is a counterpart to Projection, called Retrieving," the young elf explained. "It is an ability that under normal circumstances is forbidden from being learned, but in this case I think we're going to need to make an exception and teach you guys. The ability allows the user to go into other people's minds and seek out information."

Jason shifted on the balls of his feet. He did not like the idea of going against the mage's wishes.

"Well jeeze, that doesn't sound like violating someone's privacy at all," he muttered through his teeth.

Darius exhaled deeply, not sure how else to convince the others, "It is, and that's why it is usually forbidden, and Puc never meant to teach any of you. To use this ability means you would be hunted by the host of the Unknown."

"You mean angels?" Jason asked.

"Yeah, angels." Darius nodded. "To be able to peer into someone's mind is one of the greatest sins, for it is to level yourself with the Unknown. It is the ability to know only that which he who created all worlds does, and that is blasphemy."

Jason looked down at his feet. His mind raced back to the story he had been told by his own father, and the information Puc had added afterwards. His heels screamed at him to run, but where? He looked over at Annetta, who had never felt the consequences of such a thing, and he wanted to tell her, but his voice was trapped within him. He needed to obey.

"How are we even supposed to do this?" Jason questioned after the long pause. "We never even attempted that retrieving thing when we were training."

"I guess this is one of those times we don't have training for it. We need to just go and do it," Annetta told him.

The Hurtz scratched his ear with a clawed hand, causing his earrings to jingle as he did so.

"I still don't agree with this plan completely, but I suppose I got no choice." Brakkus crossed his arms over his massive chest. "Alright, would-be mage. The stage is yers."

"Thank you, Brakkus," Darius said. "And Jason does have a point. You don't even know how to try doing it. How about...how about one of you try on me? I'm a Water Elf, so my brain will probably be the same as everyone else's there."

296

"But what if we hurt you? You're our only guide here now," Annetta reminded him.

"She's got a point. Since I've done the least here, you should try on me instead," Link stated, "If you fry my brain, at least you won't lose magic or muscle."

"Don't be so hard on yerself, lad," Brakkus laid a paw on his shoulder, "Yer more useful now than any of us."

"And your brain won't be fried. Worst case scenario, you black out for a bit," Darius reassured him, before turning to Annetta and Jason. "You'll need to try one at a time. I don't think two at once is a bright idea, and once we go in there you both need to acquire different targets so you don't go for the same mages at once."

Darius looked around at their surroundings. They were in the middle of a busy street, hardly ideal for trying to hone new psychic abilities, let alone forbidden ones.

"Let's get out of here first. Find a room at an inn." He pulled a small pouch with money out of his cloak, and motioned the others to follow him.

They continued to walk through the busy streets until Darius stopped them having found a familiar sight, 'The Steam Whistle'. Were Annetta and Jason walking alone through the city they would have discarded it completely and kept moving along for the inn was nestled tightly among other shops and housing units as though it were part of them. The aged exterior of the structure did not help either in making it seem as though it were one with the others. Only the faded wooden sign hanging by two chains gave it any sort of distinction.

The interior of the structure seemed to be the complete opposite of the run down outside. Clean bright wooden panels beamed to the companions as they strode in and the smell of freshly cut timber filled everyone's nostrils. Darius walked ahead of the others and immediately headed for the bar, where the tall, thin male innkeeper with dark hair was cleaning a tankard with a rag.

"I need a room for five for the night," Darius said, and put down five gold coins on the table before him.

The innkeeper's pale eyes went wide at the sight of all the money.

"Sir, a room is only one silver piece." He swallowed.

"My friends and I intend not to be disturbed. We have traveled far and we're weary," he said. "This is simply to ensure that peace."

He slid the coins towards the innkeeper, who put his long, slender fingers on them, taking one into his hand to examine it.

"I will make sure such service is provided, young master." He nodded. "Shall you like any dinner sent up to your room?"

"No we have an appointment later on, we simply need to rest for now," Darius told him.

"Yes of course," the innkeeper retrieved a large brass key from behind his desk, "Right this way."

₨₩

Once Darius was sure that the innkeeper was gone and out of hearing range, he locked the door and turned his attention to his companions, spread out around the room. Brakkus leaned against the wall closest to the door, propping himself up on the hilt of his sword, while Annetta and Jason sat upon the beds. Link sat on a chair facing the far window, which looked down onto the town below them.

"Okay." Darius bit his lip. "In all honesty, I have no clue how to even go about this, since I've only read about it. So this is going to mostly be you guys at work with Brakkus and I supervising."

"Hmp, if by supervision ya mean guarding the door when the screaming starts, then I can do that, lad." Brakkus smirked, "But I'm even more useless when it comes to this stuff than you."

Annetta and Jason looked at one another. The anxiety was written clearly on their faces. It made the plain room with pale sheets and light wooden boards seems to darken around them.

Darius turned his gaze to Link, who sat facing the window. From the side of his face he could see that his eyes were closed, as though he were in deep meditation.

"You sure you want to go through with this?" Darius asked him.

"No, I don't. But what other choice do we have?" He turned to look at the elf, his half crescent scar darkened by the shadow of his hair.

Darius's shadowy eyes locked with the blue ones of the youth in a heated challenge for a few moments, before he turned his gaze back to Annetta and Jason who looked down at their feet.

"Are you guys okay to start?" he asked, noting their unsure expressions.

"It's like Puc said, the longer we take, the longer we make him wait in that cell." Jason sighed, rubbing the sweat off his palms before he stood up.

298

"Can we just start instead of doing this drawn-out nervous thing?" Annetta finally snapped, getting up. "You guys are acting like Puc's dead or something. It doesn't even look like there's a death penalty for this."

"Annetta-" Darius snarled.

"No, listen. We've been doing this psychic thing for a while now, and every time we approach a new skill, Puc makes it seem like the biggest thing in the world, then after it all, he just says 'hey, you learn on the battlefield more than with me'. He said everything he taught us was a base, and you said it was a combination of projection and telepathy, so let's try it."

"But how do we...even begin to do that?" Jason raised an eyebrow.

"We experiment with it? You think I know?" Annetta groaned. "Puc said something before about a fighter only knows what weapon he's good with by knowing about all of them and choosing a favorite. I think, whatever weapons we were supposed to know about, he taught us before bringing us here. I mean I know this isn't part of what we're supposed to know, but it can't be all that different."

The entire rest of the room stood in silence.

"Orbeyus' granddaughter thee be." Brakkus chuckled. "I would have expected fear, or panic, but a speech, ho! Never."

Annetta lowered her head a little, blushing slightly as everyone else in the room came back to life.

"She's right," Link said, getting up from his seat by the window and walking towards them. "We're scared of the unknown and nothing else."

He stopped in front of Annetta, he expression neutral, hindered into anger only by the scar across his eye. Darius clasped his hands together loudly, sighing and turning attention to himself.

"Right then. So, Annetta, when you're ready, you can start first and take your time. I know this isn't easy regardless of the speech you just gave. Trust me, learning some spells is pretty tough. I can't imagine what harnessing psychic abilities must be like."

Annetta ignored the ranting, still looking at Link with full attention and pushing aside any signs of nervousness into the back of her mind.

"Ready when you are." The Gaian exhaled, looking down at his feet and then back up at her.

"Uhm...you know you don't need to stand so close," she said with a grin.

"Oh…right…well doesn't it help?" He shifted his weight on the balls of his heels and moved back, feeling embarrassed.

"No, it doesn't make a difference. You might want to sit on the bed in case I do knock you out by accident," Annetta said.

Nodding, Link lowered himself onto the bed and waited.

Annetta closed her eyes and relaxed her muscles. She then pictured Link in her mind's eye and attempted to send him a message.

'Can you hear me?' she asked.

The voice made Link jump from his seat as he looked up at her. Annetta opened her eyes for a moment to see his shocked face and smiled, closing her eyes once more.

'I'll take that as a yes. Let's see now.' She recalled in her mind's eye the use of projection, the ability to place information into another person's head. This time, however, the goal was to take information from someone.

She put herself in the role of being the one to receive information from someone. But instead of a connection with Jason, she pictured the bond with Link and waited.

Nothing seemed to happen at first. But then she felt it. Emotions that were not her own began flooding her like a fog that moved in slowly. It was almost not noticeable at first and then it hit her. Faster and faster like a thundering train, she found herself surrounded by memories and feelings that were not her own. It was like being in a file room or watching a flipbook going by.

The easiest memories to see were the freshest, like the walk through the woods and the unicorns. There were a few she could pick out that looked like Link training with a group of other youth, which she assumed to be his military companions. She felt almost as if she were there with him reliving them for herself. In addition to those, however, was something menacing. At first it was subtle, like a light pounding in the depths of her head, and so she ignored it, going through more of the memories. But the feeling progressed like the steady beating of a war drum, getting ever louder as it approached. In an instant, everything turned dark in her mind's eye, and a pair of burning red eyes and a flash of razor-like teeth blotted everything out into black. It was so sudden and terrifying that it forced Annetta to open up her eyes and gasp, in need of a grip on reality.

"You alright?" Darius gripped her arm. "What happened?"

"I...I don't know. I saw something." She shook her head, putting the image out of her mind. "It was awful, some kind of monster."

"Sometimes people's memories take things and twist them to their own perspective, or things can be symbolic of different things." He helped her sit down.

Annetta rubbed her temple and looked over at Link to see that he had already risen in an effort to help her.

"You okay?" he asked. "Did...did my brain do something...bad?"

"I don't know." She shook her head, which now pounded with the memory, "That must have been some monster you faced...was it a monster?"

Link looked like he was about to say something, but instead closed his mouth in order not to look like a gaping fool and turned away from her.

"Yeah, it was pretty bad," he said, then turned his attention to Darius. "What's the plan? Do you want them to continue?"

"Jason still needs to try," Darius replied, "but I don't think it's such a good idea for you to be the lab rat for the experiment. We don't-,"

"I think if anything it ought ta be him at this point," Brakkus interrupted. "Nothing seems to have happened to him. It was only Annetta that got affected by what she saw. I don't think whoever the robber is'll have pretty images floating about in their heads. Ya need to be able to act normal in these situations. So, Annetta, take a break and let Jason try."

Annetta did not argue and sat down on the bed without further discussion. Link took his place again and Jason turned his attention to the task at hand. She watched as Darius instructed Jason a bit, encouraging her friend. She found Darius a much easier teacher to get along with than Puc, who continuously chastised them for their faults.

"I thought you didn't know anything about psychic abilities, Hurtz." Darius looked up at the giant after a moment.

"I don't, but I know war and I know that acting like yer scared will draw attention to ya. One needs to be able to keep a cool head," he grunted, shifting his massive blade from one paw to another. "And that can be learned with practice. So, practice on, because we don't have all day."

Darius nodded and turned his attention back to his other friends. The trio gazed back at him with looks of eagerness.

"Okay, let's learn to put on a poker face then, shall we?" he said, clasping his hands again and they continued.

స‌ిCR

After a few hours of practice, just enough to get both Annetta and Jason comfortable with some of the images they might see when they enter a person's head, Darius and Brakkus decided it was time for them to go and visit the Mage Academy.

Leaving Puc's horse with the innkeeper and taking their own, they rode to the Mage Academy on the other side of the city, isolated from the bustle of the central area. Though it was called the Mage Academy, it was also where soldiers learned their craft and others who wished to advance their knowledge went. It was most famous for training mages, so the name stuck. Surrounded by a smooth white stone wall, the structure very much reminded Annetta of pictures she had seen of one of the old universities in Toronto. There was a dignified air to the mass of vine-crept buildings that were spread out all along the open field that was encased by the wall, unpolluted by the streets of the city.

Arriving before the main building, a tall structure of dark brown wood and grey stone, which looked much like an old gothic mansion to Annetta and Jason, the companions got off of their mounts and began to have a closer look around at their surroundings. The area seemed dead with no signs of movement anywhere. Their scouting however, was interrupted by the sound of boots thundering across the stone paths towards them moments later.

"Halt! State your business at the academy!" Two sentries at the front of the gate stepped before them, wearing the same uniforms as the ones that had arrested Puc, their staves aimed at the group threateningly. Noting the guards' distress at the newcomers, Darius stepped forward, taking charge as the representative for his group once more.

"We are here to see Nathaniel Guildwood, concerning the case of Puc Thanestorm," Darius stated, stepping forward from the group. "I am the apprentice of Puc Thanestorm, Darius Silver, and these are my companions Brakkus the Hurtz, Lincerious Heallaws, Jason Kinsman and Annetta Severio."

Hearing the two last names, the guards muttered something to one another, then frowned and turned back towards them.

"Very well." They lowered their staves.

Darius nodded watching the two lookouts return to their posts. He then turned to his companions, motioning for them to follow him further with the

302

wave of his hand. After locating the stables to have their horses taken care of, they ventured back to the main building. Inside it was crowded with elves both young and old, dressed in robes similar to that of Puc and Darius. Many were bent over thick books or running from one place to another, completely oblivious to their presence, or very good at hiding it.

"Man, it's like we're surrounded by thirty-six flavors of Puc," Jason whispered to Annetta, who giggled a bit.

"Not quite, but everyone would wish to be as great a mage here as Thanestorm was," a male voice interrupted them.

They turned around to see the source of the voice, a man in brown and green robes with a thin face and a long black beard lined with silver hairs. Darius recognized the man instantly and bowed.

"Master Guildwood, " the youth said with his eyes to the ground. "These are my companions here, Brakkus the Hurtz, Lincerious Heallaws, Jason Kinsman and Annetta Severio."

"A pleasure to meet you all, and to finally meet the heirs of Orbeyus and Arcanthur." Guildwood smiled at the others who stood there. "Welcome to Aldamoor. And you can get up, boy. I'm not your master anymore. I'm just an old school teacher. And just where is Thanestorm?"

"That is why we are here, sir." Darius rose to his feet. "Puc has been accused of stealing Chiron's Toolbox, and the First Mage said if we wished to help, then to come here and investigate."

"What? That is an outrage! Thanestorm would never... how is that possible? The last time he was in Aldamoor was before the death of Orbeyus, and he said he would not come back until the heir of Orbeyus and son of Arcanthur would return." Guildwood stopped and looked at the shield Annetta still held in her hand. "I refuse to believe it was him. I've known him since he was a boy. I trained him through all his years. Thanestorm was many things but the thief of the Toolbox, never."

He began pacing back and forth, his brow furrowed, speaking mostly to himself. "He wanted me to be there with you when he asked to renew the alliance. I was the only one who knew of his arrival in advance. Unknowns bane! It does not make sense! He didn't even care when he was finally granted permission to be allowed to see the Toolbox. He said he had learned enough from other books alone, and there was no point in him unearthing the mistakes of the past, for some things are best left forgotten. He said those words!"

"Was there anyone who didn't like Puc, or could have wanted to frame him?" Darius asked.

"I can think of a few people," muttered Jason quietly, only to feel a slap on the back of the head by Brakkus.

"Well what? It's true," Jason insisted. "The guy is about the grumpiest person I know, constantly snapping at us with sarcasm. I mean, let's be honest. We only need the guy as a guide."

"Ye'd understand why he is the way he is, lad, if ya spent a day in his shoes," Brakkus grunted at the boy grimly before turning his attention back to Guildwood.

"Didn't like him?" Guildwood ran a hand through his beard. "He was considered a legend after the Great War, and a key help in bringing down Mordred. There isn't a mage here who wouldn't have wanted to be like him."

Guildwood looked around at the busy hallways, distracted by the sight of his students, gaping at his ranting. Feeling their eyes on him, he cleared his throat surveying the room as everyone returned to their tasks and he turned back to the companions.

"Perhaps we could go to my office and speak there, it will be slightly quieter," he offered.

"That would be much appreciated, sir." Darius nodded as they followed the old man up the stairs.

୫୬୯

Much like the rest of everything in Aldamoor, the gadgets in Guildwood's office were all powered by water and steam, or possibly magic. Tall wooden shelves with massive leather bound books filled every wall from top to bottom, and the smell of old paper and pine filled the air. Seating themselves on the chairs provided, the companions looked upon Guildwood from behind his desk.

"Is there anyone at all you can think of that could have had something against my master? Maybe a rival from his own days of being an apprentice?" Darius asked once more. "When I saw him before coming here, he mentioned wanting me to look into all those registered for excelling in transformative spells, in case someone took his shape to steal the book."

"Hmm," Guildwood looked into the ripples inside one of the water filled contraptions on his desk. "Now that I think about it, Kaian was never very fond of Puc when they were training together. Kaian believed in being the strongest while Puc always took a more patient approach and wore out his opponent, outwitting him. We will always have rivals, it seems."

"Wait, the same guy who is on the council?" Jason raised an eyebrow. "That Kaian?"

"Well there isn't a fairy godmother out there, if that is what you are asking," Guildwood replied dryly. "Kaian is the descendant of the mythic figure of Chiron. He has always stressed that. He reveres in the fact that he is of such an important bloodline, and it killed him that Puc was a more skilled mage than he. Puc being so talented meant he could have become the First Mage had Kaian proven insufficient at his art, and for a time he did. It was a great burden riding upon the shoulders of Kaian, for his family has held the seat for...well since the great city first came into being. You have no idea how much he loved it when Puc was chosen by Orbeyus to be his advisor. He was practically jumping for joy, knowing his rule would not be threatened."

"So could he have done it then?" Link asked. "He seems to be the prefect guy."

"Why would Kaian steal something that he practically owns? It is lunacy," Guildwood replied. "As the descendant of Chiron, he essentially has sole ownership of the tome and could take it whenever he wants. He would gain nothing from stealing it, and could not have done so to place blame on Puc, as he did not even know Puc was returning."

"Did he know my master was coming here?" Darius suggested. "Maybe he got someone to frame him because he was scared that Puc would challenge him for the right of being First Mage."

"No one aside from myself knew," Guildwood said to the apprentice. "I was the only one who received the letter from him, and that letter has remained here in my custody the entire time."

"So if he didn't know and had no reason to steal it..." Annetta concluded before retreating completely into her thoughts.

"It was someone who may have wanted to get back at Kaian." Darius looked up at him and bit his lip in remembrance. "I think I may know who did it and I know for a fact he was pretty good in the transformative arts from our classes together. Does Kaine still go to the Academy?"

"Kaine? No, he dropped out a few weeks ago." Guildwood stopped as his eyes widened. "About the time the tome went missing, now that I think about it."

Darius rose from his seat as though he were struck by lighting.

"Where is he?" he questioned.

"Kaine? Possibly by the airship docks, I'm not sure now that he is no longer part of the Academy. You know how much his father hated his desire to become an airship pilot. He said all those from the line of Chiron had been mages, and nothing would change that because it was their responsibility to keep up their heritage." Guildwood paused. "You're not thinking he would have actually…"

"I don't know, sir. What I do know is that we need to find him." Darius gritted his teeth with impatience.

"Even if you do find him, how are you going to get a confession out of him?" the older mage asked.

"We won't get it out of him through conventional means, if that is what you are asking." Brakkus flashed him a grin, to which Guildwood's face paled.

"You're going to torture him?"

"No," Darius sighed, shooting Brakkus a glance. "Not really, anyways. I plan to bind him and use a truth spell to get it out. Annetta and Jason can help with the binding, as they are psychics."

Guildwood's beard glided across his robes as he turned to Annetta and Jason, who sat quietly on the two stools they were given beside Link and Darius.

"You both have the gift?" he asked, to which they nodded. "You've been taught how to use it?"

"Puc has been teaching," Jason stated. "Well, more like drilling us to learn it."

"Do you know how to create psychic fire yet?" Guildwood ran his fingers through his beard, twirling the ends.

"I…no we haven't." Jason looked down, feeling somewhat ashamed.

"Hrm. No need to feel bad, young one. Most psychics don't learn how to use psychic fire until they are old men and women. From what I've been told, it took Arieus and Arcanthur well into their prime to learn and control it. I'm surprised you both know how to use any abilities as it is," he said, his gaze turning back to Darius, who looked as though he were being bathed in boiling water. "Dock one fifty four. Speak with Captain Weaver. He is a close friend of Kaine's. It might be a good starting point."

306

"Thank you, sir." Darius nodded and after a bow headed for the door without further conversation.

Chapter 30

Once out of the mage training quarters, Darius wasted no time in leading them straight to the docking area for the airships, a collection of platforms located high above the city. Leaving their horses behind, they walked up the rickety ramps. The majority of the crafts looked like old zeppelins Annetta had seen on television or in books, only these ones looked far less glamorous, with large mismatched patches where holes had been mended and rust had begun to form, most likely from the overexposure to the water from the falls.

"Most of these are cargo ships. They're not exactly the pride of Aldamoor," Darius told her. "If we have time, you should go see the military ships. Those are a sight to behold."

Darius looked up at the signs above that indicated which port they were at as he continued to move forward, searching for dock area one fifty four. His mind was so focused on the task at hand that he almost ended up passing it, had Brakkus not grabbed him by the scruff of his robes and placed him in front of the sign with a massive swing.

"When yer looking for something, make sure ya find it in the end." The Hurtz grinned.

"I'll keep that in mind for future reference," Darius responded snidely, and walked onto the platform to which the dock was connected.

"He's really taken this mission to heart," Link said, looking up at the Hurtz.

"Puc is the only kinda family the lad has." Brakkus looked over at the youth searching the docks. "His folks died, and he was sent to become a mage as an orphan because no one would take him in. When he was old enough, Puc came along and took him under his wing as his apprentice. As ya heard, Puc's a kinda hero around here. To be glanced at by someone like him, even for a second, is praise enough. To have him take ya under his wing…it's more than he coulda hoped for."

Link turned his attention to Darius off in the distance, followed by Annetta and Jason close behind. It made him wonder why he was with them to begin with. He felt the weight of Brakkus's paw land on his shoulder.

"Something ails you boy. Speak," he said.

"I don't know what my own worth in this is. I feel like a ghost," Link sighed.

308

"Ghost? Hardly, lad," Brakkus scoffed. "A ghost would not have offered to have his head pried open for the greater good."

"It doesn't feel like enough, though," Link growled. "I mean, the only reason I offered to help with them learning to retrieve was because I'm well aware that I'm disposable at this point, and someone had to do it. This is not what I was trained to be doing. I was trained to fight, to protect, and to work as a team."

"You were also, as I recall trained to know patience," Brakkus stated. "If ye've not noticed boy, I've done just as little as you this entire time, and I'm not complaining."

Link looked up at the hulking form of the Hurtz. Though he had not realized it until this moment, he had been right. The two of them had done next to nothing, except stand watch over the events unfolding before them.

"One of a warrior's greatest strength is in observing his surroundings and knowing when the time is right to strike," Brakkus continued. "To charge blindly will getcha killed. Ya must learn to control yer impulse to act before ya think. Until yer able to do that, consider yerself nothing more than brainless rabble." He turned his massive head in the direction the others were wandering as airships passed in the background, ignorant of the life around them. Link relaxed his shoulders in defeat.

"What should I do, then?" he asked.

"Follow and bare yer teeth when necessary like a good pup." Brakkus stated and took off to follow the others to their destination.

Darius had located a crewman aboard the deck, and had begun to question him.

"I'm looking for a Captain Weaver," he asked. "Do you happen to know where he is?"

Link and Brakkus quickly caught up with the group after their exchange of words, making the trio appear that much more menacing with an additional person and the Hurtz in their midst. The look on the elf's face seemed paled by the sight of the expanding group before him. Before he could respond, a voice ringed out from behind him.

"If you mean Captain Jenna Weaver, then she is here." A woman with short strawberry blonde hair and a mechanized monocle gazed down from the entrance of the airship behind her. "Speak, and perhaps I can be of service."

The companions turned to look at one another, a little shocked, not expecting Weaver to be a woman. Darius shook it off.

"I'm Darius Silver, this is Annetta Severio, Jason Kinsman, Lincerious Heallaws and Brakkus the Hurtz. We're looking for Kaine Chironson to ask him some questions about the disappearance of Chrion's Toolbox, and his whereabouts when it happened," he explained.

The captain came down from the platform and strode towards the group in a challenging tone, stopping right before Darius. She was no taller than him, but she appeared a giant in the way she carried herself with her broad shoulders out, blue cape flowing behind her and the natural scowl on her face.

"I've not seen him for a few days, to be honest," she said. "Last I saw him he was planning a trip to the falls to collect herbal samples for the mages."

"Were you aware that he had left them?" Darius looked her directly in the eye.

From behind, Jason nudged Annetta quietly.

'Look into her mind.'

She glanced at him with a frown, wondering what he could be up to, but did as he said. She bent down as if to tie her shoe, and once she was masked by Darius's cape, closed her eyes and began the process of entering the head of the woman before her. The first thing she realized was that Weaver was not a woman at all. It took her only a few moments to realize whom it was from the memories unfolding before her, like pages of a book. She caught a quick glimpse of the taking of the tome before she was forced to stop. She exited the mind before her, and stood up as casually as possible.

'Did you already go in?' She looked at Jason.

Jason looked her from the side and nodded slightly.

"No, I had no idea he'd left." Weaver smiled calmly.

"Darius, that's not the Captain," Annetta interrupted.

"What?" he turned around.

Before anyone could say anything else, Weaver pulled a pistol from her back and opened fire at Darius, who ducked out of the way, but not enough. The metal ball from the pistol lodged itself deep inside his shoulder, splitting bone and flesh as he howled in pain. Weaver ran for it as those around them began to panic from the sound of a gunshot.

Annetta knelt down beside Darius, helping him up.

"Stop wasting time, Anne! He's getting away," he growled. "I can heal this! Get a move on it!"

She rose and looked around, seeing that Link had already taken off in a dead run with Jason in an attempt to keep sight of Kaine. Saying nothing more, she raced after them, her heart pounding in her chest.

୫୦୧

Kaine, who at this point had changed back to his normal self, ran past the various docks, winding, creating the path of greatest difficulty for his pursuers. Entering a crowd of people who had begun fleeing when the shot went off, he paused, no longer seeing his opponent, slowing to the pace of the masses around him.

'Damn outsiders. No doubt father's work.' Seeing no one following him, he continued along in a more relaxed manner to further lead them away from his trail.

୫୦୧

Running like mad and breathless because of it, Annetta came to a halt, her brown hair matted with sweat from chasing Kaine. Jason and Link stopped alongside her, seeing their friend catching air in her lungs.

"We won't be able to find him like this," Link breathed, leaning against one of the buildings.

"Damn it! There has to be a way," Annetta snarled, as she got ready to take off again, "We almost had him…"

The trio ran until they were engulfed in a crowd of elves, and slowed their pace so they wouldn't bump into too many people and acquire more rude stares than they already had. Leaving the tiny streets, they came into a larger opening. From the many stalls and massive crates dispersed around them, it looked to be a market. Moving from side to side, they finally slinked out into an area that was a little less crowded to stop and organize themselves.

"Well, this is just peachy," groaned Jason, throwing his arms up in defeat. "We're never going to find him."

Annetta ran her fingers through her tangled mass of hair. "There's gotta be something else we can do."

"Like what?" Jason questioned. "I mean, I can't tell you where we are, or what direction he could have gone, because we're surrounded by people."

Link moved to the side as a man in a top hat and cloak ran by him without a word. "Okay, if he's here, then he's in the same predicament, since we're not seeing anyone thrown aside in order to escape."

"So, he's hiding?" Annetta said, putting it together. "But if he is, then maybe he changed back, and then we don't even know who we're looking for."

"Even better," muttered Jason.

As the two of them talked, Link spotted a familiar blue cape, and tapped Annetta on the shoulder. "I think we may have found our shape-changer."

Annetta and Jason turned their attention to the tall blonde man walking away briskly, his white shirt ripped in the seams and a cape seeming a little too small for the massive figure.

"J.K. go around on the other side to cut him off. Link and I will take the back," Annetta instructed formulating the plan in her head.

ॐ

Kaine walked past the crowded streets of Aldamoor when someone blocked his path.

"You know, where I come from, people don't take it well when you shoot at them." The youth with shaggy brown hair grinned at him.

Kaine snarled, showing a mouth of teeth, and pulled out the pistol once more. As he was about to fire, it flew out of his hands into the air. He looked to the side to see the young girl and the other boy with her. The people around them began scattering like frantic ants upon seeing the gun in the air, which landed upon the cobblestone ground some feet away from Kaine. The life in the market place died, and the elf found himself alone surrounded by the foreigners.

"Disarming me doesn't mean a damn thing." Kaine brought his hands together and muttered something, sending a wave of what appeared to be shards of glass at them.

On instinct, Annetta stretched her hand out in an effort to stop the shards, but when nothing happened, leapt behind the closest stack of crates, taking Link with her.

"What the hell? Why didn't it work?" There was panic in her voice.

"Nerves maybe?" Link suggested, to which Annetta frowned. "Or a protective charm," he offered. "He is a mage in training. Or was."

Annetta furrowed her brows as the assault continued. It was not a good enough explanation for her, but they had no time to dwell on it. Glancing back, she noted they were close to the end of the market. After that, it broke off into an enclosure with buildings. Gears turning in her head, Annetta turned to look over at Link.

"Can you sneak up behind him or something?" she asked. "Looks like there might be a way around those buildings where he won't see you, like the shortcut we take to school."

"I don't know. I'll try." He nodded.

Annetta turned to where she thought Jason was, focusing her thoughts. *'Can you help divert Kaine's attention for a moment? I want to get Link to try and sneak up on him.'*

'On it,' Jason informed her, and stuck his head up when the rain of glass stopped, "My little brother has better aim than you, and he just uses elastic bands!"

"I'll show you aim when I tear off your face!" Kaine sneered at the insult, and sent another stream of glass at him.

Link took that as his cue to leave, and headed off into the streets.

'So Anne, what's plan B?' Jason sent the message from the other side, glancing at the side of the box. It was beginning to come apart under the constant beating of glass.

'Haven't thought that far ahead.' A sigh filled her thoughts as they were assaulted again, and she noted the condition of the boxes she sat behind. *'How about you toss 'em left, and I toss 'em right?'*

'Better than getting a piercing sitting here.' Jason shrugged and turned his attention to their foe. *'Makes you think. Where's this whole army Kaian has searching for the book too, eh? Anyways...On three?'*

'With the amount of people you saw running,' Annetta replied, *'it might take them a while to tear through the crowd. We're on our own now. And yeah. Three!'* She then used psychic force to toss the crates she had hidden behind at Kaine, while Jason did the same.

Sidetracked, the mage was forced to give up on his spell and block the objects thrown at him, causing them to explode into splinters that scattered all over the square. Gritting his teeth, he created what looked like a ball of electric energy, his eyes filled with its reflection as he glared at the two of them.

Annetta and Jason looked at one another, and with a quick nod both disappeared from Kaine's sight.

"Over here!" Annetta called from the left side of Kaine's peripheral vision.

Kaine turned around and threw the ball of electricity at her, but she was gone before it reached her. The elf hissed, watching the blast explode and hit nothing more than an empty shop, its contents flying through the air and scattering on the cobblestone. Turning around again, he looked behind him, wondering if she was there.

"Look up! Waaaaaay up!" Jason yelled from one of the rooftops behind him.

"Hold still, you runts!" he snarled, creating another ball and throwing it at Jason, his effort again in vain as he vanished before the ball collided with him. The roof shattered and sparkled with the impact of energy.

This cycle of evasion lasted for some time longer. Annetta and Jason seemed to dance around the market, teleporting from side to side, up and down, never in the same pattern, while Kaine tried to take them out with blasts of electric energy that destroyed all they touched.

Meanwhile, Link positioned himself in one of the dark alleyways, watching the battle dart back and forth, waiting for his opening so he could immobilize the mage. The longer he waited, the slower he seemed to move, as though he was being worn out. The fight seemed to come to a momentary halt as Kaine ran out of energy, panting heavily. Annetta and Jason teleported to a rooftop directly facing the elf some distance away, and waited for his next move. Link looked up to where they currently were, and smiled.

"Come down and fight me!" Kaine howled, puffing like a mad beast.

"Make us." Annetta stuck her tongue out at him and giggled.

Kaine gritted his teeth, ready to throw another blast when Link appeared and snatched his wrists, holding them behind his back with all his strength. Annetta teleported down and looked at Jason.

"Go back to Darius and Brakkus," Annetta formulated the next part of the plan. "Tell them we got him here in the market, and try getting them here if Darius is okay. I'll stay here with Link and make sure Kaine doesn't get away."

"Right, on it." Jason nodded and was gone.

314

It did not take long for Jason to return with Brakkus, who carried Darius in his arms like a child, running at full speed.

"Ya kids alright?" Brakkus asked, coming to a stop and letting go of Darius, who marched straight over to Kaine and began padding down his pockets.

"Er, what are ya doing, lad?" Brakkus asked

"Finding the amulet," Darius hissed, as he found a small pendant carved from wood resembling a small straight spiraling horn, and pulled it free. "Now try restraining him using your psychic abilities."

Annetta turned her attention to Kaine and focused on binding all his muscles to be frozen the position they were at. It was no different than moving the stones when they practiced, except now the object she had in mind was a body, and she did not want that body to move.

"You got him?" Link asked, feeling Kaine freeze up under his grip.

"Yeah, I think so." She nodded.

Moments later, guards had arrived the vicinity, surrounding them.

"Arrest them! These foreign-," Kaine began to snarl.

"What is the meaning of this?" Kaian's voice echoed from the crowd of soldiers, seeming to part it as he stepped through.

"Sir!" Darius started, while applying pressure to the wound on his shoulder, "We have information about the Toolbox. We know for a fact that it is your son who stole it, assuming the guise of Puc to pin it on him due to your history with him."

Kaian looked at his son, hot fury pounding through his pale face. He walked closer to the young man and looked him in the eye.

"Is what Darius saying true?" he asked.

"Father, who are you going to believe? Your own son or some children who just waltzed in?" Kaine snapped, unable to move.

Kaian turned to look at the group standing opposite to his son with the Hurtz towering behind them.

"Sir," Darius started, "I saw with my own eyes that he can shape shift. He was hiding in the docks under an assumed identity, having left the academy the same time the Toolbox went missing, according to Guildwood. Were he innocent, what reason would he have to shoot me and destroy half the market while trying to kill my friends?"

"You can shape shift? You know this is truly a rare gift in our people. Why did you not say anything?" he snapped, letting go of his son's arm.

"Because I knew the moment I spoke up, you'd insist on making me join your stupid council!" Kaine hissed. "I never wanted to be a mage, and yet you forced me to go to your stupid academy, because that was what was expected. You didn't even bother to listen to my dreams. All you cared about was what was expected of me. You want to know why I stole your precious tome? I did it with no other motive than to seriously wrack your nerves."

Kaian's gaze turned back to his son, his pale eyes fixed on him like a rabid animal. He reached out and grabbed his son by the arm, locking eyes with him and muttering an incantation no one could hear. Kaine could do nothing more than stare into his father's eyes as all his secrets came undone before him.

Annetta felt goosebumps form on her arms as she watched what was happening. She came up close to Darius and whispered in his ear, "I thought reading someone's mind was forbidden."

"The First Mage acts as an agent of the Unknown. He's pretty much got free reign to do as he likes. Which is why you don't want to get on his bad side."

Seeing the last part in his minds eye as he read his son's mind, Kaian's lips curled. The composed elder released Kaine, a note of failure visible in his eyes, and turned the legion of guards surrounding everyone.

"You three, take him away to the prison. Have Puc Thanestorm released and brought to the council meeting room. Brakkus, you may take Silver to the infirmary at the academy. He will be treated there by a medic. The rest of you, follow me," he ordered turning on his heel with his staff in hand.

As everyone went their separate ways, Annetta, Jason and Link stood routed to the ground, uncertain of where to go, watching Kaian leave.

"By the rest of you, I meant everyone at the scene, heir of Orbeyus, son of Arcanthur, and he who is cursed." Kaian's voice rang from the distance.

Without needing further prompting, the trio rushed after the small platoon of guards. They did not need to walk long, for Kaian paused at what looked like a small shack, meant to hold supplies for the airships. Grabbing his staff in both hands, Kaian broke through the rotting wooden door then unlocked the lock from the inside. Throwing open the door, he marched in without so much as a flinch from the flying dust. Gliding past the assortment of mechanical parts, ropes, and other odds and ends he came to a large chest.

By this point, Annetta, Jason, and Link had managed to get around the soldiers, and ran inside after Kaian, who stood in front of the trunk that lay on the ground before him. The only thing that could be heard inside the room was the elder's breathing, still full of rage, unable to come to a normal pace.

"I knew he was unhappy where he was," he said, quietly. "I myself never wanted to accept the responsibility when I was younger. To be of Chiron's line means you have an inescapable duty. Others view you as the icon, the founder of civilization, and an uncrowned king."

For a moment, Annetta felt a heavy wave of thoughts crush her. Being one man's descendant had forced her into the responsibility that lay ahead. She was not much different from Kaine.

"Sometimes we don't have a choice," she said. "We just have to work with the cards dealt to us the best way we can, and hope that we can do what was asked to the best of our abilities. Your son didn't want to do that."

Kaian's eyes widened as he looked down at the young girl standing in front of him as though a blade had struck him. His eyes then saddened, after he'd taken in everything she had just said.

"Clearly put, heir of Orbeyus." He curled his lips into a faux smile. "You are very perceptive for one so young, but you lack the experience of years in order to truly understand the way it all works."

Kaian unlocked the chest, and pulled out a large leather-bound book. He ran his hand over the inlaid gold words on the cover, exhaling deeply.

"This lack of experience. I will try to help fill in on your quest," he stated. "You may go now and meet with your friends in the mage training grounds. I will summon for you once the tome is secure in its rightful place, and once I have had a chance to apologize to Puc for my rash thinking."

Chapter 31

Upon his release, Puc was escorted to Kaian's office by two guards on either side. He had been told very little, save that the true thief had been caught and the tome restored. After knocking, he entered the office of the descendant of Chiron. Kaian looked out the window of the tower with his back turned to him.

"I could have foreseen many things, but the betrayal of Kaine was not among them," the elder said after a moment, before turning to face Puc, who stood in the doorway, both hands on the neck of his staff.

"Kaine stole the book?" The mage said with a look of surprise, "But why? He was your son, wasn't he in training to become a mage and your successor?"

Kaian lowered himself into his chair with the weight of the world on his shoulders as he looked up at the younger-looking mage. Though they were the same age, Puc had chosen to remain youthful, while Kaian had allowed time to eat away at him. Inside them both, however, dwelt the same amount of knowledge and power.

"He was. But it is not that great of a loss. There is always someone else that can be seated upon the First Mage throne." Kaian sighed, taking a few pieces of parchment and shuffling them around his desk. "Chironson blood is plentiful in Aldamoor."

"You speak as though Kaine is already dead," Puc said, leaning against his staff.

"He is dead to me after the atrocity he brought about," Kaian snapped, "To hate the duty of becoming the next leader of Aldamoor is one thing, to steal Chiron's Toolbox is another. Now, this is not the reason I brought you here. Tell me, why have you brought these children into my midst?"

Puc strode closer to the desk and produced a photograph from his robes, handing it to Kaian. On it, barely visible in the dark of space, was an enormous fortress. Kaian only needed to glance for a moment before recognizing its shape. He dropped the picture onto his desk, staring in disbelief before he looked back up to face Puc.

"When was this taken, and under how strong of a telescope?" he asked.

"It is in the orbit of the Earth. Undetectable by human eyes, but my apprentice was able to unmask it. We prepare for war with he who should have died years ago. I warned Orbeyus this would occur. Mislantus returns

318

for vengeance, to rule all worlds. A Leonemas attacked the boy a few days ago. Those don't just appear at random. They are brought into the world by someone who can summon them, someone who wants access to the Eye to All Worlds."

Kaian looked down at the photo again in silence, taking in everything Puc was telling him.

"Kaian," Puc added. "I do not come here to make games. You know how dire the situation can become if he is not stopped. Vengeance is not a sword with a dull edge."

"I know you would not come without such a purpose, Thanestorm. I simply now worry," Kaian's pale eyes met with Puc's own as he smiled bitterly. "You didn't think I would continue to harbor all that hate from those years when we trained, did you? The way I see it, you got the short end of the stick, babysitting brats for Orbeyus and living in that forsaken base you call The Lab."

Puc smirked, hearing Kaian's summarization of his duties. The elder handed the photograph back to Puc.

"I swore to Orbeyus years ago that I would trust the words of his advisor as though they were his own. The way I see it, you still are, considering his heir walks with you." He stated. "I simply wanted to test her and the boy, nothing more. What better way than to help with events that were already taking place?"

ഇരു

After Darius's wound had been tended to, the group took the time to fill in Guildwood, who was impressed by the quick thinking of the trio. Shortly after, Kaian summoned them to the council's headquarters. Puc was already waiting for them, standing beside Kaian. The elf mage wore the same cold demeanour on his face as always as he watched them enter the room, his hands no longer bound in cuffs like when they had last seen him.

"Those of us gathered today take part in a monumental event, which will shape the course of tomorrow," Kaian spoke, in a fluent and clear tone. "Many centuries ago, a man by the name of Adeamus Severio and his friend Demetrius Kinsman happened upon us in their journeys. They asked for the help of the elves, for our assistance in the preservation of the freedom of all worlds. And so it was for centuries that we aided the Severio and Kinsman warriors. It was not long ago we stood by Orbeyus Severio, a warrior the world will never forget, and his son Arieus, from whom today comes

Orbeyus's heir, Annetta Severio, accompanied by the son of Arcanthur Kinsman, comrade to Arieus, Jason Kinsman. I now ask on behalf of the Water Elves of Aldamoor, what is it that you seek, young Severio and Kinsman?"

Annetta and Jason froze, unsure of what to say and taken aback by the professional tone which Kaian was addressing them in. They were expecting a simple swearing in, not an entire ceremony. They looked at one another and nodded.

"We come here," Annetta started, "like those who came before us, for your help. Mordred had a son, Mislantus, who my grandfather spared. Now it looks like he might be back to finish what his father started. I need to free Severbane from its resting place, and reunite the Four Forces once more. So I'm asking, and I know I don't look like someone who knows much, but that's why I'm here in the first place, for the old ways to be restored. I need the help of those who do know."

Kaian looked over at Puc and nodded. He rose from his seat followed by all those were seated in the rows around him. Coming down the stairs, Kaian came towards Annetta and Jason and knelt before them, the other mages kneeling beside their seats right after him in a single motion, like waves on a sea.

"In the one who is severed we trust. Our lives to you until we are dust. What is ours we give onto you to use. Our strength and wisdom, use as you choose," the multitude of voices echoed in the room around them.

Annetta felt a chill go down her spine as she looked around the circular room at all the mages standing in their long robes, each with their own ornate staff. It had finally hit her, the seriousness of the situation at hand. This was no longer a dream, or a figment of her imagination. She was standing in a foreign land.

"It is done. We will take up arms against Mislantus when you've reunited those of us that created the Four Forces. Good luck, young warriors, and may the Unknown watch over you." Kaian spoke for a final time before taking his seat. "You are free to come and go to Aldamoor as much as you like. Do not feel estranged from us."

Puc descended from where he stood beside Kaian to join his comrades.

"We thank you Kaian, descendant of Chiron who created this world. We will return when time allows." He bowed before the council.

Jason and Annetta bowed right after, so they would not seem rude. The others in the group followed their lead.

∞🞔

The way back to Severio Castle was filled with more chatter than when they arrived, this time about the events that had transpired in the short time they had spent there. The day was coming to an end around them, with the sun setting behind the waterfall.

"Uhm, so how do we find the portal for the way back?" Jason said, interrupting the chatter. "Like, I know some portals are tears in the world and whatnot, but how do we find one to get back from here?"

Everyone drew their horse to a halt except for Puc and Brakkus, who continued on going as though they had not heard Jason's comment.

"Uhm...is there something we missed?" Annetta raised an eyebrow.

"We need to find it," Puc called from up ahead.

"Man, are you saying we're stuck here until we find a portal to take us home?" Jason whined, until something tapped him on the shoulder. "WHAT?"

Link pointed silently to what looked like a stone arch, barely visible from beyond the trees. Jason urged his horse to the other side to see it was similar to the arch in the castle. Brakkus and Puc's horses stood beside it, waiting for the others to catch up.

"Well, that wasn't there before," Jason said, dimly.

"No, you are just not very observant. It was here. This arch has stood here for years, but the portal within it only becomes active once the oath is sworn to the new Severio," Puc explained. "Hurry up, now. We haven't got all day."

Urging their horses, the group descended down the slope to meet with the elven mage and the Hurtz. Charging through the gate, they made their way back. In an instant, the forest scenery faded as Annetta opened her eyes, seeing that they were back in Severio Castle once more.

Puc descended from his horse and grabbed the reins of the animal, patting its muzzle. He turned his gaze to the gates, which gave off a faded blue glow. Saying nothing, he proceeded to walk his horse down the ramp. Instead of going all the way down, he stopped and went into the room where the sword was stored.

Annetta followed to see the room filled with the same dull blue light that surrounded the arch where the portal to Aldamoor was. She peered closer to see the symbol on the pedestal that looked like three rain drops was lit up with the blue glow.

"Water, the first element restored to the Four Forces," Puc stated. "Our next mission will be to the Minotaur clans in Morwick. Tonight, however, you will need to rest. I dare say our expedition has been tiring, to say the least."

Annetta simply nodded, entranced by the shining symbol in the stone. Her shaggy head shifted down to look at her feet moments later when she remembered something else she had wanted to say.

"Puc," she said.

"Yes?"

"I'm sorry...if it seems like Jason and I take what you tell us lightly or for granted at times. It's just that...well," she tried to find the right words to say.

"You're a juvenile delinquent. It's what you are supposed to do," he said wryly, looking down at her. "You're not much different from your father, and I remember him when he was just your age."

Annetta raised an eyebrow and turned around to look at Puc, only to see he was already exiting the room.

"I know I was told not to ask, but how old are you exactly?" she called after him.

"Very. Let's leave it at that, young Severio."

க்இ

Once in the Lab, everyone dispersed in order to set to the tasks that needed doing before they retired for the evening. Annetta, Jason, and Link had headed off to the armory in order to put away the shield, then walked together to the exit, while Darius went to put away the potions he and Puc had taken with them. Brakkus attended to the horses while Puc sat at a distance on a chair, watching his companion deal with the beasts.

"Ya sure ya don't want to come here and try?" Brakkus teased his companion, knowing full well Puc's unease around the creatures due to an accident in his youth.

"No, and a thousand times more, no," Puc answered in a casual manner.

"I don't understand ya, mage." Brakkus shook his head. "Ya ride the bloody beasts, but anything more than that, and ya won't stand within ten feet of them."

"I never said I enjoyed it, Hurtz. I do it because it is a necessity," he responded, adjusting his grip on the staff.

"Bah," spat Brakkus. "I bet yer way over that whole ordeal, and ya just don't wanna have to deal with the horses, because ye don't want to dirty yer pretty little hands."

Puc rolled his eyes upon hearing the comment. "Oh yes, just as you don't enjoy wracking your brain when you're injured by looking through the potion cabinet. Instead, you're at the infirmary trying to patch up a wound with a band aid when it needs to be sewn shut."

Brakkus gave a hearty laugh, hearing the thick sarcasm in the mage's voice, and turned back to brushing out the horse's coats.

"I have to say," Puc began again, changing the subject, "I did not expect things to sort out as rapidly as they did. It was sheer luck for them to have found out who did it, and so quickly. The Unknown alone played his hand in it."

"Yeah, them kids be lucky for it." Brakkus nodded absentmindedly.

"I mean, for them to have found Kaine based on the simple fact that he could shift...there were hundreds of candidates in those papers, it was not just coincidence." Puc continued rambling mostly to himself. "It should have taken days. Tell me, who was it that decided to go after Kaine?"

"That would have been your apprentice," the Hurtz answered.

"Darius came upon the conclusion?" Puc furrowed his brows. "Well, I suppose it would make sense. They were both, after all in, the academy at the same time. Still, it seems very odd to me. It's as though something does not add up quite completely."

Puc crossed one arm across his chest while he used the other to prop up his chin with his thumb, balling up his fist as though his jaw would dislodge at a moments notice. He could feel the grit of newly grown facial hair under his thumb, a sure sign it had been a long day. The more he focused on the problem, the more he could not comprehend why it had been so easy when it should not have. Kaian had sent his entire force out to find the tome, so why should they have been so lucky? The more he thought, the more the fire of curiosity burned him, until the mage stood up, unable to find his answer. Leaving the Hurtz without another word, he walked in the direction of the infirmary, where Darius was.

His apprentice was absorbed in the tasks given to him, and did not notice his master's entrance until the tip of Puc's staff barred him from putting away any further supplies. Darius turned around with a questioning look.

"I came around to acknowledge you for what you did," Puc said in a neutral voice. "I would have rotted in that cell had I remained there much longer. Brakkus tells I have you to thank for figuring out Kaine was the one behind it all."

"It was nothing," Darius answered, and began to stack the shelves once more.

"Nothing?" Puc raised an eyebrow. "I would hardly call it nothing, considering I am no longer accused of a crime I never committed in the first place, wouldn't you agree?"

"Yeah." Darius nodded quietly. "I guess so."

Puc narrowed his pale eyes as he looked at the boy. He grabbed the youth's shoulder. "Darius. Is there something you are not telling me about all of this?"

"It's not important, master. It was all solved," the youth responded in a stern tone, only to feel the iron grip of the mage spin him around so he faced Puc.

"And what exactly am I to make of such a notion, Silver?" Puc looked straight at him. "Tell me, and by the Unknown's bane, boy you'd better be honest. How did you come to know it was Kaine who took the tome?"

Darius felt the life be drained from his arm as Puc held onto it, his master's eyes the portals to the final judgment by the Unknown as they watched him, stripping him of any resolve he had.

"Answer me," hissed Puc, shaking life back into his apprentice.

"Now look, I only did it because you know how Kaian can be with his mood swings," Darius began.

"Did what?" Puc demanded a clear conclusion to the situation.

"I taught them to retrieve." Darius clenched his jaw as the words passed his lips.

Puc let go of his apprentice, anger and fear creeping through the mage like scalding hot water as his face froze up in shock, only to be replaced with a snarl erupting from the mage's throat. "You what?"

"Like I said, you know how Kaian gets." Darius tried to explain himself.

Puc pressed a closed fist to his mouth as the rage continued to burn within him. Giving himself a few moments to cool, he waited until he was able to think again, "You know the magnitude of the atrocity you have committed? You are very lucky we are all not dead now. You know what happened the last time."

"The last time, no one was trying to save the world," Darius reminded him. "Maybe the Unknown cut us some slack."

"Were you there?" Puc asked, earnestly.

"What?"

"You must be a lot older than I thought," Puc replied, dryly.

"Master, you know what I-"

Puc silenced him, raising a finger in his direction, "Be as it may, something like this cannot go unchecked. The power will need to be bound in order to prevent future use, for I doubt the Unknown will show mercy for committing such a sin a second time. That power was not meant for any mortal realm known to us to use freely. You had no right awakening it, especially in children, because that is exactly what they are, no matter what lens you view them through."

Before Darius could say anything else, Puc was already racing out of the room.

"With me, Silver," the mage called after his apprentice.

ಶಿಡಿ

As Annetta, Jason, and Link approached the teleporter, the distinct sound of feet could be heard from some distance behind them. Link stepped in front of the group, his guard only faltering when he saw Puc and Darius emerge.

"Uhm, hey," Annetta said, curiously. "What's up? We put everything away like you asked us."

"This is another matter entirely." Puc silenced her with a raised hand, and then looked at the group. "I need you all to come with me before you leave."

"Man, we're tired," Jason groaned. "I just wanna go to bed and-"

"This is not a request, but an order." Puc shot a glare at the boy, and then turned to everyone. "It has come to my knowledge that you have been taught retrieving. Is this correct?"

Annetta glanced at Jason, raising an eyebrow and faced Puc. "Uhm, yeah. Darius taught us, and he was actually pretty nice about-"

"I care not for your opinions on teaching techniques," retorted the mage. "Listen to me, and listen well. You were never meant to learn that ability, and for a good reason."

Annetta growled and rolled her eyes in frustration. "We know. Darius told us that it's because the Unknown's host-"

"Then you understand that we are playing with fire." Puc interrupted her again. "Fire of the most deadly kind, and you should all consider yourselves very lucky to not have been discovered using it."

The youth all looked at one another, their eyes shifting away from Puc's judgmental gaze, including Link, who felt he should have objected more strongly to their using the ability to begin with.

"Look, it seemed like a good idea at the time," Annetta sighed. "We just wanted to help, that's all."

"We were aware of the consequences." Link put in his own thoughts. "Saving the life of a friend seemed a valid enough reason to break the rules."

Puc sighed, the hardened creases on his face softening slightly as he found himself looking at the children. "I understand your concern, and thank you. However, next time remember that when something is forbidden, it is with good reason, for your own protection, and the protection of others. I will need to perform a binding of the ability. The Unknown is generally merciful only once."

"Couldn't you have bound it before we learned how to use it?" Jason asked. "And why didn't you ever bring it up if it's so forbidden?"

"You need to know the ability before it can be sealed from being used again," Puc explained. "If I'd attempted sealing it before you learned, I could have hindered other abilities in the process. As to why I never said anything about it beforehand, I didn't think you would ever learn it under my tutelage."

Annetta and Jason shot Puc a glare, to which the mage responded, "I only impose as much as I think you are both capable of handling. It is never more and never ever less."

The mage adjusted his grip on his staff, allowing the information to seep in before he spoke again. "Now, follow me. The sooner it is done, the sooner we can all sleep more soundly."

೮ンೞ

As soon as they entered the library, the mage set everyone to work preparing the ground and moving everything out of the center of the room until there was a large space. Annetta noted that the ground, unlike everywhere else, was stone.

"Concrete. It is steel beneath," Puc assured her, noting her glances. "Sacred circles are used for incantations, and larger spells cannot be drawn out on steel. A stone base is needed."

Saying no more, Puc motioned for Annetta and Jason to go into the center of the room, while Link and Darius stood at the door, their task of helping prepare completed.

Puc exhaled heavily, mentally preparing himself. He began by taking his staff and dragging it behind him as he walked in a circle around Annetta and Jason.

He chanted as he walked in the circle, quietly at first, so none could hear what he said, but then getting louder as he began the circle anew. The words made little sense to Annetta and Jason and sounded foreign in their origin.

They continued to stand in the middle of the circle, confused by what was happening. Nothing seemed to change, and they were beginning to feel silly about it all. The incantation continued to escalate, the words blurring into a constant rhythm. Just as Jason was about to put in a snide comment, the ground Puc had been tracing with his staff began to glow red. Sparks formed upon the third passing of the mage, and leaped alive into a circle of flames. The three of them then found themselves trapped within the ring of fire, the mage standing before them.

Putting the staff down on the ground, Puc then placed his hands on their heads, closing his eyes as he continued to chant.

Jason felt his knees almost buckle beneath him when the mage placed his hand on his head. A wave of dizziness spread through his body as he felt the hand press him down. Shutting his eyes, he tried to find a center to secure himself. He felt as though the hand was crushing his skull. He felt a hand grip him in time, steadying him. Opening his eyes slowly, he saw it was Annetta, her hand gripping his sleeve, holding him up, but not dragging him down in her own moment of weakness. He could see that she was in no better shape than he. Lifting his own hand, he gripped her wrist in the same silent promise he had made when they had first come to Q-16.

Chapter 32

Annetta awoke the next morning at home in her bed, having strategically snuck in while everyone else slept. Stretching, she headed straight for the kitchen to see her entire family waiting for her at the table, glaring at her with shocked expressions. She stopped dead in her tracks, looking back at them in confusion.

"Uhm. Morning everyone?"

Immediately, her mother threw her arms around her, embracing her in a tight hug, her father rushing up to do the same.

"Ow...being crushed," Annetta murmured, pulling back. "What's the matter? I was only gone a day."

"Sweetheart...you were gone a whole week!" her mother exclaimed before she pulled her back to get a good look at her.

"What? No I wasn't. We were in Aldamoor for a day," Annetta said, still at a loss.

Arieus gazed at his wife, a questioning look still lingering on her face. He shook his head and sighed.

"Did Puc give you C.T.S.'s?" he asked.

"What? No, what's that?" Annetta looked up at her father.

"You were traveling into another reality, another dimension sometimes time doesn't flow equally between them. C.T.S.'s are supposed to prevent you from skipping time in your own world. It synchronizes the amount of time a person stays in a place to their home," Arieus said to her daughter. "I've been trying to contact you down there somehow. After you didn't come home the same night, we feared the worst."

"Everything is fine dad, we all go out okay. Really." Said Annetta then added, "So does this mean its Saturday again?"

"Yes. It also means you have a pile of homework Xander has been picking up, because you apparently have strep throat." Aurora pulled out a large binder with photocopied papers as she spoke. The sight of it made Annetta sink her head below her shoulders.

"No matter what you were up to," Aurora continued, "this needs to get done."

"Yes mom," Annetta sighed.

ജൻ

328

Having been called by Annetta to come over despite being grounded by his mother for having been missing, Jason walked over to the apartment building. He had his headphones on when a form caught the corner of his eye. He turned around to see Sarina waving at him madly, trying to gain his attention. He pulled out the ear buds and turned off the music.

"Hey! Where have you been? I missed you at school." She beamed.

"Oh, hey Sarina," he replied with little energy to his voice, "Uh...you wouldn't believe me if I told you."

Sarina looked at him in a teasing way, almost saying 'try me'. Jason knew she would, but he wasn't in a talking mood after having fought with his mother and slamming the door on her. He could still feel her judgmental eyes on him as she told him how much of a problem he was, and how he would end up like his father. Her enthusiasm died down at bit when she saw he would not elaborate.

"Well, I guess I won't bother you if you don't want to talk about it. Where are you off to?" she asked.

"Annetta's," he said. "We're just gonna hang out a bit. Her dad is taking us to a conservation area outside of Toronto so we can go hiking-"

Before Jason could continue with his alibi, he felt another pair of eyes watching him. Looking behind Sarina, he saw Matthias in the distance, his lean but imposing frame blending against the evergreen he was propping his arm up on. He studied Jason with the intensity of a hungry wolf, giving him chills down his spine. Sarina looked back to see what had stolen her friend's attention.

"Oh, that's just Matt. You remember him, right?" she smiled and waved for him to come over.

His eyes still fixed on Jason, Matthias walked towards them, allowing Jason to get a better look at him. Though his hair was tousled and he wore no glasses, Jason recognized him as the man who had been speaking with one of the teachers in the hallway the day Sarina had first come to class.

"Matt, this is Jason." Sarina introduced him once Matthias stood behind her. "You saw him before, remember? He's the one I told you about. He's like you."

"Prove it." Matthias continued to eye him with his carnivorous gaze.

Jason's eyes found a discarded plastic bottle that lay close to the road. He glanced sideways and caused the bottle to dance upward in the air, as though it were a plastic bag on the wind.

'And I can do much more than that,' he let the man know.

'I see, but can you do this,' the young man reached his gloved hand out in front of him. As Jason looked closer, he could see what looked like a small flame spark from the middle of Matthias's palm and grow rapidly. Once it was about the size of a basketball, Matthias braced it with his other hand. Grunting, the youth aimed his arms upward, coiled back, and shot the flame up, watching it disappear into the sky.

"Was that?" the boy pointed up.

"Psychic fire," Matthias said, "Sarina tells me you have not learned how to use it."

"No, and some people told me it takes forever," he sighed, thinking back on his conversation in Aldamoor.

Matthias smirked. "I could teach you, if I had the right space to do so," he said. "The rooms in the safe house would not be able to withstand a blast from an inexperienced psychic. It would be like setting off a small bomb."

"Could you...at least tell me how you learned?" Jason pleaded.

Matthias regarded the boy with the same predatorily look in his eyes as when he had first approached.

"You must learn to channel true hate into a physical form," he said to him. "Only when you have found true hate, can you ever hope to create psychic fire."

Jason absorbed the words as soon as they hit him, and nodded once Matthias had finished. Something about his tone, and the requirements needed to unlock the ability didn't sit right with Jason. It reminded him too much of the stories he'd eaten up over the years where someone tried to attain a power and ultimately became evil. It struck him too close to home since his father had ended up this way. Jason shifted uncomfortably and stored the information in his head.

"Are you ready to go home, Sarina?" Matthias looked down at her.

Sarina slightly inclined her head and murmured a goodbye as she began to walk in the other direction with her brother, leaving Jason on his own.

೫೦೦೩

Once they were far enough, Matthias dropped the act and a wide smile appeared on his face.

"Power. The simplest way to a young man's heart." He chuckled.

Sarina raised an eyebrow and looked up at Matthias, who seemed all too happy.

330

"I don't know if I fully understand what the point of that encounter was," she stated flatly.

"You saw the way his face lit up when he saw that ball of psychic fire, like a moth to a flame." Matthias's grin continued. "I know what it is like to be the one who has nothing to offer, the one who continually takes orders. You dream of nothing more than to rise above the benign tasks you are assigned. Jason feels this. He doubts his place among his friends, unsure of why he is really there, aside for being the son of someone who was once important. He is also plagued by the fact that should he step out of line he has no defense against those who call themselves his friends, as was the case once with his own father. But Arcanthur at least knew how to use the fire. I showed him psychic fire, and showed him someone who could teach him to harness it if they had access to the proper equipment, like in Q-16."

Sarina's eyes widened as she stared at him.

"In those few minutes I gave him a proposal. Bring us to the base, shelter us, and I will teach you how to use psychic fire."

"But if he does not let us into Q-16, then what?" she asked. "You know my father is growing impatient."

"He will let us in sooner or later." Matthias's eyes shone in the sunlight. "Any man, young or old, can only stand so long to be in the shadow of someone else. That is the type of man Jason is, no matter how well he masks it."

Matthias spoke no more and continued on his way back to their house, silently striding across the pavement in broad daylight. Sarina frowned, not fully satisfied with the revelation.

"You put too much faith in your ability to read people," she muttered, but got no response from him. In his mind's eye the plan was already set in motion.

෫൪ඟ

After clearing everything up with her parents, both Jason and Annetta wasted no time in heading down to the Lab, intending to confront Puc and the others.

Puc was in his usual spot in his room, bent over a book, when Annetta and Jason came to a halt at the door.

"If this is about the headache after going through the portal, then take an aspirin and carry on, I'm not your nanny," he stated, not bothering to look up.

"It's about a bit more than that," Annetta said. "It's about us missing a whole week of life here and getting bombarded with assignments!"

Seeing no reaction at all from the mage, the girl felt her face heat up and snapped. "Why didn't you tell us time was...all screwed up in other worlds?"

Puc finally looked up at them, his mouth hanging open for a split second as he contemplated what to say.

"It...oh," Puc pushed back a mass of black hair from his face as he stood up, "Well, that is a mess."

Brakkus popped his head in with the large rabbit ears bobbing in tow behind.

"Oi, you two, something the matter?" he asked striding inside.

"We forgot about the watches." Puc sighed. "It was never my job to deal with that before. I merely acted as the guide and advisor. Usually it was a tech specialist who made sure everyone had one."

Annetta and Jason simply glared at Puc, demanding a better answer from him.

"Well, what do you want? I am not some guardian angel, or an all knowing god," he growled, the book falling shut before him as he grabbed his staff and strode out of the room.

Exchanging only a quick look with one another, the children and Brakkus followed him, trying to match the inhuman speed of the mage and the rhythmic beating of his staff against the steel floor.

"Where's Link and Darius?" Annetta asked, seeing as Darius had never left with her when they had returned.

"Darius is at Severio Castle doing research for me, while I cannot confirm Lincerious's whereabouts," Puc stated as they reached their destination, a room that appeared to be sealed off by a steel door. Puc typed in a code that caused the door to creep open mechanically.

Stepping inside, Annetta noted the large assortment of workstations upon which were situated various gadgets. Puc ignored all of these and headed straight for the back, where a locked cage stood filled with racks of weapons. Pulling a key from his robes, he unlocked it and walked inside. He came back holding six thick black leather wristbands with large digital clock faceplates on each of them.

"These are the C.T.S. watches," he began. "Communications and time synchronizers. By wearing one of these, time becomes synchronized and flows evenly in all dimensions. This way, you end up coming back the day you left instead what happened to us. These are particularly crucial if one were to end up traveling into a dimension where one hour is equal to one hundred years here on Earth. They can also be used as a communications device, seeing as not everyone is a psychic, and getting split up is inevitable on the course of our journeys. You simply press the number corresponding to the watch and it will link you to that person. I grabbed whatever numbers were first visible. Your number is engraved on the back."

Annetta took one of the watches and looked at the back to find 01 neatly engraved into it, and showed it to Jason who exchanged his number of 02 with her.

"Ya found 06 for me again, how sweet," Brakkus chuckled, strapping the watch to his massive wrist, the metal buckle clicking in place.

"There was only one I spotted big enough to fit you," Puc said. He then turned to the others. "Remember when using these to only refer to yourself as the number you are given, especially when we visit technologically advance societies. You never know if there is someone listening in. My number is 05 while Brakkus is 06, and I have one here for Darius that is 117, and 106 for Lincerious."

"I can go and find Link to give him his," Annetta said, taking the watch labeled 106. "Will we be leaving today? I mean, to see the Minotaurs?"

"Tomorrow, young one," Puc said. "I think it is safe to say that we all need a days rest and preparation before we tackle the next task. For now, you may try to find Lincerious and give him his watch. Jason, if you wish, you may journey with me to Severio Castle."

Jason only nodded before exchanging a quick glance with Annetta and leaving with Puc. Brakkus stood by her side, quietly watching them go.

"Do ya want me to go with ye?" he asked, "If not, I'll go make sure Puc doesn't stir up the horses too badly."

"No, I think I'll be okay." Annetta said. "I think the horses need saving more than I do."

"My girl. And don't go wandering into the biospheres alone, alright? No telling what sort of things still be out there since the blackout. Ya want to go in, ya know how to call." Brakkus chuckled, patting her on the back, and adjusting his belt as he followed after Puc and Jason, leaving Annetta alone.

She stood silently and looked around for a moment, taking in the cold blue metallic interior. She looked over the work stations in particular, littered with half finished projects, as though the place was simply shut down for the evening while everyone had gone home. Picking up a clump of wires and metal parts that lay twisted on a nearby desk, she examined it, wondering what it was meant for and knowing she had no way of finding out, because the person who could tell her was gone. Placing the contraption down, she felt her loneliness sink in.

"Just what went on in here, gramps?" she asked quietly, knowing no answer would ever come.

ജോ

Mislantus, seated in his throne, waited with drawn patience for the transmission to come through from Matthias. His nerves were at their limit. It should not have taken this long for anything to unravel. Every day since the shuttle had taken off and landed on Earth, he had waited to hear of the penetration of the base, the death of the heir of Orbeyus, and the cue for the march into Severio Castle to begin. The image on the screen resolved itself into the face of the young man he had put his trust into.

"Speak, and I do hope you have something of value to present this time," the tyrant said in a low, mechanical voice as his cat slit eyes gazed at the screen.

"I do, my lord. I have made contact with the son of Arcanthur." Matthias smiled slyly. "Our alibi as two refugees on the run has worked, and he now knows I am a psychic like him. He knows I have the ability to teach him to use psychic fire, but cannot do so without the resources in the base. It is only a matter of time before he breaks."

Mislantus glared into the face on the screen, his pupils dilating and contracting as he analyzed the plan.

"You are certain that he will allow you in?" he asked.

"Yes, my lord," Matthias assured him. "He yearns for a purpose among his allies, something that sets him apart. To know how to control psychic fire would give him that purpose, especially when set against the heir of Orbeyus. Not to mention it has become clear to me that the information retrieved about his father can be used to fuel distrust between him and the heir. Who knows? If I'm given enough time to play my cards right, we could have a potential ally. At least in destroying those in our immediate line of opposition."

334

Mislantus's face showed nothing, the cat eyes lost in thought as the information formulated, turning the gears in his mind. He had never considered using the Kinsman boy as a weapon, but if Matthias succeeded, it would save him much cannon fodder for other conquests.

"Very well. Proceed." Mislantus folded his clawed hands before his face. "But note that I am still not happy with how long this is taking."

"I apologize, my lord," Matthias said, "but this is something very delicate. They are children, and their trust needs to be earned. Time is the one thing that allows us to do this. I cannot simply go in, kill them, and hack the portal that leads there, like on Derune."

"And what fine work it was on Drerune. Accomplished in thirteen hours flat." Mislantus grinned, his wicked fangs exposed. "I expect no less of you once you have access to the Eye to All Worlds secure."

"I will not fail, my lord. I only ask for your patience until I have been able to secure what is necessary. I can assure you that my work is closer to being finished than it was before." Matthias bowed his head on the screen.

"I will try to keep that in mind. It has been a lifetime of waiting, gaining strength to return and deal back the blow that was once dealt to me. I intend to dance on the crushed skulls of Orbeyus's descendants, and all those who once stood with him on the battlefield." the tyrant's eyes flashed dangerously. "Carry on."

෮෬

The screen went dim for Matthias. Rising, he turned off the monitor and proceeded to close the dresser where the device was hidden. As he closed it, he felt a pair of eyes on his back, burning into him. He sighed, knowing exactly whom they belonged to.

"Amarok. It's been a while." He smiled lightly under his breath and turned to face him.

The older, armor clad assassin strode forward from where he stood in the doorframe of the spacious living room. His beige trench coat fluttering on the wind as he moved slowly towards him while his silver mask gleamed from the sun.

"I thought for a moment you may have let your guard down. I would have skewered you like a piece of meat," the white haired elder assassin stated.

"I was taught better." The youth smiled darkly. "So, who sent you? Mislantus? Or did you come because you missed having me as your dog?"

"Oh, I wish it were the latter, but sadly it was our dear lord and master who sent me," Amarok chuckled. "But he did send me to observe, and not reveal my presence. I came bearing a message because I grow bored of watching you in the shadows, knowing that you never knew I was there to begin with."

"If you want a more interesting game, just say so. I can give you a matching set of scars on the other side of your face," Matthias spoke coldly.

"Oh, very good boy, very good, makes my heart sing for joy hearing the taunts." Amarok stifled a laugh, then stopped. "The message I come with is this: I can see you are becoming overly comfortable in this world. If I sense this in any way, shape, or form you will betray the cause, then Mislantus has given me permission to execute you on the spot."

They stood facing one another after the threat, their eyes locked. Amarok's cheeks tightened into a smile under his metallic mask and he dropped his gaze, knowing full well who would win if he were to actually challenge the young man. He shoved his fists into the pockets of his coat.

"Heed my warning, and just do your job. The game is on," he sneered. Teleporting, the masked assassin was gone just as quickly as he had arrived.

Matthias looked around at his surroundings, wrinkling his nose in disgust at what Amarok had said. What ties would he actually have to a place such as this one? It was true that he was becoming closer with Sarina, and knew the moment this mission was over that they would not be able to speak to one another as they did now, as siblings, but he knew above all that was the way it was meant to be.

A sister...he remembered vaguely having one once, and having loved her, but he was too small then to hold any lasting memory. It could even have been a figment of wishful imagination from a life he had never lived.

"Game on, Amarok. Just remember, I only play to win," he spoke to the empty walls of the house. Somewhere in the dark, the silver mask smiled back.

Chapter 33

After having received her C.T.S., Annetta made her way around the Lab, trying to find where Link might be. She had already checked the training grounds, and given a quick glance to the outskirts of the forest biosphere, but did not go in further due to the past encounter with the giant. Brakkus would not be happy either to learn she had gone off alone again. He and Puc were sure there were more unwanted creatures lingering, possibly in the Lab itself. Annetta did her best not to think of that when moving through the isolated steel halls. The silence did not help. Aside from the buzzing of the high voltage white lights, there was no sound. It was unnerving.

Suddenly, Link appeared around the corner, walking casually with his hands shoved into his jean jacket pockets, his sword hung over his shoulder. The crescent scar on his face looked deeper from the shadows cast by the light. His sudden appearance caused the girl to jump.

"Hey!" Annetta called, waving as soon as he was within hearing distance.

Link stopped in his tracks and waved back at her as she came across the hall to him.

"I've been looking all over for you. Puc wanted me to give you this." She handed him the watch she had been fidgeting with in her hand. "It's supposed to synchronize time whenever we go through portals. A week passed here when we were only there for a day. Also, you can contact people if you type in the number of their watch."

Link put the watch on his wrist and examined it. There were two times written on it, one at zero and one stating the time, date, and year. He then flipped open the small compartment holding the number pad, looking at how they fit into the whole octagonal faceplate.

"Want to go and test them out?" He looked at her.

"Uhm, sure." Annetta nodded.

Following Link's lead, the two of them went in the direction of the Lake biosphere.

"We can't actually go in this time," she said as they came to the entrance. "I promised Brakkus I wouldn't."

"We won't go far. We can stay close to the opening," he reassured her as he held the door open.

Annetta groaned, knowing the Hurtz would not be happy. But the look on Link's face teased her to give in. She was beginning to trust her abilities a bit more also, becoming confident that should a situation arise, she could handle it well enough to get away. After all, the one time they'd been attacked, the odds were in their favor. Reluctantly she stepped through the door.

They walked out onto the grassy area that started right at the door. The sun was setting overhead, creating a fuchsia tint on the horizon. Ahead, the riverbank beckoned at them.

"Okay, so how about you close your eyes and I go hide, then you contact me so we can see if they work," Link proposed. "I'll try to make sure I am out of hearing distance."

"How am I going to know when you're far enough?" she asked.

"Simple, I'll contact you. Now close your eyes so you don't know where I am."

Annetta frowned, not really wanting a corny element like that as part of the test, but she said nothing.

Link took it as his cue to leave, and took off in a run to one of the large collapsed logs on the other side of the riverbank. Flipping the keyboard compartment on the watch, he typed in the code for Annetta.

On the other side of the riverbank, still closing her eyes, Annetta heard a faint beeping coming from her wrist. She opened her eyes and saw a light glowing green on the faceplate. She tapped the button on the side with a small diagram of a megaphone with soundwaves coming from it.

"Can you hear me now?" Link's voice came through with a tinny radio distortion to it. Annetta almost jumped back upon hearing it so clear.

"Uhm…yeah, I can hear you really well," she answered.

"Oh, wow. These antiques work better than I thought," his voice replied. **"I assumed Puc was joking when he gave these to you. This is actually kind of neat. I could be half way around the world and you can hear me."**

"Don't you guys have phones where you came from?"

"Fones?" Link tried to pronounce the word, causing Annetta to sigh on the other end of the speaker. Link chuckled moments later. **"I know what they are, and we do have communication devices, just nothing this primitive you know?"**

338

"Yeah, we don't have anything like this in our world either," Annetta said absentmindedly. She sat down on the grass. "I don't know if I ever asked you, but how different is your world from ours?"

"People wise, or weather, or what?" he asked.

"Everything. What kind of things do your people believe in? What are they like?" She grabbed some blades of grass and pried them from the stems.

Link smirked and stretched out against the log on his side of the stream, looking at the sunset, trying to think of a good answer for her.

"Well, I guess you can say we're a warrior nation. Everyone learns to fight. It's what we pride ourselves in. To be a Gaian means to be a warrior, and everyone is subjected to the same training when they're young. That's what I was doing when I came here," he explained. **"We're ruled by a king, and just because we're warriors doesn't mean that we go out and fight whoever. We have a very strict code that says that we are sworn to protect the weak. It's believed that is the task the Unknown appointed our people with at the beginning of time. We are meant to help others."**

"Is the Unknown like a god? I hear Puc and Brakkus use his name all the time." She sat up straighter, trying to pay attention to the voice in the watch.

"Yes, the Unknown is exactly that, the creator of everything. Different races know him by different names and faces, but in the end he, or rather it, is this unifying force from which all good comes from. That's why no matter where you go there is a universal good," he continued. **"Of course, not everyone knows of his existence, because he has so many names. But in the end, the good of a person is what determines if they know what the Unknown is."**

Annetta silently nodded her head, trying to understand what Link was saying, but the information was seeping out the sides of her head. She looked up into the sky again to see it lit up with dozens of stars and a brilliant crescent moon hanging in the midst of them.

"I wonder if that moon is actually real. What do you think?" she spoke into the watch.

For a moment, she heard nothing from the other side, and then came the inhuman scream she remembered hearing once before coming through. She turned it off instantly, but could still hear the screams, and raced in their general direction, thinking Link was under attack. Teleporting across the riverbank to avoid being soaked, she looked around frantically in all directions.

"Link! Where are you?" she called out.

There was silence and something shuffled in the tall grass. Annetta turned in the direction of the noise, her heart pounding with fear.

"Link?" she asked.

There was no answer again, and this time nothing moved in the grass. Annetta's fists balled up as she got ready to throw the fallen tree to where the grass had moved before. She knew it might do little good, but it was better than nothing. Bracing herself on the ground she took a deep breath.

"Whatever you are you better come out! I'm Annetta Severio, and I am not afraid of you!" she spat gritting her teeth.

"Annetta, I need you to leave," a gruff and barely distinguishable voice said from the grass.

Annetta paused, her reflexes relaxing, but remaining confused upon hearing the voice. She took another step towards the grass to reaffirm her confidence.

"Who are you and what have you done with Link?" she snapped.

The voice sighed. "I am Link."

"Well, unless you caught a cold, you have some explaining to do." She frowned, not really buying it. "Come out then, Link, if it is you."

"Okay, but promise me one thing," the voice said.

"Fine?"

"Please don't run away when you see me."

"Okay, but why would I-" The grass began to move Annetta's eyes widened.

Instead of the form of the young boy, a creature that seemed too surreal to be a living thing stepped out. For the most part, it looked like a giant brown wolf wearing the tatters of Link's clothing on him. The only things that remained intact were Link's gauntlets, which had somehow managed to stretch to the size of the wolf's massive forepaws, and the watch that had done the same. The creature had the antlers of a stag. Despite having the body of a wolf, it moved like a large ape would, on its knuckles with its upper body slightly raised as though challenging its opponent. A part of Annetta, the one that was still grounded in her old life, wanted to run, but the rest simply stood and watched. As she got closer, she noticed the spot

340

where Link's scar had been across his eye there was now was a golden crescent moon tattoo and a red wicked orb stared back at her. She recalled what Puc had said about cursed scars, and how he had been worried when Link first came to the Lab. The creature moved out fully from the grass and stopped some distance away from Annetta, lowering its head as if ashamed.

"Link?" she looked questioningly at the beast and started to walk towards it.

"Don't come any closer," he grunted, moving a few steps back. "I never wanted anyone to see me like this."

Annetta stopped in her tracks. She felt sorry when she heard him speak. The creature lowered its head in further shame, the antlers touching the ground.

"Is this the curse?" she asked. "You're not a werewolf of some kind or something, are you?"

"I guess I sort of look like one, don't I?" The creature raised its head. "But no, I'm not a werewolf. At least, I'm not someone who was bitten by a werewolf. The curse placed on me was transferred from my father, who dishonored himself in battle. In turn, his commander gave him the same scar I now wear on my eye. Through generations, let the taint of your deeds be seen under a moon incomplete."

"So the curse makes you turn into this under a crescent moon? You don't loose your mind or need to kill a person or anything?"

"No. I keep my mind as it is," he answered. "The better to know exactly how frightening I look. And I can change at will as well, not just at this time. But this form is cursed and it's not normal. I hate it. In Gaian society, to change into such a creature is seen as the biggest taboo. It shows you are unclean, impure, bad blood."

"So you mean it's common for people to turn into-?" Annetta motioned to him, the words stuck in her throat. "Like, you and Darius?"

"Darius uses a spell, but yes, there are many races that can shape shift. But it is seen as horribly wrong when you cannot fully phase into a pure form." He explained.

Annetta nodded, looking at the creature, its animalistic eyes meeting her own, but darting away whenever they almost made contact.

"Well, the way I see it, it could have been a lot worse," she said. "You could lose your mind and hurt someone."

She walked closer to him. The muscles in Link's legs tensed up as though he would make a run for it, but Annetta ignored it and kept going.

"Besides, you think this is bad, what about Brakkus? He looks like that all the time, not just under a crescent moon. He's not exactly friendly looking either, but we all like him because of who he is, not how he looks. You could have just told us about the curse. Maybe even Puc could help and find a way out of it or something."

Annetta stood in front of him and put a hand on one of the massive antlers on his head, feeling the velvelt texture under her fingers. Link's eyes finally met her own. The red orbs watched her.

"Besides, I don't find you scary like this, you actually look kind of cool." She smiled.

"I've just...well, where I come from, something like this is very frowned upon." He sighed. "You said you wanted to know more about Gaia? As I said before, to be turned into a beast like this is the highest form of disgrace in our society."

"Well, you're not on Gaia anymore."

The creature hesitated. In truth, Link was horrified that anyone had even discovered him like this. The one thing he had been taught all his life was never to allow this exposure to happen. But seeing the girl standing there with no fear in her eyes sparked something within him that made him see another side to it all. His muscles relaxed as he forgot what he was, and only remembered who he was on the inside.

"I guess I should keep that in mind." the creature grinned its razor sharp teeth. "Want to see something cool that I can do when I'm like this?"

"Sure," she nodded.

"Okay, then climb onto my back and hold on tight." Link lowered himself closer to the ground. Annetta, feeling a bit nervous hopped onto his back as though she were getting into a horse, and grabbed into the antlers.

Link coiled up like a spring, and then launched himself into the air. Annetta held onto the antlers for dear life as the creature ran full force. Never in her life had she wanted the safety of a saddle more than this, and she usually felt like she would fall off of one. The sea of grass brushed against her jeans like the bristles of a broom, but became fainter as they raced on into the night. Once she was certain she would not fall, she opened her eyes to see how quickly they were running. The entrance was a little blur on the horizon behind them, and the trees were getting thicker as they went on, the grass becoming shorter.

"Keep holding on. We're not done yet," he grunted. With another leap, he grabbed one of the thick branches of a tree, jumping from one tree to another using his massive forearms.

Annetta closed her eyes yet again to prevent the pieces of bark and dirt from flying into her face. She was starting to feel queasy, as though she were on a roller coaster. The girl could feel them being propelled higher and higher, the feeling of jumping and swinging going on as she held onto him. A few moments later, all movement stopped aside from a light breeze that went through her hair. She opened her eyes to see they were in one of the tallest trees in the biosphere. Her jaw slacked.

"How big do you think this place is? Does it ever end?" she asked.

"I honestly don't know. I've never traveled very far here, mostly because of Brakkus's warning about not knowing what's left over from the blackout," he said, supporting them by holding onto the trunk of the tree with one arm, sitting on the branch.

"I bet right now most things would be scared of you instead," Annetta said.

"Just because I'm big and hairy doesn't mean I'm the absolute scariest thing around," he snorted.

"And before you were saying you were," Annetta continued. "Oh, I'm so ugly I can't show myself to anyone in fear of breaking a mirror," she said in a rasp.

"Yeah, well, I'm pretty sure a drake or giant spider would be much scarier to come face to face with." He tilted his head slightly back to face her as much as he could. "I don't breathe fire or spit acid."

"Wouldn't that be something." chuckled the girl.

Chapter 34

The ride to Severio Castle with Puc had been a silent one for Jason. Much danced in his mind as he reflected on his meeting with Matthias, the psychic warrior. He remembered the tense look in the young man's eyes as he approached him. But most of all, he remembered the glow of psychic fire at his fingertips as he wielded it. Jason wanted the same, part of him wanted to be in Matthias's position instead of the life he was in now. He pictured himself as the runaway psychic, protecting a defenseless girl, being the hero. It was not that he did not enjoy what he did here, but he wanted to be his own man, able to operate independently. It seemed like Annetta was more recognized than he was, and it stung him.

He was also concerned about how things would play out on the day the others would learn of Sarina and Matthias. He knew Puc in particular would not be thrilled about the idea of him bringing them to the Lab, and he feared a conflict would occur because of it.

"Puc, how long does it take to learn to control psychic fire?" he finally asked, as they stopped and dismounted in front of the castle. The elven mage shot a look of surprise at him.

"Guildwood asked Annetta and I when we were in Aldamoor if we had learned to use it already or not, that's why I ask," Jason said, a technical truth.

"Well, that truly varies by individual. Regardless, it is not a fast process, or something that there are real exercises for, which is why I have not taught you or Annetta," the mage answered.

"Well, what can you tell me about it?" he probed further.

"A person needs to draw upon the purest form of hate in their heart," Puc spoke as he tethered his horse to the post before the castle. "They need to be able to channel that in order to create the fire. Sometimes it takes years before a person can realize what it is they truly hate above all else, and learn to unleash that hate without destroying everything around them. In your case, I would not worry about it for a long time. You are still young, and have other things to learn before that even becomes something to tap into."

"Why hate, though?" asked Jason, "I mean, why not love? It seems so dark when you think about it."

"Hate is only dark when aimed in the wrong direction," Puc explained as the two of them walked up the castle steps to the main door. "Hate is an emotion. It is only when you attach negative connotation to it that it becomes a vile thing. You can hate war and love peace, and there is nothing wrong with that, is there?"

"I guess that makes sense. I never thought of it that way. And what if we encounter someone who can use it?" Jason questioned. "I mean, we aren't the only ones that can do this, right?"

"You learn to block and bounce the attack back. Psychic fire is like any other attack," Puc assured him. "Why do you worry about this all of a sudden?"

"Because of what happened when we were in Aldamoor with Kaine. You weren't there, but, well it could have come in handy," he grumbled. "I haven't felt that helpless in a long time, and I just didn't like it. I couldn't do anything to stop him."

"Neither could Annetta," Puc stated, opening the door. "And Kaine was wearing an amulet to protect him from psychic energy, neither of you could have done anything. Only wit alone saved you."

Jason nodded his head as they walked up the stairs together. Puc's answer had not been what he'd hoped for. In his heart he was beginning to consider the possibility that Matthias could help him learn to wield psychic fire. After all, he was only a decade or so older than Jason himself. But he had told Jason that it was dangerous to teach him out in the open. He sighed, internally giving up for the moment before following Puc to where Darius waited for them.

ഇന്ദ

Darius sat in a large wooden chair with red leather cushioning, bent over a massive book. He was completely oblivious to Puc and Jason's entry. The two stood over him for a good minute until he realized there was a shadow being cast over his page.

"You forget to be vigilant." Puc scolded his apprentice. "What if someone had managed to get in?"

"Well, then we'd all be dead, wouldn't we?" Darius stated dryly. "I found the records for the time flow in Morwick like you asked. It might be a couple of hundred years on their end since anyone made contact with them. I wouldn't be at all surprised if every general who ever served under Orbeyus is dead by now."

"That's the problem with mortality." Puc sighed. "At least they'll have records, be they etched in stone or metal. They will have recognition of what happened, and they will remember."

Puc turned his attention to Jason who, seemed out of the loop. "Time in the world of the Minotaurs flows much faster than here. One year here equals ten there. The Minotaurs are above all else known for their craftsmanship in stone and metals. They have a love of sculpting in peace, and a love of weapons in war."

Puc strode closer to the records Darius had been pouring over and scanned quickly through them.

"If you wish, you may take a break, Darius," he continued. "I will examine these for myself."

"Yes, master." he nodded and turned to Jason. "Wanna go out on the balcony? I could use some fresh air. I'm starting to see letters dancing in front of my face."

"I don't blame you." Jason laughed as they exited the room, leaving Puc to his piles of books.

୪୬୧୪

"It's sort of sad that it ended up being Kaine who did it." Darius said once they had made it outside.

"Did you know him well?" Jason asked. "I mean you immediately jumped to thinking it could have been him. Were you just going on the hunch of the whole shape changing thing and him knowing about Puc and his father?"

Darius shook his head, his shaggy black hair massing before his eyes as he turned to look at Jason. "No. There was something else that made me think it could have been him."

Jason formed an 'o' shape with his mouth and looked out over the balcony, watching a pair of sparrows flutter from branch to branch in one of the nearby trees.

"When you're at the academy, you meet everyone who studies there," Darius explained. "It's such a tight knit community that at some point you end up bumping into everyone. I befriended Kaine when I first got there. He was a few years older than me, and protective of those who first came to the academy and were picked on by other seniors. He became kind of a big brother to me until I was able to fend for myself. We both came to the academy unwillingly. People are sent there because they are talented, or it is required of them. It's hardly ever by choice. I remember my first years there, when I wanted to leave more than anything in the world. When Puc came, it was like a blessing. In those years, Kaine fueled my imagination with the world outside. I remember him talking to me about how he longed for freedom from his father's plans. He told me he wanted to fly an airship, and he wanted nothing to do with becoming First Mage. What struck me most about the conversation was his tone, how serious his words were. And at the end, he asked me if I would go with him if he ever planned an escape."

Jason felt a pang within him. Something about the scenario made him remember his encounter with Sarina and her brother. He wondered if the time ever came to bring them down to the Lab, what everyone would think, and who would they side with. He swallowed hard, suppressing the thought and focusing on the conversation. "And what did you tell him?"

Darius sighed, running his hand down the stone railing. "I told him I could not, because my place was there."

"But if he was your friend and he wanted you to go with him, why didn't you?" he inquired further. "I mean, if he had a plan and all that."

"Because I had a responsibility to stay at the academy, and he had an even bigger one due to being a pureblood Chironson."

Jason furrowed his brows. "But he was your friend, and he stood by you when you needed it. If you both felt the same way, then why not?"

"It wasn't the right thing to do." Darius said firmly, his voice strained.

"Okay, what if, though," Jason continued. "What if it was, like, a matter of life and death? If he was sentenced to death, and all he wanted was for you both to escape so he could live the rest of his days with his best friend."

"Now you're stretching it." Darius gritted his teeth, but then relaxed a bit. "Besides, it was my choice to stay. He could leave whenever he wanted, and eventually he did. He did shoot me when we met again probably as payback, but that's beside the point. At any given time, only you can decide what feels right, and if your friends are really your friends, they'll accept your choice.

The light thud of wood on the stone ground could be heard as Puc emerged from inside, holding a book under his free arm and his staff in the other.

"Finished airing out your brains so we can head back?" he asked.

Darius locked eyes with Jason before turning back to his master and nodding. The two then began to walk while Jason took a moment to stay back.

He was still torn about Sarina's situation. What Darius had said made sense. His own choices should feel right to him, and the others would have to accept them if they were truly his friends. He sighed, wasting no more time on his thoughts and shoved his hands into his pockets. He then followed the two elves out of the castle.

ଛୋଷ

Upon returning to the base and having the horses set back up in their respective stalls, Puc pushed ahead to find Brakkus. Darius and Jason walked at a slower pace behind him, the constant rhythmic thudding of Puc's staff on the metallic surface giving the feel of a slow marching party.

The feeling was interrupted when he stopped, and with a quick gesture lifted the screen of the watch and pressed the numbers corresponding to Brakkus.

"Oi, you called?" The Hurtz's voice came through the watch.

"Where are you, 06? More importantly, is 01 with you and 106? I need to brief them about tomorrow."

"Actually, that'd be the problem at hand," Brakkus said through the speaker. **"I got no message from Annetta about leaving, and the boy's nowhere to be found. I've traced their scent to the Lake biosphere, though."**

"What? She was told not to go in alone!" Puc hissed, furrowing his eyebrows.

"I know, but the matter of the fact is she done it," Brakkus sighed.

Puc ran his hand through his hair, feeling a headache form at his temples.

"Did you smell any blood?" he asked with defeat.

"No, but I smell something else out there with her," he answered. **"Can ya make it here soon? Where are ya?"**

"Corridor closest to the stables," the elf told him. "I will be there with Darius and Jason in less than five minutes. 05 out."

Shutting the watch, Puc turned to the two boys with him.

"You heard Brakkus. Annetta may be in trouble. Move!" With those words, the mage strode off in a pace so quick, Jason was sure he was using a spell. He wasted no time in attempting to match the pace and before he knew it, they were beside the imposing frame of the Hurtz, who stood at the entrance to the biosphere with his massive blade drawn, and a scowl so venomous it could kill.

"You are certain you smell no blood?" the mage asked yet again.

"Would I have any reason to lie about something like this?" Brakkus turned to him.

"I should think not," Puc stated, his grip tightening around the staff until his already white knuckles began to show blue veins. "Whatever we encounter, we fight it, no hesitation on anyone's part. Annetta's life may hang in the balance."

Nodding in agreement, they all entered the biosphere. The night was clear upon the artificial horizon, and there seemed to be no signs of disturbance anywhere. The only thing they had to go by was that Brakkus had smelt something. The party advanced towards the river leading to the lake. Brakkus stopped, pointing out the sets of prints in the muddy sand beneath them.

"Lincerious is here with her," he pointed out. "But his scent gets lost…"

Before the conversation could carry on, something moved in the tall grass across the river. Coiling into defensive positions, everyone got ready to strike. Moments later, out came Annetta, riding on a beast the likes of which none of them had ever seen. It had the antlers of a stag and the head and body of a large brown wolf, but carried its forearms like that of a gorilla. The creature stopped when it noticed everyone on the other side of the riverbank.

"Annetta, get away from that thing!" Puc snarled, raising his staff.

"Whoa! Time out guys! Don't be so quick to jump to conclusions!" Annetta waved her hands in protest. "It's just Link."

"Lincerious?" Puc raised an eyebrow, staring at the beast, and then noticed the crescent scar and gauntlets. His jaw dropped slightly, but he composed himself quickly. "I will assume this is the nature of the curse, correct?"

Annetta slid off of Link's back and stood beside him, running a hand through his fur.

"Through generations, let the taint of your deeds be seen under a moon incomplete," the gruff voice of the creature spoke. "A curse laid on my father, then transferred to me."

Puc nodded his head, while the others simply stared. Link's scar, now golden, glistened as he watched them, his eyes cast downward.

"As someone who has dealt with Gaian culture," Puc spoke, "I understand this to be a disgrace of the largest kind. I know why you hid this from us for so long." The elven mage straightened his posture as he spoke. "However, you are not among Gaians here, so you should have nothing to fear. Shapeshifting is a common thing. As you have seen, Darius is one as well. We've all encountered our fair share of beasts. I've seen a lot worse than you."

"That best not be referring to anyone standing here, elf," Brakkus sneered playfully.

"Friend, you can't argue that you look like a fairy princess, if that is what you are asking," Puc stated, looking at the Hurtz sideways. "But I can say I've grown used to your face."

"Aye, thatcha can." Brakkus chuckled, sheathing his sword at the remark.

Annetta teleported herself to the other side of the river in order to join her friends, while Link leaped across, clear over the water.

"Seeing as we are here and on the subject, is there anything else we should be aware of at this time, Lincerious, or is this the worst of it?" the elf asked, leaning on his staff.

"No, this is it," he replied. "I can do this at will, but I choose not to. The only time it's involuntary is under a crescent moon. I know I should have mentioned it before, but it's not something I was proud of sharing."

"As I said, it is understandable, coming from where you do." He nodded before turning to the others. "We will leave tomorrow at dawn. Bring warm clothing with you. Morwick has long winter months, and we will most likely arrive in such conditions."

"What about missing more school?" Annetta asked with a worried tone. It was not that she particularly cared about her grades, but she disliked the idea of having to do piles of homework when she got back.

"I do not foresee it taking that long, and we now have the watches. Two days will be no more than two days. A year here without them is ten years in Morwick."

Jason cringed at the idea of coming home ten years later after only spending a year in another world. "And you're sure these things work?" he asked.

"Are you sure I'm an elf and not just a man pulling your leg? Who led you through a mirror into another world?" Puc looked at the boy, who was about to answer, but hesitated. "Have some faith in me, Jason Kinsman. It will do your future self some good for his blood pressure."

"Well, I mean, you forgot last time, and we lost like a week, so I think I'm justified in asking," muttered Jason.

"An error. One that will not happen again," Puc sneered to silence him.

Jason growled, but nodded back at him. He then turned his attention to his other friends.

"I guess I should head back home to pack my stuff," he said.

"I will walk you back to the exit," Puc said, stepping forward, "Seeing as the mystery here is solved. Will you be back to your normal self by tomorrow, Lincerious?"

"Yeah, I'll be ready," the creature nodded and stood up on its hind legs, "If you don't mind, I would rather wait out the rest of my night in my room. It's still uncomfortable to be like this, no matter what."

"Of course," Puc nodded and watched as the beast exited the biosphere. He then turned to Jason. Nodding silently, they moved to the exit. Annetta, Brakkus, and Darius lingered.

"Lass, I told ya not to wander off alone," Brakkus's voice rang the moment Puc had left.

Annetta lowered her head slightly, leveling with her shoulders upon hearing the words. Somehow, she knew this would happen, and she would be the one to take the blame.

"We weren't going to go far. Link just wanted to test out the C.T.S. watches," she argued. "We were going to stay right here, close to the exit in case anything were to happen."

"My point is, lass, ya went in when I told ya not to," the giant snapped. "Do ya have any idea what this could have cost us? I don't think ya realize yer own importance to all of this at times."

"I do, it's just that… well I didn't think it would be that big of a deal. I mean, how was I supposed to know about the crescent moon thing when you guys didn't either? Besides, it's not like Link tried to hurt me or something," Annetta growled in frustration. "And both you and Puc keep telling me how I'm supposed to be some great psychic warrior. How can you have any faith in me if you won't ever let me go off alone anywhere because you think some monster is going to pop up and eat me like I can't take care of myself?"

Brakkus's ears flattened against his skull, and it looked as though he would pounce on her.

"We were charged by Orbeyus to take care of ya as soldiers of his, to serve those of his bloodline that came after him. It's our job to worry and if ya had any respect for all that your grandfather's given ya, then you would maybe understand and appreciate the hard work that we do trying to ensure that for him. For you!" He snarled, and stomped out of the biosphere.

Annetta felt a tinge of guilt wash over her as she stood alone, with only Darius left beside her.

"I will say this. Not the best time to stand up for yourself," Darius said, shoving his hands in his pockets.

"I sort of get that." Annetta frowned.

⋔⋕

Jason could tell the elf had much on his mind as they walked. Despite this, part of him had a question of his own he wanted to ask. Taking a deep breath, he went over it in his head before speaking.

"Hey, Puc, are Annetta and Darius's apartments the only places with access to the Lab or are there like…other ways to get there?" he said quietly with hesitation.

The elf stopped, turning his full attention to Jason, who stood beside him with his hands crammed into the pockets of his hooded sweater. He then turned his gaze back, facing the dark of the room.

"Seeing as you do ask, there is one other way, but it has not been used for years, and I'm not sure if the entrance even works anymore, to be honest," the elf stated. "As I said before, I am not one of the technicians who looked after this. I was Orbeyus's advisor in battle, magic and diplomacy; where my skills lie."

"Well, if the one at Annetta's house worked after so long, then shouldn't this other one, too?" He probed further. "I mean, the reason I'm asking is because I was wondering if there's one closer to my house. My mom has really been getting on my case lately, and it's not like I can always slam the door in her face in order to go to Annetta's."

"Yes, I understand your concern." Puc nodded, thinking hard for a moment. "There is another entrance in the woods behind your home. It's

352

more fixed than the ones in Annetta and Darius's apartments, which are a device that can be taken down and stored anywhere."

Jason looked at the elf hopefully, absorbing all the information he had for him about this new form of entry.

"Again, if I knew more about the technology stored here, I'm sure I could locate another device which you could store in your room. However, the machinery was left a mess. Perhaps in time we can find another. Or use one of the rooms to have one created though I would not know how to install it." The mage rambled and then stopped, going back to his original point, "If memory serves, the one Arcanthur used was in a very particular tree, which the appearance of would be unchanged due to its artificial nature. He would have marked it, somehow, as well."

"Could it be a dead tree?" Jason asked, his memory flashing to the forest area around his house, trying to think of any trees that would fit the description.

"Yes, it could be, But Jason. You must remember that if the device is faulty then none of us can really help you," Puc reminded the boy.

"Don't worry, I think I can handle it." He smiled, sliding his card key into the teleporter home. "Like I said before, you need to have a bit of faith in us, Puc."

"It is not you I doubt, young Kinsman. It is time, and the infliction of time upon machinery," the elf stated. "Now, remember to bring a parka for tomorrow, we're not going to the tropics."

"You don't have to tell me twice. I live in Canada." Jason chuckled.

Chapter 35

The next morning, the group had gathered on the sofas in the meeting room. Upon hearing they were going to Morwick, Annetta's father had insisted on her wearing two sweaters, a heavy winter jacket, and tights under her jeans. By the time she entered the Lab, she was sweating up a storm and barely able to move because of all the layers of clothing.

"Hey Eskimo girl, how are you alive in that right now?" Darius raised an eyebrow upon entering to meet with everyone.

"I am buff tha doesn mean I wiff be fo lon." Annetta's muffled voice came from behind the large wool scarf her mother had wrapped around her face, "Can youh helf me ou of dis?"

"I'm sorry, what?" Darius chuckled, causing whatever was visible of Annetta's face to turn redder.

Puc entered with Brakkus, closely followed by Link behind them. The elf stopped the moment he saw the absurd sight.

"I hope you know whatever you bring you are responsible for carrying, Annetta." Puc eyed her up and down. "I said it would be cold, but I did not mean we were going to the arctic."

"Iss ma dadz ideha." Annetta tore off the gloves she had, and pried the scarf from her face, gasping for air. "It was my dads idea. The moment he heard Morwick, he started going on about how cold it was, and how him and grandpa got lost once with no way to make a fire-,"

"Annetta, he does know there are two mages coming with you, correct?" Puc raised a hand in protest.

"Yeah, well, you were supposed to be with us in Aldamoor, and look what happened." She crossed her arms. "Plus, once my dad has something planned, you can't talk him out of it. It was either getting the clothes superglued to me, or putting them on willingly."

"She's got a point, ya know," Brakkus said in a somewhat detached tone.

Annetta fussed, removing the jacket first and letting it fall to the floor before she tackled the two sweaters, leaving only her t-shirt. She then reached into her backpack and pulled out her jean jacket, stuffing the other clothing in its place.

"Okay, that was liberating." She sighed, adjusting the jacket on her shoulders.

Jason walked in moments later, carrying a portaging backpack with a winter jacket slung over his shoulder, and his scarf hanging loosely around his neck.

"How did you get past my dad without him telling you to bundle up?" Annetta raised an eyebrow.

"Oh, he saw I had a jacket and scarf, said I would be fine," he said. "He did tell me to make sure you had gloves on so you wouldn't catch frostbite."

Annetta sighed, lowering her head in defeat while Darius and Link stifled a laugh. Puc shook his head at the situation, while Brakkus stood in silence. Annetta could tell he was still angry with her about the night before.

"I would like to proceed, if that is at all possible," Puc said after a moment. "We are wasting precious time."

They all nodded in agreement and shouldered their backpacks as they set out for the stables.

"So, are you okay after last night?" Annetta asked Link, falling behind a bit from the group in order to speak with him.

"Uh, yeah, I'm fine. Why wouldn't I be?" he asked.

"Well, I mean, when you changed there was this awful scream I heard and... doesn't it, like, hurt for your whole body to change into something else?" She looked at his crescent-scarred face.

"It's a bit draining, but the thing is, once you change back you fall asleep in order to recharge, right? So the next morning, it sort of feels like all your muscles are sore, but that's it. Puc gave me one of his potions to help a little bit, getting rid of the pain, so I'm okay now. It feels better when I'm on the move."

Annetta nodded. Out of the corner of her eye, she saw Brakkus striding along. "I have to go. There's something I need to do. You sure you're okay?"

Link noted her eyes when they moved to Brakkus, knowing what she meant, for he too had noticed the mood of the Hurtz. "I'm fine. Go talk to him."

Annetta gave a quick bob of her bushy-haired head, and headed towards Brakkus, who strode in silence, without his usual loud chattering.

"Brakkus, can I talk to you for a moment?" she asked.

The giant stopped in his tracks and turned to face the young girl, his ears flattened against his skull.

"Aye, speak what it is ye have on yer mind," he said crossing, his arms as he waited.

"I just wanted to say I was sorry for what I said yesterday. You're right, we shouldn't have gone off like that, but we're kids. We don't always think about the danger of a situation, just the fun."

Brakkus's gaze remained hardened for a moment, but then softened. Seeing the sincerity of the girl's words to him, his arms dropped to his side as a sign of acceptance.

"It's alright, lass. Just try not to do it again, ya understand?" He looked down at her. "Now come on before we lose 'em. I don't think the elf will do too well on his own in the stables."

Annetta nodded, a smile returning to her face as she followed the giant through the halls.

಄ಇ

Once everyone was set with their horses, they moved out for the castle. Puc was already in a sour mood because of how long it had taken for everyone to assemble. Brakkus argued that if he was so worried he should have given them all a more specific, less poetic time than 'at dawn.'

"A soldier works on time, not verse," the Hurtz stated again. "Ya want us all gathered at a particular time, name the time, and don't beat about the bush like a maddened goblin."

"We will do it your way next time, Brakkus," the elf said once the rant had finished and had reached their destination. "The Morwick portal is located in the lower level of the castle. The simplest way will be to go from the rear entrance where the cave is."

"Ya sure that's a good idea? There may be something lurking in there," Brakkus protested.

"Please, that wyvern was disposed of years ago, and the entire cave was checked for any eggs that could have survived," Puc informed him, before turning to the others. He noted the now uneasy expressions on their faces.

"Orbeyus was a little fond of wyverns," he explained. "He tried to tame one, but once he passed away, it became feral and we had to dispose of it with Brakkus, in fear it would destroy the castle. We had to then search the cave, because wyverns reproduce asexually, meaning they don't need to mate with one another."

"And they're tricky little blighters," Brakkus added. "That one almost tore my arm off when we fought it. Got lucky Thanestorm shot a spell when he did."

Once inside of the cave they walked beside their horses, and were it not for Puc's staff giving off light, they would have tripped all over one another. The smell of damp rock was all around, and from the light hitting the inside of the cave, Annetta could swear that walls glistened with water but, when she touched them the stone was dry.

"Years of erosion," Puc said, catching her out of the corner of her eye as he led the way to what looked like a wooden door placed in the middle of the rock. "This entrance was built as an escape in case the castle was ever overrun. It was also used for guerilla warfare during the Great War by Orbeyus and his forces."

Reaching into his robes, Puc produced a large set of iron keys. Selecting one, he carefully placed it into the lock. There was a click, and moments later the mage pushed the door open after removing the key. Muttering something, torches lit up instantly in the hall before them, and he continued to lead the way.

After walking some distance, the hall before them widened, coming to an end. Annetta noted the doors that stood locked before them.

"Now, can ya remember which one?" Brakkus teased. "I'm surprised ya remembered as much as ya did so far."

"When you've seen these halls the amount of time I have Hurtz, you do not forget," Puc stated bluntly, causing Brakkus to chuckle as he inserted the key.

But the door did not creep open. Puc pushed as hard as he could. It was as though something was blocking the path before them. Brakkus patted his companion on the shoulder, and Puc stepped aside. With one heave the giant forced the door open, taking a good look at the lock mechanism before letting anyone through.

"It's rusted over from the all the humidity," he said, running a clawed finger along the deteriorating metal. "I'll need to come back later and put in a new one."

Jason pulled his attention away from the rusted lock and walked his horse into the room. Above them on the doorway was a massive stone arch, similar like the ones in and out of Aldamoor. On this one, there were two massive Minotaur guardians engraved into the stone. They were clad from head to hoof in what looked like heavy armor, and held a warhammer in their hands. The portal within the room looked similar to the one leading to Severio Castle, appearing to be made of liquid, only blue and brown instead of red and black.

"I would suggest that now is the time for you to change into winter gear," Puc said. "As I said, Morwick is shrouded by an almost eternal winter, and there is a good chance we will arrive in the midst of it. We will also need to set our watches once we cross there..."

Puc rolled away the heavy sleeve of his robe and looked at the watch for what seemed like a good few minutes, clearly trying to work something out.

"Well, so much for not forgetting." Brakkus snickered as the elf continued to stare in silence at the watch, and only briefly glared back at his companion with a disapproving scowl.

Fiddling with one of the knobs on the top of the watch, he turned back to the others. "This one here, if you move it clockwise, will line up the time with the one here. You need to press the knob down before you go through the portal, so that time will stay the same once we go there. Once in the Morwick portal, it will sync the time in the watch to the place you are in, grounding the time here to the one in Morwick, so that it flows equally."

"Well wait, once we leave won't, like, ten years start passing there again when it's only one day here?" Jason asked.

Puc pulled out an extra watch from his robes and held it to Jason's face.

"As long as someone there has one of these, our times will be synced," he stated. "I will need to go back this week and give one to Kaian as well."

"So, wait, all it takes is just one little watch to synchronize time in different dimensions?" Annetta tried to grasp it all herself, looking at the device on her wrist. "That's a lot of power for a little thing like this. How does it work?"

Puc paused, closing his eyes as he tried to steady himself. His shoulders slumping beneath his black cloak as he exhaled.

"Miss Severio, have I ever in all this time here stated that I am a scientist?" Puc shot a narrow eyed look at the girl, who shook her head. "Then you will agree that I am not the creator of such a contraption, and therefore have no knowledge of how it works, so do not ask me. I'm sure it's written somewhere in the library, and if you wish, you can look it up at your leisure."

Brakkus pressed a large paw on the mage, gripping him firmly as if to remind him of his place. Annetta noted the reaction in Puc to her question. "I'm sorry. I was just curious."

"No need to be." Puc sighed, as though something sat at the back of his mind, but quickly dismissed it. "Everyone set the C.T.S.'s as I've shown you, so we may be off."

Annetta, Jason and the others set the times on the watches as Puc had shown them, and threw on their winter jackets, waiting for further instruction.

"Aren't ya going to throw something else over that?" Brakkus looked at his companion, putting on a thick fur cloak.

"Do you have any idea how many layers of clothing I'm already in?" Puc raised an eyebrow at the Hurtz. He then turned his attention back to the others. "Saddle up."

"Lock and load," Jason grinned, only to have Puc glare him down. "What? Oh. Sorry."

Getting on the horse as quickly as he'd shot the look, the elf took off and disappeared into the portal. Annetta could tell that Puc felt they were wasting time standing around and talking. Taking his lead, she closed her eyes and whispered into Bossman's ear to fly. The horse bolted straight ahead into the blue and brown water wall.

She had expected to feel some kind on sensation to overtake her like in the other portals, a smell or a taste, but nothing seemed to happen. It was only when the horse finished running that she felt the cold hit the skin on her knuckles, causing it to instantly become stiff and leathery. She felt something touch her cheek and turn to water, and opening her eyes, she found herself in what looked to be another setting out of a fairy tale.

For miles around them stretched cliffs and mountains of deep brown stone, capped with snow. As far as Annetta could see, there was no vegetation of any kind, save for some sparse grass that grew on the ground beneath her among the snow and dirt. A sharp wind passed by every so often, blowing stray snow from the ground, causing her to wish that her grandfather had made an alliance with a race that resided in warmer climates. She hid deeper in the hood of her parka. Brakkus, Darius, Jason and Link emerged through the portal moments after.

"Holy...sweet...what in the world?" Jason clung to the sides of his jacket as his whole body shook with the shock of the cold.

"It's not so bad, lad. Ye'll get used to it." Brakkus slapped him across the back, causing the boy to straighten in the saddle. The Hurtz turned his eyes towards his elven companion, already studying a map in his hands. "Where to from here? There was once a city, right?"

"This map is now over a hundred years old," Puc said, neatly folding the parchment and placing it in his robes. "If it's still relevant, Morwick lies west, so west we shall go." He gently urged his horse onward.

"Is there any telling what we'll find?" Brakkus questioned, following his lead with the others.

"I cannot honestly tell you, friend," Puc replied. "What I do know is that last we were here, all was stable between the Minotaurs and giants."

Puc turned back to the younger members of his party. "There is an eternal rivalry in this world between Minotaurs and giants. When Orbeyus and I first came to this land, we needed to help the Minotaurs beat back the giants that had taken over their land in order to get them to join us. It was a bloody account, one I will not soon forget."

"Nor them giants," Brakkus said with a chuckle, "We gave 'em a damn good thrashing with Lord Orbeyus."

"That we did, old friend." Puc smiled faintly, then continued on leading them through the snow-covered grounds.

"So is this whole world like this?" Jason asked. "Covered in snow I mean?"

"From what we have explored and what we know, yes," Puc answered the boy. "You have to understand that going through a portal is like going into another entire existence. It would take a thousand lifetimes to know everything that goes on in each universe completely, including that world's solar system and stars."

Jason felt very small upon hearing this, and it made him think back to what he had heard about Mislantus. How could one person want to control so much when he would never know the full extent of knowing everything he would conquer? His thoughts were quickly shaken off by the cold wind blowing in his face, causing goosebumps to form on his neck.

"How far away is Morwick?" Link looked over at the elven mage who rode at the front.

"About an hour's ride from the portal. At least, it was," Puc stated. "City boundaries could have either fallen in, or..."

Puc stopped at the edge of a cliff and looked downward, a perturbed look on his face.

"Expanded." He finished his sentence.

Annetta, Brakkus, Darius, Jason, and Link came closer to the edge and looked down at what Puc had been staring at, a massive maze made of black stone. Though the structure did not rise above the mountains, it stood out, an imposing force of power on the landscape that seemed to suck the beauty out of everything around it and encased itself as the center of everyone's attention.

"Someone likes mazes..." Jason tried his hand at sarcasm and failed, particularly since no one else seemed to be really listening.

"It is a war tactic used by Minotaurs," Puc explained. "Trapping their foes who have no sense of direction. Minotaurs can find their way out of even the most complicated labyrinth. It is how they survived in a landscape that looked so similar. Morwick was known for having its outer walls be composed of a maze of black stone, which means the city must have grown since we have last been here."

"And it looks like we know who kept their land," Brakkus added. "The question is, will they remember us?"

"Only one way to find out. We move forward." Puc veered his horse around and onto the path that led down towards the labyrinth.

The closer they got to the structure, the larger it appeared to be. Annetta got a sinking feeling as they came closer. This was not a place she wanted to end up in alone, and she had no idea how they would find the front gate once they entered. They dismounted their horses and had a look around.

"There, in the center of the city, should lie Stoneberg Castle," Puc said, pointing to what looked like towers rising even higher than the monolithic walls of the maze before them. "But seeing as the city has expanded so, it will take time to get there."

Before anyone could react however to what Puc had said, the clattering of chain mail and hooves could be heard drawing nearer from behind the walls of the labyrinth. Feeling uneasy, Jason summoned his mace with a quick uttering of the word, while Annetta drew a sword she had been given from the armory to use in place of Severbane, putting the shield out before her in case of an immediate attack. Link too placed a hand on his sword, but did not draw it, while the others stood unmoving.

"You can relax. This is only protocol," Puc assured them.

Out charged two large black Minotaurs, armed with twin headed battle axes. They were covered from head to hoof in armor, and upon their chests gleamed dark blue tabards, almost blending in with the silver chain mail. Annetta and Jason nearly fell over in fright seeing the two creatures, but kept their ground, holding their weapons at eye level.

"State thyne business on cloven hoof ground, flat footers," the one to the right spoke, holding his axe in a battle ready position, "Be forewarned, we do not take kindly to strangers."

The second Minotaur stood in silence, ready to strike. Upon locking eyes with Annetta's shield, however, the giant fell to his knees, pressing his hands upon the hilt of his axe and bowing his head.

"Long live the Lord of the Axe and his son, the Hand of Death," he spoke, no longer able to look up at those before him.

The first Minotaur looked at the shield cautiously, and in realizing his flaw joined his comrade.

"Long live the Lion of Hell, warrior above warriors," he added, seeing the mace.

Annetta and Jason dropped their guards a little, looking at one another in confusion over what had just transpired,

"Rise, sons of Votan." Puc gestured with his hand for them to get up, and strode forward before the others. "I am Puc Thanestorm, known to you as The Mage. I come with my companions, Brakkus the Hurtz, Lincerious Heallaws, and Darius Silver, my apprentice. We come in peace to renew the old ways, and honor old friends. I bring to present to your king the daughter of the Hand of Death, and the son of the Lion of Hell."

"Then our king will be right pleased to know such warriors walk in his midst," the first Minotaur said as he rose. "I am Hideburn, and this is my brother Bonebreak. We are the guardians of the front gate surrounding Morwick. You must forgive us for our gruffness, but tragedy has struck within the city, and every outsider is a suspect. Please, come with us quickly, so we may bring you inside as friends and guests should be brought."

Puc narrowed his eyes upon hearing the word tragedy, but inclined his head, and mounted back on his horse. They followed the two guards, who managed to stand as tall as the mage sitting on his horse, further into the maze.

362

Breaking the silence, Puc looked at the guards. "What tragedy is it that has befallen these walls, if I may ask?"

Bonebreak tilted his head back slightly to answer, "The Crown Prince has been taken by one of the giants. Our scouts have told us rumors that Yarmir the Firstborn plans to resurrect those of his kin by sacrificing the young prince, filthy flatfooters and their magic. Most of our forces are deployed in search of him, but no news has come as of yet. The whole city is in a state of alarm. Don't let our own steady dispositions fool you."

"The training of a Minotaur." Puc nodded, finishing the thought.

It was quiet for some time as they moved through the labyrinth. The imposing black walls made everyone feel uncomfortable. At times, it seemed as though they would start moving in on them. It gave Annetta and Jason a sick feeling, and they tried to focus on the path, even though their eyes wandered from side to side.

"The walls are meant to draw the attention of the enemy and cause paranoia," Hideburn explained. "There is nothing worse than fear in a place that looks exactly the same all around."

"How do you not feel that way?" Annetta asked.

"When we are young, all Minotaurs are trained to be able to maneuver in mazes. It is a right of passage in our society. Going through mazes is repeated multiple times with the young, until they are no longer afraid of the possibility of becoming lost, and are able to find their way through the most difficult of webs. In the final test, for a period of forty days, we are placed in a labyrinth built for the event with a ration of food and water to last us the time expected to complete the task. We are then required to find our own way out of the maze, or die in it."

Annetta nodded. She still hoped she would not have to go through a maze to prove her worth to the Minotaur King with Jason. She could barely maneuver her way around downtown Toronto, even less in a maze.

After walking for some distance more, they came to an imposing front gate. Beside each door were carvings of the same guarding Minotaurs as the arch in Severio Castle.

"We bring guests to the halls of Lord Ironhorn," Bonebreak roared to the observatory tower, his breath visible on the wind that was now laced with small flakes of snow.

"You know the orders! No one in or out, unless it is the warriors returning home!" the sentry barked.

"We bring the daughter of the Hand of Death and the son of the Lion of Hell," Hideburn retorted. "So I would suggest you open the gate before we ram it down and tell the king of your insolence."

There was silence and the wooden gates slowly crept open before them, the sound of rusted iron from the hinges creating a screeching noise as the slabs of wood moved along. Annetta had expected the city to be as busy as it had been when they had come into Aldamoor, but the streets before them lay empty. The only signs of life were the soldiers posted around the city that moved from time to time as though on duty, staring at the newcomers on their horses.

"Pay no heed to them," Hideburn assured them as they moved in the direction of the towers they had seen from beyond the maze. "They have never seen flatfooters your size. We are much more accustomed to seeing them on a larger scale, with a more threatening disposition. And we are all on alert."

"Is it always this quiet in Morwick?" Darius asked his mentor. "It said in the chronicles that the streets were always bursting with life even in the darkest winter days."

"That they did, young master," Bonebreak replied instead, "but we are currently involved in a crisis. Our prince has been taken hostage, and orders are for all who are not of the army to stay indoors in case others fall prey."

The buildings they passed by were not like in Aldamoor, for everything in Morwick seemed to be carved in heavy stone. Even shop signs were carved in stone slabs. In the distance, the monolithic black walls of the maze lined the city, guarding it from any intruders who would dare come near its borders. Annetta tried to get a good look at all the architecture around her, but with the wind howling more and more, it was impossible. She tightened her hoodie around her head to keep the wind from rushing to her ears.

"I take it yer not fond of the winters back home?" Brakkus noticed her fidgeting.

"If I had one wish, it would be the weather always stayed above twenty four degrees," she muttered, to which the giant gave a hearty laugh.

They rode past an assortment of buildings, some of which looked older than others, until they came to an opening in the streets where paths from multiple directions joined. Annetta could see the steps leading towards the castle, but what caught her eye before that was the immense statue in the center of the square. There before them, standing over ten feet tall in the same pose as his portrait in the castle was Orbeyus, his black alabaster eyes gazing out at them.

"A tribute to one of our nation's heroes," Hideburn said. "Made by our finest craftsbeasts from the same stone which protects our lands. May his spirit watch over us for eternity."

"But were there no other heroes who helped as well?" Jason asked.

"There were, and their images all lie within Stoneberg's walls," Bonebreak answered. "But the Lord of the Axe is known best to our people. It was he who led our armies against the giants and drove them back, saving our lands from their rule."

"We may take your mounts and store them in stables if you like," Hideburn suggested. "It has been a long time since anyone has seen horses here in Morwick, but I am sure we can find someone to care for your beasts."

"That would be good." Puc dismounted as the Minotaur guard came to take the reins from him, and proceeded to take them from everyone else gathered.

"I will see to this task before returning to the wall," Hideburn said. "Bonebreak will lead you to Lord Ironhorn. Of fast speed, my friends." He inclined his horned head before leaving.

Puc tilted his own head to the Minotaur before turning on his heel and following Hideburn towards the steps to the castle. Annetta and the others followed, not knowing what to say about the situation unfolding before them. Bounding up the grey stone steps, they came before massive twin wooden doors and waited as they swung open at the Minotaur's command with a single gesture of an iron clad fist. Once inside, the doors closed, and their bodies were instantly hit with goosebumps from the heat of the many fireplaces and torches burning within. Everywhere Annetta looked, an orange glow filled the crevices of the rough stone walls.

Jason warmed his hands by rubbing them together, and removed his hood to get a better look. It seemed darker than Severio Castle. The walls seemed to compress the hall around him, but unlike the maze, it felt more like they were old relatives coming in for a hug.

Hideburn led at the front of the group, guards and servants from the castle parting as he walked with Puc at his side.

"Is Lord Ironhorn able to hold an audience?" the soldier asked a Minotaur dressed in a red garb with twin golden axes embroidered on it.

"He is in the throne room," guard in red replied. "I will inform him of your presence, but I highly doubt it considering what is going on. And these are?" He eyed Puc and the others.

"Tell him I bring forth the descendant of the Lord of the Axe, and the son of the Lion of Hell. It was long foretold that they would return in our time of need," Hideburn announced.

The red clad Minotaur said nothing more. Vigorously nodding his head, he rushed forward ahead of them to announce their arrival. Hideburn turned to the group.

"His majesty is to be addressed only as Lord Ironhorn. He does not take kindly to other titles," he explained. "It is seen as a mark of respect to address the king by his title and name. It shows that he is a compassionate ruler, and not a tyrant without a soul."

Annetta raised an eyebrow, looking at Link for answers and receiving a blank stare as she tried to figure out why a race of fearsome warriors would be concerned about their soul. She remembered what Puc had said about technology and spirituality and figured there would be enough time later for him to clarify the customs of the Minotaurs to her. She was also uneasy about Hideburn mentioning a prophecy of their return. It put a chill in her spine, despite the warmth of the room.

Jason looked up the walls of the castle while walking beside Brakkus. It was then he noticed the massive shelves carved into the walls. Upon them, in the same black stone as the one in which Orbeyus was immortalized were other sculptures of creatures and men he could not recognize.

"Are those the statues you spoke of?" he asked their guide.

"Yes," Hideburn assured him as they neared another twin set of doors, before which stood guards and the red-garbed Minotaur he had spoken with earlier. "They stand in commemoration of those who were there during the Great War, and have done so for over a hundred years now, watching all those present inside these walls. If you look for your father's image, you may need to keep following me."

Exchanging quick nods, the crimson clad creature turned around and went in first, slipping through the door more gracefully than Annetta thought possible of such a large beast.

"Lord Ironhorn," the voice of the Minotaur boomed from behind the wooden doors, "I present to you Puc Thanestorm, leading his party of Brakkus the Hurtz, Darius Silver, Lincerious Heallaws, Annetta Severio, the

366

granddaughter of the Lord of the Axe, and Jason Kinsman the son of the Lion of Hell."

There was a long silence. Puc's grip on his staff tightened as though he were ready to cast a spell at a moments notice. Brakkus also coiled in a defensive position along with Link and Darius at either side. After their encounter in Aldamoor, it was an expected reaction. Even Annetta and Jason found themselves reacting similarly.

"Let those who come with Thanestorm enter," a deep and rich voice instructed as the doors instantly opened.

The chamber, brighter than the halls they had just walked, lit up with life the minute they peered inside. Tapestries of gold and sapphire decorated the walls, before which stood more black statues. Within the center of the room stood a throne of white marble. Above the throne hung two single bladed axes, crossed and suspended by large chains to keep them from falling. Upon the throne a Minotaur resided, clad in gold chain mail and a sapphire tabard. Upon his brow rested a heavy golden crown lined with blue gemstones. His light brown fur seemed even lighter in the bright room as he observed those who had just come into his abode. Annetta also noted the fact that his left horn was not real, but made of a silver metal. She wanted to chuckle at the irony, but instead said nothing, not wanting to offend the king of the castle.

Ironhorn's gaze pierced those standing in the doorway as though he were searching for answers in their faces. As soon as his eyes locked onto Annetta and Jason, he rose from his seat.

"I would recognize both those pairs of eyes anywhere from the stories written within our chronicles. Venture forth, that I may have a better look." Ironhorn motioned for them to come forward.

Annetta and Jason looked at Puc with a questioning glance, to which the elven mage nodded his head in approval as they went ahead. The Minotaur King stood before them, elevated on the steps leading to his seat of office, his sharp clawed hands hooked into his thick belt, as his azure eyes watched the two youth in curiosity.

"Lord Ironhorn." Annetta stopped at the foot of the steps and bowed to the king as low as she could go without losing her balance with the massive shield she carried. Jason followed her lead, a bit out of step.

"You carry the shield of the Hand of Death," Ironhorn said, "therefore it is my right to assume that you, m'lady, are the descendant of the Lord of the Axe." He smiled and then turned to Jason. "As I can see from the pendant around your neck that you are the son of the Lion of Hell."

The king looked up beyond them, at the other companions.

"And those who know the legends know of the wisdom of Puc Thanestorm the Mage, and the courage of Brakkus the Hurtz, who stood with my grandsire in driving back the forces of Yarmir. And though your stories both go unknown to me," he said to Darius and Link, "I am sure that whatever they may be, you come of good blood with those here that I know from scripture as though they were my own kin."

The Minotaur Lord then sat back down upon his throne and rested his chin on a curled fist, gazing upon them all.

"To what pleasure is it that the halls of Stoneberg give visiting rites to ones such as yourselves in these dark times?" he asked.

Puc took this as his cue and strode forward, his cloak and robes billowing behind him. He placed a hand upon Annetta and Jason's shoulders, getting them to move back.

"We come, Lord Ironhorn, to revive old alliances. To bring back the Four Forces that once were responsible for protecting the Eye to All Worlds. Those of the Water Kin have already sworn alliance, and we come now, humbled, to the race of Stone to ask to lend us their firsts in a time of impending war." Puc spoke with the same confidence he had shown at the gate, clear of any of the sarcasm his friends knew him by within the halls of the Lab. He was on a mission here, and it was clear by his disposition that he would not falter until his quest was complete.

Ironhorn took in the words, and savored them as though they were a well flavored piece of meat. He locked eyes with Puc before moving his gaze to the two youth, and then to the others gathered.

"It is to my knowledge, Thanestorm, that an alliance has mutual benefits on both sides. I cannot focus on any other cause of war with the knowledge that my son is missing," the Minotaur Lord sighed. "You come in a time of our own need, a need which in days of old, the banners of Lord Orbeyus would have answered. It was foretold that his forces would one day return in our darkest hour, and I believe this meeting is not without a tinge of fate. What better way to resolve the question of heroic lineage than this?"

The words pierced the entire party. Even Puc stood rooted to the spot.

"If they truly are who they say they are, then this should not be a difficult task, am I correct in assuming so?" Ironhorn inquired, breaking the silence.

"Indeed, Lord Ironhorn." Puc nodded in agreement.

"Good." The Minotaur Lord acknowledged. "Then here is my task for you. Bring back my son from Yarmir's mountain, and a discussion shall be taken up when the prince is safe."

"As you will it, we shall see it done." Puc inclined his head again in an emotionless bow.

At the sound of those words, Annetta wanted to get up and protest. But the decision had been taken from her. Puc had already spoken, and the only thing she could do was bundle up in her parka and ride on to wherever the road led them.

"We will head out at once," Puc continued. "I will, however, request a map, or someone to act as a guide to Yarmir's lair."

"We have maps which may be provided by merchants within the markets. The giant's territory will be marked on them. I may lead you to them if you like," Hideburn offered.

"But don't you need to get back to your post?" Annetta let her anxiety get the better of her and spoke out.

"My dear young one, we have more than just a pair of Minotaurs guarding the front gates," Ironhorn chuckled.

"Oh." she felt herself blush a bit and noted Puc's head shaking from the corner of her eye.

સ૦ભ

Upon leaving the presence of the Minotaur King and being set in the right direction by Hideburn, the companions set off to the market for Puc to acquire the necessary maps. From what he remembered, the mountain where the giants had once taken refuge lay to the north of the city, and it would take them a day of riding in order to get there. Hearing this was not what Annetta had wanted. She knew full well the sort of hell that would erupt in school once she got back from being absent, and the piles of homework she would have to catch up on. There was also another tension that lay with the group as they pressed on through the nearly abandoned streets, and the only soul among the brave enough voice the thought was Jason.

"Okay, now that we're far away enough, what was that all about? All that 'it was foretold' garbage?" he vented.

Annetta looked over at her friend's sudden burst of words, which caused them to stop.

"I mean, I get it. We're descendants of those two, but, I'm sorry, this is too much," the boy shook his head.

"Aye," Brakkus spoke, trying to calm the boy. "I do agree ye were sort of put on the spot, but it happens. Ye just need to make the best of the situation at hand."

"He's right, though," Annetta added. "We might be related to them, but we're not actually legendary heroes or anything. We're just kids. I mean, we go to a highschool in the city, play video games, we daydream. And don't tell me none of you think this kidnapping isn't bit suspicious. We just had to find a lost tome in the last place we were at."

Link smiled a bit, looking down at his boots as he tried to cover up the slip of emotion. He could not help but agree with the point she was making. His eyes turned to Darius, who stood beside Puc. The elven mage halted upon hearing the words, and drove into action right away upon the finishing of the last sentence.

"The Minotuars and giants have been at war for thousands of years," Puc replied, "So no, I do not find it suspicious. Well, the timing perhaps, but not the situation. As for your whining, I suggest you leave it behind. If you think this is difficult, then I can only laugh at future tasks that will come before you and your reactions to them."

Annetta wrinkled her nose in anger. "What's that got to do with-"

"It has everything to do with the situation." Puc cut her off. "It has everything to do with what will be happening in the years to come, in the battle that lies ahead. Yes, it's unfair they put you on the spot, but considering your ancestry, this will happen more often than not. You need to accept it, and accept it with the grace and dignity that is befitting who you are meant to be."

"But we're not-" Jason snapped.

"You are to them," the mage interrupted again, causing the boy to frown in defeat. "You are a symbol of hope, something that says there are those who will stand and defend the future. They do not see children who go to school. They do not see the boy and girl who pay little attention to their lessons, and chase dragons in their dreams. They see hope, and the ones who will not bow to shadow."

"Okay, but that doesn't change the fact that-" Annetta growled.

370

Puc raised a hand to silence her. "It changes everything. You are not on Earth anymore. Annetta. I understand it is hard for you both to accept. You think it was easy for your fathers? They were boys that were your age once, who were just about as unruly as you are, and they didn't spring out of the ground. Neither did Orbeyus. I remember him as a wild-eyed boy who said he would unite worlds to help others, and everyone laughed at him. But he did it, and saved thousands. You know what they all had in common?"

"I bet you're going to tell us," Jason muttered.

Puc narrowed his eyes into a glare upon the comment, but continued. "They cast off any mantle placed upon them, and plowed on ahead without complaint. It didn't matter if they were expected to be great heroes. They simply went and did the best they could."

The last words cast in the midst of the empty stone streets left silence among the companions, the cold wind blowing past them personifying the sudden conflict that had arisen.

"Even the smallest person can make a difference if they believe in themselves," The elf said once more with a scowl on his face, and stormed on ahead with his staff in hand, leaving the rest to contemplate while he entered one of the small buildings.

Another bout of silence ensued. Annetta felt the weight of the words sink into her like the chill that was slowly overtaking her face and hands. Jason felt less burdened with the explanation of the elf, even if it had been somewhat harsh in its tone. Another gust of wind passed by them, blowing stray snowflakes into the boys face.

"Man, do we even have like, tents or anything?" Jason grumbled, covering his head with his hood.

"That's what caves are for." Darius snickered as Annetta glared at him. "What? It's true."

"We done it plenty of times here before," Brakkus stated. "No point in carrying something that won't even provide shelter from the wind. Rock is sturdier."

"Right... I kind of hadn't thought of that." Jason shook his head. "Still, though, we don't have sleeping-"

Before he could finish the sentence, a stack of what looked like heavy furs landed in his hands, almost crushing the boy from the impact. Annetta chuckled at the sight, only to be saddled with the same load moments later.

"I cannot keep listening to you babble and complain so make yourselves useful and carry your sleeping hides." Puc growled from beyond the mounds as he paid the merchant and threw the same loads to Brakkus, Link and Darius. "Unknown's bane...are you really who they say you are sometimes?"

"I don't know, you might want to check it out with a more reliable source," Annetta said sourly.

Puc was about to retort at Annetta's comment, but upon hearing Brakkus burst out into laughter, he decided to let the young girl win the spat.

"Alright ya lot, come along. We're wasting daylight," The mage threw his own sleeping hides over his shoulder with his free hand, and began to make haste back to where they had left their horses.

Chapter 36

Sarina woke up hearing the rain rapping on her windows, and the wind through the trees. It looked so dark that when she first opened her eyes, she thought it was still night, and would have gone back to sleep had she not seen the time on her alarm clock. Sitting up, she stretched and went about to start her daily routine of showering and getting dressed. Picking out a pair of dark blue jeans and a button up green shirt, she headed downstairs to where she could hear Matthias listening to the television.

The assassin sat on the black leather sofa, absorbed in what he was seeing on the screen. Sarina looked over to see he was watching the news channel.

"They're such a destructive species," he mused. "It's…it's wonderful. Fascinating that an entire world can be so violent to one another, without knowing that just overhead there is a threat that could end it all in a heartbeat."

Sarina glance again at the screen to see something had been set on fire. Statistics flew by underneath the picture as a voice both dispassionate and explanatory spat out information about what was going on.

"They're a young world though, aren't they? It's kind of to be expected," she said, dismissing what she saw on the screen. Grabbing a box of cereal, she poured it into a bowl and went to get some milk from the fridge.

Matthias smirked in agreement and flipped the channel to something else.

"Do you think he will be back in school tomorrow?" Matthias said, trying to sound idle. "I don't want to keep reporting to your father that we have no progress on this. I think we may need to push things to the next level and play on his emotions a bit more." He looked at the young girl. "The next time we see him, tell him there was an attack. Tell him it is no longer safe for us to reside where we do, and that we must move. The severance of that connection should push him to the breaking point of do or do not."

"Understood." She nodded.

Matthias's face darkened further, and after a pause, he spoke, "I never told you, but your father sent Amarok here."

"Amarok? But didn't he-" Sarina raised an eyebrow in surprise.

"Oh no, he's very much alive, and in his own words, he will remove me and take you back should it seem like we are straying from what we need to do which is why we must push things along." The young assassin turned to face her.

"What? But it's not your fault it's taking so long! Becoming friends with someone and gaining their trust enough to know their secrets takes time," Sarina protested, dropping her spoon in her bowl.

"You are speaking to a professional killer. I know what it takes, and how long it takes, but someone who is not trained does not, and when you don't have things to report they get mad," Matthias snarled, feeling frustrated. He turned off the television and walked into the kitchen.

"Then why does father trust you so much?" She watched him come closer. "He always said you were the best."

"I was not always the best." He sighed. "Do you know how I became the best, and how Amarok ended up the way he did?"

"No, how?" she asked sarcastically.

"I did it to him, and took his place as your father's top assassin," he snapped. "I was in Amarok's shadow for years, from when I first came aboard Valdhar. It took me a lot of time to get to where I am now and it was never easy."

Sarina's eyes widened upon hearing this, his blue eyes piercing her gaze in an almost animalistic manner. Matthias had always been the one who came and shared his stories with her about his missions and the things he saw. But she had never heard about him being Amarok's apprentice. He had always seemed invincible to her.

Matthias sighed, looking down at his feet as his shoulders slumped down.

"I never wanted you to know about that, you who were always filled with wonder about the things I'd seen and done. The truth is that your father's only number one is himself, and everything below is whoever fights to get to the place they are." He gazed back into her eyes. "That's all I lied about. I am loyal to him. Tyrant and cold-hearted bastard as he might be in his own right, he still gave me everything I have today instead of leaving me for dead. That's worth being loyal to someone about and I will continue to carve out my place at his side."

Sarina nodded, hearing what Matthias had said to her. Still, something stung in her heart listening to him speak, and it had nothing to do with the

374

way he had addressed her father. She felt the same way he did about Mislantus. There was only one number when it came to who survived, and it was not his little girl, a fact she was realizing the more time she spent with Matthias.

"I'll do what I can when he gets back," she said quietly. Taking her bowl with her, she went back to her room.

Remaining behind, Matthias sank back on the couch in front of the television, but did not turn it on. His mind wandered elsewhere, to something more nightmarish than the news channel could produce.

ℰᑎᎶᎡ

Four years before arriving on Earth, Amarok stood with his back to a youth, looking down at the ravine below. The sky around them swirled a mixture of red, brown and orange as the flames from the battle died down, another conquest for the flags of Mislantus the Threat.

"Is it not a glorious sight, my apprentice?" the elder assassin spoke, the wind blowing through his mane of white hair. "Death is the one thing that reigns supreme over all creation. Without it, our lives have no meaning. We would simply exist in a world without end, were mortality not present,"

Matthias stood some distance behind him, the blood where the nation's leader had attempted to plead for salvation decorating his chest plate. He watched Amarok Mezorian, the head assassin of his lord and master, contemplating his next action. Finally, he spoke.

"Then, as you know, my next move should not come as a surprise to you," he said, breaking the prolonged silence.

Amarok smirked. His eyes closed as dust and debris did what it wished around him, the scent of burning buildings ensnaring his nostrils.

"Let me guess. I have two options. I may step down, or you will fight me." He chuckled. "No, no, that would not be your style. You simply challenge me for the title. Am I correct, Matthias Teron?"

The veteran assassin turned around to face the young man in black armor, their cloaks already in battle stance as they floated and snapped on the wind.

"Only thing you've ever been right about, old man." The claws on Matthias's gauntlets extended as he took off in a charge towards him, roaring in anger.

Amarok smirked as he awaited the impact of the attack. Matthias leaped through the air, about to collide with him as Amarok's armor sprang to life, spikes arising all over his arms like on a hedgehog. Steel clashed on steel as Matthias's claws collided with Amarok's spiked shell. He bounced back, circling his mentor as he looked for an opening.

"You're quite the predictable lad," Amarok said. "Yet I still wonder, did I not teach you all you know? Take you in when you were just a babe and show you all I know?"

"You did. But all children must surpass their parents, and I grow tired of being the shadow at your heel. I want to carve out my own name, starting in your dead flesh!" Matthias snarled as he leaped once more at the white haired assassin.

"Bold words for one so inexperienced," scoffed Amarok as he took each attack with grace, bracing his legs on the shattered earth below him. "Are you done yet, pup?"

Matthias retreated back to his original position and watched his mentor, no signs of fatigue visible on him. Amarok glared at the youth as a laugh broke over his face.

"Now, will you survive the storm you've brought on, Teron? Or will it be your end once psychic fire is brought into play." Amarok grinned, bringing up his right hand, palm up, as sparks of purple and blue energy began to leap around his fingertips.

Matthias pulled back his left fist, claws extended as though he were getting ready to land a punch on Amarok, but the youth had a very different reason for doing so. His right hand came up to eye level as a ball of energy began to simmer and dance within the center of his palm, glowing dark purple as sparks of blue zipped all around his arm.

The world around them seemed to slow down and tense up as the balls of purple and blue flame grew larger in each opponents grasp. Their eyes were locked upon each other. All else ceased to exist.

Matthias made the first move, throwing the ball of flame straight towards Amarok. The elder assassin dodged the blast with little effort, twirling on his heel. They exchanged three more rounds of flames, each slightly nicking the other and proving that neither was greater. Amarok finally shot his own psychic fire, but controlling the form, he caused the flames to come out of his hand in a long barrier instead of a sphere. Matthias leaped away from the wall of fire, hiding behind the demolished foundation of another structure.

"What's the matter pup? You grow tired of your own game?" Amarok hissed. "Well you'd best know that a game started is not a game finished, and I finish all my games!"

"Has anyone ever told you that you like to talk a lot?" Matthias snapped, creating another ball of energy within his hands, nursing all his anger into it.

"I have a right to brag, don't I?" Amarok chuckled and shifted his position lower to the ground. He focused his mind, causing the spikes on his arms to curve forward, like hundreds of little knives. "Now, come out. I don't have all day with that lovely reception waiting for me back in the fortress."

Taunted, Matthias leaped from out of the debris and shot the blast, a move that cost him dearly in the battle. Expecting the move, Amarok teleported and was upon him instantly, his cold fist gripping Matthias by the throat and slowly squeezing.

"You are still the same old Matty I took in all those years ago, hungering for a fight wherever he looks." Amarok chuckled as the spikes on his arm stretched further, towards Matthias's face like a pack of snakes. "It is a shame that this time marks our last battle. I should very much have liked for you to have been around after my death, and carry on in my place. You have what it takes for this job."

Matthias swallowed hard as the spikes came ever closer. He knew of the deadly poison applied to those barbs. He knew he was a dead man if he did not act quickly.

"As I said before Mezorian, seeing as master no longer fits, you talk too much!" Matthias snarled as he lifted both hands to Amarok's face, full of psychic fire, releasing the flames onto his body. Breaking free of his grip in the chaos, Matthias stumbled to the side, catching his breath and checking his neck for bruising as he watched his master howl in the pain of the psychic flames, fire created only out of hatred.

಄

Matthias stared out the window blankly after reliving the memory as rain gently landed on the glass. His expression livened as he realized something. Why should he fear Amarok's return when he could use it to his advantage?

"Game on, indeed." He chuckled. "But don't think I will ever play fair."

Chapter 37

Having been led out of the maze surrounding the city, Annetta and her friends bid farewell to Hideburn and Bonebreak, who had returned to their posts. Turning their attention to the north, the horses began the course that would take them deep into the heart of what was once giant territory.

"The majority of the giants were transformed into statues made of a crystalline form within what once was Yarmir's lair," Puc explained to his younger companions. "I'm actually quite surprised that Yarmir is still alive. I would have thought the giant would have been vanquished by now."

"Aye, but he was a crafty son of a wench," Brakkus added. "And I recall him claiming was the first giant in this world."

"First giant?" Jason raised an eyebrow.

"In this world, giants are spawned, not born," Puc stated. "It takes a great deal of magic to spawn a giant. Yarmir was the first giant spawned by the ancient Minotaurs of this world, to serve and aid them in the building of their cities, as were others who came after him. But Yarmir, being the first, saw that there was something more in the world, freedom, and so he revolted with the others. It was how the war between Minotaur and giant started. When we came to this world with Orbeyus, it was already in full swing, and the Minotaurs were losing. We vowed to help drive back the giants from their lands in exchange for their help in overthrowing Mordred's forces."

"I thought you said a world can either have magic or technology, not both," Annetta interrupted.

"They evolve one way or another, but all worlds start off with a bit of both," Puc said. "It depends on the experiences of a given world which way it will go in the future. As you saw with Morwick, the Minotaurs have stayed far away from magic after the war with the giants, and instead have become masters of stone and iron."

Annetta nodded, tightening the grip on Bossman's reins in order to regain some feeling in her slowly numbing fingers. The further away they got from the city, the more confusing the landscape became. Every cliff staring down at them had the same snow-capped ledge, and every small tuff of string-like grass below them the same shape. The monotone clopping of horseshoes added to the unchanging pace of the journey. She could only compare it to a rural form of Aldamoor, which had had the same effect on her of not being able to distinguish one street from the next.

Link wrapped his scarf tighter across his face to keep the cold breeze from penetrating his skin. He kept close to Brakkus, with whom he had spent a great deal of time. Though he did not share it openly, a friendship based upon understanding had formed between him and the formidable warrior. Both had a single desire, and it was to protect those closest to them out of a fear of loss. It was not something either would admit to those they traveled with, but they both knew it was there. It made Link feel distanced from Annetta, Jason and Darius. Pry as he tried, he could not reach the same level of closeness he truly yearned for. It was a triangle of friendship he seemed to be forever locked out of, even if he had gotten closer to Annetta.

"What weighs on yer mind?" Brakkus noticed the frown forming on Link's partially covered face.

"Huh?" the youth looked up, "Oh its nothing."

"Ya looked like yer contemplating sending the remnants of a dying army into the gate of hell, and ya tell me its nothing." Brakkus chuckled. "I think I have the right to say that I know ya better than ya likes."

"It's really nothing, Brakkus," he snapped defensively, feeling his face heat up despite the cold.

The Hurtz snickered as they came to a stop, while Puc checked his bearings on the map some distance in front of them. Annetta, Jason, and Darius all huddled together, chatting. Brakkus caught Link's eyes wander towards them.

"Ye feel like ye don't fit in," he summarized.

"I know we talked about this before, Brakkus, but I still feel like I don't really have a place here. Sometimes I wonder if my coming here and following the vision I had was a mistake," he growled.

"I wouldn't say that." Brakkus shook his massive head. "Take a look and tell me what ya see there."

Link glanced a second time and looked back at Brakkus, confused.

"Yer missing in the picture," the Hurtz grinned. "Ya need to understand, lad, we are all one of a kind, and nothing can replace someone, but our presence can add to the overall picture. So, stop yer moping and go over there."

Before Link could retort, Brakkus slapped the horse's rear, sending Link's mount bolting forward.

Annetta turned around to see Link's horse charging towards them, and veered Bossman out of the way as the other horse came to a startling halt.

"You okay, man?" Jason asked withholding a laugh at seeing Link's frazzled expression.

"I've been better, thanks," the Gaian youth sighed, his eyes trailing to Brakkus, who rode over to join Puc.

"You know once you're out here long enough and bouncing about on horseback, it's not so bad," Annetta said. "The cold, I mean."

"I wonder if you'll be singing the same tune tomorrow when we've been inside a warm cave all night," Darius said.

"I'm not thinking about then. I'm focusing on now," she huffed, crossing her arms in the saddle.

"Well, we can do the same thing I did every morning back home and run a mile in the morning as a warm up," Link added.

"Before or after I dump a bucket of water on Annetta for sleeping in?" Darius grinned wickedly as a noise of protest emerged from Annetta, but no recognizable words formed.

"There will be no pneumonia on this journey, Silver," Puc's voice rang from behind his apprentice. "Everyone is to be fit. We've no time to waste on sickness because of horseplay. Save it for a later date."

Darius sighed, but nodded in obedience to his master, veering his horse around in the direction they were heading.

"Don't worry. If he did that I'd throw him in a lake," Link whispered to Annetta, causing her to smile.

"I heard that! And don't think I wouldn't do the same right back!" Darius threatened from the front as they all headed out once more.

"Challenge accepted, after the quest!" Link called back, and urged his horse into a dead run to match the pace of Puc, Brakkus, and Darius.

Annetta chuckled, looking at Jason, who shook his head as they took off.

As they travelled they saw no forms of life at all, except for Link once spotting what looked to be a pack of a sort of deer with goat horns and a thick white fur textured with specs of brown.

"Mountain deer," Puc said, upon catching sight of them. "The Minotaur's primary food source, as it was the giants. In the war, they were hunted to near extinction, sometimes being mistaken for Minotaurs by giants. But I can see they are now thriving."

"I could go for one over the fire tonight." Brakkus eyed the creatures. "Shall I bring one down?"

"We will go hunting later," Puc replied. "For now, our main focus is to find a cave to stay in and cover the most ground before the sun begins to set. Carrying a carcass of that size will likely slow us down and attract fenrikin in the process."

"Fenrikin?" Jason asked.

"A species of wild dogs that reside here," Puc explained. "They are sometimes trained as guards. They are incredibly vicious, and can take off a person's head in a matter of moments if given the chance. They were often used in the war as a distraction, as cannon fodder, usually by the giants."

They continued onward, until Puc came across what he saw to be a grotto large enough for them to fit in comfortably. Dismounting, they strode towards the entrance, led by the elven mage. Coming to the mouth of the cavern, they could instantly feel a rise in temperature, as though they had stepped into a well warmed home.

"Okay, I take back what I said earlier," Annetta announced, taking off her gloves and rubbing her hands together. "It's still cold outside no matter what."

Brakkus scanned the cave with his eyes. The walls seemed to be adorned with strange, barely legible scribbles in a language he was not familiar with, accompanied by drawings. He was about to say something to Puc, when his train of thought was interrupted.

"And Fefj does not likem when visitors brings coldsome into nice warms cave," a voice from the dark spoke.

Puc gripped his staff as Brakkus and Link unsheathed their swords, readying themselves in defensive stances. Darius's fingers sparked with magic, while Jason called upon Helbringer, and Annetta drew her sword.

Out of the shadows hobbled the strangest creature Annetta or Jason had ever seen. It had a grin so wide and a face so wrinkly that were it not for the shaggy brown hair atop its head, she would have had difficulty recognizing where its face started and ended. In one tiny, withered, barely useful hand, it seemed to be carrying what looked like a small stone that had one side worn out as if it had been used for scraping against rock.

"Now what's be so important that yous has to interruptem Fefj in making his master arts?" the thing growled in an angered tone, indicating at the carvings on the wall, which Annetta deemed almost child-like in appearance. But as she looked closer, she noticed the subject was far from the imagination of a child, due to the violence and other unseemly subjects depicted in the scenes. It made her want to turn away, and she lowered her head.

"Whats? You no liken dem?" The thing walked straight over to Annetta.

"Uh, no. They're very lovely." She responded almost automatically from being put on the spot.

"What is that thing?" Jason asked off to the side, looking at Puc, who stared back at it, stone-faced.

"That would be a troll," Puc said quietly under his breath.

"Fefj Rebry no besome thing! Fefj troll-folk." The troll, obviously hurt, scoffed, then turned to look back at what seemed to be a crudely set up fireplace with multiple fish roasting on it. "I also happens to be troll-folks withs delicious foods and fire. Wonderfuls life, is it nots?"

"Thanestorm, we ain't got time for this." Brakkus hovered over the shoulder of the elf, "It's going to get dark soon and we need to find shelter."

"He's right, master." Darius added. "The temperatures will drop to a point where the horses could die on us."

"No speaksome when Fefj talks! That bees Fefj rules here. Don't makeum send Fenrikin's after yous!" the creature warned as he continued his rant, having gotten everyone's attention once more. He sat down on a rock before the fire and began gorging himself on one of the cooked fish. "Too bads you don't has lovely caves like Fefj does, with oh so cozy fire and fishes for eatsin."

"This is ridiculous, let's just go," Annetta said not enjoying the troll's attitude. "I bet there are hundreds of other caves around here."

"You cans if you likes, but no caves for another hundred leagues or so," the troll said nonchalantly, cleaning off the fish bones on the stick and tossing them into the fire before grabbing another, "Mmmm fishes so tasty and juicy. Such goods foods."

"Can't I just kill the thing and put it outta its misery?" Brakkus squinted as the troll continued to ramble, mostly to himself, on the other side of the cave. "All them wrinkles are hurting my eyes."

"Whats em matters, rabbit-wolf flatfoot? Mads from colds?" The toothy, wrinkled grin glared at Brakkus, making the Hurtz flatten his ears in a threatening manner. "Now speakem! Whats brings you to here?"

"We are off to find the son of Lord Ironhorn of Morwick, who has been captured by Yarmir and the giants," Puc began.

"Oh, I hopes the little cow gets eaten by them." The troll grinned widely in delight, watching the reactions of all those around. "Anything mores to story?"

"We're on a journey to unite the Four Forces," the mage continued in the same steady tone, "races from different universes that once stood together and vanquished the armies of Mordred the Conqueror. After many years, his son Mislantus has raised another army, and plans to accomplish his fathers dream to rule all universes. Lord Ironhorn is in no state to speak with us due to the grief caused by the capture of his son, and so we must find him. We must get him back if there is to be any hope of us bringing together those who once stood against those who threatened the lives of all living things, including your own."

There seemed to be a moment of connection as the crumpled face blinked and looked up at the mage with sympathy. Puc's shoulders relaxed, seeing his task accomplished, only to have the thing begin to laugh in a shrill tone, throwing its wrinkled head back.

"Heh! Nice stories, buts Fefj has more importants stuffs to consider, likes which fish to eats next. Has fun with quest! I hopes the dark one wins." The troll chuckled and went back to his business.

Puc placed a hand on Brakkus, who was clutching his sword, then strode towards the self-proclaimed Fefj Rebry, facing the creature with the same stony face, before bowing.

"Master Rebry, my companions and I are not from these parts, we are travelers from a far place and we look for shelter for the night. Would it be possible to share a fire with you in exchange for some more tales? I see you yourself are a master storyteller." The mage tried to appeal to the troll.

"I don't knows. Thisum be far more entertaining than stories. I has to think about it while I eats another fish," Fefj grinned as he cracked open another flaky morsel and began stuffing his face.

Link stepped towards the mage with his hand on the hilt of his sword, having had enough "I don't think this is going to go anywhere, if I may say so."

Losing his temper as well, Darius strode forward to solve the conflict. "Hey, listen buddy! It's cold outside, we're tired, and we need a place to stay. I don't think you need all this space anyways, so if you-."

Before another syllable could be uttered by the youth, a slimy object collided with his face, causing him to fly back and land on his rear. Scrambling up, startled by the assault, Darius curled his fists, noting the large fish that had just hit him on the floor.

"I has herring, your argument invalid," the troll replied, flatly.

Puc shot a look at Darius to keep his resolve, and looked back at the troll. "Perhaps we could come to some sort of agreement, something that can benefit us all."

Fefj hunched over on his rock, twirling hair in his fingers as he contemplated his next move.

"There be some no visitors in Fefj Rebry's cave. Nope, nopes! Not without some taxes to be paid." The wrinkly thing folded its arms across its massive belly.

The troll looked around the cave, stroking his creased face until his eyes landed on Annetta. Picking off a piece of the fish in his hands he slowly placed it in his mouth as he eyed her from head to toe, a rumbling, low chuckle erupting from inside of him. In response, she immediately flung a rock using her psychic abilities, knocking the fish from his hands.

"Shes touchem me!" The creature began to wail hysterically. "Nasty little girls!"

Having taken a few steps back, Puc retrieved something from his pack, while Annetta provided a distraction. The mage then strode forward, stepping in front of Annetta.

"You'll have to forgive her, she's a little bit feral. We usually keep her caged up, but she was sniffing out game. We will gladly pay the tax you require, in exchange for the hospitality of your home," the elf said, keeping his bow low.

The troll muttered for a few moments, rubbing his hands together as his mind registered what had just been said to him, and turned to the mage, stroking his face once more.

"Hmmm, sees, dis tone Fefj likes." The troll grinned impossibly wider. "Whatsum gots for Fefj as taxes?"

"As you know, we are but humble travelers, and though we have not much aside from weapons and the clothing upon our backs, we do hold one thing that we prize above all else," Puc said, and pulled out a modest parcel from his robes. "This jewel-encrusted mirror was given to us by the First

Mage of Aldamoor for services performed for his lands. We offer it to you, and hope it is sufficient for what we require."

"Oooo," Fefj reached out his tiny, crooked arms, leaning forward as he did so, since they barely reached past his head, and pried the parcel away from Puc, to open and admire the mirror on his own. "Fefj likes shiny mirror."

Annetta, Jason, Link, and Darius were not sure what to make of the scene as Fefj fussed over the mirror. As soon as the creature turned the mirror around to look at his reflection, however, he froze, and turned to stone.

"What? What just happened there?" Jason gasped as he walked up to the statue of Fefj, who was still looking at the mirror with his overly creased grin.

"That, my dear friend, would be a Medusa hex," Puc said, and pulled the mirror free, looking at it. "Though it needs to be cast each time on an object, and only works once. For creatures like trolls, it is by far the most effective method in making them shut up. Their society thrives upon infuriating others and exaggeration of their exploits. There is just no reasoning with them because they always want to have the last word."

"Oh…so that's why," Annetta muttered to herself, thinking of a book she had read once with trolls in it.

Brakkus burst out laughing, slapping his knee and planting his giant sword in the ground beside him.

"If ya just wanted to shut his trap by turning him into a garden gnome, ya shoulda just said so," the giant said between chuckles.

The corners of Puc's mouth slanted upwards slightly, and it would have seemed as though he was attempting to smile, but it quickly faded.

The troll having been eliminated, Link and Darius began looking through the cave, searching for anything else lurked within. Their eyes, however, were drawn to the scribbles on the walls.

"I have to ask, what's the purpose of all of these?" Link asked, staring down the carved pictures.

"Trolls, as I said, love to boast," Puc said from behind them. "The pictures on the walls tell of his exploits against foes and with female trolls. All of which are most likely fictional. It's another troll pastime. We will stay here tonight. It grows dark, and with darkness comes even colder temperatures, ones that neither the horses nor we would last in. I will place a magical barrier before the entrance of the cave for the night, so nothing will get in. We should be safe enough till morning."

"The creature mentioned something about setting fenrikin on us. Is that something we should concern ourselves with?" Link asked as he walked over to Puc.

"We would have heard them the moment the creature turned to stone, and a troll is hardly a creature of intelligence, let alone skilled enough to control fenrikin."

The youth nodded, having his question answered. Turning back, he offered to take the reins of Annetta's horse, to which the girl smiled and gave them while she slid her sword back into its scabbard and moved the shield to its normal resting place on her back.

"Do we have to stay here with the creepy troll statue?" Jason groaned, "That's not exactly a sight I want to wake up to next morning."

"Would you prefer the live thing then?" Puc asked as he lit up the top of his staff and led his horse further in.

"Well, no, I-," Jason stuttered, following the elf's lead.

"Then do not complain," the mage sighed.

Jason frowned as he watched the elven mage push onward, but followed his lead along with the others. Though Puc had reassured him that there would be no fenrikin hiding in the cave, he could not help but worry about the possibility.

As they walked, the cave seemed to widen around them. They came to another area that looked as though it was used as a fire pit, with stones all around as seats. Brakkus set down his heavy pack and began to unpack bundles of sticks.

"What's yer plan now?" Brakkus looked up at the elven mage.

"Seeing as you wished to go hunt, you may do so but be back before the sun sets completely. I will get things ready here with Darius, and make sure there are no other tenants in the cave. You may take Annetta, Jason and Lincerious with you," Puc said, taking off his packs from the horse and setting them carefully on the ground.

To this news, Brakkus's fangs glistened brightly in delight, as he began to quickly rummage through his pack to produce a crossbow and bolts.

"I knew these would come in handy!" he grinned as he checked the weapon to make sure it was working. He then turned to the trio. "I'll teach ya how to bring down a big one. Nothin to it!"

"Bring down what? Mountain deer?" Annetta raised an eyebrow, watching the giant stand back up once he had gathered all the equipment needed.

"Course I mean mountain deer. Ever tried to eat a fenrikin? Toughest meat this side of the world!" The earrings on Brakkus's ears jingled as they twitched animatedly when he spoke, watching the two children's uncomfortable expressions.

"I generally buy my meat prepackaged," Jason said. "I don't know how to go about anything when it comes to hunting."

"Me neither," Annetta quietly added.

"Well, bout time ya both learned. Link, ya got yer crossbow?"

"Loaded and ready, Brakkus." Link smiled, showing the projectile weapon to the Hurtz.

"Come along then lads and lassie, no time to be wasting sitting here with the elves." Brakkus chuckled, gently placing his paw on Annetta's back and pushing for them to get out of the cave before anyone could say anything else.

∞⟨∞

After spending an hour or so doing some target practice, they set off tracking down a herd Brakkus had seen. Despite it being Annetta and Jason's first time doing anything of the sort, the hunt had been successful, but mostly because of Brakkus being able to hear anything within a hundred foot radius about them and Link's precission. They'd managed to capture a big stag, which Brakkus carried over his shoulder back to the cave.

"Ye both need more practice with targets once we get back. Yer aims are terrible," he said to them, before nodding his chin towards Annetta. "I won't make ya gut it this time, but next time, yer not getting out of it just because yer a girl."

"Never said I wanted to get out of it. I just…don't know how." She put on her bravest face despite the concept of pulling out guts churning everything in her stomach. She knew worse things were to come, especially if there was to be war. She would just have to get over it, though the idea was much different than being found in the situation itself.

When they returned, they were pleasantly surprised by a campfire, and what looked to be a cauldron hanging from a makeshift spit. Puc and Darius already sat around the pit, pouring over the map.

"Yer supper has arrived," Brakkus announced triumphantly, as he dropped the dead animal in front of Puc, who had been engrossed in his parchment. The elf looked at the carcass, then back at the grinning Hurtz.

"Good, then can my supper be turned into something that looks more edible than roadkill?" Puc replied, turning to another map, not bothering to look at the deer anymore.

Brakkus chuckled, knowing the elf was masking his disgust for the carcass. Picking it up, he went back outside to skin and gut it.

"He does that every time," Puc sighed.

"It's because he knows it gets on your nerves," Darius smirked. "Same as when he set the horses loose in the library just to see the look on your face."

Puc flipped the maps and folded them as he eyed him, clearly not amused.

"Did I ask for your opinion, my apprentice?" scoffed the mage as the younger elf smiled lightly and continued on with his work.

෫෬

After the group had eaten their supper, prepared by none other than Brakkus himself, they stayed up a little longer to exchange stories. Annetta and Jason listened with intent as Puc and Brakkus relayed tales of the times when Orbeyus's banners flew high and the Four Forces rode alongside him to them until Puc deemed the hour to be late, and declared it to be time for everyone to sleep. Casting a protective shield around to cave to prevent anything from getting in, everyone settled under the massive sleeping skins that proved to be a lot warmer than they looked.

Unable to fall asleep as the roaring fire died down to nothing more than embers, Annetta looked up at the ceiling of the dark cave, fear and excitement from the day still pulling her apart from the inside.

"Anne, you still awake?" Jason's voice whispered.

"Yeah, why?" She turned to the side, barely making out the silhouette of her best friend.

"I just needed to hear a familiar voice is all," he said quietly. "It's all...still kinda much for me at times, you know?"

Annetta nodded, pulling up the covers over her neck until her face was the only thing visible.

"Yeah, I feel like that too sometimes, but I'm trying my best to cope with it," she said. "It's tough but we don't have much choice but to move forward. It's like Puc said, there is no turning back now."

She shifted in her sleeping skins, changing the subject. "The world's a lot bigger than we thought. Sometimes it kinda feels like a dream come true."

"Or a nightmare." he added.

"Yeah that too," Annetta said, quietly.

"Hey Annetta?" Jason's voice rang from the dark.

"Yeah?"

"I know Puc already talked about all this stuff before, but I don't know. Do you honestly agree with him about the whole sucking it up and just doing what's expected thing?" he asked.

Annetta shifted under the covers again, unable to find a comfortable spot for too long.

"I don't, really. Not all of it, anyways. I mean it makes more sense the way he put it. We all have to start somewhere. But at the same time, I think he still missed the point. We weren't born into this stuff. We've been learning it for a few months, and that's all."

"It really feels like we're just stuck doing what we're told," he continued, half rambling, "and if we don't, then terrible stuff is going to happen. It's just like when the angels showed up. We don't have a say in any of this."

"See, this is true. But we can mope about, it or just push forward." She glanced in the general direction of his voice. "I guess that's why stories are told about people after the adventures are done. They take out all the gritty parts, and no one really asks how scared they were at the time."

"True. I never thought of it that way," Jason spoke softly, seeing the people around them begin to stir. "Maybe every one of them felt just like us, then."

"That's the way we gotta start seeing it, I guess," Annetta yawned.

"Yeah." Jason nodded. "Hey, Anne?"

"Yeah?" she asked sleepily.

"I'm glad you're here, with me."

"Same. Night, J.K."

"Night Anne," he replied. Closing his eyes, he allowed the darkness around him to take hold in sleep.

Chapter 38

As soon as the light of day touched the inner cave walls, Puc was up and awake, preparing everything for the remainder of the journey.

"Oi! Lassie! Time to wake up." Brakkus's massive paw shook Annetta gently as she stirred under the covers, hiding her head. The Hurtz's ears flattened at the sight, "Miss Annetta, if ye don't get up, I can throw ye in them deer guts I buried outside the cave last night."

Hearing the proposition, Annetta bolted up from her bed. "No need! I'm up! I swear!"

Brakkus chuckled, holding his thick belt, then left to check outside the cave from within the protective barrier, while Puc and Darius looked over the maps once more to reaffirm their bearings. Jason sat, half unconscious on one of the rocks around the fire pit, while Link was off doing what appeared to be sparring exercises.

"How are you...so awake?" Annetta yawned as she watched Link cut down another invisible foe.

"I don't know. I slept like a rock. Plus I'm always wide awake in the morning," the youth said, stopping what he was doing and sheathing the sword.

"Oi! We got a bit of a problem." Brakkus ran back from the entrance towards them.

"What's wrong?" Puc stood up.

"I don't think our little garden gnome was joking about his bodyguards," the Hurtz said as he turned to head back to the entrance. Puc snatched up his staff and followed his lead along with the others.

When they arrived they saw all around the entrance of the cave slept what looked like giant white hyenas with massive saber fangs protruding from their slack, open mouths as vapors of hot air rose from them. The only thing separating them from the beasts was the protective spell Puc had placed on the cave, which now looked like a glass bubble over the entrance.

"Unknown's bane! The troll was telling the truth! They must have tried to get in last night after having been on a hunt," Puc said as he scanned and counted the fenrikin.

"Either that or the smell of roasting meat brought 'em here. Ya said yerself no stinking troll coulda had a pack of fenrikin under his command," Brakkus stared intently at the fight before him.

"Unless that troll was working in co ordination with Yarmir," Puc thought out loud. "But he would have said something about that. That is their way."

"How are we going to get out?" Annetta looked at all of the creatures.

"You need to wake up and pack up," Puc said. "We may just need to bolt past them. There is no way they will remain asleep once they hear horses."

"Don't you have a spell to keep them asleep or something?" Jason asked.

"I know a lot, Jason Kinsman, but I am not all knowing, nor can I remember everything I read. Now come on. We need to be ready to break out of here and run like the wind, or worse, fight." Puc strode back to the inner cave, followed by Annetta, Jason, Link and Darius.

"I love the smell o' blood in the morning." Brakkus chuckled, following his companions.

"Will we be able to actually outrun them, or is that just something you're hoping for?" Darius questioned his mentor.

Puc stopped dead in his tracks as he gazed upon the ground. He'd meant for this to be a quick, easy trip, but it looked like they would have to shed blood sooner than he'd like. Sighing, the elf resigned himself to the notion that he'd shielded the children as much as he could from harm's way, but it would now be time to face the reality of the world they had entered.

"We will ride out with weapons drawn," he announced, strode to his horse and mounted up, "I will go first and deactivate the shield spell. The moment this happens, they will most likely all awaken if they are not already, seeing as the shield is not sound proof. Brakkus and Link, you will ride at the back, seeing as your sword arms are strongest. Annetta and Jason will be in the middle with Darius."

"I can fight as well," Darius protested.

Puc grabbed his apprentice's shoulder, and pulled him aside, "Which is why I need you protecting Annetta and Jason."

Darius's dark eyes met Puc's pale blue ones. He nodded, and mounted his own horse, getting into formation with the others.

Annetta drew her sword with her free hand, holding the reins with her shield arm, the adrenaline beginning to course through her from the impending events. Her arms barely felt the weight of the weapons, as though they had melted into her hands, simply becoming extensions of herself.

Having called upon the mace, Jason gripped the weapon, feeling his other hand naked as he held the reins. Helbringer was meant for two-handed combat, and in truth, neither him nor Annetta had ever been taught to fight on horseback. He hoped now would not be a crash course.

"We ride forward!" Puc called out, raising his staff high as his horse beneath him bolted in a pace that seemed all too fast for the small enclosure of the cave.

With weapons drawn, the others charged out, not bothering to try for silence in their approach to the mouth of the cave. Already the fenrikin stood alert, watching from behind the wall of protective energy, their fangs glistening in the winter sun with saliva.

The moment Puc's staff collided with the shield, the barrier came down, and the ice hounds were upon them. Brakkus and Link slashed back and forth from horseback as Puc and Darius cast spells to repel the approaching swarm before them. Holding the reins of their horses tightly to try and control the panic in them, the companions found themselves quickly surrounded by the horde.

"I say we take 'em here and now!" Brakkus called, his voice edged with bloodlust as he hacked at them, veering his horse as it whined.

"If that is your wish." Puc crashed his staff into the head of one of the disoriented creatures he had set on fire, putting the brute out of its misery. "Then let's have one for the Axe once more."

"And many more after," the Hurtz shouted. Roaring, he loped off the heads off of two more creatures, charging into the fray.

Finding themselves separated from the veteran warriors as the pack closed in, Annetta and Jason held their own as well, though more than a few times the creatures had managed to jump up on their horses, or nick them and almost land a blow. Were it not for the psychic abilities that let them throw the beasts over a hundred miles from where they stood, they would have easily been overrun, and they found themselves thankful for the lessons. The mounts did their own part as well, trampling the beasts that came too close with their massive hooves out of fright. Darius lent his own hand to their defense, sending waves of spells at the creatures from his horse. But the more fenrikin they seemed to kill, the more came back in their place, angrier and more vicious than before.

Link cut through every foe that came before him, his sword waving from one side to the other as he struck down each foe. The more he did it, though, the more came, until the sheer force of the creatures around him pushed the youth from his mount, onto the ground. Getting up, Link snarled as he stood before the horse, brandishing his sword and holding the reins in the other hand.

The fenrikin circled around him, their bloody maws with massive fangs glaring at him in a frenzied look. Each time a beast leaped for the horse, Link's blade found him in turn, the horse behind the youth dancing with fear at the sight of the creatures that stood ready to end it. Suddenly, one of the creatures leaped at the youth, knocking him down, causing the grip on the reins to slip.

Pinned down by the foe and unable to help, Link watched helplessly as his mount was torn to shreds in a bath of blood and foaming spit, the screams of the animal fueling the horror of the carnage around them. In a spurt of rage, the young Gaian warrior drove his sword through the beast that held him down. Kicking the thing in the gut with both his feet, he managed get up from under it.

Finishing with the horse, the other creatures then turned to face him. Armed with only his sword, Link stared back in animalistic fury, his grip on the blade becoming tighter as he placed it back in the scabbard and focused all his energy. Letting out a howl, his scar glowed a blinding gold, his form changing into that of the cursed creature. Claws arched and fangs exposed, he snarled as he attacked the beasts on equal footing.

"Something is wrong! Their numbers should be lessening!" Darius called from amongst the chaos surrounding them.

"Oh no, you honestly think so?" Puc drove the end of his staff into the gut of a fenrikin who tried to leap at him. "I'm starting to suspect these are Yarmir's hounds and he's got a hydra spell cast on them."

"What ye be thinking we do then?" Brakkus shouted breathlessly. "I'm not complaining if we stay and fight 'em-,"

"We won't be able to, Brakkus. Each time we kill one, two come back in its place. We must flee!" Puc informed him, to which the Hurtz whined a bit, having his fun spoiled.

"We flee this battle. There is no winning it!" Puc yelled at the top of his lungs, making sure everyone heard him. Veering his horse in the direction of their destination as he remembered it from the maps with Brakkus at his side, the mage readied his staff to cast as spell.

Annetta, Jason, and Darius joined moments after on their horses, followed by Link in his cursed form, his sword between his teeth, and the remnants of his saddle and backpack on his back.

"Stay behind me, everyone," Puc instructed as he readied the staff, pointing it at the approaching horde, the weapon's tip beginning to glow a faint blue as he measured his opponents with precision. "And you fly when I tell you to."

The beasts came out seconds later behind them, jaws snapping at the air, an assortment of chaotic howls. Wasting no time once they were in range, a blast of pristine pale blue light spilled forth from the staff in the shape of a massive tidal wave, causing everything it touched to slow down until it stopped.

"Now we fly!" Puc veered his mount around again, as his companions took off. "We only have about ten minutes, but the spell will give us some lead on them."

Catching up to the elf and Hurtz, Annetta wheezed, "What do we do now?"

"Haven't thought that far ahead. I'm working on it," Puc snapped.

Frantically, Annetta looked around. Seeing the cliffs on either side, an idea came to her. Despite them putting much time behind them and the beasts, she knew they would catch up or their horses would tire.

"Well, if you don't have a plan, I do," she shouted back. Stopping her horse, she turned the beast of burden around, leaping from the saddle and dropping her weapons.

"Annetta, what are you doing?!" Jason's eyes widened in panic as his friend closed her eyes and stretched out her arms.

Jason then realized what she was attempting to do. Jumping off his horse, he put the mace back to its dormant form, and ran over to her.

"I'll get one, and you get the other," he said, to which she nodded, more than happy to have him with her.

Puc stopped his horse, looking back, every fiber in his body screaming in anger and fear.

"Severio! Kinsman! You get back here right now!" he yelled.

"Just watch, and if you won't help, then stay out of it," she said. Taking a deep breath, she focused on the cliff to her right. If ten minutes were all her and Jason had, then they would make it count.

Silence and the feeling of impending doom froze everyone who stood before what they knew would be a wave of oncoming fenrikin, the only thing between them a young boy and girl barely old enough to make their own decisions. Still they stood, unwavering, as the world around them began to tremble.

Snow fell from the mountains around, as did loose stone. They thought it was metaphoric at first. That it was their minds playing tricks on them, but then they realize that it really was happening, and they looked beyond Annetta and Jason's small forms. The two mountains seemed to be rising up from the ground, as though someone were pulling out a plant by its roots.

Annetta felt the world begin to spin around her as she did her best to hold her ground. But the more she focused, the more her temples were beginning to pound, like muffled drumming that was not able to fully come into its forte. Still, she would not falter, knowing their time was running short. Despite everything Puc had said to her about never letting the enemy know what one was doing, she raised her hands to the sky, closing her eyes as the mountain rose more.

Jason too felt overwhelmed by the task at hand, but he tried to remember what Puc had been teaching them the entire time. A person needed to erase the size of the object. Only then would they be free to do as they pleased with it. Instead of the wall of stone, Jason pictured the blocks he had been playing with in his room with his brother, and how they had floated through the air. Despite this, he felt his knees get weaker.

"Don't think about the size, Anne. Just go with it," he muttered out loud, more for his own sake than hers.

"What are they doing?" Brakkus blurted out.

Puc felt his blood boil as he watched. He knew exactly how much time was left before they were overrun, and as the clock came to an end, he felt the weight of it all begin to set in on him. He would not run. His honor prevented him from doing so, and he knew the Hurtz would not falter, either.

The mage's hand went into the folds of his robes, and traced the hilt of another weapon, a last resort that he had not unsheathed in well over a decade. The closer he looked at Annetta and Jason before them, the more he saw someone else standing in their place, and his hand went back to the reins.

"Master, what now?" Darius questioned.

Puc continued to observe, the mountains rising higher and higher as debris from the stone formations swirled upon the icy wind.

"For once, the answers are not in my grasp," he stated. "They lie with those who stand before us."

Then it came, the howling and the charge. Puc and the others watched, gripping their weapons, as the mountains hung in midair, and the horde came around the bend of the trail, jaws snapping and eyes blazing as they locked with their targets.

Opening their eyes, the boy and girl viewed the oncoming storm, their breathing heavy with the labor of their deed, their minds strained with the task. When they were sure of their position, they sighed in release as the behemoths fell, crushing the wave of beasts in their entirety, for how could something come back twofold if it lay buried beneath stone?

Annetta looked at Jason with exhaustion and gave a faint smile, then fell to the ground, drenched in sweat mixed with blood from the minor scrapes she'd acquired during the fight. She could not remember feeling that weak since her first visit to Q-16. Everything began to spin as she heard people calling out for her. Before she knew it, her world turned dark.

∞∞

Annetta awoke to find that night had fallen again. Sitting up and stretching, she noticed that her jacket had been taken off while she was sleeping, and was folded up neatly beside her. She also saw that the right sleeve of her shirt was torn off, and her upper arm was wrapped in bandages, along with her left leg. Looking around she saw that she was back in a cave. The heat of a fire licked the side of her, and turning to face it fully she saw Puc staring back at her from beyond the flames, his pale eyes invisible in the shadows.

"Did I? Did I sleep the whole day away?" she asked, feeling guilty.

"Well, it's not like I sped up time," the elf responded. "And what you did was incredibly reckless. It could have cost us our lives."

Annetta got that same feeling she always did of her ears going flat against her skull, even though it was not humanly possible.

"But I will also say this, it was the right thing to do," he added afterwards. "You used your training well, and for that I commend you. But next time, warn us."

A heavy thud of boots could be heard from the other side of the cave behind Puc. Brakkus's massive form then became visible.

"Ah, the lass's finally awake, I see." The Hurtz flashed a toothy grin. "Ye gave us quite a scare back on the road, ya know."

"Yeah I probably did." Annetta smiled, rubbing the sleep from her eyes. "Where's Darius, Link, and Jason?"

"I sent out Darius to scout out the perimeter of the lair. Lincerious is still unconscious after changing back, and Jason is in the same state as you," Puc answered.

"He took a right down beating as well," Brakkus jumped in. "We didn't realize it till after, but he lost a lot of blood after being bitten by one of them fenrikin."

"Is he going to be okay?" Annetta jumped awake upon hearing her friend was injured. Looking around the dark cave, she searched for him until her eyes fell upon his sleeping form with a bandaged arm.

"He will be fine. He just needs to rest," Puc said to her.

"But what about the rescue mission? If we don't get Prince Snapneck back, then what chance do we have of-,"

"I have decided to wait a few more hours into the dead of night. Yarmir will most likely be sleeping, and it will be easier to penetrate the defenses, or at least to try and catch him off guard," the mage explained.

Darius then walked into view, apparently out of breath, judging by the fumes rising from his mouth quickly due to the cold.

"I've got some good news and some bad news," he said, walking closer to his master and inclining his head slightly to Annetta. "Good news is, Snapneck is alive, because Yarmir needs him for some kind of ceremony. Bad news, the place is swarming with fenrikin, and I think the ones we saw before are the same as what he's got on his mountain."

"Then you don't bring me much good news." Puc frowned and turned to Annetta. "You may go back to sleep. We will wake you once we've come up with a plan. There's no use in draining your strength in staying up when it is needed to recover."

"Recover? I feel-," Annetta tried to jump out of her sleeping skins in protest, only to have her knees buckle underneath her, and land face first in them with a growl.

"As I said, go sleep." The mage smirked lightly and watched as the girl grumbled something under her breath before closing her eyes and drifting off again. He then turned his attention to his apprentice. "You should do the same. I know how draining shifting into a werepanther is on you, and we may need you to shift if we encounter trouble."

"Master?"

Puc's gaze pierced through Darius. "This quest is no longer as easy as I thought it would be, but despite turmoil, one needs to use a steady head. Go rest. I give this as an order and also as a request from a friend."

Seeing that he could not argue, for the conversation would only progress in that manner until Puc got his way, Darius nodded and walked off to lie down where his sleeping skins were spread out. Within moments, the young elf was in a deep sleep from which very little could wake him.

Puc continued to watch the fire while all of this went on. His mind raced as it replayed the events that had occurred within the last two days, calculating the next moves that were to come. His jaw clenched tighter, drawing in the contours of his face to become harder than they already were.

"What be on yer mind, mage?" Brakkus walked up to his friend and slumped down on a rock beside him.

"I just needed to think," he said. "If Yarmir has a hydra spell on all those fenrikin like he did the others, then we are done for sure."

"Can ya counter such a spell?" Brakkus asked.

"I would need to find the original fenrikin upon which the spell was cast, which, as you saw, can be a problem with a few dozen snapping mouths coming at once." Puc rested his knuckles over his lips, combing through his mind for a solution. Watching the flames a little longer, his gaze lingered on the sleeping forms of Annetta and the others, when it came to him, "I might not be able to fully put them to sleep depending on how many there are and the layout of the inside of the fortress. However, I could possibly slow them down enough to be able to locate the original. You and the others will have to keep them occupied as long as possible."

"And how will we get to the young prince?" Brakkus questioned. "Yarmir may panic when he sees us and just kill 'im then and there."

Puc huffed, shoving a log into the fire, another roadblock in his plan. He pushed back his hair with his free hand, the other gripping his staff as his mind swam in strategy. He was trying not to split the party, and what frustrated him most was not knowing the inside of the mountain. His brows furrowed together as he gave up. "Then we may have to have Annetta and Jason go retrieve him."

398

"Yer wanting to send them up against Yarmir alone?" Brakkus's ears rose. "Are ye bloody mad?"

"Would you prefer for me to go and leave you all to the mercy of multiplying fenrikin?" Puc snapped at him. "I've thought it through. We can buy them the time that will be needed. I am including you in this plan so that you are well aware of what the situation may be, and so you can help me execute it with the precision necessary."

"I've still got a right not to like it." Brakkus's ears went back flat against his skull like a threatened animal, his multitude of earrings jingling as they did so. "The lass may have proven to be quick on her feet, but she ain't no seasoned fighter, and neither is the boy. Ye should send Darius or Link with them-,"

"It would leave less of us to fight the fenrikin." Puc sighed. "Now please, I wish not to talk of this anymore. There are still a couple of hours until midnight...I-,"

"Ye want a friend to be here?" Brakkus finished the sentence. "I can do that."

"Thank you, warrior." The mage acknowledged him. Watching the fire, the two companions waited until the alignment of the stars and moons in the sky signaled the hour of their strike.

ജഇ

Annetta was woken by the sound of multiple voices chatting in the cave. It was still dark, but she remembered what Puc had said about wanting to go in at night. With a huff, she threw off the sleeping skins, and sat up. Puc was explaining something to Brakkus, Darius, and Link as they sat around the fire.

"Hey, you're up," Jason's voice called from beside her.

Annetta turned around and smiled at her friend, taking a quick glance at his bandaged arm. "How are you feeling? That looks pretty bad."

"It's just a lot of cloth. The scratches weren't even that deep." The boy lifted his arm, moving his fingers around to show her. "It'll look pretty cool when I go to school, though."

"Yeah, how are you going to explain that? I don't think anyone will believe you if you say you got mauled by a cat," she said.

"Well, it's lovely to see yer all up and ready." Brakkus crossed his massive arms as he looked at the two of them from beyond the flames.

Annetta got up and stretched. She felt the strain on her whole body as she got a better look at the bandages on her.

"Man… just…what happened to me?" she asked.

"Battle scars," Puc stated. "Or as we like to call them, scrapes of experience. I managed to salvage your jacket."

Annetta could only picture so much of how her mother would react to her being missing for multiple days and returning with the injuries she had sustained. Sighing, she moved in for her jacket, put it on, and zipped it up all the way. She was only now beginning to register how painful her cuts were in the cold air around her, as she fully awoke from her slumber.

"Ready yourselves quickly." Puc rose from his seat at the fire along with the others, as they walked off to where the horses stood resting. "We must leave if we hope to catch him at least a little off guard,"

Annetta rolled up her sleeping skins with Jason. Packing them up like Brakkus had shown them on their horses, they saddled up, making sure they left nothing behind. They were both feeling stiff from the many hours they had spent riding, but neither complained. They knew it would do no good.

"We will need to leave the horses some distance away from the mountain," Puc warned them. "We don't wish them eaten by fenrikin. The way back to Morwick would take us at least twice as long, if we're not frozen during the trip. We've already lost one, and that is more than we can spare."

Jason cringed at the image of the group being turned into miniature icebergs. He was also unhappy with the idea of parting with his horse. Part of him worried it would wander off, or some troll would cook it for dinner if they left it alone too long. Though he was not as attached to his horse as he saw Annetta was, he still liked it, and didn't want to see it get hurt, especially after seeing what had happened to Link's during the battle.

"There was another cave I passed not too far away from the mountain. We could try there," Darius informed him as they headed out.

"Yes, but did it have any inhabitants?" Puc inquired.

"I heard nothing inside the cave, if that's what you are asking," his apprentice replied.

"But you did not go in," Puc stated firmly as they continued to ride through the dark and rocky landscape.

As they continued their arguing about where to place the horses, Annetta took the time to step out of the cave, and look around. There were no artificial lights of any sort, but the world around her still seemed to be lit up by the light of the stars, and the three moons she now saw. She paused upon seeing the three spheres all in different positions in the heavens. They seemed so surreal to her. She had a hard time realizing she was actually looking up at the sky, and not a manipulated photograph. The sky itself was not a dark blue, but purple, as the light from all three moons made it impossible for it to be completely dark, leaving the heavens in a state of perpetual twilight. Though it was cold, and her body ached from riding, she could not help but find peace looking up, even if it all seemed strange.

Going back into the cave, she helped everyone pack the horses as they set off. Once she was back on horseback, she could not help but look back up at the night sky. She forgot all about where they were heading, until a voice brought her back to the present.

"We stop here. Annetta, quit daydreaming." Puc stated, a line Annetta heard all too many times.

They stopped beside the cave Darius had indicated and waited while Puc went inside alone. Brakkus had tried to protest, but all efforts were in vain. Once the elven mage made up his mind, there was no changing it. Almost as soon as he went in, he came out.

"There is nothing inside the cave now, but I will still place a shielding spell on it once the horses are inside to prevent anything from getting at them," he announced. Grabbing the reins of his mount, he led it inside, followed by everyone else.

They unsaddled their horses, leaving their packs securely on rock ledges, taking only what they needed most with them. Annetta walked over to Link, who seemed more quiet than usual, and she could only guess why.

"You feeling alright?" she asked.

"Yeah, I'm fine I guess," he responded with a huff as he examined the saddle from his devoured horse, fumbling with the ripped straps.

Annetta sighed, kicking up a few loose rocks with her shoes. "Link, you gotta remember that you're not on Gaia anymore. We're not going to judge you, okay?"

"Look, I know, okay? It's just easier said than done." He glanced at the girl.

Before Link could say anything else, a baritone voice echoed through the cave.

"I'd love the see what them Gaians would think of me." Brakkus gave a toothy grin from beside them, which caused Annetta to snicker at the sight.

"A picture of grace and charm, what else?" Puc threw in his comment from the other side of the cave, having secured his horse.

"Why thank ye kindly, master elf." Brakkus bowed to him, to which the mage only shook his head as he headed back out.

⚜

It did not take them long to reach the mountain. It was hard to ignore the set of enormous steps that led the way to a gate flanked by two chained fenrikin, gleaming at the dark in alertness.

"He must really love those things." Jason sighed in defeat upon the view.

"The front gate is not our best option then. We will need an alternate way in." Puc analyzed the mountain, then turned to Darius, who nodded without saying anything.

Within seconds, Darius's body melted into the form of the same creature Jason and Annetta had seen him shift into when they'd gone to the movies. With unnatural speed, the creature began scaling the walls of the mountain, looking for good footholds for the rest of them before it disappeared behind the mass of rock. After a few minutes, he came back and leaped down to land on all fours nearby.

"There's what looks to be a balcony that was a natural cave on the other side," the werepanther said in a gruff voice. "It's not too high up, but it is still a fair climb."

"We will not need to climb as long as the platform is visible," Puc said, as he looked up to examine the opening. "Your next test will be teleporting to the top of that ledge, once Darius checks to make sure it is clear."

Jason and Annetta took a good look to see where they were going, committing the place to memory like they had been taught. Despite what Darius had said about it being an easy climb, there were very few ledges that could be seen. Without claws like the werepanther, it would have been a very long night of bleeding and broken nails. Darius launched himself onto the wall without further commands from Puc, and disappeared into the balcony.

Silent tension built among the party in the time Darius did not emerge. Brakkus's ears twitched as he tried to hear some sound of movement, while Link's grip on his sword tightened. Annetta felt her stomach clench as she waited for the signal to go. She was nervous about having to teleport someone along with her, seeing as she had never done it before. Despite her brain telling her to trust Puc's judgment, her body did its own thing, and the butterflies continued to build up. Jason's own unease meant biting his nails, a habit he never quite grew out of. The only one in the group showing no emotion was Puc, who closed his eyes and breathed slowly, ignoring the cold.

Just when Brakkus was about to blurt out that they should go up anyways, the black panther popped up from over the side of the stone railing and looked down, signaling that it was clear.

Annetta looked over at Puc, who had opened his eyes, "Is there a limit as to how many people I can bring with me at a time?"

"How many do you believe you can bring is the question." The elf inclined his head to the young girl. "If you feel comfortable bringing only one at a time, then that is how many you can bring."

Annetta nodded. Placing the shield on her back, she grabbed both Puc and Link's wrists, leaving Brakkus with Jason. She took a good look at the balcony. Looking at the part of the floor she could see, she began to concentrate. Leveling her breathing to almost nothing and closing her eyes, she began to feel the familiar sensation of her body heating up. Within moments it was done. She let go of Puc and Link, only to feel lightheaded and begin to stumble backwards.

"Whoa there!" Link grabbed her firmly as she took the extra support as cue to regain her footing.

"First time is always the worst," Puc assured her. "As it is with most things."

Jason appeared moments later beside them with Brakkus, who immediately unsheathed his massive sword as soon as he was fully materialized.

"I forgot how sick bloody teleporting makes me," he growled. "I never did like when Arieus done it. Make ye feel like ye can do nothing to prevent it from happening."

"Now is not the time for reminiscing. We need to get moving." Puc turned to Annetta and Jason. "No matter what happens between now and getting to Snapneck, you both need to press on. It is important that you are the ones responsible for his rescue."

Jason did not like the tone Puc was using with them. He'd heard it often from his mother when she spoke about what had to have been done with his father and when she talked about sacrifices. It brought a small sting of pain to him thinking about her. He was starting to miss home despite only having been away for two days.

"Puc you say like you guys are going to-," Annetta didn't want to finish the sentence. Though she had known them all a short time, she was beginning to admit to herself that they were all becoming like her extended family.

"That is not what I am getting at. I am simply saying that should there be a fight, try to escape beyond it," the mage stated, and then turned to his apprentice. "Did you smell any fenrikin?"

"On the lower levels," the werepanther spoke. "There seems to be nothing up here. I think it's primarily used to allow smoke to escape, and as a lookout during clear weather."

Puc stepped towards the stone railing and peered over it. After a few moments of carefully scanning the heavens, he then withdrew.

"We have to hurry. If I am correct, Yarmir is using the alignment of the moons to solidify the ritual," the elf said as he began to make the descent down a flight of stairs. "Which means there is no time to waste."

The rest in the group drew their weapons and stormed after Puc's billowing robes on the stairs. Torches vaguely lit up the walls on either side as they descended further into the mountain, the sounds of thudding feet made on stone echoing around them.

"Shouldn't we be...you know, stealthy or something?" Jason asked.

"If we draw the attention of the majority of the fenrikin guarding Yarmir, then will that not leave him vulnerable?" Puc glanced backwards at the boy.

"Yeah, but won't that mean more for you guys to fight off?" he replied.

"Kinsman, you have not yet seen the full wrath of a cornered mage. Or a Hurtz for that matter," Puc assured him with a smirk as they continued to press on, the temperature dropping each time they descended another flight, their breath becoming visible on the air yet again.

As they reached the end of the stairs, Puc raised his fist up to signal for them to stop. He then turned to Darius, who slithered around the wall of the grotto, going deeper inside. The mage's knuckles turned white as he gripped the staff, listening for any signs of movement while everyone remained still, mentally preparing the first spell he would need to administer on the creatures that would come at them and at the rest of the plan he had in mind. There came the hiss of a large cat creature from the dark, and something smashed into the wall of the cave.

"Now!" Puc shouted as his staff came to life with light and he charged forward, the others close behind him in tow.

The walls around them seemed to tremble as a pack of fenrikin came towards them, fangs glistening and eyes glowing in primal rage. Darius roared among the pack as his claws made easy work of the foes.

"Darius, fall back!" Puc ordered. "I have a little gift for our friends, and it's best you not be affected."

The mage turned quickly to Annetta and Jason. "Once I cast this, you must teleport to the other side and run. Do not hesitate or look back, do you understand?"

"But won't they notice?" Annetta protested, to which Puc lifted a finger.

"For once, Miss Severio, I should very much like if you were to trust my judgement as much as your grandsire once did." The elf turned back to the battlefield to see his apprentice using the sides of the walls to outmaneuver the enemy and leap effortlessly behind them. Puc pointed his staff at the approaching horde. "Get ready."

A blast of energy, so bright that it lit up the entire room a brilliant shade of white, hit the fenrikin head on. It shrouded their bodies in light, only to make them reappear afterwards when the light dissipated. When the fenrikin came back into view, they were moving so slow it seemed like they were barely stirring.

"Forward!" Puc snarled the command as Darius, Link and Brakkus let loose from their restraint into the fray, an array of swords and claws making a crimson mess on the ground as they tore through. The mage turned back to the boy and girl. "It is time for you to go. The spell will not last long. Make our efforts not in vain."

Dazzled by the display of light, blood and battle, Annetta and Jason merely nodded to the request, and teleported to the other side of the fenrikin mob. They pressed on to what appeared to be another flight of stairs leading down.

೨೧೪

Annetta and Jason ran until they saw the end of the stairs. Pausing to catch their breath, the two friends took a moment to look at one another in the dark.

"Man, you ever thought something like this would happen when we signed on?" Jason asked.

"No, you?" Annetta labored over her breathing as she watched it rise up in puffs of smoke.

"Why do you think I asked?" He laughed softly before he was cut off by the sound of a foreign language being chanted.

Stopping close to the foot of the stairs and hiding behind the corner of the wall, they could see an eerie blue light illuminating the room beyond. A shadow could be seen animatedly moving in rhythm to the words being spoken, becoming louder each time the verse repeated. Jason grabbed Annetta's sword hand as they snuck close to where the light began to touch the sides of the stone. Stretching their necks enough to see but not be seen, they looked inwards.

Before what looked to be a massive stone altar stood a large human-like being dressed in a golden ornate robe, with long brown graying hair, and a thick beard. He seemed at least ten feet tall if not more, comparing him to Brakkus who stood close to seven.

To the side, in a cage big enough for a large bird, Annetta made out what looked to be an incredibly small Minotaur whimpering and holding the bars of his entrapment. In the dark beyond the altar, stood what looked to be hundreds of giants all lined up in rows, their grotesque faces frozen in the pale stone that imprisoned them.

Seeing no threats aside from the giant, the two nodded to themselves and stepped out from hiding.

'*If we get close enough, we can open the cage and get him out,*' Annetta thought to Jason at her side, not wanting to betray their position by speaking out loud.

'*Right, but then what?*' the boy looked over at her, only too late to realize he had stubbed his foot on a rock that then went flying in the direction of the giant.

The chanting giant stopped and turned around to face them, his complexion blue like the light around him, sawed-off horns protruding from his forehead, his lower fangs jutting forward from constantly pursed lips.

The creature was ugly enough to almost make both of them shiver, but knowing better, they stood their ground.

"What? Who are you? Who is there? Who dares to enter the lair of Yarmir the Firstborn?" The creature spat, looking everywhere to see where the stone had come from, his gaze then shifting to where the children stood before him. "And what is this?"

Annetta felt as though she was a deer caught in headlights as soon as the two yellow eyes found them. She gripped her sword tightly, and put on her bravest face. She stepped towards Yarmir from the shadows so he could see her better.

"I am Annetta Severio, heir of Orbeyus." The words echoed in the cave around them.

A laugh, terrible and shrill, erupted from the giant so powerful that Snapneck hid in the shadows of his cage.

"Heir of Orbeyus? My, my, what titles for such a little runt," he scoffed. "Tell me, and do so quickly. How it is you even got in here?"

"I have some powerful friends." Annetta continued the small talk.

In the meantime, Jason slipped away, focusing his mind on the small cage. Slowly, it began to move away from its original spot.

"And why, if I may ask, is it that you happen to be here, little girl?" the amused giant asked.

"Oh, you know, I got bored in my world, so I came to kick some evil giant butt," Annetta smiled back politely, and noted the cage was gone.

The giant laughed. "Well then, you will just have to wait until I awaken my brethren, and-"

The giant paused, noticing something had changed out of the corner of his eye. Turning his head slightly, his instincts were confirmed. The cage was missing. The titan snarled in fury, bared its fangs, then launched itself at her, clawed hands first. Annetta instinctively slashed blindly with her sword, hitting the creature's knuckle, and splitting the skin open, causing it to jump back. She then focused as hard as she could, throwing the giant into the far end of the cave, past all the statues, causing some to collapse onto him.

"So… did you think of anything past this?" she questioned Jason.

"Nope, why?" he asked, setting the cage down. He then bashed the lock open to let the creature free.

The tiny Minotaur hopped out and looked up at Jason, giving a high-pitched squeak of fear, its brown fur ruffled from the cold as it held onto its tail with both hands.

Yarmir groaned, which then turned into a howl echoing in the dark as the giant gripped his head, and looked at the sight of the collapsed giant statues in terror.

"My kin!" he shrieked.

"You gotta get out of here little guy, go up the stairs," Jason said to him as Yarmir regained his footing, and charged once more at them.

"I have waited over a century for this, you pests will not ruin it for me," he hollered, charging at Annetta and Jason.

The two looked at one another. Jason grabbed Snapneck, and made way for the maze of statues, knowing Yarmir would not risk going after him.

Meanwhile, Annetta pulled her shield out in front of her, and waited until the last moment, teleporting right from Yarmir's grasp, causing the giant to trip and headbutt the wall she had stood against, the impact causing a few loose stalagmites to begin falling from above them. The creature screamed, grabbing its injured forehead. Shaking off the pain, he turned around in pursuit of the children, trying to find them.

Annetta and Jason had taken the time to hide behind the stone statues of the other giants, their hearts pounding with adrenaline. Snapneck began to whine once the sound of the giant's wails had gone away, causing Jason to shush him.

The giant snarled, "Come out and face me! You've nowhere to run from there. I can just lock you down here until you freeze to death."

Annetta and Jason looked at one another. Their options were running low, with the giant having the upper hand. Even if they teleported, they would still likely be pursued.

'*You think we can take him?*' Jason turned to Annetta.

'*We can give it a try, but I don't know,*' she replied in telepathy, '*It might be best to run for it.*'

'*But he'll follow,*' the boy protested.

Yarmir paced the lair, the blue glow of the walls still prominent as he observed every corner. He began feeling more and more helpless by the moment, as there was little the giant could do in the room without injuring his frozen people. Yet he knew that they had not yet left the room. Arming himself in patience, the giant stood before the door and waited.

"You've got no other way out, so stay here and die, or face me and die. Either way, I will get what I want." He hissed.

Annetta frowned, looking at Jason. Tightening her grip on her sword and shield, she walked out from among the giant statues.

Jason looked down at the Minotaur in his hands and placed him on the ground. He whispered, "You get to the stairs without him noticing you, got it?"

Not convinced, Snapneck made a small nod and scurried off into the shadows. Jason then turned to join his friend

"Glad to see you both came out to play," Yarmir grinned. "And who is your little friend, runt?"

"I am Jason Kinsman." Jason stepped forward, saying his name loud and clear.

Yarmir made eye contact with them both, his pupils becoming smaller upon recognition of events past.

"I never forget a Severio. Neither shall I forget a Kinsman wielding that mace. What good fortune it is that brings you both here, so I can suck the marrow from your bones with my kin!" The giant lunged at them once again.

Annetta and Jason did not run this time, but instead charged to meet the creature head on, their weapons raised in attack.

Clashing, the trio locked claws and weapons together, trembling from the impact. Withdrawing, they slashed at the giant with every bit of strength and precision they had.

Yarmir did not falter, sending his own claws to try and find the children, successfully ripping through their already torn jackets more than once, as they blocked with mace and shield.

After a series of volleying blows, they locked weapons again, and tried to push forward, hoping to throw him once again into the cursed giants. But Yarmir's strength was too great, and the giant sent them flying with little effort towards the altar.

Annetta tumbled to the ground, rolling until she hit the foot of the altar, soon after joined by Jason who experienced a similar trip. The boy groaned, running a hand through the hair on the back of his head. Annetta scrambled to her feet, gripping sword and shield, feeling the exhaustion.

They were both still weary from the fight with the fenrikin, their injuries still raw from the night before.

Wasting no time, Jason sent Yarmir flying into the midst of the statues, while Annetta sent the altar overtop of him, hoping to buy them some time as they regrouped their strength. It was then that she noted Jason's wound on his arm starting to seep through the bandages.

"J.K., get Snapneck out of here," she said.

"Anne, I'm not going to leave you here," he snapped at her.

Admittedly, part of his reply was composed of the need to be in the fray. He needed to stand by her side against the enemy at all costs, and show that he wasn't weak. Was this what rivalry felt like? Was it the desire not to give up in front of the one who seemed to be better than you? He shook off the idea. Annetta was not his rival, and he had no idea where such dark thoughts manifested inside himself. She was his friend, and no matter what comparisons he made in their lives and the stories they read, their friendship was the reason he did not want to abandon her. She was always there for him when he needed her, and he had promised to do the same when they had first come into the knowledge of their heritage. His true reason then was failing his friends was not an option, not ever. He gripped the mace tighter as he looked at the direction in which Yarmir had fallen.

Annetta noted his determination, and had an idea what he was thinking, "J.K., this isn't about pride, okay? Damn it! You're bleeding, and someone needs to get Snapneck out."

Yarmir growled as he threw the slab aside, wiping the blood from his bruised brow. With a roar, he leaped from where he fell towards the children.

Annetta leaped back instinctively as she blocked the onslaught of claws coming her way from the giant, when an idea came to her.

Focusing, she let her psychic energy flow through her sword. It was as if the weapon became an extension of herself and as she slashed at Yarmir, the blows pushed him back each time. Experimenting further, she teleported behind him, embedding her blade in his calf before the giant could turn around to face her. Howling with pain, Yarmir returned the blow, swatting Annetta across the room.

Jason watched, mesmerized, as everything began to tremble around them, and this time it was not the giant running. Snapneck came out of his hiding place and huddled beside Jason, wringing his tail in his hands with fear. The boy placed his arm protectively around the small Minotaur, watching his friend combine psychic abilities with swordplay. Losing footing, she got knocked back right beside him.

'Listen,' her voice rang in his head as she got up, facing her foe, 'I need you to go warn Puc and the others, but at the same time, I need you to keep communicating with me, do you understand? I have a plan, but if I faint, I need someone to get me out of here. The only person I can count on is you.'

Grabbing her blade, she turned to the giant, panting from the effort of the fight. "Hey ugly! What? That it?"

She turned her head lightly to the side to face him, 'I don't have much time to pull this off, just please get moving while he's busy. This is a team effort and I can't do it without you.'

Roaring, the girl ran at the giant yet again, her sword leading the way.

Jason lingered a little longer, watching his friend, but her words rang truth. Picking up the small Minotaur in his arms, he ran up the stairs, not sure if he would be able to teleport multiple times in his condition if he needed to get Annetta out. His mind replayed the events that had happened moments ago as he tried to make sense of his behavior, but there was no use. It felt like his personality was being split into two, one half still loyal and following Annetta, the other seeing her more and more as an opponent, and he was not sure why. Annetta was his best friend, and always had been. They'd met in kindergarten, two misfits that played with plastic dinosaurs pretending they were dragons and using the farmhouse as a castle. Shooting back to reality, he focused on the task at hand and kept going.

೮೦೦೪

Slaying the final fenrikin with the swing of his mighty double edged sword, Brakkus growled as the head of the creature rolled on the ground.

"Was that it? HUH? Come at me, ye flea biting pooches!" The Hurtz' deep voice rumbled as he slammed his sword down into two of the dead creatures, freeing both arms.

Puc looked away from dressing Link's wounded arm, only to shake his head. In truth, he was glad to see the Hurtz in good spirits despite the situation. The Hurtz were a tough species, and war seemed almost to come as second nature to them.

Darius stood off to the side with his arms crossed and eyes closed as he tried to focus his energy on something else aside his stinging wounds. His concentration was broken when the sound of footsteps on the stairs below became louder.

Jason emerged with blood on his jacket, carrying a small Minotaur in one hand and the mace in the other. He stopped at the top, out of breath.

"What happened? Where is Annetta?" Puc rose from his task, gripping his staff.

"She's...she's fighting Yarmir...told me to get Snapneck out," he said in between breaths.

Puc moved forward and examined the wound on Jason's arm. Frowning, the elf pulled a vial out of his robes.

"Take this. It will stop the bleeding," he said.

ഇരു

Meanwhile, Annetta continued to assault the giant with every bit of strategy she could come up with, combining what she had learned with her psychic abilities and sword lessons. She knew she would be no match without the ability to knock the giant back as far as possible.

At long last, the giant made a mistake, driving his arm into a hollow stone wall and trapping it there. Annetta made quick use of the opening, and hacked away at the limb, severing his arm in a few blows, just as the giant withdrew it in the hope of saving the damaged appendage. The giant's limb fell to the ground, still wriggling around.

"Looks like you need a hand," she smirked.

The giant smiled maliciously at her. Within seconds his arm began to grow back, fingers forming as though he were made out of liquid. To Annetta's greater horror however, the arm on the floor began to grow and expand. A moment later, another giant stood beside Yarmir, his exact replica.

"A nifty little spell I found. Quite similar to the one used on my fenrikin," said the original. "The more you hack and slash at me, the more of me there are. I just had to wait till your little friend was gone so I could take care of you."

The two giants laughed as each began to circle the girl, faster and faster until she lost track of which was which.

"Great...they didn't warn me about this," she sighed.

ഇരു

"I say we go and kill him!" Brakkus roared, freeing his sword, ready for another fight.

"He's too strong, Brakkus," Jason said, taking the potion and grimacing, "Plus Annetta said she-,"

412

'*J.K, can you hear me?*' Annetta's voice rang in his head.

'*Yes I can, Brakkus is ready to fly downstairs and take on Yarmir all by himself,*' he replied.

'*Not happening. I'm collapsing the foundation,*' she notified him.

'*What? Are you out of your mind?*'

"She's contacting ye?" Brakkus noticed the expressions change on Jason's face as he sent messages back and forth.

"You need to work on hiding those facial changes Jason," Puc stated.

"She's collapsing the mountain." Jason's face turned white as he announced it.

"Oi sorry...she what?" Brakkus's eyebrows knotted.

"Tell her she can't do that! We are still inside," Puc snapped.

'*Annetta we'll all be crushed if you do that.*' Jason repeated Puc's worry.

'*Get them out. Yarmir can duplicate himself. He waited till you were gone, and he's got a spell on him that's just like what he used on the fenrikin. If I cut any limb off, it turns into a double of him,*' she explained.

Jason frowned. "She says Yarmir has some kind of spell placed on him where he duplicates-," Jason felt the ground underneath him begin to shake.

"Confounded girl! Why does she not listen!" Puc snarled. "She'll kill us all if she does this."

"I can get us out," Jason said. "But only if we hurry up. I don't know how much longer I can hold on."

"Unknown's bane! Why can't I just go down there and finish him?" Brakkus growled, looking at the mage.

"Because we are dealing with adolescents, Brakkus," Puc reminded him before he turned to Jason. "You're sure you can teleport us all out?"

"Doesn't look like I have a choice." The boy cringed as he recalled the mace back into its pendant state, the world around them shaking increasingly violently, rock beginning to fall around them.

§○Q

Annetta faced the two giants, her heart pounding with adrenaline as the four pairs of yellow eyes grinned at her fiercely. She gripped the sword and shield desperately as she relayed her plan to Jason through telepathy.

"Scared of the fight you've found yourself in, little girl?" the creatures chuckled in unison, closing in on her.

Annetta went into the fighting stance Brakkus had taught her, with her shield forward and her sword tightly against her side, like a large spear. It was the easiest way to either become defensive right away or offensive if need be. Annetta, however, had a much more complicated plan.

Springing to action, she charged between the two giants with her arms outstretched. Bashing one with the ridge of her shield, and the other with her sword, she teleported, reappearing some distance behind them where the altar had been. Flexing her arms into a fighting position, she steadied herself, watching her foes. The giants wasted no time in retaliating, claws extended, one leaped right at her, full force. Teleporting again, she reappeared closer to the stairs, only to have a fallen rock hurled at her from the second Yarmir incarnation that stood behind its brother. Her shield did little to lessen the impact, and the girl hit the floor. She rose, however, with a roar of determination, and charged once more.

Her aim was different the second time. Teleporting, she whooshed past the giants, towards where the statues were, and sent two of the fallen their way. Before either giant could respond, they were forced against the wall, pinned by their stone kin. Trapped, they could do little to Annetta as she slammed her blade into the ground. She focused all her energy into it, picturing the vibrations of the blade plunging into the ground as they collided and magnified, until everything around them began to shake. More and more violently, everything began to tremor.

"What are you doing?" the first Yarmir shrieked as he struggled to break free of the statue holding him.

"What does it look like? I'm bringing down the mountain!" she snarled, as stalagmites collapsed around them, shattering into pieces.

"You foolish runt! You'll kill us all!" the twin hollered.

Annetta's grip on the sword became numb as she held on, continuing the effects of earthquake, her first phase of the plan. Defiantly, she locked eyes with the creature, a smile spreading across her face. Only she knew what would happen next.

"No, just you." She grinned wickedly as her body began to fade from the room.

Her last view of the giant was one of fear. It was a face Annetta did not wish to see on any of her friends. But at the moment, it sated her need for power over the enemy.

Chapter 39

Jason had managed to get everyone out on time, though it had taken a major toll on him, leaving him barely able to stand. The group watched in terror as the entire mountain seemed to disappear underground in a cloud of dust and snow, leaving a deep canyon in its place. At first, not seeing Annetta anywhere caused panic among them. Calling through the wilderness at the top of their lungs, they stopped upon hearing laughter only a few feet behind them. The companions turned to see the girl lying on the rocky ground on her back, sprawled out like she was lying on a feather bed.

"What on Earth?" Brakkus's ears pricked up at the sight of Annetta.

"Anne! You okay?" Link asked, helping Darius carry a half conscious Jason by resting his arm over his shoulders.

Puc remained behind all the others, fury building within the mage, not because the enemy had been taken down without the help of the group, but because of everything that had been at stake. He gave himself a moment before moving forward to Brakkus's side. Seeing the girl laughing, however, brought his rage right back up.

"ANNETTA SEVERIO," the mage snapped, grabbing the girl by the scuff of her jacket and hoisting her up like she weighed nothing at all, "Do you have any idea how irrational your actions were back there? You could have been killed in the process! Were you even thinking of the magnitude of danger you placed yourself in? Placed all of us in?"

Annetta had calmed down from laughing upon seeing the enraged face of the elf snarling at her. However, she started laughing again once he had finished.

"What in all of the Unknown's domain is so bloody funny that you cannot absolutely stop just for one moment!" The mage ordered an explanation and then turned to Brakkus, "I do believe she has gone mad."

"Oh, well, you know how when you cut down a tree you tell timber?" she choked out of herself through chuckles. "I should have yelled something like… boulders."

Puc's eyebrow went up, as did everyone else's around her, not understanding the joke. The mage was not amused, as he set down the girl on her two feet. Unable to stand from the energy she used, Annetta tumbled forward, only to be caught by the elf's iron grip again.

"That was truly the most irresponsible thing I have ever seen anyone do," Puc hissed at her. "We could have died, you could have died, and everything would be for naught. It was also the most Severio thing I have seen you do."

Annetta grinned upon hearing the last bit, only to have Puc eye her more fiercely. "Next time," he said, "allow others to aid you. It is what we are here for, to call upon the strengths of one another. Together we form a powerful force, alone we are vulnerable. Do you understand?"

Annetta lowered her head and nodded. Puc noted that her shield was still attached to her arm, but her sword was missing from its scabbard. He said nothing. He had a bit more faith now that with or without a weapon, she could take care of herself.

"So what do we do now?" Jason asked, looking at Snapneck, who was now sitting on Brakkus's beefy shoulder, happy as a clam.

"I think the little one wants to go home to his dad, don't ya?" Brakkus looked over at Snapneck, who chirped in agreement in his squeaky voice.

"My question is how does a little guy like you get a name like Snapneck?" Annetta asked looking, at the mini Minotaur.

Snapneck puffed out his chest as he leaped to the ground. Grabbing a nearby stick, he let out a high pitched snarl, and snapped it with all the savageness the little being could muster. He then turned to look at Annetta with his arms crossed and gave a huff that he had proven his point.

೫೦೦೪

The journey back to Morwick was slightly more strenuous. Their original path had been blocked when Annetta and Jason had knocked down the mountains in order to rid them of the charging pack of fenrikin. Due to this, they had to lead the horses across the jagged rocks instead of riding.

"I still don't see why we can't just move them again, or you could blast through it with some magic," Jason growled, his fingers scraped to the point of being raw from falling down multiple times on the rocks and leading the reins of his horse.

"Did you see how much rock that was?" Puc glared at him. "It all has to go somewhere, and I would rather not risk you and Annetta fainting yet again from the effort. It's too dangerous. You both need to realize that even though you have this great power within you, there are limitations. You are not gods as you like to think from the mountain fight."

Annetta felt the words sting at her pride, though she knew it to be true. Since she stood against the pack of fenrikin armed with only her powers, something had been born inside her, a sort of resolute fearlessness that stood in the face of danger. The emotion was too complex for her to dwell on and shaking her head she thought of other things, like the little Minotaur that was hopping along the rocks happily, throwing pebbles before them from time to time and watching them roll downhill with satisfaction.

"I say ye'll bring down the mountain if ya keep doing that," Brakkus said, watching the little creature giggle and hop about.

"I think we have had enough of that this trip," Puc added, not the least bit amused, to which the Hurtz chuckled.

Snapneck, as they found out, could not yet speak, and so only produced squeaks, laughs, and the odd strange combination of half words the Minotaur had picked up from their speech. He was for the most part chipper in their company, amusing them by trying to show off his non-existent strength by snapping twigs and trying to pick up rocks that were bigger than he was. Being no bigger than a soccer ball also made him easy to carry when he was too tired to press on with the rest of the company.

"He's a cute one." Link grinned watching Snapneck mutter something at a rock before he headbutted it.

"Thinking of taking him home? I don't think his father would approve." Annetta smiled, seeing the young warrior's amusement.

"I'll pass on the kidnapping, thanks," he replied as they descended. "Plus, carrying one beast around inside is enough."

Annetta only smiled lightly back after hearing the last part. She knew it hurt Link to think of his curse, and she wished there was something she could do to convince him that it was not so bad, but all attempts were futile. She pressed on ahead to where Darius and Puc were at the foot of the mountains, looking through maps. By Puc's scowl, she could tell something was not right, and the moment she got there she would hear of it.

"What's wrong?" she asked, prompting conversation.

"Nothing really. It just looks though like we're close to another wall of the city. Look over there." Darius pointed behind him.

Annetta squinted her eyes, trying to look on the horizon. Barely visible was the massive black wall of the maze protecting Morwick from intruders. A smile spread on her face, seeing the end of their journey draw near.

"So it's a good thing we took down the mountains with Jason?" She looked at Puc, half grinning in triumph.

"Don't get ahead of yourself, Annetta. It won't work in every scenario. We just got lucky." The mage rolled his eyes, folding the map and saddling up.

Chuckling, the girl waited for Link to catch up with her on foot. They were both riding together now, since his horse had been killed in the fight. Watching his footing cautiously, the youth descended down the rocky path until he found himself on smooth ground beside her.

"Look, I'm sorry about what I said before," she said to him, seeing the withdrawn look on his face when he came closer.

"It's nothing. Don't worry about it. It's just something I need to get over on my own," he answered, getting on the horse and extending a hand to her.

Annetta hoisted herself up in the saddle with some difficulty. Though she could ride alone without any problems, having someone else there was awkward. She especially disliked not having any reins to hold onto, save for holding onto Link in front of her. Waiting for the rest of the group to catch up, they made their way to the black gates.

છબળ

When they came to the gates with Snapneck, the sound of great horns blasting could be heard. A small squad of guards came out to escort them into Stoneberg, where Ironhorn awaited them with his officials, clad in the blue garments and gold chainmail he had worn before, a large golden hammer before him which he leaned on, watching the companions enter the room. Seeing his father, Snapneck dashed up before him with high pitched yelps without any concern for bowing to the King of Morwick.

Ironhorn too forgot his role and scooped up the small Minotaur into his arms, then held him closely before placing the youth on his shoulder, leaving Snapneck to hold onto his sire's horn for stability.

"You have done well. You bring much joy to me in returning my son from Yarmir's grip. Tell me, what was the fate of the giant?" the king asked, taking a seat on his throne while Snapneck played with his father's crown.

"He is slain, Lord Ironhorn," Puc explained, moving forward before the rest of the company, "by Annetta Severio and Jason Kinsman's hands. They rescued your son as well, while we held off the fenrikin which the fiend had employed into his ranks."

418

Ironhorn twirled his beard with his clawed fingers as he listened, completely oblivious to what his son was doing. Annetta could not help but smile upon seeing the father's tolerance of his son's playful behavior even in receiving news as important as this. It made her wonder if her own grandfather had been like this with her father. Perhaps if things had gone differently it would have also been her fate. As a little girl, she could have run through the castle walls, known each corner of the woods and the mountains. If things had gone differently, would everything have also come easier to her?

The great Minotaur shifted in his chair, his eyes upon Annetta, making her snap back to reality. His gaze also went to Jason.

"You have done a father the greatest service that can be provided, and an even greater one to our kingdom by returning its heir unharmed, and ridding us of an ancient enemy." The Minotaur King stood up once more. "In times past, we the Minotaurs served Lord Orbeyus of the Axe for his own great deeds to our people. We were the stone upon which his army was built, the crafters of great weapons and warriors, the likes which few have seen."

Ironhorn stepped down from his throne and set Snapneck on the ground to stand beside him, still holding the crown in his hands, muttering to himself. The great Minotaur then raised himself to look at those before him and at his advisors and generals who were present in the room. Slamming the hammer face down onto the ground, Ironhorn bowed before Annetta and her party, as did all of his subjects.

"In the one who is severed we trust, our lives to you until we are dust. What is ours we give unto you to use. Our strength and wisdom use as you choose." The hall around reverberated with the sound of thick, gruff voices reciting the vow.

Annetta and Jason felt a chill go down their spine hearing the words spoken a third time. At that moment, something caught their eyes as they noticed the two statues guarding the throne.

"You did not think that the Lion of Hell and Hand of Death would get places of honor with their visages?" Ironhorn got back up, and seeing the faces of the two, smiled. The statues were images of their own fathers. "For all eternity will they grant the courage and wisdom to all who reside in the throne of Morwick, until The One comes to pass judgement in the end days of this land."

Annetta and Jason simply nodded, not fully understanding the mythology the king had just recited, but still feeling a little prouder of who they were none the less.

Ironhorn then inclined his head to one of the guards, who retreated from the room. "A warrior should never be without a weapon Lady Annetta," the king said.

Annetta looked down at her empty scabbard and blushed a little.

"I lost it in the mountain, Lord Ironhorn. It was the only way to bring it all down and to be able to escape," she answered bashfully.

The Minotaur Lord bobbed his head as the guard came back, holding something wrapped up in a deep navy silk. Unraveling it, Ironhorn produced a sword the likes of which Annetta had never seen. The blade itself was pure black, with the edges lined in gold, the hilt decorated with fur and what looked to be two silver Minotaur horns.

"Until the time Severbane is unleashed from its resting place, you may use my dagger, Fearseeker, to serve you wherever your journeys may take you, young Annetta Severio." Ironhorn took the weapon from his servant and walked up before Annetta to place it in her hands. "It should suffice as a sword to your small hands. Try not to lose it."

Annetta examined its details in her hands. The weapon was light in her grip, despite how large it was. She placed it carefully in the scabbard. It fit like a charm, "Thank you, Lord Ironhorn," she said.

Annetta took a step back as Puc made his way forward.

"We too have something for you, Lord Ironhorn, in order to keep our worlds aligned so that we may stand united when the time comes." The mage reached into his robes, producing one of the C.T.S. watches, its strap much larger, designed for a creature the size of a Minotaur. Some of the Minotaurs gasped, wondering what it was. "If you've any written records anywhere, these devices were used by Orbeyus in order to keep our times synchronized."

Ironhorn nodded, accepting the watch and placing it on his wrist, "I do remember reading of these strange devices Orbeyus brought, and if necessary I shall wear it. There is writing that once the war had finished, time needed to return to normal in order to avoid damage to the veils that separated all worlds from one another, and so once the Four Forces were disbanded. These had to be returned for fear of the worlds collapsing from the great pull they had on time. Strange little devices, that they should hold so much power."

Puc simply nodded in agreement, making Jason look down at the watch on his hand in alarm.

"It won't cause a black hole, if that is what you are thinking, Jason. You may stop turning into a shade resembling my own." Puc noted his reaction, causing the boy to turn a little red and Annetta to snicker.

"I should ask that you all stay for our feast tonight in your honor for returning Prince Snapneck to us." Ironhorn sat back down on his throne.

Annetta felt her stomach growl at the mention of food, causing her to go red at the ears from embarrassment. She glanced back at her companions to see similar looks on their faces. The last time they'd all eaten was the previous night when they'd captured the mountain deer.

"We really should be going-," Puc began only to be cut off by a glare from Brakkus, who was not about to pass up a meal. "Perhaps for a little while, then."

Chapter 40

After spending some well earned time at the feast, Annetta, Jason and the others saddled up on their horses. Following Puc's lead, the group headed for the portal that had now opened to lead them home. Dark was fast approaching, and with it, colder temperatures that Annetta had never been more glad to leave behind for the approaching summer in their own world.

"To have to go through a Canadian winter is one thing, to have to go through two in a row is another," she stated as they crossed the portal. She checked her watch to note the day and time. "Man, we missed more school. How am I going to catch up with all this homework?"

"A trinket in the span of the larger things at hand." Puc looked back at the girl. "And your homework is nothing compared to what you would be getting at the mage academy."

Annetta simply growled under her breath, not wanting to picture anything more complicated. She found herself understanding more and more why some people would want to forget their life in the real world. One was not stuck beside a burning lamp writing equations that meant nothing out of context.

"You worry too much about school, Anne," Jason said, seeing his friend's expression. "I mean, you missed, what, three weeks when you had chicken pox?"

"Yeah, well, blame my dad for instilling it in me." She frowned and then added, "That was back then. This is high school."

Link watched the scene as he stripped out of the winter jacket, allowing his body to breathe the warm air around them. Puc had assigned him to start going to school with the others once they came back from Morwick, due to the attack on Jason. It was not something he was looking forward to, and from what Annetta was saying, it made him want to do so even less. He had been trained to use a sword, not a pen.

"It's not as bad as she makes it out to be," Darius said walking by Link and seeing his expression. "I mean, if she would actually do her homework and not have her head in the clouds, it would all be done quicker."

A bloody winter jacket smacked Darius in the side of the face as he laughed, catching it and looking at Annetta.

"I do not daydream!" she snapped. "Besides, that was before I knew about...all this."

"Whatever your heart desires, Anne," he chuckled throwing the jacket back at her and continuing out of the castle, leaving the growling and muttering girl behind with Jason.

ର

Making sure everything was secure, the company retreated back to Q-16, where the horses were placed in their appropriate stalls and examined by Brakkus.

"I say the next time we leave the horses in the castle," the Hurtz stated, looking at the hooves of one of the beasts. "I'd rather not lose another in a fight, and they need a rest as it is. All of them are gonna need new shoes, and that takes time to make."

"I dare say we will not need them when meeting with the Soarin," Puc stated. "But yes, I agree with you, we will need the horses alive and well. How many spares have we left?"

Brakkus looked through the stalls, counting the horses.

"Seven," the Hurtz said, looking back to the mage. "A lot of them are getting old, not good for riding. Ye think ye'll be able to pick up some fresh ones in Aldamoor when ya go to see Kaian?"

"How many do we need?"

While Puc and Brakkus discussed the matters of bringing in new horses, Annetta took a moment to sit down with her friends outside of the stable, and look at the portal leading to the castle before them.

"I don't know about you guys, but I'm beat," she said with a huff.

"I think we're all in the pretty much in the same boat." Link chuckled lightly.

Annetta smiled back at him, the wind blowing gently through his dark blonde hair as he closed his eyes. She looked over to Jason and Darius, who also looked like they were on the verge of falling asleep. She too was beginning to feel tired.

"I think we need to finally get home to our parents," she said, standing up. "I don't want to think about how worried mine are."

Jason's eyes instantly opened as he bolted up. "Man, I don't even want to think what my mom is going to say. It's bad enough she doesn't want me down here in the first place ... but it's been..."

"Almost three days." Puc's voice came from the doorway making everyone turn around. "And that is a wise choice, Annetta. I'm sure Arieus and Aurora are worried about your whereabouts, as is Talia about your own, Jason."

"I guess we should get going then," Jason sighed.

"I'm right behind you," Annetta replied.

Puc nodded. "I will be gone tomorrow. I need to return to Aldamoor to give Kaian one of the watches, and to purchase some fresh horses. I will probably need some help in securing them."

"I'd be more than happy to accompany you if you like," Link offered. "I hear from Brakkus you're not a fan."

Darius chuckled, to which Puc only shot him an angered glance.

"Very well then," the mage nodded.

"Can I come along too? I mean, if my parents won't skin me alive tonight?" Annetta asked, wanting to go back and see more of Aldamoor.

"I assure you, the only skinning that could happen is by Mislantus's hands, not your parents," Puc stated. "And yes, you may come along. Jason, do you wish to accompany us?"

"No thanks. If it's all the same, I kind of…need a break from all of this," the boy said putting his hands in his pocket.

Puc nodded and then turned to Darius. "I will need you to stay behind and help Brakkus. There are also some potions and spells I will show you later that I want you to prepare, just in case we run into any trouble. Though the Soarin are not as heavily armed as the Minotaurs, they are not to be taken lightly if for some reason we are not welcome."

"I'll get on it, master," the apprentice nodded.

With those final remarks, the companions parted ways for the approaching night.

෨ଓ

Though Arieus and Aurora were well aware that whatever Puc would have set up for Annetta and Jason to tackle would take time, it was parental instinct which drove them to worry when their daughter did not surface from the underwater base for near three days. On the first, they told themselves that there was a lot of travel involved. But when they woke up on the third day and Annetta was nowhere to be seen, both had trouble concealing their feelings from one another. Pacing around the kitchen with strained conversation was how the majority of the day passed.

"Perhaps we should go down there Arieus?" Aurora finally said, unable to hide her worry anymore "It's been too long, even if they were traveling to Morwick-,"

"You forget that they could be caught in a snowstorm and walled up in Stoneberg. Or maybe it's taking them longer to convince the Minotaurs. You remember how stubborn they were whenever we tried to negotiate with them," Arieus cut in, putting down his mug of tea on the kitchen table.

"Well, you seem incredibly calm despite everything!" she huffed. "Arieus, there could be a war. A war we should be fighting, not them."

"We're not as young as we used to be," Arieus reminded her.

"Well, she's too young, and so is Jason," she protested.

"And how old were you when you raised your sword with my father's army? Fourteen, maybe fifteen years old at most? Not much older than they are now," Arieus rose from his seat snapping, "We knew what they were getting into."

"She's your daughter Arieus, does worrying for her mean nothing to you?" Aurora glared at her husband.

"I worry as much as you do, if not more," he sighed, sitting back down, "But there is very little we can do, except pray that the Unknown keeps her safe. Besides, I have great faith in both Puc and Brakkus. She's not completely alone out there."

Aurora nodded upon hearing those words from her husband. It brought comfort to her knowing that the Hurtz warrior and elven mage were both by her side. She remembered all too well what great fighters they were, and how much faith Orbeyus had placed on the both of them. Sighing, she sat down beside the man she had married and placing her hand in his, gave it a good squeeze.

The couple basked in only their own presence, a silence that had become much appreciated in their years of raising a family. Xander was gone for the evening at a sleepover with a friend, so not even the clatter of a remote control could be heard. It was broken with the familiar sound of the teleportation device. Rising from their seats, they rushed to the room to find Annetta standing in its midst, tattered like she had been in a fight that had not ended well.

"Annetta, sweetheart what happened?" Aurora shrieked, grabbing her daughter by the arms and examining the many bandages and bloody winter coat. "Are you alright? Is Jason-,"

The sound came again, and Jason appeared, not looking much better, bandages covering his arms. Together the two of them looked like they had gone through a war, the only things betraying their feelings being the look of innocence in their eyes.

"Should we be concerned?" Arieus's eyes widened. "I'm... I'm not sure how I'm going to explain this to Talia..."

Jason raised an eyebrow and then remembered his arm. "Oh, it's not as bad as it looks, sir. Puc gave us a few potions to take before bed. He said if we'd taken them earlier they would have knocked us out flat, and he didn't want to risk that on the journey in case anything happened."

Arieus sighed heavily as relief flowed through him, and then looked back at Annetta's jacket. "Looks like you'll need a new one come next winter."

Annetta flushed crimson, which made her father chuckle.

"Well, we're glad you're back safe," Arieus said, walking out the door to grab his shoes and jacket. "If you want, J.K. I can drive you back home. You must be tired from everything that happened."

"If it's okay J.K., I think I might sit this one out. I'm feeling pretty gone," Annetta said looking over at her friend.

"You and me both," the boy replied, putting his tattered winter jacket over his shoulder. "Good night, Mrs. Severio. Later, Anne."

"Night," her and her mother both answered as the door shut behind them.

As soon as they left, Aurora wrapped her arms around her daughter tightly, pulling her close. Though she did not cry, and she knew she could not show her daughter fear, her body trembled all the same against the girl. Annetta wrapped her arms around her mother, resting her head on her shoulder. It was then that she realized how home sick she was. The long hours in the Lab, the traveling, and school left little time for her to see her parents. This was when she felt she needed them most, parents who had always been supportive of her, no matter what happened in school, or with friends. The parents she came home to each day after school and she could tell anything because they would, unlike many, listen. She wanted to tell them of all she was learning and everything she saw and let them know that no matter where she was she would always miss them. Despite Aurora showing courage, Annetta could not hold back as tears formed in her eyes, streaming down her cheeks.

Feeling something dampen the shirt on her shoulder, Aurora pulled back to gaze into the girl's eyes. Despite what Arieus had said to her, she saw no warrior but a child who was in need of her mother.

"Sweetheart, what's wrong?" she asked.

"Sorry...I just... I missed you mom," Annetta sobbed.

"You have nothing to be sorry for, Anne. Don't ever apologize for something like that." Her mother smiled lightly at her. "Though I will not lie to you. You've made your father and I worried sick about you."

Annetta pulled back a little, wiping her eyes on her sleeve as she looked down, not knowing what to say back to her mother. "I'm sorry..."

Aurora sighed and shook her head. "It's not your fault either, sweetheart. We just need to adjust to the fact that you'll be home less and less. That's what happens when you grow up. It's the natural order of things."

"Yeah, but I don't think going off to other worlds fits into that natural order," Annetta stated.

"In this family, I'm afraid it does," Aurora sighed. "Like I said, your father and I just need time to accept this. We thought we had left it behind, but it seems that sometimes destiny cannot be changed."

"You mean the prophecy that Puc told us about? Through the sword of thy sire, that one?" Annetta asked.

Aurora nodded her head, "Your father knew of this prophecy for some time. It had been thought to be about him and Arcanthur. But the lines did not match up, because it talks about how Orbeyus would no longer be alive."

Annetta looked down at her tattered boots on her feet, another thing that would need replacing, then back up at her mother.

"Do you think you and dad will ever come down to the Lab again?" she asked.

"Only time will tell, Annetta. For now, we are not ready to go back to that life. Your grandfather's death still weighs on your father's conscience, and any reminder of that life would make it haunt him even more so. We made a promise to one another, to escape that life so that we could build a safer future for you and Xander."

"Speaking of Xander, where is he? I missed him too," Annetta asked seeing the room empty and the television screen blank.

427

"Over at Kevin's for a sleepover because he couldn't sleep in his room without his big sister." Aurora smiled, thinking of her son and how close he was with Annetta. But she feared the day she would have to tell him everything about where his older sister, the hero in his eye, went after school, and why she no longer had time to play video games with him like they once did. He was still young, and so many things could be simplified for him. He would no doubt follow her if he found out the entire truth, and she wondered how long she could keep him from that world.

Annetta yawned, rubbing the sleep from her eyes. She pulled out the vials Puc had given her.

"I think it's time for you to shower, and then take those and get to bed." Aurora kissed her daughter's forehead. "You have school tomorrow and a lot of homework to catch up on."

Annetta frowned the moment homework was mentioned. Taking down a mountain was one thing, but a mountain of homework was a whole other battle.

೩೦ೞ

Talia stood outside the complex with a cigarette in hand, letting the fumes rise up in the twilight that was gathering around her, turning everything deep blue. It was not often that she turned to the little sticks of tobacco for comfort. Unlike Aurora, she did not have the comforting hand of her spouse to rest on her shoulder. For Talia, the day she found her son levitating objects in his room was her worst nightmare come true. It was the day that everything she had pushed back from her past came welling back up, telling her there was no escaping.

She had never wanted Jason to meet Annetta at all, and had severed all ties with Arieus after his fight with Arcanthur. She'd needed her husband put away so her sons and herself could lead something of a normal life. Still, the fear lingered for her sons ever being in the same situation, trying what Arcanthur tried and ending up the way he did. But fate had planned differently, and it did not take long for Talia to pick out the offspring of Orbeyus Severio when she saw the little girl's eyes in the schoolyard playing with her son.

She had known she could not simply go out and tell her son not to be friends with the girl because her father had been responsible for sending his father to the mental hospital. She had instead endured and learned to tolerate what formed into a deep friendship, seeing no threat from the girl herself.

428

She knew Annetta could not help being who she was, but Talia still feared her, and so tried to limit Jason's contact with the girl, giving him other obligations. When she had entered that room on that day, everything changed, her planned future crashing and she knew there was no stopping it. Instead of even fighting, she washed her hands and turned a blind eye. Being a mother, however, she could not be blind to her son's absence, and this was now what lay in the center of her heart.

It was a huge relief to her when a familiar set of headlights pulled into the parking lot, belonging to a beat up minivan, the kind a devoted parent would drive. Extinguishing the hardly touched cigarette, Talia watched as the door slid open and Jason came out with his backpack in hand.

"Mom?" Jason raised an eyebrow, surprised to see her. He ran towards her, embracing her.

Talia wasted no time wrapping her arms around her son. Whatever anger she had harbored moments before dissolved, replaced only with gratitude that someone out there had allowed him to come back home safe. She looked up, away from the embrace, to see a pair of the same blue eyes she had seen in the schoolyard watching her. She noted however that these eyes had seen much more in life and were tired of its burden, Arieus.

'Why did you not stay? Why did you not protect them from this fate?' the words telepathically transmitted to Arieus.

'Talia, sooner or later it would fall to them. It is an inevitable fate, one we were all born into. All we can do is embrace it.' Arieus watched her from behind the dark of the glass.

'But it could have been prevented for a little longer, until they were old enough.' She closed her eyes and let go of Jason, trying not to seem suspicious by lingering too long.

Arieus lowered his head behind the glass with a sigh, and put the gears in reverse. *'I'm sorry, but I'm just a man, flawed as any. This is how it was meant to be.'*

The car pulled out, leaving a light trail of dust behind as Talia watched it disappear. She then turned to her son, finally conscious of all the bandages. Her jaw dropped.

"Jason? What...what happened?" her eyes widened as she examined the wrappings on his head.

"The short version, I got slapped by a giant," the boy said calmly. "Long version, we had to rescue a Minotaur prince from a ritual being performed by a giant in order to gain the trust of Lord Ironhorn so he would renew his race's vow to the Four Forces."

"And you expect to go to school like this tomorrow…how?" She waved her hand up and down, motioning to his bandages. "You look like a half finished mummy."

Jason pulled out a few vials from his pocket. "Puc said to take these before I go to sleep and I should be fine tomorrow morning. He said I couldn't take them earlier because it would knock me out."

Talia shook her head. Were any other parent hearing the story, they would have thought their child had fallen from a tree and bumped their head too hard. But she knew better thanks to the many things she had seen in her own lifetime.

"Well, let's get you to bed then," she sighed, putting her arm around him. "And maybe tomorrow you can tell me about what you saw."

Though worry had just occupied her mind seconds ago, the stress of it was gone, and something Arieus had told her had taken hold. She had to embrace it. She had to embrace the fact that her son was now aware of the world she had tried to leave long ago, a world of monsters, magic, and psychic warriors. She did not have to like any of it, in fact she would still stay very much away, but she would endure, for that was what a mother always did best for her child.

Chapter 41

Annetta woke the next morning, feeling as though all traces of her battles in Morwick had been erased and the events of the last few days were nothing more than a figment of her own imagination. She smirked to herself, the overnight healing reminding her of something out of an RPG video game. At least Puc's potions had worked, she told herself. Noticing the time on the alarm clock beside her, she rushed to get ready for school.

Walking into the kitchen to get a bowl of cereal, her hair flying in all directions, her pajamas still on, she did not notice Link sitting on the couch with her brother watching television until he spoke up.

"Morning, Anne." he looked in her direction with a smile.

Startled by the voice that was not part of her usual morning entourage of sounds, she jumped awake and glanced back to see his crescent moon scar and blue eyes watching her.

"Oh, hey Link." She flushed red trying to fix her hair a little. "When did you get up here so quick?"

"Uh... Puc sent me up after I got a military wake up from Brakkus, which included my bed being flipped over upside down," he answered.

Annetta chuckled, picturing the massive Hurtz flipping over a bed with a sleeping Link in it, but shook off the thought when she saw the minute hand on the clock creep closer to eight thirty. Her parents had already left for work, leaving just the three of them in the house. There was so much for her to do and so little time. It was times like this that she wished she had been born a boy, so she could stick on any pair of jeans and slick down her hair to be good to go.

Scrambling out of the house after Annetta had finished getting ready, the trio met up with Darius downstairs.

"When did you get up?" Annetta yawned, still somewhat sleepy, seeing him waiting in the lobby for them. "Didn't Puc have you doing stuff for him last night?"

"Same time as you and, there's nothing coffee can't fix." Darius smiled. "Now come on. We gotta get there earlier so Link can go into the main office and pick up his papers."

"Crap, right," Annetta muttered to herself, almost forgetting it was Link's first day of school. Sighing, she looked over at him. "You ready for this?"

"I just fought a pack of fenrikin yesterday, and you're asking me if I'm ready for math equations and grammar?" Link paused rethinking his words. "On second thought, I will take the pack again from what you tell me."

"It's not so bad." Darius chuckled. "Plus for us bodyguards... well...we sort of get to cheat with our homework."

"Really? This job comes with benefits? Pray tell." Link said looking at the elf intently.

"Man, I'm the one who is supposed to save the world, and you guys get to fake your homework? What gives?" Annetta growled.

"Because we know most of this stuff already, and it's not our world, but yours. If you do save the world, you'll still have to go and do finals, but for us, it doesn't matter," Darius said, to which Annetta simply growled again, and pressed on.

৪৩৫৪

Arriving to school early, Jason sat on the saltbox beside the drop off area, waiting to see Sarina. He knew he could speak to her without hiding the part of him that seemed so vital to his existence, but at the same time needed to keep it suppressed from the world around him. He had Annetta, Darius, and Link at school now, but somehow it was not the same. They were all in it together, but he needed someone on the outside who could understand. Though he had not known Sarina as long as Annetta or Darius, something about her made him calm when he spent time with her, like time stopped and everything he had to worry about no longer existed. He liked that feeling, and could not wait for it to happen again.

Winding around the side of the school, came a familiar small figure, her almond shaped eyes lighting up when she saw him.

"J.K.!" Sarina grinned as she raced towards him. "Are you alright? They were saying you were really sick... strep throat or something like that."

"I'm fine, actually," he said. "I was gone on a mission with my friends."

Jason's train of thought was cut off when he felt a pair of eyes watching him from the shadows. He looked up to see Matthias. He was dressed in the same outfit as the day he had brought Sarina to school, with glasses and his hair slicked back, yet he looked different. It took Jason a moment to figure it out, but he then noticed there were cuts on his face, and his arm hung in a sling with a cast on it.

Sarina turned back to look at Matthias, and then back to Jason. Her facial expression changed as soon as she saw her brother.

"Uhm, Jason, I need to tell you something. I'm going to be moving schools again, once our new safehouse is secure, and our new papers done up. We got attacked two days ago. It's not safe for me to stay here." She lowered her head. "In fact, I can't even talk to you really anymore. They might see us, and they'll come after you as well."

"What? But...but how?" Jason felt his jaw drop.

"I'm sorry Jason. It was nice to have a friend for once." She smiled and then walked past like she never knew him.

Jason stood as if he'd been cemented to the spot. He looked up to meet Matthias's gaze for a split second. The young man simply shook his head and disappeared. Jason curled up his fists, gritting his teeth. He wanted to go and tear out the man's throat for failing, but knew it would do him no good.

Growling, he stuffed his hands in his pocket and feeling the card key dig into his palm he remembered the other entrance to Q-16. He still had one more chance to make it right. He knew the risks, but he also knew somewhere deeper inside him that he had to do this for Sarina and her brother.

"I just need time," he muttered to himself. Shouldering his bag, he went to meet with his friends.

ഇരു

Link had expected a much darker place from everything Annetta had ever said about her school. He was surprised to see kids chatting and laughing in the schoolyard, waiting for the day to begin. After they'd gone to the main office to get all of Link's papers sorted, the trio came back outside to the schoolyard to wait for the bell and to look for Jason. Leading the way as she always did, Annetta walked to their usual corner, eyeing younger students who had attempted to take over their spot. It made Link snicker a bit to see her do this. There was something adorable in the glare she gave, even though it was meant to be lethal.

"Just act normal. If people stare at your scar you need to ignore it," Darius reminded him as they came to a stop beside the fence to lay down their backpacks. "I'll back you up on the story we worked on before."

Link nodded as he adjusted the bag he had been given. His gaze turned to Annetta, who leaned against the fence, watching the track and the soccer game that was going on in the middle of it. A boy came running towards them, his face as red as a beet.

"Hey Darius, could you lend us a hand on the field? We're short one offense player," he asked, panting.

"Uh...yeah, sure I guess I can go." He turned to Annetta and Link. "Would you guys mind looking after my bag?"

"Yeah, no sweat," Annetta said, and watched him take off with the other boy.

Link observed as well, and looked to the girl questioningly.

"He's always been a drifter, even though he doesn't show it as much now because his secret is out," Annetta explained. "It's why Jason never got along with him before. Darius always led on that there was more to him and it bothered us, especially when we made plans and Darius would cancel last minute because someone else invited him to a party or something cooler than what we were doing. That's not what friends do, right?"

"Right." Link nodded.

"I guess it all makes sense now," she continued. "He was probably doing stuff for Puc. Though seeing him run off that way makes me doubt it."

"Well, everyone needs to have some time off," Link said to her.

"True, but why he enjoys kicking a ball around for fun is far beyond me," she huffed, crouching down as she began picking at some of the longer strands of grass the lawnmower had missed.

Link followed her lead and took a spot beside her, watching her small fingers pick up the blades one by one and twirl them in between before letting them drop.

"Listen, I just wanted to say thank you," he said.

"For what?" Annetta looked up at him.

"For believing me right away, then later for believing in me," he told her. "Not many people would do that, especially today."

"You make it sound like chivalry is dead." The girl continued to play with grass.

Link smiled faintly, hearing the words come from her.

Annetta stopped pulling at the grass and looked up, turning in the direction of the corner to her right that was located by the parking lot and generally belonged to the younger students. At that moment however, Finn was having his way with them, taunting a younger student by taking his hat and threatening to throw it over the fence to the backyard of the house beside the school while other students stayed farther away, not even looking to help their friend. Never before had she turned a blind eye to Finn, and she was not about to let it go now. A very different spark glistened in the girl's eye as she got up. Taking her bag, she strode over at a confident and fluid pace.

"Why don't you pick on someone your own height, Finn?" she called, still standing some distance away from him. "It would make for more of a challenge. Unless you're afraid."

The bully cocked his head to the side, seeing Annetta and lost interest in the hat. He threw it into the muddy moat that separated the track from the grass, causing his victim to scramble for it. Disposed of his latest toy, he faced the girl.

"Back from your little vacation? I heard you got sick. But let's be honest, you were just at home crying." He grinned viciously.

"Like I'd waste a precious resource like water for someone like you." Annetta rolled her eyes. As she spoke, she noted how inferior Finn looked to Yarmir, it having only been a day since she returned from Morwick. Part of her wanted nothing more than to throw him against the fence and into the mud with her abilities. But she knew better. She had to live her role in this world.

Closing in, the pair circled one another like two cobras ready to tear each other's throats out, but neither made an effort to strike. Annetta's eye's flashed back and forth from the track to her opponent, making sure no teachers were in sight, in case Finn made a move. She always let him make the first move. She never allowed herself to seem the violent one, in case they got caught. Most of the time, it worked.

Link grabbed his and Darius's bag, moving closer, watching what was going on. He found it curious that Annetta had chosen to go out of her way to confront the other boy. On a deeper level, he knew why and what drove her to do it. It was the need to protect and stand up for those who could not do so for themselves. It was that same drive that caused him to join the militia back on Gaia.

He watched as Finn lowered his huge frame, curling his fists up while Annetta remained upright, not even flinching. Link was unsure of what she was trying to do, but did not interfere. Setting down the bags closer to where the two were, he leaned against the fence, watching. Then it began.

Finn charged at Annetta, oblivious of whether or not he would actually hit the girl. It was only then that Annetta showed any recognition of the boy and went into her own fighter stance before leaping out of the way of the shot. He spun around like an enraged bull, his dark eyes fixed on the girl.

"Coward! Fight back," he snarled, launching himself at her again.

Annetta did nothing of the sort. In fact she had no intention of really fighting him, except to humiliate him while he tried to assult her. She had noticed all the running around with a heavy shield and sword had made her lighter on her feet without them, like there was more bounce to her step when she walked. The ease with which she dodged that attack fueled her imaginary suspicion. She grinned, watching Finn lose control of his emotions.

"If you're gonna be all talk and no show, you shoulda stay out of it. Now fight me!" he sneered, and raising his leg, aimed it right at her midsection.

Unable to move out of the way in time fully, Annetta grabbed her opponent's foot after he landed the blow on her bracing forearms, pushed him forward so that he landed on his back on the mud.

"That look suits you," she said, coldly.

Some of the students who were standing by watched the encounter and laughed, only to be shot angry looks from Finn, who was now covered in mud. Taking her moment of triumph, he grabbed hold of the girl, trying to wrestle her into the same filth.

Annetta however, who was no ballerina, roared and shoved Finn towards the fence, trying to gain some advantage by twisting one of his limbs into a submissive position and end the fight early. Finn blocked each assault and when she least expected it, landed a punch to her gut, sending her off balance.

Annetta groaned, clutching her midsection but not falling to the ground. She tried to shake off the pain as quickly as she could, knowing another attack was mounting, but when nothing happened, she looked up to see Link grabbing hold of Finn's arm.

"Hey what gives, buddy?" Finn snapped as Link continued to hold his arm at bay.

"Didn't they ever teach you it's impolite to hit a lady?" Link asked calmly.

"What?"

436

"I said, didn't they teach you it's impolite to hit a lady?" Link shouted more ferociously the second time around and threw Finn's hand back to make him lose his balance, almost sending him to the mud again.

Link turned back to look at Annetta who was still trying to stand upright after the blow that had been landed on her.

"You okay?" he asked.

"Yeah, I'll live," she answered.

Before Link could say anything else back, something hard collided with the side of his face, almost making him trip. He turned around to see Finn attempting to jump on him and drag him down into the mud.

"What is going on here?" a stern voice from the track called.

Link, Finn and Annetta turned around to see Ms. Quixote, the English teacher.

"Nothing," Finn muttered.

"I don't think it was nothing. You three, to my room. Now," she ordered them.

The trio followed her inside the school to the English room. When she had closed the door and seated all three of them before the front of the class, she began.

"Finn, were you picking on our new student?" The flame-haired woman glared at the boy, who seemed to shrink tenfold in her presence.

"No, miss." He shook his head.

"Funny, because I could swear I just saw you punch Mr. Heallaws." The woman's sharp eyes seemed to pierce through clothing and flesh when she eyed him, her gaze then turning to Annetta.

"And you, Miss Severio. I assume were trying to play the part of a hero. Well, let me tell you something, young lady, if I can even call you that. The heroes you read about in your books are dead and gone for a reason or fictional. It's great that you love to read stories about them, and write about castles, but there is a time and place for everything. Society cannot tolerate vigilantes, and neither will I. In our world there are rules that must be obeyed, and it doesn't matter how much you think you can help. You see a fight happening, you go and report it. You will not get involved in this business anymore, or I'll have to call your father again, and Lord knows that man has had to deal with enough of you picking fights. Were it not for Mr. Breezone, I would have had you expelled with Finn long ago. Now go and put your things in your lockers. I expect you here once the bell rings, and go clean yourself up, Finn. You look like a swamp monster."

Dismissed, they left the classroom, parting ways the moment they were out. Annetta and Link headed over to her locker. Darius and Jason came running towards them. Seeing Finn across the hall covered in mud only quickened their pace.

"What happened?" Jason asked as soon as he was within hearing distance of them.

"I leave for ten minutes at most and you get in a fight?" Darius shouldered his bag, nodding a thank you to Link for not abandoning it.

"Man, Finn was picking on one of the younger kids, I wasn't going to sit by and watch it happen," Annetta growled, annoyed.

Darius sighed, shaking his head in resignation, and watched as the girl walked ahead of the three of them.

"Has she always been like this?" Link asked as they made their way to their lockers.

"Ever since I can remember," Jason said. "She's always fought against people who pick on others in the school. She would go up against the kinds of things teachers were oblivious to. The fights that they don't hear about, that's where Annetta always was. She always says, if she doesn't fight, then who will?"

Link nodded as he watched the girl disappear into the crowd gathering in the halls. From afar, she looked no different than any of those students who chatted in line, a young girl in a baggy jean jacket with shaggy hair. But the trio standing and watching saw the girl who had traveled to foreign worlds, who held a shield and sword in hand, and who risked it all because no one else would.

From where Annetta stood, however, she felt something else, different from what her friends thought. She felt something dark, something she had not experienced before, when she had confronted Finn. It was a feeling that made it seem like all emotion was switched off, and it swam in her like a poison. It scared her to no end.

⁖⁗

The day had passed quicker than any of them had expected. Thankfully, they hadn't missed as much as Annetta had anticipated, and all she ended up having to do were three summaries.

438

Shouldering their bags once the final bell rang, they headed out of the classroom until they got to the back gate.

"So, I guess we split up here for today," Annetta said, standing at the crossroads of her apartment building and Jason's complexes.

"Yeah, sorry I just... I need a time out to be with my mom and stuff." Jason looked at his feet.

Annetta nodded in understanding, "I'll see you tomorrow at school."

"Yeah, see ya later, Anne." Jason waved lightly as he turned around and headed for home. But his intentions were different, and his first course of action was to walk straight to the forest behind his house.

ഇരു

Entering the wooded area and proceeding to his favorite rock, Jason set down his backpack on the mossy boulder. His green eyes scanned the area around him as he tried to think of where to look first, a tree that never changes. He pursed his lips. Why did there have to be so many trees?

Thinking no more on the issue, he set out with card key in hand to turn every stone and stick before darkness claimed the woods. His only comforting thought being that his efforts might let Sarina find a permanent home among his friends.

ഇരു

Once everyone had made their way down to the Lab, the trio headed towards the stables where they had agreed to meet Puc and Brakkus the previous night. Both mage and warrior were busy with their own tasks in the stable, Puc looking through scrolls while Brakkus worked with the horses.

"When are ye gonna get over that horse buckin' ya off so things can go faster here?" Brakkus grumbled at the mage.

"I was not "bucked off" as you say, Brakkus. I was thrown and then attacked by a vicious beast." Puc didn't even look away from his papers as he spoke.

Annetta put her arms up on the railing of the metal fence isolating the horse pens from the blacksmithing area before lifting herself up to she could rest her legs on a lower bar to see over it. Link stood beside her, not needing to do so due to his height.

"Hey guys, what's this about Puc falling off of a horse?" She looked at the mage, who only shot her an angered glare.

"Reason he hates 'em," Brakkus said. "Multiple times it happened actually, all with different-,"

"Brakkus, you finish that sentence and I'll turn you into a carrot and have them nip at you," Puc snarled.

The Hurtz stifled a laugh before he went back to putting saddles on the horses.

"I can help, if you want. It could move things along faster," Link offered as he came around the fence and grabbed another saddle.

"There's a lad," the Hurtz grinned, watching the boy work. He then turned to Annetta. "I should be making ya do this, not him. Ya need to be more proficient in putting on saddles."

"What's wrong with how I put them on now?" Annetta asked.

"Nothing, he just has little else to prod at." Puc stated.

"Oh," Annetta uttered quietly, and looked down at her feet hanging on the fence while Link and Brakkus worked away. She then turned to the mage, "Puc, can I talk to you about something without getting a response covered in sarcasm?"

"Only if you don't ask me to saddle a horse," the mage responded, rolling up the parchment he had been studying, turning to the young girl.

"Well, I got into a fight with Finn again," she said, to which the mage's jawline twitched. "No, I didn't use my powers. I swear. It's just that when I approached him, I felt different."

"Well you faced a giant and fenrikin." Puc studied the girl. "I fail to believe he is more frightening than those."

"I know that. But just when I fought him, when I was actually going up against him, I felt different. Like I didn't care, you know?"

Puc sighed, "You faced, as I said, a giant and fenrikin. What you are feeling is numbness to the everyday life you are used to. Anyone who travels to different dimensions feels it at first. Anyone who fights a foe greater than what they are used to, and then comes back to their old life, feels it. It's nothing unnatural. You're not becoming a sociopath, if that is what you are trying to get at."

"Is that why J.K.'s dad became how he is?" she asked.

Puc sighed, standing up from his seat and walked over to the sad-eyed girl that still sat on the fence. "There were many things that led to that, and believe me when I say this, you will be alright. But you must stop being hotheaded, unless you wish to get yourself killed."

Annetta looked up into the pale eyes of the elf, and nodded. "I'll try to remember that, but it's easier said than done."

"As is the way with all things in all worlds," he replied.

"They're ready for ye," Brakkus called.

Puc turned to face him. "We should be back before nightfall."

"Ya think I actually know when that'll be in this dungeon?" Brakkus indicated the lack of windows in Q-16. "Ya might as well say next year."

"Point taken, friend." Puc nodded and slung a pack with scrolls over his shoulder before turning to Annetta and Link. "Are you both ready?"

Annetta and Link glanced at one another before scrambling onto their horses.

"Remember, no horses over six years!" Brakkus called after them as the trio headed out, with lengths of rope attached to their saddles for new arrivals.

∞☙

The journey to the castle seemed quicker the third time around to Annetta, as they came to the front gates of the white fortress. Climbing the stairs with their mounts, they came to the archway of the door that had led them into the homeland of the elves. Without so much as a thought, they headed through the portal to Aldamoor. Puc said almost nothing the entire time they rode, aside from spewing out instructions about what needed to be done.

As soon as they passed through, Annetta took the opportunity to look around the massive plains as they pressed on towards the city, framed by a waterfall with tiny airships floating about like bees.

"So I've been meaning to ask, did you and my grandfather explore all of this world, or do you just know Aldamoor? And is it the same with Morwick and the other universes?" she said, breaking the silence.

"I'm afraid it would take many lifetimes to explore all the known realities, ones which no being aside from the Unknown has," the mage spoke. "Granted, I have been fortunate enough to see much of this world, it being my own, but to answer your question more directly, no, your grandfather did not explore all the worlds he visited. Aldamoor is just one city of many, and the Water Elves are one of many different races of elves that exist on this world that is called Teralim. Morwick is most likely the same, being located on a world called Aerim, from what we learned from the Minotaurs."

Annetta tried to wrap her head around the concept of this city being just one part of an entirely different world with its own solar system, and other planets in it. The thought of never being able to see it all made her a little sad, but she quickly shook it off. If she could not see it all, she would at least see a small part of it.

"It must make you feel very small to know of so many worlds." Link voiced Annetta's thoughts as though he had read her mind, before turning to Puc. "I mean you know there is so much out there, more than you can imagine..." His thoughts trailed off as he lowered his head and closed his eyes in contemplation. The mage turned to face him, his black hair gliding over his shoulders as their horses continued to trot.

"Yes?" he looked at him.

"I just, I still don't understand why Mislantus wants the Eye to All Worlds," Link blurted out. "It's not like he's immortal, and his influence will not be eternal. He will not rule all worlds forever. It's not possible."

Puc could not help but laugh out loud, something neither of the children had seen the elf ever do around them, at least not as fiercely as he did then.

"My dear Lincerious, if we sat you down with Mislantus in a room over a cup of tea we could just end the impending war then and there." Puc chuckled and then sighed, his face going back to the same neutral look it always had. "Alas, greed knows no logic, it knows only to climb, horde and collect. It is only upon its death bed that it analyzes its own stupidity."

Link frowned, and said no more. Nearing the outskirts of the city, the small figures of soldiers patrolling the border could be made out with their bayonet-like weapons.

"Halt! State your name and business," one of the guards shouted, lowering his weapon before them as others followed his lead, surrounding the trio.

"I am Puc Thanestorm, this is Annetta Severio and Lincerious Heallaws. We have come here to acquire horses and speak with Kaian Chironson."

The lead soldier, a man in his late thirties with a thick trimmed beard and brown cropped hair, lowered his weapon. A surprised look came to his face. The other soldiers followed his lead without question.

"Thanestorm?" he inquired repeatedly.

"Last I checked, that was my name," Puc stated bluntly.

The guard chuckled, taking his mustache and curled it upwards, "And you don't remember me?"

Puc raised an eyebrow, watching the man's gesture. He got off his horse to get a better look at him.

"Iliam? Iliam Starview?" he asked, regarding at the man, who grinned back with a chuckle.

Puc smiled back lightly, giving the man a quick and firm brotherly embrace. Link and Annetta watched the encounter, never having seen the mage behave in such a way, even when around Brakkus. Not forgetting himself, Puc turned to the two of them.

"Iliam is a close friend," Puc said as introduction. "We grew up together on the streets of Aldamoor."

"And would have remained here, if you hadn't gone all magical on the guards." Iliam chuckled, turning back to his friend. "I heard you were held responsible for the theft of Chiron's Toolbox but a few days ago. I hope you're not back to whip up more trouble."

"Nothing of the sort, though trouble does stir in the dark." Puc inclined his head and then turned to Annetta and Link. "This is the heir of Orbeyus, if you've not met her yet. And this is a companion of ours, Lincerious Heallaws, a warrior in the making like you once were yourself."

"Oh yes," the elven warrior said, motioning to the others to disperse, "Brakkus tossing him around then I suppose,"

"It's more like full out flaying." Link sighed.

"Well, that's what being a warrior is all about." Iliam smiled, then turned back to Puc. "What is it you need to speak to Kaian about?"

"We forgot about the communication and time synchronizers," he answered stiffly, "But issues pressed us to Morwick first before we could return to Aldamoor."

"Ugh, you were making an alliance with those smelly cows?" Iliam wrinkled his nose, to which Puc shot him a glance, causing the man to crack an embarrassed smile. "I will not cause a scene, I swear. But I am entitled to my opinion on those creatures."

"As they are to their own about you," Puc warned him.

"Touche." The elf nodded.

Puc looked at Annetta and Link then back to acquaintance. "How long are you on duty here until? I would have a favor to ask of you if possible."

"I am the leader of these platoons," Iliam assured him. "I come and go whenever I please. I'm soon to become vice general of Aldamoor's forces, actually."

"My congratulations to you, then." Puc inclined his head lightly. "I was wondering perhaps, if you have time to spare, you could show Annetta and Lincerious around the city. They're curious to learn more of Aldamoor, and I can think of no one better for the task than yourself."

Iliam looked at the girl and boy, continuing to curl his mustache, a low approving sound coming from his throat as he grabbed his weapon, placing it over his shoulder.

"I can indeed help with that." The elf smiled. "But you owe me an ale and time to catch up on old glories in the Great War. I've not seen you in years! Where have you been hiding all this time?"

Puc cracked a small smile, but nothing more. "There is much for us to discuss, old friend. When Orbeyus passed away I was charged with watching Q-16 until his heir and the son of Arcanthur were old enough to take up their respective posts. I'm sure you remember how time passes differently in our world compared to theirs. That is the reason for visiting Kaian as I said earlier to begin with."

Puc produced the watch from his robes to show Iliam, who nodded his head as he took in all the information. His gaze then turned to Annetta and Link, still on their horses, wondering what came next.

"You lot even been up in an airship?" the elven warrior asked with a grin on his face.

৪০৫৪

The group parted with their horses and left them in the care of the military stables. Iliam led Annetta and Link back to the familiar docks where they had fought their battle against Kaine. Iliam seemed most at home on the platforms leading to the different ships, stepping lightly over ropes and crates that lay in his way as though encountering them was an everyday thing for the guard squad leader.

"All of these ships are powered by steam created from water vapors. The zepplins you see? Those are filled with hot air," Iliam explained as he continued to lead them until they stopped at one platform and headed towards the ship docked at it.

Annetta and Link marveled at the size of one of the vessels, and how air and water alone seemed to power it. The ship they eventually came to a halt at was of the smaller variety. The lower area reminded Annetta very much of old pirate ships she'd seen in books and paintings. The zeppelin attached to it had the same emblem that resided in the High Council chamber, an airship with an open tome beneath it, with three drops of water falling onto the book.

"This is one of our scouting vessels, we call her Tessa," Iliam continued to speak as some of the crew saluted him when he came on board, "She's not a fighting ship as you see from the lack of cannons and balconies for mages in the lower decks, she was designed for observation and of course for pleasure travel. She can fly higher than most and steer away from danger almost as quickly as she senses it."

Link examined the rails of the ship to one side, looking over the edge at the city below while Annetta took her time examining the ship as a whole. She'd never been on a ship of any sort, not counting the ferry she took one year to Toronto Island for a school trip. The detail in the wood was overwhelming to take in, and it felt as though she could spend a lifetime just studying that alone.

Iliam spoke with a woman in a leather vest, white blouse, brown trousers that were neatly tucked into her boots. She had aviator goggles propped on her head, combing back an impressive head of deep chestnut hair and a wide pleasant grin across her broad yet finely featured face. Exchanging a few nods, they headed over to Annetta and Link.

"This is Captain Maria Gladiola, my fiancée, and the captain of this ship," Iliam introduced her, the woman saluting Annetta and Link with a smile.

"Pleasure to meet you, Lady Severio and Mr. Heallaws," she said. "I served with Iliam and Puc in the Great War under Lord Orbeyus."

"You all knew my grandfather?" Annetta asked after she bowed, exchanging a greeting in the manner Puc had taught her to be appropriate.

"Aye, and quite a man he was," Maria said. "I've been told by a little bird in blue uniform you lot have never flown in an airship before. Seeing as they are the pride of Aldamoor's army, and myself being Captain to one, I am obligated to help eliminate such lack of knowledge. That is, if you should like."

Annetta exchanged a glance with Link, who simply shrugged, having no opinion on the matter.

"If we're not too much trouble." She nodded shyly.

"No, certainly not." Maria smiled. "And I owe Puc a few favors from saving this girl in the war. About time I started paying my dues."

With a whirl of her brown hair, Maria turned to her crew to let them know they would take off with a hand gesture. Men and women began untying knots and making sure everything was secure.

"What's the course, Captain?" a woman with an eyepatch called from behind the helm of the ship.

"A quick trip round Aldamoor. We've got the daughter of Arieus Severio aboard, and a friend of hers. I'd like to show them the city on behalf of Puc Thanestorm," Maria called out in a voice both friendly and commanding.

The woman from behind the helm nodded upon hearing her captain's command, and moved behind the wheel, to a row of levers with various colored pieces of cloth attached to each. She pulled a few back and a few forward, then returned to the helm and began to steer the ship away from the port with effortless ease. Annetta felt the craft move under her feet, as though the entire wooden beast had sprung to life beneath her.

"Whoa!" She grabbed hold of one of the beams that supported the ship's upper dock. Link chuckled at Annetta's reaction, only to be shaken himself moments later when the ship seemed to hit a bump, causing him to grab onto the railing.

Maria walked the ship with no fear of falling over when turbulence occurred. She found it amusing when people who had never been aboard an airship came on and expected to feel nothing at all as they floated through the air.

"If you'll come with me, I can give you a better tour of the city from the upper deck," she said as she casually walked past them with Iliam at her side.

Annetta pried herself off of the wooden beam, seeing it was safe to walk without fear of being bucked off the large wooden structure. She made her way upstairs, followed by a reluctant Link.

Maria already stood facing out into the open world below them, her hair flowing gracefully on the wind. Iliam, on the other hand, stood with his back against the rails, hands in his pockets.

"I'm guessing you don't have anything like this in your world by the looks of worry on your faces?" he said, seeing how unsure they were. "Don't worry. Luna over at the helm is one of our best pilots. She competes in our annual race each year, and won the last five in a row."

Maria grabbed a handful of Iliam's hair and pulled back as thought she would throw him overboard, causing the elf to chuckle and swat her hands away.

"Of course Maria here is the best captain, so she won't let anything happen to you." He grinned as she let him go with a satisfied smirk visible from the side of her face.

"Come closer to the rails," she said, looking back at them, "Don't worry, it's not in our best interest to throw you overboard."

Annetta and Link moved up beside her. Taking a deep breath and closing their eyes, they peered down. It looked as though they had climbed higher into the sky. The world below seemed composed of little toy houses with occasional wagons moving around, and dots of people on the street.

"Aldamoor is the capital city of the Water Elves," Maria said, looking over at the two. "I'm not sure how much Puc has told you about us, but this city has stood for over ten thousand years, if not longer. It was said to be the home of Chiron, whose descendants became the leaders of the High Council and the guardians of Chiron's Toolbox, which from what I heard, you did a grand job of retrieving. The large central structure is where the High Council meets. Further to the Great Falls is the Mage Academy, which I believe you had a chance to visit. In addition to Water Elves inhabiting our world, we share it with our cousin kin, the Forest Elves, Fire Elves and Dark Elves. We stay out of one another's business for the most part, although sometimes we do trade. The Dark Elves are exceptionally good at mining and creating metals, though they are not as pleasant in demeanor. Forest Elves stay within their woods, but are excellent guides and know all herbs found in the land. Fire Elves are next to the Dark Elves in lack of manners. They are a savage race who loves combat and domination, it is with them we are generally most at war when they are done licking their wounds from the last."

Annetta did her best to absorb the information, nodding her head where it was necessary to show she was paying attention while the ship continued to sail lazily through the air.

"So this ship is part of the military? Who do you report to, then?" Link asked, finally more at ease on the moving vessel.

"The High Council decides if we are at war, but we ourselves simply report to the general," Maria answered him.

"Ah, so you don't have a king." Link nodded. "Where I'm from, the king is the one who rules pretty much everything."

"That amount of power in one person? That cannot be a good thing." Iliam turned his head towards them and cut in. "The council was created because people feared the descendant of Chiron would have too much power over them."

"It's in my knowledge that anyone with power becomes corrupt at one point or another," Link stated. "It's a survival instinct for anyone to be the best and give the best to his kin. But what a person can do is try to see their faults and listen to the voices that echo in the void below. Our king, thankfully, is such a man."

Both Maria and Iliam glanced at Link. "Well, they'd certainly make a mage out of you were you born in Aldamoor," Maria said.

"Did you both know Puc and my grandfather before the war?" Annetta asked.

"I grew up with Puc," Iliam began. "We were both street urchins, believe it or not, abandoned after a war with the Fire Elves that nearly destroyed all of Aldamoor. We were taken to the academy when our talents for magic were discovered during an attempt to steal some food from a local shop. I signed up for the military after a few years, though. Sitting around books was never my thing. But Puc, he could go for hours at it. As for your grandfather, when he first came to Aldamoor, he was maybe a little older than you were. He came as an explorer, curious of the world he had stepped into. He said he was Lord of the Eye to All Worlds, and he wished to make alliances with people of different realms so that if one day evil were to descend, we could fight back. At first no one took him seriously, but he proved us wrong to doubt him. When the Fire Elves attacked again, he risked his own people to help us. Help is not something our kind are used to getting when we're all so divided. In the end, Kaian's father agreed to the alliance, and the first of the Four Forces was born. I'm pretty sure it went the same way for the other races. Your grandfather, when he walked into the room, you could sense the nobility that came forth from him. He meant business, and you could tell great things would come of him, no matter how doubtful."

Annetta nodded. Having seen the painting of him in Severio Castle made it hard for Annetta to picture him as a young man, but she understood the feeling Iliam spoke of. She hung her head, looking down at the city below.

"What's up?" Link asked, seeing her looking upset.

"Huh? Nothing really. Just thinking about some stuff," she muttered back quietly as the wind played with her hair.

"Sometimes sharing helps, they say." He smiled back at her.

Annetta heaved heavily as she turned around. "It's nothing, really. Just, sometimes when people talk about my grandfather, he just doesn't seem human, you know?"

Link raised an eyebrow. "Technically, I'm not human."

Annetta glared at him jokingly. "You know what I mean."

"Yeah, I do. You're intimidated by your grandfather's reputation, right?" Link completed the thought.

"Wouldn't you be?"

"Intimidation by reputation should not be a worry of yours, young one," Iliam's voice rang out from the side. "No two lives are the same. We each write our own stories in the pages of the great tomes of time."

Annetta turned back to look at the elven warrior and nodded. "Still, it is sort of intimidating, no matter what."

The airship continued to sail onwards through the sky, occasionally passing through clouds that caused a mist to sweep the deck, obscuring the positions of the crew. The longer they remained in the air, the calmer Annetta found she was becoming, until something hit the ship, causing everything to shake.

Link grabbed hold of Annetta's shoulder instinctively with one hand, and the railing with another.

"What's the trouble?" Maria yelled to the crew member in the observation deck.

"Rainbow serpent!" a young man from above called.

Maria gritted her teeth at the news, and hoped for it not to be true. Iliam placed his arm around her, trying to comfort the captain as best as he could. Annetta and Link, on the other hand, had their eyes going in all directions, hoping to spot the creature.

"They're usually not dangerous," Iliam assured her, rubbing her back.

Maria frowned, muttering something under her breath, when the ship was hit yet again, causing anything and anyone not tied to the deck to go flying in all directions.

Annetta shut her eyes as her hands dug into the railing. She had not planned to die on an airship in another world.

"What in the Unknown's bane is going on?" Maria snarled to the observation deck yet again.

"We might be in the center of its territory. It might have expanded outwards from non-traveled routes since the last time we flew here, and it's trying to defend it," came a reply.

"Damn it." The captain turned to the helm, "Can we outmaneuver it?"

"I will try, but I can't promise anything," Luna replied as she began turning the wheel furiously. "We may need to call for backup,"

"At least get us further away from the city," Maria instructed, to which Luna nodded and began again maneuvering the ship through clouds and wind.

Annetta continued to hang onto the rails as she felt the ship move faster and faster, the city below becoming more and more distant. She then notices a massive, multicolored, scaled tail beneath them, moving back and forth as though it were slithering on solid ground.

Beside her, Link also saw the tail and turned his gaze to face her, looking for some confirmation of his own sanity.

"Is there anything you need me to do?" Iliam asked, going down from the upper deck as Maria paced the lower levels furiously, ordering her crew about, each elf scrambling to secure any loose items as the serpent continued to ram into the ship.

"Love, just sit back and relax, and let me fight this battle," she stated, barely paying attention to him.

"But this ship is not equipped to fight!" he protested.

"Well, I cannot just sit and look pretty while an annoyed flying snake tries to tear Tessa apart!" Maria snapped, glaring at Iliam with her pale blue eyes.

Annetta heard the commotion below. Summoning her courage, she pried herself away from the railing, holding onto Link's arm for support as they walked down to join everyone else. The further they got from the city, the more distinct the rain clouds forming upon the horizon became.

"Captain! Storm ahead of us!" Luna called in warning.

"Blast it all to hell. This was supposed to be an easy trip," Maria growled as she pushed her hair back from her face. "Go around it if you can!"

450

"This is not what I pictured for my day off." Annetta sighed in resolution as she held onto Link.

"At least you can't say you're bored." He tried to laugh lightly.

Then they saw it, the coils of the great beast that had been stalking them from below. It was the biggest snake Annetta had ever seen in her life, and as she continued to look at it, the coils seemed to engulf the ship from all angles, multicolored scales glistening in the sun. Fear began to paralyze any rational thinking in the girl and the crew that danced around the deck, trying to fight off the coils.

Link was also feeling less confident upon seeing the creature. He would be lucky to do some minor damage to it, let alone kill the thing. Becoming restless at the thought, he reached the blade strapped to his back, against all logic.

"There's no point, Link. You couldn't even hit it without falling below," Annetta reaffirmed, watching his arm muscles tighten as he gripped the sword.

"Not to mention the hide is too thick for a blade to do anything to it," Iliam added. "We usually need magic to bring one down when they go rogue and get too close to the city. I'm not the greatest spell caster, though. It was the reason I dropped out of the academy."

Annetta bit her lip, trying to think of a solution. She then looked around for Maria.

"Is there anything that can be used as a spear or harpoon on board?" she asked the busy captain.

Maria and Iliam looked at one another as they frowned at the question, trying to figure out what was on the girl's mind. Iliam looked at his staff he carried, examining the bayonet on top.

"Would this suffice?" he asked as he handed it to the girl. "Mind you, I need that in one piece."

Annetta took the weapon in both hands and examined it.

"Yeah, this will work fine," she said. "And don't worry, I'll get it back."

She turned around and made her way as quickly as she could to the upper deck.

"What are you planning on doing, Annetta?" Link asked, trying to be included in the plan.

"Just watch. When it gets close, can you stab it?" She looked over at him with a serious expression.

"I thought you just said-," he began.

"I need to get its attention," Annetta said, holding the staff firmly. "Can you do that?"

Link nodded his head and began observing the coils around the ship. Finding a length of rope, he began tying it around his waist, using the knots he'd been taught in the military. He hopped onto the railing, holding onto it with one hand, his sword in the other, watching. Seeing an easy spot to pierce the scales, he lunged with his sword using full force. Metal puncturing the flesh, the serpent began to squirm, its coils a convulsing mess of reds, greens, blues, yellows and oranges.

Annetta stood her ground at the deck, adrenaline pumping through her entire body, causing it to shake with excitement as the clouds before her parted to reveal a massive serpentine head, wings of feathers to either side of its body as it lunged for the girl without any thought. Annetta hurled the weapon at the open mouth of the snake. But her plan did not end there. She focused on the weapon, placing psychic energy into the weapon to drive it home. Colliding with the snake's sensitive upper jaw, the bayonet tip of the staff drove straight through, and did not stop until it emerged on the other end, between the creature's eyes.

Losing his balance on the railing from pulling his sword out, Link began to tip forward, his only comfort a prayer to the Unknown until he felt the rope tighten, and looked around to see Iliam pulling him back up.

Hissing its last breath, the creature stiffened, and plummeted to the ground, its last testament in the world a thunderous crash onto the rocks below. Annetta recalled the weapon to her hands, dripping in a mixture of saliva and blood that made the girl cringe to even be holding it.

"Well, I would not have believed it had I not just seen it with my own two eyes," Maria said, coming up to the deck to join them once everything was secure. "It seems I now owe a debt to the granddaughter of Orbeyus as well. Many thanks, m'dear. We'd have been long dead and crushed in the belly of the snake were it not for your quick thinking."

Annetta felt her face go a little red, and the expression on Link's face did not help either as he watched her, untying the rope from himself and sheathing his sword.

"Still doubt your abilities?" he whispered, as he walked by her.

She watched as the young man continued to walk to the railing on the ship, his back towards her. She turned her attention back to more pressing matters, like the blood on her hands dripping from the weapon.

"Uhm… you wanted this back," she said, gingerly handing the staff to Iliam, who produced a large handkerchief from his pocket, and began wiping down the weapon as best as he could.

"Generally it is customary to wipe the blade clean before returning it to its owner," he chuckled. "But thank you."

࠾ଔ

Awaiting them when the ship reached the docks were Puc and Kaian, along with a squad of guards. News of the Rainbow Serpent attacking the ship had gotten out through the sentries that prowled the city towers, and it was not until both mages saw the girl and boy emerge that their expressions relaxed a little.

Annetta and Link walked out of the ship, followed by Iliam and Maria. They paused upon seeing Puc and Kaian standing before them. The younger-looking mage strode towards them.

"What happened?" Puc questioned. "Are you alright?"

"Your little Severio here proved to be quite the fighter," Maria said "She took out the Rainbow Serpent with nothing more than wits. I can see you've trained her well."

"Well I…hello Maria," Puc acknowledged the female captain's presence with a bow. "I've done my best with the student given."

"You sure she can't just win whatever war we get into for us?" Iliam chuckled, only to get an angered glance from Maria.

"Afraid not. She's not that good yet," Puc replied. "And the skill of one psychic warrior will not be enough against Mislantus's forces, not if I am even close in estimating what he will bring to try and capture the Eye to All Worlds. Mordred's forces were tough enough to take out, driven by pure fanaticism. This army will be different, driven upon the principle of both vengeance and extremism. I dare not think what lies ahead, and what will be needed."

"You've a suitable start." Kaian nodded, turning his attention to the girl. "How do you like the airships?"

"They're like nothing I've ever seen, sir." Annetta made a small curtsey upon being acknowledged by the descendant of Chiron, which made the elder mage chuckle.

"There's no need for formalities with me, young one. Kaian is and always has been my name." He smiled, and then turned to Maria. "Was there any damage to the ship? Did everyone make it?"

"There was not enough time for damage or lost members, I'm afraid," replied the captain. "Our young Severio and Master Heallaws saw to that."

Annetta noted while Maria and Kaian continued to speak that Kaian now wore the same watch Annetta and all her companions had. She looked at Puc with a questioning glance, wordlessly asking if they were going soon. The excitement of the day was beginning to wear on her, despite her not wanting it to end.

"By your leave, Kaian, we should be getting back once we aquire new mounts to replenish the stables," Puc said, catching the signal from the girl. "They have schoolwork that needs attention, and the rest of the week still beckons us in our world."

"Of course. Iliam?" Kaian turned to the warrior, "Once they have secured the horses they need, will you escort them to the city gates?"

Exchanging silent goodbyes in the forms of bows, they headed out of the docks.

ഇരു

Before Annetta knew it, she was heading out of Aldamoor, through the portal, and on the route leading to the entrance gate of the castle with Link and Puc beside her, leading a string of young and fresh horses. Annetta could tell from the displeased look on Puc's face that he was not having fun surrounded by so many of the beasts of burden, particularly ones that he'd never been around before. Each sudden movement made the mage hold the reins of his own mount tighter.

"Whatever happened to overcoming your fears at the onset of battle?" Link smirked, seeing Puc's reactions.

"You keep your focus on yourself before you preach to others, Lincerious," the mage sneered.

Annetta only chuckled, seeing them bicker as she opened the great doors to the castle. The trio then headed out to the front, stopping before the stables.

"I suggest you see if Brakkus is able to come and lend us a hand. Traveling flat ground with so many horses is one thing, uphill is another," Puc said, looking at the young warrior, who nodded in response and veered his horse around. He hurried off into the distance to the black and red wall overlooking them.

Puc dismounted the beast and tethered it to a post with the others before he turned to the girl. "There's something I've been meaning to show you for quite some time. Come with me."

Annetta did as she was told and tied up her own horse to a post before she followed the mage's casual pace. His steps turned to a part of the castle Annetta had never entered before, a set of stairs leading downward. Puc began to descend, but the girl paused, waiting for some clarification as to where they were going. To her knowledge, the only thing that lay below a castle was the dungeon, and that was not a place she wanted to see.

"You've trusted me thus far, Miss Severio. Will your faith falter now?" came the flat tone from Puc, who waited for her.

Hearing the words, Annetta began to make her descent down the stairs to join the mage. Once at the bottom, Puc pulled out the same key ring with hundreds of keys he always had with him, and taking his time to find the right one, inserted it into the lock to open the doors. With a rusted click, he removed the key and pushed it open, lighting his staff at the same time in order to keep light with them. The inside of the cavern smelled of mold and dampness, not something Annetta found pleasing at all. Her displeasure was doubled when she realized where they were.

"These are your family catacombs." Puc confirmed her suspicions as they neared the first sarcophagus.

Her initial reaction was to wrinkle her nose and run out of the vicinity with all speed. The last place she wanted to be in was a place of death. The lingering effects of horror movies where hands grabbed onto people's ankles suddenly surfaced, and she could not help but think at any moment that such a fate would befall her. With the many things she had seen up to that point, why were the undead, after all, not a possibility? The more she stood at the mage's side, however, the more she realized she had nothing to fear, nor was there a point for her to show fear to the sardonic elf. The more they pressed on, and the longer she kept going, the more she was filled with a gothic sense of wonder at the sarcophagi surrounding her instead of fear, each bearing the image of its dweller, like that of kings from long ago.

"Ever since the creation of the Eye to All Worlds, its overseers and rulers have been buried in these tombs you see before you," Puc said. "They can be traced all the way to Lord Adeamus, the original founder, and your ancestor. But more importantly for you..." Puc stopped at a particular sarcophagus and moved no further into the dark.

Annetta stopped as well, and she could see why. A double bladed axe in the hands of the stone visage gave it away. The look upon Orbeyus's face was that of peace, and his closed eyes made him look as though he were simply sleeping, covered in a thin blanket of grey. She turned to the mage, whose expression was blank as ever.

"Why did you want to show me this?" she asked, still not understanding why she'd been lead there.

"They say that the soul is always attached in some way to the final resting place of its body, and that should you come and speak with it, and the soul can hear you. I have always found it a comforting thought to be able to come here and speak with Orbeyus years after his passing," Puc said. "I'd hoped it could perhaps serve you one day, if not now, to know of such a place. My other reason for bringing you here is to reveal to you the nature of your grandfather's passing from this world. I'm not sure what your father told you, but it was not a natural death. Your grandfather was wounded with a poison so powerful that I had neither time nor the skill to pull it from his body. It was the work of an assassin who entered Q-16 by means that I have never been able to decipher. We did change the code for the card keys right after, but the fact remains, and it was something I felt you should be aware of."

Annetta looked once again upon the image of a man who looked unlike someone who could be related to her, but a king from one of her stories. The thought of an assassin having killed him made her feel even more humble, despite everything she had achieved in the short time she had been aware of her heritage. It made her wonder what chance she would stand if someone like that got in.

"Puc, is there a point in all this training if we won't even be ready for Mislantus?" she asked looking down at her feet.

"What do you mean by point?" The mage looked in her direction." You've learned so much already. Why doubt yourself now?"

"I dunno, I guess just," Annetta tried to speak, but every word after her opening remarks became barred up in her throat.

Puc glanced at the stone sarcophagus. "Annetta, allow me to divulge a little secret to you. Do you know what makes a great warrior?"

The girl's blue eyes glanced up at him for a brief moment, but then she shook her head in resignation.

"Reflex and instinct," the elf spoke, "It is not necessarily a matter of how much one trains. Instead, importance lies in the ability to use common sense, and to react at the right moments. I think your little adventure with the rainbow serpent proved that you have plenty of both."

Annetta could almost see a sincere smile on the mage's ever-serious face, which only faded once more when he began to speak. "Each warrior is mortal, and we all die at some point. It is part of life, be it naturally, or by error. Your grandfather had a long life. I know, I was there with him for much of it."

Annetta said little else. A multitude of emotions rushed through her as she thought of the man in stone. Abandonment, anger and sorrow were just a few of the feelings that welled up inside her. She simply stood, rooted to her spot, watching the tomb.

"We should be getting back," Puc finally said. "I'm sure Brakkus and Lincerious will be here in no time. You will have time to catch up with Orbeyus at another date." With a whirl of his cloak, Puc began moving towards the entrance. "That is, unless you wish to become a statue yourself, Lady Annetta."

Annetta frowned at the title Puc had bestowed on her. She took another quick look at the visage of her fallen grandsire, placing a hand on his and feeling the cold of the stone beneath her fingertips.

"I'll try to make you proud, grandpa," she whispered.

Chapter 42

That evening, when Annetta had already headed home after having helped with the horses, Puc found himself completely alone in the solace of his room. Though electricity was something he could use, he preferred to sit by candlelight while reading. It had been so since his academy days, and it always reminded him of the pleasant part of home. His peace was broken by the sound of knocking on the door. The elven mage looked up to see his apprentice, carrying a large sack.

"I finished with the potions and spells you asked me to prepare," he said, setting down the parcel on the corner of the mage's large desk. "Is there anything else you would have me do before I retire?"

Puc looked up and studied the face of the young man. Were it not for the fact that Darius chose to dress in human clothing, a black dress shirt and jeans instead of mage robes, he would have seen a ghost of himself there.

"No, I believe that will be all," he answered shutting the book before him, "Have a good night, Darius."

Darius nodded, and began to turn around to leave, but he still stood in the doorway. Something nagged at his gut, and he needed to tell someone before it got the better of him.

"Master, what if we fail, or Mislantus attacks before the Four Forces stand united again?" he asked, not bothering to turn around and face him.

"Darius, we have two options when thinking like that," the mage answered. "One is to sit around and cry, and the other is to press onward. I personally prefer the latter option."

"For now everything is going according to plan, but any plan can be foiled. You taught me so yourself." The youth finally turned to face the master.

"Which is why we are working at the fastest pace possible, Darius," Puc replied. "It is not possible to disrupt their lives completely, not yet at least. Normalcy needs to be kept for the sake of their appearance on the surface. Which is why the angels should not have come to them at such a young age, but the Unknown has his reasons for doing so, and we must trust him to it."

"You talk of the Unknown as if you have met him," Darius growled under his breath.

"Do not blaspheme, Darius Silver!" Puc snarled. "I will tolerate all else from you, but that; I will not and cannot."

"I have my views as you have yours, master. You cannot force them upon anyone," Darius spoke softly, not losing his edge. "That includes religious views."

Puc stared long and hard at the young man he called his apprentice. Despite being obedient almost to a point, Darius did have his own view of the world, a view in which religion of any sort, or belief in a power above did not fit. He understood where this despair of his came from. It was the feeling of abandonment, a feeling Puc was all too familiar with. Perhaps this was why, out of the hundreds at the academy, he had chosen Darius. He exhaled quietly, letting the harsh lessons he might throw at Darius leave his mind. Now was not the time for it.

"Well, when we die, if the Unknown is there to greet us, you owe me a pint of ale. As for the present, good night, Darius." the mage turned back to his books, but saw from the corner of his eye the bewildered expression of his apprentice as he left the room. Once gone, Puc took time to reflect upon the words of the younger man. In truth, he had his own moments of doubt, but he had something more than the others prodding him on, and it was responsibility.

೩ೞ

After leading Annetta back to the exit of the Lab, Link found himself making his way back to the armory. With everything that had been going on, he'd had little time to himself, and little time to work on a certain project he'd wanted to tackle for quite some time. Stopping in his room to grab the degraded scabbard, and winding down the monotonous corridors, he entered the room. Thinking he would be alone, Link was surprised to find Brakkus in its midst, sharpening his sword on a whetstone. The Hurtz looked up upon hearing him enter, his earrings jingling on his large rabbit ears.

"Sorry, I didn't meant to intrude or anything," Link said, breaking the silence.

"Intrude? What are ye mad?" he scoffed, "I'm surprised ye didn't bring yer own sword to sharpen after all that fighting. Gotta keep the edge fit somehow, after all."

"I was going to, eventually, but..." He bit his lip, "I remembered I had something I wanted to start on."

Brakkus noted the scabbard in the boy's hand, and grinned. "Ah, almost forgot ye'd taken that thing with ye." Finishing with the blade, the Hurtz ran a finger down its edge lightly to test it, and slid the double-bladed behemoth into its scabbard, "I'll show ye where the supplies are I suppose. Ye said you've done this before?"

"Yeah, there's just one problem, though," Link said. "I've always had the sword before for measurement."

Brakkus headed to the far back of the armory, where swords hung upon a weapons rack. The contrast of the swords hanging up against a metal wall seemed awkward to Link, but he understood the use of a blade was more reliable than most ranged weapons, particularly when dealing with magic or psychics. The Hurtz came back to him, carrying a simple longsword with a curved guard.

"Closest one I could find in length and blade width," he said, handing the weapon guard first to Link, "Ye'll need wood first for the core."

Link followed Brakkus as the Hurtz gathered up the supplies needed for creating the first component of the scabbard, thin slabs of wood that the Hurtz had stored in a corner of the room. Selecting ones that were in better shape, he handed them to the boy.

"I've seen yer fighting on the battlefield when we were in Morwick. Ye've been learning fast from all the lessons I've been given ya," he said, then added, "Best we get these to the smithy. Gotta steam and wrap the wood around the blade."

Link nodded as they left the room, and moved down the corridors to where the blacksmithing area was set up, next to the stables. They walked for some time before the Hurtz decided to speak again.

"Yep, them fights in Morwick did ye good. Yer understanding what I was telling ya all along, ye need to learn to fight as a unit. Ye remember what I said when ya first came here, lad?"

"Yes, I do," he said as he continued walking.

"And?" The Hurtz prodded more.

"And you were right?" he said shortly. "But it doesn't change what I feel when it comes to wanting to protect people from harm."

"I never said it would change." He chuckled. "But ye understand why it is important to be able to fight with others now, I hope." He eyed him, awaiting an answer. "Being a hero don't always work best in war."

"Worked for the many Hurtz I've read about." Link gave a small smile.

"Aye, but I'm a Hurtz, and yer a little scrawny Gaian twig I can snap in half if I like." Brakkus made his threat legitimate by flashing a row of sharp teeth.

"Yeah, but only if you're fast enough." Link proved his own point by snatching the old scabbard the Hurtz was holding before the giant could even react, causing him to chuckle.

"I'd still squash ya, lad."

ଚ୦ଔ

Miles above the surface and far away, Jason collapsed on his bed, covered in dirt and mud from having scanned half the forest behind his house for the tree that held the gateway. He'd done everything from digging up roots to climbing up top, with falls and scrapes acquired in the process.

"I'm never going to find it," he growled at himself, as he sat up on his bed and began picking at the dirt under his nails.

The frustrated teenager glared at the only photograph he kept of his father as a reminder of happier times. It was of his parents before they had him, in a park of some kind. Arcanthur's face was not lined with the same torture as it was in the asylum where he'd last seen him. He held Talia in a piggyback and his free hand pointed a camera upwards at them. Jason could almost see his father spinning his mother on his back as she tried to tackle him with a hug. It was a scene he wished he'd known in his lifetime. The only images he'd ever associated with his mother were anger and sorrow. He could only even closely link images like that to Arieus and Aurora, Annetta's own parents. It was what he envied, and had come to envy even more about Annetta in the last few months, that her father had been strong where his had not. Though it pained him to no end that he had no father so to speak of, he knew there were others that were worse off. He knew there were those who did not even have a home, or a place to call their own, and this was why he had to help Sarina.

As he continued to look at the photograph, something caught his eye. He picked up the frame from his bedside and studied it intently. He turned it around and opened the back of the frame to take the picture, and looked where his eye had led him: the corner of a mossy rock that was most intimate to him. Curling his lip and furrowing his brow, the youth continued to stare.

He tapped the photo over his fingers as he lay down on his bed. It would be too hard to find so late in the night but, Jason could swear the very same tree was still in that spot. It would all have to wait, however, as darkness fell.

Chapter 43

The next morning, bright and early as Puc had instructed them, everyone gathered where the couches were located. Having received no special instructions, everyone came dressed in casual gear, Annetta sporting her signature jean jacket, Link dressed the same, Darius in black, and Jason in a hoodie and t-shirt. Puc came in much later than he said he would, followed by Brakkus in his stead.

"Early, he said," Jason grumbled while the others chuckled.

Puc ignored the commentary and shot Jason a glare that indicated his words were not needed as an opening statement.

"We travel today to the Trafjan Cliffs in the world known as Eolastin to meet with the Soarin, or Sky Wolves," he announced. "Their time flows in accordance with our own, and so we will not need use the C.T.S.'s. Their leader is Entellion Windheart, a Soarin most distinguished for his prowess with the bow. The Soarin are known for their marksmanship, and there is yet a target they have failed to hit, unless it is a psychic warrior."

"So are there any kidnappings or stolen books that could get in our way when we get there?" Annetta asked.

"Yeah, seriously, if we walk in there and there's a civil war going on, or some kinda disaster..." Jason trailed off with a laugh.

"Maybe there will be a giant purple dinosaur that breathes fire," Annetta added.

"None to my knowledge," Puc cut in. "Although there is the Eternal Hunt, which, should they choose you participate in, you must. They are very particular when it comes to their customs."

"Do we have to skin it?" Annetta cringed, thinking back to Brakkus's threat in Morwick.

"How about ye cross that bridge when ya get there?" Brakkus chuckled.

"I guess that works." Annetta sighed as she got up and followed the pace of the mage and the Hurtz.

Before they knew it, their weapons were all accounted for, the fresh horses that they had acquired in Aldamoor the day before were saddled, and the companions rode off again to the gates of Severio Castle. Stopping their horses, they waited for word from Puc, who knew where each portal lay hidden within the Eye to All Worlds.

"Where to from here?" Link asked as Puc trotted his horse closer to the entrance.

The mage veered around to look at those who awaited his instruction, still uneasy on the newly acquired stallion he'd been given since his old mount was still recovering from the hard ride in Morwick.

"Where it is most appropriate for the Sky Wolves to have their portal, the tower," he stated, pointing to the tallest part of the castle.

"Does every room in this castle just have portals?" Jason asked as they entered the entrance hall once more.

"No, but many do," the mage said as they climbed the stairs with their horses, holding the reins so the animals would relax, "and as I said before, had you been paying attention, they are marked so none will enter unaware and end up on the far side of some unknown reality."

Annetta, having left Bossman in the stables to recover from Morwick, held the reins of her new horse tightly. Her new mount was a calm chestnut gypsy vanner with an oddly colored yellow and black mane. The unusual color was what first drew Annetta to him, for she had never seen a horse like it on Earth. She had been told by the handler in Aldamoor that the coloration was very common, and that he was called Firedancer, for when he ran, it looked like his whole body was on fire from the mixture of orange and yellow in his fur. From there it was just a matter of her and Link convincing Puc that the horse had all the qualifications Brakkus had asked for, an easy enough task when the elf disliked being around them, and wanted to leave as soon as possible.

Reaching the top, Puc produced his familiar key ring, and went for the door closest to the window in the tower. The arch of the doorway was decorated to look like two mountains standing to either side like sentries. Above each mountain were strange creatures that had the faces of wolves, but the bodies of men, and held longbows that were ready to fire. At the top of the arch, a double spiral adorned the peak, completing the stone collage.

"Was this done by the Minotaurs?" Annetta asked, touching the stone.

"Yes, they are responsible, as they are for all the carvings in Severio Castle." Puc heard a click in the lock and withdrew the key as he opened the door.

Peering inside, Annetta and Jason thought they would vomit at the sight as their equilibrium adjusted to the view. It appeared as though they were looking through a glass floor onto a world of miniature hills and rivers.

"This is a joke, right?" Jason swallowed hard, "None of us can exactly fly."

"Not to worry. I've got that covered," Puc told him calmly.

"What? Are we going to sprout wings?" Jason bared his teeth. "Or do you have some fairy dust, and I have to think a happy-,"

"Jason Kinsman, calm yourself before I push you into the portal without further ado," the mage snapped, shutting the boy up instantly.

"I don't mean to be the bearer of bad new Puc but Jason is right," Annetta agreed. "I don't know when you last checked, but we can't just sprout wings and fly."

Puc sighed and growled something in a foreign tongue under his breath as he looking into the pack on his horse, pulling out a piece of parchment.

"I am well aware of the human anatomy, and I have a Pegasus spell prepared," he said, "which is why I will go through the portal first, and cast it on everyone as you go through."

"Well, why not just do it here?" Link asked.

"It's not a particularly powerful spell, and going through the tear may disrupt or even disable it, and I can only cast it once per day on any given subject," the elf answered. "Any other doubts or nay sayers, speak now or forever hold your peace."

Puc looked around the silent room and then nodded in approval. "Good, we carry on then."

Backing up his horse without further words, the mage charged forward, holding his staff like a lance as he pierced the portal with its tip before disappearing. The remainder of the companions looked at one another, despite Puc's assurances that they would be fine on the other side, the idea of falling to one's death gave them pause. Brakkus was the first to move without hesitation, and disappeared as well. Annetta, Darius, Jason, and Link crept to the edge of the portal, trying to see if they could spot Brakkus and Puc falling but nothing seemed to be appearing.

"Well, I am his apprentice," Darius said. Pulling his horse far enough to get a good trot from it, he urged the beast forward.

The remaining trio simply looked at one another, silently asking who would go next, each wearing their heart on their sleeve as to how much they dreaded what could come to if Puc's spell did not work.

"Well, gentlemen, it was nice knowing you both." Annetta sighed as she began to pull Firedancer back so they could charge.

"Hey Anne, if all else fails, you think we can teleport to the ground below?" Jason asked as she continued to move back.

The girl stopped the horse and furrowed her brows in thought, it had never occurred to her.

"We'll cross that bridge when we get there. If so, we're wasting time where we can help the others. Fly!" She kicked the horse's sides, causing it to rush forward. She closed her eyes waiting for the portal to consume her.

It took a moment to kick in, but before Annetta knew it, the feeling of massive winds coming from all directions came over her, the sensation of falling and being lifted all at once by an unseen force. It ended as quickly as it started, replaced with a momentary feeling of falling. This too, however, vanished as an all too familiar voice spoke words that made no sense to the girl, stopping the feeling. Annetta opened her eyes to see Puc, Darius and Brakkus on their horses, standing on air.

"What…what in the world?" Annetta said, a delirious tone to her voice.

"Careful, lassie, ya best move. I think we got another coming." Brakkus motioned with his meaty fist.

Annetta quickly urged her horse out of the way as Link came charging through. Puc was ready with the spell, and within moments uttered the same incantation, causing the young man to stop falling and simply float up to their level.

"What in the name of the Unknown?" Link looked about, turning white upon seeing the ground below.

"Pegasus spell, also known as the levitation spell," Darius informed him as he signaled for Link to get out of the way, the sound of a panicking Jason coming through.

As soon as Jason's horse came crashing through the portal, the boy, with his eyes closed, began screaming and cursing. Even after his horse was on the same level, he continued to scream for a good few minutes, until he realized he was not moving, and opened his eyes. "Oh … I… I thought I was gonna die."

"Not today, Mr. Kinsman," Puc stated. "There is much to do and see here. I welcome you to Eolastin, the home of the Sky Wolves of the Trafjan Cliffs. We will not see the world below for the most part, because of the Eternal Hunt that goes on there, unless you shall participate. The Soarin make their home upon mountains high above."

466

"I was gonna say, big land mass, no occupants, what more does one want?" Annetta raised an eyebrow.

"You shall see," the elf said. "Follow my lead, and we shall be there soon."

They rode, or possibly flew onward, passing the peaks of hills, which stood upon wisps of clouds that looked like blankets of white. The horses did not seem to mind the sight of the ground below. Their riders, however, were a completely different matter, each having their own reaction. Puc and Brakkus were the only two who showed no sign of discomfort.

It took some getting used to, but Annetta was soon able to look down, as was Jason and Link. Darius seemed to be the only one who could not do so without turning slightly green each time his eyes made contact with the ground below.

Before they knew it, Puc had directed them towards a patch of mountains. From afar, fortress walls made of what looked like sharpened wooden spikes could be seen, topped by banners of green and grey floating upon the wind.

Annetta adjusted her shield to keep her balance, as she looked to see the reactions on Jason and Link's face, wondering what their own thoughts were. To her, the day was getting stranger by the second, and the more she stopped thinking about the logic of the situation, the more fun she had from it all. She even urged her horse to go a little faster. It was not every day that she got to fly on a horse in the middle of nowhere.

Closer to the gates, the natives became visible. Their names were well earned. From afar, they looked like wolves standing upright, with giant feathered wings on their back and the tails of lions. Their fur was white, save for their manes, which varied in color from blue to purple, and were braided. Stripes on their arms matched the colors of their manes, and the two small horns that curved forward at the top of their heads. Each sentry carried a magnificently carved bow.

"I warn you not to stare too much," Puc muttered. "It is, after all, impolite in any culture as the visitor."

"Oh, so it's okay if you're the native?" Jason said, sarcasm in his voice.

"It is fine if you are the one asking the questions, such as what a strange being is doing in your homeland," the elf hissed as they came within hearing range. Coming to a halt, they stopped at the front gate on solid ground.

"Who dares to come to the foot of the Trafjan Cliffs, ruled over by the mighty Entellion Windheart?" A swaggering, young, white and teal Soarin leaned over the gate, glaring at the intruders with his good eye since his other was covered with an eyepatch.

"My name is Puc Thanestorm, once advisor to Lord Orebyus Severio of the Axe. I come here with his granddaughter, Annetta Severio, and the son of Arcanthur, Jason Kinsman, as well as our other companions, Brakkus the Hurtz, Darius Silver, and Lincerious Heallaws."

The creature seemed to raise a nonexistent eyebrow for a moment. Stepping over the barricade, he parachuted himself down using his wings to break his fall, and landed on the ground before them, towering over the party at seven feet.

"Puc Thanestorm?" he asked, coming closer to get a better look. "Is that really you?"

"Last I checked," the elf stated coolly.

"You don't remember me, do you, dude?" The wolf chuckled. "I'll give you a hint. I blew up the enemy caravan with a firework attached to my arrow when I was a cub."

Puc searched his memory as he studied the face of the young Sky Wolf before him.

"Doriden Windheart?" He squinted.

"About time you remembered, dude," he said with enthusiasm. "Most people call me Doriden Deadeye, or-,"

"Dori! Where in Orion's fury are you?" a female voice called from behind the gate, causing Doriden to flatten his ears and sigh.

"I'm down here, sis," he growled. "What did I tell you about calling me Dori in front of the soldiers she-wolf?"

"Well maybe I would stop," a smaller, more agile white wolf with fuschia hair and markings said as she glided down beside him, "if you stopped going to fight every intruder we have."

"And this would be Amelia, if memory serves." Puc looked at the female Soarin.

"Yeah, what's it to you?" she huffed, glaring at him. However, her expression changed when she noticed the staff. "Puc the Mage?"

"In the flesh, or so the story goes." He made a light bow.

"It's been so many years," she began. "We feared something happened."

"Something did indeed happen," Puc replied, "and it was the reason the Four Forces were never summoned again. Orbeyus of the Axe was slain, and his son refused his post."

"What? They got the Lord of the Axe? No way! Who?" Doriden questioned him.

"We never caught the bastard," Brakkus said, getting off his horse and standing almost at eye level with the two.

"You should have let my father know!" Amelia continued on her rant, almost oblivious to everything else. "He would have had trackers crawling all over Q-16 had we been informed."

"I had no command nor orders to do such a thing," Puc explained. "As soon as the events occurred, Arieus disbanded the Four Forces.

"Man, why would he do something like that?" Doriden crossed his arms, trying to wrap his brain around it all. "Didn't he know how much was at stake in doing something so...rash?"

"Arieus was more concerned with protecting who you see in front of you." Puc tilted his head in the direction of Annetta, who got off her horse, a dwarf compared to the great Sky Wolves before her.

"Aww, well aren't you the darn tiniest human I've ever seen." Doriden grinned, squatting down to Annetta's level, "I just wanna pinch those cheeks and-,"

"Oh, Dori, grow up, will you? She's not as young as you think." Amelia growled, bearing her teeth at her brother before turning to Puc. "You'll excuse our lack of manners. You will most likely wish to speak with my father about whatever business brings you to here."

"If he is indeed still the ruler, then yes. I should like to," he nodded.

"That old wolf is still up and running." Doriden rose back up as he turned to the others.

Amelia smiled lightly, then turned her gaze upward, "We have guests. You may open the gate. Puc Thanestorm is here to see my father, along with his companions."

"Yes my lady," another of the Soarin nodded and disappeared behind the barrier.

The wooden structure crept open, the sound of logs stressing from being pulled and compressed dominating everything else. Doriden and Amelia entered first, and with a wave of their arm dismissed any suspicious archers who were still readying their bows.

"He's most likely in the main longhouse," Doriden said to them as he and Amelia led the way through what looked like a large nomadic village. The tops of the longhouses were covered in animal skins, and everything was tied with organic rope. There was hardly any sign of any metal, from what Annetta could see.

Young Soarin watched from the sides of the houses as the riders and their horses made their way further in, curious of the strange beasts that had come into their home. The older Soarin paid hardly any heed, most remembering the days of the Four Forces, but were still a bit curious as to why so many years had passed since a horse and humanoid creature was last seen in their midst, so they did glance sideways at the new arrivals. Doriden motioned for them to use one of the posts to tie up their horses, while Amelia went inside to locate Entellion.

"Are there many villages like this on your world? And what of the surface below?" Link tried to make conversation.

"Yeah, there are different tribes all over where mountains are," Doriden replied, perching himself like a bird on one of the wooden posts beside the house. "Surface, ain't a pleasant place with all the beasts that roam around. We use it mostly to gather wood, and for the Eternal Hunt,"

"What is the Eternal Hunt?" Jason asked, hopping off his horse.

"It's the hunt for the everlasting boar, Orion," Doriden explained. "Orion is a one of a kind boar, a gift from the Great Provider, given to the Soarin to be hunted as a food source. The only condition was that when Orion was hunted down, his bones were to be returned to the earth of the surface world, so the next day he could be born again. Hunting Orion is now done only as a rite of passage for young Soarin who wish to declare themselves adult in the eyes of our society. We hunt other stuff too, but there was a time when the boar was hunted each day. I guess it kinda just became a bore. Get it?"

"Are you telling the boar joke again, Dori?" Amelia's head poked out from the door.

"Sis, do you have to keep at it with the nickname?" Doriden groaned.

"Till the Great Provider takes my last wind." She literally grinned wolfishly, then turned to the others. "My father is inside and ready to receive you."

They entered the main chamber of the long house. Its interior was intricately carved, and looked nothing like the outside of the weathered

470

dwelling. The warm light of a fire at the center of the quarters burned brightly, causing everything to give off an orange hue as they came closer. On elevated steps, an elder looking Soarin gazed down at them, his partially braided cyan mane turning orange from the fire.

"Hey Dad, check out what we found with sis at the front door." Doriden grinned, motioning to his companions.

"Thanestorm?" Entellion rose from his chair, his voice weary with age. "Is that you, or do my eyes deceive me?"

"Yes, Alpha Windheart, I have returned." Puc bowed deeply, "My highest respects to you. I understand from Doriden and Amelia that you were never informed of the events three years after the Great War's conclusion."

"Indeed." Entellion stepped down to join them. "We never heard from Orbeyus or any of his envoys since your previous visit to inform us that an heir was born. How is the Lord of the Axe these days?"

"My lord has been dead for almost two decades now, Alpha Windheart. He was murdered, and the Four Forces disbanded, but the heir and firstborn, for Aurora later bore a second child, a boy, was never harmed, and neither was the firstborn son of Arcanthur, who I hope you should remember well," Puc said, before turning to Annetta and Jason, who came forward, Jason with his mace out and Annetta with her shield at her side.

"This is Annetta Severio," Puc continued, "daughter of Arieus, and this is Jason Kinsman, son of Arcanthur. I have come with them and our companions, Brakkus the Hurtz, whom you should remember from the war, Darius Silver, my apprentice, and Lincerious Heallaws, a warrior from Gaia to aid them in restoring the Four Forces. We fear a new war is dawning on the horizon with no one to protect the Eye to All Worlds."

"They're a little young to lead an army, don't you think, Thanestorm?" Entellion studied the girl and boy. "Neither has likely had their first taste of drawn blood, much less planned a war."

"They are young, but they are not alone for Aldamoor and Morwick stand behind them," Puc replied, causing silence in the hall, "Our lives onto them until we are dust and our strength and wisdom is theirs to use as they choose."

Hearing the paraphrased words of the oath, Entellion continued to look at them both, his light blue mane and white fur rising and falling as he breathed in and out, weighing the consequences of his future actions.

"Hey, Dad, here's a thought." Doriden squinted at the girl and boy. "If you think they're too young or whatever, why not have them participate in the Eternal Hunt? I think they're about the age Amelia and I did it. How old are you in moons?"

Annetta and Jason shot each other a glance, not knowing how to respond to the question. Before they could reply, Puc stood in front of them, blocking their view.

"They are indeed old enough to take the test in accordance to Soarin law. If it would please you to have them show their competence with a bow before you decide, to renew your oath to the Four Forces, then they stand ready to take the test," the elf interjected before anyone else could get a word in.

Entellion stroked his mane and knotted his brows in confirmation of the mage's words. He then descended the stairs and walking around Puc looked at both of them in inspection.

"If you say they are, then it must be so," Entellion spoke. "One who carries a weapon in our society is not marked as a minor. Doriden, I would ask that you accompany them to the surface as our elder warriors helped you and Amelia when you first participated in the Hunt."

"Yes, Alpha." Doriden nodded to his father, then turned to Annetta and Jason. "So, you ready for flying down to the surface?"

"Uhm, we can't fly, remember?" Annetta swallowed hard.

"We will have a band of our Soarin help you descend," Entellion said. "After that, you are on your own."

Entellion turned to Puc and Brakkus. "You will understand that I cannot have you both participate, for reasons of tradition."

"Understood, Alpha Windheart. Is it the same for Darius and Lincerious?" Puc questioned the elder.

"If they wish, they may participate as well. They are of age." Entellion nodded, looking at the two of them. "They are, after all, warriors with whom we will fight, should they succeed in bringing down Orion."

"Then the four of them shall descend together." Puc turned without consulting the two of them, and with nod communicated that they had no choice in the matter.

"Very well. Doriden and Amelia, you may choose two more warriors to go with you," the elder instructed.

"Yes, Alpha." Doriden answered once more obediently.

"Good, you may select bows from our armory to assist you. Amelia and Doriden will help you find a longbow suitable for your heights, though I dare say that may prove difficult." Entellion frowned.

"If necessary, and with your permission, I may adjust the bows down to the needed size with magic," Puc offered.

"Permission granted. Now, go. And may the Great Provider be with you." Entellion nodded, giving the cue for everyone to exit the room.

Chapter 44

Darkness crept through the chambers of Valdhar as the fortress moved to the dark side of Earth. As all creatures do, many of its inhabitants found themselves floating off into sleep. This pattern of mortal life was no different for Mislantus, who after many hours of meetings and planning, was taken with exhaustion in his throne room. Feline face resting propped up on a fist, the Lord of the Castle in the Sky found very little peace in his dreams.

∞Ω

Glowing cinders danced on the warm breeze as feet crunched through the burnt debris. The smell of all matter burning filled his nostrils as Mislantus crossed the field of battle. He was still humanoid then. His broad face was clean shaven, with platinum locks of hair that seemed grey from the ashes around him. It was someone he had long forgotten had existed, and the only thing that remained even remotely familiar to his present self as he carried on were the yellow and green eyes that danced along with the dying flames. He was unaware of his destination, but it came to him upon seeing another figure, cloaked and silhouetted against the dark red sky. His feet moving in its direction, the man roared a victorious cry from deep within his throat.

"It is done father!" he proclaimed. "All worlds, every single edge of the multiverse now bows under the banner of Mordred the Conqueror. There is no one left who does not yet know the banner of the seven headed beast."

The figure, still a shadow, did not respond. The cloak continued to billow on the wind, uninterrupted by the words of the man. It seemed indifferent to all around it, a part of the scene. Mislantus shifted uneasily, the lack of words unnerving him.

"Father, the castle is taken. We hold the Eye to All Worlds," he continued, licking his lips from the dire heat around him. Still, there was no response. "Father?"

Moving forward again, he came closer, his hand outstretched to tap the man he called his sire on the shoulder, thinking he had simply not been heard over the carnage of the flames.

"And what of the banner of Mislantus, the son of the Conqueror?" a voice spoke from where the figure stood.

Mislantus withdrew his hand, curling it into a fist. "What...what did you call me?"

474

"Son of the Conqueror," it spoke again. "That is who you were, was it not? An empty threat in the shadows of a far greater man."

Mislantus felt himself shrink to the level of a boy as a pair of deep set green and yellow eyes he had known his entire life turned to face him. A face, powerful and proud, with a lion's mane of golden hair, gnarled and weathered by the storms of a hundred wars looked upon him in that moment. It was the face of a warlord before his time.

"That is what they call you now, is it not? A threat? My legacy, a simple threat," The man spat. "You are the descendant of Freius, a Freiusson, the enslaver of Korangar. He, that gave us mastery over life and death of all worlds."

"It is a name, and I am the Lord of Valdhar, just as you were," Mislantus said, having regained some courage looked him in the eye.

"A lord who cannot even dispatch of children." Mordred laughed in a booming tone, "A lord who is opposed by the weakest of foes, but does nothing aside from sitting on his throne. I would have taken the whole planet, and damn the billions who inhabited it, until I had what was meant to be mine by divine right. By the will of the Unknown."

Mislantus felt his blood boil as he looked at his feet, "You know full well the penalty for touching the blue planet, you know as well as I that the price is too high."

"You must make sacrifices if you're ever to claim your birthright," Mordred sneered.

Mislantus recoiled repetitively. It had always been his father's way to interfere with his plans, and make him do things the way he saw fit. His first curled around the saber at his belt. Within seconds of securing the handle in his grip, he drew the weapon, striking at his father with a single vicious snarl.

"I am my own master," he breathed, as the form of his father crumbled onto the floor and shattered into a million embers, becoming part of the ground around him. "As I will be master of all worlds."

There then came a familiar thundering, the sound of armor clanging, like an army on the march to the sound of a drum. Veering around, Mislantus glared into the distant flames as a single figure returned the gaze, marching towards him. It did not falter in the least bit, marching onwards with a tower shield at its side.

"Arieus." Mislantus's eyes narrowed as he gripped the saber with more ferocity.

As it passed through curtains of fire, the figure, the one he thought to be Arieus, became visible. It was clad from head to toe in a suit of armor, silver plate mail that shone blue in the blazing orange and red flames. Mislantus snarled and prepared for the encounter, but then he realized how much smaller the figure before him was than the man he had faced many years ago. Straightening himself, he could not help but chuckle at the sight.

"My, Arieus, age has gotten the better of you," he said with a smile.

The suit of armor did not respond, and instead went into a fighting stance, shield raised before it, blade poised to strike. It seemed to taunt Mislantus, like a beacon. The warlord did not miss a beat, and launched himself at the foe, steel ringing as weapons collided. Faster and faster his arms pumped the blows, only to be blocked by the enemy. Withdrawing away from it with a quick slide of his feet, Mislantus took a moment to analyze the situation. Something did not sit well with him, for he remembered well the fighting style of the gallant young man named Arieus, and the one before him, did not have it.

"Who are you?" Mislantus furrowed his brows.

The armored assailant did not answer. Stepping towards him, it struck once more with the blade. Mislantus teleported behind him, and with the heel of his boot, kicked the shorter fighter to the ground, causing the helm to be knocked from where it had been locked in place. Chuckling, Mislantus watched as the fighter rose. As it did so, however, the glee of battle faded from his eyes, only to be replaced with horrid realization. From behind a cascade of copper hair, the face of a girl glared back at him. His mind flashed back to a memory from a battle many years before, where the same expression had belonged to a man with hair of a similar shade, just moments before it happened.

"Well done, Annetta," another familiar voice rang from behind Mislantus.

"We will take it from here," a third rang.

Turning, the warlord was faced with two other ghosts from his past. The first voice belonged to a mountain of a man with a double bladed axe, who wore a thick black and grey beard, while the other belonged to a smaller man with sharp features and dark hair, who carried a staff, a weapon that was all too well known to Mislantus. It was then that he realized he had been cornered once again.

"What shall I do with him, my lord?" the voice of the elf rang out.

Mislantus felt the saber drop from his hands in paralysis as his gaze met with Orbeyus. The blue eyes of the man fell upon him in judgment, like ice biting at him in the midst of all the flames.

"Do what must be done." The words rang like a bell. "Spare the life, but not the shame."

The mage then stood before him, a towering being with flames dancing around him. The staff tipped downwards, pointing at the fallen warlord, and the rest of the scene fell to darkness.

ℹℹ

Waking with a startle, Mislantus stirred from his seat, noting that it was still night upon the ship, and all who could have seen him withering in his slumbers were nowhere to be found. Exhaling, the warlord stood up and strode to the massive glass panels separating him from the vacuums of space, and looked at the blue planet. It was not the first time the dream had surfaced, and of late it was happening more and more frequently.

Cat ears flattening in disdain, he thought no more on what had taken place, and the terror he felt each time he was forced to relive his humiliation in his sleep. He had vowed to get vengeance on the mage, but he also vowed to prove to his father that his name was whispered in fear as much as his had been. But he meant for his own to last forever. The path of all out war had not worked for Mordred, costing him his life, Mislantus sought to achieve the dream instead of only swim in it, and if it meant hiding in the shadows for a little while longer, then he would endure. There was after all, no sense in wasting cannon fodder.

Chapter 45

After selecting the bows, and having Puc adjust them, the company split up to their next destinations. Annetta, Jason, Link and Darius waited near the entrance of the village on some discarded logs for Doriden and Amelia to get them. Puc and Brakkus were off speaking with Entellion, informing the elder of everything that had taken place since their last visit to the city above the clouds.

The youth sat in silence, picking at the loose splinters of wood on the logs, simply observing the tall and graceful creatures running back and forth. Everything around them smelt of fresh cut trees and the aroma of sap. It reminded Annetta and Jason of bringing in a tree at Christmas each year. Despite the pleasant smell, tension was mounting among them. The idea of going down after a creature such as the boar vaguely terrified each and every one of them. From what Doriden had said to them in the armory, the beast was over twenty feet long with razor sharp tusks, and huge fangs for teeth that could snap trees like twigs. Of course, each time he spoke of the boar, he received a good whack over the head from one of the bows Amelia was holding, and was told to grow up. It made the tension lessen, but the fact remained that none of the four gathered had any true experience in hunting anything at all. Target practice lessons in the Lab with Brakkus did not exactly count.

Amelia and Doriden emerged from the shadowed entrances of one of the longhouses, followed by two other Soarin, one sporting a purple mane with multiple small braids, and one with a deep green mane, cut short at the sides but left long down the middle of his head. Each was armed with a bow and quiver of arrows, their sleek and muscular anthropomorphic bodies betraying each slight movement as they all walked in unison towards them.

"You pups ready for this? You know it's considered a great honor to participate in the Hunt." Doriden crossed his arms as he studied the four of them with his good eye.

Amelia simply rolled her own eyes at her brother trying to act cool in front of the children and prodded his elbow with the end of her bow, causing him to lose balance and nearly topple over onto Darius.

"These are Alterin and Ephaziel," she introduced the two male Soarin who stood behind her and Doriden, "they are two of our leading huntsmen.

They will help you get to the surface, and will be with both Doriden and myself tracking your movements as you go after Orion."

"They are the ones who go after Orion?" the purple haired Alterin asked, eyeing the four skeptically. "They will be lucky if they survive the encounter, let alone get a shot at him."

"Is that a judgement based on size?" Darius glared at the Sky Wolf. "Because in my world, they say the bigger you are, the harder you fall."

The comment caused both Alterin and Ephaziel to pull back their gums and show a dazzling display of white fangs. Darius did not back down from the challenge either, and from the look in his eyes it was obvious he would change into his panther shape and challenge both Soarin to a fight without second thoughts.

"Hey dudes, chill. There's no need for a fight here." Doriden stepped in the middle of them. "They don't mean nothing by it, Darius, and you guys need to act a bit more your moon cycle. Yeah, they're small, but they're also a different species. If you remember Orbeyus, the man never could look me in the eye."

"If you say so, Doriden. I simply speak the truth I know." Alterin lowered his gaze to where Darius stood. "I am sorry."

Darius stepped down, his back muscles loosening and he exhaled. Link placed an arm on his shoulder in a premeditated effort to hold him back if another duel of words occurred.

"Apology accepted," The young elf broke free and walked to the entrance without another word. It was clear, however, that his pride had been stained not matter what he said to the Soarin hunter.

"He's a really proud guy," Jason said to the hunters, trying to diffuse tension that had just mounted. "So, how are we going about this descent business?"

"Simple, dude. We go down." Doriden motioned to the gate and watched Jason's eyes bulge out of their sockets, causing him to chuckle and Amelia to prod him again. "Okay, okay, I'm just kidding. We glide down dude."

Jason sighed in relief, not wanting to think about jumping all the way down. He was not afraid of heights, but the concept of becoming a pancake did not come as a pleasant thought.

"Well, if you boys are all done sorting out your differences, are you ready to make the descent?" Amelia spoke up as she motioned for the guards at the gate to open the massive wooden structure.

"Now or never, I guess." Annetta slid off the pile of logs she had been occupying, doing her best not to get any splinters in the process.

Amelia turned to Doriden and the other two hunters, her eyes watching them like a hawk for any unfavorable gestures in their body language, mostly from Alterin and Ephaziel.

"We go where the future Alphas of the pack lead us," Ephaziel answered, having been silent for most of the spat. He turned to his companion to see him nod in agreement.

"Good. Now as penence, carry the youth you just offended," Amelia said in a stern tone, and nodded to the others to get ready.

"You may wanna climb onto my back and hold on tight, little dudette," Doriden said to Annetta, lowering himself.

Annetta looked at the Soarin and felt her face flush hot from anxiety as she tried to figure out how to climb on without hurting the creature. Muttering words of encouragement to herself, she grabbed hold of one of the shoulder blades connected to his wing, and hoisted herself up, unsure of what to do with her hands. Her error was corrected moments later when Doriden reached back and pulled her hands around his neck.

"There, all secure. You dudes ready to take the plunge?" Doriden turned back to see everyone ready.

"Uhm...have you guys ever actually done this before with humans on your back?" Jason asked from behind Amelia.

"Not in our lifetime," Alterin answered him, leaving the gate with Link on his back.

"Well, that's comforting," Darius sighed, a thick cloud of sarcasm lacing his voice.

"Should you like, I can let you go down the natural way." Ephaziel eyed him from the corner of his eye.

"Thank you, but no, I would rather keep my limbs intact. Carry on," the young elf spoke in the same steady tone he'd kept throughout the whole encounter.

"Dude got an arrowhead stuck up his rear end or something?" Doriden asked Annetta quietly.

"If he does, it's been there a long time." She grinned, answering him back, causing the Soarin to chuckle.

Going to the edge, each Soarin made sure to have enough room on either side, then spread their wings to full span, the feathers alternating between white and the shade of each of the Soarin's mane.

"You want to go first, or should I?" Amelia looked at her brother.

Doriden turned around to face his sister, a smirk on his face as he shifted his foot backwards. Annetta clung onto him for dear life, not sure of what the Soarin had in his head.

"As they say, ladies first. But you ain't no lady." He gave her a mock salute before taking another step back and beginning the drop.

Annetta closed her eyes, not sure if her breakfast would stay in her stomach much longer. She clutched tightly at the creature as though she were glued to him, the wind whipping her face.

"Whoooo! Alright!" Doriden shouted as he shifted his weight, causing him to spiral a bit and make Annetta hold him even tighter. "Uh...you okay back there?"

"Not exactly, if you haven't noticed," the girl snapped. "I've never done this and it's scaring the living daylights out of me!"

"Right! Uhm, well, let's see, then." Doriden began to slowly open his wings, causing them to begin to slow down in the air. "Better?"

"Yes, thank you," Annetta wheezed.

"You scared of heights? Your eyes are closed," the Soarin asked trying to make conversation.

"No I just...I don't like the idea of falling. No human would," she explained, opening her eyes.

"Yeah, I keep forgetting about the no wings thing. Sorry, dudette," the Soarien said, flexing his wings as he began to spiral down like a great vulture, the surface becoming more visible by the second.

Annetta managed to keep her eyes open, the fear of falling passing, but still present enough to keep her filled with adrenaline the rest of the way down. Another part of her, the one that was removed from her bodily fear, was enjoying the trip, but it was still not enough to convince the rest of her that everything was going to be okay.

Doriden touched down upon the surface smoothly, his great paws coming down on the grass beneath him. A breeze passed through the area from his powerful wings before he folded them back up neatly. The Soarin let the girl down off of his back, then waited for the others to join them.

Annetta looked down at the grass below her worn running shoes and torn up jeans. It looked no different than the grass around the track of her school where she hung out with her friends. She looked up at the surrounding trees and landscape. It looked the same as what surrounded Severio Castle, and what filled the biospheres in Q-16.

"Have you ever seen any of the other dimensions?" she asked Doriden.

"Nah, I saw the Eye to All Worlds briefly as a pup, but I never traveled outside this one. Why you asking?" The Soarin crossed his arms, looking out for his comrades.

"Oh nothing, I was just curious. This world doesn't look much different from the one I live in. I wonder if there's just a universal design to how a world should look," she said as she gazed at her surroundings.

"Well, it would make sense, I guess." Doriden nodded. "I mean, doesn't everyone want the same things no matter what species, world, or reality they come from? We all want for goodness and peace. That's what the Great Provider instilled in the hearts of every living creature. That's what Orbeyus told us about his own god, the Unknown. He said that it's hate that corrupts that need into something darker. I'm no philosopher, I just kinda remember the gist of stuff. I still believe the will of every living creature plays part in what they do."

Annetta nodded, then turned around to see Amelia, Alterin and Ephaziel land with Jason, Link and Darius. Her three friend's expressions ranged from terrified to exhilarated, Darius seeming to be the most pale, and Link to having the most fun out of the three.

"Can we do that again?" The young Gaian warrior grinned as he leaped down from the back of the Soarin.

"Can we just teleport on the way back?" Darius gasped, trying to return pigmentation to his naturally pale skin. "Seriously, I never want to go through that again."

"It wasn't so bad. Grow up, Darius," Jason said in a neutral tone. "It was kinda fun towards the end, like a roller coaster."

"A roller what?" Doriden asked.

"It's, uhm," Jason tried to explain to the best of his abilities, as the Soarin looked at him like he had fallen out of a tree and was talking gibberish, "a machine people go on for fun to go really fast and stuff. We

482

can't fly, but being on one of those thing's feels pretty close to what I just felt now. It's a form of entertainment."

"One that not everyone enjoys," Darius added, slowly starting to look better.

"Why do humans torture themselves? What is the point?" Amelia cocked her wolfish head to the side. "I mean, if you get no satisfaction out of some form of entertainment, then why do it?"

"Competition to show who is the braver one," the young elf answered.

"Oh, so you mean like…going into the eye of a cyclone, or teasing a sleeping boar by pulling his tail?" Doriden asked, trying to understand.

"Something like that, just not as drastic." Annetta made a face trying to imagine both scenarios, and the massive amounts of bruising that would occur.

"Humans are a strange species," Alterin sighed, making his conclusion before he turned to Amelia. "What next?"

"A few pointers in tracking, for they have never hunted and then we go to our posts." Amelia crossed her slim and powerful arms. "Am I correct in this assumption?"

Annetta and Jason turned to one another and nodded in agreement, while Darius and Link said nothing, both watching the female Soarin with little enthusiasm.

"I have hunted before in the woods where my father and I lived," Link assured them. "I can and will if necessary teach what needs to be taught. Your Alpha did specify not to help us at all."

Amelia looked over at Doriden for confirmation, her brother simply shrugging his shoulders.

"Very well," she said. "We leave you on your own. Use whatever skills you know and have earned. Be warned that Orion generally travels with a pack of other boars that are his family. Once you track the boar, you must somehow isolate the beast before delivering it to its death. When you have done that," Amelia trailed off and reached into a pouch on her belt to produce a small bone whistle, and tossed it to Darius, "use this to call us so that we may assemble the Alpha and other elders for judgement of your kill. Good luck, and may the Great Provider be with you in your time of the hunt."

The Soarin spread their wings and all took off, disappearing high above the clouds. Suddenly, Annetta and Jason felt very alone. It was the first time they were in a world not their own without both Brakkus and Puc. They turned to Darius and Link, the two of them watching the woods.

"Now what?" Jason asked, throwing his hands to his side.

"We have to track it, which would have been easier if we knew what we were looking for," Link said with a frown. "I can only imagine how many boars actually roam this forest."

Darius nodded in agreement, biting his lower lip as he tried to come up with a solution to their problem. His eyes then lit up. Stripping out of his shirt and boots, he phased into his panther form.

"What are you doing?" Annetta raised an eyebrow. "We're not fighting anyone yet."

"No, but an animal's sense of smell is better than a human's. We can at least try to track more effectively like this," the panther spoke in its gruff tone, then turned to Link. "You too, buddy. On all fours."

Link turned to Annetta and Jason with a pleading look, not wanting to change. There was a tinge of betrayal that cut at him when he saw no support from the two of them, but he knew at the same time it was what needed to be done. Taking off his jacket and pressing it into Annetta's hands with his bow and quiver, he let out a howl of agony that caused all the small animals for miles around to stir at the unnatural sound. Dropping on his massive front paws once the transition was complete, the creature turned to Darius.

"Have you smelt a boar before?" the panther asked.

"An animal like any animal, isn't it?" Link responded.

Darius dropped his head and sighed. This was going to be more difficult than he thought. He wanted to scream and bring the Soarin back down in his frustration at the situation, but instead he kept calm and simply took a few raspy breaths. Like it or not, they all looked to him when Puc was not around, and if he panicked, then the rest of them would follow.

Jason had noticed something in the bushes during their conversation, and began to drift away from the group. Using the end of his bow, he peeled away the layer of leaves and branches.

"Hey guys!" he called. "Guys!"

Link and Darius turned around to face the boy.

"I think I found something," Jason continued pulling away the thick branches to reveal what looked like a really old boar carcass beginning to rot away. "You think that will help?"

Annetta's lips curled in disgust at the sight, while Darius and Link stepped forward to examine what Jason had found.

"This will give us a good lead," Darius said, inhaling the aroma of the carcass. "There's enough of the animal odor left on it that we can track down more of the same scent. Can you smell it, Link?"

"All the way from over here," Link nodded, not going any closer. He leaned over to Annetta, who still had a disgusted look on her face. "Trust me, it smells worse than it looks."

"I can't even begin to imagine," she muttered back quietly. Sucking up the remainder of her revulsion, she turned to everyone and drew an arrow from her quiver. "So...we gonna hunt or what?"

Darius moved away from the dead animal. He raised his great black furry head into the air and began sniffing. Link did the same, lowering his wolfish snout to the ground instead of the air. Moments, later both creatures were on the move, Annetta and Jason following closely behind.

"So...do we even know how we distinguish Orion from other boars we come across?" Jason asked Annetta as they followed their friends in a light jog.

"You're asking me? Only place I've even seen one of these things before is at the zoo," she grumbled as they continued onward.

Link was completely absorbed in the scent of the woods. Every aroma seemed to come alive before him. The shapes of leaves and animals danced before his dazed eyes as he ran forward, trying to distinguish the smell of the boar from everything else, the undergrowth of the woods becoming denser as they left the grassy area and went further in.

Darius ran beside Link, turning from time to time at his companion, who seemed completely at home with his senses, in a state of absent bliss. Darius wished he could let himself go the same way, but he knew that he needed to make sure he did not lose Annetta and Jason in the back, since it was them that would need to take down the boar if they were to have an allegiance of any sort with the Soarin.

Puc had explained the situation and how it would most likely play out. If he or Link poached Orion, there was a chance that an allegiance could be considered null and void, because it was not those who were being sworn to that proved they were capable of battling the fierce boar, but two of their underlings. Darius's sole purpose in this mission was to sit back, watch and to make sure neither Jason nor Annetta failed. His youthful appearance had once again made him the eyes of Puc Thanestorm where the mage could not venture.

"Man! Can you guys slow down?" Annetta panted as Link and Darius began to speed up. "Our legs aren't that long!"

"Stop, Lincerious!" Darius used the young warrior's full name to get his attention, the creature coming to a halt. "They cannot run as fast as us."

The creature groaned in resignation and looked at both Annetta and Jason, panting as they finally caught up with them and began catching their breath.

"I want...whatever fuel they put in you guys," Jason gasped, holding his knees.

"Yeah, seriously," Annetta muttered beside him in between breaths.

"We cannot wait for them to keep catching up, otherwise we will lose the trail," Link protested to Darius.

"Then we only have one choice. We will need to carry them," the panther indicated, "Unless you stop acting like a scent-driven mutt."

Link flashed a set of long fangs at Darius and then turned to Annetta, indicating for the girl to get on his back. She nodded and climbed onto the creature, securing her bow and arrow along with her pack. Grabbing onto his horns, she waited for him to take off again, all too familiar with how fast he could go. Link wasted no time diving back into top speed, his feral senses taking over as he lost himself once more in the woods.

Darius and Jason watched him take off, the panther growling and waited for the boy to climb on. Jason did what was required, but then realized he did not have anything to grab onto once he was on Darius's back.

"Uh...how do I stay on?" he asked, dumbfounded.

"Arms around my neck, and no funny business," he responded. The werepanther then launched himself with a roar in pursuit of Link.

Annetta felt the wind tearing through her hair with vicious speed as the horned wolf-like creature charged ever faster in pursuit of its invisible target.

"How do you know if it's Orion you're going after?" Annetta called past the wind to him.

"You'll just have to trust me," Link responded almost absentmindedly as he continued to charge, every muscle in his body working to maximum capacity.

Moments later, a massive black panther leaped out and joined them with Jason flattened against its back as it pushed past the trees, trying to catch up to Link.

"Not as fast as I thought you'd be," Darius smirked at him through labored breaths.

"Wanna make a bet on that one?" Link taunted, glancing sideways. "I bet I'll get to the boars before you even catch sight of my dust."

"Your funeral," Darius grinned wickedly and kicked up grass and dirt as he shot past Link.

Gritting his teeth, the creature snarled and sped onward. Annetta held onto him for dear life, no longer confidently holding onto the antlers, but flattened out against him, holding onto his neck. She struggled between her own grip and the possibilities of choking the great beast, which she doubted she had the strength to do even if she tried.

"Link, please, slow down," she cried out from behind.

But the youth was too far gone, his instinct having taken over completely, the thrill of the hunt pounding through his veins. There seemed to be nothing left of the young man within the beast but the pure primal urge to run forward.

Annetta felt every tendon in her arms set on fire as she continued to hold on, her grip slowly slipping. Regardless of the pain, she continued to hold on, hoping if she kept calling him he would respond or stop. Maybe she just needed to be louder, maybe the wind was preventing her from getting through. But her body began to fail where her spirit did not, and all too soon Annetta found herself letting go and falling off the charging beast, her body tumbling on the ground like a rag doll before coming to a halt against a tree trunk with a thud.

The girl picked herself up painfully, noting her jeans were torn, as was the sleeve on her jacket. But she was more concerned with the stinging cuts on her elbow and knees, and her right hand on which the skin on her fingers and palm were torn. Though her hand was not bleeding a lot, it stung and it took away from her concentration, something Puc had instilled in them from the beginning was necessary in all tasks. Ripping off a piece of her t-shirt, she wrapped it around her hand as best as she could, wishing she at least had some water to put on it. She had an even bigger problem than her sores, however. She needed to somehow find both Link and Darius. On top of that, she checked to make sure her bow was still in useable shape, and noticed her arrows had flown out of her quiver, leaving her with no ammunition to use. Looking around she managed to recover a few that had fallen when she took the tumble to the tree but it was not enough for what she was going to face.

With a final sigh of frustration, Annetta took up her bow and continued onward in the forest, doing her best to follow the tracks left by Link and Darius from their claws digging into the ground as they had raced along. In due time, her anger at the situation subsided and Annetta was able to immerse herself in the woods around her, almost forgetting the task at hand.

She had always envied Jason for living so close to his own little woods, while she was stuck in the industrial forest of towering buildings. It always made her feel like her own life would never know peace of any kind, because everything moved so fast. But whenever she was there, she marveled at how everything stopped.

After some time, she heard raised voices and began to run in their direction. Coming to some bushes that obscured her from whoever it was, she peaked from behind them to see Link and Darius, fangs barred and claws at one another's throat.

"You were responsible for her!" the monstrous werepanther bellowed. "What the hell is wrong with you, Heallaws? I suppose we should have listened to you before we uncaged that mindless thing."

Link drove his antlers towards Darius, the panther dodging with feline agility, snarling at the beast.

"Guys, stop!" Jason said, trying to get them to stop quarreling. "This isn't going to get Annetta back. We just need retrace our steps and find her."

"It doesn't change the fact of what he did!" Darius howled in rage at Jason and then turned back to Link, "You have just cost us everything, you pathetic excuse for a-,"

"That's enough, you guys." Annetta emerged from the bushes.

The trio of boys froze and turned to face her as though she were a forest specter come to haunt them.

"Annetta! You okay?" Jason finally kicked himself into gear when she was within hugging distance, and threw himself on his friend, giving her a good squeeze.

"No, I'm dead, I snapped my neck in seven places and have come back as a zombie to eat yer brains," she said seriously, diffusing the tension, even causing Darius to give a pleased cat-like noise.

"What happened to your hand?" Jason noted the poorly tied up piece of cloth and torn shirt.

"It's just a scratch, painful as hell but nothing deep I think," she flexed her fingers.

Link continued to look at her for a few moments, then lowered his head and raced off into the woods.

Before Annetta could react, Darius caught her by the shoulder with his huge paw. The girl turned to face the green eyes of the great cat, looking at her with concern.

"Leave him be. He will join us again when he is ready. He has proven himself a great enough tracker," he stated. "At the cost of almost losing one of our needed hunters," he added, sourly.

"It could have still happened to anyone," she muttered.

"Not to me," Darius snapped. "Not when you know you are part of a team that needs you. If you cannot be a team player, then you're better off dead when it comes to war. I was taught that, I was fed that from my very first days of being a mage's apprentice. It is crucial to work as a team, to remain in control. Even when playing fun and games or people can get hurt, seriously hurt."

"You do remember the age difference between us, right Darius?" Annetta bit back, fed up with his repetitiveness. "Yeah, I get it. We all need to work together and put our pride in the gutter. But we all know about Link's curse. We all knew…well, we didn't even know something like this could happen, that he could lose control. But my point is, accidents happen."

Darius frowned in resignation, seeing no point in arguing with Annetta. In fact, there never was much point to arguing with her, because she was so stubborn. It was a trait he admired about the younger girl, but it drove him insane when she did not take his advice when it was meant to benefit her. This trait had been ever present in her from the first day Darius met her. At first, it was simply having her way with whatever they did after school but it escalated later into fights with kids who picked on others. Darius would always have to watch as Annetta took the fall and he worried that one day things would get too far and then he would have to smile and tell Puc that the heir was killed in a school fight. He had resented having to watch her on Puc's orders because of this, and tried to be the distant sort of friend. But later, as he got to know her more, he found he could not keep away. Perhaps it was that in some twisted way, she was no different than Puc, a mind that never faltered or perhaps it was the words she spoke each time he tried to stop her, I fight because nobody else will.

"Do what you want, but be quick about it," the panther spoke in resignation. "We found a pack of boars, and one that matched Doriden's description of Orion, but I'm afraid Link and I scared it off when we got into a fight. They won't have gone far if you hurry."

Annetta gave a firm nod, and ran off in the direction Link had gone, once again following the markers of ripped grass as an indicator.

Darius growled, watching the girl leave, hiding his frustration as best he could from Jason. He knew they could not afford to waste time that could be used in taking the creature down. Noting a change in the altitude of the land before him Darius walked over to the low growing bushes to see that their path ended and a cliff separated them from a less dense area of forest below. It could have almost been said to be a meadow, were it not for the sparse trees growing all over.

"You okay?" Jason asked, trying to break the silence.

"I've been better," the panther noted. Getting down on all fours, he stalked off down the ledge of the cliff, contemplating his next move.

Chapter 46

Running, running and continually running, Link finally stopped upon reaching the edge of a riverbank. Hunching over on all fours and sitting like a common house pet, he stared down into the water, the head of the massive wolf with antlers staring back at him, the voices of all those who had drawn back in fear upon seeing him the way he was echoing back at him from beyond the rapidly running water. Freak, monster, animal, half-breed, thing, the list of names went on. They were names that were viler in their meaning on Gaia than on Earth.

He looked down at his massive ape-like paws, with claws long enough to be small knives protruding from where his fingernails should be. He curled them inward aggressively until the points began to sting his palms. He had been reckless, and it was unforgivable. He could have killed the girl he had sworn to protect and help. It was not just an oath to anyone he'd made. It had been an oath to the messengers of the Unknown itself.

He heard a faint voice from the distance calling for him. Though far, it was strong. He realized moments later that he wanted nothing more than to hide his face, whatever form it took.

Getting up, Link began to make his way towards the river, getting ready to cross it. Weighed down by his mixture of emotions, he was only half way through the shallow bank when Annetta ran out from the clearing. Link did his best to ignore the girl's arrival and kept on moving, as though it was simply a curious deer that had emerged to watch him.

"Link! Hey!" she screamed after him at the top of her lungs, catching her breath. "Wait up!"

Unable to not respond, he turned around, still on all fours in the water, his crimson eyes and golden scar focused upon the young girl holding the bow. The wind gently ruffled her hair, causing it to look like a lion's mane as she watched him.

"Finally. I thought you might have gone deaf or something," she said, quietly.

Link growled, looking back down at the water running past him.

"Leave me alone, Annetta. I can't even look at you right now," he said in a low voice, and continued to trot through the river until he emerged on the other side.

"Link, look, it's okay. Darius isn't mad at you anymore. I talked to him," she began, running up to the waters edge, about to go in after him.

"Annetta, no! Just go away and leave me alone, alright?" he snarled viciously.

About to say something, she drew back a little as she watched the beast with her blue eyes, a hurt feeling emerging behind them.

"Darius is right. I'm a liability, okay?" he spat.

"That's not true, you helped a lot in Morwick, and when we were in Aldamoor," she began again.

"Yes but when I'm given a bigger task, something that's my own to carry out, I screw it up. It happened when I was trying to protect you from the giant, it happened with Darius, and it happened now, and you know what? It could happen again, and you could not be so lucky next time. Don't you see? I'm no good at this. You wanna know why I probably got picked by the Unknown? I kept praying to get off that damn planet day in and day out because of what I am."

"Well, if you keep telling yourself that, then nothing will change," Annetta snapped back at him. "Link, no one is perfect. The sooner you accept that, the better it will be. I mean, Puc forgot about the C.T.S., and we missed a whole week on Earth. But he admitted he forgot about it, and that was that. He's still, like, the smartest guy we know, and he is still a mage, a pretty good mage, considering his reputation. As for Brakkus, I'm sure he's had his bad days too, but we just haven't seen them, because he works hard at it. When you work hard at something, you get better. That's what all of us have to do. We have to keep trying until we just become good. If we don't try, how are we ever going to improve?"

They continued to glare at one another for a very long while, their gazes unwavering, until Link finally gave up and looked away. Though it stung his ears, Annetta was speaking the truth. Everyone had their problems, and they just had to accept it and do the best they could.

"Well? Are you coming or what? We have a really big pig to roast!" Annetta growled crossing her arms over her chest as she watched him with raised eyebrows.

"I'm, sorry but I can't." He shook his head. "The fact of the matter is that I did endanger your life, and I can't forgive myself for that, no matter what kind of sympathetic talk you try to give me. I'm too dangerous, Annetta. It will have to be you, Darius and Jason that go after Orion."

Annetta's jaw dropped, her face turning red as she got ready for the rebuttal of her life, when Link leaped over the stream and landed beside her.

"You would do me a kindness, however, if you gave me my clothing back for when I change back. I don't think these pants will be much good for anything except a dusting cloth, and even that's going to be a high calling for them." The wolf flashed its wide, pearly grin at her.

Annetta took the backpack off her shoulder and then threw it to Link. Anger boiled inside her for a few more minutes as she did her best to calm down.

"You're not a liability, if anything it's me for being who I am," she said quietly and walked back to where Jason and Darius were waiting for her.

Link turned his head around after he was sure the girl had left and watched her until the figure faded from sight. He then disappeared into the forest.

෨෬

Jason leaned against a tree trunk watching the woods where Annetta had last been seen, while Darius, still in his panther form, continued to gaze out to where he had last seen the boars.

"What's taking them so long, dammit." Darius furrowed his black furred face, his lips curling in a snarl. "We're going to lose them. Each moment is precious."

"Relax, for all we know she could have run into Orion, and his boars and will be calling us via telepathy any second now." Jason glanced over at the ever-worrying elf. "Honestly, you need to chill, or you may actually start looking your age."

"Funny, Kinsman," the panther spat.

"I try to be," Jason answered, when the sound of a breaking twig gave away Annetta as she emerged from the foliage.

"Where's Link?" Jason asked.

"He said he wasn't going with us because he feels he'll be to much trouble," she answered. "I tried to convince him, but he wouldn't have it."

"Silver tongue not working for you?" Darius quipped.

"Can it, furball," she growled. "Now let's go find this boar."

"Finally talking some sense." Darius grinned. Leaping down the ledge, he began to sniff at the ground around him, making out the pattern the animals had left scattered behind.

Annetta and Jason took the time to find a way to climb down safely using stable crevices in the small rocky slope without twisting an ankle. Though they could have easily teleported, energy was one thing they did not want to waste.

"Hey Annetta, where did all your arrows go?" Jason noticed her almost empty quiver.

"I lost them when Link went out of control," she said, twisting her head back a little to look at them. "Could have been worse though, right?"

"Yeah, I guess." Jason nodded as they reached the bottom.

"I found them," Darius announced as they approached him. "I'll go on ahead to scout them out, but slow enough that you can still see me. You guys should be okay that way. If anything, just yell if you're in trouble."

"Darius, it's not exactly our first day doing this," Annetta said wearily. "Well, this maybe, but not the whole adventure thing."

The panther nodded, and before they knew it, he was on the move. The two of them took off in a sprint, everything around them becoming a blur as they went, the small form of a black cat their only guiding light in the green.

It did not take long for them to notice that the panther came to a halt, a cue for the pair to slow down. They had come close enough.

"Be as silent as you can," Darius whispered as he crouched low to the ground. He crawled to the edge of the green blocking their path. Annetta and Jason also went down on their bellies and crawled to the edge of the bushes, peering out from between spaces in the branches to look at what lay on the other side.

They were unsure at first which of the many brown haired short and stocky animals was Orion. Each of the beasts looked almost identical, until they noted the behemoth that rose above them all like a mountain. The creature looked more monster than boar, with a set of tusks, like two white swords curving out of its mouth in a vicious smile, a grin of death. Annetta began having second thoughts about the challenge of the hunt as she looked down at the bow that rested on the ground beside her. The sting from the sweat in her covered hand also reminded her that she had a problem that would be hard to forget.

"So this little dinky toothpick has to take down that thing?" Jason whispered, pointing at Orion.

"Don't shoot the messenger, but yes," Darius answered as both Jason and Annetta's heads hung low. "You need to understand, there's usually more hunters participating, and it sort of doesn't help that you're a lot smaller than the Soarin."

"Haven't you ever heard, size matters not?" Annetta said. "Yeah it's bigger than us, but...uh..."

The girl looked back at the massive boar and stuttered, thinking of what to say.

"Hey, Annetta, you think you can do what you did back in Yarmir's mountain with the sword, but this time do it with an arrow? Focus your energy into it?" Jason asked as he began to put together a plan.

"Yeah, why? What's up?" She looked over at him as the boy took out an arrow and got into a crouching position, pulling back the tip.

"I've got a idea," the youth grinned.

ⅎ℣

Puc looked down from the walls of the village barricade into the drop where Annetta and the others had descended. Though no emotion was readable on his face, those around could tell that the mage was worried.

Brakkus sat on the logs below, resting his great paws and leaning on the hilt of his sword, which he'd dug into the ground, his eyes upon his friend, watching his back. It had always been this way as long as Brakkus had known the Water Elf. Though Brakkus knew they were safe where they were, it was a reflex after years of having been down in the Lab, and the years before that spent with Orbeyus on his various campaigns where danger could come at them from anywhere.

Entellion emerged from his long house, his tabard-like tunic billowing from the movement as he approached the seated Hurtz, who was in deep study of his friend on the wall.

"He cares for them more than he lets on," the Soarin elder finally spoke, when he was sure Brakkus knew he was standing beside him.

"Ye'd be surprised," Brakkus nodded. "I think though, it has something to do with the guilt, even though we all tell him it wasn't his fault that Lord Orbeyus passed from our world. Angels that were sent visited him from the other side on Orbeyus's orders to train his heir, and the son of Arcanthur, to make them ready. He feels responsible for them."

"So he worries due to a promise," Entellion concluded.

"Aye, Alpha, that he does." The Hurtz answered.

Entellion nodded his head and left Brakkus to his thoughts. He went to the stairs leading up to where Puc stood, looking downward.

The mage seemed to be in another world entirely, gripping the staff in his right hand with such ferocity that his knuckles turned white, his pale blue eyes focused upon the ground below. It was as though someone had propped a corpse up in his place like a scarecrow.

"They say worry is the death of all teachers, parents, and guardians," Entellion said as he looked out over the wall, towering well over the mage as he did so.

"And what makes you think worry even crossed my mind?" The mage glanced up at the Sky Wolf.

"The way in which you hold the staff of your office, the way in which you look down, hoping to spot the hunt though we are above what even you can see, and the way in which you answered me now, Puc Thanestorm," Entellion replied to him with the same regal tone in his voice as when they first arrived.

Puc huffed as he loosened the grip on his staff and began pacing away from the elder Soarin, anger swelling up within the mage for his actions betraying how he felt.

"Brakkus told me of your spiritual agreement with the Lord of the Axe," Entellion continued, causing Puc to stop in his tracks.

The mage spun around, his deep green and black robes following his trail like a faithful dog as he looked back at Entellion, who was standing as though he had simply bid him a good morning.

"When one is asked from the other world to complete a task, one must treat it with utmost respect. Failure is not an option," the elf answered coldly.

Entellion shifted his weight from one paw to the other as he continued to look at the mage who had once again focused his gaze downward. Moments later, a Soarin tore through the thin veil of clouds and landed on the ground below the timber wall.

"Alpha Windheart, the one named Lincerious has split away from the group and is on his own. Shall we retrieve him back to Trafjan Cliffs?" The Soarin knelt from the other side of the gates upon seeing Entellion.

"Leave him where he is, Alterin, and tell the others to do so as well," the elder informed him. "No one is to be moved until Orion has breathed his final breath."

"Yes, Alpha Windheart," Alterin nodded. Swooping down, he was gone as quickly as he had come up. Puc looked over at Entellion, demanding an answer for his course of action.

"It may be a plan and we know it naught," Entellion began. "That is the rule with most youth. Though we think them dim and inexperienced, we must learn to trust what it is that they are trying to do. As we grow older, we forget we were once like them, and we too made mistakes. It is in mistakes we grow, and from mistakes that we become wiser. If all is handed to us on a plate, then we will never truly know the extent of our own prowess."

Entellion turned to face Puc, the grip on his staff still very strong, blue veins visible on his knuckles where they were whitest, his eyes fixated on the ground.

"This is the same when speaking of the heir of Orbeyus and the son of Arcanthur. In personal knowledge I think it is most important above all else. You need to let them go, Thanestorm. What if this final battle comes with Mislantus and one of them dies? Will you spend an eternity in mourning, blaming your inability to teach them? That the great Puc Thanestorm failed? No, you did not fail, it was their lack of experience from not allowing them to fail that will have gotten them there." The Soarin elder finished and began to move away, seeing he could not get through to him.

Puc remained where he stood. Though he had heard every word the Sky Wolf leader had spoken, and agreed with it, he could still not help but think of every scenario that could happen below that he was useless to prevent. That was what haunted the mage. It was the same emotion he had felt when he had come upon Orbeyus's body, and it had welled up inside of him today when he had been told to stay behind. He was Puc Thanestorm, one of the most skilled mages in the known magical world, and mere words had halted him from performing his duty, a command he knew he had to obey, but he had the choice of not liking. He exhaled in anger, and went to join Brakkus on his stoop of logs.

෴

Annetta crawled backwards out of the bushes into the clearing, making sure to be as silent as she could, and began moving sideways to the left. Darius was already positioned on the other side of clearing, ready to herd the beasts whichever way was needed for her and Jason to have a clear shot at Orion. Annetta and Jason had split the remaining arrows from Jason's quiver equally, in order to give each of them enough ammunition to take the beast down. They had also agreed to try and avoid the smaller boars, which would most likely charge at them or run away. The latter was what they were hoping for.

Taking out one of the projectiles, Annetta focused as best as she could, remembering what Brakkus had instructed her to do in all their lessons. She pulled back the arrow on the bowstring close to her face, her hand throbbing from the sweat and dirt stinging at it from the cuts. Panic began to surge through her as she was fairly confident in her inability to hit a target from the injury. She looked down to see Jason glancing back up at her sideways for a signal. Exhaling, she nodded. It was now or not at all. She focused her psychic energy on the arrow to direct it before letting it fly. It began.

One arrow hit Orion in the shoulder, while the other missed the mark completely, landing right beside him. The animal went into a frenzy, squealing and causing all the others to rampage, dirt and grass being kicked up as the boars began to scatter into the woods. Orion continued to scream in pain, warning his kin to save themselves before he spotted Annetta readying another arrow from beyond the bushes.

"Run, Annetta!" Darius yelled getting the girl's attention.

Annetta looked up, her gaze locking with that of the boar. Fumbling, but doing her best to focus on the plan, she pulled the arrow back again, still glaring at him. Orion gave a roaring squeal and charged towards her.

"Dammit Annetta, get out of there!" Jason called after her, but the girl did not move, instead she let the arrow fly, hitting the pig straight in the eye, teleporting out of the way before the behemoth would collide its tusks with her.

Jason wasted no time in catching a breath of relief when he saw the boar howling in pain. Pulling back his own bowstring, he let another of the projectiles whistle through the air and hit it. The creature veered around in his direction, and charged for Jason.

"Uh." Jason panicked as he tried to think of what to do next.

"Get into one of the trees!" Annetta called from above, readying another arrow, her hand throbbing more and more. She let it fly, regardless of her improper form.

Her arrow missed the massive creature as Jason quickly picked a branch and teleported to the sturdiest looking one beside Annetta, nearly losing his balance when he made it there.

"We can't stay up here forever. We gotta get back down there." Annetta looked down at the raging animal, trying to figure out where she could teleport.

"Go back down? You nuts?" Jason shot her a look of concern, "Also are you insane? Waiting till the last moment like that to hit him in the eye."

"I don't need a lecture, I need a plan, okay? Now help me think of something," the girl growled in frustration.

"Uh…uh…right," Jason nodded as he tried to think, coming up with a blank.

Orion slammed his massive tusks into the tree moments later, splintering the lumber into a million pieces from the collision, wood flying in all directions as the tree began to fall.

Annetta and Jason quickly had their decision made for them. Splitting up, they teleported to two different trees, their previous stoop falling to the ground with a crash.

Darius raced out of the woods, and leaped onto the back of the creature, slashing with his powerful claws at the thick hide, trying to keep Orion's attention to himself. Orion squealed in pain and started bucking, trying to throw Darius off, causing him to land beside Annetta's tree on the ground.

"I'll distract it! Aim in between the shoulder blades where the nerves are," Darius instructed as he leaped down and began to run, faster and faster, driving the creature in a circle like a sheepdog.

Annetta pulled back her bow again and fired, the arrow missing its mark. She drew again without hesitation.

Before Jason knew it, he was on his last three arrows. Cursing to himself, he looked over at Annetta, also nearing the end of her ammunition.

"I'm almost out, now what?" he looked over at her.

"I don't know, arrows don't seem to do any damage to him at all. He's too strong," she yelled back over the squeals of the monstrous boar.

Darius was also beginning to tire from rounding up the creature. His arm and leg muscles were on fire as he continued to press onward, doing his best to avoid both the flying arrows and the sharp tusks of Orion at his heels. He swerved in and out among the trees, causing the boar to knock down a few in the process, making their circle that much larger. But he was running out of time, and was reaching the point where his body would become numb from exhaustion.

Jason let his last arrow fly, watching it land in the flank of the boar as it continued to rampage.

"That was it. What do we do now?" He turned to the girl who had already used up her own final arrow, and simply watched the events below.

"I don't know, but I think the fact that we are smaller than the Soarin does make a difference." She frowned and looked down at the dagger Lord Ironhorn had presented her with. "They didn't say there were any rules about only using arrows, right?"

"I don't think so. Why? What are you thinking?" he asked.

Darius finally lost his footing and tripped over a root, tumbling into the bushes and landing against one of the fallen tree trunks. Pain shot through his entire body as he struggled to catch his breath. Covering his face, Darius's body coiled up for the impact of tusks, but nothing happened. Instead, the howl of a creature that was not of the natural world echoed, and the snapping of jaws to hide could be heard. Darius opened his eyes and looked up to see Link wrestling with the boar, tearing at the skin upon its back, slashing with his sword-like claws and fangs.

Orion shook and shrieked, trying to get Link off, but the creature was suctioned to him with his claws, only ready to let go when he breathed his last breath.

Annetta and Jason were shocked to see who had come to the rescue of their friend, thinking Link was completely out of the hunt. They wasted no time teleporting down to the earth below, Annetta drawing her blade, and Jason calling forth Helbringer from its pendant.

"On three, we throw 'em!" she hollered to Jason as they ran. "One...two...Three!"

Link leaped off of the boar. Before the creature could see what was heading his way, both the mace and sword hit the creature, penetrating its thick skull. Orion gave one more death cry and collapsed to the ground.

Annetta and Jason watched as the beast stopped moving, blood beginning to stain the grass around it. Shaking off the initial adrenaline, they rushed over to Link and Darius.

"You guys okay?" Annetta asked.

"Been better," Darius replied faintly and pulled out the whistle he had been given to blow on.

Jason took the time to circle the boar, examining where each arrow had fallen, then carefully he grabbed the hilt of Helbringer and pulled it free, stumbling back from the force needed to take the weapon out.

"So. Where we gonna barbecue this one?" he asked with a grin.

"I don't think we have a spit big enough." Annetta raised an eyebrow as she looked back at the boar. She then turned to Link and nodded a thank you.

Before Darius could blow the whistle, Amelia, Doriden, Ephaziel and Alterin all landed around them and the corpse.

"Whoa, that was some mad hunting, dudes," Doriden congratulated them. "I haven't seen a show that good since Amelia and I had to participate in the Hunt."

"You mean never, brother. Even we had it easier than they did." Amelia glanced over at her brother with a chastising look and then turned back to them. "That was well done, as quick and swift as any Soarin."

"Thanks, I guess." Annetta scratched the back of her neck, feeling cornered by the large creatures. "So, did we pass?"

"I'll say, with flying colors." Doriden smiled wolfishly before noting Darius lying on the ground in panther form. "Uh, you hurt dude?"

"No, just exhausted," the panther breathed heavily.

Doriden looked in Ephaziel's direction. "Take him back with you to make sure he gets rest, and send for the retrieving party."

"Right away," the Soarin warrior nodded. Scooping up Darius as though he were a small kitten, he shot up into the air, disappearing among the clouds.

Annetta walked over to where Fearseeker protruded from the head of the boar, and gripped the handle, tugging to pull it free from the bone. It didn't budge, so she placed a foot on the side of the boar and pulled with all her might, not realizing how far the weapon had gone in.

"Your grandfather had the same idea when he was hunting Orion to prove his loyalty to the clan," Amelia said, watching the girl free the Minotaur dagger.

Annetta stopped, and only smiled lightly in acknowledgement, continuing cleaning the blade, and placed it back in its scabbard. Getting up, she looked over at Amelia, who eyed the strange instrument in the girl's hands with curiosity.

"A Minotaur Lord lent me this. I sort of want to keep it in the same condition I got it," she explained.

Amelia nodded back and looked to the skies, hearing the sound of multiple wings overhead, like the hoofbeats of a hundred horses. A dozen Soarin landed around them and began lining the boar with ropes, securing each section.

"Your task here is now done. Come, and let us got back to the Trafjan Cliffs," Amelia spoke, turning to the remaining trio.

ဢၢ

Brakkus and Puc waited at the main gates when Annetta and her friends burst through the clouds and landed on solid ground on the backs of Doriden, Amelia and Alterin.

"HAH! I knew ye'd do it! Not a doubt!" Brakkus greeted them with a wide grin as he scooped Annetta into his arms and pulled her into a bear hug.

As soon as he was on the ground, Link began to retreat to find a place to change back and into his clothing. He felt the pressure of judgmental eyes, and looked to see whom it was. His gaze was caught by Puc, who eyed him with the same stare he gave when he was trying to get someone's attention without directly calling him or her out.

"Your lone wolf attitude got in the way again, Lincerious," Puc spoke in an even tone. "Be sure it does not happen again, lest you wish a muzzle and chain to be secured on you at all times."

The creature sighed and nodded, turning away towards the shadows.

"Oh, Lincerious," the mage called after him yet again, the beast turning to face his back, "That was well done."

Link nodded as he turned away. He knew he had a long way to go before he could fully control his attitude in battle, but a complement from Puc was a good sign.

ဢၢ

Once the boar had been brought up and was prepared by various cooks in the village, everyone began gathering in the main longhouse. Tables were pushed together to form a rectangular shape, and long benches were provided as seating. The smells coming from the main pit were richly intoxicating, and the dishes of fruits and vegetables were already being brought out further reminded everyone that they were indeed hungry.

Entellion was already in his seat of office, Amelia and Doriden on either side of him. Annetta, Jason and Darius had been instructed to stand beside them with their bows in hand, as was customary for successful first time hunters. Link came to join them soon after the preparations began, having recovered from his transformation enough to be walking about without fear of stumbling.

"You feeling okay?" Annetta whispered to him.

He nodded. "Yeah, thanks."

Puc and Brakkus remained at the side entrance of the longhouse, observing everything. Well versed in Soarin culture, Puc knew his place as an outsider, and did his best to stay out of the way while the Soarin prepared, Brakkus following his lead. It was not until Entellion made eye contact with the mage that they made their move, coming forwards.

Entellion raised a hand to all those who had gathered in the hall, an immediate silence falling when he did. The elder rose in a firm but fluid style from his seat and outstretched an arm to Annetta and her friends.

"I give you those who left as cubs and return as wolves to us!" he called out, and the sound of howling and the banging of tables was the reply. Annetta cracked a small grin, but stopped when Entellion made another silencing gesture to the hall. "For those who know naught, I received most sad news today. Our good friend of old, Lord Orbeyus of the Axe, has moved on into the light of the Great Provider. But I also received news that he did not leave us alone, for he left behind new warriors to follow in his stead. They are those whom you see standing before you. Like Orbeyus before them, they have slain the mighty Orion in the Eternal Hunt. I turn now with all of you to them, to Annetta Severio, Jason Kinsman, Lincerious Heallaws, and Darius Silver; the slayers of Orion in this day, and those that will now lead the Four Forces. For those here who do not know, the Four Forces were the armies of collective races who stood as a shield against foes who would take the fortress known as the Eye to All Worlds, and use it as a key to enslaving different universes. Orbeyus created this army in order to prevent such a thing from happening. This army was composed of four elements corresponding to nature: water, stone, wind, and fire. In days past we were the wind, the unseen tempest. Rise with me now to bend knee in oath."

As soon as everyone rose, they fell to one knee. Entellion moved before the four of them and joined the others, his eyes cast down as he began and the others followed in a mantra like manner, "In the one who is severed we trust, our lives to you until we are dust. What is ours we give unto you to use. Our strength and wisdom, use as you choose."

Annetta felt goosebumps appear on her skin underneath the torn jean jacket as she stood there. No matter how many times she heard the words recited, there was something powerful about them that transcended what she in her short life understood. She looked over at her three friends. Today it was not just her that they were swearing an oath to but to all four of them, they were equal. It made her grateful that she was not alone but in the protection of her own little pack.

Entellion rose as did everyone else in the room, Brakkus and Puc among those who had just sworn the oath, blending in with the white furred creatures.

"With that, I open our mid-spring feast," the elder concluded. Through the doors, Soarin carrying various trays of meats emerged.

Entellion turned to the youth and nodded, giving permission for them to take a seat with Puc and Brakkus, who were already at the spots given to them. They bowed back and made their way over to them.

"Naturals ye be," Brakkus chuckled, beaming as they came closer. "How ye young hunters feeling?"

"Like we ought to have had more practice." Link sighed shaking his head, causing the Hurtz to chuckle a bit more.

"It was well played," Puc said, "and we are just that one step closer to reuniting the Four Forces, so long as no more lone warrior acts surface."

Link felt the sting of the mage's words, but he made quick eye contact with Puc to confirm he was simply being his snide self, and went back to taking his seat at the table.

Annetta sat down quietly beside Puc, the mage catching sight of the tattered jacket she now wore. Now that she had time to think, she felt rather upset that it was ruined, especially since it was a gift from her father. Her thoughts lingered on the events she had just gone through, and it was not until the mage placed a hand on her arm that she snapped out of it.

"It's just a jacket, nothing stitches won't fix. Better that than your head," he stated plainly, and turned back to his conversation with Brakkus, soon joined by Darius.

504

Annetta paused at the strangely warm words thrown from the usually distant elf, trying to figure them out, but was interrupted when the meat arrived in front of her.

"I'm going to need a lot of stitches before this is all done," she muttered in resignation as the feast begun.

๛๏๙

The return trip was slow, filled with nothing that stood out as noteworthy in Annetta's mind, who was drowsy from all of the food that was eaten at the feast. As well, on Brakkus's insistence, the cup of mead given to each of them to, in the words of the Hurtz, put some fire in their bellies. Annetta was beginning to agree with Puc that it was not a good idea when riding was to come after, as her head drooped in the saddle with want of sleep.

They'd had to stay longer, as the Eternal Hunt demanded that the bones of Orion be returned to the ground for the mighty boar to be reborn on the first light of the new day. Doriden and Amelia had gone down with them to show how the rite of burial was performed, ordering them along in the process, giving them first hand experience in the cultural practices of the Sky Wolves. When all was said and done, they saddled up the horses, and were off.

Reaching the gates of Q-16 after crossing the final portal, they all dismounted, groggy from the events.

"You may have the day off tomorrow. You've exerted yourselves as it is," Puc announced once they left Brakkus and Link in the stable to deal with the horses, still humming the tune the Soarin bard had played last before they departed.

"I'd still like to come down a bit later after school, if that's okay," Annetta said, surprising the mage. "There's something I need to work on."

Puc and Darius both wore a surprised look on their face when they heard what the girl said. She had always been the first to grin at the words free time.

"Are you well Annetta?" Puc asked.

"I'm fine Puc, seriously. Just doing all this stuff has made me kind of, you know, want to know more about what I can apply my powers to. Mostly, though, how to use psychic and melee fighting as one."

"Melee and psychic as one?" Puc leaned on his staff, intrigued by what the girl was saying.

"When we were in Morwick, I was able to channel my abilities into the sword," she explained. "I'm not sure how exactly I did it, but if I could learn how to do it proficiently, maybe it could be useful in the future. I mean, even during the Eternal Hunt, I channeled my ability into the sword to have that extra force in it against Orion."

Puc listened to the girl. "Practice is the only thing that can help you in that. Some sparring exercises should help you get a better feel for it."

"That's it?" the girl asked, catching herself yawn. She put a hand over her mouth.

"I think rest is what you need most now," Puc stated. "If you encounter anything with Jason on your way to the exit, you know what to do."

Annetta furrowed her brows, not used to Puc letting her go alone anywhere without either him or Brakkus in their tow. Nodding she turned to go with her friend.

Puc sighed heavily, still leaning upon his staff as he watched them fade into small shapes the further they went.

"Looks like someone is learning to let go," Darius said.

"Through the sword of thy sire shall be born battles ancient desire," Puc recited the words from memory. "It is not Severbane the words speak of. The words address the psychic sword, the abilities passed down from father to daughter. The more she uses it, the more she comes into awareness of what they can do when combined with the discipline of weaponry, the more useful it can become in the trials that lay ahead. It is not in causing battles that this desire comes out of, but out of the simple need for self preservation and the preservation of loved ones."

"You got all of that out of two little lines?" Darius looked over at his mentor. "Is it not a little overkill to think so much about a little phrase from some old book?"

"Words spoken by a prophet and recorded well before either my time or yours, young friend. Words not everyone has the gift to understand," he said, then straightened his back and began walking away, calling after his apprentice. "Now, don't you have a spell to be preparing somewhere?"

Darius groaned and rolled his eyes, knowing full well Puc had seen his face, but he did not care. He knew his master simply meant to keep him busy in fear of boredom and the imagination setting in.

&0C&

The next day, Darius had already had his newest task assigned to him and trudged towards the stables with a list of herbs he needed to acquire for the upcoming trip to the Yasur Plains. Since there would be time left over if he got there early, he had decided to visit the Academy and catch up with some of his old classmates. Pacing the plain steel corridors, he came upon Link.

"You seem to be in a hurry," the Gaian greeted him as they came to a stop before running into one another, "Puc found you something else to take care of?"

"He's always got something for me to do," Darius huffed.

Link looked at the young mage in training in question. In his short time in the Lab, he had never spoken to Darius alone. He took the opportunity to see the haggard look on Darius's face, that seemed more overworked than his own, and was accentuated by the dark cloak that was draped over him. Link shifted a few paces back, noting he was still invading Darius's space.

"At least you are occupied." The Gaian attempted to make the conversation go further.

"Yeah, I guess you're right." Darius's shoulders relaxed, no longer feeling the need to be on edge. "I mean, I don't mind it, and I still find time to do what I want, like go to some of the parties people throw at school, but sometimes I just feel like a drone."

"To be honest, you kind of are," Link replied. "You're always off doing the bidding of the amazing Puc Thanestorm."

"I guess, if you put it that way," Darius muttered. "Still, I can't imagine any other life. Puc has given me everything I know."

"You've never thought of being a soldier or anything?" Link asked.

"I didn't have much of a choice. I was an orphan raised at the Academy, surrounded by other mages, so I guess for me, becoming a mage was the obvious answer to what I should do. Then I met Puc, and, well, here I am. What about you?"

"I wanted to help protect people," Link said, stretching his arms. "I've always had that drive in me. I can't explain why, but it's just always been there."

"You sound like Annetta when you say that," the elf said, then impersonated the girl. "I must stand up for those weaker than myself!"

Link laughed a bit, the imitation was eerily correct. "Well, we can't all be mages," he said. "Unknown makes many people with different talents."

"It would get pretty boring if we were all the same." Darius nodded. "Not to mention, I can only handle one Puc."

Chapter 47

Matthias examined his face to see the last of the self-inflicted scars healed. It would take time, however, to see if his plan had worked, and the boy would find a way to get them into the Lab. He would soon be free of the threat of Amarok coming back to claim his old place at Mislantus's side, and he would be able to breathe easy again. He checked his face once more to make sure he had not missed anything and then turned away from the mirror to see Sarina.

The girl sat in her room upon her bed flipping through report sheets with photos of Annetta and Jason. She kept flipping back and forth, reading the words on the pages over and over, particularly stopping at the photograph of Jason. Matthias watched in silence from the doorframe, until he saw fit to interrupt.

"It's a hard job, going after a target. But you must never forget whose side you are on."

Sarina bolted up as soon as she heard his voice and turned around, still startled.

"Uh? I was just reading over, you know, in case we missed anything important," she stammered.

Matthias studied the girl intently as he came into the room, no longer acting in stealth, allowing each footstep to be heard on the wooden floor as he sat on the corner of her bed. "I remember my own first mission, where I needed to get close to the target. She was a princess of a planet, and a person so noble, it was hard for me to justify her death. I had to spend time with her, get to know her, and earn her trust. I began to like her, but I knew that I needed to do what was asked of me in order to secure my place. In the end I took her life, and the moment it happened, it was like something inside me fell away, like a new door was opened in my mind. I realized after that I was able to simply shut off the emotions I felt. I have done so ever since. I now only allow the sound of death to pound in my ears as my claws rip the life from my victims."

Sarina flinched, hearing the story for the first time. Though the assassin had shared many of his accounts with her, he had never told her of his first kill.

His eyes turned back to her. "We have come this far Sarina. Do not begin to doubt what must be done. They stand between you and your father.

You cannot see them as living beings, but as pawns to be knocked out of the way for the king. Do not make me doubt having brought you along."

"I'm fine, I promise." She nodded her head. "I was only seeing if there was anything else we could use, that's all."

Her gaze locked with his, doing her best to remain strong in front of the assassin. When he was satisfied he got up and walked out of the room. Sarina sighed and closed the door behind him, not wanting to be snuck up on again.

She was beginning to lose her resolve for what they were doing. It was not because she was disloyal to her father, but because she had finally found a friend who did not judge her. She had to lie about whom she was, but she got to be herself around him. Her eyes turned to the photograph of Jason she had lying on her bed, his green eyes watching her. Her friend, someone she wanted to tell everything to, but could not, because her father's name had yet again trapped her. Worst of all, he desired Jason dead. Crumpling up the paper in frustration, she tossed it into the garbage. It missed, and partially unfolded, a distorted image glaring back at her. Could she ever be free? When her father ruled all the worlds, would she then be able to have friends, even love? Or would her father continue onward like a black hole?

Sarina paced around the room, burying her hands in her thick hair as she looked out the window into the world beyond it, a world that did not know the threat that was coming.

She dismissed the thought as quickly as it came to her. She had not chosen to be the daughter of a warlord. It was simply the circumstance she was born into, and if she could, she would have changed it in a heartbeat. Sarina glanced once more at the crumpled photograph on the ground, and turned away. She would need to do as Matthias had told her. She would need to forget he was there, that he was a pawn, and that it was all part of a game to make way for the king. And the king was near.

೫೦೧೩

Jason ran through the woods with the photograph in one hand and a folded swiss army knife in the other as he searched for the spot that matched. The day off from Puc was a blessing. Coming to his usual spot, he climbed onto the boulder and began to study the image. He was so close he could almost see the tree he was looking for. Holding up the picture before him, he began to scan, turning slightly every few moments to make sure he missed nothing. Finally the boy stopped, having found what he was looking for.

Jason examined the photo before sliding off of the rock and moving closer to the ancient tree. Unlocking the knife, he began to scrape at the moss-covered bark along a particularly deep groove, when he felt his knife hit something metallic. Putting the knife on the ground once most of the dirt was cleared away, Jason began clawing away at the remaining moss with his own fingers like a dog in search of a bone. Once he was satisfied with what he had uncovered, he drew the card key from his pocket, a moment of anxiety coming over the boy. He knew the risk, but he also knew if he did not do it, Sarina would continue to be hunted.

"Here goes nothing," he breathed quietly, and slid the card down the groove as quickly as he could. Nothing happened. The reaction in Annetta's apartment was always instant. Jason sighed, dropping his shoulders in defeat.

He turned around and began to walk away, pausing when he remembered he had left his knife, and turned back to go get it. Coming back, all color left his face as he saw that the tree had shifted, It did not look like the teleporter in Annetta's apartment, made of dark metals. Instead, it blended in with the surrounding, looking to be made of rock and trees. Jason stepped onto the pad to make sure everything was there, a smile spreading on his face. He had done it on his own, without anyone's help.

"Now comes the big question, does it work?" he muttered to himself, looking down at the card key in his hand.

It took the boy a moment to orient himself to where everything was on the camouflaged structure. He pressed the "1" button on the keyboard, and prayed he would not end up in a wall somewhere in the Lab, or split into a million pieces. Closing his eyes, Jason waited for something to happen. And waited and waited. He opened his eyes to see what was going on, when the sensation of swimming in intense waves took over, and darkness shrouded his vision. Though he knew the feeling well from all his trips before, somehow this time it was more intense. Jason felt himself choking on the masses of water all around him, and then it stopped.

The first thing he felt was the familiar steel floor beneath him. Opening his eyes, Jason looked up to see the twin behemoth doors smiling down at him. Getting up, he staggered back, and grinned at the sight. He was close.

Opening the gates as quietly as he could, he looked around and shut them, making sure he was indeed at the main entrance.

He now faced a second problem, not ending up in Annetta's room and having to explain what he was doing there. He looked around where the teleporter to the surface was located. Running his card key through it the slot, it appeared before him. Taking the time to focus, Jason scanned the information on the number pad, noticing the arrow keys going right and left. He watched the location on the screen flipping between three options, 'Forest', 'Mobile 01' and 'Mobile 02'.

Taking a deep breath and selecting 'Forest,' he closed his eyes. When the feeling passed, he opened them once more to the sound of the birds and wind in the trees. Hope in his quest restored, he deactivated the teleporter and raced home, forgetting the knife once more.

₭ℂ⃫

The sword danced in Annetta's hand as she swung it, slashing at the defending blade of the Hurtz. It had been a while since the girl had time to spar with him. There was a sort of tranquility she enjoyed when pitted against someone in the arena in Q-16. Though she played with a sharpened blade, she felt safe, as the fight was in her own control. Stripped down to her t-shirt from the battle-worn jean jacket that lay at the side of the arena as a spectator, she circled the giant, never allowing her eyes to leave her opponent, the first rule ever taught to her.

An opening being left on her part, Brakkus took the initiative, the girl dodging the attack by rolling out of the way, her shield before her in a defensive stance, awaiting the next blow as she came to her feet. As soon as the shield was struck, she made her move again.

Brakkus took each blow the girl offered him, his own massive twin bladed sword working quickly to parry each movement, not being given enough time to fight back. The moment another opening presented itself, though, he struck the shield, causing the girl to be knocked over like a turtle on her back. He went for the metaphorical kill to finish the duel, intending to position his blade at her throat in order to end the fight, but the blade was knocked back, flying from his hands and landing on the floor some feet back.

Annetta wasted no time after the forcefield she had envisioned had knocked away Brakkus's sword, and launched herself at the Hurtz's neck, trying to wrestle him to the ground.

"I win!" she declared with a laugh, holding onto the giant.

"Oi, that ya did. I yield," Brakkus chuckled. Grabbing hold of the young girl, he placed her down on the ground before him.

Puc watched from the side with Link, the younger warrior awaiting his turn to lock swords with the Hurtz and continue his training. The elven mage examined what had occurred in his mind, before getting up and striding over to the edge of the arena.

"Might I have this next fight?" he asked, looking over at the girl.

"I...uh..." Annetta shifted uneasily on her footing. Puc had never taken an interest in her weapon training before. "Sure."

Brakkus looked at the elf, somewhat surprised, and retreated from the arena to stand beside Link, still seated on the bench.

Annetta's eyes focused from the rush of joy to the elf standing before her, his stature nowhere near as imposing as the one of the Hurtz, though his grip on his staff was firm, and the look in his eyes was one of war. The girl shifted into her defensive stance, her feet apart, the shield before her like a wall with her sword arm tucked in beside her body, waiting.

Puc smirked and threw his staff to Brakkus, who caught it with ease. He reached into his robe, producing a sword from the long folds. The blade wasn't silver like a metal's natural coloring, but blue. It was nowhere near as broad as Brakkus's and it retained a grace about it unlike the heavier weapons the girl was used to seeing the Hurtz use. The cross-guard curved upwards towards the blade, ending in spikes with flames engraved on them, while the wire-bound grip turned into a pommel that looked much like a clawed hand grasping at a crystal orb.

"This is Tempest," the mage said. "It is a weapon I rarely draw, for when it is so, it is the last thing an opponent ever sees. Let's see you prove that wrong, Severio."

Without so much as a warning he came at her, the blade slamming into the shield with such force that Annetta thought her arm would come out of its socket. The girl pushed the shield forward as best as she could, her arm going numb in the process as the elf slammed down again and again until she finally could not feel her arm at all. Casting the shield aside, Annetta gripped the sword in both hands as Puc's blade relentlessly pursued her own without mercy. She could not catch a break if this continued, or have any chance of winning.

Taking a quick glance at the floor, Annetta noted she was being driven straight into the wall, and that there would be nowhere else to run after that. She needed to think fast. Regaining a little of her composure, she focused her energy on her blade, feeling her will flow into the weapon. The next strike seemed to slow its pace tenfold as Annetta took the last possible step back. Using the entire momentum of her body, she swung forward, blades colliding, focusing all her thought into the swing. Puc staggered backwards, losing his balance temporarily, giving the girl the perfect opportunity to teleport out of the way and onto the other side of the arena. Picking up her shield, she wasted no time getting back into a fighting stance.

"You're holding back, Annetta. I do not appreciate that," Puc snarled as he drove the sword toward her yet again with the same power as before.

Annetta felt her entire being shake with the continuous assaults, and had little time to react when the slim blade curved under the edge of the shield, slashing her wrist so deep she dropped it, curling back her bleeding hand.

"I thought ya said no blood!" Brakkus began to protest, not liking where the fight was going.

"Silence, I am teaching a lesson here," the mage growled, looking at the confused girl before continuing his course of action.

Annetta had no time to react between each blow, feeling herself grow more tired by the second, unable to focus with the stinging wrist she now cradled close to herself. She worked her feet back and forth, the routine never the same one as she tried to maintain her ground, parrying and slashing when she had an opening, but never even landing close to the fast moving elf. His style was unlike the one Annetta was used to fighting, and it was sorely showing.

"Stop contemplating, and fight," he ordered again, this time landing a gash across her shoulder, then jabbing the girl with the hilt of his sword he knocked her to the ground.

The blade fell from her hands with a clash, and before Annetta could begin to think to grab it, Puc had already kicked it clearly from her reach, pointing his own sword at her throat, the signal for submission.

"Yield, you are done for." he spat.

Annetta stared up into the pale eyes of the mage, feeling the heat of his words burn at her more than the cuts she had rightfully earned. How could she ever hope to live up to the expectations of her grandfather, or even her own father? She was hopeless, but she was not broken yet.

Something inhuman seemed to take possession of Annetta's body as she felt psychic energy course through her body, a force so strong that it sent Puc flying across the room, knocking him flat on his back. Annetta called her sword to her hands, and with demonic speed she projected herself towards the still recovering elf, stepping onto his hand, grasping for his own weapon, and commanding the blade so it slammed into the ground, not to be withdrawn until she saw fit. She aimed her weapon towards her teacher, still in a frenzy, Puc's eyes wide open.

"I yield mistress Severio, withdraw your sword," Puc said in the same level tone, as Annetta came to and withdrew the sword, sheathing it immediately.

"What in blazes were ye tryin' to do?" Brakkus rushed up with Link to the elf as the fallen fighter propped himself up on his staff the moment it was in his hands.

"To prove a point that anyone at any time can become the enemy," Puc said as he straightened his robes and moved over to where the sword was planted neatly in the ground. "When one trains, they must do so with all of their heart, regardless of their opponent. One cannot improve through training if they hold back. The enemy on the battlefield most certainly will not."

The elf grasped the hilt of his sword, but was unable to move the blade from where it stood rooted to the ground, no matter how much he pulled at it.

"Miss Severio, if you would so kindly let go of my sword."

80CR

Jason did not stop, his legs pounding the pavement, until he reached the townhouse complex he knew Sarina and Matthias lived in, almost twenty minutes later. Coming to a rest, he began catching his breath, but realized when he looked at the houses that they all seemed the same to him. He had never paid particular attention to which one Sarina went into, knowing he would never get an invitation in with everything that was going on. It seemed a huge mistake on his part.

"Great, now what do I do?" he gritted his teeth as he tried to come up with a solution, his eyes catching a bright red minivan which sat in the driveway of one of the houses.

His thoughts turned to Matthias's black car. It was a vehicle Jason could hardly forget, being a teenage boy who could not stop to look at a sports car when it passed by him. He began looking around for any sign of it and then realized the houses all had garages, some not showing any cars at all.

"Wonderful," he muttered to himself, lowering his head in resignation as he recomposed himself for the next idea.

The more he thought, the more he doubted his course of action. He was going against Puc, against Annetta, and all the others that awaited him in the Lab. Below the surface beat his own desire, to help Sarina. Like Annetta, he shared a love of fantasy. When he came to learn of his heritage, he longed to embrace the wondrous roles that came with the world that had unfolded before him. He wanted a quest of his own and everything that had happened between him and Sarina pointed to just that. Yes, the more Jason Kinsman thought about it, he admitted to himself that this was his own heroic quest, without Annetta or Darius or anyone else in the spotlight.

He looked once more at the identical rows of townhouses with their neat reddish bricks and white mortar fillings. He could not tell one lawn from another with their front gardens not yet in bloom from spring showers. There was one, however, which stood out to him above the others, a house with an object under a blue tarp sitting in the driveway. From the bulky shape he could make out what looked to be a car, and taking a closer look, he noted it was the one Matthias had driven.

Running up to the front porch, he rapped on the door madly, composing himself so that he would be prepared for any sort of answer.

A middle-aged man opened the door and looked down at Jason, who turned incredibly pale and began stumbling over his words.

"If you're selling chocolates, we're not interested thank you," the man responded, and began shutting the door on a stuttering and protesting Jason who was trying with lack of words to get answers.

"Jason?" a familiar voice came from behind.

Jason turned around to see Matthias with his arm in a sling, a leather jacket over his shoulders, and mail in his good hand as he stood on the front porch of the house beside the one Jason had gone to. The boy sighed in relief and trotted over to the man without even taking a second glance at the other house.

"What are you doing here? I told Sarina specifically not to..." Matthias knotted his eyebrows as he began.

"It wasn't Sarina who invited me here today. I came of my own will," he interjected quickly. Taking a deep breath, he continued, "I have a place, a place where you'll both be safe."

"Safe?" Matthias laughed in his face. "Let me guess, your basement, boy?"

Matthias's laughter stopped when Jason let go of the chain and allowed the card key dangled before him. The man's eyes were drawn immediately to the words on the card.

"You wanna live in peace? You come with me."

80Q3

Sarina woke up to hearing voices downstairs. Stirring under her covers, she turned to the other side, covering her head to muffle out the noise, wondering why Matthias was listening to the television so loud. Coming more to, she realized whom the second voice belonged to and jumped out of bed, rushing to get dressed.

Coming down the stairs, she saw Matthias and Jason hurrying to pack supplies in large duffle bags, sputtering out instructions and short phrases as they worked. The sight baffled the young girl so much that she sat down on the stairs and watched them work before she announced her presence with a small cough.

"Sarina, pack your essentials. We're leaving," Matthias instructed nonchalantly. "I put a duffle bag beside your room."

"What's going on?" she asked.

"I'm taking you guys to a safe place," Jason said, helping stuff the last of the clothing and other items Matthias had given him to pack. "It's a place I inherited from my father. Trust me, no one will be able to find you there."

"Uh, okay." She nodded, still playing the part of the confused younger sister.

She went upstairs and began to pack the bag Matthias had slumped at her door. As she packed, she began to doubt whether this was the way things were supposed to go, or if she should run downstairs and tell Jason it was all a trap, to run, to hide and never look for her again, or her father and his assassins would cut him down because their plan on infiltrating Q-16 had failed. But she saw her own life being taken in the equation, and was not sure if she was capable of such sacrifice on her own part. Dying scared her.

Finishing up with what she thought was essential, she grabbed the bag and hurried downstairs to see Matthias and Jason standing at the door with the two other bags. She allowed the façade of the role she had to play take over, and turned to Jason.

"Where to now?" she asked.

"Since you guys haven't been there before, we can't teleport, and I don't know where you could leave your car there," Jason thought out loud as he tried to formulate more of a plan in his mind.

"Then we walk." Matthias shouldered one bag with his good hand. "We are wasting time standing around when the most obvious solution is before us."

Jason opened his mouth to say something back, but closed it, only nodding to the older psychic warrior. Grabbing the other bag, he headed for the door, pausing before it to look back at Matthias.

"You both wait outside for me," Matthias stated. "I must make sure everything is turned off. A fire is not a good way to make ourselves invisible to the enemy."

Matthias watched as both Jason and Sarina walked out. The assassin moved to his communication center, opened it up, and typed in the code needed to contact Mislantus. The impatient cat face was visible upon the screen seconds later, glaring back.

"I hope you bring news worthy of interrupting my time, Matthias," the voice hissed.

"Do I ever report if there is not something worth reporting?" Matthias bowed to the screen, "I am moving into Q-16. We leave with Sarina now, and will contact you once we are inside."

"At last, news I wish to hear." The face grinned. "And I hope contact will not take as long this time as the last."

"No, my lord. But I do have one request of you." Matthias kept his face low as he spoke.

"And what would that be, assassin?"

"I want no sign of Amarok following me to my kill." Matthias raised his eyes to meet that of the tyrant. "He has confronted me, and I know he is here, my lord. I understand your frustration with the duration of this mission, but I need you to trust my judgement. His presence will cause conflict with that which I have tried to build here."

518

There was silence between the both of them, an exchange of glances as each tried to test one another's resolve. The servant was testing the master and the master getting a read on the defiance of the servant and his intentions. Mislantus's cat slit eyes widened back to their regular size as he closed them, making his final analysis.

"You play on dangerous ground, Matthias. I have always liked that about you. Done, I will make sure Amarok does not bother you on this venture," the tyrant looked back at the assassin, who bowed his head in return.

"You will not be disappointed, my lord. I will ensure that with all my being," Matthias answered, looking back down.

"Good, then carry on." The screen went blank.

Matthias closed up the cabinet quickly and joined Sarina and Jason outside. Closing the door, they began the journey to forest behind Jason's house. Matthias slung the bag over his shoulder as they crossed the first set of lights, and began walking down the sidewalk. His eyes wandered all over in case any eyes pursued him, but he saw nothing. He exhaled after awhile, with his mind finally somewhat at ease. Little did the assassin know, something in the shadows was grinning back in malice.

⁝

Annetta and Puc watched from the bench as the duel between Link and Brakkus came to a sharp end with Link sprawled out on the ground, Brakkus's blade at his throat, his own sword meters away.

"Do ya yield, lad?" The Hurtz watched from beyond the pummel, the blade not even beginning to shake from the effort of keeping it straight as long as he had.

"Do I have a choice?" the youth managed to say between labored breaths, his eyes fixated on the razor sharp tip that could easily rid him of his eye, or worse.

"Ya do," Brakkus said, withdrawing his blade and placing it back in the scabbard. "Ya can keep fighting, though I wouldn't recommend it."

He turned to Puc. "What say you, elf? We keep these whipper snappers fighting, or we give 'em a breather?"

"I believe that is enough thrashing for now," Puc stated, rising from his seat and grabbing his staff. "Perhaps later. I grow tried of sitting here and watching barbaric swordplay, when there is more important work to be done."

"You mean getting prepared to meet with the Ogaien?" Annetta asked, following him.

"The Ogaien are unlike the three races we have met so far," he said, leaving the training grounds, "and their landscape is not as friendly to the flesh as the others have been. There is more spellcasting involved than before if we want to survive walking the Yasur Plains,"

"How bad can it be?" Annetta raised an eyebrow.

"Do the words burned alive bring anything to mind, Miss Severio?" The mage looked down at the girl whose curious expression almost instantly faded. "I thought so."

Brakkus and Link followed the pair out of the training room, the two still engaged in conversation about how Link could have beaten Brakkus if he had wanted to. The Hurtz did not believe a word the boy was saying, giving him multiple theories of his own about what he could do to prevent it.

"Fact is, lad, ya can't beat me, not yet at least. It'll be long years before ya can." Brakkus grinned in victory, finishing off the conversation.

His expression changed however as his ears twitched, turning in various directions as though he were trying to pick something up. It was a sight that made Annetta want to laugh, since he resembled a startled rabbit. Puc turned around to regard the now silent Hurtz.

"What is it?" he asked.

"J.K. has come down, but…" Brakkus's ears continued to twitch and pan from side to side. "I think someone else be with him."

"What?" Puc's eyes widened. "How can you be sure?"

"I can't," Brakkus told him. "They're too far away to make anything out."

Puc furrowed his eyebrows and made for the main gates without another word, his robes flowing behind him like a general's cape on a battlefield. Annetta, Link, and Brakkus trailed behind him, hoping what Brakkus had said was not true. Perhaps the Hurtz was just becoming hard of hearing as he got older, or Jason was talking to himself again.

ജരൂ

Sarina felt the sensation of being crushed by waves stop as she found herself on a steel floor, completely dry. Her senses returned to her body, and she rose to look around. When she turned around she saw the enormous doors displaying the words 'Q-16' across them. The size of them was overwhelming.

"Where are we?" she asked, knowing yet not knowing.

"We're under the ocean," Jason explained. "This is a base my father and his friend owned, called Q-16. My friend Annetta and I inherited it from them. This is where I go after school. It has a foolproof place to train using psychic powers, along with a lot of other cool stuff."

Matthias was completely taken aback by the structure. Though he had spent most of his life on Mislantus's fortress, Valdhar, the feeling of being completely cut off from the world under the ocean was far different than the realization that one was in space. Still, he did not allow it to trouble him openly, and he turned his attention to Jason, who used his psychic abilities to open the massive gate before them with little effort at all. The assassin had to admit the boy was a quick learner, and it was a shame that their time together was coming to an end. He could easily picture himself training the youngster as his own apprentice.

The trio walked in without without saying anything else. The sound of footsteps and a thudding object on the metallic floor quickly overpowered their own. From the distance came the girl Sarina knew as Annetta, the boy known as Link, and two others she did not recognize.

Matthias, on the other hand, knew whom the two were, having read the full report multiple times. There was no mistaking Puc Thanestorm, the right hand of Orbeyus of the Axe, with his staff and robes of office. There was also no way the sight of Brakkus the Hurtz could go unnoticed by any mortal who wished to see the light of another day.

"J.K." Annetta began greeting him. But her eyes fell upon that of Matthias and Sarina, causing her to fall silent.

"Who are these people, Jason?" Puc, the only one rational enough to keep speaking, addressed the young boy.

"They are my friends Sarina and Matthias Repronom, and they need help," he explained. "I didn't know where else to go. They're being hunted."

"Wait," Brakkus cut him off, "I'm sorry, lad, but ya brought people down here who ain't supposed to know about this place, and ya didn't think to consult us about it?" Brakkus summarized while Puc eyed the two new arrivals, trying to keep his own anger internal.

"It's not what you think. Just listen to me!" Jason cut in.

"Then what is it Jason?" Puc sneered, "for betrayal likes to wear many guises, but at the end of the day it's the same foul excrement one produces when one cannot keep their mouth shut." Puc walked closer to the boy, and cornered him against the wall. "Do you have any idea what you have done at all? Then again, I should have guessed. Like father like son."

"Look this seems to have been a bad idea," Matthias said, a startled look on his face. "Maybe it's best if we leave." He grabbed his bag and began to turn around.

"No, stay." Jason reached out his hand to him and then turned back to Puc, "They're my guests. Last I checked, I got the keys to the Lab, not you."

"I was the advisor of Lord Orbeyus of the Axe, you little whelp." Puc flashed his teeth in anger.

Jason felt the assault of words crash down upon him.

'*Jason, can you hear me?*' Matthias's voice echoed in Jason's head, '*Do not let him frighten you. As you vowed to help us, so I vow to help you, and be your shield.*'

'*But you don't know him. Puc isn't someone you want to mess with,*' Jason continued.

'*He is not psychic, and so does not understand our sacred brotherhood,*' Matthias rebutted. '*Who he once was is not of any concern to us, for it does not apply to him in the present. What is important is that we are brothers. Bound by a power few will ever understand.*'

"Correction. You were the advisor of Orbeyus. And he isn't around anymore," Jason lashed back challengingly.

"J.K., what's gotten into you?" Annetta stepped forward.

"I'm trying to do the right thing, Annetta. They need our help. Can't you understand that?" Jason motioned to Sarina and Matthias. "I thought you out of everyone would. I guess you just want to be the hero like always. If it's not your quest, it's not important. A warlord, who wants to kill them because they're from another planet, is pursuing them. It's no different than someone being picked on in the schoolyard."

Annetta felt a jolt go through her body when Jason accused her of trying to be the hero. Link wanted to throw himself at the boy and tell him to take it back, but a look from Brakkus put him in his place.

Puc exhaled roughly, drawing attention back to himself. "Heir or not, you are not of age yet, leaving me as the guardian in charge. Risk your own safety if you will, Jason Kinsman, but I will not allow you to risk the safety of those around you." The mage then turned his gaze to Matthias and Sarina. "You two will come with me, and we will discuss the matter of your stay here, and I will be the one to judge whether or not what you say is truth."

522

"As you will have it, master mage." Matthias bowed to Puc, who was unable to get a read on the man's address, and if it had been mockery or sincere. With a whirl of his robes, he began making his way towards his quarters with Sarina and Matthias behind him, with Brakkus at the back of the group as guard.

Annetta, Link, and Jason watched as the crowd began to split up at a fast pace. Jason took off, going after Puc and the others, while Link and Annetta remained behind before taking off after the boy as well. The girl could not find any words inside her until they were already in the common room.

"Jason. I never wanted to be the hero." Annetta paused in the midst of the couches, and looked at her friend. "And I thought we both were."

Jason stopped in his tracks, watching the group before them become smaller and smaller. He turned to look at the girl he called his friend, blinded by anger. How could she, out of all people, not understand why he was doing this? He had hoped with all of his heart that she would have stood by his side in his decision to bring Matthias and Sarina down to the Lab, but he could see that his friendship with her did not matter, and that the Gaian warrior who now stood beside her had replaced him.

"Don't kid yourself, Anne," he spat. "You always take the glory as the heir of Orbeyus. I'm just the son of a guy who was there."

The boy and girl locked eyes; Annetta's filled with sorrow, while Jason's were lined with anger. She looked away, taking a step back to stand beside Link, deep in thought about what Jason had said about the two new arrivals.

"Then I don't want any of it, if it means we have to fight," she said quietly.

"I don't buy it." Link spoke up after a moment. "If they are being pursued, it seems too lucky that they happened to come across you. And who's the warlord pursuing them? They could have fled to Gaia. We've a very strict policy when it comes to dealing with people like that. Earth isn't exactly..."

He paused where he was, for the group had not gotten so far away that Matthias could not hear the conversation being held. The psychic warrior spun on his heel and looked back at the trio.

"It was out of the way of any who would try to infiltrate the safe houses of a higher planet," Matthias spoke in the same silky and eloquent tone as before.

"No offense to Earth," he added.

Surprised to hear Matthias, Annetta, Link, and Jason turned to the group before them, who had stopped.

"No one gets past Gaian defenses," snorted Link. "Either you're lying or you're just not as well educated about the universe as you ought to be."

"Then perhaps you don't know your people as well as you think you do," Matthias snarled.

Link got ready to throw himself at the young man, when the immense paw of the Hurtz came crashing down on his shoulder like a brick and slamming into place.

"And who is it that pursues you?" Puc looked at the man, his anger not completely gone, merely faded into the back of his mind.

"He's called Mislantus the Threat, and has hunted us here," Matthias explained. "We have been moving from safehouse to safehouse, but we cannot stay in one place too long. It was by chance that Sarina met Jason when the Leonemas attacked her."

Puc showed no reaction to the familiar name. Instead, his eyes landed on Jason once more in accusation, but then turned back to the young man. "Regardless of your tale, we are not very trusting of strangers, and until you prove to be friend, we will treat you as an enemy here. That is our way."

"Then allow me to be of some service. I am, like Jason, a psychic warrior, and one that can use psychic fire," Matthias explained, "If allowed, I can teach him to harness it."

He turned to Annetta, her blue eyes now locked with him in question of his intentions. It made the assassin almost want to kill her then and there.

"I can teach the girl, of course, with your permission," he added, flashing a smile at her.

All eyes found themselves upon Puc, who stood in silence, gripping his staff as though he would break the wooden object from sheer force. He was betrayed, and despite his thick hide, the words from the boy had left a gash across his pride. His icy stare bore into the youth he had done so much for. It seemed he had been cast aside like a rag that was too old to be considered a shirt any longer. Remembering who he was, his grip loosened on the staff as his thin lips tightened to bring feeling back into his face. His eyes fell upon Annetta, her small fists curled up into balls as she looked back at him in hope of an answer. Collecting his thoughts, the mage turned to the new arrivals.

"You are the enemy in my eyes, and so you will be treated as such until I trust you, meaning you will not come near my charges. You will now come with me, and answer all questions asked." He glared at Matthias, and turned back to head in the direction he had been facing before. "I still leave as planned for the Yasur Plains at the end of this week. Those who wish to come with me and see the reunion of the Four Forces through with Annetta, feel free to do so. I grow tired of telling you all what to do. My place was, as marked by a certain individual, by Orbeyus's side, and not yours."

Matthias nodded his head. Feeling the vicious glare of the Hurtz, he continued on his way following the mage with Sarina, whose eyes went back to Jason in a silent plea. The boy, seeing the look in her eyes, only needed to glance once to know his course of action, and began following the group, hoping he could be of use in pleading their case.

Annetta watched as the shape of the mage grew smaller and smaller in the distance, Link by her side. She wanted to run after him and scream that Jason was wrong for what he had said. She even felt she ought to give Jason a good thrashing for the way he had acted towards Puc, but knew it would do no good. She looked over at Jason in resignation, much like Puc had moments ago. She too felt a pain inside her, but it was a different kind. She felt she had lost a friend.

Chapter 48

Matthias and Sarina followed the mage to his quarters without a word, trailed by the Hurtz, whose palm rested constantly on the hilt of his sword. Behind all of them, in the distance, shadowed Jason. His cause, however, was blocked when the Hurtz stood before the door to the room.

"And where do ya think yer going, laddie?" Brakkus asked.

"In." Jason answered without hesitation, as he looked around the giant to peer inside. "I need to-"

"Ye've done enough today." Brakkus shifted his weight on his legs to prevent Jason from seeing anything. "Honestly, I don't think Puc wants to see ya right now and, ya got all the reasons as to why."

"But Matthias and Sarina-."

Brakkus interjected by shifting his ears, causing the earrings to jingle as he did so. "They won't be harmed, ye have my word. Now, if ye have any common sense at all left in yer head, I would say get out of the mage's sight."

The two of them continued to stare one another down, until Jason saw there was no point in even attempting to persuade the normally gentle giant. He sighed, and turned around in the direction of the exit. Watching the youth leave, Brakkus exhaled, and turned around to enter the room, where Puc was already seated behind the massive wooden desk, with Sarina and Matthias in the seats before him.

"Has he left?" the elf asked.

"Aye, he has." Brakkus responded, re-sheathing his sword.

"Good, then we can begin this." Puc's eyes fell to the two newcomers who sat before him with neutral expressions on their faces. "As I said before, I am not very trusting of any new arrivals. In fact, it almost seems too convenient for you to be pursued by Mislantus the Threat, when we are in the midst of preparations to fight against him, as well as your being warriors with psychic abilities. If I had less of a skeptical mind in such situations, I would say you are both spies, and you should be both put to death."

Matthias's muscles coiled as he got ready to strike at Puc while Sarina's arm, wrapped around his to stop him.

A wiry smile crept onto the mage's face as he watched the spectacle before him unfold with amusement. "I do, however, use common sense and therefore will not jump to such conclusions. I will give you fair time to prove your story's truth. There are, however, some conditions which you will need to abide by."

Reaching into a drawer in his desk, Puc produced two wide silver cuffs, plain in design, with a single rectangular black screen on each of them.

"As I said, until you prove otherwise, you are the enemy, and will be required to wear these in order to neutralize any psychic abilities you have. I will not risk having two untrustworthy psychics running around here unchecked."

"So, we are to be your slaves, then?" Matthias picked up one of the cuffs and examined it.

"No, you are guests that are not allowed into the private spirits stash, simple as that," Puc retorted. "The second condition is that you will both be under a tracking spell, meaning I will be able to know where both of you are at all times, as well as who you are with. This is not only for the protection of those who are already here, but for your own protection. This is not a safe place to be, due to some of the creatures still lurking within the deepest parts of the Lab."

"Creatures?" Sarina looked at the mage in a panic.

"A story for another day and another time." Puc stopped the question in its tracks. "The story that is most relevant now is your own, and so I strongly suggest that you begin spinning the tale from beginning to end."

၈၁၈

When all was said and done, night fell upon Earth, leaving Puc and Brakkus as the only ones awake, with Annetta and Jason gone home, Link had retired for the night, and Darius was off at Severio Castle for errands Puc had sent him on. Brakkus had made sure the two new arrivals were locked in their rooms. Still, neither of them could sleep when those they could not trust paced the halls of Q-16 unwanted, even in a confined area and with all their magic and technology hindering any possible talents that lay within them. They sat by candlelight, just like before Annetta and Jason had arrived. Puc had cast off the heavy mage robes for the evening, and sat backwards on a wooden chair in a simple linen shirt and pants, his eyes watching the candle, his head resting on his folded arms across the headrest of the seat he occupied. Brakkus sat on the ground cradling his sword, eyes also focused upon the flame, but with a less intent look than that of his companion. The Hurtz finally broke his gaze from the orange light, and shifted his eyes to that of his friend, swimming so deep in thought he seemed to be dead aside from the slow steady breathing as his shoulders rose and fell.

"Ya can't still be thinking of what the boy said, are ya?" He broke the silence, causing the mage to snap out of his daydream as well.

The elf's straightened from his resting position, the black hair framing his face so it appeared to be almost floating on its own in the darkness.

"He disobeyed the most sacred commandment, Brakkus, never let anyone know of the Lab. Not under any circumstances. Perhaps the battle in Morwick did more damage to his skull than I anticipated originally." Puc gritted his teeth, spewing out the last of his sentences.

"I think the damage be elsewhere, if I can be bold enough to say so," Brakkus stated. "I've seen that look he had in his eyes. I've seen it in Orbeyus's eyes. I've seen it in Arieus and Arcanthur's. I saw it once in my own reflection, and I remember seeing it in you, mage."

"What are you blabbering about Hurtz?" Puc snorted.

"I mean the look of love." Brakkus decoded his own words, seeing he had to be straightforward tonight with his companion. Usually it was the other way around with them. "I think J.K. has some ties to the, girl and I don't think he quite realizes it yet himself."

"Brakkus, you're spewing nonsense," Puc growled, rising from the chair, and walking out of the glow of the flames. "He's too young for that sort of thing."

"Oh? And you and what's her face weren't?" Brakkus teased, only to have a book thrown at him from the dark, which he caught without effort. "I think ye simply forgot what it was like to be young, and have a pretty little thing look at ye in a way no other friend ever did. To look at ye as something much more. If it had a feminine form, ye were a slave to its will, and that was that. All logic flew out the window. I remember when ya met-"

"I do not wish to dwell on such things, Hurtz," Puc's voice rang from the dark. "And as I said before, he made his point clear about my place. He can stay here under lock and key with those two learning to use psychic fire until he obliterates himself in the process. It seems the only sane one left is Annetta."

"Aye, but ya need both of 'em, not just one," Brakkus reminded him. "And I don't think Arcanthur is in any sound state to disown his firstborn so that his next in line can become heir."

528

"And what am I to say to a fool who brings wolves in sheep's clothing to his home, and offers them his own hand?" Puc came back out of the shadows.

"Ya let him get bit, but make sure he still uses his left hand to take out the garbage." Brakkus grinned.

Puc couldn't help but smile at the frank comment of his friend. Sooner or later he would need to compromise in order to get Jason to go with them. His threats to leave him behind had sadly been empty. In order for the oath of the Four Forces to be valid, both Annetta and Jason needed to be there, the right hand and the heir combine. That was the catch of freeing Severbane from its resting place. The only way that could ever change was if the heirs were disowned by their fathers. This would leave Annetta and Jason's siblings as the ones to become the heirs themselves. It was a form of magic that went far back in history. Though few realized how powerful the words of an elder were, it was there. The problem, of course, was that Arcanthur would never be convinced to do something of the sort to Jason. Puc knew this full well from his last encounter with the mad Kinsman.

"My pride does not allow me to do such a thing so freely," he stated out loud after the thought had passed through his head.

"Well, I don't expect the boy to come and apologize when cupid's got him through the heart with an arrow," Brakkus reasoned. "Ya need to be the responsible one, elf and ya gotta-,"

"I grow tired of being the responsible one." Puc sat back down in the chair, resting his arms on the headrest. "He stated his mind. Whether it is sound or not is another question entirely. Now, a more important question, Hurtz, who takes the first watch?"

"Well, I could arm wrestle ya for the privilege, but would there really be any point to that?" Brakkus grinned at him dangerously.

Puc's pale eyes took only one glance at the huge arms of his companion to note he would be no match.

"Too right, and happy watching." The tired elf got up once more and lay down in the cot, staff and sword within arms reach, allowing Morpheus's spell to cast its charm.

෨෬

The next day, no one seemed to come up to bother Jason at school. Even after he came down to the Lab, no one came to greet him. It was as though the boy was being ignored by the world.

He adored it. No Puc telling him he needed to train, no schedules of any kind. He could go as he pleased and best of all, Sarina and Matthias waited for him down in the Lab in the lake biosphere once he got there. They explained to him that Puc had allowed them to stay under the condition that they both wear the power binding cuffs and had the tracking spells placed on them, which, they reassured Jason, were a small price to pay.

He had never stopped to consider how the biosphere worked, but he always found it bizarre how it seemed to be eternal summer whenever he went down there. The sky was always a bright blue with while rolling clouds, and the blades of grass below were a radiant green. Amidst all of this, Sarina sat on a log, looking out into the river that divided the biosphere.

"Was this all made by someone?" she asked as Jason came closer.

"Annetta's grandfather. Though if you ask me how. I have no clue," he said hopping onto the log beside her.

"Her grandfather made this?" she asked, looking around. "It's beautiful."

"And real, too." Jason picked up a stone and skipped it across the water.

Sarina gave a faint smile, watching the rock disappear beneath the rumbling stream, then lost herself in her own thoughts, thoughts that had begun to invade her head the more she got to know Jason. Why did her father want to badly to conquer everything and to kill someone like Jason? Why had her father never sought to build anything in the ruins he created, and left smoldering ash in its stead? These and more flooded her head until a tear of confusion gathered in her eye, and rolled down her cheek.

"You okay, Sarina?" Jason asked.

"Yes, I'm just," she sniffled, "I'm very happy to be here, and to have a friend like you."

Jason went a little red, and he turned away, not looking at the girl in his vulnerable state. He did not understand these feelings he had for her, except that they were different than the kind he had for Annetta and his other friends. With Annetta, he did not really feel like he needed to protect her. She did that for him most of the time, like a big sister would. With Sarina, he felt he could play that role of the protector instead.

"I'm very happy to be your friend, too," he whispered quietly.

ℂℂ

Annetta came down to the Lab the moment she finished her dinner. Her mood was foul from Jason's mouthing off to Puc, and the way he had treated her. Despite it only having been words, she could not help but replay the conversation, and his accusations. Her fists were curled almost all day as though she were biting down on nails. Even Darius had given up trying to convince her to relax, after she told him to shove it because he had not been there to see it. The only one who had not gotten on her nerves was Link, who'd kept silent, following her wherever she went.

It was no surprise to her when she finally came down that he was waiting for her in the common room, seated in one of the armchairs, his sword propped up against the armrest.

"Hey," he said quietly in greeting.

"Hey," she answered back, shoving her hands into her jacket pockets before flopping down on one of the couches beside him. "Where's Puc and Brakkus?"

"I think Brakkus is in the stables checking on the new horses. Puc is with Darius at Severio Castle working on something," he answered. "I'm not sure. I went to grab some food from my room and then came here to wait for you."

"Oh." Annetta finally began to snap out of her hate-filled shell a little, having had a warm meal when she came home, "You didn't have to, you know. I mean, I'm sure you have training and stuff you want to do, especially now that you're stuck at a desk for six hours during the day."

"Nah, I'm okay. Besides, Brakkus bosses me around plenty enough I don't need to train all the time." Link flexed his arm. "And it's paying off, too."

"Well, I'm glad," Annetta chuckled. "Still though, you didn't have to wait for me."

"I wanted to wait, though," he said in a serious tone, looking her in the eye. "I mean, Brakkus always states the importance of not wandering around alone in case anything is still lurking around. Besides, I know what J.K. did wasn't easy on you. I don't think you should be alone right now."

Annetta frowned and slumped her shoulders forward. She leaned into a sitting position on the couch, looking down at her shoes.

"It still kinda hurts, you know, to have someone like that stab you in the back." She looked over at him. "I mean, I didn't ask to play the part that was given to me, it's just who I am. I was that weird girl who read fantasy and loved medieval movies and got into fights at school because I didn't like it when people got picked on. I don't want this anymore though, not if it means hurting my best friend in the process."

Link watched as she threw her hands up each time she listed all of the things about herself, and could not help but smile, finding her frustration comical the way she presented it. Of course, his smile vanished when she looked back at him each time.

"I wouldn't say you've lost a friend yet," he reasoned. "When people get into fights they don't hold back, they use everything they have to hurt the other person. It's like if you held back on your punches when dealing with Finn."

Annetta only looked over and glared at him for bringing it up.

"Okay, I meant before you knew about your powers," he protested.

"I guess you're right," she sighed. "Still, it doesn't make me wanna thrash him any less. It still hurts. I feel like I've lost a friend, and I can't help it."

Link nodded, hearing her out. He had no idea what else he could say.

"I know I'm not Jason, and we haven't known each other for long, but I was sent here to help you in whatever way you need," he said, the girl looking over at him as he spoke, his palms sweating under his gauntlets. "If it's a friend you need, then I'm here for you."

Annetta could not help but grin at the sincere offer.

"Thanks, but do me one favor, okay?" she said.

"Uh, sure, what is it?" he asked leaning closer as though she were about to convey onto him the secrets of the universe. He was severely surprised when she grabbed him by the ear and tugged.

"Be yourself, and none of this servant crap." She smiled, letting him go. "You're either my friend, or that dude who follows me around, you gotta decide."

Link rubbed his sore ear as he watched Annetta get up from her seat.

"I'll race ya to Brakkus," she said, taking off.

ഇരുക

Annetta thudded to the floor and was forced to look back up at the boot of the Hurtz warrior. She groaned and picked up the sword, then went back into a fighter stance.

"I think ye've had enough, lass." Brakkus chuckled, sheathing his blade. "I don't want ya turning blue and black, so ye'll have to explain to Puc what happened."

"Yeah, but we won't have that option when it comes down to facing Mislantus," she said as she was pulled up by the massive paw of her trainer.

"Ye got a point, but I'm standing by my own." He grinned and then turned his gaze to Link. "And I think yer getting bored just sitting here watching me smack the light outta her."

"I guess a little," he replied, observing with one knee brought up to his chest, resting his chin on it.

"You seem really happy, despite what happened last night with J.K.," Annetta said to Brakkus as she straightened out her jacket and shirt.

"Those two can't be any trouble even if they tried," Brakkus answered, "Not after Puc dealt with 'em. He's got a tracking spell on 'em both, and no matter what, he can sense where they be with it all the time. He was thinking of putting it on all of us."

"What for?" Annetta raised an eyebrow. "We have our C.T.S. watches with us."

"Extra precaution I guess," Brakkus mused, "Point being, they ain't gonna be no trouble, because they can't leave the Lab if they tried. Not even with J.K.'s card key. He found our old prisoner cuffs we used back in the good old days. Neutralizes any powers anyone might have."

"Sounds like it'll be fun running around with hostile hostages," Annetta thought out loud. "I guess I'm gonna go to the lake for now. If you want you can come find me later. No, I will not wander far. I learned that the last time we wandered off. Maybe I'll run into Jason and we can talk a bit. Maybe sort this all out."

"Atta lass, you show 'em who's the more mature one." Brakkus nodded.

Annetta gave a small sheepish smile in return and sheathed her sword. She walked off in the direction of the lake biosphere at a slow and weary pace, having given it her all in the ring with the Hurtz warrior.

To her disappointment, she did not see Jason, or the girl named Sarina, but she found another unexpected visitor by the river. It was the one who had introduced himself as a psychic warrior, Matthias Repronom.

The young man wore a dark green tight sleeveless top and a pair of jeans as he gazed out into the open. She noted the singular silver cuff around his right wrist that had replaced the thick gauntlets he had worn the day before. Annetta stood at a distance, not sure if she should bother him. Making up her mind, she began to turn back.

"You can come closer if you like. I don't bite, last I checked." Matthias rolled his head slightly to the side to look at the girl.

"Oh, sorry, I didn't want to bother you or anything," she replied, turning back around and walking towards him.

"You can't, really. I have nothing planned," he answered, going back to his original position.

Matthias watched as the girl sat down on the log beside him. How he longed to stick his blades into her and be done with it. The innocent smile on her face made his insides churn in anger. He wanted to distance himself from it all. He was so close, he could taste victory, but the interrogation by the elf the night before, and the slapping on of the cuff that now bound his powers proved to be a new thorn in his side. How he hated Orbeyus for using both magic and technology. Still, he had no choice now but to wait for an opening and play the part he had assigned to himself, big brother Matt. Still, if he was here with her, he would get to know his enemy more. Crushing her would be all the more satisfying in the end.

"So, how did you come to know of all this?" he asked nonchalantly.

"Hm? What do you mean?" Annetta inquired.

"This place. I'm assuming not everyone knows about it on Earth, otherwise I would have seen more people around here," he stated.

"Oh, well, my grandfather gave it to me. Well, not exactly. You see, earlier this year, these two birds came and they said they were angels sent by him to give Jason and I the keys to this place. They said it was our destiny."

"And you just up, went and believed what they said? That sounds a little rash to me." Matthias flexed his muscular arms as he stretched. "I wouldn't just believe what some stupid fowl tells me."

"They weren't stupid. And they weren't ordinary birds, either." Annerta furrowed her eyebrows and shot Matthias an icy stare. "They were special. You would know if you saw them."

"Whatever. Call me skeptical, but I've seen too many things in my life to trust anything right away. It would take something far more convincing for me to accept that legacy than two special birds giving a proclamation about what my birthright is. It's just all very suspicious. What if they struck me dead if I said yes?" the psychic warrior reasoned.

534

Annetta took in all of these questions like a child would take a whipping, and sat quietly in her thoughts. She was really starting to dislike him, and she barely knew him. What angered her most was that his points made sense. Her answer came to her a few moments after.

"I did it because I believed," she said. "I did it because when you spend your whole life reading, watching, playing games involving fantastic possibilities, and then all of a sudden you are given a chance to be part of a world greater than the grim reality before you, something makes you want to believe that chance before you wasn't something that was placed there to cause harm. That chance was given to you to believe in it. Otherwise, if chances like that were passed up all the time, I don't think anyone would do anything extraordinary in their life and the world, no, the whole universe, would be a really boring place. So if that makes me dumb, reckless, then whatever, go ahead and laugh, but I stand by what I did. I did it because I believed in taking a chance."

Matthias was about to ask her how old she was, and then stopped himself, the look in her blue eyes saying it all to him. Belief was something he had never allowed himself to have. He had stepped into a world he did not understand at all, and it did not even take a portal for him to do so. All it took was a girl from Earth. He smiled at the challenge before him, and also at the recognition of an old soul.

"You'll do something great someday Severio," he replied, finally.

ଚଠଘ

After walking Sarina back to her room, Jason walked through the halls, going over everything they had spoken of in his head. Their conversation had strayed to the events of the night before, and the fact that Sarina and Matthias now were basically prisoners of Puc and the Lab. He would have to speak with the mage about it when he saw him, and it was his hope that the elf was in the common room. Mentally sharpening his tongue, he almost slammed into an unsuspecting Annetta.

"Watch it," he growled at her and continued forward.

"Is this the way it's going to be, J.K.?" Her voice rang out from behind him.

The boy turned around, the girl's blue eyes watching his own green ones from across the steel corridor, where the light of the halogen lamps did not extend. An angered look manifested his face, as he got ready to retreat.

"Look, I just want to talk okay?" She approached non-threateningly. "I can't speak for everyone else who was there, but I can speak for myself, and I can say that I'm sorry. If I have seemed like I was trying to play the hero, it was because I didn't want to see anyone else hurt, and that's the only reason. It's just an instinct thing for me. It always has been, you know that."

Jason's face softened a little. His memory took him back to school, to all he had been through with her before they knew about the Lab. Not much had changed, really. She was, at heart, still the girl that always wanted to help. He'd forgotten she didn't think of herself as a hero, but as someone who prevented others from being hurt. Focusing on the present, he saw the same girl in a beat up jean jacket.

"I know you can be mad at me and stuff still," she continued after a pause, "but if it's all the same to you, I wouldn't mind if we all could try to be friends together. I just wanted to throw that out there as an option. Like I said, I understand. You can still be mad and-,"

"No, I was wrong." He shook his head, interrupting her. "And to be honest, I should have at least told you about it. We were put in this mess together, and I promised to follow you to the bitter end. You've been my best friend for years, and I treated you like crap. It's not fair to you and I'm sorry. You don't deserve someone like me."

Annetta walked closer to Jason, coming out of the darkened area, her brown hair messed up from training, wind, and the stress of daytime. There was a calm look to her face, like a burden had been taken off of her shoulders.

"Well, news flash, you're stuck with me, and you're still my best friend, screw up or not," she said. "But best friends talk to one another, okay? I know I'm a stuck up bulldozer sometimes, but give me a chance at least."

"I'll try to keep that in mind," he said with a wry smile.

୫୦୧

Annetta and Jason made their way back to see Matthias sitting within the training grounds, seemingly to be meditating within the center of the rectangular battle arena. He was completely still until the two of them passed the Calenite diamond walls, and his eyes opened.

"Can I help you?" He stood up, towering over both of them, his messy brown hair and goatee adding to his imposing presence.

They stood rooted to the spot. Annetta turned to look at Jason. They had both agreed on coming to find Matthias, who had made a promise to teach them to harness psychic fire.

"I think you know why both of us are here," Annetta stated defiantly.

"Ah, business then," Matthias said pleasantly, not missing a beat. "The question is are you prepared to handle the blows dealt out to you?"

"Last I checked, you couldn't deal any blows, so there won't be a problem," Annetta replied, casting a glance at the large metallic brace encircling Matthias' arm. "So teach. What's first?"

Matthias gritted his teeth silently, wanting to slap the girl across the face for her tone. Seeing as he was on her turf, he relaxed his shoulders and allowed the mask to take over.

"Indeed, I promised I would teach you both to use psychic fire, though I warn you now that such a feat is not something achieved in one day. In fact, I wouldn't be surprised if you do not learn to use it for many years to come," he began explaining, folding his arms across his chest as he did so. "There is one key thing you need to know about psychic fire. It is an energy produced by hate, and because of that, is a force of destruction which you need to be able to aim at whatever it is you plan on attacking, otherwise you can kill yourself and those around you. The reason it takes so long for anyone to learn to use psychic fire is not because it is hard to control. Rather, it takes a person a long time to understand what it is that they truly hate. Sometimes, it boils down to the simplest things, hating an abusive parent, hating a ruling power, I've even heard once someone was able to unlock it because they admitted to themselves they hated a certain type of food. Many times people back down in the quest to attain the power, because they fear discovering the person they truly are. To know what it is you hate means you also know what you love and cherish most. There is nothing more essential and also nothing more powerful in all the multiverse."

"That doesn't sound that hard," Jason blurted out. "I know what I hate already."

"Oh? Do you? Care to share?" Matthias said, bitter tones in his voice.

"Sure thing," Jason replied, missing the hints. "I hate being told what to do all the time. I like to be free to make my own decisions."

"Okay, go on then, tough guy," the older psychic mused, pointing to the arena. "Let's see what you got."

Jason marched to the center. He realized seconds later in his own pride that he had no idea what needed to be done.

"Uh, what now?" He looked at Matthias questioningly.

The psychic scoffed, shaking his head as he looked down at his shoes, then back at the boy. "Focus your energy into your hands as though you were trying to create a sphere within them using only psychic energy. At the same time, however, you must evoke your feelings of malice for that which you hate most."

Jason nodded, spreading his feet apart so he could get good footing on the concrete floor. He took his arms and raised them before his chest, the same way Matthias had done at their first face to face encounter, his fingers out as though he were cupping an invisible ball. He closed his eyes, focusing. He had to admit, Puc's training had made the task much easier, otherwise it would have taken twice as long for him to understand the basics. Closing his eyes, he let himself go, recalling all the times his mother, teachers, Puc, and others told him he had to follow rules. He imagined being chained to a rock, unable to move forward. He pictured his friends in trouble, the Leonemas being the easiest enemy to remember, charging for them, with nothing he could do. The helplessness welling up inside of him as the creature got closer with each moment, its half visible claws ready to launch themselves into the throats of those he held dear.

From the other side, Annetta and Matthias watched as Jason's face contorted in such rage and anguish that it was hard to look at. Annetta was ready to turn away when she saw small blue sparks begin to surround Jason's arms and hands. She was unable to look away in anticipation, hoping that maybe her friend had proven the overly cocky Matthias wrong. All too soon, his knees buckled under him, the sparks disappearing as the boy collapsed, only stopped by his hands hitting the floor before him.

Matthias still looked down at him, unimpressed. Annetta, however, was wide-eyed, never having seen psychic fire.

"Did he do it?" she asked.

"No. Sparks, but no fire. You've still a long way to go," Matthias said, then turned to the girl. "And you, Severio, do you know what you hate so much in this world that you would set it ablaze?"

Jason's eyes fell to Annetta, joining Matthias's, the two of them awaiting an answer.

538

Annetta felt like a deer caught in headlights. She had never given much thought to what she hated most. There were many things she hated to many different degrees.

"I don't know," she finally responded, feeling the back of her neck heat up. Noting the triumphant expression on Matthias's face only made her add, "But you're definitely on that list."

Matthias's smirk deepened. He hoped once they got rid of the cuff on his wrist he could have an honest fight with the girl. It was rare to find an opponent with the flare she was proving to have.

"Good start," he finally said, "but I'm afraid it will take more than words for you to realize what it is you truly hate. For now, you will meditate on the subject, and Jason will continue once feeling returns to his limbs."

Jason nodded and reverted to the same position he was in before and closed his eyes. Annetta seated herself on the bench outside of the arena and crossed her legs. She had been taught that hate was wrong, yet here, in order to unlock this ability that could help her, she needed to do just that to channel it. She continued to sit quietly with her philosophical thoughts.

Chapter 49

The next day seemed brighter than the two previous ones, though Jason still did not speak with Darius at school, or with Puc. The younger elf, having heard of the backstabbing Jason had committed, found it inexcusable. Because of this, he spent most of his day with other students during breaks; the other three at the school, only catching glimpses of his black hair among the crowd. The remaining trio spent their time walled up in conversations about their past, and of what they would do once the day was done, the final bell ringing just in time to signal the end of the school day and the beginning of life outside of it.

They walked together among the slowly awakening world, green buds penetrating from dark branches and adding a shade that seemed almost alien to the gloomy earth.

"Should we wait for Darius?" Annetta asked as they exited the back gate.

"No point," Jason said as he shouldered his bag. "He's probably already down at the Lab, or at least left the school. And I think I'm gonna take the entrance by my house, and meet you guys down there later. I wanna swing by and see how my brother is doing, since I haven't been spending much time with him lately."

"I hear ya. See you later, then." Annetta waved him off as she watched Jason turn around the corner. She sighed and turned to Link, who leaned against the red brick wall of a parking lot, watching her. "You ready?"

"Yeah, let's get going." He straightened his posture and put on his bag that rested by the wall.

"I wonder what Brakkus is going to have us do. Or if Puc is going to fight us again," she spoke out loud as they passed through the residential area that was a shortcut between the school and Annetta's building.

"I wish they would have us fight one another, or switch up techniques more often than they do," he responded. "I feel like I'm fighting too much against the same style all the time. I mean, look how easily Puc took you off guard just because he uses different moves than Brakkus."

"Not really." Annetta wrinkled her nose as she thought back to the fight. "He was quicker. I didn't expect that, but that was an error on my part. A sword fight is a sword fight, no matter how many fancy moves someone throws in. At least, I see it that way."

"I guess so," Link muttered, "I just sometimes feel like we haven't been in a fight against a real opponent, and we're not prepared."

"What? What do you mean real opponent?" She raised an eyebrow as they paused to cross the street. "There was the whole thing in Aldamoor, all the fights we got into in Morwick, and-"

"That's not what I mean," Link said with a sigh. "I'm talking about fighting another conscious being, someone who means it when they point a sword at our neck. I don't think you realize it's a lot different to kill a rational being than a beast."

"Yarmir was sentient," Annetta said after a moment, still not understanding Link. "He could talk, and he was thinking about what he was doing."

"Yeah, but when you looked at Yarmir, did you think he was a monster, or did you think he was someone like you?"

Annetta paused as they exited the shortcut through the maze of townhouses. She was having a hard time trying to comprehend what Link was getting at. She watched as the youth walked ahead of her, his backpack draped over one shoulder, while his hair, tied in its messy ponytail, hung on the other.

"I guess he was a monster. But still, an enemy is an enemy," Annetta responded, only to have Link come up right in her face without warning, the scar on his eye blurring with the rest of his features, the prominent gray-blue eyes the only thing in focus.

"This isn't one of your video games I've seen you play with your brother on your free time." he glared at her. "Imagine your face this close to someone else as you plunge your sword and then twist so hard you see the life flee from their eyes, that one spark that sets us apart from other forms of life. That is a lesson no one can teach you, but has to be learned."

Link pulled away and crossed the street, leaving Annetta behind on the other side of the road as she allowed his bipolar behavior to swim around in her head before she followed him.

"And let me guess. Mighty Lincerious Heallaws actually had to kill someone face to face?" She came up behind him, her eyebrows furrowing at the boy.

Link stopped dead in his tracks and looked over his shoulder. "It's a feeling I never want another person to experience, because nothing will ever prepare you for it."

Annetta's expression softened. She felt as if a heavy stone had slipped from her hands and fallen to the floor. From the corner of his face, she could see he was not taking any of what he had said lightly.

"I'm sorry, I didn't-" She tried to form a sentence, but nothing came out.

Link exhaled, his bangs falling in his face from having hung his head low. He looked at the copper-haired girl and the world surrounding her, a world grounded on blissful ignorance to the things that happened all around it, and the worlds beyond. At that moment, he longed for nothing more than to remain confined to the Lab, and never have to enter the world he saw before him again. His vision moved from the urban setting to the girl standing ahead of him, a horrified look on her face.

"Its fine, I just don't want to talk about it, if you don't mind," he responded.

Annetta nodded as the two of them stood facing one another. Adjusting her bag on her shoulders, she decided to change the subject for both their sakes.

"I wonder what mom made for dinner today," she said as the two of them trotted off, the building towering above the trees in front of them.

∞Ω

After what Annetta had deemed to be the best glazed chicken with wild rice she'd ever had, she and Link bid her parents a goodbye for the evening as they retreated into the depths of the Lab. Picking up their swords from the racks they always left them on, they made their way to the common room to find it completely abandoned.

"This is weird." Annetta looked around, suspicious of the mage's absence. "Puc's usually here by now and yelling at us about being late. And where's J.K.? And Sarina and Matt?"

"I wouldn't be surprised if J.K. and those other two are already off in the training room," Link said as he chose his direction and began walking in it. "As for Puc and Brakkus, maybe they had something they needed to take care of that couldn't wait until we got here. Come on, let's do some exploring. There's this one cool place I found I wanted to show you. It's another biosphere I came across. I'm not too sure where it's supposed to be on Earth. I've never seen anything like it myself. It's ridiculously warm."

"What about Brakkus and Puc?" she asked as she began to follow.

542

"They can get through to us using the C.T.S.'s and besides, it's not too far out of the way," Link assured her as they kept going. "I don't remember it being, at least."

"Should I worry about the last part of your sentence?" Annetta sighed.

They walked down the monotonous corridors for what seemed like over ten minutes, until Link stopped, the passage fanning out into a bigger area. There was no lighting coming from the large halogen bulbs that hung overhead.

"There was light here the last time I came." Link frowned walking forward.

"Maybe it's motion sensitive?" Annetta suggested as she followed, waving her arms around to see if the lights would turn on, but nothing happened.

"No, they were on the last time. I'm pretty sure of it." Link pursed his lips as he looked around, confused.

Annetta was one step ahead of the young Gaian warrior. As she was accustomed to living on Earth, she looked to the nearest wall, noticed a switch, and flipped it, flooding the massive room with light. Closing her eyes, she waited until the inverted colors disappeared from before her lids, and opened them to get a good look at her surroundings. It looked to be another common room area, but much larger. There were many object covered in blue tarps, some resembling furniture, others simply polygon shapes. In the middle stood a large raised metallic table with a black glass top on it. It reminded her of something that would be found on board a spaceship in a movie.

"What is this place?" she asked, running her hand along the smooth tabletop. "Looks like a command center or something."

"You're asking me?" Link snorted, "I have less of a clue than you do but it's a good guess. Come on, it's just beyond this part."

"Right," Annetta nodded and went after him. She took a few more steps, but then she heard something from behind, a low gurgling rumble.

At first, Annetta thought it was one of the overhead lights dying out, and they would need to come back to change it. As the noise continued however, a knotted feeling in her gut grew stronger then finally escalated, turning to goosebumps, when the noise became a full out reptilian snarl.

"Link," she could barely speak, paralyzed, feeling the warm breath behind her getting ever warmer.

One step ahead, Link had begun to draw his sword and spun around. Her fear was justified when he stood face to face with a very angry giant reptile, its horned face hovering above Annetta's with a set of jaws filled with sword-sized teeth, ready to swallow her whole.

"Run, Annetta!" he whipped out the blade from its scabbard as Annetta teleported behind him just in time to see the creature clamp its maw where her head had been.

Removing her own sword from its sheath, Annetta stood beside Link, wide eyed. Though she had seen many strange creatures over the last few months, never had she dared to dream she would stand so close to something as vicious looking as that.

The reptile eyed the two hungrily, its dark green and brown scaly skin betraying even the slightest movement of muscle on its snout as it snarled, curling back its lips to reveal the teeth yet again. It came forward, a machine of doom, without any hesitation in the steps of its two clawed feet, wings flexed onward with hooks pointed ahead like lances ready to spear either one of them.

"Is that what I think it is?" Annetta asked, trying to get her mind working.

"Wyvern. And it's really mad," Link answered, his sword raised and his second hand feeling the absence of a shield.

The wyvern wasted no time, and lunged at them full force, wings spread like a great net on either side to obscure the possibility of escape.

Annetta and Link dodged to opposite sides, the beast stopping itself from sliding on the steel floor and veering around charged for them. Annetta took the initiative, focusing on the nearest sofa, and willed it to fly at the wyvern, hitting it square in the head. The massive creature did not stop, simply shaking its impenetrable skull and howled. Out of ideas and in the line of fire, Annetta rolled out of the way as the thing came at them, crashing into Link in the process. Jolting from the shock of contact, she did not miss a beat. Seeing the behemoth about to descend, she hurled two more tarp-covered pieces of furniture, causing it to temporarily collapse. Using the opportunity, the two of them hid behind a large rectangular object.

"How the hell do we kill that?" she asked.

"You think I know? We don't exactly have wyverns running free on Gaia," the youth retorted, his words silenced by the sound of the wyvern.

"Well, we need to figure something out," she snapped.

Link bit his lip as he tried to quickly come up with a plan. The wyvern having recovered, however, heard Annetta's voice and swooped up, crushing the tarp covered object, nearly impaling them with its massive claws. Link managed to push Annetta out of the way, causing them both to crash into the wall.

"Running isn't going to work," he said. Picking up his sword, he turned towards the beast, whose red eyes gleamed back at him like two balls of flame.

Annetta wanted to follow his lead, but as she got up, something began to sting at her arm, and her sleeve became very wet. She looked down to see her whole upper limb covered in blood, a massive gash quickly turning her whole jacket crimson. The pain made her drop the sword, and forced her to pick it up with her good arm.

"Not good," she muttered to herself, and looked over at Link, who was already circling the creature like a boxer in the ring.

The nightmarish beast circled Link, its crimson eyes fixated on the boy, reptilian lips curled back in an eternal snarl as it followed the steps of his dance exactly, tail lashing behind it like a sword of its own.

Link watched his opponent with labored thinking, not knowing what to expect. He deflected the blows of the barbed tail each time they came at him with a sure hand, but his problem remained that he needed to land a hit on his opponent, and fast.

He noted from the corner of his eye the bleeding gash on Annetta's arm, a setback that could escalate, judging by how she was covered in blood. He needed to get her to Puc, but he was unable to do so with the wyvern. He had thought of telling Annetta to teleporting to safety, but now that was not an option. Her strength was being drained at a fast enough pace from loss of blood. She would most likely faint before she got anywhere, leaving her more vulnerable than she already was. Gripping the sword tighter, he lowered his gaze for the chest of the creature. Driven by desperation, he charged blindly for his target a haggard war cry erupting from his lungs.

Annetta watched as sword clashed with scaled armor, her willpower overcoming the sensation of weakness in her body. She too charged for the beast. Launching herself from the table and teleporting mid leap to confuse the creature, she landed on its back and wrapped her bleeding arm around the creature. She began stabbing with all her might at the tough armor with her good arm, hoping to get through the hide and do some damage before she was too weak to hold on any longer.

The wyvern began to buck and shake, trying to get Annetta off, in the process paying no attention to Link, who repositioned his sword, and plunged upwards into the belly of the beast, finally lodging a hit. But in doing so, he brought the jaws of death back onto himself, and noticed the girl fly off into another direction, hitting some of the sofas that were blown into the wall.

"Annetta!" Link cried out. Turning back, he continued to assault the wyvern slashing mindlessly. Logic had left the warrior, for if Annetta had died, then his sworn duty to help the girl that had been given to him by the Unknown was forfeit.

His lack of reason inadvertently cost him his balance, and the young warrior soon found himself on the ground from one whip of the great creature's tail, its jaws leaning in upon him, ready to claim what it had came for. Link gritted his teeth, holding up his sword before him.

An inhuman cry rang out of the darkness, and a blurry shape launched itself at the wyvern, bringing the creature to the floor with a crash. Link only had seconds to see that it was Brakkus, the massive two-handed sword before him aimed at the creature. The wyvern recovered, a shriek erupting from its reptilian face as it bared its teeth and charged for the Hurtz.

"Get Annetta out of here, lad!" he shouted as he ran for the wyvern, an unstoppable force of fury.

His blade quickly collided with the creature's wing, crippling the beast as it sliced through bone with minimum effort. Grabbing hold of one of its horns he hoisted himself onto its back, gaining the upper hand.

Link ran to where Annetta lay while Brakkus battled the wyvern. He found the girl unconscious on an overturned couch, the majority of her jacket now stained red. He checked her pulse and pulled out a handkerchief, wrapping it around the wound, hoping it would slow the bleeding at least a little. His next course of action, contacting Puc, was interrupted when he saw the Hurtz crash to the floor only a few feet from them, the leather armor on his chest pierced from what looked like teeth marks.

Brakkus rose from his landing point, giving another beastly shout as he darted at the creature the second time, his sword lost to him in the fall. He was now armed only with his own hands, landing an uppercut on the wyvern's horned face, the sound of bones cracking echoing as the creature fell back. Brakkus wasted no time in retrieving his weapon. Coming at the fallen creature, he drove it into the same spot Link had landed his original blow, urging his blade upward with all his strength, slicing through the ribcage.

Nearing the heart, hearing the death cries of the wyvern, Brakkus felt all his senses become overpowered by the thundering sound of a heartbeat, the same sound emitted by the war drums he had been around for so many years. They were peaceful, and the marker of a battle won, this however was not to last.

A sharp pain erupted from the Hurtz's stomach, the metallic taste of blood surging in his mouth as he looked down to see the barbed end of the wyvern's tail sticking out of the front of his armor. He looked into the creature's vicious eyes, a smile of conquest visible.

"I ain't going if you ain't coming with me to hell!" the Hurtz snarled dangerously. Inhaling one final powerful breath, he shouted and drove the sword home, destroying the heart of the beast. The wyvern flailed, pulling out its tail from Brakkus, sending him to the floor as it died.

Annetta had come to, and seen the ending of the spectacle. Weakly pulling herself up with help from Link, she stumbled towards the fallen warrior. Link did his best to keep up with her, helping her along as they came to Brakkus's side.

The Hurtz wheezed helplessly on the floor, clutching at his torn stomach, holding firmly in his other hand the hilt of his sword. He tried to straighten himself into a sitting position but failed, his strength leaving him.

Link knelt beside him along with Annetta, holding up the Hurtz's head in his arms.

"Annetta, call for Puc," Link ordered as the girl opened up the watch and began putting in the code. Link turned his gaze to the Hurtz. "Hang, on Brakkus. We're gonna get you out of this mess. I swear."

"No point in swearing, laddie, I made my choice," he responded weakly. Holding up a weary bloodied paw, he rested it on his shoulder. "Ya did good, lad. I'm proud to have called ya a student."

"Don't say that. I'm still your student." Link grabbed hold of the hand, his eyes lined with tears as he looked into the great amber eyes. "I'll still be for a long time, same with Annetta. Right, Anne? Say something."

"I can't get a hold of Puc. I don't know why!" the girl said, panic taking hold of her as she looked over at Brakkus. "But Link's right, you're the toughest one here. You need hold on, you-,"

"Lass, sweet lass, ya gotta let me rest my eyes," the Hurtz breathed deeply. "My time has come and passed, yers is about to begin."

Brakkus's gaze turned to Link, the youth's face streaked in tears as he cradled his head upwards.

"Cryin' ain't befittin' a warrior," he grumbled. "I've one last thing I need ya to do for me before I go to the halls of the eternal. I was the sworn protector of Lord Orbeyus long ago, and after his death, I became the protector of Annetta an Arieus. I need someone to take me place, and I got no one else to trust but you."

"But Brakkus, I'm not as great a -," Link almost had the wind knocked out of him as Brakkus's fist landed on his chest over his heart.

"I'm a Hurtz, the most feared thing on the field of battle, a beast like none other. You, Lincerious, I've seen yer also a beast like me, a force the enemy'll cower before. Don't doubt what you have inside you. I never have." He breathed heavily as he forced himself up a bit more. "Now kneel before the Lady Severio, and repeat after me: I, Lincerious Heallaws."

Link propped Brakkus up against one of the destroyed couches, and took out his sword, lying it flat across his palms, knelt before Annetta, who was barely able to keep herself up, let alone listen to any oath.

"I, Lincerious Heallaws," he repeated, wanting to get it over with as soon as possible.

"Swear by the Unknown, and all that is right and just, to defend tha honor of her ladyship, Annetta Severio."

"Swear by the Unknown, and all that is right and just, to defend the honor of her ladyship, Annetta Severio," Link reiterated.

"To be the shield where armor be missing, to be the sword in times of darkness, and the friend in times of light. The unstoppable force under banner of truth united, my services and strength unto you I give until the time death release me from mortal grip."

Link concluded the oath, looking up at the weary Annetta. Their gazes then turned back to Brakkus, who looked at them both, his eyes becoming smaller.

"I see me little girl. My Nara calls for me," the Hurtz whispered in a hoarse voice, his heavy head sinking to his chest.

It was those final words that broke down any resolve, any strength either Link or Annetta had. They watched as a silver film settled over the eyes of their friend, signaling life's end. Sinking to her knees and caught by Link's firm grasp, tears rolled down the girls face as she buried her face in her blood stained hands.

A frazzled and exhausted looking Puc dashed in, his black hair matted with sweat as he examined the scenario. His reaction was not clear until his gaze fell upon the vanquished warrior and the other two, drenched in blood and tears at his heel. Dropping his staff, the mage rushed to the Hurtz's side, checking for any signs of life, shaking the corpse to try and wake it. His efforts in vain, he retreated for a moment, his world shaken.

"What in the Unknown's bane happened?" he asked, attempting to remain calm, the sobs of Annetta driving the patience out of him as he turned to face them. "Answer me!"

"A wyvern attacked us," Link explained as the more coherent of the two. "We were just exploring the corridor and it came out of nowhere."

Puc looked over at the dead creature, a mass of scales, muscle, and bone now lying on the steel floor, drenching it in blood. He turned back to his fallen companion, a warrior who had lived through more than his share of battle. This was not to have been his end. There was only one logical explanation for what had happened. He intended to get answers. He turned back to Annetta and Link, noting Annetta's arm and fished out a vial from his pocket.

"Take this. It will help you gain your strength back," he stated, pressing it into her hand. "Go to the hospital wing, where Lincerious can properly have that patched up. When you feel better, I need you and Link to go to the control room, and check the cameras to find out how this thing got in here. I will take care of this mess, and then I have some business to attend to."

"How can you just say that? Brakkus has died!" Link snarled.

"Do not question my orders, Lincerious. You will do as I ask, and then there will be time for mourning," Puc hissed back at him, his feral eyes boring into Link.

Annetta was confused by Puc's reaction. He seemed so calm, as though nothing could touch him. They had lost a close friend, and he just expected them to follow orders? Knowing more arguing was not an option for her with all the lost blood, she rose with Link's help, still in tears and the two of them made their way to the hospital wing.

Puc watched them disappear into the depths of the Lab, then turned his gaze to where Brakkus lay, a collapsed pile of flesh. Sure that they were gone, the elf slid down to his knees beside the Hurtz. Though tears formed in his eyes, he did his best to keep his sorrow silent. It was not appropriate for a mage to weep, though he could not help but feel the same emotions that welled up inside of him when Orbeyus had been found. If he'd been there, perhaps Brakkus would still live. A lump formed in his throat as he choked, tears rolling down his cheeks. He quickly brought the sleeve of his robe to his face, ridding himself of any signs of weakness, sadness replaced quickly with anger.

"You will be avenged, friend," he whispered.

Chapter 50

His feet and staff working rhythmically as one, Puc made his way to the training grounds, not bothering to stop and check on Annetta and Link, who watched him pass by the room they both sat in, his face alight with the need of answers.

It did not take him long to reach them, the elf's long strides splitting the journey in half and soon he heard the voices of Matthias, Sarina, and Jason. He stopped beyond the Calanite diamond walls and glared, his eyes set ablaze, wanting his enemy to spot him before he charged.

As soon as Matthias felt the gaze upon him, Puc entered, and with demonic speed pinned the younger man to one of the walls, his staff constricting Matthias's windpipe.

"Puc what's going on?" Jason asked, watching the mage's rash actions, actions that seemed fueled by something he was not aware of. Sarina hid behind the boy, not wanting to be next in the hurricane of fury.

"Can I help you with anything, Thanestorm?" Matthias spat, trying to pry the staff away from his throat as he continued to lose breath.

"Give me one good reason why I should not pop your head off here and now like a cork," the mage cryptically snapped, holding the staff to his neck with inhuman strength. "Tell me, how the hell did you managed to set a wyvern loose on the premises without anyone noticing? I'm curious. I want to see the answer leave your lips as you die."

"What the are you on about, mage? I set nothing loose within-," Matthias felt the wind knocked out of him as Puc slammed his staff harder against him. Now the psychic warrior began to worry if he would survive. He could feel strength in the grip of the mage, and knew the cuff restricting his psychic abilities put him at a serious disadvantage.

"Puc, answer me. Matt was here the whole time," Jason furrowed his brows.

"I advise you to stay out of my way while I extract justice." Puc's tone of voice went back to being level-headed as he spoke, but turning his gaze to Matthias as he suffocated him, his expression read something different.

"Justice? This isn't justice," Jason sneered at the accusation through his teeth.

"What's going on here?" Annetta and Link arrived, watching Matthias and Puc.

"I was wondering the same thing," Jason said, then looked back at the mage. "Puc, this isn't like you, and I know we have our differences but, what's Matt got to do with any of it?"

"He knows exactly what he has done," Puc snarled. "And I thought I told you both to check the cameras for proof."

Annetta noted the madness in his tone of voice. She turned her head slightly to Link. They would need to restrain him. Puc was in no emotional state to be left alone, that much was clear to them. The orders he had given had been to get them out of the way while he went to go 'take care of things'. They began moving slowly behind the mage in unison.

"We'll go, Puc, as soon as you let Matt go. This isn't how you do things," Annetta said.

Jason watched as they moved in slowly, but he was more concerned with Matthias at the moment. Each second led closer to his death as the mage pressed the staff harder and harder.

"Stop it!" he snapped, and using his telekinetic abilities, threw Puc out of the training room, into the depths of the Lab.

Matthias fell to his knees, gasping for air as he held his neck, Sarina joining him at his side as he choked. Jason took a quick glance backwards to make sure his two friends were fine, but stood guard in case the mage would charge at him again, his hands curled up into fists.

Annetta and Link rushed to where Puc lay in a heap of broken tarp-covered objects, blood clearly visible running from his forehead. Annetta lifted up his head to see if the spark of life still ran within his eyes. Seeing this recognition, she felt every fiber of her being begin to burn with rage. She turned around and teleported back into the training room to face her friend.

"What the hell is wrong with you, J.K.? You could have killed him," she snapped.

"He would have done the same to Matt if I hadn't stepped in," he retorted.

"We were going to stop him," Annetta protested.

"At the cost of killing Matt." Jason bared his teeth. "That's something I can't let you do."

"What's gotten into you, J.K.? We've known Puc way longer, and he's taught us so much." The girl moved towards him, tears forming in her eyes.

552

"Without him, there's no one left because…well… Brakkus just died protecting us."

Jason felt his guard drop upon hearing this. He felt his blood drain from his face as images of the Hurtz warrior flooded through his mind, a being that was so familiar to him, he found it impossible to believe he was gone. It could not be. Yet, seeing the girl before him in tears, he felt the truth, and another feeling took the place of his sorrow.

"No. He died protecting you, Annetta! You, always you!" Jason gritted his teeth. "If it wasn't for you then he would still be here, but he had to protect the great Annetta Severio, heir of Orbeyus. I'm tired of being the little sidekick, okay? I am just so damn tired of being 'son of Arcanthur,' whatever that title is meant to be, and I am tired of being second best. I am Jason Kinsman, and I am going to be number one!"

Annetta felt the weight of every word hit her, like a crowd hurling stones at an accused prisoner. She reached for the hilt of her sword, reason leaving her as she went into a battle stance. It was the same feeling that took over whenever her and Finn had an encounter at school. It was the feeling of setting things right, and her mind flashing back to the image of Puc on the floor beside Link did not help quench the fire from her gut.

"To some extent you're right, but it was not just me," she spoke, calmly at first, but more agitated as she continued. "It was Link and I that were attacked together. You are not my sidekick, and you never were. We choose our own roles in life. If you want more, then you go for it. Yeah, I had a title handed to me, but I never expected it to come my way. It just did, and I rolled with it. We all need to make due with what we get. If you think in your twisted version of the world you can become number one by defeating me, then come and claim that right, but don't you dare say that I was responsible for Brakkus's death!"

Jason let out an animalistic howl as he summoned Helbringer from its pendant state, and charged at his once best friend, both hands upon the weapon, ready to prove his worth no matter the cost.

Annetta rushed into the fray, not wasting a single second. Part of her screamed at herself to stop, but the heat of the moment overwrote everything else. Her hand fingered the hilt of Fearseeker. In an instant, she released the black blade from its scabbard, rushing to meet her rival with her own war cry. The two collided and it began, a frenzy of psychic throws mixed in with the clash of metal on metal.

It was like a dance they had been rehearsing their whole lives. When Annetta turned one way to strike, Jason was right there to block and to try and push her against a wall to knock her unconscious. It was the fight of their life, one born out of friendly rivalry until friendship had been severed.

ഇരൽ

Having helped Puc to his feet, Link made an effort to bring the mage over to the hospital wing. Their route colliding with the training room, and Link watched the scene from outside as the two titans unleashed their fury in a combination of sword fighting and teleportation, which made both seem to float in midair with the weapons they wielded.

"Will you be alright?" Link asked the mage.

"I will live," Puc answered, still shaken from the impact he had suffered.

Matthias exited the training room to see Link and Puc. The psychic warrior walked in a quick pace over to them.

"Is he okay? I didn't think J.K. would have-," Matthias began, only to have Link step in his line of sight, blocking him from the mage.

"You stay away from him," the youth grunted.

Matthias could not help but smirk at Link's actions, "Let me guess, you think I did something as well. Tell me, what is it that I apparently did?"

"Brakkus was killed defending Annetta and Lincerious from a wyvern," Puc explained as he walked around Link to face Matthias. "A creature we would have caught purging the Lab when the power went back on. So there is only one way such a thing could have eluded us for so long here. It was a new arrival."

"And you think I apparently brought this...what did you call it? A wyvern?" Matthias raised an eyebrow. "Is that a sort of plant?"

"Don't play coy with me, Repronom," Puc sneered.

Matthias glared at the mage, "You know, Jason always said how wise and understanding you were. He told me how you took him to see his father when no one else would. But I don't see any part of the wise Puc Thanestorm here, except a maddened elf. You deserved what you got just now."

Puc's grip on his staff tightened, but his view of Matthias was obstructed by Link.

"What did you say?" Link growled.

"I said he got what he deserved," Matthias stated. "I was here the whole time, and I had no reason for killing the Hurtz. I guess he got sloppy taking care of kids all the time."

"How dare you!" Link bared his teeth. "Brakkus was our friend!"

"Friend or not, he's six feet in the ground now, and the only one you have to blame is yourself," he stated, "He ought to have watched out more."

"You." Link felt the rage pump to his brain. "We just saved your life, and you insult the memory of my friend? Brakkus was a great warrior, more than you'll ever be."

"Jason saved my life. You stood by and watched," Matthias retorted. "And a true warrior does not let emotions get in the way of his better judgement. That is a weakness that is unforgivable. A weakness I can clearly see you exhibit this very moment boy, same as your mentor."

The last note was too much for Link. He let the beast take over, phasing as he charged at Matthias, ignoring Puc yelling at him to stop.

Matthias watched in fear and awe as the youth turned into the werewolf-like creature with antlers. The event triggered something so deep within him that it had lain forgotten for years, long before he had come into the service of Mislantus. Closing his eyes, he allowed his own internal senses take over. It began.

₧₧₧

Blades and war cries collided with each attack. Leaping back, their movements enhanced by focusing their psychic abilities into their bodies, Annetta and Jason circled one another.

Jason wasted no time renewing his assault. He charged, lifting the mace over his head and trying to crash down, hoping to land another injury to the girl.

Annetta leaped out of the way, the mace hurtling to the floor. Mockingly, she kicked Jason in the rear, causing him to fall on the floor, but he teleported out of the way, reappearing behind her.

"You think this is a game?" He snarled.

"I'm just doing what you asked for, kicking your ass," she mused through labored breaths.

Jason gritted his teeth, and flew at her, readying his mace like a baseball bat. The girl stood still until the last moment, teleporting just before the weapon collided with her. Stopping himself, the boy turned around to see the girl behind him, going back into her battle stance.

Annetta lashed out at Jason, her sword striking the ground as he teleported out of the way and behind her. He almost had her, the mace thundering down, but she teleported once more, and emerged to his side, locking the sword within one of the lion-head-shaped blades that made up the mace.

"Are you going to kill me? Is that it now?" she spat, having a moment to corner him while their blades remained locked.

Jason did not answer back. He stepped backwards, strategically slipping the mace out of the sword, continuing to charge blindly. Anger pounded in his head like the rhythmic beating of a drum.

Bracing herself, Annetta took the blow again, pushing Jason across the room. Teleporting upwards above him, she tried to slam the sword down, hilt-first, into his back. Despite all the turmoil and rage within her, she still could not come to terms with the possibility of having to kill her best friend, nor would she. Her lack of offensiveness, however, cost her a blow to the same shoulder the wyvern had slashed, reopening and deepening the wound. Angered, she sent Jason full force into the Calanite diamond wall behind him. She had been holding back, hoping to knock some sense into her friend, but the wound had made her let go completely.

Jason raised himself from where he lay. He felt every part of his body go numb with bruising as he looked at his rival, her arm covered in fresh blood, his handy work.

ഇ൩

Link froze on his warpath, and watched as Matthias transformed before their eyes, the humanoid form melting away, rippling and changing as thick brown fur sprouted everywhere. Moments later, before them stood what looked to be a half-man and half-bear hybrid that reached over seven feet.

"What in the name of the Unknown?" Link stopped in his tracks, his thoughts blotted out by a snarl from the creature. He wasted no time in returning a roar as he attacked.

Link and Matthias clashed into one another, claws and fangs flying as they alternated hits, ripping and tearing at any part that would give advantage to either of them. It was not until Link managed to dig his claws into Matthias's chest was there a break in the string of monotonous assaults for either side.

Lowering his horns like a bull, Link charged forward. Matthias grabbed at the antlers to flip his opponent belly up, then slammed into him, knocking the wind out of Link, cracking a few ribs in the process.

Link cringed before recovering enough from the blow to wrap his jaws around Matthias's neck and press hard until his opponent got up, reeling Link along with him. Both returned to their positions, standing slightly hunched over with claws bared before them.

"Do you honestly think you can beat me even like this, boy?" the werebear spat. "Think again. You thrive on your emotions. It will get you nowhere."

Link grabbed hold of his ribs. It was getting harder for him to move. He noted the multiple cuts on his body, but ignored them, staring into the eyes of the enemy. The fight would not last much longer unless he found a way to surprise Matthias, who was proving to be faster and stronger than Link. His gaze turned to Sarina, who had come out of the training room and stood some distance away, a distressed look upon her face, watching everything as it occurred.

"I may thrive upon emotions, but you are no different than me!" he snarled, and charged for the girl.

Matthias raced after Link, never having thought the Gaian soldier would even think of it.

₨₧

Farther beyond all that was occurring, Puc watched as both scenes unfolded before him, the dazzling display of weapons and teleportation within the training grounds, and the bestial spectacle outside. He was still in pain from the throw, and was sure he had broken a rib or two in the process. Cringing to ignore the pain, the mage pressed on into the training room, knowing his attention would be most needed there. He had to try and do something to stop the carnage, which was in truth of his own making, he now realized. There was too much at stake.

His gaze, however, turned to Sarina, who stood outside the room with a look of fear in her eyes, watching the two beasts. Knowing flight from fright when he saw it, Puc wasted no time in weaving a spell for sleep, in order to avoid the girl possibly fleeing in the chaos.

₨₧

"How dare you hold back on me!" Jason spat. "Are you mocking me, Annetta?"

557

Annetta glared back at Jason, pain shooting through her arm once more as she watched him from the other side of the arena. His face was curtained partially with brown hair, his green eyes observing her in defiance, and the reason behind it all was a name she held, and a title that had been thrust upon her without consent. She thought back to the day the angels had appeared and cursed it all. She tossed Fearseeker to the ground, her strength failing her as she looked upon him.

"No, I quit," she said, stretching out her arms. "So go ahead and kill me, because that's what you want to do."

Jason stopped himself upon hearing the word 'kill,' his eyes wide as he looked down at his hands. He looked back at the girl on the other side of the arena, half her arm drenched in blood, looking back at him in resignation. No matter what it came down to, she was his friend, and his intent was never to kill her. She was the girl he hung out with at recess, the girl who trudged through the snow with him each year on the way back from school, the one he laughed with, and the one he confided in. He lowered his gaze to the weapon that had drawn her blood, and dropped it with a thud. It was not right. It then hit him again, full force. Brakkus was gone, and the one to blame was before him, no matter what way he tried to look at it. Tears welled up in his eyes.

"That's right, let it all out," Annetta said, weakly.

"Damn it, Anne. Is he really gone?" Jason exhaled heavily. "He's dead?"

"I'm sorry, J.K...like I said, he died protecting-" Annetta cut herself off mid-sentence when she noticed Jason as he lowered both his hands to one side as though he were holding an invisible basketball.

"What's going on?" Annetta asked, confused, "What are you doing?"

"This is your fault," he shouted through his tears. "Brakkus would still be here if it wasn't for you!"

His anger reaching his limits, Jason visualized throwing all the frustration he still had left into his hands, the heat rising from his palms.

Annetta watched in dismay as in Jason's hands formed a ball of purple, blue, and black flame. It was the most beautiful thing the girl had ever seen and she felt so drawn to it that she could not look away. She knew what it was, and knew it was deadly, but somehow, nothing in her body seemed to be working against the pull.

Jason looked down, amazed. He had finally done it, in all his anguish and torment he had produced psychic fire. He, not Annetta, had succeeded. Taking a step back, he launched the ball of flame.

"Feel what it's like to be on the other side!" he shouted.

Snapping out of the trance, Annetta panicked, seeing the ball of fire flying towards her. She was fortunate enough to still remember what Puc had told them long ago, and raised her hands towards the approaching projectile, praying it would work.

Lost in his victory, Jason did not notice the approaching ball of flame until it was almost too late. He would have been lost were it not for a pair of hands that saved him from the inferno at the last minute and teleported him out of the way, allowing the Calanite diamond walls absorb the shock.

Confused, Jason turned around to see Annetta standing behind him, a hand still on his shoulder, her face pale and drawn of blood.

"Good job," she said, before the two rivals fell unconscious to the floor, exhaustion from the use of psychic energy having taken its toll on them both.

❦

On the other side of the arena, Link charged towards the girl, only to be intercepted by Matthias diving before him, antlers tearing into his gut and shoulder. Coming to a stop and depositing Matthias on the ground, Link stood up on his back legs, looking down at his fallen opponent. The werebear withered in pain as Link bared his claws, ready to deliver the final blow.

"That is enough, Lincerious," the voice of Puc rang from behind. The youth turned around to face the mage, standing despite the injuries he had endured.

Link turned back to Matthias, who was fading out of consciousness, and phasing back to his human form. He remembered the girl, and looked to see she had fainted. His eyes fell back upon the mage in questioning.

"Worry not about the girl and I want him alive," he stated, standing beside the beast.

Chapter 51

His tasks complete, Darius returned to the stables of Q-16 after making sure all was in proper order in the Eye to All Worlds. Securing his mount to its post and taking off the saddle, he could not help but notice how empty it all was.

"Brakkus? You around here?" he called, hoping to hear the Hurtz answer.

There was nothing. The longer no response came, the more uneasy Darius grew. He checked his watch, noting the time of day and knowing full well that the Lab, though massive in size compared to the companions that inhabited in the evenings, should be teeming with life. Hearing footsteps, the young elf curled his fists defensively, in worry of a fight, but found no one standing in the doorway except for Link.

He noted the battered demeanor of the Gaian youth and chuckled, "Well, at least I know the Hurtz is cleaning his blade from giving you a good thrashing."

Link lowered his head upon hearing the laugh escape the youth.

"I'm sorry, did I say something to injure your pride?" he asked, gathering his pack with supplies he had bought.

"Darius," Link exhaled, "Brakkus has been killed."

The mage apprentice felt something hollow within him break, only to realize a broken jar of herbs lay under his feet. He felt unable to comprehend the words, or the situation they pertained to. Stepping closer to the door, Darius noted how aged the words made Link look as he stood there.

"How?" Darius questioned.

Like a marionette come to life, Link looked up from his feet at the elf. "I don't know, but I intend to find out, and I'm going to do just as Puc asked me. Come with me to the security room. I'll fill you in on everything on the way."

Chapter 52

The humming of electric lights overhead was the first thing Matthias heard as he came to. Opening his eyes to stare directly into the source of the noise did not help him regain his sense of self. The thundering feeling in his head did not help either, and upon trying to lift his hand to shield himself from the light, he realized he had been tied down. Coming to his senses, Matthias took note that he was strapped down with belts to the bed he lay on, and like any free being who had been restrained he began moving around, trying to break free of his bonds.

"I'm afraid that will do you nothing in your current situation," a voice rang said from the shadows. "Strange how circumstance led us back here. Then again, I always felt it would."

Matthias turned his head to see the outline of Puc, sitting in a chair, gripping his staff from beyond the bright lights that shined down upon him. It all came back to him, the fight between Annetta and Jason, his own duel between him and Link, and Puc's furious arrival which had brought on the storm. He noted he had been dressed, and his wounds attended to, but looking into the eyes of the mage, which shone in the darkness, he knew there was a good reason for the preparation.

Puc got up from his place in the dark, and moved into the light, a bandage wrapped around his head, and a heavy, old book in his left hand.

"Do you know what I have here?" he asked Matthias. "It is a book filled with torture spells by my cousin race, the Fire Elves, who are masters of inducing pain. What makes this book all the more enticing is the fact that each of these spells, if not cast correctly, will still inflict pain upon the victim, some spells greater or lesser than intended. You see I chose this book because I have never been one for torture spells. I have specialized in battle and healing all my life, therefore with a book like this, I will not fail either way."

Matthias felt a chill go down his spine, only now fully beginning to understand the formidability of the mage that once served at the side of Orbeyus of the Axe, and the danger the elf evoked.

Puc pulled up a chair beside the psychic warrior, and setting down his staff he cracked open the book. He began flipping through the pages with a blank but amused glance, scanning the words on each.

"Now here is an interesting one. It begins with breaking the bones in your fingers apart into dust and then continues upwards on your arm should you not answer. What do you think of that?"

"I never killed the Hurtz," Matthias said through his dry throat, "I was with my sister and Jason the entire time, and you won't get a different answer than that."

"Yes but there were many hours that day," Puc snapped. "And I think being able to phase into a werebear proves you still have a few tricks up your sleeve. So we begin with the obvious question. Who are you, really, because I fail to believe you are a runaway prince from a planet far away."

"What? What reason would I have to lie to you about my identity?" Matthias growled in protest. "I mean, yes, I can phase, but I did not even know about that. It just happened. I guess it's a genetic trait that was passed down. It does not mean I can use magic. There are many races who can do that."

"Wrong answer," the infuriated mage snarled as he looked down at the page. "But I will have the right one."

"Puc, wait!" Link's voice came through the dark as he entered the room with Darius.

Puc turned to regard both the youth, still engulfed in his anger.

"Speak." The mage went back to his usual calm tone.

"We just checked the cameras, master, and he never let the wyvern in," Darius began. "The wyvern was an egg we never saw while purging the Lab with Brakkus. It had been hidden in the tropic biosphere. We checked with Link once he called me. The door of the biosphere is torn off. We went back a few weeks in the video, and the creature had come through from there, way before Matthias and Sarina arrived."

Puc felt the last of his anger flee. Ashamed, the mage closed the book that lay in his lap, staring at the floor. It was not the man that lay before him, but his own error that had contributed to Brakkus's death. He had come rushing as soon as he had heard the commotion on his C.T.S. coming from the other end of the line, but he had not come fast enough, and it had cost him all too greatly all over again.

"We're sorry, Puc," Link added after a moment.

Curling a fist around the staff until he felt most of the blood rush from it, Puc grabbed a dagger from his sleeve and sliced open the belts that had held Matthias down. He left the room without another word, shoving past Link and Darius.

Matthias rose from the bed wearily, making sure everything in his body still functioned, his eyes falling to Darius and Link. Before he could raise his arms in gratitude, an unexpected hand struck him across the face so hard he staggered back, almost falling to his knees. Recovering, he looked to see Link retracting his hand, the youth's crescent scarred face appearing all the harsher in the aftermath.

"Never speak ill of Brakkus again," he said. Having made his point, he followed the departed mage out of the room with Darius, leaving the baffled Matthias to contemplate the events that had transpired.

ೋ೧೪

Link and Darius traveled down the hall out of where Matthias had been held, deciding to go visit Annetta and Jason, who had still been unconscious. The Gaian warrior and apprentice mage moved through the steel corridors side by side, the only sounds heard around them the buzz of halogen lights, and their footsteps. Neither of them had the will to speak after what had transpired. For Link, the events had been all too real. For Darius, it was an awakening into a harsh reality.

"I still can't believe he's gone," Darius said. "The Hurtz seemed invincible."

Link walked on in silence for what seemed almost an unnatural length of time. The youth was doing his best to suppress the tears he had not had time to shed for the fallen warrior, and every mention of the event drew them closer to the surface.

Darius noted the silence, and stopped speaking. His own way of dealing with the events was to retrace them, trying to bring it all to life in order to understand the loss. He could scarcely begin to imagine what his own mentor was enduring, or worse, what he would have been feeling should it have been Puc slain in the event.

Recovering from his emotional fall, Link straightened himself up and looked at Darius. "He was not just a Hurtz, his name was Brakkus."

ೋ೧೪

Annetta woke up, feeling the light from the lamps above sear her eyelids with an assault of pink and red. Opening them, she found that she had been strapped down with belts, and was unable to move anything but her head. The last thing she remembered was deflecting Jason's psychic fire, then teleporting him out of the way. Cringing, she tried to slide up under the straps so she could move her head around more. Seeing a familiar counter to one side, she realized she had been taken to the hospital wing. She turned her head to the other side to see Jason, still peacefully asleep, his many cuts and bruises dressed, also strapped down to his bed. His eyes began to flutter.

"What? Where am I?" he asked in a dazed state.

"Hospital wing from what I can tell," Annetta answered as Jason's head turned to face her.

The two locked eyes in what seemed to last an age, but in that brief moment, more than any words could say transpired. Feelings of regret, sorrow, and a wish for reconciliation poured forth from them. Turning away, both allowed themselves to regain some level of clarity.

"I'm sorry, Anne," Jason's voice rang out on other side of the room.

"For what?" she asked, still turned away.

"For attacking you like that. For lashing out at Puc. There's been a lot at war inside me." He sighed. "I wasn't thinking at all."

"You're right you weren't," Annetta said, finally looking at him. Jason turned to face her as well, briefly, then turned away again, unable to look her in the eye for too long.

"I've been so consumed with trying to be better than you, that I lost sight of our friendship," he blurted out.

"Better than me? Why? What's so much better about me?" she asked.

"Because wherever we go, you're the granddaughter of Orbeyus Severio, and I'm just the son of Arcanthur, another one of his soldiers who happens to tag along." Jason turned to her yet again. "I'm a sidekick don't you see, and I don't want to be just the sidekick."

Annetta sighed as she turned her head upwards toward the ceiling, allowing her vision to be flooded by light.

"You focus so much on what we were given that you don't even look at what we have to do. You think it's easy for me to be 'the heir of Orbeyus' and have all of these expectations put on me? Every place we go to it's just, hey, you're the heir. Do something about this thing going on now. Prove yourself to us, because you're the descendant of this person you don't even know, but that's okay because you're their flesh and blood. I don't want any of this, and after a while it just wears at you, and the way I look at it, you are as much involved in this as I am. We don't have the Four Forces following us around just because we are the descendants of someone. Everywhere we go, they ask us to prove ourselves, so really, what they call us, our titles, they're just empty words."

Jason nodded, hearing the speech wash over him. For so long, he had been throwing the excuse of titles at his problem, and all it took was a few simple statements from Annetta to make him see, oddly, that they were just words.

"It still hurts, I mean. Being called that. No matter how you say it," he said.

"Never said it wouldn't." Annetta shook her head. "But we can maybe hope someday people will call us Annetta Severio and Jason Kinsman, leaders of the Four Forces."

"I kinda like the sound of that more," Jason replied quietly.

"So don't worry about it so much," she said. "You're not alone, okay? I'm in the same boat as you are. There is no better or worse. Plus, I think you creating psychic fire before me kinda proves that, right?"

"Yeah, I guess I did beat you in that," he said, smiling despite himself.

"Yeah, and you don't see me moping about it, either," Annetta replied.

Jason nodded his head, his mind turning to another subject, one that had been the primal fuel in his rage.

"Did Brakkus really?" His face calmed from its previous joyful expression.

"He did," Annetta sighed. "The wyvern got him."

Lowering his head to his chest, Jason took in the news. Though he had not been the closest with the Hurtz, he would miss his bright attitude. On top of that, Jason was now beginning to feel the guilt of having thrown Puc as hard as he did when the elf had sacrificed so much for him. He had gone to great lengths to take him to see his father, something that he had wished for his entire life. Jason began to move around, but noted the belts strapping him down.

"Uh, what's up with the straight jacket stretchers?" he asked.

"All the more to keep you in place, my pretties," Darius cackled.

Annetta and Jason turned to see both him and Link at the door. The two of them seemed like old companions, and not the bitter enemies they were on their first encounter.

"You both seem on better terms than when I last saw you," Link added, following Darius in.

"I can say the same for you," Annetta replied. "We had a bit of time to sort our differences out."

"Where's Matt, Sarina, and Puc?" Jason asked, noting their absence.

"We put Sarina in her room after she fainted. Matt is recovering from his injuries. And as for Puc, I think he needed some time to himself," Link answered. "How are you guys feeling?"

"Tied down," Annetta mused, looking down at her strapped form. "Help would be appreciated."

"Are you guys okay with one another, though?" Link raised an eyebrow. "I mean, that's why Puc had us strap you down to begin with."

"Yeah, we're okay now. Honest," Jason said. "Plus, I think if we weren't, we could teleport from under here anyways."

Darius shook his head, then tapped on the cuff each of them now wore, the same one that Puc had placed on Matthias. "Not until the next time we see him. Besides, I don't think you guys would be able to even if you tried."

"What's that supposed to mean?" Annetta glanced at the elf while Link began undoing her buckles.

"You'll see," he said, crossing his arms.

Annetta wasted no time once the last belt was undone. While Link went to free Jason, she leaped to her feet, only moments later realizing what it was that Darius was getting at. Feeling all her strength leave her after the initial jump, her knees buckled underneath her. She grabbed the bed in the nick of time, and sat down on it, causing Darius to chuckle. Her entire body felt numb with the feeling of torn muscle.

"There's a price for using psychic energy to the point you guys did back there," Darius explained, "though I did not see it first hand. It's the same when I use a lot of magic. Your body needs to recover."

"You weren't kidding," she said, sucking in some air as she tried to stand up again with the support of the bed. "J.K, get up slow."

Their laughter was interrupted when everyone's eyes fell to the shape in the door. Puc emerged from its shadows, his pale face was more drawn and weary than usual, a halo of bandages adorning his head. No one dared to speak, not knowing the state of the mage.

"It is good to see you all well," he said, his tone empty of emotion.

Jason ignored his pain and stood on his feet. He locked eyes with Puc and limped towards him.

566

"Puc, I owe you an apology," he managed to say, before tripping and beginning to fall forward.

Surprisingly, Jason did not hit the ground face first as he was bracing himself to do. Instead, an iron grip caught him and hoisted him upwards until he stood face to face with the mage, the void-like eyes observing him yet again without a trace of the earlier outburst.

"We all harvest weakness within ourselves, Jason Kinsman," Puc said, holding the boy up. "The question always remains, are we willing to rise above it, or fall into its abyss? Even the most wise and controlled of us can fall prey to it. I am a testament to that, but I refuse to let mistakes rule my life. I will move forward."

Helping Jason steady himself on the bed, Puc turned towards everyone else gathered in the room. "As we all should do."

Seeing them give an acknowledging nod, his eyes fell once more to the boy. "I do forgive you for your misdeeds, if you are willing to forgive me for my own. It was wrong of me to assume Matthias had let the wyvern in, simply because he is new."

Jason bobbed his head. "I forgive you."

Puc then turned his attention to the others. "I leave in the evening to lay Brakkus to rest at Severio Castle. Those wishing to come with me, feel free to do so. For now, rest," the mage spoke, and left the room.

Ⅎ℧

The road to Severio Castle that night was a soundless one as Annetta, Jason, Darius and Link trotted on their mounts following Puc who rode his carted beast with Brakkus's body in a wagon. Tethering their horses in the stables, they entered the catacombs where Puc had once shown Annetta the resting place of Orbeyus, the light of torches leading their way. There, laying the body of the departed Hurtz on a stone tablet with no image carved into it, they gathered. Aligning the corpse so it gripped its sword blade downward as it did in life, Puc took a step back.

"Here lies a warrior who carved out his name from nothing into greatness," the mage intoned. "Born a slave, freed by Orbeyus to live as he chose. And choose he did. Surname from sire never known, he lived his life by his own unnamed blade, known only as part of the race called the Hurtz. He was once father and husband, teacher and friend. There is so much I could say, but nothing would ever be enough to portray your prowess and life. Here in immortal visage lay with the lord you swore to protect until the

567

Unknown call you from eternal sleep." Puc came forward. Lifting his staff upwards, he slammed it down with full force, creating a light so bright that it blinded everyone gathered. When their sight returned, Brakkus's body had turned to stone like all the others around them.

"Sleep well, my friend," Puc said. "We will see one another again."

The deed having been done, everyone began to disperse out of the catacombs. Annetta lingered behind, looking upon the stone face of the now stern-looking Hurtz.

"Come, Annetta," Puc's voice rang from behind her. "The longer you dwell, the harder it is."

"I know. It's just, I never knew." She furrowed her brows, trying to give a clear and concise answer. "I feel like I never got to know him as well as I should have, as a friend."

"No one ever expects to leave the world in the manner they do, so not everyone shares their life story to the fullest," he explained. "I assume you are addressing Brakkus being a slave, and him never having mentioned it before."

"I mean, that's kind of something significant, right?" she said as they turned to leave.

"Sometimes, despite the past shaping us into who we are, it is difficult for us to look back to," he answered. "Brakkus had a hard life, but he laughed when he could in order to hide his sorrow. It was a trait many admired in him, myself included."

Annetta lowered her head, watching her feet work the rocky steps leading up, contemplating what was said. What bothered her even more was that this fight would not get any easier for all of them. With their friend having died, Annetta had been forced to finally face the facts. This was not a game. It was war.

⋙⋘

Having stayed behing under the pretex of needing to rest with Sarina, Matthias snuck out of his room, and silently slipped along the shadows to Sarina's quarters. He knew the risk of being caught by Puc, but it had to be done. Without warning, he entered.

Sarina rose from the bed, half asleep, astonished to see the assassin lurking within her chambers.

Matthias looked around, having learned that the room took the shape of what the resident desired their perfect habitat to look like. Sarina's room resembled the one she occupied on Valdhar, dark green walls that seemed to close in on a person, and looked almost black in their tinting. A tall dresser stood guard on the far side of the chamber opposite to her four-post bed, and a bookshelf guarded the other wall close to the door, filled with an assortment of literature. It was simple, like a prison cell, but he knew this was what she was most familiar with. He noted one thing he did not like, though. Sarina had the photograph of Jason from the mission files on a wooden nightstand. His blue eyes gleamed as he gazed at the image and then turned to the girl standing before him in a long grey bathrobe.

"Are you alright?" she asked.

"I'm fine, though I dare say I overestimated the bookworm and the beast boy," he said, lifting his shirt slightly to show the intricately interwoven bandages. "A mistake I cannot and will not make again. This is why I am here. I have decided the moment we strike comes soon, for we now know what is needed in order to come and go to the Eye to All Worlds. There is no reason left to keep at this game."

"Oh. I see," Sarina said, seating herself on the bed as she mulled it over. "Will Puc not be more on his guard? I mean, after the wyvern attack, and after he saw that you can phase?"

"His eyes are set to the fourth task, a perfect time to strike," Matt replied. "I will say we should go with them. And when they are most vulnerable, isolated, I will pick them apart like wild animals."

"But Matt, you can't even use your powers, you have no advantage, and you saw how easily Link was able to-," she began to protest.

Matthias noted her eyes when she spoke, her gaze shifting back and forth from him to the photograph. Annoyed, he moved swiftly and slammed it down onto the wooden table, silencing her. Closing his eyes, the assassin took a deep breath.

"It does not take a scientist to figure out that you are infatuated with the boy," he said. "But let me say this. I will not let you jeopardize this mission on account of some ill-placed feelings. You are the daughter of Mislantus the Threat, one who would rule all worlds and he is the son of a warrior who opposed your grandfather's will."

"Rule or destroy?" Sarina snapped back, only to be pinned against the wall as quickly as she had delivered the line from her lips.

"You dare say something like that?" he sneered, withdrawing his position, folding his arms across his chest. "We all think he's a tyrant from time to time. That's just the way with rulers. I tell you now that you will not ruin this for me. I have been your friend for many years, and if you are mine you will grant me this one request and resist jumping in the way when my blades find the curve of their throats."

Sarina looked down at her feet, still feeling the grip of Matthias's hands where they had ensnared her arms. Raising hers hands to the heated areas she nodded. He had never in her entire life lashed her out at her, and the shock was still new.

Matthias, having seen his point made, gave a swift nod, and exited the room, leaving the girl.

Chapter 53

The end of the school week seemed to pass by quicker than expected, fortunately, for it was like there was a large void with the absence of Brakkus. The Hurtz seemed to have been the vibrant life of the base, and with his death, it appeared grayer each time the friends made the descent. The trip was now more of a blessing than a perilous journey into the unknown, as everyone busied themselves with preparation, Puc and Darius worked at their potions and spells, while Annetta, Jason, and Link helped with preparing the horses.

Annetta worked quietly, putting on the saddles and securing the straps. The last time she had done the task, Brakkus was right there beside her, chuckling and instructing her with the same wide monstrous grin he always wore. She realized now it did not scare her as much as it had upon first arriving to the Lab. She had grown fond of it.

"All the shoes are checked. No signs of any loose nails or anything that could hinder us," Link said, walking over to her from the other side of the stable.

"Sounds good," Annetta nodded, finishing up with the final knot. "Saddles are set as well. J.K? You got the supply bags ready to hook on?"

"Yeah, they're good to go," he said, lifting two up, handing them to her, then grabbing two more before going over to one of the other horses.

Annetta accepted the bags, and began attaching them to the saddles, lost in her own thoughts once more. She could not help but wonder if she might have prevented Brakkus's death if she had been faster, if she had thought it through. The problem was she could not turn back time, there was no save point, and she could not do it over.

Link noted the weary look in her eyes as she focused on the task. Similar thoughts poured through his own head as he tried to replay every scenario. He placed a hand on her shoulder, stopping her.

"You're not alone," he said quietly. "Even if the thought doesn't help much, we're in the same boat."

Annetta turned around to look at him. His face seemed to have aged a decade from the dark rings under his eyes and the blonde facial hair that beginning to line his upper lip and chin. She sighed, looking down at her feet, then back up at him.

"Thanks," she said. "It still doesn't make much of a difference in what happened."

"Sometimes knowing you're not alone helps," he said after hesitating. "If you're feeling the same way I am, you're thinking of every possible way you could have saved him, what you could have done differently."

"It doesn't change anything." She paused, curling a fist at her side. "What I can change is this. I will never again underestimate my opponent, and I won't let anyone die again. This I swear."

Link admired her words, but something inside of him still wanted to retort, but his train of thought was broken.

"Hey Annetta, are you okay?" Jason asked, catching on that something was going on.

"I'm fine, J.K." She gritted her teeth, suppressing tears and turning away from the boys so they would not see.

"You don't sound it," he said, walking over to stand beside Link.

"That's a big promise you're making Annetta," the Gaian warrior spoke, having collected his thoughts, "and one that even I can predict will someday be broken. No one can save the whole world."

"Well, I'll be the first one to prove that wrong," she muttered under her breath, composing herself so her eyes would dry.

The familiar thudding of a staff came from the outside of the stables, and soon Puc and Darius stood in the door, holding two backpacks, Puc adorned in a deep blood red and black robe, and Darius in his usual black jeans and dress shirt.

"Red? Really, Puc, it's not your color," Jason said, looking at the eccentric outfit.

"It is not mine to choose, Jason Kinsman," the mage snapped back. "I wore them when discussing matters with the Ogaien, and they are a symbol of my office, which far exceeds yours when it comes to negotiations."

"Ouch, the elf bites." Jason rolled his eyes.

Annetta could not help but crack a smile while finishing up with the saddle. Puc and Jason's quarreling meant some sign of normalcy was back.

Another pair of visitors entered the stables in the form of Sarina and Matthias, immediately grabbing the attention of everyone there.

"We wish to join you on your quest," Matthias stated boldly. "Though we do not know much of it, if it is indeed linked with the defeat of Mislantus then, it is a cause that is dear to us as well. And I wish also to prove myself friend instead of enemy in your eyes, mage, despite our past disagreements."

Puc strode forward to face the young man, his pale eyes boring into his soul as he searched for answers about his behavior, but could find nothing. In fact, he liked the idea of keeping those he deemed his enemies close rather than letting them stay in the Lab unchecked.

"You may come along. Annetta, Lincerious, ready two more horses," he instructed. Turning away, the elf went to attach his bag to his saddle without further conversation. Finishing preparations, they mounted and rode off.

Coming to a halt before the first portal leading to Severio Castle, each of them charged in head on, disappearing behind the red and black wall until Matthias, Sarina, and Puc remained.

"You can go ahead. It will not kill you, you know," Puc stated.

"It's just that I've never seen a portal before in all of my life," the young warrior said, wonder on his face. "It's one thing to read about it, but another to see it." It wasn't a lie. The more he gazed upon it, the more he felt it overwhelm his senses.

Sarina too could not stop looking at the imposing black and red wall of what looked like water. Her heart seemed to want to leap from her chest with panic. She had seen many things while traveling the universe with her father, but the sight of the portal had not been what she was expecting at all.

"They are indeed something to hold with reverence," the elf replied, adjusting his grip on the reins as his gaze turned to Matthias. "The eye to another world is what they are called by my people, hence the alternate name of Severio Castle, the Eye to All Worlds. Built in the exact location where tears in reality occur, and have been protected for generations by Severio lords and ladies past. It is usually best to first close your eyes, and charge ahead until you are on the other side."

Matthias could feel the distrust in Puc's tone of voice, but said nothing of it to the elf, for he knew he could not win. Exhaling roughly, he tightened his grip on the reins of the animal he had been given, and straightened his back before he grunted the command for it to move forward.

Sarina watched as he disappeared to the other side, and only quickly exchanged a glance with the elf before she went after Matthias.

Puc waited as everyone went through the portal, and suddenly felt completely alone. It was a sensation the mage had not felt in years, the kind that made the joints of ones bones grow stiff with cold despite there being no chill. He ignored it, however for he had to press on. There was no other way.

 howkra

Reaching the front gates, the entire party stopped and dismounted. Sarina and Matthias looked around, confused, but did as everyone else had.

"You must swear the oath in order to be able to enter the castle without being killed by the magic placed on the gate," Puc stated, as he motioned for them to get off their mounts. "Now, on your knees before Annetta."

Everything within Matthias ordered him to spring up and choke the life out of the imposing mage. There was only one he would ever bow before, and that was Mislantus, to bow before anyone else was blasphemy. Still, he knew that with his powers blocked off, he stood little chance of doing anything, and it was not until he had the right opportunity that he could hope to lay waste to the mismatched little band. Exhaling, proud Matthias bent knee before Annetta, followed by Sarina.

"Now repeat after me," Puc said, towering over them from behind. "In the one who is severed we trust, our lives to you until we are dust. What is ours we give onto you to use. Our strengths and wisdom use as you choose."

Matthias reiterated, knowing if he did not then the mage would have reason to suspect him. He tried to make it sound as authentic as possible, though the words felt like ash falling from his tongue. He reminded himself that oaths could be broken as he finished, rising upon completion on the mantra.

No further exchanges were made between them as they walked inside, leading their horses up the specially designed ramps. Daylight shone through the large open windows, causing every stone within the walls to give off a pale silver glow.

Puc led the way and stopped at a door. He pulled out the same large key ring he always had on him, rummaging through keys in order to find the right one.

Annetta looked at the arch that guarded the door, adorned with horses that seemed to be set ablaze as they reared and at top of the arch, a great dragon's head leered down at her.

"The sight on the other side may be shocking, I warn you," Puc said. "This world is unlike any you have ever seen."

The door opened, silence falling among the companions as the peered through to the other side. No mirror or wall of water faced them, but a simple window into where they would step next. From what they saw, fire blazed all through the great plain before them, a magma-like floor, fissuring and glowing. What looked like orange and yellow grass grew in clumps along the flat surface as towering black volcanic mountains blotted out much of the red sky. Hell incarnate.

"This some kinda joke?" Jason asked his eyes wide open.

"I'm afraid not," Puc said flatly.

"Does the phrase fried chicken mean anything?" Annetta muttered.

"Don't worry. We got it covered," Darius said pulling out a vial of purple fluid from his pack and tossing it to her. "Cloaking potion created using Beta Dragon blood, and other odds and ends."

"Where did you get Beta blood from?" Link asked, knowing the species to be native only to his home planet.

"You're not the first Gaian we crossed paths with," Puc answered casually, and pulled out another vial. "You and your mount will need to ingest this. It will give you the properties of a Beta dragon, and shield you from changing conditions in your environment."

"Aren't our clothes gonna burn off?" Jason asked.

"The potion protects everything around you within a two foot radius, so there it no need to worry about anything you own going up inflames." Puc went into his pack and produced more of the vials, handing them out.

Annetta sighed, looking at the purple liquid inside of the vial, flipping it back and forth as she watched it splash inside the glass.

"Won't they not work if we take them here?" she asked, remembering what Puc had said about magic before.

"Good memory," Puc answered as he finished handing out the bottles, "but no, you are ingesting the potion, and that is different from having something cast on you. Think of casting as an odor that follows you around. But once something is in your system, it would be the equivalent of removing a lung. They will last for a week. I do not expect us to be there any longer than that."

Annetta dwelled no longer on the subject, and uncorked the potion, then downed it. She was left with a burning aftertaste in her mouth, as though she had taken a spoonful of wasabi and hot sauce mixed together.

Burning all the way down, the potion left tears in the girl's eyes as she tried to mask the pain.

"Well, that will put some hair on your chest," Matthias said after finishing his. "I think it's stronger than Seraphim Tears. Could probably get drunk off of this if you tried."

"All the more reason simpletons are not taught magic." Puc sighed and took out a syringe to feed the potion to his horse.

Before Matthias could retort, Puc was on his horse and charging through the portal.

"He grows on you after a while," Darius said with a sigh. "You just gotta give him time and a reason to like you."

"I'm starting to run out of them," Matthias replied. Mounting his horse, he followed in the mage's stead.

めのの

As soon as Annetta crossed the other side of the portal, she thought she would be burned to ashes. Closing her eyes and shielding her head, she waited for fire to begin combusting on her body, but nothing seemed to happen. Opening her eyes, she looked around to see the blazing inferno. She came to realize it was beautiful. The red sky, the strange glowing grass beneath her feet, and the magma-like ground made the world look like it was being seen through rose-colored glasses. Even the trees, their trunks like ebony and leaves glowing like a flowing river of molten rock looked like something from a dream. Snapping out of it, she remembered something and pulled up to Puc's horse.

"We forgot to set the C.T.S. watches," she said to him.

The elf rolled back his massive sleeve to show his watch to the girl. He peered at the gadget, looking at the various small screens.

"I must have set mine without telling everyone how to set them," he muttered mostly to himself, then turned to see everyone had come through the portal. "Time in this world passes slower than in our own. Here, only a few hours will have passed since our last encounter with the Ogaien. My watch is already set to keep time synced. In order to do so, you need to press the green button twice on the bottom left."

Jason groaned. This was not the first time Puc had forgotten to mention something about the watches. Despite all that had transpired between him and the mage, he found it hard to forgive him for that error.

Puc did not miss a beat, and glared at the youth. "If you have not noticed, larger things have come into the forefront of my mind of late. Mourning for a lost friend being one of them."

He turned to Sarina and Matthias, pulling two more C.T.S. watched from his robes and tossing one to each of them. "These are how we communicate when we are separated. Each of us has a numerical code assigned to them."

Before Puc could continue speaking, the sound of thundering hooves could be heard in the distance, and everyone's attention turned to the oncoming storm of clouds on the horizon. Moments later, a black steed wreathed in a mane of flame came into view and halted before them. The rider was a strange creature to Annetta and Jason. It appeared to be a woman with reptilian featured face, scales covering all of her body, carrying an ebony spear, her green saucer eyes looking upon the new arrivals. Long black hair that went past her breasts lay evenly against her pale hide tunic, contrasting with her red and orange scaled skin.

"Was it but not an hour since our last encounter, Thanestorm?" she spoke in a calm voice that almost did not suit her vicious appearance.

"Greetings once more, Anuli." Puc inclined his head to the woman. "In your world it has indeed been no less than an hour since the parting of ways for what we thought would be a long time. But in ours, fifteen years have passed."

The serpent woman called Anuli blinked a few times, a forked tongue emerging from her lips to sample the air as she tried to comprehend what had happened.

"And Lord Orbeyus is where, then?" She looked among the crowd.

"I'm afraid he is no longer with us." Puc shook his head.

"I see." She lowered her head. Taking her two clawed fingers, she drew a symbol in the air before her. "May Tiamet, Mother Goddess of All, watch over his soul. I did not expect Lord Orbeyus leave us so soon, though I was aware of the changes in time once our times were unbound, I did not think they were that severe."

Puc nodded solemnly. "No one expected to have him pass so soon from our midst. I do, however, bring with me a new generation of Severio, which I wished to present to your Great Mother, Natane."

Puc motioned for Annetta and Jason to come forward, though Jason's expression clearly said he wanted to do otherwise.

"This is Annetta Severio, granddaughter of Orbeyus, and this is Jason Kinsman, the son of Arcanthur." He introduced them as both nodded their heads in a bow, then turned to the others. "With them ride their companions: Lincerious Heallaws, a warrior from Gaia, Darius Silver, my apprentice, and Matthias and Sarina Repronom, those hunted by Mislantus the Threat."

"A female Severio? You ignite intrigue, mage." Anuli grinned. "Come then, ride to the Yasur Plains. I will ride ahead to inform the Great Mother of the circumstances and I will assume your memory is not rusted."

"Not in the least bit, Anuli." Puc smiled back out of politeness, and watched as Anuli veered the flaming steed around, disappearing behind a cloud of flame and sparks.

"Vicious looking dragon lady on a flaming horse. How much more metal can it get?" Jason waited to say anything until she was just a blur on the horizon.

"No commentary needed, Jason." Puc shot him a look. "I would appreciate it if for all of our sakes you keep your wisecracking mouth shut. The Ogaien are a matriarchal society. To them a male is seen as inferior. The only reason I commanded any respect from Anuli was due to years of laboring for it with Orbeyus."

"Okay, okay, no need to strangle me." Jason frowned. "I was just trying to lighten the mood."

"Save it. Lest you wish your family jewels removed," Puc said, and urging his horse into a trot.

Jason wrinkled his nose and shook his head as he followed, admiring the strange world of chaos they had walked into.

୭୦୯୫

It did not take long for them to notice the shapes of yurt huts on the flat terrain before them, nor the banners flying in the air at the entrance of the camp, warding off intruders with horse skulls hanging at the top of each like trophies. Behind them, the mountains were in full view, acting as a wall protecting the back of the village. Herds of horses with flaming manes roamed around freely in the background of the village.

Annetta could not stop looking at the graceful creatures. They seemed like something out of a dream. They looked like regular horses, but their manes were set ablaze in a variety of colors ranging from red to green flames, their eyes corresponding to the color of their mane.

"Those are the Aiethon," Puc explained, "the fire horses that roam the world of Salaorin, and the most prized possession of the Ogaien."

"They're beautiful, even if they are kinda creepy," she said as they came to a halt in front of the first set of banners and dismounted.

"And they are not to be taken lightly. Each is as deadly as its rider," the mage added, taking his reins and leading the way into the central part of the village, where more of the Ogaien seemed to be assembled around the largest of the structures.

In the center, surrounded by two fierce warriors wielding spears, stood an older member of the tribe. The fine silver hairs on her head were interlaced with black and her eyes told a story of experience in life.

"Greetings, Great Mother Natane." Puc bowed, going to his knees immediately, prodding everyone else to do the same as he had done out of the corner of his eye.

"Rise, Thanestorm and companions," she spoke calmly. "I take it peace came to an end in your world already, as is the case in worlds of male dominance."

"Fifteen years," Puc answered, rising to his feet. "And yes, war will be upon us. Orbeyus, out of the kindness in his heart, spared the son of Mordred. Now it seems Mislantus follows in his father's footsteps."

"I see," she said, noting from the corner of her eye the scowls of her female warriors. "Error can befall anyone. Who is this now you bring before us?"

"I have with me Jason Kinsman, the son of Arcanthur, and Annetta Severio, the granddaughter of Orbeyus." He motioned for them both to take a step forward. "With us ride my apprentice Darius Silver, Lincerious Heallaws, a warrior from Gaia, and Matthias and Sarina Repronom, who are hunted by Mislantus, and wish to aid our cause."

"Understood." Natane nodded her reptilian head to Puc, but her attention was already drawn to Annetta as she walked towards her. "A female Severio to unite us? My, Puc, you are trying hard this time."

"She was Arieus's firstborn, and as Orbeyus willed it, his heir," Puc answered, somewhat stiffly. "The Lord of the Axe did not discriminate when it came to gender."

"Nor do we. But women in this society garner more respect than men," Natane hissed at him, sensing the hostility.

She turned back to Annetta. "Tell me, child, do you have any idea why it is that females here hold higher station than males do?"

"No, Great Mother." Annetta shook her head, feeling singled out by the serpent-faced woman.

"Well, we should correct that, then." Natane grinned, her forked tongue flickering. "It is this way because it was Tiamet, the Great Dragon and our Mother Goddess, who gave birth to our race after being wounded in battling Pioren, the Lord of Thunder. It was female that gave birth to male, and so as the life form that grants life, we are to be revered. Without us, life would never have begun to exist. Do you understand, young Annetta?"

"Yes. I do." Annetta bobbed her head, not wanting to offend Natane in any way.

"Good. Then we are of equal understanding," the woman replied, looking the girl deep in the eyes before she turned her attention back to Puc, allowing Annetta to catch her breath in the shadows of the group. "Speak, mage. What is it that brings you here this day yet again, and over a decade for yourself, as you say?"

"I come here seeking to renew alliances with the heir and son of those who you fought with not so long ago, those who you learned, despite gender, to call brothers with fondness, and not distaste. Mislantus is at our doorsteps, and Severbane needs to be lifted in battle once more. After his father's death, Arieus disbanded the Four Forces, wishing to save his children." Puc wielded his words like a finely tuned blade, as he awaited a reaction from Natane and her kin.

The Ogaiens looked at one another, chattering. Some were outraged that war was upon them again so soon. Some angered at Arieus's decision, while others had no opinion at all. There were also a few that made it known they would stand and fight. Natane took all these words in, and upon the arguments reaching their pinnacle, she raised the massive ebony spear she was resting her weight against, and slammed the object down to create silence. She looked around at her kin, her large green saucer eyes flecked with orange, passing judgement.

"We have always known the day would come when war would come again. Tiamet taught us to live ready for battle with spear in hand and Aiethon at side, but never provoke battle where it is not necessary. What's more, she taught us never to abandon a sister in battle. We will rejoin the Four Forces, for you have brought before us hope that in your world, a

580

female may stand among males in the same position. Orbeyus honors our people in doing so, but none may stand as one of us without undertaking the Visium, the journey to discovering the truth of one's weakness. That way, in battle, one may overcome this obstacle, fight with valor and face life, stripped of lies. It is our right of passage to be considered an Ogaien, and all must undergo it. You will travel into the mountain temple of the Dragon Goddess, where in its heart you shall breathe the fumes of the mountain, and there, in clarity of mind, face your true self."

"Understood, Great Mother," Puc nodded.

The Ogaien, seeing the choice made, turned back to their tasks, leaving the companions still standing before Natane with her two guards, one of them being Anuli.

"My daughters Anuli and Amayeta will lead you to the mountain," Natane said. "I must move ahead to prepare. A Visium of this size has not happened since the day Orbeyus and you first arrived on our plane."

"I remember that day well," Puc mused.

"I meant to ask, but what of the Hurtz, Brakkus?" Natane inquired as Amayeta brought a white mare with blue flames surrounding it to her.

"He was slain in battle just this week," Puc sighed. "A wyvern killed him."

"I see. It is misfortunate that a kin of Tiamet would take so great a warrior from this world. Alas, the goddess giveth and taketh as she sees. None can understand her chaotic ways," Natane spoke, then urged the mare into a run, and disappeared.

"So we're going into a mountain to get high and see the truth about ourselves?" Jason summarized what he'd heard as Puc began walking back to where he had left his horse tied up.

"Is this wise, master?" Darius began, running up beside the mage. "I've heard these quests take months sometimes. People can even die during them. To agree to something like-"

"Those are very rare cases." Anger glazed Puc's words as he spoke, cutting his apprentice off. "We have no choice, Darius. The Ogaien have made it very clear what it is they want us to do, and there is generally no arguing with them."

"Well, I can only guess what culture you adopted that practice from," frowned Darius.

The mage glared at him. "You need to trust my judgement when I say that this will be both the easiest and hardest of tasks, but no one will fall to injury. I will also not tolerate your questioning me in this, apprentice."

Darius stopped, allowing Puc to walk the rest of the way himself. Though his master often mentally slapped him in the face when he spoke out of turn, he felt this time that Puc had taken things a little too far.

"What crawled up his butt and died?" Jason asked, walking over to Darius, who looked forlornly over at his master, who was busy reviewing something on parchment at his mount.

"I think Brakkus's death affected him more than he wants to admit," Darius said. "Like it or not, they were companions for many years, and something like that leaves a void."

"Yeah, I can't imagine how I would feel if it happened to you or Annetta." Jason nodded, feeling a lump forming in his throat, as he thought back to the fight between him and his friend. In his rage, he'd almost killed her. Darius peering over his shoulder with puppy dog eyes interrupted his train of thought.

"What?" Jason raised an eyebrow.

"I didn't know you felt that way about me, dear," Darius said, as he tried to grab Jason in a hug.

Jason shoved his arm. "You know what I mean."

Darius chuckled at him. Back at the front of the hut, Annetta and Link still stood close to Anuli and Amayeta, who seemed like breathing statues, neither uttering a word, causing both the girl and boy unease. Link lowered his gaze from the women, while Annetta could not help but admire the weapons each carried. Their spears were not made of wood or metal, but seemed to be one fluid ebony material, which shone against the red sky. On each, intricate designs representing battles were etched into the shaft.

"I'm sorry to bother you, but what are they made of?" she mustered up the courage to ask.

Amayeta stood silently, ignoring the girl, while Anuli sprang to life, her face seeming more human than dragon. Switching the weapon in her hands, she held it out, allowing Annetta to touch it.

"It is carved from the trunk of the Ignibrite trees," she explained, "which are found on the Yasur Plains. Strong as the steel you wield, it will not break like the spears your kin would carry. An Ogaien is given one of these after their Visium, and upon it are carved the vision they have, so each shaft differs. It is always easy to tell whom the weapon belonged to, or if a weapon was stolen, for an Ogaien without their spear is as useless as a lame Aiethon."

"Are those the trees that look like they're on fire?" she asked, the Ogaien nodding in response.

"You ask many questions human child," Amayeta said, finally looking at her. "Did they not teach you anything?"

"No, actually," she admitted. "In my world, no one has heard of the Ogaien. This is the first time I've ever seen a place like this. My grandfather knew, but he died when I was a baby."

Anuli looked at her sister with shame in her eyes, both having heard what Puc had said about the girl's origin. Amayeta bit her serpentine tongue and lowered her head as she exhaled a breath, gathering her thoughts. Looking back up she was finally able to see the girl for who she was, and not a stranger who had simply come into her land.

"I am sorry for your loss," Amayeta replied, looking down at the girl. "I saw Lord Orbeyus but a few short hours ago standing here as he thanked us and left, severing the link between our worlds until it was needed again. I will say this, Annetta Severio, you do have his and your father's eyes. Never have we seen eyes of such coloration here in our world before Lord Orbeyus's arrival."

"Uh, thank you." Annetta blushed a little as the two Ogaien women chuckled upon seeing the flush of color. She then turned her gaze to Link, who silently leaned against one of the huts with his arms crossed.

"You seem real quiet," she said.

"I'm just not stupid enough to speak in a society where males are viewed as canon fodder, that's all." He grinned. "Gaians made that mistake on Vena over a thousand years ago. It didn't end well for their army at all. Not for the guys, at least."

"You are wise then, young Lincerious," Anuli said, teasing, "But fear not, I know of what you speak, and it will not come to that. We heard that story from one of Orbeyus's men. It was quite fascinating around the fire."

Annetta cringed, not wanting to picture what happened, then turned to Link, who still stood quietly, not replying as the two women kept laughing.

Matthias and Sarina watched everything from a distance, standing at their saddlebags, while Matthias pretended to look through them. The girl seemed distracted with something else, looking around at the sight of the village in the strange coloured land.

"So what's your plan?" Sarina asked, watching everyone off in their own circles.

"Oh, this has played out far better than I could have expected," Matthias replied, eagerly. "Now that the oath is sworn, and we can pass freely through the Eye to All Worlds, I will use this vision quest to my advantage. I will slaughter them in their sleep, and come out the victor."

"And just how do you plan to do something like that?" she raised an eyebrow.

"Quite simple," he replied, and produced the hilt of a small dagger from his saddle bag, careful to keep its view hidden from anyone but the two of them. "A miracle what those rooms in the Lab can produce. I shall have to ask Mislantus to grant me permission to use one as an armory."

"You're going to be drugged," she reminded him.

"It's called holding your breath," he stated. "And I can hold mine for a very, very long time."

"I still don't think it will work, but fine." She sighed, turning away, only to feel Matthias's hand grip her arm.

"It will not fail. I swear." His eyes bored into the back of her head as he whispered the words, a truth he was willing to risk everything for.

ℴℴℴ

The party set out not long after Natane had departed. The Great Mother was waiting outside the temple, dressed in what looked like white linen robes laced with gold, the emblem of a dragon in their center representing Tiamet. The temple was carved into the side of a mountain of red-brown stone. Were it not for the ragged stairs and the two sculpted images of dragons guarding the entrance, it could have easily been mistaken for a regular cave.

"The temple of the Dragon Goddess welcomes you, travelers of other worlds," she spoke. "As I am Great Mother, I also undertake a role as head priestess of this temple, and one who speaks for Tiamet. I ask now as I ask all who come here, are you ready to undertake that which will lead you to understand the truths hidden in your soul?"

"Yes, high priestess," Puc replied, formally. "We do come here for this purpose." He kneeled, and the rest of the group followed suit.

584

"Very well," she said back to them. "Our male servant Quadan will lead you to the entrance of the heart of the mountain. From there you will walk till sleep takes your soul into Tiamet's plane where truth be shown. When you awaken, you will be able to exit the cave without fear of falling asleep again, for your quest shall be completed. Should death take you, may the Dragon Goddess judge your souls."

Natane motioned to where a male attendant in a loin cloth stood at the side entrance of a cave shaped like a dragon opening its mouth to swallow the one entering whole. From behind him, fumes of white smoke emerged, obscuring the view of the inside.

Annetta looked to those gathered, and to Puc, who nodded for her to go forward. She then made her way to the entrance, and followed the male Ogaien.

Natane then looked directly at Puc. "You will go as well, though you have already done the test, for I sense much troubles you, Thanestorm. A demon that has burrowed deep into your soul."

Puc looked down at his staff before facing the great mother again. "Do we not all carry them?"

Natane grinned a draconic smile, exposing her teeth. "Yes, but we learn to carry them as though they weighed nothing at all, and not the weight of the world. Go forth, Thanestorm, and cleanse that which has become tainted again."

Puc wanted to retort, saying he was fine, but seeing the look on her face, he knew there was no arguing. Tightening the grip on his staff, the mage proceeded entered the cave. He noted Darius's snicker from the corner of his eye, and shot him a glare just before going in. "Don't stick your nose where it is not welcome, Silver."

"Yes, master," the apprentice replied.

Quadan led the way through the lit cavern, torches flooding the narrow passage with orange lights as the companions went after him, until they came to an opening. The Ogaien male stood and waited until everyone had assembled.

"Man, I was starting to get claustrophobic in there," Jason said with a forced chuckle, trying to break the tension.

"I leave you here," Quadan said. "Behind me is the passage that leads to the heart of the mountain temple. Go forth and fear not when sleep grasps your soul. It means the beginning of your Visium. Safe journey, travelers of other worlds." Quadan bowed and left them the same way he had just led them in.

"Uhm. Okay. Now what?" Annetta raised an eyebrow, directing her gaze to Puc. "Didn't you do this already with my grandfather?"

"Natane requested I go with you," he responded, then turned to the others. "We go in together."

The mage wasted no more words, the thud of his staff on the stone floor overpowering any questions anyone could have raised in the time between him being visible and disappearing into the fog, which came from their destination.

Annetta did not dwell on the conversation, and marched right in. She had no idea what to expect, and did not like it when fog began enveloping her entire body. It did not take long for the girl to begin to feel the shield she held on her arm weighing her down. She looked back to barely see everyone stumbling in after her through the rising smoke. For some reason, she did not choke. The vapors smelled sweet, not from a fire. Soon, unable to keep herself upright, the girl fell forward to the sandy floor, followed closely by her companions.

❧◆☙

Matthias struggled to keep himself awake as he walked in, last to go into the passage. He had them alone, all of them in his grasp where no magic, psychic powers, or anything else could stop the assassin. Should he emerge the only one, he could blame the visions for killing them all, and ride away before their bodies were discovered.

The hunter pressed on, a scarf covering his mouth, preventing as many of the fumes as possible from getting him. He then came upon her, the target he wanted most, Annetta Severio, sleeping without a care in the world in the sand. There was something about the girl that bothered him more than any of the others. Her innocent defiance when she spoke with him was something he loathed. He could not pinpoint why. It unsettled him to hear her speak with such a naivety that it could only belong to a child. As he looked down, that was exactly what he saw, and he watched as the girl's torso rose and fell with the rhythm of sleep. He smiled.

Unsheathing the dagger from its hiding place, the assassin stood over his prey. Running his fingers over the smooth hilt of the blade and clutching it tighter, he raised it skyward.

❧◆☙

Sarina awoke in a familiar setting. It was her room in Valdhar. There was something different about it all, though. Looking out the window, there were no stars visible. Instead, she saw a green sky with what looked like purple snowflakes falling from it. She gazed questioningly, knowing full well where she was. Beginning to get out from under her covers, she froze upon hearing a faint chirping noise coming from the foot of her bed.

Peering over the ledge, the girl nearly gave a yelp upon seeing the creature looking up at her with its lavender eyes. It was no bigger than a kitten with brown hair that seemed to be made of feathers. It would have looked to be a kitten as well, were it not for the tiny cherubic wings and small yellow beak that peeked out from among the fur, squeaking to the girl.

Sarina remembered the creature she had found upon one of the planets her father had conquered. It was a Griff. She scooped the creature into her arms, looking at it in disbelief.

"Rumples, what are you doing here?" she asked.

Before she could think further, there came a knock at the door. The creature whimpered, cuddling up against the girl as she wrapped her arms around it tighter.

"You can come in," she answered, still seated on the bed.

"Lady Sarina." A soldier's voice came from the other side of the door in a demanding tone. "Your father wishes to see you in his chambers. I am to escort you there, and he requested you bring your pet with you."

"I will be out in a moment," she said mechanically, unable to stop the words coming from her mouth. Quickly getting dressed, she took Rumples under her arm and followed the soldier.

Mislantus sat in his usual place. Beside him stood Amarok, his prized psychic assassin, dressed in the tabard of his station, long white hair going down to his chest, no silver mask yet covering the haunting sharp face that seemed ageless. Coming to a halt before them, she curtsied. As she did so, she became fully aware of what was going on, the lack of Amarok's mask being the indicator to her that something was amiss. She remembered the chamber of smoke, the mission to the Yasur Plains, and soon she knew what would happen next, what was going on at that very moment.

"Sarina, it has come to my attention that you have broken our agreement." The cold words emitted from her father's feline lips, and echoed throughout the room.

"What is it that I have done to wrong you, father?" The words again found their way to her lips without her wanting it.

"You have, against my wishes, been sneaking your pet from its cage and bringing it into your room. Am I correct?" The silky voice posed the question as Mislantus examined his pointed claws, paying little attention to her.

"It was only for one night, father. He was scared." She furrowed her brows, the dialogue still pouring forth from her involuntarily.

"Scared is what you both should be, knowing the consequences of these actions." Mislantus's cat-slit eyes turned full force upon her. Rising from his throne, the warlord strode forward, his cape billowing behind him. "When I allowed you to keep the thing, I made it very clear that you were not to become too friendly with it, due to the species having to be put down upon reaching adulthood. You, however, chose to go behind my back, bring the creature into your living quarters, and befriend it, so I am going to do what any caring parent will do for their child."

Mislantus pulled a small silver dagger from his belt and handed it to the girl.

"You will learn that disobedience comes with consequences. I will watch you here and now put the thing to death, instead of having a soldier destroy it out of sight once grown, as we agreed." Her father glared, holding the knife out.

Sarina's heart sank as she recalled the whole scene in its entirety, everything about the room becoming more and more realistic. It had happened just a few shorts years ago, before they had set out for Earth, the day she had been forced to watch Rumples die by her own hand.

What had hurt most about it was that the small creature had been more to Sarina than just a pet. It had been her first true friend. Before she had become close with Matthias, the Griff had been the girl's only comfort on the ship, something that was still child-like, something that had a heart. She looked down at it for a second time in her life, its eyes pleading with her to not abandon it, the hilt of the knife poised towards her from her father's grip. Regaining control of her body completely, her eyes snapped up to meet her father's.

"No," she whispered.

"What did you say?" Mislantus's feral pupils diminished in size as he glared at her.

"No, I will not give up my friend." She stood firmly in place, saying the words louder. It felt good to her, and so she continued. "I will not be your good little girl who always follows orders because of who you are. I am not a princess locked up in a tower, someone you come to see when you feel like it. I have a name and feelings, and I want to be around other people who care about me, so I can be free to be who am I, and not a statue!"

Mislantus gritted his teeth and flipped the dagger around, readying himself to plunge the instrument into the heart of the girl. There came an animalistic scream from the Griff in Sarina's arms as Rumples threw himself at Mislantus, the creature melting away into a massive beast over eight feet in length, with an eagle's head covered in a thick mane of red and orange feathers, and a lion's body covered in grey scale-like feathers, with broad wings to match, and claws large enough to tear through stone with ease. The beast landed on Mislantus, pinning the warlord to the ground. Sarina watched in fear as the scenery around her faded, turning to a shade so white, neither sky nor ground could be distinguished from one another. Before her, the beast still stood, a lion tail swishing back and forth.

"Rumples?" she asked, once she had cleared her throat.

"Never forget," a deep male voice came from all around her.

"Never forget what?" She spun around, trying to address the voice.

"Never forget who your true family and friends are. They are the ones who show kindness, compassion, love, and understanding. They are the ones who offer everything, with little in return. That is a true family. It is not simply a matter of which loins we come from." The creature turned around to face her, its owl beak fully visible from the now matted brown fur. "You have learned much since we last met, Sarina. I wish I could have been here to see you as you are now."

Sarina felt her lips begin to tremble as hot tears ran down her face when she looked upon it.

"Rumples, I'm sorry. I didn't know what to do. If there was another way, I would have chosen it. I-," she began.

"Cry not for the dead, Sarina, for we are already gone." The creature shook its impressive mane of feathers. "Besides, were it not for my death, you would have never met Matthias, who waited just outside the chamber when you came out, and in doing so, would never have met Jason as well."

"But we need to kill Jason. That's what my father wants," she sobbed. "And I can't show my father I am friends with Matt. He'll kill him as well. I am alone, and I always have been."

"Wrong, Sarina," he spoke. "You are alone because you choose to be, because you choose the easy way out. I tell you this now. You have a choice between blood and family. It is you who will choose who means more to you, and you have the power to do so."

Sarina felt the words hit her like a wall of water, causing her to shake her head with the invisible effort of the wave. Closing her eyes, she pictured her father, looming over her and opening them once again she looked over at the imposing beast.

"You don't know my father. He is like a shadow that eats everything and leaves nothing good behind," she cried out as everything around her became black.

"That may be so, but you have something he will never have," the Griff's voice boomed even louder. "You have friendship, should you choose it, and with that you do not need to face the shadow alone."

Sarina turned around to see Matthias, Jason, Annetta, Puc, Link and Darius standing behind her, filling the girl with a sense of belonging. She turned to face Rumples once more, the creature stretching its enormous wings and flapping them a few times as the black of the world around her diminished.

"To walk alone is a difficult path indeed," Rumples spoke once more as everything around the girl began to dim, "but never forget that those who are in need may find friends to aid them should they be open. Farewell, Sarina. And may you never forget."

෫൫൘

Jason woke up feeling the cold sting of the floor against his cheek. Getting up, he looked around to find himself inside of a cave. It was dark, and he found no matches or flashlight in his coat pockets. Finding the wall of the cave, he began to feel his way around, trying to figure out how he got there, and why it seemed so familiar.

"Yousum gots a problem?" a gurgling voice said from behind, stopping Jason in his tracks.

Summoning the mace to his hands, Jason gripped it tightly, every muscle in his body beginning to coil, ready to pounce at the intruder.

"Who's there? You better show yourself," he snapped.

"Tsk, tsk, tsk. Notsa way to speaksum to Fefj after all he dones for you," the voice said again.

Jason quickly sidestepped, spinning around to see the fat troll leering down at him with the same ridiculous cheshire cat grin he had when they had first met. He was quite thankful he could only make out his outline in the darkness, and not the entire creature in detail.

"But you were turned to stone," Jason began to protest.

"Yessum, but I is your spirit guides," the troll replied, its grin cracking even wider, "So ya stucks with me."

Jason then realized where he was and what was going on. He remembered the cave with the fog and falling asleep as he had walked through it. He looked down at his mace, then at the creature.

"Why, out of all the people and things I could have had to guide me, do I get a giant stupid blundering troll?" he asked out loud. "Did I do something in a past life to deserve this?"

"Or dids yousum do something in this life to bees treated thisum way? That is you question, methinks," the troll retorted in the same amused tone.

"Ugh! Why are you even here?" Jason gritted his teeth. "I want out of this damn cave!"

"I is here becausum you has somethings to learn from diss." Fefj waved his thin, almost vestigial limbs in the air as the cave lit up around them with light.

Jason cringed as he was forced to stare into the face of the grotesque wrinkly creature standing before him with a grin, tiny arms tucked to either side like a plucked chicken as it observed him with its huge eyes.

"And what could I possibly learn from something like you?" He snorted defiantly.

"How sky is not always blue," the troll grinned. Seeing the angered face of the boy, he brought the smile down a notch, decreasing the permanent wrinkles on his face. "Fines, yousum think you no needs Fefj, den Fefj sing in corner whiles yousum think of why silly little Ogaiens broughts you to Fefj."

The fat creature waddled over to the corner and sat down with a thud. He began humming a melody so horrendous that Jason thought his eardrums would start bleeding at any moment.

"Fefj! Fefj! Fefj is the best! Fefj! Fefj! Fefj so better than the rests!" he belted out, trying his hardest to snap his fingers but failing each time.

"Okay, I get it. You are really annoying! Jeez!" The boy covered his ears.

"Why you no likes beautiful song about maiden?" Fefj looked at the boy questioningly.

"Okay, look," Jason sucked in some air to prevent himself from screaming. "I don't want to be here, but if I have to choose between poorly put together rhymes and having you as my spirit guide, then I chose the latter. So what do you have to-"

FWAP!

Before Jason could utter another word, he felt something cold and slimy hit him in the face. Peeling it away he, looked to see it was a dead fish. Cringing, he threw it to the floor in disgust, and looked at the grinning troll.

"Respectsum first. Leave fishy business with fish, Fefj likem fish but only cooksum." He wrinkled his face even further and got up, then waddled over to the boy. "Come, I shows you something."

Jason kept still "How do I know you won't either throw a dead fish at me or start singing again?"

Fefj walked for a little longer and paused upon hearing the end of the sentence. "You donts."

Sighing, the boy shook his head and put the mace away into its dormant state before he followed the troll to the mouth of the cave. On the other side, however, did not lay the snowy mountain landscape that he expected. Instead, he found himself in the familiar setting of the schoolyard he was used to seeing each day. He sensed something different about it, but he could not make out what it was.

"Nonesum can see yousum or me. We be completely invisibible to them unlessum you wants to be seen. I donts." Fefj waddled beside the boy, explaining. "Dissum be what to you exactly?"

"It's my school, though it looks different," Jason furrowed his brows as he turned, to where his usual spot with his friends was beyond the school track. He began walking, seeing someone in the distance sitting there.

"What yousum need schools for? Sounds like waste of time." Fefj continued to speak, despite Jason not paying attention.

He pressed on until he was halfway to the field, then stopped, the troll waddling to his side at a much slower pace.

"I need to be made visible," he announced.

"What? What's for?" The troll raised a wrinkled brow.

"Just do it, and stop wasting my time," Jason said as he began running.

"Okay okay, sheesh. Stupidsum boy," Fefj muttered waving his hand in a disappointed manner.

Jason had long forgotten about the troublesome troll as he ran and stopped just before the jump across the moat to the outskirts of the track. He could not believe his eyes, but there sat Annetta on the grass, with her nose in a book, or so it appeared to be Annetta. The girl uncharacteristically sat alone. The book she held was still a fantasy title, but there was something about her that did not feel right.

"Annetta?" he asked.

The girl, startled, dropped the book and backed away upon seeing someone. She then did the strangest thing of all, and coiled up defensively, eyeing Jason in a suspicious way.

"Uhm...Annetta what are you doing?" He raised an eyebrow.

"Oh, you're not with Finn. This book was from the library. I can't really afford to have it thrown in mud like the last one he got a hold of." The girl stood and snatched the book, still backing away, making sure Jason had no room to strike at her.

"What's wrong with you, Annetta? You're acting really strange. Where's Darius and Link? Are they in this vision as well?" he asked.

"What? What are you going on about? Vision? Darius and Link? You part of some role-playing club?" She looked at him as though they had never known one another.

"Hey! Who's the new kid? And what's he doing in our corner?" The all too familiar voice of Finn rang out like a bell from the track. Jason turned around to see him standing some distance away with his hands in his pockets.

Jason watched painfully as Annetta's whole form curled at hearing him. This was not the Annetta he knew. Feeling his whole body freeze on the spot he watched helpless and in silence from the far side as Finn took his time in humiliating the girl, first by snatching the book and taunting her with it, then tearing it to shreds and throwing it into the moat around the track. Panicking, the girl quietly went to go pick up the pieces of the book sinking into the boggy moat, when Finn pushed her into the water, causing her to get covered in mud.

"Why are you showing me this?" snarled Jason. "What does this have to do with me?"

"Thissum has everythings to do with you," the troll said, having finally waddled over to join the boy, huffing from the exertion. "Bleh, why youssum has such far place you needsum to be showed? Why cants it be outside Fefj's cave. Or betters, insides it?"

"Can you just stop, and tell me the point of this?" he growled, annoyed, pointing at the scene while Annetta wrung out her jacket.

"Points is, you not see your own worth." Fefj pointed a grubby finger at the boy. "You always compareum to An...er... to girl. Lookie what missing there. Who not there?"

"I'm not there." Jason frowned, having noticed that from the beginning. "Okay, but how does my absence have anything to do with Annetta not being able to defend herself?"

"Sometimes, power there buts not seen by persons whom has its," Fefj managed to say.

Jason looked back to the scene as it faded away, changing to a memory more familiar to him. It was the day he met Annetta. He had been picked on by Finn in kindergarten, and Annetta came out of nowhere like a hawk, chasing the boy away.

"You okay?" she asked the younger version of himself.

"I think so," he said, blinking as she handed him the toy car he'd had taken from him.

"My name is Annetta Severio. What's yours?" she asked.

"I'm Jason, but everyone calls me J.K., cuz that's what my mom writes on my lunchbag." He introduced himself to her.

Jason watched as a small smile spread across his face, remembering the fated day well. He still kept the small toy car as a symbol of the day he met a friend who never abandoned him.

"Yousum not know diss," the troll concluded as everything around them began to fade to dark, "but girl find reason to fightsum when she see someone in need. Your meeting ignite fire, and dissum fire cannot be extinguished."

☜☞

Link found himself stumbling and darting through a thick forest in the middle of the night. He was not sure why he was running, but it had been this way for as long as he could remember, and something was chasing him.

He could hear the cracking of branches breaking from behind. Coming to a clearing that ended in a cliff, the young Gaian warrior was forced to stop. His heart pounding in his chest, he turned to face the oncoming storm. He noted quickly that he was dressed in his trainee armor, and located his attached sword and shield. He readied himself into a combat position.

Out it came from the thicket, a beast so large it blotted out the starry sky and crescent moon overhead. Roaring on two feet it then hunched on all fours, its red eyes glaring at him and its canine lips pulled back in a snarl.

He could scarcely believe it, for Link found himself staring at his own occasional reflection, the beast. He could not understand with how it was possible, his father was long dead, and no one else carried the curse. It then came to him in a flush of memories, his trip to the Ogaien, and going to the Visium. His grip on the shield and sword tightened as he glared at the creature, not knowing what to expect.

The boy and the beast circled one another for what seemed like ages, neither flinching nor giving any indication of wanting to attack one another, save for the threatening look in the other's eyes. Finally, the beast raised its head up from the defensive position and glared at Link with its red feral eyes.

"You fear me," the deep guttural voice spoke.

"I've never feared you but I have always hated you." Link let out a howl, then charged head on at the beast.

The creature stood rooted in its spot until the last second. Then with demonic agility, it moved aside, causing the youth to tumble into the growth. Link quickly recovered his wits, holding the shield above his head for cover. He spun around to see the beast standing by the cliff, observing him.

"Don't mock me and attack! That's what you want to do, isn't it?" Link snarled, his unease upon seeing his alter ego clouding everything else.

"What gives you that idea? Is it simply what you think I should do?" the thing asked.

"You were always my mark of shame on Gaia for something I never did. Worse yet, when I was sent here, you almost killed Annetta!" Link screamed with primal furry and charged yet again, blindly against his enemy.

The blade collided with the horns of the creature, Link's entire body shaking with the impact as he used all his force to cut the things from the creature's head. But the beast had its own agenda, and flexed its powerful neck muscles as it flung the boy into the air with his sword, causing him to fall on the other side of the opening, closer to the cliff.

"These things are indeed true, but to every being there is light and dark," the creature spoke, its back still towards the boy. "You can blame me for all the wrong you want, but I have also done good. Together we fought against Matthias and won, we tracked Orion, and helped in taking the boar down. So you see, I have done good as well as harm."

"You're a wicked thing, and I want you purged from my body." Link cringed, getting up, feeling his ribs were bruised, "And maybe this quest is meant to see it done!"

Before Link could take another step to charge, a powerful gust of wind blew him away, knocking the youth from his feet repeatedly, causing him to land painfully on his injured side. Link turned around to see a wyvern standing at the edge of the cliff, its massive bat wings spread in triumph as it screeched. Fear gripped the youth as he remembered the outcome of the last battle he held with such a creature, the grip on his weapon beginning to slip as his palms sweat.

"Now what do I do?" he asked himself, glaring at it.

The wolf-like creature beside him hunched on all fours, its liquid steel muscles coiling, biding time until the appropriate moment to strike came. Link watched his alter ego, how gracefully in the face of danger it moved. It did not for even one moment allow itself to be seen as prey, but as predator. It was a power the youth was realizing he had craved all along, to not falter and be like the heroes in tales he had heard back on Gaia. They had inspired him to strive for greatness, but the more he tried, the less it seemed likely he would ever reach anything close to them. He was Lincerious Heallaws of Gaia, a militia boy. Worst of all, he was cursed. He sighed in resignation. If he could not reach it, then he would aid it. The two of them locked eyes, the boy and the beast.

"I've not your strength or agility," Link replied, "But the odds of two against one are better. Should you wish it, my sword is at your disposal."

The beast continued to glare at Link, its crimson eyes fixated on the boy. A sense of understanding passed over them both.

"Together as one, for that is what we are," the creature spoke. Turning back towards the wyvern, they let out a war cry, charging as everything around them became irrelevant.

Darius found himself walking through the streets of Aldamoor. His destination was the Mage Council, and his goal was to be analyzed by its members for the right to hold the title of a mage. It was a day he had long waited for, to be recognized as more than an apprentice. It was the day many young Water Elves waited for. Some, left to pursue other occupations, but not Darius Silver. With confidence, he strode into the building of the tower, and walked towards the main audience chamber that was guarded.

"I am here for my session with the High Council concerning my appointment into magehood," he said, doing his best to contain his excitement.

The nondescript soldier standing before him gave a nod, and opened the door. Darius did not need any other gestures to tell him what to do next, and walked inside, the doors shutting behind him. There was an unusual calm within, and when he looked up into the seats, he realized the entire chamber was empty. His heart sank in fear, wondering if Kaian and the rest of the council had forgotten what was to happen on that day.

Out of nowhere, the world around him seemed to dim, and the voices of the council could be heard muttering above as each of them faded into place. Kaian strode into the room, seating himself upon the throne of the First Mage. The elder looked down, raising an eyebrow upon seeing Darius.

"I was told this meeting was for the induction of the one named Darius Silver, not a meeting with Puc Thanestorm," the descendant of Chiron said.

"I am Darius Silver, though," the young elf spoke.

Those within the chamber roared with laughter. The only one who did not seem amused, aside from Darius himself, was Kaian. One hand rested on his intricate staff with moving gears, the other against his mouth as he observed Darius's reaction. The First Mage rose, and used the stairs located to the side of his private box to descend to meet him.

"Thanestorm, you were injured during the Great War. Do you not remember anything?" Kaian asked, a genuine look of concern on his face.

"My name is Darius Silver," the boy said, aggravated. "I am Puc's apprentice, not Puc himself!"

Kaian shook his head, and with the tip of his staff created a mirror made of water from one of the decorative fountains within the chamber that stood close to the wall. He drifted the mirror over to himself.

"I'm afraid it is you who is mistaken," the First Mage spoke, and moved the mirror before Darius.

Darius felt his entire body go numb as he stared into the reflection. Tracing the contours of the face, there was no denying it that it belonged to his mentor.

"What? But how? Who did this?" the youth questioned. "I am not Puc Thanestorm."

"You are the one and the same, the one who allied himself first with Orbeyus of the Axe, the one who has been his advisor, the one who is destined to one day reunite the Four Forces with the help of his heir. This is who you are," Kaian spoke.

"No, I am not Puc Thanestorm!" Darius snarled once more. "I am Darius Silver!"

"Who in all the realms of hell is Darius Silver? What are you babbling about?" Kaian asked repeatedly, and motioned for two of the guards at the door to step forward and restrain Darius.

"I am the apprentice of Puc Thanestorm. I am the-," He spoke with confidence at first, but the moment the first sentence passed his lips, no other words found their way to them. He was at a loss. Who indeed was Darius Silver? Looking inward, Darius was forced to face a horrid truth. Despite all the things he had learned from his time in being Puc's apprentice, he could not find himself among the well of knowledge that dwelt within him. He was ever the mage's errand boy, the one who stayed up doing research, the one who did as he was told. It was not that he was unhappy in his role. He held a great reverence for the mage, but the realization hit him like a cold blade in the chest, the moment Darius Silver truly realized that he was dead to the world.

Standing in silence, he was soon held down by the guards, their grips crushing his body that suddenly felt vulnerable. He was no one, and no one would ever know of Darius Silver.

He then found himself back in his old room in the Academy, his hands resting on the small wooden cabinet before which stood a mighty mirror, in which his own face now was present.

"You're sure you wish to leave with Thanestorm this early in your training?" Nathaniel's voice came from the doorway. "I can deny his request to have you as his apprentice, you know. You're far too young to be going off in the care of a full mage. You still need to learn the basics. To find yourself."

Darius's memory jogged back to the day the event took place. It was the day Puc had come to the Academy in order to select an apprentice. The Great War had ended, and peace had been restored to the multiverse. It meant time to begin anew.

The young elf looked down at his hands, curling them up into tight fists as a million questions pounded through his head. The most furiously persistent one was why these events above all others were present in what he now realized was the Visium.

"Why shouldn't I go with him? He chose me above all others. He is the greatest battle mage to walk all the worlds of the Four Forces," the words came automatically from his mouth, echoing what he had said that day.

"Yes, but don't you want to see who you will become?" the elder elf spoke.

Darius froze, further thoughts piercing his already confused demeanor like a hot blade.

"Was it my mistake in going with Puc at such a young age?" he breathed quietly, looking into the mirror at his reflection. "Did I lose sight of who I was to be by following in the footsteps of Puc Thanestorm, and in so doing erasing any trace of who Darius Silver was?"

Before he could question any further, his world began to disappear around him, evaporating like steam that rose towards the sky. Looking at his hand, Darius watched as it faded from existence, along with the rest of him. No questions had been answered, and no more could be asked.

ഇരുഭ

Annetta woke up to find herself in a dark room. Letting her eyes adjust, she found herself lying on a bed with soiled tattered sheets, and before she could think about how she'd ended up there, the sound of creaking wood caught her sensitive ears.

"Who's there?" She perked up her head, sitting up and looking around.

The entire room was a ruin. Rotting beams seemed to be falling from the ceiling and parts of the plaster were eaten away. Before she could notice anything else aside form the crumbling drywall she spotted a silhouette standing in the doorway, watching her intently. She rose from the bed and walked in its direction cautiously, her hand gripping her sword hilt.

"Who are you?" she asked.

The figure stepped out from the darkness of the archway. The woman was dressed in a suit of silver plated armor, her hair in a disheveled ponytail, tied loosely to allow the long brown hair to flow wildly, like an extension of the red tattered cape she wore. Her visge was unnaturally pale, a face that was haunted. Her eyes, invisible to Annetta from the dark circles and shadows of her brow, bore into her nonetheless, staring the girl down with furious intent.

Annetta shifted, her palm on her sword as she got ready to draw it, realization dawning on her that this was the Visium, and that she would perhaps be required to fight this figure before her.

The woman made no move to harm Annetta. Instead, she raised a hand to motion for Annetta that she did not mean to fight. Annetta dropped her hand to the side as she followed the woman, not sure what to expect. It then dawned upon Annetta, the cape, the hair, the armor, she had seen it all before somewhere. She had dreamed it. She continued to observe her as they walked through another desolated room, this one with a burned sofa with beams sprawled out all over it. Annetta felt like a massive fire had caused the place they were in to look so. Her gaze then turned back to the figure, which pressed on, not glancing back.

"Um...So, who are you anyways. Are you my alter ego or something?" Annetta looked her up and down, "Because you look like the drawing I used to make whenever I was daydreaming in class."

The woman said nothing, and continued walking, moving out of the burned room onto a balcony. Annetta turned from facing her and looked out to see what lay before her. The breath in her body halted as she looked out from what once was, she realized, her balcony into a wasteland of ruins that once was the skyline of Toronto. Jagged buildings stood out against a dusty sepia sky. Even the C.N. Tower stood as a ruined monument, its proud pointed tip torn off, smashed as though a toddler had had its way with it, and then put it back for all to see.

"What happened?" she asked, wide eyed.

The figure looked down at Annetta, her eyes still obscured by shadow. The muscles in her jaws loosened and clenched as she opened her lips.

"We did not believe, and we failed," a fluid and confident voice spoke.

"Who?" Annetta asked in confusion.

The woman said nothing else as she looked down at the girl, unseen eyes penetrating into her.

600

"Who, me? What did I not believe?" Annetta questioned, pointing a finger at herself.

The figure said nothing, but took the young girl's hand, and placed it on Annetta's chest, leaving it to rest there. It took Annetta a moment to realize what the figure was trying to get at.

"You mean in myself?" she asked, as the figure nodded, "What does believing in myself have anything to do with any of this? What does the world getting destroyed have anything to do with lack of faith in myself? Let me tell you, I do not lack any faith in-,"

She did not finish the sentence, her own hand still resting on her chest as she spoke. The girl looked down at the hand, and then back up at the figure before she dropped her hand to her side.

"I just don't know if I can do what grandpa did is all," she spoke quietly. "I'm not really a warrior, I'm just me."

"You are only as much as you think of yourself," the figure spoke again, the half shadowed face turning down to look at her. "And I would think that one who said yes that day would not think so. I, in my circumstances, had no choice, but you did, even if you thought you did not. You could have walked away. That is what you must remember, little Annetta. There is always a choice, but you must first choose to see it."

Annetta felt a lump grow in her throat the more the figure spoke. It was as if someone was holding her neck, crushing it more and more with each word. She was unsure of the feeling within her. It was like uncertainty, but the more the figure burrowed its gaze into her, the more she felt something else surface from deeper within. Anger erased any trace of the previous emotions, and it rang like a thundering drum beat in her ears.

"That doesn't matter, I'm still just a girl!" she snapped, "And I can't be expected to know everything about all of this! I can't lead armies, I'm not that good of a fighter, and I can't even create psychic fire!"

The figure watched, unmoving, as tears of frustration began gathering in Annetta's eyes, unable to hold in the whirlwind of emotions she had kept bottled up for so long.

"Grandpa and Dad left me alone with all of this," she choked out of herself as she looked up at the warrior woman. "I'm a sixteen year old girl from the city. In the last few months I've had to learn to fight with a sword, ride a horse, use psychic powers, and they tell me there is a warlord on the way to kill me and my best friend, and we're alone in this mess. It was cool at first, yeah, we all wanted magic and fantasy to be real. But in reality, it is just…it's hard. It's not like in the stories I read about. People everywhere always expect something from me because of who my grandfather was, like I'm some deus ex machina who'll clean up all their problems. And stories don't tell you how to deal with actually fighting, because there it's cool, and they don't tell you how much it hurts to lose a friend. I'm frightened, I-"

An ironclad hand landed upon her shoulder, stopping Annetta mid rant. The girl looked up at the woman who knelt before her, drawing her sword and planting it in the ground, as she looked Annetta in the eyes.

"In the one who is severed we trust, our lives unto you until we are dust. What is ours we give unto you to use. Our strength and wisdom use as you choose," the woman spoke, her blue eyes now visible. "Though the path is full of obstacles you are never alone and never stop believing in who you will be tomorrow."

⬦⬥⬦

Puc walked in the Lab. He did not remember when he had returned, or what the outcome of the meeting with the Ogaien had been. All he could recall was entering the mountain temple, then finding himself here, walking towards the Lake biosphere. He could not remember why. His body moved of its own accord as though he were on an airship descending from its voyage in the clouds getting ready for the plunge to lower atmosphere, and he could not escape it. It all made sense, however, when he entered the biosphere and saw a familiar figure sitting upon the log, broad shoulders and back turned towards him, massive rabbit-like ears hanging from either side of the furry head, decorated with multiple silver earrings that jingled like chimes each time they twitched.

"Brakkus?" he said in disbelief, stepping closer to the Hurtz.

"About time ya showed up, mage," he responded, teasingly. "I was thinking ye wanted yer beauty sleep more than ta see me."

Puc swiftly came around the log and sat down, looking at his companion the way he last remembered seeing him alive. Though he was shocked, Puc knew full well Brakkus was not alive, and so he remained impassive as he joined him on the fallen tree.

"What?" Brakkus raised an eyebrow.

"Nothing, it is just good to see you well," the elf spoke.

"Pffft! Save it. Ya sound like a love stricken school boy." Brakkus swatted his hand in front of him. "Now, I believe I'm here for a reason, and it ain't playing the remember the old times game. Ya got something ya need ta tell me."

Puc smiled at his friend's straightforwardness. Even as a ghost, the Hurtz still refused to beat about the bush when something important needed to be done. A task was a task to him, and no questions were ever asked. He sighed, looking at the setting sun reflecting on the steady river that flowed before them. It felt good to have the giant at his side once more, like in all the years they had spent in the Lab awaiting the return of the heir of Orbeyus and son of Arcanthur. Their cares had been their own, and all they had to keep each other sane were the unbreakable spirit of friendship they had forged in times of war years before. In truth, Brakkus had been Puc's oldest friend next to Iliam. They had fought and outlasted many of those who had been part of the Great War, and now it seemed Puc had outlasted them all. The thought left the elf truly feeling the weight of his years. He looked over at the Hurtz, Brakkus's eyes staring into his like a faithful dog.

"I'm sorry I let you die," the mage managed to say. "It was my fault. If I had been waiting for Annetta and Lincerious, they would have never gone exploring, and none of this-"

"Stop beating yerself with that stick ye call a weapon, elf. It ain't befitting ya in the least," Brakkus growled. "Aye, I'm gone, dead, but the bloody thing was running loose in the Lab, and I guarantee sooner or later it would come looking for snacks, and we woulda had ta confront it."

"But we could have done it together. I should have-," Puc began.

"Ye should have, but ye weren't, alright?" The Hurtz glared at him. "And stop it, cuz yer making me sound like an incompetent minor! I ain't an infant ye needed to shield. I'm a Hurtz, and a Hurtz I always have been. Ours is a warrior race, and ye best never forget that about me. I died fighting, not on me death bed, and that was how it should have been."

"I should have died before you," sighed Puc. "I have lived for so long, seen so many people come and go, do you have any idea what that does to a creature of rational being? It destroys us, tears a piece of our soul away until we are just tattered rags."

"Yer also the most resilient bugger I ever met, and the foundation that kept us both sane during the blackout," Brakkus interrupted. "Thanestorm, ye've got ta get over it. I mean...ye can't save the whole world. No one can."

"I never wanted to save the whole world. I just wanted my friends and my lord to still be walking in the plane of my existence," Puc snapped, rising from his seat. "Is that so horrible a thing to desire?"

"Thanestorm," another voice said from behind him.

Puc flinched upon hearing a voice so well known to him. He turned around to find Orbeyus standing only a few feet from them, wearing his chain mail and cloak, with his double bladed axe loosely hanging in hand. None of his potency of spirit was lost in the vision, and none of his strength as he strode towards them, both companions falling to their knees and bowing.

"Rise, you know better than to bow to me," he spoke, words he often said when someone showed any sort of reverence towards him.

The companions rose, staring into a face that seemed to have been dead to them for an age. He looked younger than they remembered him, his beard and black hair only beginning to show the silver tint they had in old age. His eyes then focused on Puc, resting a powerful hand on the mage's shoulder, as he looked his once trusted advisor and right hand in the eye.

"You were one of my greatest companions in life, and together we did extraordinary things. This is why I chose you above all others to take care of those who would come after me, and you knew full well I would never live as long as you are meant to, Puc Thanestorm." The words seemed to echo with bittersweetness to them as the man spoke. "We all have a purpose in life the Unknown gives us, and when it is done, we return to the eternal where our souls remain."

Puc felt his being tremble slightly, but he would not show emotion in the face of his lord, and nothing living or dead could compel him to do so. He lowered his head, regaining control before facing Orbeyus.

"How much longer must I endure this?" he asked.

"That I cannot tell you, for only the Unknown knows the hour and day of each creature's demise. What I can say is this: you are not at fault for my death, nor for Brakkus's. We served our purpose. It was our time to leave and make room for those who hold the future in their hands, and I ask you as I once did, Puc Thanestorm, will you take up arms with Annetta, my granddaughter, and Jason the son of Arcanthur, to help destroy who I could not?" Orbeyus's eyes searched for an answer within Puc's as he spoke.

The mage remembered the words well. They were the same Orbeyus had presented him in the vision he received a few days after the warrior had been murdered.

"My words, my lord, stay as they have always been. My life to the Severio clan until I am dust," he spoke.

"Then go, and do not mourn for our death, but rejoice in knowing we shall all one day meet again," Orbeyus said in a thundering tone. They were the last words the elf remembered before falling into the same blinding light as he had in his previous encounter with Orbeyus. Before Annetta and Jason had come to the Lab, Puc had dreamed of his sworn lord standing beside the two birds who had called themselves angels. There it was that the mage had sworn to not leave, to stay behind and wait for the next generation that was to take its place as the defenders of earth, a generation that he was meant to train. This he had sworn to his lord, and he now remembered his vows to the Lord of the Axe.

ഇരുൽ

Matthias held the dagger firmly with the blade facing down as he stalked through the rocky corridor. Something did not fit. He had been sure before that he was right in front of Annetta. The brown stone walls wound around him like the coils of a great serpent as he ran. Finally, he saw something through the smoke, a figure lying on the sandy floor in the distance, fast asleep. Clutching his dagger, ready to strike, he began creeping up, the sand beneath his feet making not a sound as the muscles in his legs worked in unison to keep it so. He had not been able to use his true skills in this mission as an assassin very much, and now it was time. He glanced at the sleeping form of the girl, her chest rising and falling. Wishing a silent mocked goodbye, the assassin raised his dagger.

The small figure began to move however, twitching as though waking from a nightmare. Matthias noticed that the girl before him was not Annetta Severio, but someone else.

"What in the stars?" He blinked, watching as the girl awoke before him. Without him noticing, his surroundings shifted into something Matthias had thought would never return to him. A burning inferno he had long put out of his mind.

The girl rose, her clothing tattered and worn, and her face smeared with ash. Her tiny hands reached out towards him, pleading.

"Matti, where's mommy and daddy? I'm scared," she sniffed.

Matthias's feet began to shift towards her automatically, like a puppet on strings. Kneeling down, he reached for the girl and embraced her. For some reason, she felt so familiar to him and then it all hit him. He was far from being awake. He was now a passenger on the ride.

"Dana, it's alright, you're safe," he whispered. The words coming from his mouth sounded different, not that of a man, but of a boy. He then realized his entire body had changed into that of his ten year old self, as old as he had been when it had all happened.

"But where are mommy and daddy?" the girl sobbed into his chest

"I don't know, sis, but we're going to find them, okay? I promise," he said, pulling back to look into the little girl's round face, tears glistening all over her pale cheeks.

The girl sniffled, trying to pull herself together. She was only a year younger than he was, but to him she had always seemed the more fragile. Her pale blonde hair cascaded all around her from the top of her head, and now lay in tangles, her blue eyes watching him through a curtain of tears. She nodded upon hearing him. Her mouth opened ever so slightly as she was about to say something, but instead of words, her body jerked violently, blood began pouring in a single stream from her lips, her eyes filled with shock. The boy did not let her go, clutching his sister's shoulders as if trying to force life back into her, only to notice the single metal spike going through her chest. The object slid out of her as the girl fell to the floor.

Matthias held onto her the whole way, cradling her in his arms as he tried to comfort her.

"Dana, don't go…stay awake." His lower lip trembled as he watched the silver film of death form over her eyes, everything else in his world becoming blurred.

"Well done in finding the boy Amarok," a familiar voice said from above.

Matthias then found himself looking at the hem of a black cloak and boots right before his face. His bloodstained face and tear streaked eyes moved upward to face the source of his grief, the being he had come to know as Mislantus the Threat. He was not Mislantus as he was now. Instead of the face of a cat, he had the face of a man, though twisted by his desire to please his father. His green eyes were fixed upon the boy, peering from beyond his brown eyebrows, his forehead knotted in thought, making his short cropped receding hairline to be even more noticeable. Even before the curse, he still had the demonic aura of the animal. Another man stepped out of the shadows, his long tangled hair and armor making him distinguishable to the young boy as his future mentor, Amarok Mezorian.

"As instructed, I have disposed of the parents," he quietly informed Mislantus.

"Good, take this one into custody," Mislantus grinned, pleased with the assassin. "Someday, Amarok, when I rule in my father's stead, you shall inherit the post as my right hand."

It all came hurling back into the forefront of his mind. The years he had spent burying the truth about his parent's murder by Mislantus and his men for the simple fact that they had been born with psychic abilities and refused to bow to the warlord. Hearing the words exchanged by the two brought bile to Matthias's throat, and he turned away from the corpse of his sister and vomited onto the barren ground, charred by the fires of war. Coughing up everything that was lodged into his throat, the young boy felt an iron grip land upon his shoulder.

"Rise, child, for there is nothing left for you here now but death and despair. Come and follow me," Mislantus said in a voice so gentle, it was unbefitting to the tyrant Matthias had grown up beneath.

Matthias stopped, looking up at the man. He couldn't tell if this was all fact or fiction. He wanted to shout and scream that this was not what had happened, that Mislantus had taken him in when he had defended him. That another dangerous foe had raided his home and killed his family.

"This is all a dream, a really bad dream." He shook his head.

"No dream, I am afraid, but the truth." Mislantus shook his head as he extended his hand to the boy. "Now come and follow me, young Matthias, and in blood drown out the sorrow for your family. Kill and kill and kill until bloodlust is satisfied. I give you the option between life and death. Choose now, boy. You can join your sister, or become one of the greatest warriors that ever lived under the banner of Mordred the Conqueror."

There were now two identities within Matthias, the man of close to thirty years witnessing events over again that had been purged from his consciousness, and the little boy who lived it all for the first time, terrified of everything that was going on around him. The man could only helplessly watch from afar as the boy chose the only answer that would ever make sense in the eyes of a child. He reached out his hand. He could do nothing but scream and howl inside a body that was not his own and never was since that very day.

಑ಒ಩

They each awoke at different times, and crawled out of the tunnel, then waited in the room they had been left in by Quadan. They were all shaken for different reasons, but one thing was clear, they had come to a new understanding within the mist of who they were. Jason was the second to emerge from the chamber, and upon seeing Annetta stumble out from the corridor, ran to her, embracing his friend who was still coughing the smoke from her lungs. Annetta returned the embrace lightly, confused about what was going on.

"Don't ever change," he managed to say, hugging her.

"Uh. Okay. I won't," she said blearily, and pulled away. "You look like you saw a ghost."

"Something like that," he smiled weakly, dropping his arms to his side. "Just promise me you'll kick the crap out of Finn next time we're in school okay?"

Annetta smiled lightly, still shaking off the effects of the mist. "As long as I know you're there to back me up, dude."

Puc and Link sat wordlessly off to the side. The Gaian and the Water Elf watched the reactions of those in the room, only guessing what they had seen. Link sighed, shifting his weight as he used the hilt of his sword to prop himself up on the rock he was sitting on, causing Puc to glance over at him, a smile drawing itself lightly on his face.

"Were I to give you rabbit ears and a snout, I would say you remind me of a certain Hurtz I once knew," he said, finally beginning to understand his own vision with more clarity.

"Well I hope you don't decide to do so. I think my alter ego may be a bit jealous if someone else came knocking on the door," the youth retorted with a grin.

Puc said nothing more but nodded. He was feeling much lighter, as though a load had been taken off of his shoulders, despite knowing what lay ahead of them. He had forgotten the feeling since the last time he did the Visium. It was meant as a time of reflection, even if the images themselves were painful to behold at the time of the trance itself. He looked over at his apprentice to see him leaning against the stone walls farther away, a scowl on his face as though he were in deep thought, and decided it was best not to disturb him. Everyone took in what they saw differently.

It was no shock when the last of them, Matthias, came out with his face completely pale, and eyes rimmed in red from tears. He sat down heavily beside Sarina, not saying a word.

Though strain was visible each of them even if they tried and hide it, there was a sense of peace and resolution that seemed to radiate through the room until the thin, muscular form of the Ogaien male emerged from the other side of the cave, followed by Natane and two other priestesses.

"The Visium has come to an end," Natane spoke. "Tiamet has breathed her wisdom into you, so that you may with clarity approach your lives from this day forth. How feel you warriors from the world of a blue sky?"

Puc, who spoke for the group on such occasions, showed no fire to address the Great Mother. His gaze instead turned to Annetta, and the girl rose in his place.

"My friends and I are tired, but..." She looked around at everyone, not sure if she was saying what was appropriate, "But strength that was lost can return. Weariness is weakness leaving the body to make way for more strength."

The draconic woman smiled, happy with the answer provided by the girl, and looked beyond her, locking eyes with Puc. The mage inclined his head slightly before standing and walking over to Annetta's side.

"We are ready to press onward," he said. "It is as Annetta said. Weakness will be replaced with strength in due time."

"Then come, rise all you that have fallen as fire does rise upon the horizon," Natane spoke as she watched the rest of the group get up and begin to leave the cave.

Matthias, last to come out of the trance, was the last to exit. Stopping before Natane, he touched the Ogaien's arm, trembling from the fear that ran through him like a cold fever, despite the heat of the mountain.

"I...I'm sorry. I need to know something." He swallowed hard, tripping over his words. "Do the visions show fiction or fact only?"

"Whatever do you mean, male?" Natane raised an eyebrow. "The visions show what we lack, what we must see."

"Can they show the past? A past that we have tried to forget?" He licked his lips nervously. "Look, I need to know if what I saw was real, or a trick of Tiamet, or some apparition from my own perverse mind."

Natane turned to fully face him, and her fierce reptilian features seemed calm and almost lovely to the assassin. Reaching out both her slender arms, the priestess laid them upon his temples, and closed her eyes, chanting a mantra to her Goddess.

Matthias felt his whole body sweat as the chanting became louder, more labored and exhausting until the prayer seemed to reach its end. Silence occurred for after, the closed eyes of the Ogaien seeming to shift beneath the lids before they opened, Natane gasped for air after coming out of the trance, falling to the sandy floor.

"Bathed in the blood of a loved one," she panted. "No pain can be greater, and one would wish to forget. I am sorry for your loss. She had a beautiful soul."

Matthias did not need the priestess to elaborate anymore on the subject, his suspicions having been confirmed. Hoisting the woman up with a single pull from his arm, he left the temple without saying anything else.

The others waited outside with Natane's daughters, and what seemed to be a few thousand riders with spears in hand standing beside their Aiethon, waiting for the party to assemble. Puc shot a glance to Matthias, wondering what had taken him so long to emerge with Natane, but said nothing, knowing it was not the time to scold the young man. The riders hollered their war cries upon everyone emerging from the cave, their ebony spears lifted towards the sky. Natane raised her arms in an effort to calm the horde. Once silence fell, she pointed to Annetta and her friends in a swift and powerful motion.

"They arrived as children, and come now as one of us, having walked to smoke of Tiamet. They come as Ogaien!" she called out as those before her went into another frenzy of cheering.

Amayeta came towards her mother and handed Natane her spear, reaffirming the leader's role as both Priestess and the Great Mother. Natane raised an arm again with a smile in order to silence the crowd, and turned towards Annetta and her companions. Her look fell most intently upon the young girl in the front, a sword strapped to her side, her father's shield held in hand.

"You look not much different than a certain young man I met many years before. He led armies, slew monsters, and carried a weight unlike anyone in all the worlds has ever seen. Are you truly ready to undertake a burden like this?" she asked.

610

Annetta looked back at those who stood behind her, then back at Natane, not needing much confirmation about what her heart told her at that moment.

"Alone I don't think I can, but a burden can lessen if you share it with those who are there for you," she replied, a small smile spreading on her face. "I like to think I have a few of those."

"More than a few, little Annetta," Natane nodded, and leaning in, whispered to the girl. "I watched your vision as you went through it. Remember well the words."

Kneeling on one knee and planting her spear into the ground before her feet, the Great Mother set the example for all those behind her to do the same.

"In the one who is severed we trust, our lives unto you until we are dust. What is ours we give unto you to use. Our strength and wisdom use as you choose," the sound of a united chorus of voices boomed from all around.

Rising, Natane took a step back as Anuli and Amayeta brought the horses of the company forward.

"They will escort you to the portal," Natane said to them, "for I have many preparations to attend to, warriors to be gathered, and other Mothers to inform of the situation at hand. It will not be an easy process, but I will see it done."

"Let this be of some help in providing time to heal wounds." Puc handed one of the time synchronizing watches to the Great Mother. "I will be back upon having sent word to the others so that we may all meet."

"Agreed. I look forward to riding into battle with you once more, Thanestorm," Natane said with a fiendish grin.

Puc felt a pain in his heart upon hearing the Great Mother speak of war. He looked upon the reptilian face of the woman, the draconic eyes glaring at him with a fire he had only known two other people to harbor in times of war, friends he would miss dearly. He mounted his horse.

"We will meet the enemy before the season sets. Be ready," he spoke, and veering his horse around, thundered off with the others, the sound of cheering Ogaien echoing in his ears as they left.

Chapter 54

Upon arriving back in the castle, the companions made their way towards the armory wing after leaving the horses at the stables. The day was in full swing with the sun shining through the windows, causing the stones of the mighty fortress to glisten as though it were lined with thousands of diamonds. Running up the multitude of stairs, Annetta led the way, followed closely behind by everyone else. Coming into the room with the tapestry surrounding the pedestal, she froze, and everyone in turn stopped behind her as soon as they reached the top.

"Well, come on, Anne, what's the hold up?" Jason asked. He plowed through to the front to stand beside his friend, who stared at the sword. "What's wrong?"

Annetta snapped out of her trance and looked over at Jason, then back to the sword sitting in the pedestal that looked no different from a simple stone that had been rolled into the middle of the room. But now, the four etched symbols on it glowed in their respective colors: the water drops in blue, the mountain in black, the wind in green, and the flame in red.

"Nothing. It's just that…well." she swallowed hard, walking up to the sword. "Here goes nothing."

Having seen too many movies and video games in her spare time, Annetta half expected to end up in an alternate universe, or feel completely different, or for time to race forwards, but nothing happened. The leather on the hilt felt soft as she gripped it tightly, and began pulling upwards. At first it was as though the mighty blade was caught in the stone, or it had all been a big gag set up by some team from a television studio who would jump out at any moment, but after hearing the gritting of steel against stone, the blade began to smoothly rise up, so much so that Annetta nearly fell back upon withdrawing the blade completely.

Catching herself just in time, she looked down at the fruit of her labors with her friends. The sword hilt looked plain to Annetta, but she found it complete and beautiful. It sported a wheel-shaped pommel instead of an elaborate design. Crisscrossed leather covered the hilt completely, and a straight silver guard led into the two-edged blade. Looking even closer, she noted huge embossed letters on the sword.

"Severed be he whom forgets." Puc read them out. "Words all Severios learn to hold dear. From what early texts say, they are the words Lord

Adeamus told his army before their battle with Galtevor's forces, the man who betrayed him. People teased him about why his surname was Severio, meaning 'cut off,' or 'severed.' He would use the words to illustrate that the only ones who were indeed cut off were those who had forgotten who they were, who had forgotten responsibility and who had forgotten themselves."

Annetta held up the sword before her, admiring the gleaming of the blade in the sunlight as she took in the etched in words, feeling a chill go down her spine. The same amazement filled her as it always did whenever she discovered something new about the life she was in now. It was a feeling that she was part of something greater than herself. She looked at the blade once more as she tried to comprehend the history it possessed, and the amount of lives it had touched, both in the act of taking life, and as a symbol to the wielder. Link came up beside her quietly, holding an empty scabbard and belt in his hands.

"I found these behind where your father's shield had been," he said, handing them to her. "I've been working on restoring them, since the leather was so worn."

Annetta accepted the black leather scabbard into her free hand, and slid the blade in with ease. Somehow, holding it in her hands felt more right than anything else in her short life ever had.

"Thank you. For everything," she said, looking around at those who were in the room. Little did the group notice that two of them were missing.

೩೧೮

Matthias had been present at the drawing of the sword, but having remained silent the whole journey, it had been easy for him to slip out onto the balcony in the vast library to contemplate more on the haunting images that had been reawakened by the vision quest. His conscience stirred like the heart of a twister as he weighed his options. Mislantus had made him live a lie, had used him as a tool. Now, having been given the truth, he had a choice. Would he leave, or would he stay?

The choice was more than obvious to the assassin, but there were other factors involved. He was just beginning to gain the trust of the other Q-16 inhabitants. How could he now tell them what his true intent had been? But he knew that the longer he allowed his deception to go on, the more there was a chance that he could be discovered, and from what he had seen of the mage's behavior, that could mean death for him. His thoughts were interrupted by the sound of footsteps on the marble floor. Turning, he saw

Sarina. The assassin rose on instinct in the presence of one who was technically his commander.

"Matt, I need to tell you something important," she said firmly.

"Good, because I have something I must say to you," he replied.

"I'm not leaving Earth," she said promptly, before he could say a word. "I've made up my mind. Valdhar was never my home. In fact, my father, well, I bet he wouldn't even care if I was missing. All he has ever cared about since grandfather was killed was conquering the Eye to All Worlds. He doesn't care about me, and I want my own life. I want to have friends that I don't need anyone's approval for, and I don't have to be scared about having to kill them because he does not like them."

Matthias sighed, his own confession having been made that much easier.

"I'll stay as well," he said in a grave tone. "I have my own reasons, though, and a score to settle with both Mislantus and Amarok."

Sarina, despite being unsure of what Matthias meant by the second part of his announcement, could not have looked happier. She ran over to him and embraced him tightly. Matthias winced a little from the sudden rush of emotions, but returned it with a light pat on the back, still not comfortable with showing much affection towards his adoptive sister. Pulling, away the girl looked at him with a worried gaze.

"What do we tell the others?" she asked, a question both of them needed to discuss in detail.

ഽരുൿ

The assassin prowled the bowels of the shadows within the fortress's structure. Amarok, a man of many resources, had never given away the secret of his responsibility for the murder of Orbeyus Severio. He knew it was in his favor to always have some tricks up his sleeve against other warriors of Valdhar who wanted to take his place in case another opportunity were to arise, and there were many opportunities for an assassin as skilled as himself in the depths of space. After the defeat in the Great War, when all of Mordred's forces had scattered in the panic, the crafty warrior had taken the time to loot the rotting corpses on the field. In his toils, he had been able to recover a single card key, with the letter and numbers 'Q-16' on it. He knew their meaning, and so his planning began, watching and waiting for the right moment to end the life of the wretch known as Orbeyus Severio, the one responsible for having destroyed the one chance all worlds had of being united under a single iron grip.

Though it was true he did hold an allegiance to Mislantus, and always would, he was ultimately concerned more with his own standing. He would always be number one, no matter what it took. Now, as before, the tattered card key had served as his way in. He would never bow to any other assassin as superior, especially one he had trained. Mislantus's growing displeasure at Matthias, fueled by Amarok's reports, had only brought the aging fighter back to his true place. Finally, it had all fallen into place when neither Amarok nor Mislantus had heard anything from the young assassin upon his entrance into the base with Sarina, and they were presumed killed in action.

Taking his time, slipping through the base, he made his way through from memory. He had spent two years mentally mapping out the layout, hiding, observing. This time, the preparations would not need to be so grand.

He had been given instructions to return with Sarina if she lived, and with matter from the 'Eye to All Worlds,' which could be used in Valdhar's prized portal cannon, the Pessumire, now fully operational after years of reconstruction.

It had been destroyed in the Great War, and it had taken many years and many great minds to get the magnificent device to work again. But in order for it to create portals, it needed somekind of molecular particles from the material plane it would make its way onto.

Traveling through the red and black portal that led to the castle, Amarok quickly eyed a small shrub. He pulled a branch from it before heading back into Q-16, where he could better await his prey, and slip away even quicker by teleporting back to Valdhar from the base. To Amarok, physical distance and size were not a restraint when it came to his abilities. He was past the boundaries of physical thinking, a feat few psychics ever truly achieved.

Noting that no one was around, the assassin took his time in looking around all the known places that captives had once been held in, searching for the daughter of the warlord. His searching came to an end as he heard voices begin to echo down the metal corridors. Coiling and stretching the muscles in his body, the assassin retreated to his hiding spot beside the main gate.

Having returned to the Lab, the companions separated for the evening. Darius still seemed withdrawn, and went to his room while Link stayed back to attend to the horses, which were weary from the travel. Annetta, Puc, Jason, Matthias and Sarina headed to the main gate together, Annetta still holding Severbane's hilt tightly, almost like a security blanket.

The girl had worked so long and hard for the weapon, she didn't like having to leave it behind with Puc, and wanted to protest, saying she would leave it in her room. But she knew all too well that the mage would never allow it. They stopped before the great doors of the base that led to the teleporters, and it being Annetta's turn, she opened the behemoth gates.

"I should like to speak with you, mage, once they are back safely in their homes," Matthias whispered to Puc from the side, to which the elf nodded, his gaze still fixed on his young charges at the same time.

Annetta took the sword belt off from her waist, holding the weapon in her hands.

"Doesn't Severbane have a spell on it like Helbringer?" she asked, regretfully handing the weapon over to Puc.

"It does," the mage answered. "Your father would know how to put the blade in a dormant state."

Before Annetta could respond with even a nod, the blade flew from Puc's grasp as if hit by an arrow, and landed some feet away with a clang. The mage shifted into a battle stance, drawing Tempest, and readying a spell to fire from the tip of his staff. A flash of silver appeared before him. The mage let the blaze from his staff go. In need of reassurance that the mark had hit home, he struck with his blade, only to find air in place of the shape.

Readying a second blast, Puc spun around as he tried to locate the target. In what seemed a split second, the blur of silver appeared once more, the staff and blade colliding with an ocean of metal spikes. The metallic extensions seemed to come to life as they extended out from Amarok's body in the dark, swaying and targeting both the sword and staff simultaneously. Succeeding in knocking the staff from Puc's grasp, the spikes then began to concentrate upon the sword, extending and combining in front of the motionless Amarok, coalescing like liquid into a single silver spire as they aimed to break the weapon. Fury taking over the mage, Puc wasted no time in gathering his wits in retaliation, and readied a blast of white energy with his free hand. Before he could unleash it, however, the spikes vanished, causing further chaos among the gathered.

Sarina screamed helplessly while Annetta and Jason turned around to face the invisible foe, Jason readying a batch of psychic fire while Annetta covered his back, ready to send their opponent into one of the steel walls around them. Faster than anyone could predict, a form teleported, grabbing hold of Sarina, then knocked Jason from his feet from behind and grabbed him, teleporting some feet away from Annetta. The girl gritted her teeth in anger and began focusing her mind on the shadow before her, but found she was unable to do anything, her whole body paralyzed. It felt as though someone was holding onto her, not letting her make her own decisions. She could feel from her deeper subconscious that someone was responsible for the sudden lack of power over her senses. There was a malignant trace to their intentions, and she did not like it one bit. She looked over helplessly at Matthias, who also seemed stunned by a mental attack, his body shaking, trying to break free form the assault.

The only one from the group who was still moving was Puc, the white ball of energy present in his right hand, and the blade in his left. His eyes darted wildly as he searched for the perpetrator. As if in answer to his challenge, the spikes appeared from the dark, their origin point invisible, and Puc released the blast from his hand upon them.

"Run, Annetta. Get out of here, the lot of you!" Puc ordered the group. But as the smoke cleared, his concentration on his companions diminished as he was faced with another onslaught of spikes that threw him against the nearest wall, shaped like a club. Before Puc could recover, a vine-like extension then came off of the club and took advantage of Puc's fall, slinking into his robes and pulling out a small wooden pendant with markings on it. It then crushed it, and the extension slithered back into the dark.

"Anti-psychic charms. You were prepared, mage. And well done, Teron." A voice Matthias had heard only too many times answered from the darkness. "I will admit, when Mislantus gave the order to pronounce you dead in action, I did not mourn his decision. Yet, here you are."

He stepped out from the shadows, into Annetta's line of sight. The armor on his arms was covered with silver spikes, which were all curved and pointed towards his two hostages, Jason and Sarina. On his face, a broken star-shaped mask glistened back at her, long locks of white hair protruding from it. Her gaze then turned back to Matthias, the one the comment was directed at, his face white with shock.

"You," Matthias managed to utter with a struggle. "You wanted this all along, didn't you?"

The assassin chuckled, striding towards him, standing an inch from the young man's face. Commanding one of the spikes with his mind, it sprang to life and slithered forward, shaping itself like a human hand that cupped Matthias's face. Amarok noted a change in the eyes of the younger man, as if the hate that was there before had built up even more over the short course of time since they had last spoken on Earth.

"I can see Earth has made you soft. Am I correct in this assumption, Teron?" Amarok's eyes glinted behind the mask.

"Then you are a fool in thinking so, for the only thing it has done is made me see the truth," the younger man spat.

"Ah, but there is only one fool when betrayal of the master is concerned, and it is he who carries out the crime," Amarok spoke as he continued to hold Sarina and Jason in his grasp. "Shame on you for kidnapping the daughter of Mislantus. But never fear, I will make sure she gets home safe and sound."

Everyone's eyes widened at the declaration except Matthias, who was still focused upon Amarok.

"I hope you burn someday," Matthias gritted his teeth, venom searing from his eyes.

"Already have. You made sure of that," Amarok said.

His gaze then lingered on Annetta. "And you must be the little Severio everyone is talking about, I am correct? Annetta, is it?"

Annetta felt her blood boil as she looked helplessly, still in a state of paralysis as she gazed at Jason who looked paler than she had ever seen him before. Amarok saw the connection between their lines of sight and smiled beneath the mask.

"Well, Annetta, if you would like to see your friend here again, then I propose a deal. You surrender the Eye to All Worlds to my lord and master, and I will see to it that you get him back," Amarok explained. "If, however, you choose to play the part of a hero, and stand and fight, then I will make sure that he remains as a decoration for our dungeons. You have till midnight."

618

Moments later, he had teleported from before their eyes, with Jason and Sarina still in his grasp. Released from the being's invisible grip, Annetta flew forward, the pressure from her wanting to tackle him still present in her body after the fact. Matthias showed no such will, simply falling to the ground. Puc then came towards them, Severbane slung over his shoulder. Handing the blade back to Annetta, the mage turned to the man.

"Who in all the infernos of the known worlds was that?" he snarled.

"Amarok," Matthias said, the color drained from his face. "Amarok Mezorian."

Puc froze. He had not recognized the assassin in the silver mask. The name, however, had been well known to him. It was a name the mage had learned to fear and respect. His gaze then turned to Matthias, his ears having picked up something among the chaos. Without warning, the mage slammed the man to the floor, pinning him with a spell.

"Puc what are you doing?" Annetta's eyes went wide.

"He is a spy! He always has been," the mage spat, causing the tip of his staff to light up like hot iron in front of Matthias's face, "I warned you of the fate you'd face should you prove false... Teron."

ନଙ୍କ

Darius stood in front of the mirror in his quarters as soon as the door shut behind him. A million thoughts rushed through his head as he tried to grasp every single one of them, a herculean task even for a mage's apprentice.

Apprentice. Could he even consider himself an apprentice, or was he something else, something lower? His dark eyes glared from behind a curtain of black hair, his face wrinkling in disgust. His eyes fell upon a dagger lying beside him, a new addition to his room that he did not recognize. Had he conjured it up to end his own life in his despair upon unlocking the door? He shook his head. No, he was never one to have even contemplated such a notion.

His hand reached for the brown leather sheath. Sliding the blade out, he studied its perfect edge. Darius's gaze then shifted to his own visage in full with the blade as a thought came to his mind. Grabbing hold of a lock of his hair, he pressed the blade close and began sawing away. Severing it, he reached for another and another. Once finished, he looked up at the work of art he had created, running a hand through it.

"Better," he breathed quietly, only to have someone knock on his door.

Turning away and opening it, he found Link standing in its midst, his bangs and braid in disarray as though he had been running a marathon.

"Something is wrong," he panted. "Something is not right with Annetta. I can feel it."

"What are you talking about, Heallaws?" The elf raised his eyebrow. "How can you feel something is wrong? Did someone place an empathy charm on you?"

"Something is not right, damn it!" he snapped, and with a hiss, he grabbed his forehead. "I don't know, it's been like this since I swore that oath to Brakkus. I can't explain it. It's like I can sense what Annetta is feeling, just not direct thoughts."

"You sure you just didn't get kicked by a horse or something?" Darius questioned him, finding the claim ridiculous.

"No, I didn't. Just trust me!" he snarled. "We have to hurry."

"Okay, okay. I'm going," Darius waved his arm, trying to calm down the panicking warrior. Stepping out of his room, he went after Link.

By the time the two of them arrived, Matthias was pinned down on the floor by Puc with the mage's staff in his face, while Annetta tried to stop the assault with words from the side. Jason and Sarina were nowhere to be seen.

"Master!" Darius called, running over to him. "What's wrong? What happened? Where are the others?"

"Taken. And this fool is a mongrel spy!" Puc sneered, threatening Matthias with his molten staff tip. "I should have killed you the moment you set foot in the Lab!"

"And I tell you, I did not lead Amarok here!" Matthias called back.

"Mark my words, I will break you and you will tell no more lies." Puc's vicious demeanor did not fade. "I should have known you were one of Mislantus's cronies. I should have known from the bloody start."

Link ignored the banter between the two, and walked over to Annetta's side. Touching the girl's arm, he looked for a sign that she was alright. She only looked at him briefly before turning her attention back to the others.

"There is no need to break me, mage. I'll tell all willingly," Matthias said finally with a defeated sigh but smirked after, "Not that you'll believe me anyways."

"You're right. I won't believe a word of it without spilling blood," Puc hissed. Conjuring chains around Matthias's wrists and legs, he pulled the man up. "I will get the answers I want. The choice on how it plays out is yours alone."

The mage's awareness then turned to the youth standing around him, their eyes fixated on his.

"Stop looking at me like that, and go back to your rooms," he snarled at the two boys, before turning to Annetta. "Don't even think about doing anything rash. We will figure this out. In the meantime, you will stay confined to your home and go nowhere until I call upon you. Is that clear?"

Annetta could do nothing in return but nod, in a state of shock at the mage's outburst.

"Good, then we are agreed." Puc gave a single gruff nod, and pulled Matthias along. The two of them became mere dots in the distance as they pressed on to their destination.

Annetta blinked a few times as she tried to take in everything that had just happened. In a matter of seconds, her best friend had been kidnapped, and now the one person she had counted on to have a plan had told her to go to her room instead of help find him. Tears of frustration began to gather in her eyes. Holding them back, she faced the two standing before her, knowing this was neither the time nor place.

"We have to do something. We can't just leave him," she said to them.

"Yeah, but where would we even start?" Link asked.

"I have a fair idea of where Mislantus's fortress is," Darius said as he ran a hand through his new short hair subconsciously. "Puc had me mapping it through a telescope from the apartment building. I think our main problem will be getting there."

The trio's eyes wandered from one another as they tried to come up with a solution. Link's lit up shortly after.

"Follow me," he said, and took off.

"What? Where are we going?" Annetta put the sword belt on.

"I think the Dutchman needs a night out!" Link called back to her.

"What? Are you crazy! That thing is an antique!" Annetta's eyes widened, as her memory flashed back to the ancient sea galley that was said to be a space vessel by the Gaian youth. Her gaze turning to Darius, who stood beside her with his hands in his pockets. She saw something different about him, and it took her a moment to realize from all the commotion as to what it was. "Nice hair cut. It suits you better."

"Really? Thanks," he replied. "I wanted to try something different."

"Well, you picked one hell of a time." She shook her head and ran off after Link, who already had a head start on them.

Chapter 55

It had only taken Amarok moments to get back to Valdhar. Years of training had made him proficient in teleportation, and it now came to the assassin as second nature. His grip on Sarina and Jason remained firm throughout, the deadly metal spikes honed in on their necks through the use of his psychic abilities as he rose from his kneeling position with them, watching the disoriented staff staring.

"Well, don't stand there, you imbeciles. Notify Lord Mislantus that I have returned with his daughter and a hostage!" He roared the command as the closest soldier scurried off into the depths of the fortress.

Jason, still in shock, began coming to, looking around at where he was, and at the assortment of strange creatures dressed in grey tabards bearing the emblem of a seven headed dragon with ten stars. Looking out the window, he saw something even more frightening, like something out of a science fiction book. The light of a multitude of stars flickered in a black dotted sky. Shocked, his mouth opened.

"Don't even think of escaping. You will be dead in seconds," the elder assassin growled. Prodding him, they walked towards their destination.

›‹

Informed of their arrival, Mislantus waited in his audience chamber, his eyes closed and ears flattened, only becoming alert when the doors opened and the sound of feet could be heard.

Jason came into the room, fitted with a cuff suppressing his abilities. The boy stopped when ordered by Amarok, to stare at the cat-like face of the tyrant. Looking at the strange being, Jason had a hard time coming to terms with it being sentient, only believing it when he began to speak.

"So, you are the son of Arcanthur?" Mislantus questioned, his glowing feral eyes fixed on the youth.

"I am and I always have been," Jason spoke defiantly. "What's it to you, tabby face?"

Mislantus bared his teeth in anger. He wanted to strike the boy, but he had other plans for him. He needed Jason to lure the others so he could dispose of the would-be protectors of the Eye to All Worlds. Withdrawing his fangs, the warlord turned his attention to Amarok, who stood behind the boy.

"You returned with my daughter, I presume?" He cocked his head to the side, resting his chin on two curled fingers.

"Yes, my lord. She is locked up in her chamber as you requested," the assassin responded with a bow.

Jason felt part of him crumble upon hearing the confirmation. He had been hoping since the accusation had been made in the Lab that it had been false, that Amarok had somehow made a mistake.

"Good. And there she will stay until this is all over," Mislantus said, dismissing the matter. "Now, do you have what I asked you to acquire?"

Amarok stepped past Jason and produced a single small twig decorated with a few leaves to the tyrant. Grabbing the thing from his hand faster than the assassin could hand it over to him, the warlord hissed in glee, caressing it with a joy he had not known since before his father's death.

"At long last, my father's dream shall come true. The banner of the descendants of Freius, the enslaver of Korangar shall reign upon the heavens of all," he said in a faint whisper, closer to his goal than he had been in years.

His eyes then shifted to Jason, who still stood in the room, having listened to everything that had gone on. "Take him to the dungeon. I will have someone bring him to me when the time is right."

"As you will it, my lord." Amarok bowed once more.

Mislantus closed in on the boy and looked him in the eyes, Jason glaring back rebelliously. It intrigued the warlord immensely for it was not often that someone dared to face him.

"Ah, little boy, what do you truly know of the world?" He grinned. "You've no idea what is about to happen here, do you? You have never had the chance to witness the glory of an army in full regalia as it marches to victory."

Jason said nothing as Amarok's hand found its way to the youth's shoulder, and began steering him to the door.

"Jeez, you're really full of it, you know," Jason called as the door opened. "If you think my friends are just going to give up without a fight, you have no clue what you are up against."

Mislantus smirked, turning away, twirling the twig in his hand. "Oh but I do. A little girl with a pony, and a sharp object, nothing more."

ⅾↃ

Matthias hollered in pain as the staff tip crashed down against his naked torso, sizzling the skin from his ribs. It was an agony unlike any the assassin had ever felt, and he had felt much pain in his life.

Puc, sitting on a chair opposite of him withdrew the weapon once he knew that the skin had been burned raw. He had never been overly fond of torture, but it was a means to an end and he wanted answers. How long had Mislantus been watching? How had Amarok gotten into Q-16 again? Most importantly, what role had Matthias played in the whole plan? A darker, more primal side to Puc was enjoying the screams coming from the psychic warrior, as the sound of skin frying sang in his ears.

"Now then. Will you tell me your part in the scheme of things?" the elf asked repeatedly as Matthias withered in pain, suspended from the chains Puc had strung him on like a sack of dead meat.

"I already told you! What more do you want me to say?" He snarled, receiving another wound to his stomach, this one cutting deeper than the others.

"I want to hear the truth, and I would like it now, for I am not a patient mage when the lives of my friends are concerned," Puc said in his usual calm tone, pale eyes glaring at Matthias.

"You want the truth? Or your own damn version of the truth!" the assassin spat blood, having been struck multiple times in the face beforehand by the enraged elf. "Okay fine, I led the whole escapade. Mislantus has been watching for years, and I'm the Unknown himself!"

The final comment landed Matthias another smack across the face, sending his whole body to one side with the force of the blow. Laughing, for he could do nothing else, he looked up with bloodshot eyes at his captor.

"Good enough, elf?" he sneered.

Puc lifted his staff backwards, preparing to hit him with another spell. The mage's patience drawing closer to its end hearing the mocking laughter echo in his ears but he was stopped by a hand falling on his shoulder. Puc turned to see Darius staring back at him, the angular cut of his jaw now more visible with the shorter hair.

"I think that's enough for today. Wouldn't you agree, master?" he asked.

"I think I will be the judge of that," Puc said darkly, breaking free of the grip.

"No, wait!" Darius stalled him. "Annetta sent me for you. She wants the Four Forces to be alerted that Mislantus has found Q-16, and plans to attack soon."

Puc stopped mid spell and turned back around to face his apprentice, leaving the sagging assassin to wallow in the aftershock of his torture.

"Yes, you are right. They do need to be notified of all of this," Puc said, spacing out and analyzing what needed to be done. "I must let them all know in order to give time to prepare."

"Do you want me to come with you?" Darius asked.

"No, there will be no need. I will get Kaian to lend me messengers in order to begin moving the chain. I need you to stay here, make sure Annetta doesn't do anything rash, and keep an eye on our prisoner. Notify me if you see anything in the telescopes. I want to know if Mislantus begins mobilizing troops to attack Earth itself instead of going straight for the Castle, which he may be doing. If that happens, this may be the battle of the end times for the human race."

"Everything will be fine, master." Darius shook his head, looking at his mentor.

Puc nodded and began walking off, not really having heard what his apprentice had said. He was in his own thoughts. War was a delicate thing, especially when an army as large as The Four Forces was to be utilized in the attack. This would be no fight for land alone. It was going to be a fight for the sake of all worlds.

"Oh, and Darius? Nice hair cut," he said off in the distance.

When the coast was clear, Darius signaled for Annetta and Link to come out of hiding from behind the wall separating the room from the vast corridor.

"I've got him to go. Now what?" he asked, looking at them.

"He's busy," Link explained, "so we need to figure out how to get the Flying Dutchman moving fast."

"Wait, I'm sorry. You expect us to fly a space ship?" Annetta snapped, throwing her arms up in the air. "You do realize I live in an apartment building in the middle of a city right? Not neighboring with NASA headquarters."

"Gaian space ships aren't hard to use," Link said, trying to calm her down, "especially ones as primitive as the Dutchman."

"You'll never get in," Matthias's weak voice came from behind them, causing the group to face him. "If you plan to go in, you need something more solid than crashing Valdhar with an antique space craft."

"You're one to talk, traitor." Darius scoffed.

"Traitor I am, but not to you. I was sent here to kill you all once I got close enough, and infiltrate Q-16. I found out from my vision when we went to visit the Ogaien the truth of how I came to be in his services. I was a small boy when it happened. He murdered my parents and killed my sister. I was going to confess and tell Puc everything before Amarok showed up. Mislantus used me, and for that I want vengeance. And I'm willing to do whatever it takes in order to get it."

Having used of the last of his strength on his speech, the assassin's head hung low as he exhaled, his wounds stinging in the cold air. It was useless, he thought, to be wasting his time telling them the same thing he had repeated multiple times to the mage. Closing his eyes, he waited for them to leave.

Annetta turned to look at Link and Darius, going over what the bloodied man had just said to them. Darius moved forward and opened a drawer in the cupboard, taking out a vial.

"Wait, you're just going to trust him based on a few observations?" Link protested, seeing what Darius was doing.

"You have any better ideas at this point, Heallaws?" The apprentice shot him a look of frustration. "I'm trying to make do with what we have."

Darius walked over to Matthias and began removing his shackles, including the cuff that was binding his psychic powers, motioning for Annetta and Link to help him.

"What are you doing?" Matthias muttered half consciously.

"I am not Puc Thanestorm," Darius said to him. "I was outside the door, listening for a good ten minutes, hearing you recite the same words over and over to him. I know very well that the spells he was using were not something a man could withhold information from. You either die or tell the truth, and when an organism faces such a choice, it chooses life. I saw the look on your face after we came out of the temple as well, doesn't take much to put two and two together."

Feeling a great weight lifted from his shoulders, Matthias nearly would have tumbled to the ground were it not for the trio catching him and easing him into the chair. Seated, a vial was put to his lips, and a liquid forced down his throat, to which he did not object, having no will power left to do so. The crowd scrambled away, leaving him room to breathe, and his wounds to begin healing from the properties of the potion. Gasping, Matthias felt life crawl back into him, the pain diminishing. Opening his eyes, he looked at the three of them surrounding him, Annetta holding out his shirt, jacket and gauntlets neatly folded on a pile.

"What first?" he asked, accepting the bundle.

෯ଔ

As soon as Matthias was dressed, they headed for the area where the Flying Dutchman was. The magnificent late eighteenth century looking vessel lay casually on its side like a discarded toy boat. The three masts of the boat were still tied up, making the ship seem to have three arms that reached for the companions as they came closer, welcoming them aboard. Annetta ran up to it, touching the cold metal panels that had been painted to look like wood. The ship still amazed her no matter how many times she passed by it.

"We're going to fly this?" Matthias said, confused. "Does it even work still? I mean…how are we going to get it out of here to begin with?"

"Leave the getting out part to me," Darius said. "We need to figure out how to pilot it."

"You mean getting it standing first, right?" Link said, walking over to the massive ship. "I don't think it'll just start up right away."

Matthias inspected the vessel, half expecting the behemoth to crumble beneath his touch should he even lightly graze it. He had only seen such ships in books. Never would he have expected to see one in person. He stepped back, getting a better overall picture. With a simple command from his mind, the ship began to turn upright. Everyone stood back, looking in amazement.

"All aboard." he grinned and teleported himself up to the helm.

Annetta followed his lead, bringing Link and Darius to the top of the ship, going after Matthias into the cabin. Though the ship appeared to be old and made of wood outside, inside it held multiple screens built into the walls, an array of knobs and switches on a panel in the middle of the cabin, a massive steering wheel, and three large windows allowing for visibility from the inside out. Link looked around with Matthias, trying to familiarize himself with the setup, checking to make sure nothing was loose or rusted from disuse.

"The Beta energy field should be a large switch. Look on the other side." Matthias spewed out a few commands as Link scrambled to find it. "Darius, I need you to be ready to get us out of here, since you claim to be able to do so. Annetta, I will need you to steer at the front."

"You sure that's a good idea? I mean, Link is sort of more qualified," Annetta said, wavering.

"He may be, but I need him in here with me. This isn't a vessel that was piloted by just one man alone. It requires a team, and we don't really have one." The assassin explained, reason enough for the girl to go to the assigned post.

"And what of when we get there?" Darius asked. "Seeing as we can't just crash the party."

"I will tell them you are my prisoners," Matthias said.

"And again, how do we know you won't actually turn us over?" Link asked, still not trusting the assassin.

"Look, I gave you my word, isn't that enough? Or do you want me to grovel at your feet, princess?" Matthias snarled, causing Link to curl his hand into a fist.

"Save your pride, Gaian," Darius interjected. "We're wasting time and energy squabbling."

Link sighed, knowing nothing would come of what he said, and stepped aside. "As you'll have it."

Matthias nodded a thank you to Darius, and noted a problem. He glared at both Link and Annetta's weapons. "Those need to be hidden, or they stay with me while we are on the ship until we get to the prisoner deck. Jason will be located there. Once we have him, we need to head back and, hope we can find Sarina as well."

"Wait, we're getting the girl too?" Link raised an eyebrow.

"For a long time Sarina wished to be free of her father. If I can help her in this goal, I will. Now hurry. If Mislantus fires the Pessumire to enter Severio Castle, it may be too late."

"Wait, whoa...what?" Annetta stopped Matthias again. "Pessum-what?"

"Pessumire, the portal-creating cannon. It emits a beam that can slice through veils and create portals. It needs matter from the other world in its core, and then it's able to calibrate itself to create a portal to that world.

That's why Mislantus wants to gain control of the Eye to All Worlds, so he can rule them all with the help of the Pessumire."

Annetta felt an overwhelming feeling come into her throat as though she were choking on air, unable to make it go down or up from her lungs. She had known for a long time what Mislantus had planned to do, but knowing it in detail created a new layer to the story within her mind. It did not help that she now knew some of the races that were within these portals. Though she could not call them her best friends, they were beings who had been kind to her, had believed in her, and had shown an inclination to do good to others. Beings like that deserved to live in peace.

"I see." Annetta answered. Turning, she headed outside for the dock, focusing on the task at hand. Part of her was feeling rather frightened by the prospect of the ship not working, or of the Beta energy field failing, but a sense of adventure overpowered this as the girl stood at the wheel, the masts overhead lowering automatically. A humming noise came from all around, which slowly turned into pumping as a field of green and yellow energy surrounded the ship in a sphere.

"Get us moving!" Link called to Darius, who did not have to be told twice.

The young elf looked up, concentrating on the task at hand, the manipulation of his element needed. He began rotating his hands before him, clockwise. The ceiling seemed to turn to sand as it shifted, in rhythm with the hand movement, disappearing before him. Faster and faster the movement went until a tunnel appeared above them, leading to the sky.

"NOW!" he shouted from beyond the chaos, as the entire craft bolted forwards.

Annetta looked ahead from the steering wheel as they shot through the tunnel. Passing the last of it, the ship did not slow. The girl only looked back briefly to see that the tunnel was gone, having vanished without a trace beneath the waves. Her grip became tighter and tighter as they climbed into the air, feeling the roller coaster effect take hold in her gut, waiting for the plunge. Pressure rose in her ears, and she really wished that she had brought a piece of gum with her to stop it.

Link and Matthias worked inside the cockpit of the ship, monitoring all the system lines, the black screen monitors flickering with green text as they went higher and higher.

"I don't think this piece of junk will hold. We won't make it past the atmosphere at this rate," Matthias muttered, beginning to slowly panic.

"A Gaian vessel never fails." Link looked over at him feeling offended by the comment. "This ship may look old, but it was taken care of. These are meant to last for thousands of years."

Matthias sighed, grumbling under his breath. He decided not to fight back, but he held strong to his opinion that this was slowly becoming suicide. But what other choice did he have if he wished to see Sarina happy once more and Mislantus vanquished?

Outside, Annetta kept her eyes closed, thinking the voyage of accelerating speed would never end. But when she least expected it, the vessel came to a halt. Nothing.

Shaken, the girl opened her eyes to see another wonderful sight. Standing on the deck of the ship and looking all around, there was nothing in sight for miles around but black space. At first, she thought she might die from the lack of oxygen, but realizing the shields were still up, she did not worry. Looking around, the stars seemed like city lights in the distance, and the sight of the Earth below her, so oblivious to the sights she saw there was a spectacle indeed, a drawing out of an atlas.

Something else caught Annetta's attention, an ominous presence that she could not describe. Turning, she saw their destination, a massive floating fortress that seemed most unnatural in the space it occupied. Its grey squat rectangular towers shot upwards from a square base. Dotting it were many small lights, windows perhaps. As they closed in, Annetta could see more and more that the fortress resembled a great castle. Unlike Severio Castle, which was welcoming, this castle was meant to inspire fear, and it did a good job, in Annetta's opinion. She turned around to see Matthias, Link and Darius all gathered on the main deck, watching it draw closer, along with the fate that awaited them.

Chapter 56

Flintz sat, watching his post at the docking station. He had been sent here in order to fill in for the usual guard, Morion, who had taken sick due from indulging in too much drink at the tavern. Being the good comrade he was, Flintz agreed to switch shifts with him, instead of having one of the higher ups find out.

It was one thing to simply drink too much and not have duty the next day, but to be hung over and on guard generally ended with Mislantus sending you to your death for lack of responsibility, if he found out. If he was in a favorable mood that day, then one got sent to the dungeon. Sighing, Flintz tightened the grip on his weapon as his mind began to doze off again, watching the twinkling stars all around him.

His drifting was interrupted by the arrival of a vessel unlike any he had seen before. Springing up, he readied his arsenal to fire.

"Halt! In the name of Mislantus the Threat, Lord of Valdhar, state thy name!" he shouted at the top of his lungs as the ship docked, without any implication of being hostile.

Emerging from the helm, waving in a sign of peace was a figure Flintz knew all too well. His wild brown hair and blue eyes were a familiar sight in the tavern. Matthias Teron, the right hand assassin of Mislantus. Lowering his rifle, Flintz waited for him to come closer to find out where the strange ship had come from.

"Master Teron," Flintz stammered as the imposing from of the assassin came forward. "I thought you'd already come back from your mission, since Lady Sarina had returned."

"Lady Sarina returned with Amarok and one of the prisoners. I was busy acquiring another." He motioned as Annetta stepped out of the ship with her head hanging low, her arms bound together with a chain, a psychic binding cuff they had found on the ship secured on her wrist. "Now, where is the other prisoner being kept, so I may add this one to his lordships collection? I want to prepare before we go and deal with this stinking planet."

"Yes, of course." Flintz nodded his head, eager to seem the good soldier he was to his higher ranking officer. "To my knowledge, the prisoner is being kept in the dungeon as of now. His lordship is preparing the

Pessumire with Abner, I think, in the main tower, to fire on The Eye to All Worlds so we may cross into it."

"Really, so soon?" Matthias raised an eyebrow and stroked his chin, then shrugged. "I suppose I will need to prepare sooner than I thought I would. Flintz, you have been a great help today. And now..."

Before Flintz could react, Matthias's fist slammed down into his gut, taking the wind out from under him. Then came a searing pain. It was one Flintz, despite his shock, was able to identify from witnessing the prowess of the psychic gauntlets used on those who had stood in the way of Matthias Teron. Sliding off the blade in one fluid motion, Flintz fell to the floor.

෨෬

Matthias turned around to Annetta, who was some distance off, watching the scene with a horrified expression. She seemed smaller against the glass dome that shielded the interior from the empty space beyond it, a speck among stars. Upon seeing the guard drop, she rushed over to him, her chains jangling.

"Did you have to kill him?" She raised her voice in a mix of horror and shock, looking down at the strange creature that resembled a man with a purple lizard's face. "You could have just put him to sleep or something."

"If I knocked him out, he would have eventually woken up," he stated bluntly, and motioned for Link and Darius to come over.

"Who's ugly, here?" Darius asked, looking down at the creature.

"Unimportant." Matthias shrugged. "But here our roles begin. Annetta, you will still be my prisoner. Do not speak unless spoken to, act afraid, and whatever happens, should we see Jason, do not say anything until I say so. It's important that no one know we are in there until it is too late for them to do anything."

He instructed her and then turned to Link. "I need you to stay with the ship and have it ready for takeoff, since you seem to be able to operate it."

"Right, how will you reach me though?" the youth replied.

"I still have the watch from the Lab." Matthias tapped on the device that encircled his left gauntlet, then turned next to Darius.

"I will need you to put on the uniform, and come with me as a guard. Say we are both taking the prisoner to the dungeon on Mislantus's orders. If anything, will you be able to charm them into thinking so, should they try to check with anyone? Word of my treason should not have reached many yet.

There is probably too much chaos aboard if Mislantus is indeed preparing the Pessumire to fire."

Darius looked down at the corpse of the creature and sighed in disdain at the scenario before him. He knew he had little choice in what had to be done. Grabbing hold of the thing, he pulled an arm over his shoulder, walking back to the ship to hide the evidence, and put on the uniform.

"Right, that," Annetta frowned, her face becoming lost as she buried herself in thought. The more she thought about it, the more her brain churned with ideas. If Mislantus gained control of the Eye to All Worlds, all he'd need to do was gather matter from wherever he wanted, fire the beam, and march through with the host of Valdhar, and no one left to stop him. Scenes from her Visium swam through her mind of a desolated city, Toronto, accompanied by scenes from the vision she and Jason had received from the angels when they had first agreed to accept the responsibility of their heritage. Goosebumps formed on Annetta's arms under the jean jacket as her mind wandered further and further. No one stood guard now, no one defended the castle. She looked down at her C.T.S. watch, her wrists still tied up.

"Before we go in, we need to tell Puc," she said, looking up at the assassin. "We have to warn them in case the cannon is fired."

Worried they were wasting time and could be caught, Matthias nodded his head, despite his instincts telling him to do otherwise. He turned to see Darius finishing up the last of the buttons on the uniform of the dead soldier he had donned, the body having already been disposed of by the mage apprentice. The assassin noted the blood and rips on the outfit, making a mental note for an alibi about them.

"Fine, we'll head back for the ship then to do that," Matthias said to Annetta, resigned. "But hurry."

80C3

Arriving in Aldamoor after the painful experience of having to saddle a horse himself before finally turning to magic in order to accomplish the task, Puc waited in Kaian's study to hold an audience with the First Mage, having been escorted there by Iliam. He was growing impatient with his aged friend, knowing Jason's life hung in the balance. It was no wonder he jumped upon the watch on his wrist going off with a series of beeps. Flipping the device open, his eyes focused in, wondering what was so important.

"05 here," he said casually.

"01 on this end." Annetta's voice came from the watch as Kaian walked in. **"Uh, don't hate me when I say this, but we're on Valdhar with Matt."**

"I'm sorry, but you are what?" Puc did his best to conceal his anger, the tone of his voice still betraying him.

"Torture later, listen now, okay? You absolutely need to get everyone ready. Mislantus plans to fire the Pessumire and create a portal to Severio Castle," she said.

Puc exhaled deeply upon hearing the news, noting Kaian had come into the room and watched as he sat down in the seat at his desk, listening in on the conversation.

"How did you find this information, and who let you free that traitor?" he asked, trying his best to stay calm.

"I did, master," Darius's voice said, **"and I'm sorry, but he is no traitor. He had nothing to do with the kidnapping of Jason and Sarina. We came using the Flying Dutchman, and are currently on board, readying to march in."**

"And what in all that is right in the world made you come to such a conclusion about him?" The elder mage gritted his teeth as he spoke, his jaw stiff from fury.

"We were running out of choices. Jason is on board, and I highly doubt Mislantus was just going to let him go if we handed over the Eye to All Worlds. Besides, if you had actually been listening to what Matthias was saying, then you would have noticed it was in past tense, an indication of something that actually happened instead of something he was making up at the present time."

There was silence on the other end of Darius's C.T.S. briefly. The apprentice was almost certain that the connection had cut off, when he heard a voice speak again. "A well deducted observation that I failed to see in the heat of the moment."

Puc fell quiet again, as he calculated everything that could potentially go wrong in the moments they spent in the enemy fortress. He was being handed a piece of hot coal, and now had to figure out the best angle to place it in his palm in order to avoid getting burned for the longest period of time.

"You are sure they did not expect you to come?" Puc questioned.

"**Negative, the grunt we ran into thought Matthias still a friend,**" Darius answered. "**Everyone is scrambling to get the cannon ready and prepare for battle.**"

"Then this is indeed urgent." Puc ran a hand through his black hair. "Even if it may be a decoy, it is best everyone is gathered and ready to strike. Annetta are you still there?"

"**Yes sir,**" she answered.

"Promise me one thing. You will come back alive to fight this war. I don't fight other people's battles and this one is most certainly yours and Jason's," he stated coldly. "And don't damage the Dutchman. Orbeyus will turn in his grave if you do."

"**Will try. 01 out.**" The transmission ended. Closing the watch, Puc looked over at his fellow mage.

"It appears I know all that I need to." Kaian smirked and turned to Iliam, who stood by the door with another of the guards. "Ready every able bodied soldier, and tell Kaine to prepare every war ship. Send messengers back to Severio Castle. There bid them to travel through the corresponding portals to Morwick, the Trafjan Cliffs, and the Yasur Plains on our fastest horses. War brews, and as sworn, Aldamoor will come to aid."

"Yes, First Mage." Iliam nodded, and was gone before Puc could blink.

"A soft spot for your son, I see, despite everything," Puc said, hearing Kaine was commanding war ships.

"I have only one son in all my long years, Thanestorm. Punishment was given as accorded, but death…not something I could deliver to my one and only son, when his sole crime was in wanting to choose his own path instead of the one dealt to him." Kaian turned, looking out his window in the tower to see zeppelins floating lazily in the sky.

Puc turned his own gaze to the window. His thoughts, however, were guided elsewhere as his prayers soared to the Unknown, hoping for the survival of a certain few teenagers who were miles away, facing possibly their most difficult battle to date, and the mage who led them was nowhere to be found.

಼ఞ಼

Annetta kept her head low as she walked in front of Matthias and behind Darius, who acted as their way in. Darius's bloodied uniform had been caused by the so-called ferocious prisoner he was leading to the dungeon, with Matthias in tow as the one who captured her. Many were too busy to bother even looking in their direction, the rhapsody of battle soaring high in the air as everyone scrambled with preparations, hauling projectile weapons, swords, and other provisions that were deemed necessary. Reaching the lower corridors of the fortress, their target was in sight, a barred door with a formidable creature that resembled a rhinoceros in front of it.

"State your name and business," a deep baritone voice spoke from the thing as it looked down, its horned face making it appear ready to lash out at any instant.

"I am here escorting the prisoner captured by Matthias Teron, and as you can see, she's a pretty vicious one." Darius indicated his bloodstained tabard.

The guard did not seem to move at all, and instead of making any indication that he would allow them to pass, crossed his beefy arms with the intrinsic weapon he bore that resembled a rifle with a blade on its tip, staring them down with his black eyes.

"What did you say your name and rank were, soldier?" the creature asked gruffly. "Last I checked, Matthias Teron was a traitor."

Darius felt his throat go dry from not having an answer to counter. Before the mage apprentice could react, Matthias had already teleported onto the thing's back and wrapped one arm around him. The gauntlet on his second arm fully extended its claws, and tore through its throat. The behemoth collapsed to the ground, still twitching, the assassin gliding down gracefully on the corpse.

"We've no time to waste. They will find us soon," Matthias told them, wiping the blood from the blades and sliding them back into their dormant state.

Annetta stared down at the body as blood began to pool from the opening Matthias had created. She froze in her tracks, knowing that before her again was a coherent being, someone who had understood everything that she had. She could not dwell long on these thoughts, as the blue eyes of the assassin, glaring at her in waiting, caught her. She took that as her cue to unwrap her arms from the chains, and dropped them to the floor along with the cuff. It was just in time to catch Severbane from Matthias, who had carried the weapon slung over his shoulder the entire time. She stood back, watching and making sure no one approached with Darius while Matthias typed in the appropriate codes to open the doors and scan the hand of the dead guard. They entered the compound of the dungeon, finding it very much abandoned.

"I take it he doesn't like prisoners." Annetta looked around.

"Majority end up dead before they reach the front doors, especially of late," Matthias answered, focused on trying to find Jason so they could leave and get Sarina.

ഈരു

Having no other means to reach his friends, his C.T.S. having been taken from him along with the pendant of his mace, Jason was left to resort to the only other thing he could do in a time of crisis, wait. He knew the depth of Annetta's devotion. She was a force to be reckoned with, especially when friends in need were the ones calling. He was, however, quickly losing hope. How on earth could he even begin to dream they would find a way to get him out? Although he had only caught glimpses of the fortress, it was clear to Jason that there was little hope Annetta and his friends stood a chance to breach it. Perhaps he was done for. Sighing he allowed his mind to wander into the void of subconscious as he sat on the cold steel floor, not much different from the Lab, save that it was much darker and he was very much alone.

He lay curled up sideways in a fetal position, trying to stay warm, but not wanting to sit anymore. He was growing tired, knowing it was way past his bedtime. But his main thought, no matter how much he tried to stray away from it, was Sarina, and the fate that awaited Severio Castle. Sarina, the girl he had wanted to save, had turned out to be the daughter of the man he had sworn with Annetta to take down. A twisted feeling sat within the boy as he dwelt on this, and yet he could not help but notice in all his interactions with her that she never once showed the spark that had lit Mislantus's eyes. He remembered well the small branch the one called Amarok had handed to his cat-faced master, and the glee it had inspired. He did not want to think what the tyrant would do once he could travel to different worlds. He had not known him long, but it did not take more than one glance at Mislantus's feral gaze to guess what ran through the creature's head. It was not what Jason stood for. And from what he saw, neither did Sarina.

Closing his eyes, his mind continued to mull over the same thoughts until he was interrupted, on the very edge of sleep, by the sound of voices and feet coming down the corridor. Opening his eyes again to see the approaching blurred shapes, he rose to his feet, the voices becoming clearer.

"J.K.!" Annetta's voice rang out. Moments later, the familiar blue eyes were looking right back at him, filled with relief.

"Annetta! How did you?" he asked excitedly, holding onto the bars. "Should I even ask how?"

"Time for merriments later, I'm afraid." Matthias interrupted, and moved Annetta aside with a gentle gesture. "We may have an angry squad of guards soon."

With a single stare from the assassin, the bars melted like icicles to the floor into a puddle. Jason stepped through to be greeted by his friend with a hug.

"Are you alright?" she asked, pulling away.

"I'm fine, but I don't have my mace or my watch," he told them. "They took it from me when I came down here."

"Those will likely be in the officer's booth," Matthias informed them as he pulled the cuff from Jason's wrist free. "We passed it back there. The moment we leave here, I want you three to head back to the ship, no questions asked. I will go to retrieve Sarina alone."

"But you could get caught, and you won't have backup," Darius protested.

"Thank you for the concern, but I'm a skilled assassin, and a master of shadows when I want to be," Matthias retorted. "I was trained to get in and out without leaving a trail, and if necessary I can teleport back onto the ship. Now, this is another important part, and you must follow it no matter what. If you see people getting curious about the ship, you get Heallaws to start that engine, and don't look back."

"But what about you and Sari-," Jason began.

"Don't look back." Matthias hissed at the boy.

Frowning, Jason nodded his head. Just as he was about to turn to his friends, he heard noise coming from the corridor where the gate was. He turned questioning to his friends.

Matthias's muscles tightened in his arms. He stepped before the others, analyzing the situation in his head.

"I'll run ahead to distract them, you get your mace, and you get out now," he snarled one last time before the assassin parted from his jacket and extended the claws to their full length before charging in.

Darius wasted no time in organizing his friends, and made his way with them to the officer's booth. It did not take long to find the pendant, discarded on the desk, but the watch was nowhere to be found. By the rising battle cries in the hallway, Darius knew they were running short on time in order to get to the ship without being noticed, possibly by higher ranking officers.

"Forget it, there are more in the Lab." Darius turned to them, bile rising in his throat from fear. "We need to get out."

Not arguing, they left the room and made their way for the main entrance. Coming around the corner, they saw six fallen warriors, including the guard from before, and Matthias bathed in their gore up to his elbows. Retracting his claws with a single thought, he looked at the companions.

"The way is clear," he said with a smile, wiping his hands on one of the dead foe's tabards and swiping a dark undamaged cloak to cover his face. "Remember, don't wait."

Teleporting, he was gone.

The trio looked at each other for answers. Darius and Annetta's eyes then fell to the mess on the floor. With their task clear, they took off, adrenaline putting a spring in their step.

Chapter 57

It had not taken long to rouse those that had called themselves the Four Forces under the banner of Lord Orbeyus Severio. In no time, armies teemed below the castle; tents lifted high, standards of each respective race floating on the wind. War was war, and the call was answered as soon as it was received, with preparations being made to allow advantage for the home team.

Puc watched the busying camp fill more by the moment, soldiers coming out of portals that were conjured by elven mages to allow larger units like airships to come through. Though it was a process seldom used due to the damage it caused on the veil holding the worlds together, desperate times called for desperate measures. He stood dressed in the battle attire of a mage, long copper tinted chainmail beneath dark blue robes embroidered with gold and copper. He sighed, the tension rising within his gut as he held his staff in one hand and his war helmet in the other, decorated with two half gears which made it appeared winged from far away. Kaian emerged from the war tent dressed in similar robes of a red coloring, which marked his status as First Mage, holding a crowned helm.

"Everything goes as planned, but where are those we fight for?" he asked.

"I have similar thoughts on my own mind," sighed Puc as Entellion, Ironhorn and Natane came forth from the tent.

"They should not have gone off on their own," Ironhorn added, the fully armored Minotaur hinging his claws on the belt that carried two large axes. "Had we been informed sooner I would have sent a score of warriors with them to put some fire in Mislantus's belly."

"They would have been slaughtered like the cows they are. Ogaien would have been better suited for the task," Natane retorted, feeling insignificant, only to have her comment answered by a snarl from the prideful Minotaur. But they were both hushed by a wave of Kaian's arm.

"Silence," the elder mage spoke. "We would all have liked to help, but we are doing our part here preparing defenses for the Eye to All Worlds. Save the fight for those you truly deem enemy."

"The elf is right, fighting will do us no good," Entellion answered. "And they had a better chance of going in alone without any of us there. A large force would have roused suspicion. They did it right."

The Minotaur snorted, eyeing the Ogaien female, but said nothing more. Natane turned away, hiding a smirk, remembering Ironhorn's grandfather acting the same way on the last campaign she had ridden to with Orbeyus. Some races never changed, she thought.

Amelia and Doriden swooped out of the sky soon after and landed before the leaders.

"As ordered, battle airships are in place, with five Soarin to each ship," Amelia reported.

"Good, if Mislantus is indeed only rebuilding his father's forces, and they expect no resistance here, we should have any small cruisers they send cornered and finished off before they can do damage," Puc nodded.

Hideburn and Anuli came as soon as the exchange of information was made between Puc and the Soarin. The Minotaur sporting full regalia, and the Aiethon, the race of horses with manes of flame, on which the Ogaien rode shimmered in black armor.

"The castle defenses are nearly complete," Hideburn reported. "Nothing shall penetrate it, or so the mages say. Do we know nothing of where the enemy will strike from? This is chaos, if I can be bold enough to say so, my lords and ladies."

"It all depends on where the beam is to be fired from," Puc stated, gripping his staff. "It all depends on what fate deals us."

৪৩

Coming to the main floor, Darius, Jason and Annetta were flooded with the disorder around them. They had a feeling it had something to do with the squad of soldiers that Matthias had killed downstairs, with the red flashing lights that now lit up the pillars to either side of the white walls.

"What now?" Jason managed to mutter to his companions, as one of the soldiers pointed at them.

"That's the one from the prison! Get him!" a creature resembling a purple lizard with a beak snarled and charged at them through the crowd, accompanied by two others.

Before either of the boys could react to the oncoming storm, Annetta grabbed them and teleported a few feet beyond the charging group. Darius and Jason jumped upon the sudden shift of ground, and whirled around to face her.

"Someone has to save your skins!" she snapped, looking over her shoulder at the confused group. Turning back, she grabbed at her

642

companions yet again. "Plus I can't remember where we parked, so this'll have to do."

Jason barely managed to open his mouth to protest before he suddenly found himself a few more feet away from where he had been, and was nearly trampled by another of the giant rhinoceros-like beings that had guarded the dungeon. He stopped Annetta right before she teleported them a third time.

"In turns, okay? I got this one," he said, focusing on the spot closest to the end of the corridor.

Darius was disoriented after the third teleportation. Grabbing his forehead, he swatted both their hands from him as he tried to find his center of balance.

"Okay, stop for one minute!" he growled. "You're giving me a headache."

Annetta looked back nervously to see the soldiers scrambling after them again. Deciding not to wait for Darius, she teleported them again a few more feet to gain some ground. Her heart was pounding in her ribcage as she tried to figure out what other options there were. She had thought of fighting, but in a whole hall of enemy soldiers, she knew they stood no chance. She turned to look at a wheezing Darius, who was starting to turn paler than his natural color.

"What other options do you see? I don't see any," she stated, still looking over their shoulder as she was handed a roll of spears from one of the soldiers passing.

"Get those to the armory! We're running short!" he called as he passed by her, not giving a second glance, after which Annetta turned to her friends in question.

Darius regained his footing. He too saw the advancing guards. Turning the other way, he saw the corridor that led to the docking station, and a plan began to formulate in his mind.

"Get us to the corridor," he ordered, as the girl dropped the bundle of spears, and teleported them out just before the soldiers came.

As soon as their feet hit the ground, they ran down the stone staircase at full speed, their legs pounding on the concrete floor. Thankfully, there was no one in the hall, which made the descent far easier. They heard the voices of pursuers closing in, and the choice of what to do next was much easier to make.

Drawing the noble weapon from its sheath for the first time, Annetta watched and waited with her two friends as the enemy came into sight. They were the original three who had begun the pursuit, a small lizard creature with a parrot beak, and two massive beasts that looked like men with leathery skin and small horns protruding from their nose ridges like a rhinoceros.

"Ya think ya can escape us?" the little soldier leading the party said, pulling out a curved blade. "We'll gut ya first."

They wasted no time in returning taunts of their own. With a feral roar, Darius shifted into his werepanther shape, and sprang upon the larger soldier that was standing closest to him and slashed at his foe. Finding an opening, he gripped the soldier's tabard with his claws and dug beneath it, penetrating the armor, and tearing skin in the process. Before Darius could land another strike, the fearful thing had fainted in his grasp. Seeing no point in the final blow, he tossed it aside like a rag doll.

Summoning his mace, Jason was no lesser as he charged at the enemy. Moments before impact, he teleported beside the fiend and swung the weapon full force into its head, crashing into the lower jaw of the second rhinoceros-like creature, stunning him momentarily. Not missing a beat, he attacked the dazed opponent again. Finishing off the job, he smashed the weapon over its head, cracking its skull, sending the creature to its maker. As soon as the adrenaline of the moment subsided, however, Jason felt immediately sick as he stood over the body, a pool of blood forming at his feet. What caught his gaze as soon as he looked down was the eye of the creature, a deep brown/gold and its pupil now covered with the silver film of death. It was not much different from the eye of a human being, he realized. He felt guilt and remorse because he realized he had not killed something, but someone.

Annetta blocked the curved scimitar, and the ringing of blade against blade echoed throughout the hall. Taking a step back to steady her posture, she found herself staring at the gleaming yellow eyes of her enemy, a creature dressed in black armor that looked like a purple lizard. She could not even begin to wonder at the strange beast, or ask where it had come from, for the thing swung at her again, causing her to block once more.

Taking another step back, she found herself not wanting to fight it. Before any final choice could be made, however, a mighty black paw swooped in and knocked the creature into the wall.

"Let's go!" roared Darius, who took notice of the look on Jason's face. He ran up to the boy, still in panther form, and grabbed hold of the boy's shoulder, smearing it in the blood that covered his paw, causing the youth to look back up at him.

"It had to be done," Darius said quietly. "If you didn't react, then he would have, and I promise you, he would not be standing there like you are now.

Glancing only once more at the look of shame on the boy's face, Darius offered no more words. Turning, he then led the way on all fours, as they made the rest of the descent to the ship, where Link waited.

 soςs

Winding around the corner, Matthias made his way to the tower where Sarina's room was. It was easy to get past the soldiers on the lowers floors, but up here, only the more privileged officers wandered, and they were the kind Matthias did not feel like encountering without need.

He could easily cut down almost any of those that stood in his path in single combat, but Matthias knew that they could prove a nuisance in a pack. He also knew he was running out of time to get Sarina away from the fortress. Coming within sight of the doors, Matthias slowed his pace and hid behind a pillar. He looked carefully, analyzing the obstacle of the four soldiers placed around the entrance. He doubly noted that they each wore the black gambeson with three metal chest plates, and red capes of Mislantus's psychic warrior ranks. It was similar to the uniform he had once worn, his only distinction being the blue cape of head assassin that he had earned. He frowned, knowing this was going to happen, but decided nonetheless to try a diplomatic approach, hoping not all of his charms would fail him at once. Dropping his hood, he strode forward with his head high and chest out.

The group of soldiers tightened around the door the moment they saw him, two of the guards already readying psychic fire in their palms.

"Amarok told us ye might be coming here." One of them chuckled as the rest of the group snickered like hyenas. "Sorry, but yer little friend, she's off limits."

Matthias glared at them, not a single drop of emotions behind his eyes as he stared down each and every one of them, each in turn becoming a little unsure of themselves. He enjoyed inspiring this uncertainty in them.

"Really? Is that so?" he said coldly, going into a casual battle stance by spreading his feet apart and bending his knees as though he were getting ready to pounce. "And which of you lovely ladies is going to stop me?"

Infuriated by the insult, the first of the four, a ruddy looking man with a medium build and a full rusty beard, sprang into action, launching himself at the assassin. He sported a fist of psychic fire that he sent his way, before extending two short swords from his hidden gauntlets and propelled himself after the blast. Matthias dodged the blue and purple flames. Twirling, his cape following him like a dance partner, the assassin extended out his claw-like blades from their dormant state and blocked the incoming swords. Using every muscle in his body, Matthias shoved his foe back full force into the wall, bending his opponent's blades with his mind so their tips began digging into the soldier's wrists. Howling, the soldier dropped to the floor as his hands were rendered useless.

The rest did not wait for an invitation as they charged for Matthias like a pack of rabid dogs upon seeing their friend fall. The assassin wasted no time, raising his hand and tearing the door from its hinges as they came upon him, the pack swallowing him in an embrace of blows.

Sarina looked out from her curled position on the bed, the same place she had been since ordered into her room, to see the commotion happening outside since her door was torn off. She could barely believe it when she saw Matthias teleport before her.

"We have to leave," he said, holding his side, where a bloodstain was beginning to form.

"Matt, how did you even?" she began to ask as the trio charged in.

Snarling, Matthias turned to face them, kicking the nearest of the three in the face and sent them flying with a missing tooth, the other two not slowing. Tackling the assassin to the ground, the battle continued to rage in a wrestling struggle between the three of them, each warrior tearing at each other like ravens at a carcass. Having had enough, Matthias extended his claws on either hand, ending them both in a single elegant blow. He then fell to his knees, the use of psychic energy beginning to wear at him.

"Matt, you're hurt," Sarina gasped.

"Good observation." He smirked weakly, his ears picking up the sounds of more soldiers coming their way. The one with the missing tooth had hit the alarm while Matthias had been busy dispatching his friends. He turned his gaze to Sarina. "Are you with me, or against me?"

Mislantus stood upon the observations dock of the tower, where the cannon was going through its final stages of preparation. The entire thing had been rebuilt from scratch upon its original destruction during the Great War by Orbeyus's army. Now, as before, the whole area had sprung to life with scientists adorned in white lab coats and red tabards, tinkering with parts and reading reports as they bustled about.

Lloyd Abner walked over to the tyrant. He'd been around Valdhar since before Mislantus was even born, and knew every detail of the ship. It was he who had created the Pessumire, from his years of researching the possible existence of other dimensions and worlds.

"How go the preparations? Will we be ready soon?" Mislantus questioned the man.

"Well that, does all depend on the where my lord does prefer to shoot the cannon," the bumbling scientist began, oblivious to Mislantus's true question. "Certainly we can fry Earth should you wish it, although I do feel that would be a waste of good timber for no more than selfish pride. I do hear Earth has some spectacular views, and-,"

"I want to know how much longer I must wait," snarled Mislantus. "That is all. I do not need a travel guide of the pathetic pile of dirt and sludge below us."

"Give or take a few hours, my lord. Calibrating Pessumire is not something that can be done right away. Otherwise, we could end up going into a black hole if we overshoot our destination," Abner continued to banter as a weary soldier ran towards Mislantus, bowing before him.

"My lord, the prisoner has been taken. I followed the culprits, but lost them in the main hall on the lower levels," the soldier said to his master. "There is also an alert that Lady Sarina's room has been ambushed by, dare I say it, Matthias Teron, sir."

"What?" howled Mislantus. "You come to tell me this, and you have not dealt with it? And what do you mean lost them?"

"I was…they…well, you see," the soldier said as he swallowed hard, saving his last breath as the tyrant stepped down before him, his piercing eyes boring into him.

"I will spare you now, but know your life is forfeit as cannon fodder," Mislantus growled, before turning to Abner. "Inform the dock to let no ship leave. Should they see anyone try, shoot without hesitation."

"Oh my, we are going to have some fireworks! How delightful." The overjoyed scientist waltzed off towards his communication device.

Mislantus buried himself in his thoughts. His gaze turned towards the little blue planet below that had cost him so much grief in such a short time. He had lost his best assassin to it, and now his daughter was defying him. He knew this was no kidnapping, but a rescue. Though Mislantus appeared to focus entirely upon his goals, he was not as ignorant of the things around his as others thought. His father had taught him one important lesson, and that was to keep eyes not just at the back of his head, but all around like in a watchtower.

଼଩

Gasping, Annetta, Darius, and Jason charged on board the Flying Dutchman. Link ran out from the cabin to see his companions sprawled out on the main deck.

"Uhm, should I even ask what happened?" he asked.

Annetta, as if hit by lightning, sprang to life, raising her sword in a defensive stance. She turned to the port to see soldiers beginning to rouse, and panicked. She had still hoped to wait for Matthias and Sarina.

"I think we gotta blast off, or whatever it is this ship is supposed to do," she said, turning to Link. He nodded and went below deck.

"Wait till the last minute to take off," she shouted as he ran off, looking at the approaching mob.

"Annetta, we need to ditch now," Jason said. "You heard what Matt said."

"We wait, damn it," she snapped, closing her eyes.

"Annetta, we should leave while we can," Darius spoke, standing beside the girl who still had her eyes closed, the breeze from the energy field ruffling her hair. "Who knows what other things Mislantus could send against us if he catches wind that we are here."

The pounding in her ears grew deafening as the crowd approached, and the odds of the return of the other two faded. Hating the feeling of defeat, she opened her eyes and arched her neck towards the cabin. "Alright, damn it, get us out!"

Link did not need further instructions. The engines of the ancient craft roared to life, and the ship began speeding along. Though he had detested staying aboard while everyone else had gotten to leave, he knew full well that no one else had the knowledge to operate the craft, and they would have been sitting ducks.

Annetta and the others watched as the ship pulled out of the dock it had been stationed at, moving faster and faster with every moment, the mob being forced to stop at the now sealed off walkway. However, their troubles were far from over, as the craft began to shake, and a bright green beam of light sliced through the main mast of the Flying Dutchman.

"They have cannons on us!" Darius called, pointing to the towers of the vast structure as another of the things headed their way.

Jason, having used the least amount of energy, deflected the beam back at Valdhar, only to see it absorbed by its protective shield. Cursing, he turned to his friends on deck for support as more of the energy bolts came their way.

Not missing a beat, Annetta threw her mental energy into deflecting one blast, which in turn hit another, causing a silent display of fireworks. The ship shook in violence again, this time as a bolt struck the side of the vessel.

Gritting his teeth, Link ignored the warning signs flashing around him and continued moving as quickly as he could, everything around him glowing crimson as he did so.

Outside, Annetta and Jason put everything they had into protecting the ship from damage. Darius, with his sharper elven eyes, acted as their sentry, pointing out each blast as it approached. Despite their efforts, it was becoming clear they were fighting a losing battle as more and more of the projectiles hurled their way at incredible speeds.

Out of nowhere, two forms materialized on the deck beside them. A bloodied Matthias collapsed on the floor with Sarina at his side. Scarcely able to believe it, Jason rushed to their side, leaving Annetta to battle the incoming assault on her own.

"What happened?" he asked.

"Pesky guards," Matthias said weakly, still smiling.

Link ran out of the cabin in a panic, sweat lining his scarred face. He noticed Matthias and Sarina on board, but turned his attention immediately to Darius.

"I honestly don't know how much more we can take," he said rapidly.

"What other choice do we have?" Darius protested as the ship rocked, taking another blow.

"Damn it! I can't hold them all!" Annetta cried, throwing everything into her psychic abilities to keep the blasts from the ship.

Matthias looked around him, his eyes growing heavy from the loss of blood and energy. Everything seemed so insignificant to him as his head began to float off to the happier moments in his life. He thought about the times he spoke with Sarina after his missions, telling her of the places he had been. She would always listen to him with those large innocent eyes, hungering for more when the story was done.

He remembered the times she would tell him of her own adventures in the schools on Earth. Though he had hated them then, seeing it all as part of the mission, he realized in retrospect that those had been his happiest memories, the act of spending time with her, the girl he had adopted as his little sister.

His real sister now lay buried somewhere. He had to avenge her. He could not die. Rising, the assassin gathered his wits together and turned to the two younger psychics.

"We're taking her home," he croaked, looking at them with bloodshot eyes, his one arm grabbing the railing, "This will take all of us. We need to teleport the whole ship to the Lab."

"What? That's suicide. We can't," Jason said, horrified at the idea.

"Shut up! This is no time for whining," the assassin breathed heavily, clutching the wound in his side with his free hand. "You're going to do this and you're going to do it now."

Annetta noted the desperation in his eyes. She was scared, but as she looked upon the man dressed in a tattered black cloak with blood all over him, she saw something she had not seen before in the assassin, faith. She then knew they had a chance of pulling it off.

"What do you need us to do?" she asked.

Exhaling with a rasp, Matthias grinned at her confidence. At least one of the two held some degree of daring.

"Grab the railing of the ship and picture the area we found it in," he ordered them, as he closed his eyes and sat cross-legged on the metal deck of the ship as blasts of energy rained overhead. "I will focus on bringing everyone on board to the same location. Jason, you help Annetta. Put your power into hers. We need all the energy we can get for this task."

Annetta looked over at her friend, her best friend for so many years she could barely count them anymore. They had stuck together through thick and thin, fought together to conquer obstacles. Despite all the change that had occurred in the last few months, he had remained.

"You with me in this?" she asked.

Jason looked at Annetta, a girl who, to him, was the embodiment of the drawings she doodled in her notebooks of fierce warriors conquering dragons and riding on horseback. She, like them, never backed down from a challenge, and was loyal to her last breath, something Jason vowed after his vision always to return tenfold.

"You never need to ask again," he answered.

Closing their eyes in unison, breathing all power into their will, everything shook around them, vibrating with such intensity that neither of them were sure if they were succeeding in the task, or if the vessel was falling apart beneath their feet. Everything turned white and became numb, but neither dared to open their eyes for fear of breaking their concentration and leaving themselves in limbo.

At last, it stopped as a final screech could be heard on a metallic floor. Both friends felt themselves tumble sideways, fearing the ship had been hit, and in seconds they would find themselves without a breath of air. However, opening their eyes, the Flying Dutchman was in the Lab, lying on its side as though it had never left. A smoldering tail of smoke was rising from the front of the ship which Link had already jumped down to inspect with Darius, while Sarina half carried, half dragged Matthias, who was slowly losing consciousness.

Jason and Annetta pulled each other up, and ran over to the fallen assassin upon seeing him.

"Matt! Matt! Can you hear me?" Sarina shook him as he closed his eyes yet again, his head bobbing from side to side.

Annetta began to feel panic rise in her stomach. She had already witnessed Brakkus die in front of her, and now Matthias seemed to be facing a similar fate. She desperately wanted to kick something and scream, because it didn't seem fair to her. It didn't seem fair that good people died and the bad lived, and not matter how hard she thought, she could not find a reason why.

Having put out the smoke, Link and Darius came over to see the assassin limp in Sarina's arms. Darius lifted the man from her arms and placed him on the ground, examining his vital signs.

"He's still alive," he reassured them. "I think he's just fainted from blood loss. I need to get him to the emergency room. He needs healing potions and-,"

"Your part in this venture is done, young apprentice," a voice from further behind them all spoke. "For another storm is brewing."

A chill went down Annetta's spine as she turned around to see Puc, with a dozen other Water Elves standing to either side of him, each dressed in the same dark blue robes he wore, lined with gold and copper designs, a robe of chain mail beneath it all, and a pointed silver helmet with two large half gears of brass coming from either side of it, fashioned to look like wings.

"I will take care of the assassin personally," Puc instructed them. "You all must prepare."

He then turned to the mages who accompanied him. "Six of you go and ride to Severio Castle, where the rest of the Four Forces wait. Make sure this lot gets there."

The party nodded and split into two groups. Defiantly, Darius stood in front of Matthias and the others, locking eyes with his master.

"And what assurance do I have you won't torture him again?" he said.

Puc lowered his gaze, meeting the younger elf and smiled. He knew full well why Darius was acting the way he did, and though he appreciated the gesture, he needed their cooperation, not their concern.

"He has proven himself to wander these halls without shackles in my eyes," he answered. "Now go and ready yourself, Darius, he who will go through the trials of becoming a full mage when he sees fit. There is little more I can teach you here."

Darius could not stop the grin that had come across his face upon hearing the words come from the one person he had come to respect as a child does a parent. He bowed in appreciation, knowing full well an embrace would be out of place in a time like this. Helping one of the other mages get Matthias up over their shoulder, he turned to join his friends and the six mages who accompanied them.

"Thank you," he said.

"Live, and thank the Unknown instead," Puc replied, turning and making his way for the hospital wing to put the fallen warrior back together.

Chapter 58

Their horses had already been prepared for them when they got to the stables, cutting the trip to Severio Castle in half. Before they knew it, the five companions found themselves riding down the rocky ridge that overlooked the fortress. Down below, the armies had already assembled, and the entire area that had always looked so barren now teemed with life. Banners from all four respective races flew high as they raced past the camps to the front gates, trumpets sounding whenever they passed by someone who recognized them was on watch.

Their immediate course upon leaving the horses tied to their posts in the stables was the armory. Passing by the portrait of Orbeyus Severio, Annetta paused as everyone else pressed on. She looked into the portrait as the man looking down at her sat casually on his throne. Feeling like she should, she saluted the painting, paying tribute to a man she knew very little about, but who had given her what seemed at times like more than she could handle.

Following everyone else into the armory, she saw Hideburn and a few other Minotaurs helping select armor for the new arrivals. Annetta barely knew where to begin. She then noticed that even little Snapneck had made his way to Severio Castle, chirping and squeaking happily at everyone who passed by, a small helmet and silver breastplate on him. The sight nearly made Annetta burst out laughing, but her joy was short lived when Ironhorn entered, causing all the Minotaurs to pause and bow before him. Everyone else did the same, until Ironhorn lifted a hand for them to carry on, his eyes fixed on Annetta and Jason as he motioned for them to step aside. Annetta and Jason nodded but before Annetta went to follow, she turned and went to fetch something from the armory. She came back to him moments later with Fearseeker in her hands.

"I don't think a Minotaur Lord should go into battle without his most trusted blade," she said, handing the weapon back to the large creature.

"True," he replied, "and a lady who leads the Four Forces should not go without proper defense, which is why I call you here" Ironhorn stepped aside, another Minotaur coming forward with a stand with armor. Ironhorn then turned to Jason as a second Minotaur came with another stand. "Neither should a lord."

The two sets of armor glistened in the sun coming through the windows. Golden chainmail outlined each set, similar to the Minotaur Lord's. On top of that rested silver epaulieres, gauntlets, and a cuirass of a simple plate mail design. With each there was a tabard, one in red with a black rampant lion on it, the other black with a red rampant lion, the trims of each outlined with gold. Never had they seen anything like it in their lifetimes despite all they had been through.

"They are made of Gyldrig, a metal mined in Aerim both for its variance in color and for its strength and resistance to damage. It is the strongest substance known to the Four Forces, and the pride of my people," Ironhorn said.

"The tabards, however, belonged to your fathers." The voice of Puc rang out from behind them as the mage stepped forward, shadowed by Matthias, who seemed to have recovered, save for the bruises and scratches that lined his face still. "The black lion of Severio, and the red belonging to Kinsman."

Wasting no more time, both were separated, and the long, complicated process of donning armor began, starting with the golden chainmail that went underneath everything, followed by the plate mail components. Annetta's hair had been put into a braid before it all began, allowing the chainmail to be slipped on her with ease. She expected to fall over when the chainmail was slipped over her head, but instead found the weight so evenly distributed that it felt only as if she were carrying a backpack filled with textbooks. When it was done, Annetta stepped down from the stool she had been placed on, testing how articulate she was in the full suit. Looking in the mirror before her, Annetta no longer saw herself, but the young woman from her drawings. Somehow, it still made her feel small and insignificant compared to the mantle she now wore as the granddaughter of Lord Orbeyus Severio.

She felt something was missing from the outfit to make it her own. Turning back, she looked at the discarded t-shirt, and her old faithful jean jacket that had already been through its own battles, clothes that had served her for years in the life she had known. Walking over, she picked up the jean jacket, unable to feel the denim texture under the Gyldrig gauntlets. The jacket had been with her to all of the different worlds she had seen, and it pained the girl to have to part with it.

"No," she whispered, "You come with me old friend"

Slipping the jacket over the armor, she found for the first time in years the coat fit instead of being too big for her.

℠℞

Soldiers scattered into their assigned positions on Valdhar as the ship reached its final mode of preparation before Pessumire was fully calibrated for firing. Mislantus, wearing a suit of blackened scalemail and his embroidered dark emerald gambeson with the seven-headed dragon on it, stood watching from his observation bridge on the upper level of the ship. Beside him, like his shadow, was Amarok.

A soldier approached them, bowing his head low as he gave the update. "My lord, the pilots for the cruisers are in place, and ready to launch on the signal."

"Good. Make sure none launch before we have passed through the portal. I want to give them a nice surprise when we get there," the tyrant replied, to which the soldier scurried off.

"How can you be sure there will even be a resistance to meet you there, my lord?" Amarok asked.

"Did you not see that boy's face when he spoke of his friends, Amarok?" Mislantus retorted. "He spoke of friendship unbending. If they have indeed escaped, and if anything Matthias has told us is true in his reports before he defected, then they were gathering the Four Forces."

"Surely you don't think a pack of children could-," Amarok began to protest.

"Children, no, but children who are more likely than not instructed by Puc Thanestorm, then yes Amarok. I do think so," Mislantus sneered, grabbing hold of the hilt of his saber firmly as he looked out at the army assembling below him in their respective formations. Once they seemed ready, Mislantus raised his arm with the saber high, a cheer erupting from the chaos. Silence then fell along with his arm, Mislantus's eyes fixed on the swollen mass below.

"For years we have toiled in the one goal that sustained us. The goal in avenging he that was Mordred the Conqueror, the unquestionable ruler of all in the universe, descendant of Freius, the enslaver of Korangar. The one who showed us even a god could bleed when he defied the council, when he defied Gaia and all other planets that called themselves superior. His life's ambition to prove he could hold all in his hands never ending, for more worlds always presented themselves to him, ready to follow the true master, the true lord. His life was short lived, and his dream incomplete when his mighty grasp fell under Orbeyus the Scourge. In his vanity, he spared me, and ever since, I have worked to avenge the dream, to take my own place as a descendant of Freius, he who held the keys to all life and death, as a god should. I tell you now that we here will see this dream through with the taking of the ultimate gateway. The Eye to All Worlds!"

The mass once again came to life as a sea of screams and shouts, a tribute being paid to the one who stood above them, their leader who would stop at nothing to see a vision through.

"They will all follow you to any end." Amarok leaned in, whispering to Mislantus. "And so will I, my lord."

Mislantus smiled, knowing his dream would soon come true, and he would walk the halls of Severio Castle as their master. No one would ever oppose him again as the true and supreme ruler of all, the goal his father had set out to achieve so long ago when he had been denied his rightful place.

Chapter 59

Annetta came out into the courtyard dressed in full regalia, the heaviness of the armor beginning to sink in as she walked. As she continued on, she neared the stables and smithy, where busy soldiers prepared their mounts and weapons. It was not until then that Annetta realized how much life the castle could hold once other beings were there. Passing by stacks of unclaimed armor and shields, she saw her horse Bossman being dressed with a full set of barding, complete with a caparison to match her own tabard. Dodging a few elves that ran by with two horses, she took two steps back to level herself, when her eye caught something another elf was carrying. At first, she thought was a lance covered in fabric, but as she got a better look at it, she saw what it truly was.

"That was your grandfather's standard." Puc's voice came from behind Annetta unannounced, almost causing the girl to jump out of her armor. "Fashioned to hold the coats of arms of all the races, like Severbane it stood in times past as a symbol of our unity."

Annetta watched one elf handing the immense flag to another, who was already mounted on horseback. The thick material unrolled in a single swift movement, like an arm stretching out to be taken. Upon it, the girl saw the four symbols that were engraved on the pedestal where Severbane had been encased: The water droplets that had stood for the Water Elves, the tri-peaked mountain of the Minotaur, the three streaks that were the wind of the Soarin, and the flame of the Ogaien. In its center, on a crimson background, were both a red and a black rampant lion that faced one another, a sword dividing them down the middle.

Puc watched the girl's reaction from the side, his own eyes lingering upon the war banner as he remembered all those who had once fought beside him under it. With a sigh, he reluctantly turned to go mount his horse.

Annetta watched the exchange of the standard between the two elves having been made. As soon as the standard bearer's horse began to move, however, something within the girl stirred.

"Wait! Stop!" she cried out across the courtyard and made her way over.

Puc urged his horse over. "What is it?"

"I can't just let this go," Annetta spoke, feeling childish. "I mean...if this is supposed to represent all of us, then shouldn't I be carrying it?"

"Annetta, I assume you will be busy fighting, the job of the standard bearer is to protect it from falling into enemy hands. If he dies and it touches the ground, then that is seen as incredibly demoralizing for the entire army."

Ignoring Puc's ranting, Annetta, with the help of one of the squires, mounted up onto Bossman. Grabbing the shield in one hand, she urged her horse over to the standard bearer. Stretching out an armored hand, she accepted the heavy wooden pole, leaning its end inside her stirrup for balance. Feeling how heavy it was, she called upon psychic energy from within to lessen the load. She then looked over at the mage.

"Then I guess this just means I can't die," she said. "Call it insurance."

The elven mage observed the stubborn girl and shook his head. "And where, tell me, are you going to carry your sword? In your teeth?" he asked with a curious half-smile.

Noting the problem, the girl looked around for a solution as a few of the assembled squires and unmounted fighters chuckled, causing the girl to flush more crimson than her tabard.

"I believe I can fix that." One of the Minotaur approached the girl. He hooked on what looked like a long, thin, metal quiver. "Had it made, on the mage's orders."

Annetta glanced over at Puc baffled, having heard his comment just moments before, to which the mage responded, "You are not much different than a certain lord I rode into battle with many years ago."

೮ාଔ

Annetta and Puc rode out to join the others as soon as everything had been set into place in the castle, protective wards cast to prevent damage to the building, and other defensive measures. The plains surrounding the castle were transformed from their green and vibrant state into a chaotic mass of trampled yellow and brown underfoot as they made their way to the lines of soldiers upon the horizon.

There was confusion as to where Valdhar would appear, but as soon as the sky began to turn grey and the wind pulled east, the mages of Aldamoor knew well where the great fortress would appear. It did not take long for each respective leader to coordinate their platoons to face where the oncoming danger would appear.

The wind, growing stronger by the moment, snapped the mighty banner on the mast back and forth beside Annetta and Jason. The two looked at each other for reassurance. Darius, Link, Matthias, and Sarina soon made their way over to them. Darius wore the same mage armor Puc had, his helmet covering most of his face and making him indistinguishable from the other mages, while Link and Sarina wore similar armor to that of Jason and Annetta. The only one differing from the group was Matthias, who still wore the same outfit he had on him when he returned from Valdhar.

"Sarina? What are you doing here?" Jason asked a little surprised to see the girl wearing the golden chainmail and black tabard.

"My friends fought to get me out. I want to return the favor," she answered.

"It's going to be dangerous," he insisted.

"Danger? You know you are talking to the daughter of the one and only Mislantus the Threat, right?" she replied, flashing her white teeth at him, to which the boy only rolled his eyes but smiled back nonetheless.

"No armor?" Darius asked the assassin.

"An experienced psychic needs no armor but his mind," he spoke in a confident tone, his gaze turning to Annetta and Jason. "Someday you will say the same."

"Each what they can by the strength of their own two hands." Puc ended the conflict before it began, and turned to Annetta. "The Four Forces will want to hear words from you."

"Wait, what?" Annetta sat up, her heart pounding in her chest.

"They are going to fight for the sake of all worlds here. You need to lead them. Go and share words with them." Puc motioned for her to move forward so everyone could see.

Annetta turned to Jason with a horrified expression. She hated speaking in public. It was her worst nightmare when she had to present in a classroom. Talking to thousands of soldiers seemed even worse.

"Don't look at me, Annetta," Jason said. "I know you can do this. If anyone can, it's you. I've been your best friend for long enough, I've seen you go up against all kinds of stuff. Those guys, they need to know what I've seen, because they haven't known you as long as I have. They need to believe it."

Believe. The word echoed a second time in her mind. She nodded, sucked in a lung full of air, and secured her shield to her back. Lifting the standard in the other hand and veering Bossman around. She charged outward and raised both Severbane and the banner high enough for everyone to see. Weapons clanged against shields and armor, wild howls rose, and the

659

sound of ten thousand voices were raised in the air, answering the beacon as Annetta gathered all attention to herself.

"To you, I have been known as Annetta, the heir of Orbeyus," she began, Bossman dancing beneath her feet as she made him pace back and forth. "But today, I come to you also as Annetta Severio, the girl. I know as well as all of you that I am not my grandfather, but someone else. I am new to all of this, where many of you are veterans to the field of battle. But I am also the future that you veterans once invested in, fighting by my grandfather's side and I come here not ordering you for loyalty, not ordering you for anything more than what you can give, but simply asking for your help, so that someday in the future, when someone else stands here in my place, they can say I am the heir of Annetta Severio, and that your descendants in freedom may say the same of their own heritage. Some of you may also wonder why so young a girl would come here to fight. The answer is this. Someone needs to stand up for those who cannot, and when I asked who defends the Earth, who defends all worlds, no one answered. Then, if you should ask why me, I answer why not? I have with me the most powerful weapon in all the worlds. I speak not of Severbane, but of something far, far greater that lies within the hearts of all of you here, and all those who will ever answer the call of clashing shields and roaring battle cries. I'm talking about belief in one's self! As long as we never stop believing in ourselves, in the strength in our own hearts, then Mislantus has nothing that can break us. He's nothing!"

A unified cry answered the end of Annetta's speech as the wind made its final round past everyone, and the sound of thunder could be heard through the sky. Swerving her horse around, Annetta turned and looked up as the clouds turned darker and darker, until they seemed a combination of black and violet, swirling in a whirlpool upon the heavens. Holding her ground, she did not back away as through the tempest of cloud and wind a behemoth appeared, Valdhar. The fortress seemed to stop flying, and crashed into the hillside of the closest mountain, lodging itself onto it like a parasite.

It all came crashing down within seconds of the fortress appearing. The charge of soldiers and the adrenaline coursing through her veins as it happened made Annetta unable to discern reality from illusion as from the ship, teleporting down onto the ground below, came thousands of soldiers, all of different races, but all banded together under the seven headed dragon

660

emblem of the warlord, their screams blending in with the pounding of rushing hooves and feet. From the sides of the fortress, small sleek vessels darted out, their bullet bodies heading straight towards the airships, many met by death before their could get within fighting distance by the colorful spells of mages and the arrows of Soarin who now flew through the skies.

80CR

Maria Gladiola, the captain of the scouting vessel Tessa, ran around her ship frantically, calculating her next move in order not to collide with an enemy vessel. But while she was measuring the course, enemy soldiers teleported onboard and began cutting down unwary crew. Snarling, Maria drew her saber and crashed into the fray, ramming through the invaders, hacking and slashing through any limb of theirs that got in the way. Allowing her crew to recover and take up arms, she dashed to the other side of the ship where more had appeared, kicking and stabbing and even pushing one of them overboard when they lost balance with the tip of her blade.

Chuckling, the airship commander seemed to have everything in hand until she was knocked to the ground by the impact of a fist to her gut. Turning she viewed her opponent, a massive rhinoceros- like creature dressed in a full suit of black armor that she remembered to be a Verden. She also noticed her sword had been knocked from her hands as the giant closed in. Shielding her head and waiting for the enormous armored fists to smash her bones, Maria was surprised when a very familiar war cry echoed, and the sound of shooting arrows followed. Opening her eyes, she watched as Iliam and Doriden took out the beast, its bloody carcass pushed overboard by the Soarin warrior.

"Bombs away, dudes." Doriden smirked, watching the body fall onto unexpected enemy fighters.

"Iliam? What are you?" Maria asked, picking up her saber, "And who?"

"Doriden Deadeye at your service. You might remember me when I was about six feet shorter and had both eyes." Doriden tilted his horned head in a bow and then rushed back into the fray as Maria chuckled, remembering the little Soarin as a pup.

"We figured you might be in need of assistance from some truly seasoned fighters." Iliam smiled as Maria shoved him playfully. Taking up positions, the two went back into fighting stance.

Down below, the Minotaur infantry charged alongside the Water Elf forces and Ogaien warriors on their Aiethon mounts, tearing through the oncoming enemy storm. Clouds of dust and heat seemed to swirl around them as the three races fought alongside one another, each playing off of one another's strengths. Among them, Ironhorn and Natane raced head on, striking down those who came in their way with acrobatic grace. The Minotaur Lord wielded Fearseeker in one hand and an axe in the other, and seemed no less agile than the smaller Ogaien on her fiery mount, who kept vigilant on his back as he did on hers.

"A fine pair we'd make in the court of Morwick, Lady Natane. No single giant would dare stand against the blade and spear combined," Ironhorn commented, driving the dagger into one of his enemies as he watched them collapse.

"Indeed, except I would never marry one as hairy and strange looking as you, Lord Ironhorn," Natane retorted, shoving her spear into the shoulder of her adversary. "More so, I would never be compliant to a male."

"Ah, but that makes you all the more intriguing in my eyes, though in truth, your strange shape does repulse me just as much as mine does to you." The Minotaur Lord roared as he head butted another unwary fighter.

"And that is a better use for that thick head of yours than the contemplations of before," the Ogaien warrior replied, watching the opponent fall as she thrust her spear through him.

"A good point indeed," Ironhorn replied.

꧁꧂

Elsewhere, Kaian was no lesser than the other leaders, fighting side by side with a score of his mages from Aldamoor, the intricate staff in his hand beaming with spells one after another as he summoned them. His goal was taking out as many of the psychic warriors as possible. Though the elite enemy fighters were a small company, they were titans on the battlefield, and they could not afford to be left unchecked. It was also easy for Kaian to locate them. Most exposed themselves by flinging scores of Minotaurs, Water Elves and Ogaien into the air, occasionally taking a Soarin out of the sky with psychic fire. The mages had not had time to prepare a vast quantity of anti-psychic charms on such a short notice, and had to deal with the hand given to them. Kaian had volunteered as one of the mages to not take a charm.

Urging his mount forward, the First Mage stopped some feet away from a small group of psychics. Raising his staff, he fired without remorse on the group as they hollered in anguish, their bodies set ablaze as they tried to rid themselves of it by rolling around. Satisfied with his ploy, Kaian smirked, only to be thrown from his horse, which took off in fright.

Hissing in pain, the mage felt the back of his armor heat up. Rising, he turned around to see an insectoid-faced creature wielding a ball of purple and blue flame closing in on him. Frowning, the mage showed no fear as he steadied himself and gripped his staff. Proud as he was of his magical prowess, Kaian refused to carry a blade, relying only upon the strength of his mind.

It was mistake that would cost him dearly. Kaian felt the mighty staff fly from his hands faster than he could react, and was sent to the floor. A second psychic appeared, a gruff looking man with a black beard and ruffled hair.

"What we got here, Minx?" he said with a chuckle, tossing a ball of psychic fire from hand to hand, "I think it's an old man that's lost his way to his appointment with death. Hows about we show him the way."

Raising his arm, the psychic prepared to fire. Kaian shielded his eyes, only to hear the thunderous roar of a great cat and the sound of a sword slicing through flesh and bone. Looking up, Kaian found his rescuers in the form of Puc and Darius, the younger mage extending the First Mage's staff to him, while the shapeshifting apprentice kept lookout.

"They always did complain at the Academy that you hated fighting with a spare weapon," Puc said once Kaian was up on his feet again, before handing him his staff.

"A true mage needs no steel to shield him," Kaian replied, a certain degree of pride in his voice as he accepted the staff.

Puc smirked, but their conversation was cut short as one of Verden warriors came charging towards them. Before any of them could react and pull away, a beam shot straight through the center of the beast, causing it to stop and slide along the beaten down ground until it stopped inches from Kaian's boots. Looking up in shock, they trio turned to see a zeppelin covering the sky above. Kaine looked down from the railings on board the ship as a ladder descended.

"You need to be more careful, father. This is not the training grounds, this is war!" he called.

"You listen to me, Kaine. Keep your eyes to the sky and don't be butting into my own business!" Kaian snarled, though he was touched by his son's actions as he grabbed hold of the ladder and began to climb, followed by Puc and Darius.

"I would, but we've got another problem," Kaine replied as they came aboard. "The more we beat them down, the more come out. Take a look." Kaine pointed to Valdhar as more and more soldiers spewed out of it. "I don't know how many more are in there but they're coming out like ants from a flooded anthill."

Kaian's pale eyes scanned the fortress as he tried to formulate a plan. "Valdhar needs to be destroyed, then. But how?"

"A self destruct button," Darius suggested. "All ships have one. That thing is first and foremost a ship, isn't it? It looked like one from the inside, at least."

"Boarding Valdhar? That's suicide," Puc protested.

"We may not have a choice." Kaian narrowed his eyes. "Mislantus has rebuilt more than any of us anticipated. Any advantage we can get will be gold."

Kaian looked down to see the six mages he had been separated from looking for him, their robes bloodied from the impacts of the war. Whistling he motioned for them to come up. He had started out with twelve, and frowned at the dwindling number. He worried he would be lucky to have three alive by the time they reached the great fortress.

"There is one problem," the First Mage spoke, finally. "If we go in, we need someone who can send the thing hurling back into space. We cannot afford to have it damage the Eye to All Worlds."

"Who better than an airship pilot, father?" Kaine asked.

&⁊⊗⊰

Racing head on, Annetta had lost track of her friends in the midst of the enemy fighters. They had surrounded her like a swarm of locusts, along with warriors from her own side, a thick veil of death and chaos. The only one she could vaguely see was Link a few paces away, thrown down from his horse and fighting on foot. Having been stopped and encircled by Mislantus's troops, Annetta had no choice but to face them with sword and shield in hand. Slashing away and constantly ready to pivot Bossman in case anyone should be behind her, the girl did her best to get away from any injury that could befall her. Her long lessons with Puc and Brakkus had helped in preparing her, honing her reflexes until she could almost detect when a weapon intended to fall her way.

Then it came, the moment that separated her from her old life. The entire time Annetta had fought, parrying and injuring the soldiers around her, trying to evade, trying to postpone. Her baptism in blood finally arrived as Severbane slid through the ribcage of one of the small reptilian soldiers with a beak who had lunged at her with his blade. Stunned, she watched the creature fall to its death. She now understood what Link had said to her before. Her stomach swam with unease as her nostrils took in the stench of fire, dirt and blood around her. Annetta's eyes focused on the gore remaining on her sword as the liquid stained the torn grass below. The mistake of daydreaming at that instant cost her dearly.

Like an angry swarm of locusts, a dozen smaller fighters were upon her and Bossman. Annetta slashed and cut and stabbed, but it was all over before it even began and there was nothing the girl could do. Within seconds, the horde had tipped the horse over, and though the girl could not see it, she was conscious of the creature's death when a gurgling whinny came from it, its throat having been slashed open. A scream of horror erupted from the girl's own lungs as the warhorse collapsed, leaving Annetta pinned helplessly beneath it. A wrath that was incomprehensible took hold of her for Bossman had been more than just a horse. Remembering her other vow to Puc, Annetta struggled with her shield arm to keep the standard from touching the ground, despite it only being inches away from the muddy grass. Ensuring the banner was safe she turned her attention to those who had caused her fall. Using her telekinetic powers, she managed to send her opponents flying. Recovering slightly, she used her energy once more to lift the standard and plant it in the ground, the flag flying upon the wind. Turning to more immediate concerns, she felt her leg, pinned by the dead horse's bulk, and she began trying to squirm out from under it, her foot caught in the stirrup.

"Damn it," she muttered, trying to move her leg.

About to teleport, she stopped as the shape of a club peered over the side of Bossman's flank. Looking up, Annetta found herself staring face to face with what looked like a man but standing at least ten feet tall. A vicious grin spread across his face as the man chuckled, lifting the massive club overhead, getting ready to turn Annetta into a pile of meaty goo. Cringing, the girl closed her eyes as she tried to think of a place to teleport, but was interrupted as a shape passed over her, blotting out the after-image of the sun rolling overhead, an all too familiar voice roaring out in a battle cry. Annetta opened her eyes and looked to see the tempest incarnate, her father Arieus blocking her from the creature's path.

He snarled as he assaulted it with a combination of telekinetic sword strokes, and finally planted his sword firmly in the creature's chest.

Wide eyed, Annetta watched. Her father stood with his back turned to her as the giant fell. She took the moment of peace to look out at the chaotic battlefield, creatures from her storybooks collided in the heat of fighting while war ships soared overhead. It all seemed so surreal to her already, and now he'd shown up. Arieus then turned around to face her, very little left of the man she had grown up knowing, replaced with everything she had ever heard about him. Without a word, he strode over to her, and with a simple glance, the horse lifted itself from Annetta, allowing her to crawl out from under it.

"Daddy?" she asked, looking at him questioningly.

"Annetta!" Jason's voice rang out from the chaos as he and Link came running towards her. "Are you alright? We saw you fall from your horse and... Mr. Severio?"

Before Arieus could reply, the soldiers Annetta had thrown back were upon them. Their shields up and swords out, the group weighed their options. Before any fighting could begin, the distinct sounds of women shouting could be heard as a ball of psychic fire crashed right through the ranks of the circling soldiers, scattering them like bowling pins.

"That's what happens when you gang up on my little boy!" Talia yelled, Aurora racing beside her to the aid of her family.

"Mom?" both Jason and Annetta said simultaneously.

"Someone needs to save you slackers." Talia winked at her son, who felt the color drain from his face as he tried to make sense of the whole scene, and shook his head.

"Have you seen Sarina or Matt?" he asked, turning to Annetta as she shook her head.

"I think I know where they've gone." Link lifted his eyes towards the great fortress that seemed to have caught fire as thousands of soldiers danced around it below.

"Valdhar," Annetta muttered under her breath, then turned to look at both of her parents.

Arieus stood beside the banner planted in the ground. He could scarcely believe his own actions, but when Puc had come to tell him of what was to come, he knew deep down that he could no longer sit idly by.

"You go, sweetheart," Arieus said, taking up the standard in his free hand. "We'll hold the fort down here. And don't worry. Your mother is a very good shot with psychic flames."

With an exchange of nods from the youth, Arieus watched with Aurora and Talia at his side as their children disappeared into the red horizon.

"Be safe, descendants of the axe and mace," he whispered quietly, before he turned to his companions. "So then, shall we slay some fiends, or not?"

Before either Talia or Aurora could say anything in return, they were caught off guard by the sound of a steam engine approaching. A ladder then descended before them. Looking up, the trio noted the underside of a wooden barge, and spotted a familiar helmet glaring back at them from the railing. Looking around to see the battle still raging, and in need of a moment to think strategy, they ascended the ladder, Arieus never parting with the standard.

"I see you got my message." Puc greeted the man with Kaian, Darius, Kaine, and the other mages close behind him, as the companions climbed aboard.

Arieus smiled, looking down at his blade, then back at the mage.

"I swore to protect my family from this," he answered. "I realize now that cannot be, so I must do all I can to stand beside them."

"That is the way with loved ones at times," Kaian said wistfully, glancing at his son in his airship pilot's long coat. "Though you set one course for them, fate wishes otherwise. I learned the hard way."

Arieus nodded at the father and son, then turned his attention back to Puc, who seemed in a hurry, "Where do you travel to now, Thanestorm?"

"To Valdhar," the elf answered him. "The fortress must be removed from its current position, put back into space where it came from, and destroyed there."

"Well, you won't be able to do that now," Aurora stated. "Annetta and her friends just went there to look for two people called Matt and Sarina. And you're not going to be blasting any ships that have my baby on board."

"Or mine," Talia added. "Besides, it's easier said than done. You want to start up Pessumire and set the ship in motion on a reverse course, without even knowing the technology."

"Where there are Water Elves, there is a way," Puc said boastfully in answer, then turned to Arieus. "We head to the fortress, and we will contact them when we are there."

"And you plan to get out how, in time, on your own?" Arieus shot back. "I know you have much faith in Annetta's abilities, and she must indeed have progressed far under your tutoring, but she has nowhere near the experience to deal with all the pressure, and there is a chance you will not run into her while aboard. Without a psychic to get you out, I cannot allow you to proceed. It would stand against all my father once held dear."

Puc was about to retort, but bit his tongue and simply nodded to the man. His gaze then turned to the metallic castle that lay against the side of one of the limestone mountains. The more his eyes traced over the contours of the behemoth structure, the more he understood he would indeed need all the help he could get.

ଛୀଔ

Slipping through the shadows, Matthias made his way towards the central bridge looking out onto the lower levels of fortress, the place he would surely find Mislantus still watching, despite the troops having all departed for the field of battle. He knew the tyrant would not leave his castle until victory was his own. In fact, his charges would prevent him from truly entering the battlefield, worried that their lord and rightful ruler could fall into harm's way. Matthias's face wrinkled at the thought of such fanaticism, something he had once possessed. His thoughts were interrupted when his keen sense of hearing picked up footsteps from behind that he had heard for some time now. He knew full well whom they belonged to. He stopped and waited for their rhythm to cease.

"Sarina, just how long do you plan to do this?" he hissed, fed up with the game.

The girl behind him cursed under her breath, having been sure she had been able to follow the assassin. Instead, she had been toyed with. Matthias smirked upon hearing the noise and turned to her, his brown hair falling into his face, causing him to have a mask over his eyes in the dark.

"You are not going with me, Sarina," he said in a low voice in case of potential guards that were still aboard. "You're already in more danger here than by being out on the field."

"Look, I don't care," she protested. "I'm not letting you do this alone."

"Oh, yes you are. Now, leave," Matthias snarled only to be cut off by the sound of a cynical laugh and clapping.

Turning to face the threat, Matthias and Sarina found themselves standing a few feet away from Amarok.

"My, you two really know how to put on the brother and sister act, don't you?" he said from behind the broken mask. "Touching indeed."

"Shut it, Amarok," Matthias snapped, extending the claws in his hands and bringing them both before him. "Where is Mislantus?"

"Oh, you won't find him here boy. He's gone." Amarok snickered, "He's up on the towers overlooking the battle, but you will never get there."

Matthias could sense the tension coming from Amarok. The two of them had never had a chance to settle the score since their initial outbreak. Now seemed a more appropriate time than ever. The younger assassin's eyes turned to Sarina for a split moment as he sent her clear instructions to get as far away as she could through telepathy, to which the girl obeyed and scrambled out of sight. Once gone, he shifted into a fighter stance.

"You think it wise to tangle with a wolf?" the elder assassin mocked.

"No, but I think it wise to kill one." Matthias leapt at him, only to see Amarok disappear before him, and kick him in the back after reappearing behind him.

Turning quickly onto his back and coiling his powerful legs, Matthias slammed both feet into Amarok's chest, causing the assassin to lose balance and fall backwards. Using the momentum gained, and manipulating it with psychic energy to make himself almost weightless, Matthias launched himself high into the air. He rid himself of the semi-levitated state once he was close to the ceiling, and rode gravity down, ready to dive blade-first into Amarok. Seeing the flaw in the plan, Amarok raised his arms before him and extended the spikes from his armor like a hedgehog. His plan having failed, Matthias teleported some feet back and threw a ball of psychic fire as quickly as his reflexes would allow him, hoping to still catch Amarok on the ground. But Amarok was already behind Matthias, the only thing saving the younger assassin in time was the sound of metal extending as the spikes threatened to reach his neck. Teleporting, he was gone again.

"You cannot win, Matthias Teron," Amarok sneered, looking diligently for any sign of the younger man. "I made you, and therefore have always been your master. Your superior."

Matthias, watching from the dark of the top railing within the observation chamber exhaled heavily as he weighed his options. His gauntlet clad fists curled up as he gathered his composure. Creating another ball of psychic fire, he roared, leaping down at Amarok, slamming the blast full force downward.

꙳

Half teleporting and half running up the hill, Annetta, Link, and Jason finally made it inside Valdhar, which, surprisingly, was barely guarded. Only a few wayward sentries stood between them and the lower levels of the fortress. Once they dispatched the soldiers, they teleported inside. When they were sure no one was around, they stopped to plan.

"Where do we go from here?" Annetta asked.

"Well we gotta destroy this thing and find Matt and Sarina, right?" Jason pursed his lips as he thought out loud. "I think I remember passing something that looked like a big room with computers and stuff. Maybe we can find something up there."

"Do you remember where that was?" Link inquired, still on his guard for any soldiers that could come their way. "They may have had the same idea we do, and we might meet up with them there."

"It was up, that's all I know," Jason said. "I say we go up, and maybe we'll run into them."

"Good a plan as any," Annetta replied, and they took off once more.

Running for what seemed like an eternity up fights of stairs and through corridors, they finally heard the echoes of battle, and quickened their steps in its direction, but stayed hidden, not sure what to expect.

Peering around the corner, the trio could see a fierce battle between Matthias and Amarok, the two clashing like a pair of wild beasts, sparks of blue and purple flying from the psychic fire each released. Neither seemed to hold the advantage, and it was hard to keep up with their movements due to their teleporting. Were it not for the sound of steel and grunts of pain each exchanged when receiving a hit, the trio would have thought them to be spirits, still warring with one another after death.

Annetta moved to turn the tables of the game, only to have her shoulder caught by Link.

670

"This is his fight, Annetta, and you can't take that away from him," he said quietly with a look of disapproval. "If you intervene in this, he may never forgive you. I'm not saying it to hurt your feelings. It's not just a fight for the sake of it. It's a matter of pride."

Annetta glanced at him in confusion.

"The look in their eyes, and what Amarok said back in the Lab. This is no ordinary fight. This is a decisive battle," Link said.

Jason nodded in agreement and added, "Now we need to find Sarina, wherever she is. We can't help him, but we can maybe help her."

Annetta shifted uneasily, but relaxed a little, and so Link's arm dropped from her shoulder. Fixing her gaze to the scene before her, she watched the fight rage on.

Each of the combatants assaulted the other with blows of psychic fire, draining their energy in the process. Breathing heavily, Amarok and Matthias snarled as their weapons clashed. Losing tempo in their dance from time to time, however, each assassin received his share of nicks and cuts until Amarok summoned up the strength of mind to curve the spikes on his armor and rake them all across Matthias's arms deeply. Matthias howled and dropped to his knees in exhaustion, glaring at Amarok like a cornered animal.

"Goodbye, Matthias Teron," Amarok said, creating the largest possible ball of psychic flame he could, and threw it at the assassin.

Instincts triggered, Annetta flew at the scene without thinking, her shield straps breaking from the combined effort of Jason and Link pulling at it to hold her back. Charging and teleporting before the flames to get Matthias out of the way, it became apparent that it was all too late. Flame and electricity tore through her, burning her tabard, jacket and searing the skin beneath her armor. Annetta felt the world around her stop and everything no longer mattered. Then there was darkness.

Chapter 60

Darkness. Jason was forced to watch as his entire world sunk into his feet when the psychic fire struck Annetta. He watched with eyes unblinking as her form crumpled in her armor to the ground beside Matthias, and moved no more. Though most of him could not comprehend it, he knew full well that she was dead. His best friend was gone, and nothing could change that. But he could get even. Tears forming in his eyes, he turned to Link, who was experiencing similar feelings. With a small nod, both of them charged out of their hiding spot, no fear present in either of them as they cried out for their lost friend.

Amarok had only seconds to take in the unexpected death he had caused before a ball of psychic fire whizzed past him, catching his shoulder and melting his armor. Now alerted, the next ball of flame was deflected to the side as the assassin retaliated with his own fire.

"I'm going to kill you! You murderer!" Jason shouted as he shot another ball of psychic fire bigger than the last.

Amarok barely dodged the attack. Worse yet, the assassin was on his last bit of energy, the fight with Matthias having drained him. He also had to deal with Link, who pursued him relentlessly with his sword, causing the assassin to have to teleport, and use up more of his reserved energy. Weighing his options, Amarok teleported to the far side of the chamber they now found themselves in, and glared at the assembled on the ground.

"I'm afraid my death will not be today, young Kinsman, for my task is not yet done," the masked assassin said confidently. "For now, I leave this chaos as it was meant to be, and I go to serve a higher master."

Not wanting to hear any more, Jason fired another ball of psychic fire. Before it could reach its target, Amarok was gone. Screaming with rage, Jason dropped to his knees, frustrated and unable to do anything more.

Sheathing his sword, Link ran over to where Annetta lay, watched over by a traumatized Matthias. Kneeling beside her, Link lifted Annetta's head, cradling it in his arms.

"Why?" Matthias finally spoke coming out of his trance, Link looking over at him, "Why did she do it? I could have blocked the shot, arms or not. Why did she?"

"Because she cared," Link answered. "Because she didn't see the danger, just the friend in need."

672

His eyes and face stained with tears, Jason crawled over to where they all sat kneeling over Annetta's body. His hands trembling, Jason reached out, touching Annetta's shoulder. It was still warm. The only indication of her not living was the fact that she breathed no more. Madness overtaking him, he began to shake her shoulder, his face contorting as he did it.

"Jason, it won't do any good," Matthias snarled.

"No! She has to live!" Jason protested, still shaking her.

"Jason, she's gone," Link said, grabbing hold of him to calm him down as the broken youth's face resorted to the only thing it had left in that moment, weeping.

₭ ‑

Darkness, darkness, darkness, and all of a sudden Annetta saw light once more. Opening her eyes and stretching, she expected to have escaped the psychic fire with Matthias. Looking around she saw neither the assassin nor anyone else, or even anything familiar that could tell her she was still in Valdhar. Instead, she found herself in a world where ground and sky blended into one in silver light. In fact, all she could see was silver light for miles around her, with no way of really moving forward or back.

"I don't think I'm in Kansas anymore, Toto," she said distractedly, trying to make sense of it all.

"Kansas? Quite far from it, actually, my dear," a male voice said from behind.

Annetta felt a tightening sensation in her chest upon hearing the voice. She had no idea who it belonged to. Turning around, she found herself locking eyes with a man of silver hair and beard who haunted her every step. There stood Orbeyus Severio. Not knowing what to do, and completely flustered, Annetta bowed before him, only causing Orbeyus to chuckle a bit more.

"Oh, my little Annetta, rise. You do not bow before anyone, especially not your own grandfather." He grinned infectiously at her.

Hearing his words and feeling a little embarrassed by it all, Annetta got up, clutching at the hem of her jacket. Gathering up the courage, she looked up at the man before her. He stood dressed in the same chainmail and tabard she wore now, a great tattered brown cape following behind him, and his mighty twin bladed axe serving him as a staff. He seemed younger, more alive than in the painting.

"Where are we exactly, grandpa?" she asked, regaining her composure, "I mean…what just happened to me?"

"Well is it not obvious Annetta? You have died, and we stand now in the afterlife, where I am meant to remain," he said to her.

"I'm dead." Annetta said the words, feeling them sink in. "Like, dead, dead and not coming back?"

"Dead, yes," Orbeyus said to her. "But the Unknown has seen it fit that you return. You are needed on Earth. There are larger things yet to come for which you must be present, and there is much more for you still to do before you come to the eternal gardens."

"Gardens? I don't see anything but light everywhere," muttered the girl.

"The afterlife is what we make it." The lord smiled. "But this will be for you to discover years from now, and not in the present."

Annetta looked down, wringing her hands as she weighed her options. The majority of her screamed to go back, to keep going, but something else nagged at her, something that for a long time, she had not been able to give a voice to. Now, standing and seeing Orbeyus, she was able to do so.

"I think I may stay with you, grandpa," she said. "I mean, look at me. I'm not like you. I'm trying to be you, and failing pretty badly at it, considering I'm dead right now. I'm not the toughest, I'm not the bravest, I'm not even that smart when you think about it. Matt could have dodged that shot probably by teleporting or deflecting or something but I got in the way anyways."

"Annetta, you are everything you are meant to be in the life you were given. You are you." Orbeyus cut her off, kneeling down beside her. "A person's worth is not measured by how strong or how brave or how smart they are. It's measured by the value of their heart. Sometimes, because of this, it is the youngest that can make a difference. Sometimes us older, wiser, stronger people, we don't see everything. We forget what it was like to be young once, and we slow down. We don't ask the simple and important questions, like who is protecting us now."

Annetta smiled a little upon hearing the last part. When she had asked her father the same words Orbeyus had uttered, who protected the Earth when he was gone, her father had said no one. From that moment on, Annetta had said that she would do it.

"Sometimes it takes more bravery, more strength, and more wisdom than anything to take a stand and ask those sort of questions," Orbeyus added. "You're being given a chance to go back and live, something I have wished many times over I was able to do. Live, little Annetta. Sooner or later, we will meet here again and the longer you linger here, the less likely there is a chance for you to return."

Annetta sighed. Indeed, the more she remained there, the more she felt like not returning. It was as if her mind was slowly floating away into a bliss she had never known before, where no pain or despair could touch her. The silver world around her shone so brightly, it was blinding her, and making it hard to focus. Her mind then rushed back to the battle below, her friends fighting by her side, and what they would think. But she lost grip for a second again, the scales in her mind tipping slowly as all earthly cares left her. She was snapped back into reality once more as the hand of Orbeyus landed on her shoulder, his blue eyes focused upon her.

"Did you hear what I said, Annetta?" he asked.

"I guess, but I just feel tired, grandpa," she said. "And I feel like I'm disappointing you down there anyways."

"Annetta, the only way you can disappoint me is by giving up," Orbeyus answered. "The world needs someone to protect it. Without you, who is left?"

Annetta's mind focused sharply on Orbeyus's words as though someone had poured new life into her. All traced of her mind wavering left her.

"You are a Severio, my granddaughter, and I could never imagine anyone else but you in that role," he said, sternly this time. "So go now, I ask of you. Fight when no one else will, and remember that I will always be proud of you."

Annetta looked once more at Orbeyus, a man who was responsible for all the adventures she had been through, a man she had never thought she'd meet. Hearing the words filled her with warmth. She nodded, and she turned to try to find her way out.

"Oh, by the way, I'm really sorry about the Flying Dutchman."

෫෨ශ෬

Puc, Arieus, Aurora, Talia, Darius (who had reverted to his normal form) and the others made their way into Valdhar, their ranks having thickened upon meeting with another half a dozen mages who had volunteered to enter with the First Mage and his companions. Their decision was to go upwards to where, most likely, the control room was. It was in their journey through the corridors that they happened to come upon Jason, Matthias and Link over Annetta.

A silence fell upon the gathered as they took in the tableau before them. Arieus dropped the standard completely to the ground as he and Aurora fell to their knees, while Talia went to her son, embracing him in a protective hug, as if trying to shield him from the death in the room. Kaian and Kaine stood back, letting the friends in first, the soldiers shocked by what they had come upon. Feeling struck by lightening, Puc looked upon the scene, taking off his heavy helmet and dropping it to the floor to see clearer. He gave a numb command to one of the mages to heal Matthias, who was still on his knees, but his mind was focused on the girl.

"Annetta?" Arieus crawled over to his daughter, taking her from Link. "My little girl...say something."

Evident to the parents that she would say nothing, they began to weep for their lost child.

Having regained some of his pride, Jason tore away from his mother, who stood holding him. Anger still filled him from head to toe, and he had an idea about how to unleash it. Taking off, he ran with mace in hand.

"Jason!" Talia tried to hold onto him, forced to watch as her son teleported mid run from before her. "Where did he go?"

"It's not back home, if that is what you're hoping for," Matthias said, his arms having been healed. "Amarok is the one responsible for this."

"I can't let him go, he'll get killed!" Talia protested as she stood up to leave.

"Not if I kill Amarok first!" Arieus snarled through his tears, still holding onto Aurora as she cried.

"Talia and Arieus, we need to keep going," Kaian said, still level headed despite the grief, making the sorrowful parent curl back a little in defeat.

Talia walked off to the side, the stress of it all building so much within her that she could not take it. Waiting for the moment to pass, she took out a cigarette from her pouch, and lit it in an effort to regain steady nerves.

The First Mage bit his tongue in shame for not having stopped to think what it was like to be in Arieus's shoes. His gaze then turned to the girl in armor, lying still on the ground as though she were asleep.

"I don't care, he murdered my little girl." Arieus gritted his teeth, speaking up once more. "I'll put the devil in the ground, you just watch me!"

"I'm with him," Link said, the father's anger infecting him as well.

"Listen," Kaian said with a sigh. "The only thing we can do now is honor her memory, and rid the world of Mislantus and his men for good. It's what she would have wanted. You must take your grief and anger with you and use it where it will do some good."

Matthias sat in silence. He felt responsible for it all. For one of the few times in his life, he felt guilt seep into his bones.

Puc continued to watch with a numbness building within him, for the scene held a resemblance to another murdered Severio's body he had walked in on many years ago, and the death of a friend he had also endured. A sick feeling of bile filled the mage's gut, and an extreme heat filled every inch of his body. He was Puc Thanestorm, one of the most skilled mages in all of Aldamoor, and he had let two of his friends die. Now his pupil, someone he had also learned to call a friend, had fallen as well.

"Was this meant to be it? Was I meant to bury my own child?" Aurora breathed heavily through sobs in her husband's arms.

There was no response for a long time from anyone in the group. No one had any words left to say to the mother in her despair. Out of nowhere, the mage and advisor of Orbeyus of the Axe sprang to life.

"Not on this day," Puc snarled, tightening his grip on Tempest's hilt as he slid the blade into the scabbard. Ordering Arieus to let go of her, the mage hovered over the body, placing his hands over her chest, and began chanting in a low voice.

"Master, she's dead. It won't do any good," Darius said.

"Not on this day," the mage repeated, and glared at his apprentice. "I have not tried to save any of those who mattered in the past. There is always hope if we choose to see it, and I will not let Annetta die, not on this day."

"Thanestorm, we are wasting time," Kaian stated. "We need to get moving. Pay your respects so we can go on."

Ignoring the First Page, Puc continued to work. He was using so much magic he was beginning to drain himself of his strength, and was slowly beginning to tap into the magic within him that sustained his life. He had to try everything possible. It was all he had left to offer the girl.

Darius tapped his shoulder gently to get his attention. "Master, we need to go."

Puc ignored the tapping, along with Arieus, Aurora, Talia and Link, who were all still on the floor around the girl.

"Damn it! We can't do anything at this point for her! She's dead!" Darius hissed.

Suddenly, as if regaining consciousness, Annetta's chest heaved and her eyes opened as wide as possible gasping for air. Darius's jaw dropped, his declaration from moments before becoming invalid as he rushed to help Puc up, so drained from his work that he nearly collapsed in a heap on the floor beside Annetta.

"Impossible." Talia's mouth hung open as she dropped her cigarette.

"By the mark of the Unknown, I would not have believed it possible had I not seen it myself," Kaian gasped.

Waking up and seeing the faces Annetta recognized almost made her feel dizzy. She tried to center her equilibrium by sitting up with the help of Link.

"You have any idea how creepy that is when so many people are staring at you first thing when you wake up?" she growled, rubbing the sleep from her eyes.

"We thought you were dead." Arieus hugged his daughter, along with Aurora.

Annetta returned the hug, but felt self-conscious about all the people around her, and withdrew quickly.

"Uhm, well I kind of was," she said, regaining footing and standing up. "Except grandpa told me something that made me change my mind about staying there."

"Orbeyus?" Aurora looked curiously at her husband who glanced back at his daughter with a blank stare, unsure what to make of the proclamation, his mind still swimming in thoughts of the seconds before, when he was sure she would never speak again.

"You saw Orbeyus?" Darius asked as he gave Puc a potion to recover his strength. "You met Orbeyus in the afterlife?"

"Yeah. He said I can't go just yet, but I guess it must have been just a dream. I mean, people don't just come back to life," she said. Her attention then focused on a certain elven mage, the first person she had seen upon opening her eyes, his hands raised over her as he chanted. "Thank you Puc, for everything."

"No, thank you, Annetta," the mage answered, "for reminding me of a lesson I forgot many years ago. To never lose hope."

Annetta nodded with a shy smile, then turned to see the massive group of people around her.

"So, uh, what are you guys all doing here anyway?" she asked, putting her sword in its scabbard and examining the shield straps, retying them as best as she could.

"An idea of assorted assembly," Puc stated cryptically, his gaze turning to Kaian.

"We are overrun down below," the First Mage explained, "and more soldiers keep appearing from Valdhar. The fortress needs to be destroyed, along with whatever soldiers remain on it."

"You guys can do that?" she replied, surprised.

"Destroy Valdhar?" Matthias said incredulously, cutting into their conversation. "The blast would kill everyone for at least twenty miles around. You'd need to-"

"We would need to activate Pessumire again, and that is precisely what we plan on doing," Talia replied, finishing his sentence.

"Good luck then," Matthias said, bitterly. "You've no idea how to use the technology on here, anyways."

"I'll have you know I'm an airship pilot by love of the trade," Kaine snapped back, feeling insulted, "and can pilot anything you sit me into the cockpit of."

"No offense, elf," the assassin said with a snort, "but Valdhar isn't your everyday little flying ship. It's a fortress meant to house thousands of soldiers, filled with chambers for science that your little nation couldn't wrap its head around."

"How dare you even-" Kaian bared his teeth as the closest six mages around him pointed their staves at Matthias.

Darius snapped out of his shock after what had taken place, and turned his attention to what was going on.

"Wait, he has a point." Darius stopped the guards and then turned to Matthias. "Can you operate any of it?"

"Yes, I know how to operate the ship," he spat, feeling insulted. "You think I'm an amateur?"

"Simple question," Darius growled, not enjoying the assassin's tone. "And if you liked your arms the way they were when we found you, then I can have the healing reversed."

Matthias squirmed uncomfortably at the thought, then replied. "I will lead the way."

Annetta nodded at the plans being hammered out. But something was missing, or rather someone.

"Where's J.K.?" she asked. "He was here before I-"

"He took off after Amarok," Talia said. "To the upper levels."

"And Sarina?" the girl questioned.

"Not a clue, but knowing that stubborn girl, her direction may not be much different," Matthias answered.

Frowning, the girl turned to everyone gathered, her decision about her own course of action made.

"I'm going to go find them. Matt, let me know through telepathy when this thing's ready to blow so I can get off," she said, gripping her weapons in hand and running off again.

"Annetta, wait!" Arieus, having picked up both his sword and the war banner, was about to run after her, when an arm grabbed his shoulder from behind. He turned to see it was one of the elves, and continued to call out anyways, "You nearly died! You're not going anywhere without-"

"Your father is right, missy. You are grounded," Aurora finished her husband's train of thought, only to be caught by one of the other elves before she could run after her daughter.

"You are not going anywhere after you-" Puc interjected, readying himself to spring, only to have Darius block his view.

"She's going to be alright." Kaian cut them all off, noticing a certain young warrior was also absent.

"But she-" Puc, Arieus and Aurora all protested.

"She will be fine. She needs our help in other ways now, and one way is to get Valdhar destroyed," he explained and then turned to Arieus. "You can't chase after her with a cloak for cold eves and a handkerchief to wipe away her tears the rest of her life."

His shoulder slumped as the elf's grip let go. He watched as the little girl, his little girl, raced off into the distance and disappeared in the ship. He remembered the first time he had held her when she was born, no bigger than his forearm. But she carried more value to him than all the riches in the universe.

"Sometimes I wish that was all I ever had to do," he sighed.

ജ‍ൽ

Jason charged like a raging animal into the fray as he conquered the last set of stairs, and emerged on the base level of one of the towers. Cold wind howled past the streaks on his cheeks where tears had fallen as he looked around. The second soldiers appeared around him, he went at them full of fury, his mace finding them no matter how they tried to avoid it. He did not use psychic fire, conserving his energy for when he would need it most. Though he enjoyed using the soldiers he passed by as a way to rid himself of the anger that welled within him from the death of his friend, Jason had a much bigger fish in mind to fry. He meant to take out Mislantus, no matter the cost. He owed that much to Annetta. Teleporting and running around the corner, he took the flight of stairs once more.

Thinking the maze of floors eternal, it came as a surprise to Jason when he finally reached what looked like the top of a tower. At the far end, looking down below stood a figure all too familiar to Jason. Gripping his mace tightly, the grim young warrior strode forward.

"You know, it's funny," Mislantus said, as though he didn't notice Jason's presence. "Wars always do so remind me of the futility of our existence. How small and fragile our lives are in comparison to the grandeur of the great design."

Mislantus smirked, his cat-like face glaring at Jason, who now stood but a few paces from him. "Wouldn't you agree, Jason Kinsman?"

Jason gritted his teeth in reply, his blood boiling within him more and more each moment he stared into the face of the warlord. Though he was not Amarok, the one he had hoped to run into, he was the cause of everything that had occurred in the last few months of his life.

"They prove that no one, in the end, is truly important," Mislantus continued, "Because anyone at any instant can become a corpse, which in turn is no different from any other matter found on the field, a shell of something that once was. But do you know what makes one immortal? Makes one champion above this infinite struggle for being noticed, being something greater than what fate designed us to be?"

Jason continued to stand in silence, not sure how to reply, and not wanting to. He used the voice of the being to drive his anger, to create more of the fire within him. He had nothing else to give his friend but a won war. He held that one image in his mind of her lying on the ground in peace, and it fueled him. He took a few more steps towards Mislantus, secretly readying himself to unleash a blast of psychic energy that, in his own ambitious mind, would shake the foundations of the earth around him. Whether he could pull it off or not was another thing entirely.

"You don't know?" Mislantus snickered, seeing the boy had no answer. "I'll divulge this little secret to you. It is the ability to make ones self seem a god!"

Drawing a saber out from its sheath, the tyrant was upon him like a great inescapable shadow, the blade coming down mercilessly in a set of heavy strokes. Jason would have been done for were he not able to focus his psychic energy into the mace, strengthening his hold on the weapon. Choosing his footsteps carefully, he circled his opponent, trying to determine his next move, ready to parry.

Mislantus wasted no time in launching his next assault, the sword coming in at Jason like an angered viper, once from the side, once straight ahead, and so on, until he could see the boy could no longer guess where the strike would land next.

Jason, however, was not about to play fair. Noticing a window of opportunity, he lowered his left hand, creating a small blast of psychic fire that he hurled at the warlord.

Dodging just enough for the ball to scorch his whiskers, Mislantus pursued Jason with the saber yet again, another blow clashing against the mace, the sound of steel echoing as the weapons slid apart. The tyrant used the opening to try and stab Jason with his claws, only to be kicked in the face by the resilient youth, who teleported behind, readying another blast of the blue and purple flames.

The warlord had a few more tricks up his sleeve, though. As soon as the ball came towards him, it stopped in midair, and flew right back at Jason, knocking him square in the chest, and onto his back. Triumphant, Mislantus slid the saber back in its place and strode over to him.

"Stupid, stupid boy," he said, standing over Jason, whose eyes had closed. "Did you honestly think that I, Mislantus the Threat, the ruler of Valdhar could not use the one ability I cherished most in my elite warriors? Pitiful, weak excuse for a-"

Before Mislantus could finish, Jason opened his eyes and rammed the weapon with full force into Mislantus's torso, causing the tyrant to topple. Grabbing his side in pain, he noted the wound and snarled.

"Don't any villains just...ever learn to shut up and finish what they started?" Jason sighed, getting up.

"What? You were hit with-," Mislantus's eyes widened.

"I made it look like it." Jason pointed over the side of the tower, where Mislantus's blast was spiraling downward into a horde of enemy soldiers. "Teleporting's great when you're too lazy to grab the remote from the other room."

As the two whipped insults and banter at one another, a third figure watched from the corridor leading up. Gripping a dagger close to its heart, it meant to end it all, and quickly. Hurtling at full speed, Sarina aimed the dagger for Mislantus's throat. Her timing too late, Mislantus's animalistic hearing picking her up as soon as she had entered the rooftop. He snatched the hand with the dagger and twisted it, aiming the weapon at her neck, holding her close to himself as a shield.

"Sarina," Jason shouted, his plan of readying another ball of psychic fire thwarted by her appearance.

"My, my, Sarina. Did I not tell you before that you never raise your weapon against Daddy?" The cat-like face snarled, his grip tightening around her wrist.

"Shove it. You never were anything close to a dad, you were only a father," She squirmed as the pain increased, the dagger pointed to her throat.

"You're a coward!" Jason growled.

"The correct term is survivalist, and I plan on living for a very, very long-," before Mislantus could finish the sentence, however, Sarina was gone. The warlord looked around frantically.

"I think anyone who picks on someone weaker than they are is a coward in my eyes," an all too familiar voice said from behind them both.

Jason and Mislantus turned around to see Annetta, standing with Sarina, her blue eyes gleaming defiantly at the tyrant.

"Annetta? How?" Jason stammered.

"Dead, came back. Long story, really." She smirked, and then turned to Mislantus. "Geeze, don't you just look ugly."

"Why, you insolent little-" Mislantus growled, readying his sword once more.

"Yeah, yeah. I've heard it all." Annetta cut him off as she positioned herself into a fighting stance, with her shield and sword drawn.

Letting Sarina go, the girl ran past a focused Mislantus to Jason, the two embracing each other, their moment being interrupted by Annetta's voice in Jason's head. *'Hey, J.K, can you do me a big one and get yourself and Sarina off of Valdhar as quick as you can? There's a bit of a surprise brewing, and I'd like for you to be able to see it.'*

Annetta focused on Mislantus, flicking her sword wrist in a taunting manner at the feline-faced opponent, pacing in a circle as each of them waited for the other to make the first move.

'What? I'm not going to leave you to fight this guy alone! He can use psychic fire!' Jason protested right back to her through telepathy.

'J.K., please just trust me, okay? Your part in this story is done. Now go on and save the girl,' she thought, wind blowing through her hair and tattered jean jacket. Not hearing a reply, she looked down. *'Go on, be the knight in shinning armor, and get out of here, okay?'*

'Annetta, I...' Jason struggled to finish his sentence.

'Damn it, move your butt and get out of here before I teleport you out!' Annetta snapped, just before Mislantus came at her with his saber, no longer having the patience to wait.

Jason watched, slack-jawed, as the battle began, the world seeming to slow down as the blades of each opponent clashed, sending sparks flying through the air. It was not until Sarina nudged him that he woke from his mesmerized state. Slipping away as instructed, heart still with his friend, Jason fled with Sarina to the lower levels of the fortress.

⁕⁖

Elsewhere, Matthias, flanked by Puc and Kaian, led the party to the control room of Pessumire and all of Valdhar, charging in a V formation towards their goal through the wide halls. They were stopped every so often by soldiers who were still making their way down to the battlefield. The sight of a band of elves and humans caught the enemy off guard, who never thought the fight would have come to them.

Finally, reaching their destination, the companions were confronted by a set of the armed Verden guards and a dozen or so of smaller soldiers, all eager to meet battle, their weapons drawn. Striding forward, one of the larger guards blocked the door, a heavy club adorning his meaty fists.

"You cannot not pass," the creature spoke in a baritone voice.

"Oh really?" Puc smirked disdainfully. Though the mage dislike much of what humanity had written, there was one piece of literature that had resonated with him. "I do believe you forgot who said that line to whom. Mages!"

The six mages readied their staves, pointing towards the obviously non-psychic guard, who panicked at the stream of magic missiles being readied at them. They stood their ground nonetheless, readying a charge towards the oncoming slaughter, each of them loyal to Mislantus to the last. When the blasts fired, however, they were no more.

Arieus quickly ripped the doors from their hinges using telekinesis, causing them to fall before him. When the dust cleared, a score of stunned scientists and engineers looked wide-eyed at the oncoming storm. The only one oblivious to it all was a white haired man still flipping through files and mumbling under his breath.

"Kretus! Keep turning that lever don't want the whole place to combu-oh. Oh dear." Lloyd Abner stopped dead in his tracks upon seeing the doors knocked down and a score of warriors standing in its midst. "My, well, this was not in the script."

"Restrain them. Let no one escape," Kaian ordered his mages as they set about the task of capturing those who fled the room. His attention then turned to Abner, who was restrained by Darius. "Now then. You seem to be the one in charge here. Tell me, how do you fire the cannon?"

While Kaian interrogated the head scientist, Matthias set about the task of going into the control room. Punching in the right codes to activate the ship was no problem. He had flown similar aircrafts his whole life, but on a smaller scale.

The problem was that it would require multiple people. Sighing, he turned around to see the majority of the crew had been rounded up by the elves and were now surrounded by glowing chains, tied down in one place.

"I'm going to need a few extra hands here," he said turning to Arieus, Aurora, Talia and Kaine. "I can't operate everything on my own. The commands are set so far apart that they cannot be reached by just one person alone."

"What about using psychic powers?" Talia asked.

"Can't," Matthias said to them. "This whole room is sealed off from using such abilities. It was always a precaution in case someone should mutiny on the ship. Last place you want damaged is the control deck."

"Does not seem to be the case with magic," Puc frowned.

"Not many worlds still practice arcane abilities, mage. It is a dying art," the assassin retorted, turning back to the controls as the others flocked around him for instructions. "Now, let me show you how to sink a spaceship."

∽∾

After the initial assault had finished, Annetta and Mislantus stared each other down, neither moving a muscle. Finally, the feline face grinned, laughing.

"Of all the champions in the known worlds, they send a female child up against me. Do you even know who I am, little girl?" he chuckled.

"Of course I do. You're a bully," Annetta said in a loud, clear voice. "And do you know who I am? Your worst nightmare. I don't appreciate it when someone pushes others around. Everyone deserves to be free and, everyone deserves the right to not have to live in fear of people who are just going to come in and turn everything they love into dust."

"Insolent little brat. Do you honestly think you can win?" the tyrant snarled, and with that, was upon her.

Dodging one attack after another, Annetta barely had an opening to land any of her own strikes against the towering behemoth of fury. His every move was calculated so she would have no gaps. Feinting an attack, the girl finally managed to roll out of the way. When the warlord came at her, spinning quickly, she slammed her shield into his face, causing him to fall back, clutching his maw in pain. Seeing an opportunity, she went in to strike at his gut, only to see him disappear moments before she got there. She felt the sting of a boot slam against her shoulder blades, causing her to fall forward.

Rising up and never letting go of Severbane, the girl pivoted around quickly to collide, blade upon blade, with the blow that was meant to end her. Taking a step back, she reaffirmed her footing, pushing the enemy strike away enough for her to coordinate her next move. Desperation drove her as her strength began to diminish slowly. She teleported above the warlord, and readied her sword over her head to slice him in two, only to see him vanish before she hit the mark.

Mislantus, seasoned veteran as he was to battle, did not slow. Seeing his opponent get worn out, he only grinned, inhaling the upcoming victory. Teleporting to the edge of the tower, he fired another ball of psychic fire.

Annetta stood, watching the ball of blue and purple flames come towards her unmoving. Waiting until the last minute, she teleported right behind the warlord and slammed the sword into his back, piercing the armor.

Howling in pain, and momentarily crippled by the sting of it escalating through his whole body, Mislantus fell onto the ground face forward, the blow having throw his saber over the edge of the tower. Turning over quickly and seeing the form of Annetta ready to pounce on him, he curled his feet and drove both of them into the girl's gut.

Annetta fell to ground in the armor like a turtle on its back. Before she was able to recover, she felt a series of kicks land at her sides. Unable to hold on anymore, the grip loosened on the sword as Mislantus kicked it away from her reach. Picking the girl up by the scuff of her tabard, he tossed her a few feet away so she lay propped up against the wall, like a sack of grain.

"Enjoy the afterlife, Annetta Severio," the cat grinned, and threw another ball of flame at her.

Annetta, however was not ready to give up just yet. Her arm, tired and bruised, lifted the shield tied to it before her as the assault came full force and slammed into the wooden guard. White light blinded everything around them as the blast collided with it.

Mislantus grinned gleefully, watching the white light diminish but his jaw ultimately dropped at what he saw when everything returned back to normal.

"What? That cannot be!" His cat-slit eyes narrowed.

Unscathed, Annetta sat still against the wall with her eyes wide open from the surprise of what had happened. Her wooden shield turned to a crystalline form as it absorbed the last of the sparks from the flame before it returned to its normal wooden shape. It was Calanite diamond. Knowing she had no time to ponder the life-saving gift, Annetta rose as she recalled the sword to her free hand.

"You know, I've learned something very important here," she began. "I think I've learned what I hate most in my life. It's people like you, Mislantus. It's people who are so full of themselves that they think they should rule over everything, who think it's right to be mean to others in order to have them submit. But you know what gets me the most? Half the time they don't even do it themselves. They surround themselves with a group of people who will just follow them around acting like they're doing the right thing. No one is ever meant to rule everything, because everyone has a right to their own life, everyone has a right to make their own decisions. No one should have to take orders from a coward."

"I am no coward, you imbecilic child," Mislantus snarled. "I'm a realist, and I do not live in fantasy. Survival is the number one objective of all living organisms. Even you have tasted fear before."

"Talk, talk, talk, talk, talk! All I hear from you," she snapped. "Just admit it and be done with it, why don't you?"

Moving her legs apart and sheathing her sword, Annetta glared at Mislantus, who was shifting to a similar position. Focusing on the words she had just spoke, she felt a surge of adrenaline through her whole body, blue sparks wrapping around her arms.

"If you are so eager to die, then so be it. I was merely prolonging your miserable existence." Mislantus grinned with both legs spread a shoulder length apart, and his arms at his side as though he were holding a basketball.

"Miserable? You're the one who ought to be miserable with a title like Threat," Annetta scoffed, and focused her fury. Her mind raced to all those she had sworn to help, those who she wanted to protect. A small ball of blue and purple flame began to swirl in her palms as she stared at Mislantus, his green feral eyes ready to tear out Annetta's heart at a moments notice. She narrowed her eyes, focusing upon the swirling and growing ball of flame in her hands.

Mislantus's own ball of flame had outgrown the original shape the tyrant had intended for it, its force prying his hands apart so much that he needed to focus most of his energy on containing the blast. He noted the small flames Annetta had managed to produce, and exposed his teeth in a vicious grin. "Sticks and stones. You can't win this one, runt. I've got your forces outnumbered, your army is dying, and so shall you soon. The survivor always wins, and once you are gone, there will be no one left to stop me from attaining what is my right. Korangar's shadow overtakes all, and it is those like me who will inherit the world."

"As long as there are people like you, there will always be people like me!" Annetta watched as the enemy's energy blast grew in his hands, her determination to not let those she cared for down creating a fire from within. Closing her eyes, she allowed instinct to take hold.

Mislantus became aware of the psychic fire growing exponentially in the girl's hands after her declaration, but he did not allow for it to sway him. He was chosen, he was the descendant of Freius, he who enslaved Korangar, who held dominion over all life and death, and so death could not touch him. But part of him began to feel very mortal.

Ignoring his fear, the warlord snarled. "Surrender! You don't stand a chance!"

The blue and purple reflection of the flames rimmed Annetta's eyes as she gritted her teeth.

"I've been told those same odds time and time again by those that want to see me fail, but I'll always fight!" Annetta yelled as a ball of blue and purple flame erupted from her hands. The girl let go of the blast as it raged forward, a storm of primal fury blotting out everything around her.

80CR

Working intently, Matthias and the other psychics under his command with Kaine worked on punching in all the coordinates for the ship to have enough time to leave the Eye to All Worlds before it self-destructed. Kaian and Puc, along with the mages, guarded the crew as well, and kept look out on the door.

"You will not get away with this, I hope you know," Abner warned them, but with a casual, carefree tone to his voice. "Sooner or later, you'll have a rather annoyed group of assassins on your back, and no one to save you."

"Whom exactly are you referring to? Amarok? He flew the coop." Matthias rolled his eyes as he continued working.

The head scientist's eyes burned into Matthias with hatred. For the first time, he was without an answer to give. He was then taken from the assassin with the prod of a staff to his ribs.

"I thought so." Matthias smiled as Abner was taken to the other tied down scientists.

Going back to his work in the control room with Arieus, Aurora and Talia, Matthias continued to give instructions, hammering in the appropriate sequences on the keyboards that surrounded him, until the main monitor before them displayed a counter.

"This baby is ready to blow!" he called to them. "We have ten minutes to evacuate."

"Good enough," Kaian called, watching the outer room with the other mages for signs of any soldiers who could come their way.

Out of nowhere, Abner ran past the crowd of prisoners. In an act of desperation, he grabbed onto the assassin from behind, squeezing at Matthias's windpipe with his shackles.

"I'll not let you destroy over a hundred years of work!" he shrieked, prying at Matthias, who grabbed at the skinnier man's arms, attempting to break them.

Before anything could be achieved, however, Matthias heard a thud as the form of Lloyd became limp and slid down. Turning around, the assassin faced Puc, his staff still pointed towards the assassin from his previous act of having bludgeoned the scientist into unconsciousness. Matthias nodded his thanks, but he could see the mage had more yet to say.

"Where is Lincerious?" he asked.

ഔ

Running as quickly as his legs could carry him, Link climbed the stairs where he had heard Annetta disappear to. Having passed Sarina and Jason along the way, he had received confirmation that he was heading the right way and a stern warning from Jason that she might blow him up if she saw him. Conquering the final steps and emerging outside, however, the scene Link came upon was one he had not anticipated.

Annetta lay on the ground unconscious, the wind blowing her hair. Some distance away, there laid the badly burned body of a man. Kneeling down beside her, Link lifted the girl's head into his arms, checking to see if she was alive. Her eyes suddenly began to flutter. Coughing a bit, she half opened them.

"I think dying once and coming back is enough, don't you agree?" she said in a raspy voice.

"I couldn't agree with you more," he said lightly.

"Hmph. Cool. Since we're on the same page, what are you doing here exactly?" she asked as Link helped her up to her feet, holding her arm over his shoulder.

"What does it look like? Rescuing you," he said, walking her closer over to the staircase leading out of the tower.

"Rescuing? I'm a self-rescuing princess, none of this-" she began, going on as she moved away from Link, nearly stumbling over her own two feet if he'd not caught her.

690

"I get it, okay?" he said. "You don't like being the one rescued. You don't like sitting around in a dress waiting for something to happen, because you want to take charge. But you just saved countless lives from him." He motioned over to Mislantus's corpse, lying on the other side, then turned back to her. "I think you can cut yourself some slack and accept a helping hand, don't you think?"

∞∮ℂℤ

Down below, Natane stood beside Ironhorn, who had been injured gravely in the last onslaught of warriors. Though it had looked like they had been losing, word had spread from Soarin flying close to Valdhar of Annetta and Jason's prowess against Mislantus, giving heart to the warriors, pushing them to new heights in battle. Looking to the peak of the castle, there came a blinding black, purple, and blue light, which could only mean one thing.

"Psychic fire," Natane whispered, her attention shifting to the beam emanating from the fortress in the opposite direction into the sky.

"What news do you have, Great Mother? Has this damned scourge won or not?" Ironhorn breathed heavily through his many wounds.

Entellion floated down on his great wings moments later, limping slightly as he walked over to Natane and Ironhorn.

"Lord Ironhorn, what happened?" the Soarin leader asked.

"A few blasts of that damn fire, and a couple of clubs, but fear ye not for me," he said through coughs. "Now, is someone going to answer me as to what in blazes is going on?"

"A blast of psychic fire just came from the roof, the largest I've ever seen," Entellion told him. "And it looks like they are retreating. Pessumire has fired once more, and is pulling out."

The three leaders watched the fortress lift higher and higher into the sky. Upon its retreat through a portal, the Minotaur Lord rose with a roar.

"Well, what are we waiting for? Let's round the rest of these maggots!" he hollered with renewed strength, grabbing his sword and axe. "I could use some new stone cutters!"

Ironhorn charged for the remaining scattered soldiers, Minotaur who had not fallen gathering behind him and following their king. Howling and shouting war cries to their deities, the Soarin, Ogaien and Water Elves followed as what was left of the armies of Mislantus the Threat surrendered to the victors.

∞∮ℂℤ

Some distance away from the battle, Jason teleported with Sarina under one of the trees close to Severio Castle, having run from Valdhar and the oncoming soldiers. Sliding down the tree trunk from exhaustion, Jason looked at the gore of battle in the distance, the plains of grass darkened by blood, broken trees and bodies of soldiers. His head began to spin with nausea.

"J.K., are you alright?" Sarina asked, watching him collapse as she reached to help him up.

"Hm? Yeah I'm fine. I just..." Jason's eyes went wide upon looking up to see Valdhar rising from its resting position against the mountain, and reversing its course back out the portal created by Pessumire. "Oh no. Annetta and-"

Before he could finish, a crowd of people began teleporting in around him, as airships approached from the distance in his direction. He noticed Puc, Darius, Matthias, Annetta's parents, and his mother among the score of elves. Standing up, he began to search for his best friend.

"Have any of you seen Annetta?" he asked, stomping right through the middle of the group before shouting even louder. "Have any of you seen her?"

Looking at one another, the group lowered their heads. Taking it upon himself as always, Puc sighed and looked upon the boy, readying himself to speak.

"We never saw her come down, Jason," he said with a heavy heart, "I'm sorry."

Keeping in his anger, Jason swallowed hard, "No, she's around here somewhere she can't be...not a second time-"

He did not want to believe it. Turning his head towards the skies, he cried out.

"Soarin! Soarin, I need your wings!" he yelled at the top of his lungs, as Amelia landed beside him.

"What is it, Jason? she asked.

"We need to find Annetta. She was on board the ship," he said in a gruff tone.

"I will send scouts right away," she said with a nod, taking off as Jason continued to go forward, marching along the field as Sarina raced after him.

"J.K., it's going to be okay," she whispered to him softly.

Full of fury, Jason spun around on his heel as he tried to hide the tears in his eyes, but he'd had as much as one could take in an entire battle. He felt as if fate was laughing upon him, his friend having been thought dead, and then returned to life, and now this. His face, stained with soot and blood, looked upon her like a black and red marble sculpture, with veins of white where the tears fell.

"Dammit, why? I promised her I would go with her on this to any end, Sarina. I said I would be there, and she made me go. I should have never listened to her. I should have..." unable to speak anymore, he broke down. Not knowing what else to do, Sarina held onto him, stroking his hair in an attempt to comfort him.

The sound then of swift wings could be heard from behind them as a strong gust blew past both huddled figures.

"J.K. and Sarina sitting in a tree!" A melodious voice interrupted the serious moment with giggling.

Jason looked up to see Annetta sitting atop Doriden's back with Link, a great big smile upon her weary face as she watched the two of them. Embarrassed, Jason's pale face turned an intense pink as the girl and boy slid down from the Soarin's back.

Amelia walked to her brother's side, seeing him on the ground with the others.

"Good catch," she said with a toothy smile.

"Thanks. I had much practice with a fledgling that couldn't fly." He grinned, only to be smacked across the face by his sister's wing.

"Annetta!" Arieus called from across the field as he and Aurora made it over, embracing their daughter in a hug. "You're alright, you're safe," he murmured to her.

"Not so alright with bruised, probably broken ribs being squished." She squirmed out from under her father's powerful grip, cringing as she gasped for air.

"Well, in any case, you almost forgot this." Aurora smiled as Arieus handed the girl the standard that he had kept with him through the whole battle, to which the girl blushed a bit in embarrassment.

"Well, if I didn't see it on my own two eyes, I would not have believed it." The voice of Ironhorn rang out from the distance, as the Minotaur approached with Natane and his kin. The rest of the foot soldiers of the Four Forces that had fought beside them also began to assemble.

Slipping down to the ground on a rope moments later from one of the airships that had docked above the assembled party, Iliam and Maria appeared, both with their share of nicks and scratches. The Water Elf warrior now carried his arm in a sling, sporting a deep cut that had rendered his arm useless for the remainder of the battle.

"A true feat. Well done, young warriors," Natane congratulated them.

"Thanks, I guess," Annetta said. "But we don't really deserve much praise. Honest, it was a team effort. Everyone did an important part. Without that, we would have never won."

"Words that far exceed your wisdom, young Annetta." Puc smiled, raising his staff while Annetta raised the war banner. The mage shouted. "All hail the Four Forces! May peace reign down for years to come in the lands we call our own!"

"Hail!" the warriors shouted back, the battle having come to an end.

Chapter 61

Collecting the wounded, organizing the prisoners to be transported back to Morwick and Aldamoor, and burying the dead had not taken as long as Annetta and Jason had suspected, thanks to the magic of the mages and the effort of those able. Before they knew it, great banners decorated the halls of Severio Castle, marking the victory of the Four Forces over Mislantus and Valdhar. The Great Hall, dormant for so many years, now lit up with the life of thousands of soldiers of the four races. After pooling all their resources together from their homelands, the feasting and drinking began. Though most stayed close to the food and drink, some wandered the halls. Among those were Jason and Sarina.

The spring weather having become as pleasant as it was, the two went back outside to marvel at the white castle walls. The wind blowing through the trees around them heralded the end of mild weather and prolonging of warmth in the promised summer months. Settling on some fallen stones from one of the walls under a great oak, the pair looked out into the green grass.

"So what do you think you'll do now that this is all done?" Jason asked finally, looking out around him.

"Well, I don't know. I've never been able to decide for myself. What do you think I should do?" she asked looking over at the boy.

"Well, I don't want to decide for you, but if you like, I think you should stay in Q-16 with us," he said, then recoiled upon hearing the firm tone of voice he carried. "That is, I mean, if you want, right? I'm totally not saying you have to. I mean, Annetta and I did kill your fath-"

"He was just blood, nothing more." Sarina shook her head. "And yes, I would like to stay. I meant what I said when I was talking about you being my first friend ever, aside from Matt."

Jason smiled a little as he looked down at his feet. Curling up on the rock, he sighed, taking in the spring breeze. Closing his eyes, he drifted off. He was brought back a few moments later when he felt Sarina's head resting on his shoulder. Opening his eyes a crack, he turned them to face her.

"I really like you, J.K.," she murmured, blushing a bit as she faced him.

"I like you too." Jason felt his ears go red as Sarina leaned in and kissed him.

"Jason!" their moment was interrupted by the voice of Puc, who stood at the front gates, dressed once more in his dark blue and black robes. "Leave the girl and come with me. There is something I need to show you."

Horrified, not wanting to dwell on how long Puc had been watching them, the youth jumped off the rock with a resigned look on his face, and trotted after the irritating mage, who walked outside the castle. They two of them walked for a good few minutes, and stopped, having arrived at an old looking rock within the foundations of the stone that lay covered with vines.

"You always ask what part, if any, you had in all of this," the mage said to the boy. "Well, I have something to show you. Something I should have shown you a long time ago."

Using his staff he pulled back the vines that covered a silver plate. Written upon it was the following:

As time once lain was, so too the stones of the Eye to All Worlds came to rest by the arms of Adeamus Severio and his kinsman, Demetrius Severio. All hail them who were severed and never forgot.

Jason read the plate and looked up at Puc for clarification about what he was reading.

"This castle is as much yours as it is Annetta's," Puc explained, looking upon the boy. "You are descendant of Demetrius Severio, who was known as Adeamus's kinsman. To avoid confusion, his last name was later changed to Kinsman, the name used by his descendants. You are Annetta's distant cousin, and always have been."

"Hey, J.K.! You done kissing the girl down there? Am I gonna need to teleport you up here? Come on you, need to see the view!" Annetta's voice rang from somewhere unseen, causing Jason's face to go red with embarrassment, making him wonder how long she'd been watching him as well.

"I'm coming, damn it!" he snapped, then turned to the elf. "Uh. I need to go. But Puc?"

"Yes, Jason?" The mage raised an eyebrow, only to have his answer returned to him in the form of a hug by the wayward youth, who took off quicker than lightening up the stairs leading to the balcony in the library.

☙❧

Annetta sat on a chair outside, enjoying the sun beaming down on her as she watched it droop lazily overhead. Her injured ribs were bound as they healed with the help of magical potions. Closing her eyes with a sigh, she waited patiently, giving her friend the time to catch up after her teasing threat had been issued. Hearing footsteps on marble floor shortly after, she turned around to see Jason, exhausted, looking at her.

"What was so important?" he breathed heavily.

"Nothing. I missed you." She smiled, flashing a grin at her friend, nearly causing him to collapse over himself and burst out laughing.

"I don't get you, sometimes, you know?" he said vaguely. "First you say go, get out of here, get the girl, now you're asking me to come up here, and you tear me away..." he gritted his teeth, causing Annetta to laugh harder and cringe as her ribs began to hurt again.

"I'm sorry, I just wanted to see you get pissed off is all." She muffled her laughing by covering her face with her hand.

Darius, who had been in the Great Hall, and had gone to search for Annetta and Jason after having noticed their absence, came out onto the balcony. "There you guys are. I've been looking all over for you. Man, it's smoldering in there. I wish they just had it all outside."

"I'll say." Jason mused, then decided to get even. "Hey, Annetta, you know what comes next, right? Warm weather means?"

"Exams," she replied, a sinking feeling in her stomach. "I haven't studied for anything with all this fighting. Oh man, I'm gonna fail math and then have to retake it in summer school." The girl turned pale as she grabbed at her hair, reality biting her where it counted most.

"Or you can study with me, and we cram last minute." The voice of Link came from behind, as he joined them with Matthias and Sarina.

"You don't even really need school, so why are you doing it?" Annetta groaned. "If I was in your shoes, I would not be going back."

"Well, I'm sure as hell done with the schoolboy act." Matthias crossed his arms. "And I'm just too old for it."

"Call me a nerd, but I like learning new things," Link said with a smile. "Come on, Anne, it'll be fun."

"I'd sooner study magic under Puc than study math," Annetta grumbled. "I can see why some people would choose to stay here instead of living in both worlds."

Walking over to the edge of the balcony, Darius chuckled at Annetta's proclamation. "Be careful for what you wish for, Annetta. You never know when Puc can hear you."

Rethinking her position on her previous comment, the girl bit her lip. "Good point. I take it back. I'll leave the magic to those who know how to wield it."

Link and Darius smiled at her sudden change of heart, causing Annetta to grin even wider than she intended. Her gaze then turned to Jason, who looked out over the balcony in a pensive state. Getting up, painfully, she walked over to join him.

"I'm still having a hard time taking it all in, you know?" he said, looking over at his friend. "I mean, with everything that's gone on, can we just really go back to math, exams, and everything else? How's it all going to turn out?"

Annetta sighed as she leaned with her elbows on the concrete railing. She closed her eyes, and focused on the feeling of the wind against her skin. She remembered the day they had found out about the Lab. Looking back, she knew they would never be the same. There was a lot she did not know about, but there was one thought that lingered on her heart. Leaning closer to her friend, she shared it with him. "I don't know the details, but I'm pretty sure everything will fall into place on its own."

A silence fell among the group as they took in the words. As they did so, they looked out into the vast plains of grass, with the mountains of white stone rising above them. Though much of it was still desolated, trampled and broken by the torrents of the battle before, already new blades of grass were sprouting from the ruins of what was lost.

Epilogue

Excerpt from the chronicles of the Eye to All Worlds:

And so the summer rolls on, with not a care to be held for miles around us, though I dare say many of us still hold our guards close, wary if any should come down the road to challenge yet again. Personally, though, I think not many shall come near Earth again for a very long time with the destruction of Valdhar and the eradication of Mislantus's troops. It has been years since I could say I knew such peace as this within my heart, and a good peace it is.

The school year has ended for the summer holidays, meaning Annetta, Jason and the other youth are home. Many days are spent simply within the Lab, or traveling to the other four known realms in visitation to the races who now try to rebuild after what has been now named the Second Great War, even though it was just one battle in truth.

Darius has resigned his post as my apprentice, and has returned to the Academy in Aldamoor, preparing himself for the final examinations before being sworn in as a full mage by the Council.

Matthias and Sarina now take up residence within Q-16. The assassin, having retired from his previous life, now helps with training Annetta and Jason, but only when the two of them do not have the excuse of 'these are our summer holidays' spewing from their mouths. Of course, even when they do, this does not stop Matthias. The man has a rule as strong as iron on them.

Lincerious (known to many as Link) has turned into an honorable man, becoming wiser each day, never failing to surprise me with his code of morals, as was once expected of many long ago. As promised to you, dear friend Brakkus, he never leaves Annetta's side while on adventure, and has even told me on occasion that he can hear her voice within his head when danger falls her way. A strange gift indeed, would you not say?

Jason and Sarina have become very fond of one another, and I dare say innocent romance will in the future years turn to something more between the two of them, though it is far too early for such conclusions, as our wise Lord Orbeyus would once say.

Annetta grows to be a more capable warrior each day. I remember when first I laid eyes upon the little vagabond, and sometimes I wonder how

I was ever able to get through to that thick skull of hers. Of course, I can say the same for Jason when it comes to their lessons.

Sadly, I ramble, and rambling is a pastime for those who have nothing better to do. But I tell you all now that there is still much wonder for this old elf to experience before such chronicles take up the rest of his days. So until the next time I pick up this ancient tome to share with the future what once was past, I tell you Adieu, and rest easy, listening to the eternal song of sky and trees. The have more to say than you will ever know, and you can only hear them if you remember to believe.

-Puc Thanestorm the Mage;
Chronicler of Severio Castle through the lives of Orbeyus, Arieus, and Annetta Severio Defenders of the Eye to All Worlds

Acknowledgements

A writer is never alone, and I don't mean we have the voices of our characters or the artistic muses that propel us into the chaotic realm of the written word. I'm talking about the real flesh and blood people who inspire and help us in achieving our goals. Should there be anyone I have accidentally omitted, I apologize here in advance, and please note that you have my eternal gratitude for having come to my aid at some point. So first and foremost, to my parents, Ewa and Wes Jankiewicz who not only raised me but allowed me to dream and pursue my passions. Thank you for the gift of life, and for being there with me every step of the way. To my brother, Adam, for always being there to support me and cheer me on when I needed it most. You're the best sibling a sister could ask for, never change. To Anthony Geremia for undertaking the herculean task of editing not once but multiple times over the years, as well as helping me catch all those stray plot bunnies. Thank you for reading my mad rants through text, those bunnies were vicious. To Ashlee Terlicher for bravely stepping in at the last minute to beta read. I truly appreciate the amount of time and effort that went into combing through these pages in catch all of the remaining plot holes/errors that may have gone unnoticed, you are a rockstar. To my teachers at Durham College; Steven Evans, Ray Gubala, Linda Cheng, Wade Clarke and Brent Hudson for not only allowing me to be able to self-publish this book as part of my thesis project but also for helping me go above and beyond what I had originally thought possible. Thank you for this opportunity, it's not an experience I will soon forget. To my classmates for all of your positive energy every day when I came into class, it was definitely a motivational factor for me. Jason Cloutier for his many smiles and encouragement and Danjiel Losic for his help in creating the flagpole for the front cover. All the people in the forums at Lulu.com for their knowledge and insights. This list could go on, but as one elf put it, "Sadly, I ramble, and rambling is a pastime for those who have nothing better to do," so until our next encounter, be it in person, on the internet or on the written page of Annetta's next adventure, keep it awesome!

About the Author

A.A. Jankiewicz (known to most as Agnes) hails from the city of Pickering, Ontario. Her debut novel 'Q-16 and the Eye to All Worlds' was published as part of her thesis project at Durham College as part of the Contemporary Media Design Program. Prior to that, she graduated from York University with a BFA in Film Theory, Historiography and Criticism. When she's not busy plotting the next great adventure, writing, doodling, tinkering in the Adobe suite programs or mellowing out with her friends, she enjoys walks with her four-legged companion Meesha. She is currently working on the next instalment in the Q-16 series.